LITTLE BLUE WHALES

LITTLE BLUE WHALES

a novel

Kenneth R. Lewis

iUniverse, Inc.
New York Lincoln Shanghai

Little Blue Whales
a novel

iUniverse books may be ordered through booksellers or by contacting:

iUniverse
2021 Pine Lake Road, Suite 100
Lincoln, NE 68512
www.iuniverse.com
1-800-Authors (1-800-288-4677)

Little Blue Whales is a work of fiction. The characters, incidents, and dialogues are product's of the author's imagination and are not to be construed as real. Any resemblance to actual events or persons, living or dead, is entirely coincidental.

ISBN-13: 978-0-595-39000-7 (pbk)
ISBN-13: 978-0-595-83391-7 (ebk)
ISBN-10: 0-595-39000-5 (pbk)
ISBN-10: 0-595-83391-8 (ebk)

Printed in the United States of America

To JaNell

*For helping to make so many of my dreams
in life come true. Including this one.*

"Wisdom is what we glean, if we're lucky, from the twisted root of the past—so that we may ignore it and proceed at once in the opposite direction"

Richard Rayner

—Murder Book

CHAPTER 1

▼

He saw them again, the two white swans, as he emerged from the cool dark shade of the towering conifers and massive old oak trees in the park, and paused at the river's edge. This time they were close by the opposite shore, twin white dots skewing their way toward the center current of the river, looming larger as they came.

They swam in graceful concentric circles, long slender necks arcing forward, heads nearly touching, as if they were decorations on a wedding cake in a store-front window spinning slowly on a motorized platter, both serenely still, yet in fluid motion at the same time.

These were the same two swans, he was sure of it. He'd first seen them here in late fall when he'd started his walks to John Grand's office every other Tuesday morning; painfully limping through the park on the shortcut he'd discovered to downtown, probing the ankle high piles of fallen oak and maple leaves with the cane he'd been forced to use then as he went, as if he was searching for land mines.

He'd seen them at Christmas time when the ground was covered with snow and they had looked like large white snow covered rocks on the shoreline until they would finally move as he approached, craning their necks, stretching and flapping their wings in warning of his impending trespass. And he'd seen them as they huddled together on the river's winter mud flats against the biting winds, and icy, slanting rains of February, and March—until the first soft days of spring had finally arrived and he'd caught a glimpse of them once again, on the far side of the park, pecking at the tender shoots of new growing grass.

They were always together whenever, and wherever he'd seen them. And they were always touching, as if their need in this regard was as perpetual and everlasting as the changing seasons they weathered close by one another, conjoined; an abiding faithfulness that survived, and thrived, in the middle of man's domain on a few acres of river bottom land that remained in may ways as wild as the majestic white birds themselves.

He marveled at the swans and wondered what it was that kept them together, and alive, in this precarious world of coyotes and foxes that slipped down from the burnt, rust colored hills above the city at night to hunt in the park. And the equally dangerous homeless men who sometimes clubbed the more docile and trusting park ducks, and geese, with heavy tree branches; grilling them after dark on the cement Hibachis left still smoldering by late afternoon picnickers. Every safe world Kevin Kearnes had ever tried to build for himself and those he loved, or those he had promised to protect, had eventually turned dark and dangerous and slipped from his hands into an abyss as endlessly deep and black as the secret he had so desperately spent his life trying to keep.

He found a big oak just above the riverbank and leaned back against its petrified leathery trunk, wanting to stay in the shade and out of the building heat of the early August morning. He watched them swim, dipping their beaks in the river and flicking droplets of water at each other as they waltzed together in the ever widening circles toward him, a joyous uninhibited dance in which they seemed to shut out all of life around them, allowing nothing in that might blur or distort their vision of perfection—the sight of each other.

People can't ever be like swans in this life, he thought. *No matter what their hearts may desire or so desperately need to keep on beating with the hope that once— when they were pure and unmarked by the terrible things that are eventually visited upon us all—they might someday, by some miracle, be that way again.* It was never going to happen for Kevin Kearnes; not now. Not after what had taken place on the rocks at the end of the jetty at Cutter Point—and then after that—when Britt had left him, too. Kevin Kearnes understood now that the only "miracle" to have ever come into his life had been Britt; and that for those few short and miraculous weeks when she was in his life, he *had* been pure and unmarked once again. And then, just as suddenly as it had all begun—he was not.

Britt, who he had needed to be his snowy white swan—something pure and clean to illuminate the dark and terrifying recesses of his mind and soul; because he wasn't well enough and strong enough to do it for himself. Britt, who was never a swan when he'd seen her through his own blurred and distorted vision then, but who had folded him inside her wings and flown him into the purity of her heart—her bravery, goodness, and decency—to a place of safety and acceptance he never could have found without the gift of her grace, and her love for him.

A bitter wave of regret began to rise inside him and he pushed himself violently away from the oak, shaking his head, a harsh, derisive laugh escaping from his mouth. He could hear the morning traffic thundering across the bridge at the edge of the park, feeding an unbroken steel chain of vehicles across the river into the belly of the small, bustling city. He walked in that direction, smelling the exhaust from the morning commute mixing with the heat that was starting to bake and soften the asphalt—a burnt, acidic odor. *You are a goddamned head case Kearnes. You should have your goddamned head examined.* He laughed again, because this was exactly what he was on his way to do. Hopefully, for the last time.

He slowly climbed the worn and cracked gray concrete steps up out of the park—his right leg aching now without the cane he refused to be seen with in public any longer—until he reached the pedestrian walkway of the bridge. He turned and looked out at the emerald green water flowing below, searching for the swans, but the river's surface was now crowded with flocks of fat tame ducks and noisy geese by the hundreds swimming in formation like miniature Battleships toward the park's shoreline. They were an amphibious invasion on the way to intercept the morning's first arriving park visitors who might feed them from sacks of dried bread, or greasy leftover movie popcorn.

He could see that the playground in the park, even though half hidden by the fortress like wall of trees, was still empty. But on his way home he knew as he passed by it would be filled with happy, shrieking kids and their watchful, attentive Mothers and he felt the regret beginning to jolt him from deep inside again, dizzying him like a punch he hadn't been quick enough to avoid. He grabbed for the steel railing of the bridge walkway in order to keep from pitching headlong into the traffic whizzing by only a few feet away, as if some subterranean channel of the river below had suddenly changed its course, moving the earth in an undulating groundswell beneath his watery, buckling legs.

It was another anxiety attack, birthed in regret and shame; an extreme physical manifestation of the absolute guilt and self-loathing he felt toward himself for having had let happen what happened to all of the dead children found at Cutter Point, and the other places. Children who by now had been grieved over and given back to the earth which they were so briefly allowed to play upon, and for whom he believed he had done too little, too late. And regret for the ugly wounds he had suffered to both his body and his soul, the scars on the inside of his leg now healed into small, thick ropes; a physical testament to the evil men can, and will do to one another. And of course regret for Britt; for what he had also done to her in the end.

Britt's heart had been like the rolling mountains of blue ocean water smashing down onto the car sized boulders of the mile-long jetty at Cutter Point; exploding into white foam and spray, and then misting down upon the sea and coming back for more.

She had always been capable of reassembling her heart in the aftermath of the many regrets and hurtful wounds she had sustained in her own life. And even when she had reached the darkest crossroads of her existence and came finally to believe otherwise…and had made a decision that only a woman completely bereft of all hope and any belief left in herself could have been capable of making; she had, in the end, found her heart still eagerly, willingly, coming back for more. That is how, and why, she had loved Kevin Kearnes. And that is also why she had left him.

He squinted against the dazzling morning sunlight and with his hands cupped against his forehead, scanned the river and both sides of the shore for the swans, but they were nowhere in sight. A large furniture delivery truck ripped past him with a *whoosh*, sucking the air away from his body and billowing up the back of his un-tucked summer shirt.

The butt of the gun he had jammed beneath his pants belt in the small of his back was exposed—the shirttail caught on its sharp, square end—and he casually pulled the shirt back down into place. It would be a portent, a sign of some sort to him to be able to see the swans one last time before he left the bridge; a good omen that he might survive this long awaited day with something to go on with in his life that resembled some kind of a future for him.

For Kevin Kearnes a sea change was coming today. And if this was the way his life had always been meant to turn out, whether by accident, or fate, the hand of God, or Satan himself in the form of the sick, depraved monster, Uriah Beek; then so be it. He was ready to transcend all. And if those who held power and sway over his life, like Dr. John Grand, could not, or would not, allow peace and dignity to be restored to him as a human being on this day, the *last* day he was willing to spend in the utterly alone and private hell he had been living in now for almost a year, then he would find that peace and final dignity himself among the stars in the summer sky overhead tonight.

In his small spartan apartment across the highway from the "Why?Not Market" in a relinquished and run-down part of the city known as Fruitdale, hidden in the bottom of a chipped ceramic flower vase where he kept his spare change, were seventeen 20mg Oxycontin tablets he had saved up from the prescription he'd been given for pain after the surgery. The old vase, which his two sons had borrowed from their Mother, had been a gift from them on his last birthday back in Kansas.

They had filled it with saffron yellow Plains daisies, Prairie violets, flowering Indian mustard vines, and delicate, pale, bluish-white Johnny-Jump-Up's they had picked in a field behind their elementary school. Alex, the younger of the two who had been only seven then, had painstakingly written on the white vase with a red magic marker, *"To our Daddy who loves a flour".* He hadn't known how to spell flower, so had asked his older brother Ethan for help. And Ethan, at age nine, always willing and ready to seize any opportunity to bedevil his little brother, had opened a kitchen cupboard and lifted out a powdery white, five pound package of Gold Medal, and pointing to the label on the front of it, had slowly spelled out loud to his little brother...*f-l-o-u-r.*

The drug which Kearnes had so carefully concealed in one of the few precious mementos he had left of his children was a potent timed release form of the powerful pain killer, Oxycodone Hydrochloride. When crushed and taken with alcohol it would triple the speed in which it would normally release its now virulent opiate compounds into a person's bloodstream, and the only thing that had kept him from emptying the vase onto his bed in the last few days, and going to the refrigerator for the bottle of Blue Goose vodka he kept there, was one simple word scrawled in a child's tentative and halting hand in red on a dingy, cracked piece of pottery—*flour.*

He looked long and hard for them, but the swans were gone now.

Britt was gone. His world back in Kansas—Tilley, his children—all gone now, as if both the choices he had made and the choices he was incapable of making in his past had swept away the landmarks he'd once been able to so clearly see in his life.

Like a fast rising tide pushing relentlessly against the shore, the terrain disappearing beneath its onslaught, Kevin Kearnes had foundered in a static, directionless landscape and lost his way from where he'd come; forever. Now this new life, this new world he had discovered and tried so hard to keep intact, with all the promise he had once believed it held—it too, now, was all but indiscernible to him. If you stand on the riverbank of your life long enough, looking for swans, he thought to himself, you will only go blind from watching the disappointment of the past flowing by. Dark, troubled waters, with undercurrents, waiting to claim you; waiting to pull you down.

He looked at his watch. It was 8:45 AM. He had fifteen minutes to make the last six blocks to John Grand's office, and he could *not* be late for this last appointment. He hurriedly crossed the bridge and pounded down onto the concrete sidewalk of 7th Street heading north, a lance of pain traveling from the arch of his right foot up the inside of his thigh where muscle, tissue, and nerves were still mending. He clenched his teeth at the sudden hurt but continued on his way, paying a price in pain for his lingering at the river watching the swans, and now having to hurry.

Waiting to claim you, waiting to pull you down.

He never looked back.

If he had, he would have seen the swans in the middle of the river now, by themselves. They were side by side, heavy angel-like folded wings touching, gliding effortlessly downstream with the slow current, making their way with certainty toward the bridge where he no longer waited for them.

CHAPTER 2

▼

He crossed 7th at "M" Street, then turned right onto 6th at the old Lincoln Cleaners building. The front door was propped open and he jumped; startled at the sudden sound of the steam pressing machine going off inside as he passed by. It was a long, hot, hissing noise; like an angry Dragon cornered somewhere in back, hidden from view by the shiny forest of hanging dry cleaned garments sheathed in plastic bags that quivered slightly each time the press was brought down, then discharged.

He moved on and soon came to a large, blue, arched metal sign suspended high above the street from steel cables that proudly proclaimed, in bold white letters, "GRANTS PASS—IT'S THE CLIMATE", and which spanned the width of this busiest of all streets in the heart of the old downtown business district. There was a Dutch Brothers coffee stand there where he often stopped for a double iced Americano to go before he walked the last few blocks to Grand's office, but on this morning he passed it by.

Fifteen minutes on the forced march in the increasingly stifling southern Oregon morning sun had painted a sheen of perspiration on his forehead and upper lip, from both the physical exertion, and the pain. Finally, he left the sidewalk and started up a fancy river rock lined walkway. It cut through the middle of a wide swath of fragrant, late blooming summer perennials, which grew lushly on both sides of the carefully placed and leveled stones, and ended at the steps to the rough cut cedar sided office building.

Kearnes admired the healthy and obviously well cared for flower garden, and in his head he began to say first the genus, and then the common name, of some of them—*Delphinium grandiflorum*, "Blue Mirror", *Aster novae-angliae*, "September Ruby", *Gaillardia*, "Summer's Kiss".

At the top of the steps was a cedar shake covered portico. It was supported by two large columns of more grey and white speckled river rocks the size of bowling balls—solidly imbedded in thick perimeters of mortar—and ahead, a massive dark mahogany door with a small engraved brass plate on it which read, "Jonathan M. Grand, M.D.—Psychiatry and Mental Health Services."

Kearnes stood in front of the scalloped antique brass door knob, pausing to wipe the sweat from his forehead with the back of his hand and to slow his breathing a little, then reached out, turned it, and pulling the heavy door toward him, stepped inside. A blast of frigid air from the building's air conditioning hit him in the face, chilling him, and his eyes resisted the sudden adjustment to the now subdued lighting and dark furnishings of the office waiting room.

He could smell the rich aroma of fresh coffee being brewed and caught the faint sounds of a coffee maker gurgling through the last of its cycle somewhere down the hallway past the front desk where Maggie, John Grand's receptionist and nurse, worked. Her chair was empty, a pink sweater draped over the back of it. He could see why she'd brought it to work with her, feeling the goose bumps on his own bare arms rising now like angry little bee stings from the frosty arctic air that was nearly twenty five degrees cooler than outside the office building.

He bent over the desk to sign his name in the appointment book and noticed it was blank, except for his scheduled session at 9AM and one other at 2:00 PM, but with no name appearing next to it. He thought this was strange, because John Grand usually saw six to eight patients in a day with appointments running from eight in the morning until seven or later in the evening.

He was suddenly aware of Maggie standing in front of him next to her chair. She set a brown earthenware mug of steaming coffee down on her desk, next to his elbow, which had a trout, rising to a fly painted on it. "Chief Kearnes!" she said cheerfully. "How about some coffee? I just made it."

Kearnes quickly scribbled his last name in the book with the pen attached to it and then straightened up, meeting Maggie's azure blue eyes that were the color of a clear, unclouded summer sky. She smiled at him, waiting for him to answer. "I'm fine," he said, picking up the coffee mug and lacing his fingers around it, the heat spreading through both his hands. "And thanks for this…what has the Doc got the air conditioning set on in here, 50 degrees?"

"60, actually, but it feels even colder, doesn't it?"

She continued to smile at him as she took her seat behind the desk and Kearnes deftly, unconsciously, moved two steps away from her, adjusting his personal space the way cops do without ever thinking about it after so many years on the job. She was married, as evidenced by the gold diamond wedding band she wore on her left hand, and in her late fifties he guessed; comely and full figured. Her long wheat colored blonde hair was streaked in places with silver gray and pulled into a bun on top of her head, revealing the downy, silken hairs on the back of her neck. She dressed conservatively and wore small, stylish, cobalt blue metal framed glasses with rectangular lenses low on her nose, peering over the tops of them at Kearnes with her perceptive and penetrating blue eyes.

Her appearance was almost matronly in a way and was probably a wise choice for a Psychiatrist's office that dealt with a plethora of the sexually walking wounded on a daily basis. There were those patients of John Grand who didn't need the further incitement of some salaciously sweet young nurse with silicone breasts in a tight uniform entering their psyches involuntarily; or consciously welcomed into their fantasies from just sheer boredom as they waited for their appointments. But older woman or not, Maggie was still quite attractive and she smelled like the lovely, soft, apricot colored blooms of some of the flowers that grew in the carefully tended soil outside John Grand's office.

Maggie had been the only woman in Kearnes' life of any importance for the past nine months other than Mrs. Schickter, his female physical therapist, whom he disliked intensely. She had a constant toxic smell of cigarette smoke that enveloped her body like a heavy smog above a smoldering, garbage strewn landfill, and he'd had to endure the very impersonal poking and prodding of her fingers—that were shaped like thick, red, German sausages—every Monday and Friday afternoon since shortly after he'd been discharged from Hospital. Kearnes had come to cherish the few private moments he usually had alone with Maggie on Tuesday mornings before his sessions began.

The brief interludes he enjoyed with her, being the first patient of the day, served to somewhat buoy up his faith in himself for a time and in the feminine half of the species he had so long been engaged in a tug of war with in his life as a man; the legacy Beek had left with him on that forgotten beach so long ago as a child. He craved the lost feeling of connectedness to women in general, the reassurance that he was still desirable as a man and had something to offer them in some way or another. In time as the empty days of his week dragged on the effects eventually wore off, and Kevin Kearnes reviled himself and was left with the belief that he in fact had nothing to offer women, or people in general, or even life any more.

But when he spoke with Maggie it was like a single, delicate, gossamer strand of a spider's web ethereally linked him to Britt, through her. It was as if he had sunk the shaft of a thin well of disciplined thought, unseen, deep into Maggie's feminine being and quietly, clandestinely, dredged up small buckets full of memories of Britt…from which he drank like a man dying of thirst. The lyrical melody of laughter in Britt's voice trailing off into the boom of the ocean surf as he played with her, chasing her on the beach at Cutter Point…the achingly beautiful swell of her breast beneath an old white cotton T-shirt of his she wore in the dimming summer light of her cabin's living room…the smell of their lovemaking on her skin and in her hair when he awoke in the morning next to her; on all those mornings after…like warmed honey.

"I heard on the radio on the way in this morning it's going to be 105 today," Maggie said. Kearnes tried to take a first sip of his coffee but it was still too hot—it smelled wonderful.

"No way," he said. "That would make four…no, wait…five days in a row that we've broken a hundred."

Maggie moved the appointment book off to one side and sat down behind her desk. "Yes, can you believe it?" she said. "And I checked the thermometer in our parking lot on the way in—it's 85 already!"

She started to take a drink of her own coffee, then abruptly put the mug back down. "Oh…I got so busy I completely forgot to tell you! Doctor is running a little late this morning and he wanted to know if you were here yet. He called in on his cell phone just before you got here. He should be here in about thirty minutes."

Kearnes blew lightly on the still too hot, steaming coffee. He repositioned his fingers so they wouldn't blister, exposing the hand painted, highly stylized chunky Rainbow trout whose wildly bulging eye stared back at Kearnes as it snapped, mouth agape, at the Mosquito pattern fly that floated tantalizingly above its head.

"Late?" he said, keeping his eyes on the curls of steam rising from his mug. "As in he had an emergency at home, or with some patient? Or late as in the fish were biting like crazy, and he just couldn't pull himself off the river, *late?*"

Maggie reached for her coffee mug again and brought it to her pursed lips. She flicked at the rim of the cup lightly with her tongue, the coffee still way too hot for her, also, and Kearnes saw her smile begin to fade into an expression of irritability.

"Late…as in fly fishing at Rainie Falls again, I'm afraid," she answered. Rainie Falls was a perilous spot on the river accessed only by a narrow, winding footpath down into the bottom of the Rogue Canyon, but just thirty minutes from Grants Pass. Zane Grey had often fished there in the 1920's and it was one of the main reasons John Grand had moved to this part of southern Oregon almost twenty years ago from Detroit—the other "reasons" being the trout rich riffles near Galice, Foster Bar, Clay Hill Rapids, and the place on the upper river everyone called "The Holy Water"—each in their own right Mecca's to many other Rogue River fly fishermen who were as passionately immeshed in their sport as he was. "Just look at this place!" she said, sweeping an arm from corner to corner of the expansive waiting room. "The man is absolutely hooked!"

Kearnes looked at the knotty pine paneled walls that held trophy mounts of fish John Grand had taken from streams, rivers, and lakes around the world. A collection of delicate split bamboo fly rods from the time just before, and shortly after, the Civil War, which included some ancient, patina burnished iron fly reels; rested in repose behind sparkling clear glass in a dark walnut display case. The display case stood upright like a sentinel between two waiting room couches that were covered in heavy, darkly tanned cowhide. The thick leather was snugly pounded into their weighty, wooden frames with brass head tacks, and the long, broad, pine arms of each couch extended outward like the arms of a resting Sphinx.

There were a few matching lacquered pine chairs with slatted backs and cowhide cushioned seats on the opposite side of the room, and on the solid oak coffee table in front of the couches were spread an assortment of men's hunting, fishing, and health fitness magazines. The magazines were fanned out in a proud array, as if every one was a winning card in a hand of poker left there when the game had, for some inexplicable reason, suddenly ended. Dr. John Grand was not only a consummate fisherman; he was also a fisher of men. Kearnes had never once seen a female patient in John Grand's waiting room.

"Hooked?" said Kearnes, raising an eyebrow at Maggie to try and soothe the moment. "Is that a pun Maggie?"

She looked up at him and saw the slight grin at the corner's of his mouth, tentatively waiting on her go-ahead to proceed into a smile. She furrowed her brow, hesitated, then made the decision to exchange her anger for exasperation—and instead laughed.

"I'm so sorry for this," she said, "and I feel like I should apologize for him." Her eyes scanned his face for both his reaction and a sign as to how she should continue. "I know his first rule for every patient is that they are here on time for their appointments...then he goes ahead and breaks that rule himself. What kind of man gets up at 4:30 am to go fishing before he goes to work?"

"Don't worry about it," Kearnes said. "Every man has the right to one obsession. Even the Doc himself, I suppose. Or so he's told me."

"It's just that I know how important today is for you," she said. "And I don't want you to think he isn't aware of that, or isn't taking it seriously." Kearnes saw her cheeks coloring a little, a pink flush starting to spread from them down to her throat. The heat from her face began to radiate her perfume in the cool air of the waiting room, and he breathed her scent in deeply. It was so *good*, so intoxicatingly pleasing. He tried to remember Britt's exact smell, but couldn't at this very perplexing moment…only that she had smelled very differently from Maggie. Britt's was an even more compelling feminine essence that had collided deep within his brain and groin simultaneously, assailing his sense of reason whenever he had been near her; igniting fires inside him that he knew one day were probably going to burn him to the ground.

But he did clearly remember the name of Britt's exotic perfume. Twice in the past six months he had driven the twenty five miles to the Rogue Valley Mall in Medford and gone to the cosmetics counter at Meier & Frank, where he had lied to two different salesgirls about shopping for a gift for a wife he didn't have. He had feigned interest in several very expensive perfumes they eagerly sprayed onto little white cardboard squares for him to sample, until finally he asked to see the small black bottle of Paloma Picasso, and a tiny spray of it was spritzed onto a new square for him. He would then thank them, ending the contact and saying he would be back when he'd made up his mind, and hurrying out of the Mall, pinching the precious sample between his right thumb and forefinger, would rush to his parked truck. Locking the doors and sitting with his head back against the seat, eyes closed tightly shut, he would hold the perfumed cardboard square jammed tightly beneath his nose, covered by his hands, and breathe deeply of the memory of Britt.

Now Kearnes began to feel a little chagrined himself. He was nervous and tired, keyed up by the confrontation he felt the morning was going to bring. "Well, you're my witness, right?" he said. "I busted my butt to get here on time…a little early even…and he's now late. The first time ever. And on my last day, too."

Maggie stood up and came around the desk. She gently took the coffee mug from his hands and set it down on the desk beside hers. She took both of his hands in hers and stepped slightly back. Kearnes tensed at first, and then slowly began to yield to the first personal, intimate touch from a woman he'd experienced since he'd been with Britt on their last night together in Cutter Point. Maggie's skin—her touch—sparked a tactile, last memory of Britt; bent over him on the rescue basket on the jetty, her mouth kissing his face, sobbing his name over and over through ragged, convulsive breaths that were swallowed up by the roar of the helicopter blades above their heads. Britt holding his face between her hands tenderly; her mouth working in a tortured communication he could no longer hear—then utter blackness.

"This is so wrong of me," Maggie said. "But in another way, it is also so right." Kearnes started to look away from her, but could not. "Just once, today, before you go…if it is all right with you…I would like to call you by your first name…Kevin…and I would like to tell you something both very personal, and very important."

Kearnes felt the soft, yet insistent pressure of her fingers squeezing his hands. He looked at her, knowing that she probably knew it all; knew everything that had happened to him—his life history, his job, Britt—everything—because she transcribed all of John Grand's reports. She *knew* him in that sense, but he didn't really know anything about Maggie at all. Kearnes had always been aware of the kindness she'd shown towards him, her sincere manner, and her seeming interest in his plight; even though his cynical and innate survivor's sense of self-preservation had intentionally positioned Maggie and everyone else he'd ever met in his adult life at a certain safe distance from him. This had all been calculated to keep his heart, and his secrets, inviolate, and it had always worked without fail with everyone. Everyone that is, except Britt—his first, and last, fatal mistake.

He couldn't answer her, didn't want to answer her. He stood absolutely still, feeling the connection her body had made with his flowing through him like a warm, low voltage current. Finally, he nodded his head slowly *yes* to her.

"Kevin," she said.

He did not respond further, and looked past her now as if she were some stranger who'd stopped and asked him for directions to a place he'd never heard of before.

"Kevin?" she said again, this time giving his hands a little tug that drew him back in.

"You are going to be OK today…you will do just fine," she said.

His eyes met hers again and he stared silently at her for a long moment, and then said, "I'm sorry. But I don't seem to have the same level of confidence in myself that you seem to have in me. I wish I did." He started to pull his hands away from her but she refused to let go of him.

"No, listen to me! You are going to walk out of here today with your life back. I've watched you since the first day you came through our front door, and you are *not* that same man."

"And one more thing," she said. "There are people in this town…just like me…who believe you are a hero for what you did! I think it's so sad, Kevin, that you can't feel good about that for yourself."

The sudden familiarity and intimacy he had with Maggie thrust him into the moment as an equal, and he felt both anger and a sense indignation take hold of him. He pulled his hands away from hers and turning his back to her, strode across the room.

"Oh really?" he said, his voice rising. "I saw the appointment book, Maggie. Is this why he's reserved half the goddamned day just for me? Because he thinks I'm such a changed man?" He both heard, and felt, Maggie swiftly cross the room to him. She put her hands on his shoulders and firmly turned him around until he was facing her.

Her eyes, no longer unclouded, began to storm over into a dark bruised, blue—the same color as the roiling sea at Cutter Point when the wind and rain would rage unchecked up and down the southern Oregon coast in the worst of the winter storms.

"John Grand is a brilliant man," she said evenly. "And if there's one thing I've learned working for him in the last eighteen years, it's that he never does anything without having a damned good reason for doing it!"

"Including being late to an appointment with a patient in order to go fishing?" Kearnes shot back.

"He's set aside half of an entire day for you Kevin!"

"He's making all this extra time for me," said Kearnes, "because he knows it's going to take him that long to explain my screwed up life to me one last time…and *then* break the news to me that my career is over, because of it."

Maggie fell silent. Kearnes saw the storm in her eyes beginning to recede now, and a shimmer of tears appear to take its place.

"If you could only see yourself now, Kevin. *Now.* Compared to how you were. You would know." When he saw her on the verge of crying, biting her lip to regain her composure, he felt the hot, hard, inner core of himself flame out. He leaned forward and touched her on the shoulder.

"I appreciate the way you've treated me, Maggie. And I am thankful for having had your friendship…for every kind thing you've done for me through all of this."

Maggie swallowed back her tears, and they didn't come. "This is going to be a great day in your life," she said cheerfully. "You just wait and see!"

Kearnes was quiet for a moment, and then the cop in him began to surface. "In all the years you've been here, have you ever seen him do something like this...for just one patient?"

"No, I haven't. But he does have another patient coming in right after you this afternoon, so I'd have to say today is going to be about two very unique people...that must both be very special to him."

"So this afternoon appointment...you're sure it's another patient?" Kearnes asked. "Do you know that for a fact? Or maybe it's someone from Salem...from the Department of Public Safety Standards. With my de-certification papers maybe?" Kearnes knew if it was in fact the latter, he would never work anywhere, ever again, as a police officer.

Maggie shook her head and smiled at him. "No, it's nothing like that. The two o'clock appointment is just another patient. Someone the Doctor has been seeing for almost as long as he has been seeing you, as a matter of fact."

Kearnes immediately felt bad about having verbally attacked her, especially when he'd seen the tears start to come, and so tried to bring back her smile. "It isn't that guy with the pool ball fetish is it? Because if it is, I want to be out of here and down the street before he even enters the parking lot."

Maggie laughed, and then began to blush. He wondered if she ever talked extensively with her husband at home about some of the truly bizarre things she saw and heard that went on in this office. Like the day "Mr. Rack 'Em" had walked in with two pool balls—the black eight ball and the white cue ball, Kearnes later learned—stuffed into his Jockey shorts and clicking together like two Spanish castanets as he made his way in a bow legged swagger to Maggie's desk to sign the appointment book. "Nope," she said, giggling, "it's not *him*, either."

She walked back across the waiting room, still smiling, and took her purse out from underneath her desk. "You'd just better hope he caught something this morning and isn't in a crabby mood because he got skunked," she said. "I'm going up the street to the Limestone Bakery for a few minutes to get some pastries for his coffee."

"OK," he said. "I'll hold the fort down while you're gone. How long before he gets here?"

"He was just leaving the wayside at Rainie when he called...maybe twenty minutes?"

"What do I do if someone comes in, or the phone rings?"

"I'll lock the door so no one will come in, and if the phone rings just let the answer machine pick it up."

"I'll even get you your favorite while I'm there, if you want."

"What's my favorite, Maggie?"

"That would be their vanilla crème filled Pershing donut with white icing and shredded coconut on top. I'll get you two...you're getting a little skinny for a man of your build."

Kearnes could not recall ever having told her that was his favorite, but being the first appointment on Tuesday and Thursday mornings every week he always had first pick from the large pink pastry box set out in the waiting room on a cart for patients, along with a carafe of coffee and paper cups. And invariably the plump, golden brown donut bursting with thick custard like vanilla crème, the top slathered with white icing and coconut, was always the one he chose. Maggie must have been watching.

"Sure," he said. "That sounds good. But I just want one." Kearnes reached into his pocket and came up with a dollar bill and started toward her with it but she waved him away—just as the phone on her desk rang. She picked it up and answered.

"Good morning, Dr. Grand's office. Yes...yes he is, but he's getting ready to...well, he is here, but...just a moment please." Maggie clamped her hand over the telephone receiver "It's for you Kevin. I think it's a policeman."

"Who is it?"

"Well, a very *loud* and insistent man," she said. "He says his name is...Thud?"

"Tell him I'm in the Men's Room," whispered Kearnes, "and that I'll call him later."

"I think you'd better talk to him now," she said, uncovering the phone and holding it out to him.

"He says he's the chief of police."

CHAPTER 3

▼

Maggie held the phone out away from her body as if it was an object that was audibly ticking and about to explode; as Kearnes came around her desk and took it from her. He could practically feel Thud seething on the other end of the line, but waited until Maggie had slung her purse strap over her shoulder, and then closed the front office door behind her as she left. When he heard the soft click of her office key on the other side of the door tripping the deadbolt lock into place, he put the phone's receiver to his hear.

"Hello?"

"Chief?"

"Yeah Thud. Hey, I've got an appointment in just a few minutes, could you call me…"

"Chief…we've got the bastards! Both of them!"

Kearnes slowly sat down in Maggie's chair, not saying a word. He knew exactly which two "bastards" he was talking about, but he wouldn't allow the excitement in Thud's voice to set him up for the ultimate emotional fall…not today…not now.

"Chief!" Thud yelled into the phone. "You still there?"

"Yeah, I'm still here Thud. But what do you mean, exactly, by *got?*"

"Got!" Thud howled into the phone. "As in they are screwed, blued, and tat-tooed! I just hung up with the Lane County D.A.'s Office and we are going to the Grand Jury next month on Mr. Roy Roddameyer and Mr. Vernon B. Bouchet´…otherwise known around our fair town here as *Fudge Packers, Incorporated.'"*

Acting City of Cutter Point police chief, Detective Sergeant Thaddeus "Thud" Compton, had a rare and unparalleled way with words for which he was renowned in local (and some even said state) law enforcement circles. It was a unique talent and characteristic which Thud had developed, and used to his full advantage, as an investigator over the years. And when other cops thought of Thud Compton, or talked about him, it was usually his skill as a self-taught police linguist which first came to mind. Followed by his manic homophobia, and his abilities as a field training officer of young police officer recruits; some of whom who had even lived to tell of their experience.

"Fucking assholes," Thud hissed. "And I mean that, literally."

Kearnes let all of this sink in for a minute while Thud, a hundred miles away on the other end of the line, recharged himself.

Roy Roddameyer, the fired ex-city manager, and Vernon Bartholomew Bouchet', Cutter Point's exposed, and now deposed, ex-mayor—and all their dirty deeds, and dirty dealings—to be paraded before a Grand Jury? And *not* a Cutter County Grand Jury either; where the "good old boy" system, as well as the many "favors" these two truly evil men still had out there in the community, just waiting to be returned, almost guaranteed their never being indicted for any criminal acts.

No; this would be a Lane County Grand Jury proceeding in Eugene, nearly two hundred miles removed from Cutter Point. Where no one knew anything about Bouchet' or Roddameyer; except possibly what they'd read about them in the papers or seen on television news. It wasn't lost on Kearnes either, that Eugene was also the Fifth District for United States Federal Court as well. A perfect place for the perfect change of venue from state criminal charges to federal racketeering charges, if the District Attorney' case began to falter in any manner, or if some ambitious and opportunistic federal prosecutor decided he wanted a career building piece of Bouchet' and Roddameyer too—just for the hell of it.

Kearnes realized he was holding his breath, wanting Thud not to say anything more, wanting so badly for all this to be true, because if it was...

"We're going to kick their asses, chief. Me and you. Kick their asses so bad, down is gonna' look like up to these two yahoos when we're through with them! And in "Roddafudgers" case, I imagine that's gonna' hurt pretty bad, considering what you did to him already."

"Thud," Kearnes said, "how did this all happen?"

"Top flight detective work is all," said Thud. "I've been on it again, for months...ever since a few weeks after you were gone. I've been digging chief. Going way, way deep. And it's finally paid off."

Kearnes was still trying to get his mind around all of this. His own investigation of Bouchet' and Roddameyer had been cut short the morning the last two bodies had been found on the beach at Pearl Cove Park…and had ended forever later that same murderously black morning on the giant rocks at the tip of the north jetty at Cutter Point.

"OK, here's what we've got," said Thud. "On Roddameyer: four counts of Official Misconduct first degree, three counts of Obstructing Governmental Function, seven counts of Solicitation of Criminal Acts, seven counts of Criminal Conspiracy, three counts of False Swearing…that's for his three recorded sessions at the Urban Growth Boundary Hearings under oath…and two counts of Felony Theft by Deception in the first degree."

"And on Bouchet'?" Kearnes asked.

"All of the mayor's charges are going to be the same as Roddameyer's," said Thud, "with the exception of the False Swearing. Old Vernon is only going down for one count of that, since he was smart enough to let his boy toy do most of the official talking in the U.G.B. Hearings; at least the three sessions we have on tape."

"Thud; who do you think you are going to find as witnesses in Cutter Point, or anywhere else in the County for that matter, who are going to be willing to testify against them?"

There was a pensive pause from Thud, and then he answered. "Well…me, chief, for one. And you. I need your testimony most of all."

And so there it was. The last thing Kearnes had wanted to hear Thud say. That he himself would have to be personally involved in any of this ever again. Would have to sit for weeks, possibly even months, in a courtroom looking at two men who had done their best to bend a small town filled with good, hard working people, to their own corrupt and depraved wills. Two men, who for the benefit of their own personal vices and financial gain, and seemingly limitless power hungry egos, had been willing to do anything; including trying to cover up a murder, and destroy Kevin Kearnes in the process.

"I don't think I can do that, Thud," Kearnes said quietly.

"Bullshit!" shouted Thud. "Chief…please listen to me for just a minute. Every charge I read off to you on Roddameyer and every charge I read off to you on Bouchet' is also going to be cross charged, one to the other, for a separate count each of Conspiracy to commit those same crimes!

"We are looking at *time* here chief, lots and lots of prison time. Even if the DA were to deal away most, or even all of the misdemeanors in a pre-trial settlement, the felony charges alone will be enough to reserve a little love nest for these two at the Oregon State Prison in Ontario, until long after you and I are both retired."

Kearnes thought about that word...*retired.* Apparently, Thud knew even less about the reality of Kearnes' life, and world, than he had imagined he did. The way Thud was talking, it sounded as if his boss had only been away for a short while—maybe on a much deserved vacation—and he was filling him in on a big case that had come into the P.D. while he was gone. But Thud also sounded like he'd done his homework, and like he was on a personal mission...one from which no one, not even Kevin Kearnes, could deter him.

"I have other witnesses, too," said Thud. "I have every member of the city council under subpoena, and every member of the Urban Growth Boundary Advisory Board, too. Some of them are dirty and some of them are just scared. But all of them, when they walk out of that Grand Jury courtroom after testifying, are going to know beyond a reasonable-fucking-doubt that if they don't tell the truth about Bouchet' and Roddameyer...their asses are going to fry right alongside them, in the same pan."

Kearnes wondered about another potential witness: Britt. Thud had never mentioned her name again after telling him that she had left town after having been interviewed for two days by both the local Task Force, and the Oregon State Police, and then testifying at the Grand Jury about what had transpired that morning out on the jetty; and the events, as she knew them, leading up to it. Including her relationship with Kearnes.

The same detectives had also interviewed Kearnes from his hospital bed at the Providence Trauma Center in Medford, as soon as he was listed as in stable condition. But their focus had been mainly on the incident involving himself and Roddameyer; and Britt's name had been mentioned only twice.

It wasn't Roddameyer who Kearnes feared confronting in court...it was Britt. He had done what he'd had to do, under the circumstances, regarding Roy Roddameyer, and he had been cleared by the Grand Jury. And even though he was relatively certain she wouldn't show up in court, now, as a witness in the case Thud was getting ready to present on Roddameyer and Bouchet'; Kearnes could not bear the thought of facing her in the physical condition he was still in. Even so, he knew she would be the first person he would look for in the courtroom.

She had never called him once, never written a single letter to him or even sent a card; and so by this time his devastation over losing her was nearly complete. How swiftly time can change things, and people, he thought. How ironic it was, he thought to himself, that even today, his *sea change* day, he would still give anything, would still do anything, including changing his plan…just to see her one last time.

"Do you have anyone else?" asked Kearnes. "Or is that your entire witness list?"

"Sure, I got some more people," said Thud.

"I got a couple of bartenders with ears like bats from two of Roddameyer's favorite hangouts, where he brought councilwoman McElvey for dinner, and drinks, of course—for about a month straight after the vote on the golf course had been postponed. Just after the bodies were discovered.

"She was so far gone with Alzheimer's, she really thought Roddameyer was her dead husband…and still does. And I know how unbelievable this sounds; but that slimy bastard was actually able to convince her to change her vote that way…by pretending that he was her husband.

"Hattie McElvey was a teacher of mine when I was in grade school. She's in a nursing home now, and will never be able to testify in court…but those two bartenders damn sure will."

Kearnes could hear the contempt in Thud's voice now. He had made no reference to Britt; but why would he? She knew virtually nothing about Bouchet' and Roddameyer's dirty business dealings; at least nothing she could effectively and directly testify to in court about. And the one criminal she did know about, Uriah Daniel Beek; she had already given her testimony to the Grand Jury on him while Kearnes still lay unconscious and fighting for his life in a hospital bed, with a post surgery infection rampaging through his body.

"Chief, look." said Thud, a touch of compassion now returning to his voice. "These assholes stole nearly six million dollars in public land and funds from the citizens to build a golf course in a town where there are more privately owned firearms, than there are four irons.

"They were willing to try and cover up the fact that we had probably one of the worst serial killers in this state's history, right here under our noses.

"They threatened to fire you if you did your job and tried to do something about it. Then, one of them tries to kill you; when you *did* do something about it!"

"I know," said Kearnes. "I was there, remember?"

"What I *remember* chief," said Thud, "is that this was *our* case from the very start…yours and mine. And I need you back on it, to help me finish it!"

"I'm sorry if you feel like I've let you down, Thud."

"Let *me* down? If you don't come back on the case, then you've let this entire town down.

"No one wants to come here any more, chief. Not to beach comb, or whale watch, or go fishing, or even play golf. We only get the film crews from 20/20 or 60 Minutes coming here; opening up all of last summer's wounds again on national television. Which scares the shit out of any tourists who thought it was safe to come back by now, and ends up bleeding this town just a little more dry than it already has been before."

"Yeah," said Kearnes, "here it is a year later and it's *still* news, Thud. And it's the very *best* kind of news because it's also the *worst* kind of news…about people's loss and suffering. You should know that about the media by now."

Kearnes knew all too well himself what Thud was talking about. The media, both national and local, had hounded him for weeks; from his hospital bed, to home. He'd moved twice already and had a pre-paid cell phone with an account that couldn't be traced, and that only Thud and John Grand's office had the number for. He never watched television any more, and had stopped reading the newspaper. Any newspaper. But Thud was *the* man. He was in charge of the Cutter Point P.D. in Kearnes' now much extended absence, and as such he had to be accessible and somewhat accountable to the media types who still encroached upon him in his job like ticks crawling along the back of a Rhinoceros.

"Yeah," grunted Thud. "You want to hear a little story about how this kind of "news" is working out for us over here?

"Well, check this out: in June we had some swinging dick Journalist from People Magazine come to town. I duck the asshole for, oh, I don't know…two or three days, but he finally hunts me down for an interview on a story he's writing about 'one of the deadliest killing grounds in the history of the Pacific Northwest'. It turns out he is some hot shot staffer who did a big feature for People a few years back on *The Green River Killer*…and won some sort of bullshit award for it.

"So anyhow, I give him his interview and he takes a few digitals and then he goes back to wherever the hell he came from; and I forget about the whole thing.

"About a month later we get a call on some type of disturbance down at the Public Restrooms at Pearl Cove. Dispatch gives it to Frick and Frack because our other units are tied up at the time, and so they start pedaling their skinny asses that way on their bikes, but they are clear on the other side of town when the call comes out…so I drive on down there.

"The guy who called it in is standing in the middle of the street, white as a sheet, and pointing to the Men's Restroom.

"So I go on in there and here's this fat dude on vacation from Vermont sitting on the can in a stall slumped over, with the last hole in his belt jammed over the head of a screw he'd backed out about half an inch from the top of the stall frame, probably with the little Leatherman tool I found on him later that's got a screwdriver blade on it. He's got the rest of the belt and buckle looped around his neck and pulled tight like a hangman's noose…and his friggin' pants and underwear are down around his ankles!

"His face is the color of grape juice, and he's got a magazine in his hands, holding it in a death grip; like he doesn't want to let go, no matter what. I get the belt loose from around his neck, get his airway open and he starts gasping and sputtering and drops the magazine…the floor is filthy in there so I pick it up. I mean, I'm thinking…what the hell kind of place is this to commit suicide, a Public Restroom?

"Then I realized it wasn't a suicide attempt…this freak was just getting himself off and it went a little too far. So I call out on my portable to get Medical started, because after seeing what I've seen so far there is *no* freaking way I'm doing CPR on this dude.

"Then I turn the magazine over and it's open to an article titled "*Murder Beach U.S.A.: Death on the Oregon Coast*". And, oh shit chief…on one page I see my picture…and on the opposite page is Beek's goddamned picture!

"Now it hits me like a ton of fornicating bricks. This asshole has been auto-eroticating in our Public Restroom!

"Whacking his weenie while choking himself out at the same time!"

What Thud described as "autoeroticating" was in reality autoerotic asphyxia, or AEA, a form of sub-intentional suicide involving sexual masochism, that used strangulation to enhance the pleasure of masturbation. Kearnes had read an article about it in one of John Grand's issues of *Focus*—the quarterly journal of the American Psychiatric Association—that Maggie had given him to look at one morning in Grand's office when he'd arrived a little early, and had tired of reading about casting for Bonefish in Florida, and trout fishing in Patagonia.

"Damn, Thud," said Kearnes, "do you think he was in Cutter Point for something that had to do with Beek? Or was it just a coincidence…I mean the magazine with *that* article in it…and opened to that specific page?"

"Coincidence?" said Thud. "No, it wasn't any damned coincidence. While I was helping the Paramedics with this guy I had Frick and Frack search his car. Want to know what they found?"

"What?" Kearnes asked.

"Sand," said Thud.

"Sand?"

"Yeah, sand. Beach sand. Dozens of Ziploc bags full of it. And all individually labeled, too," said Thud. "He had bags of the stuff from every single murder or abduction site from Crescent City clear on up the coast to Seaside."

"Do you have any idea what he was doing with it?"

"Selling it," said Thud.

"Selling it?" said Kearnes. "Where...why?"

"His laptop computer was in the car; we checked the History on it and found massive amounts of files on *eBay* that had been accessed in the previous few days, and motel and gas credit card receipts that matched his movements up and down the coast. As to 'why', I couldn't tell you...people are crazy nowadays, and will buy *anything* online I guess."

"Where inside the car did you find the laptop?"

"I didn't. Bikes R' US found it," said Thud, "A few of the sand bags were in the front seat of his rented Camry, and the rest in the trunk, along with the lap-top."

Bikes R' US was one of the tamer misnomers Thud used when referring to Frick and Frack. They were the two young summer bike patrol officers; college student interns who were back for their second summer tourist season in Cutter Point from the University of Oregon in Eugene, where they were roommates and both juniors in the University's Criminal Justice Studies Program.

He sometimes also disaffectionately addressed the pair as "the helmet headed morons," or, "the pedal files,"...a name he'd concocted to rhyme with "pedo-phile" after he'd seen the flocks of local Cutter Point teenage girls who congre-gated around Frick and Frack and their mountain bikes at the local Dairy Queen during their lunch breaks. Frick and Frack, in turn both suspicious of Thud and alienated by his at times overbearing, *ex-military*, homophobic driven ways and resentful now of his ultimate power over them as the acting chief, labeled him as "the Dick in the J.C. Penney suit," or "crew cut Cro-Magnon Man"—and now that Thud was temporarily back in uniform—"G.I. Joe."

"Did you get Tim to bring Fritz down and do a sniff of the car?" asked Kear-nes. Officer Tim Tavener was the department's K-9 handler, and Fritz was his 3 year old German Shepard police dog, who was both a "biter and a sniffer"; crossed trained to attack, and to detect drugs by scent. Fritz had bitten Thud once and now that he was acting chief it was apparent that he had not yet forgot-ten or forgiven the incident, even though those who were present the night it happened agreed Thud had brought it all on himself.

"What?" cried Thud. "That vicious animal? Hell no! I didn't want him down there. He probably would have torn that guy to shreds. Besides, I said we found sand...not dope."

"But you got a warrant first, right?" asked Kearnes. "At least for opening up the trunk?"

"Warrant?" said Thud. "Hell no I didn't get any warrant! When I saw that magazine with Beek in it, and this guy jacking off in a Public Restroom not two hundred yards away from the spot where that murdering bastard last stood, I ordered the Trike Patrol to tear the shit out of his car...to see what other weird stuff we might find!"

"Look, Thud, all I'm saying is...

"And all I'm saying!" shouted Thud, before Kearnes could get another word out, "is that things in this town, and this department, are all screwed up again! *Really* screwed up!"

Kearnes paused for a few seconds, letting Thud start to cool down a little while he carefully contemplated what he was going to say to him next. Thud Compton sounded like a man who had been pushed dangerously close to his limit; under more pressure than Kearnes had ever stopped to consider he might be experiencing in his role as the acting chief these last nine months.

The truth of what had happened that day at Pearl Cove was that when Frick and Frack had finally wheeled up to the scene—dumping their bikes on the grass in front of the Men's Restroom and running inside—they had confronted an enraged Sgt. Thud Compton, his fingers wrapped tightly in the hair of the hapless tourist from Vermont, plunging the man's head up and down inside the toilet bowl as if he were trying to unblock a stubborn clog.

They had both tackled Thud and drug him off the man, as the sound of the wailing siren of the Fire Department Medic Response Unit grew louder and louder, spiraling its way down from the Coast Highway to the Harbor area toward Pearl Cove on narrow, circuitous side streets.

"Thud," said Kearnes, "I wasn't there; so I don't want it to sound like I am judging you. But you've got to be careful. You can easily get the department sued for things like that."

"Careful?" cried Thud. "Sued?"

"Easily," repeated Kearnes.

"Let me tell you how I handled this case, chief, and see what you think: I got this guy dressed, checked over and cleared by Medical, and then had Frick pour all his sand back out on our beach, while Frack followed me into the station driving the guy's rental. I took the *jerk off* into Interrogation Room 1, and plugged in his laptop and made him watch while I removed his hard drive, and then smashed it into about a hundred pieces on the floor with a hammer."

"Then", Thud went on, "I told him to get in his car and drive east until he was across the state line, and to keep driving until he got home because if I *ever* saw his *sick*, leather belt hanging, *autoeroticating,* fairy ass in the State of Oregon again he would wish to God he'd stayed home in Vermont making maple syrup!"

Thud Compton was a former U.S. Army Ranger and past Cutter Point High School Pirates gridiron great; where he'd earned his nickname, *Thud,* from the sound he made on the field mowing down bodies on the opposing teams as he led the Pirates to victory his senior year and winning a State Championship trophy. He was a returned "prodigal son" of the community; having come back to the town eleven years ago, and had married a local girl, had kids, and eventually joined the police department as a patrolman.

He was probably not the most tactful, diplomatic, or politically correct individual to be in the position of acting chief of police; but Thud was definitely not a man you'd want to cross paths with, either, if you were a criminal. And on that final black and murderous day in Cutter Point, he'd proven himself to be a pretty damned good detective, too. It was doubtful that many more of society's vultures would be back anytime soon to land and perch at the edge of Cutter Point's misery and misfortune, surveying the tragedy that had transpired on the town's pristine, sandy beaches and thinking of how they might still make some quick, dirty money from it all.

"Now that I've heard the entire story," said Kearnes, "I think you handled it pretty well after all, Thud."

Normalcy had returned to Thud's voice again; his words no longer heated, his respirations slowing to the point where his hot, angry blasts of breath had ceased popping in Kearnes' ear like muffled gunshots.

"Yeah," said Thud, "I'm doing the best I can here, chief. And not meaning any disrespect to you sir…but *I'm* not the one who shot a city manager in the ass, either."

"No Thud, you're not."

"I only wish you'd have put one through that sorry son of a bitch's fishy looking eyeball," said Thud. "But, I guess you did stop a felony in progress; and any hit is a good hit under those circumstances. I'll bet that was the closest old Vernon ever came to getting a hole in one in his life…and using his own hole, on his own golf course, too!"

Kearnes laughed at Thud's comeback, and the tension between the two men dissolved completely. There was a creaking, grinding, metallic sound on the other end of the line as Thud Compton tipped his six foot four, two hundred and eighty pound beer barrel chested frame as far back in Kearnes' very expensive office chair as he could. The ominous sound was followed immediately by two close together, concussive *thumps*; which could only be Thud's massive size 14 Danner uniform boots hitting the top of Kearnes' very expensive and once beautiful, unmarred, executive oak desk.

"How is everything else going?" asked Kearnes. "How are you handling Polk and Downs? Are they giving you any grief?"

"Those two inbreds?" said Thud. "No, no trouble out of them. In fact, they are the ones *getting* the grief right now. The rest of the department is treating them like the lepers they are, and I'm finishing up their evaluations for you to review as soon as you get back. I'm recommending demotions for both of them…so we can yank their stripes…and hopefully they'll submit their retirement papers right after that."

"And Detective LaMar?"

"LaMar the Drug Czar?" said Thud. "Paranoid as ever! Spends most of the day in his office with the lights off, peeking out at the parking lot through his window blinds and looking for druggie 'hit men' who are after him." I let the federal grant lapse on his position last January…so him and his "program" are finished as of this coming December 31st.""

"That was smart thinking," said Kearnes.

"The asshole is now threatening to sue the department and the city," said Thud. "He's saying all the publicity on Beek and Bouchet' and Roddameyer pushed him into the spotlight, too, and now he's been 'exposed'. What a freaking mental!"

Kearnes felt strange now, as something foreign and nearly unrecognizable began to stir deep inside him. He had actually heard himself laughing at Thud over the phone, as Thud had somehow managed to engage him, drawing him back into a time, and a place, and a purpose he believed would never be a part of his life again. What was it Maggie had said to him? *You are going to walk out of here today with your life back.* What Kevin Kearnes was feeling, was *hope*.

"Are you watching out for Frick and Frack this summer?"

"OK," said Thud, "don't get me started on those friggin' Pedal Files! It's going around the department that Frick is supposedly dating some little Cutter High chick who is only sixteen…but Frack says it isn't true, and that the girl is really eighteen. He says he knows this for a fact because *he* is dating this girl's sister…who is eleven."

"Thud," said Kearnes, "they're only fucking with you."

"Yeah, I know," said Thud. "So hurry up and get back here, would you? Because I can't stand much more of this shit."

"I'm going to do my best," said Kearnes. "I should know a lot more about what's going to happen, after today."

"How's your leg?" asked Thud.

"Still healing…but a lot better," said Kearnes. "How's yours?"

"Oh, I'm all good to go again," said Thud. "Aches a little once in awhile, though."

"Chief?" said Thud.

"Yes?"

"I want you to know something. What happened that morning on the jetty…no one here that *counts* blames you for that. Not for that, or for anything else that happened before that, either."

"And chief?"

"Yes?"

"One more thing: Spenser still believes in you…just like I do. That kid has never doubted you for a second. He still looks up to you chief…still believes you're the "gunfighter" from Dodge City."

"You really think so?"

"Absolutely. You are *not* crazy," said Thud, "you've just been through some shit. We all have. You should call him sometime, chief. He's waiting to hear from you. He *needs* to hear from you."

Kearnes gripped the receiver of Maggie's phone so tightly he thought it might shatter in his fist, as he fought to choke down the lump that was rising in his throat.

There was a momentary pause, where neither man spoke. Then Kearnes said, "I will try to do that, Thud. And sometime soon."

"Good," said Thud.

"Thud?" Kearnes said.

"Yeah?"

"Do you have your feet on my desk?"

There was a sound on the other end of the line like two telephone poles crashing down in a storm, as Thud Compton's boots flew off the desk and hit the carpeted office floor below with a hollow *thump*.

"Not anymore, sir."

"Thank you, Thud," said Kearnes.

"Take care of yourself, chief," said Thud.

And then the line went dead.

CHAPTER 4

▼

Kearnes had just finished talking with Thud and hung up the phone when he heard Maggie's key opening the front door of the office as she returned from the Bakery. She was surprised to see that John Grand had still not yet arrived and apologized to him again; taking his coffee cup into the back and refilling it, then bringing it back to him along with the treat she had brought him from the Bakery. But Kearnes wasn't hungry now.

After listening to Thud and all the news he had given him from Cutter Point about the impending Grand Jury proceedings, and the possible criminal indictments which could follow, Kearnes was filled with equal parts of elation, and dread. Roy Roddameyer and Vernon Bouchet´ were venal, loathsome men; with the ethics of jackals.

They had not only harmed an entire community with their greed and insatiable appetites for power and status, but had also been responsible for setting the chain of events in motion to obstruct Kearnes and try to warn him off an investigative path he had unwittingly been on, which would have eventually led to them. And it had all ended with nearly costing Kearnes his life.

So, yes; he wanted both of these men in jail...unless the personal cost to him was something greater than he could afford. But what if this sudden turn of events was to come full circle around him—regardless of his actions, one way, or another—and because of it all, he might have the chance see Britt again? Even though he was very sure of how he still felt about her, the stark reality was that he had never seen, or heard from her again; and he didn't know how he would handle seeing her now.

He sat in the darkness of John Grand's office, having switched the lights back off after Maggie let him in, watching the blinding morning sunlight outside blaze white hot through the still nearly fully closed window blinds. They projected a pattern on the far wall of the office that resembled the bars of a prison cell, and Kearnes wondered if this wasn't more of a truth for him today, than it was just a simple irony. The once polar feeling air that hummed softly from the air conditioning vents in the floor was now starting to turn tepid, and finally becoming tolerable.

He surveyed the room—John Grand's inner sanctum—and was cognizant of how markedly different it was in appearance and décor from the waiting room on the other side of the door, which looked more like the showroom floor of a Cabela's outdoor store than a medical office. The Doctor's desk was made of heavy, dark cherry wood, its top gleaming from a recent coat of wax. It was bare except for a telephone, a sleek, black, flat panel computer monitor, and a matching computer keyboard which rested on top of a large tear off desktop calendar John Grand used to take notes on during sessions. The four corners of the holder the calendar rested in were fitted with triangles of thick reinforcing leather, to keep it from sliding off the desk.

The other companion pieces of furniture in the room were of the same kind of wood and included a mammoth book shelf situated directly behind the desk, filled with thick medical and legal volumes; and to the right of the book shelves, a credenza and hutch which held picture's of John Grand's wife and children, as well as a sculpture of a gleaming brass Dolphin, jumping high out of a non-existent sea. The guest sofa was also cherry, and as Kearnes sat rigidly on it now the butt of the weapon concealed underneath the back of his shirt sharply indented the plush green, and gold paisley sofa cushion fabric.

No art decorated the office walls. Instead, their was a multitude of framed medical degrees John Grand had earned; the U.C.L.A. School of Medicine, Johns Hopkins University, the University of Michigan School of Medicine, and other institutions…a hanging chronology in wood, glass, and paper of all the years of grueling internships, hard work, and commitment, which had resulted in his earning degrees in both psychology and psychiatry, and eventually becoming a nationally recognized expert in his field

Across the room on the wall opposite where Kearnes sat, was an antique Seth Thomas "Regulator" clock. Its original light colored mahogany wood case was shaped like a graveyard headstone. Made in the early 1900's, John Grand had retained all of its authenticity, including the black movement hands and black Roman numeral numbers; stark in their appearance against the clock's white face.

But internally he had had the clock's inner workings replaced with a modern quartz crystal movement which sounded a musical "chime" at ten minutes before the end of every hour; signaling the end of a patient's session. He had also installed a small digital movie camera, its tiny wide angle lens meticulously cut into the ornate wooden scroll work on the wooden case, and hidden perfectly.

On their first meeting in his office, John Grand had pointed out the hidden camera to Kearnes, telling him it was used mostly for his "court appointed" cases, and that he would never film Kearnes without his knowledge. John Grand had also told him none of the other patients he treated would ever be aware Kearnes was a police officer; unless for some reason Kearnes himself decided to tell them. But still, Kearnes stared at the old antique clock, and wondered.

The clock's chime began to sound; a soft *bong...bong...bong* sound, like a muffled cymbal being struck with a winter glove covered fist, and Kearnes looked at the clock's hands. It was exactly 9:50 a.m. as the "end of session" tones resonated from the clock, when John Grand opened his office door and stepped inside, turning on the lights. He was exactly fifty minutes late.

"Kevin," he said, nodding at Kearnes as he crossed the room to the office windows where he reached out and twisted the window blinds adjustment bar slightly, barely opening them just a bit further. "You look like a man in the dark this morning, for some reason. Did Maggie leave you alone in here like this?"

"No," said Kearnes. "She turned the lights on for me...I turned them back off."

"Are getting those migraines back again?" John Grand asked him, settling in behind his desk.

"No, I'm fine. I was just sitting here...thinking."

"Ah," said Grand. "Well I *do* apologize for being late. There was a hatch of *Isoperla Roguensis*..."Rogue Stripetail" stoneflies...predicted to begin this week on the river, and apparently my timing was impeccable...because I found them. The rainbows were literally rising up out the of the river after those bugs, like *The Raptured* being pulled toward heaven. I just couldn't tear myself away."

"Sounds like fun," Kearnes said, half sarcastically.

"Fun?" said Grand. "Yes, I suppose it is still fun for me after all these years. But now I seem to use the experience of fly fishing in an even more fulfilling, and productive way. It's how I do some of my most important thinking."

Kearnes stared into the gray-chrome, unblinking eyes of Dr. John Grand. They were the color of two lustrous and gleaming silver coins; and contrasted dramatically with the ruddy, deeply tanned outdoor complexion of his face. He wore sharply creased khaki Dockers trousers, and a long sleeve, light blue button down Oxford cloth dress shirt without a tie. The shirt's open collar exposed his tanned throat, and the top of his chest, where a proliferation of black, mixed with silver chest hairs sprouted freely out. His shirt sleeves were unbuttoned and rolled up to just below his elbows; where he'd left them in place after changing out of his fishing clothes and then washing up. On the inside of his left forearm Kearnes saw a single, iridescent fish scale still stuck to his skin. Caught at just the right angle by the inset bank of office lights in the ceiling above John Grand, it reflected back brilliantly; like a tiny, priceless diamond.

"But, that being said, I *do* feel guilty about being late this morning Kevin. It won't happen again."

"Again?" said Kearnes "Yeah, well, you're right about that. Because one way or another, today *is* the last day of all of this. Count on it."

John Grand smiled benignly at him. "Well yes…of course. We are finished here, as of today. I didn't mean to imply anything differently, Kevin. I was hoping, though, that we might keep in touch on a professional level with one another in the future. Just in case?"

"I think I'm going to be leaving the area, Doc," said Kearnes. "And I probably won't be back anytime soon. If ever at all."

"You know, guilt is a funny thing," said Grand, ignoring the finality of Kearnes' statement. "People generally think guilt is a bad thing; something we shouldn't ever have. But it can be a very strong force, Kevin. A *powerful* force, in motivating our behaviors…for doing either good, or evil."

Kearnes tried to will his spine to gently relax in small increments, hoping John Grand wouldn't pick up on his attempt to feign being calm and unperturbed at this typical, yet jarring, psychiatrist like comeback. But John Grand was like a janitor working on the night shift of Kearnes' mind, roaming at will through his secret corridors and dead set on finding where all of his dirty little hiding places were in there. And determined to sweep them all clean.

"What the hell is going on here today?" said Kearnes.

"What do you *want* to go on here today?" answered Grand.

"So…what is this?" asked Kearnes. "Like my final exam or something? Has this been some sort of test you've been putting me through all these months?"

"This has never been a test of any sort, Kevin. This has been therapy; and therapy is not a test. To see if a patient passes, or fails.

"Therapy is the telling, and sometimes retelling, of the *story* of a person's life. Their experiences, situations, and certain challenges they may have faced; and how they feel they have fared, either positively, or otherwise, in doing so.

"So, this last session is going to be about *your* story, and *your* understanding of it. And I suppose, to some extent; Dr. McGraw's story, also."

"Her name is Britt."

"Well, to you, yes," said Grand. "But I'm sure you understand that I must acknowledge her as a colleague, also. Much like you would another police chief you might meet. You may not know them personally, but you would only naturally extend them the professional courtesy they deserve."

"I don't want to talk about her anymore," said Kearnes, flatly. "Let's just get whatever this is; over with."

"Unfortunately...or maybe even fortunately, as the case may turn out to be, we are going to have to talk about Dr. McGraw. As well as a few other things, too."

"But first...I'm thirsty, and in need of some refreshment," said Grand. "Before we get started, would you like something? More coffee, or a soda?"

"No," said Kearnes

John Grand reached over and punched a button on his office desk phone and never taking his eyes off Kevin Kearnes; spoke towards the office phone's intercom speaker without picking up the receiver. "Maggie? I left a tray on the counter in the break room. Could you please bring it in now?" Kearnes heard Maggie acknowledge Grand's request, and less than a minute later she entered the office carrying a large circular platter containing two empty crystal tumblers, a small white plastic bucket nearly overflowing with ice cubes, and a tall, slender, green bottle of Scotch with a creamy, buff colored label.

Grand tapped the empty, expansive area of his desk in front of him with a forefinger and Maggie carefully set the tray down in that location; then looked at Kearnes and rolled her eyes slightly at him before she turned and left the office, as if to tell him now *she* wasn't so sure what John Grand was up to, either.

"Do you know what the Ancient Celts called Scotch whiskey?" he asked Kearnes. "They referred to it as "*uisge beatha*", which means, "the water of life.""

Grand reached for the bottle of twelve year old Glenlivet, and Kearnes watched as he ribboned off the green foil label on the bottle's neck in long, thin, metal Curly-Q's...then tugged out the deeply imbedded cork. He dropped four chunky ice cubes into each glass before tipping the bottle above first one glass, and then the other; letting the golden amber liquid run over and around the ice cubes until both were filled to just below their rims. He slid one of the filled glasses to the edge of his desk in the direction of Kearnes, and picked up the other one himself.

"To the *waters* of everyone's life," he said, gesturing his glass outward in a salute to Kearnes, then bringing it back to his lips and taking a drink. Kearnes stared at him as if *he* might be the crazy man, here for therapy, instead of himself.

"It's ten a.m.," said Kearnes. "I don't want a goddamned drink."

"Then what is it, you think, that you do want?" asked Grand.

"What I want?" said Kearnes. "Or what I know I'm going to end up with?"

"Want," said Grand. "Your purest, most selfish desires. Nothing held back…no obstacles in your way of any kind to prevent you from getting it. And right now."

Kearnes was bewildered by John Grand's demeanor, which had now turned uncharacteristically antagonistic, and provocative. In the months Kearnes had been seeing him they had settled into an easy, formulaic, first name basis relationship that was at times uncomfortable for Kearnes, but never threatening—like it was now.

"O.K.," Kearnes said, cautiously. "I'd like to have my badge back…my *career* back. I would like my sons back in my life; and to be able to be their Father again. I would like to see Britt…just one last time; to tell her some things that I was never able to say to her. And I would like the power to go back in time and change my life; so that none of this would have ever happened."

"Interesting," said Grand, setting his drink down. "Particularly, your desire to never have had to deal with any of your past."

"You asked," Kearnes shrugged.

"You see," Grand said, "people's attitudes toward the past are often much the same as their feelings about guilt. In fact the two often go hand in hand…and that can be a mistake, Kevin. The things from our past are in a way very much like latent fingerprints that have been left on our hearts. They are the intricate and unique patterns of the evidence of who we once were, and to some extent determine who we are now, and who, in some ways, we may *always* be.

"When people say…'what's in the past is gone, and doesn't matter anymore', it isn't just a simple lie we all like to tell ourselves in order to more easily cope with life's difficulties. It is a slander against the very existence, and worth, of the human soul.

"Do you realize that when you say you wish you could go back in time and change your life; that if you had you the ability to actually do this, you wouldn't have ever had your sons, and you would have never met Britt McGraw?"

"I wasn't thinking about it in *that* way," Kearnes said.

"Yes, I know," said Grand. "And therein lies the problem, I'm afraid."

John Grand's words sounded like a death sentence being read to Kevin Kearnes, and suddenly the air around him was filled with the smell of his own little boy fear. He waited until he was sure his doctor was through speaking, and then said very quietly, "You're not going to find me fit for duty, are you Doc."

Grand took another sip from his drink, and then set it down. He eased back into his office chair and swiveled it to his left slightly until he was directly in line with Kearnes, gazing earnestly straight at him.

"To tell you the honest truth," he said, "at this exact moment, I don't really know."

Kearnes sprang from the couch and rose to his full six foot two height, fists clenched, elbows tight in against his sides. An acute pain seared through the inside of his right thigh from the much too quick and impulsive movement, as if he had just straddled a live electrical wire. He glared at John Grand with pure, naked, hatred; overwhelmed with the urge to rush forward and smash his uncaring, smugly superior looking tanned face with his fist.

"This is finished," said Kearnes. "And by the way, one thing I left off my list of things I want? I wish to God I'd never met *you*. Good by, Dr. Grand."

Kearnes spun around and made it as far as the office door when he heard John Grand behind him shout, "Wait! I want to know about your assignment. Did you complete it?"

Kearnes stopped.

At the end of every session with John Grand in the preceding months, he had given Kearnes an "assignment" to complete before seeing him again. Sometimes it was reading material for Kearnes to take home with him. And at other times, there were odd directives. Like when Grand had assigned him to watch children at play in the Park every day for thirty minutes at a time, over a period of several weeks. He wanted to know how it made him feel; and Kearnes had sometimes had the strange sensation, while he was there, that he had been being watched by someone else himself.

But the last assignment John Grand had given him was to drive to the ocean, get out of his car at water's edge, and fill his lungs deeply with cold, salt air. And then see whether or not he would become sick to his stomach and vomit on the sand.

"I don't do beaches any more," Kearnes said, without turning around.

"Did you go?" asked Grand.

"Yes," admitted Kearnes. "I did."

"Back to Cutter Point?"

"No."

"But you went to the ocean? You stood at the edge of the water?"

"Yes."

"And you were fine, weren't you. You felt fine. No nausea at all."

"Yes," said Kearnes. "I didn't feel sick."

He hadn't been able to summon the courage to return to Cutter Point to complete this last assignment. So once he'd driven across the Siskiyou Mountains and dropped down onto the Coast Highway he'd turned left at Crescent City, CA instead of right toward Cutter Point, and had driven all the way down the coast to Trinidad, until he'd finally been able to pull his car over and get out.

"That's not only progress, Kevin," said John Grand. "It is also salvation."

He stood motionless, with his back still to John Grand. He reached for the door knob, and turned it. "Well, whatever it is," said Kearnes, "it's not enough."

Grand watched Kearnes pull open the office door and start to step out into the hallway, as he got up from his office chair to stop him. And as if he were back standing in the surging blue waters of the Rogue River with his fly rod in hand, John Grand deftly made a final, perfect cast toward Kevin Kearnes, using words of truth to conceal the barbed hook he so desperately hoped he would strike at.

"One last thing, Chief Kearnes," Grand said. "Out on that jetty; do you think you did what you did in order to save Britt...or to save yourself? Maybe to keep your secret...a secret forever?"

Kearnes froze in his steps. "Shut you're damned mouth, Doc."

"You walk out that door, Kevin, and you are *never* going to know the answer to that question. And I guarantee you that you'll spend the rest of your life, searching for the answer."

"I loved her," Kearnes said. "And I still do."

"You still love her?" said Grand. "Or you would just like to screw her again."

Kearnes slowly turned around and faced John Grand. His right hand started to go behind his back and underneath his shirt for the gun, and he saw a flicker of concern crease John Grand's face, his gray eyes narrowing and going steel blue with concentration.

"You...son of a bitch!" Kearnes shouted, as he crossed the twenty feet of open space between himself and John Grand in a blur. His knees slammed into the front of Grand's desk as he swung his hand, palm open, down and across at the full glass of liquor Grand had poured for him. The glass exploded into shards, and a mist of very expensive Scotch, mixed with Kearnes' blood, sprayed across the front of John Grand's shirt.

The office door flew open and Kearnes heard Maggie scream; he looked up and saw her standing in the doorway, her hands covering her mouth as if she was trying to stifle another scream.

"Maggie!" Grand yelled, "get some paper towels! NOW!"

Maggie ran into the office restroom down the hallway near the waiting room, and then returned to the office, wads of white paper towels bunched up in both her hands. Grand took a sheath of towels from her, folding them over the profusely bleeding gash in Kearnes' hand like a thick paperback book, and then closing his fist with pressure. "Keep your fist tight," he said. "Maggie…sit him down on the couch. I'll be right back."

Maggie guided Kearnes over to the couch, and sat next to him, searching his face for some kind of explanation. There were tears in her eyes and she used some of the paper towels she still held to blot them away.

"Well, so far," Kearnes said to her, "it's not going too well."

Before she could respond, John Grand was back, his arms full. He set a first aid kit, a tube of antibiotic ointment, and a new glass, down on top of his desk, and draped a clean, white dress shirt over the back of his office chair. Taking some more paper towels from Maggie, he walked over to the base of the Credenza where he bent over and with the towels, picked up what was left of the bottom of the broken glass where it had landed on the carpet. He walked back to his desk and dropped the fragments of glass into his wastebasket.

"Thank you, Maggie," he said. "You can go now. And whatever else you may hear going on in this office, I want you to stay out front. Is that understood?"

"But doctor, don't you think…"

"*Is* that understood, Maggie?"

Maggie looked at Kearnes, who had no expression on his face; then at John Grand. "Yes," she said. "I guess I do understand." She walked out of the office without saying another word, closing the door quietly behind her.

John Grand told Kearnes to stand over the wastebasket while he dressed the wound, letting the blood soaked wads of paper toweling drop into the wastebasket below as he worked. "You'll need some stitches in this later this afternoon," Grand said, "but it will hold until then." He asked Kearnes to sit back down on the couch while he changed into the clean shirt, wadding the dirty one up and throwing it into a bottom drawer of his desk. He poured Kearnes another glass of Scotch—this one not quite so full—and set it on a coaster on the arm of the couch next to him.

"In light of your current emotional state," he said, "I think I am going to have to ask you for the gun before we go any further, Kevin."

Kearnes now knew that John Grand knew about his weapon; had known all along that he'd had it with him every time he'd been in this office. There was no point in protesting, and even now, less point in not complying. He leaned forward slightly, then reached back with his left hand and awkwardly worked the small black Kahr P9 pistol out from beneath his pants belt, offering it butt first to John Grand who had come forward to receive it.

Grand took the gun back to his desk. He pushed the magazine release button and the magazine, loaded with seven rounds of 9mm Speer Gold Dot cartridges, dropped free, and he caught it in the palm of his other hand. Then he smartly pulled back the slide of the weapon, ejecting the live round from its chamber, which dropped onto the desktop with a resounding *plink*.

"There," he said. "Now, if you're ready; I need you to tell me your story, Kevin. One last time."

"Where do you want me to start?" Kearnes asked, resignedly. He reached for his drink.

"I think maybe the middle, this time," said Grand. "Yes...the middle. All really good stories seem to begin in the middle."

Kearnes took a long drink from his glass; the golden, smoky tasting liquor sliding hotly down his throat, spreading quickly into his bloodstream and soothing, a little, the throbbing pain in his bandaged right hand.

He sat quietly for several more minutes, drinking his drink.

Finally, he put his glass aside, and nodded solemnly at Dr. John Grand.

And then he began to tell him his story; from the middle. Of how it was he had come to live in Cutter Point, and the woman he had met, and fallen in love with there...but who was lost to him now, forever.

And of the little blue whales.

CHAPTER 5

▼

The middle of Kearnes' story had begun fourteen years earlier, when he met Tilly. He was twenty seven and she was twenty three, and he had been working for the Atchison, Kansas police department as a patrolman for two years since graduating from college in Wichita.

He was working swing shift one sweltering August Sunday night when he saw her red Pontiac Firebird parked on the shoulder of U.S. Highway 59 near the Amelia Earhart Memorial Bridge where 59 intersects with U.S. 73; the bridge spanning the wide Missouri River like the upturned palm of a giant, connecting the states of Kansas and Missouri.

She was sitting in the car with the emergency flashers on, crying, and she had a state highway map spread across her lap and an open can of Budweiser balanced on the dashboard.

At first he thought she might be drunk, but when he asked her to get out of the car her movements were fluid and unfaltering. As she stepped out the map fell away from her body and a small white tuft of fuzz drifted away from two eagle feathers that pierced the top of the back of her head, just above the place where her jet black hair was plaited in two thick braids that fell below her shoulder blades. Across her forehead she wore a tight buckskin headband, decorated with brightly shining glass beadwork, and around her throat, a hand painted necklace fashioned from the delicate, hollow bones of bird's wings.

She was the most exotic vision Kearnes had ever seen in his life; as if she were an ethereal being from the Kansas plains of a hundred years ago who had lost her way in history, and mistakenly wandered into the future. Her skin was a rich dusky brown, and her eyes stared back at him proudly through her tears, shimmering like wet, black, obsidian.

Tilly stood as tall as she could in her ankle length, hand sewn buckskin dress that was intricately beaded in the same fashion as her headband; fringed, the tanned leather the color of churned cows' cream sprinkled with nutmeg. With perfectly shaped, clean, bare brown feet flat on the warm highway asphalt, her lower lip trembling, she forced her spine arrow straight in an attempt to measure up to Kevin Kearnes but at barely five feet two inches tall her chin rose only to the level of the badge he wore on his uniform shirt, and she was forced to look up at him.

When she did, she saw a painful past dwelling in Kevin Kearnes' dark blue eyes, which were the color of a clear October sky...as well as her own expectant future. Like sheet lightning in a prairie storm, so distant that the actual strike itself could not be seen or heard, Tilly felt a sudden, velocious energy encircling her and this handsome young man dressed in blue. And at that precise moment, she knew she was going to marry him.

Traffic whizzed by all around them and the red and blue flashes of light from the overheads on Kearnes' patrol car bathed them both in eerie, revolving rainbows of color. She had stopped crying and was looking hopefully at him now. She had perfect white teeth that flashed back at him in the dark like moonbeams bouncing off a cut Kansas winter wheat field on a starry night. The expression on her face was both trusting and vulnerable, and as she gazed up at Kearnes and then moved forward close enough to him to touch, he felt his heart begin to pound.

But if either of them that night had known what the next fourteen years would hold in store for them, they might have chosen instead to run up the highway a short distance together, and holding hands, jumped over the railing of the Earhart Bridge into the dark, swirling waters of the Missouri River below. The odds of Tilly and Kevin surviving the plunge and swimming out of the treacherous currents to reach the opposite shore together alive, would have been better than the odds of their marriage ever surviving turned out to be.

"I'm lost," said Tilly. "I'm trying to get home...I live in Mercier, but I missed the exit."

"We can't stay here," Kearnes said, reaching in through her open car window and grabbing the open can of beer, which he noted was still completely full. "Get back in your car," he said, folding up the map and handing it back to her. "I'll get ahead of you with my lights on, then you follow me. I'll get you turned around in the right direction."

Tilly climbed back in the Firebird and started the engine. Kearnes set the beer can down next to the guardrail, tipped it over with his uniform boot, then got back in his patrol car and put on his full overhead lights and rear flashers as he pulled back out into traffic with Tilly following close behind.

He turned off at 14th Street and into the parking lot of a Denney's he ate at almost every night—waiting until at least 9pm to have his usual cup of coffee and piece of pie—the residual heat of the day still palpable and oppressive enough to keep him from wanting anything more.

He parked and walked over to Tilly's car where she waited for him, then leaned in through her window. "It's my dinner break," he said. "Bring your map inside, and I'll show you how to get home."

Tilly followed him inside the restaurant, still barefoot, and Kearnes met every raised eyebrow and askance look from the few customers inside with a steely eyed, practiced stare only rookie cops seem to have the ability to raise to the level of an art. They took a large booth way in the back, so Kearnes could see everyone coming and going at the entrance door, and keep an eye on his patrol car in the parking lot at the same time.

He ordered black coffee and a piece of Dutch apple pie and Tilly ordered mincemeat pie, which of course they didn't have in August, so she settled for blackberry instead. When her coffee came she put so much sugar and cream in it that it didn't look remotely like coffee anymore; more like a vanilla milkshake Kearnes thought, and he imagined it probably tasted like one, too.

Kearnes introduced himself, and she told him her full name was Tilly Elizabeth Two Trees, and that she was half Kickapoo Indian on her Mother's side, and French, German, and 'a little Potawatomi Indian' on her Dad's. She was a Pow Wow dancer then, dancing in Indian competitions around the state. It was what she liked to do for fun, and to keep herself out of the bars on the weekends.

She had been returning from a Pow Wow dance in Topeka, heading home to Mercier on the Kickapoo Reservation fifty miles north of Atchison, when she missed the exit to U.S. 73 and ended up crossing the bridge into Missouri...got turned around and made it back to Atchison, but the cars rushing past her so close cut her off and she missed the exit again. So she had pulled over to the side of the freeway and got her map out and tried to read it, but she was tired from the long drive; frustrated and scared by the seemingly never ending sea of headlights and cacophony of blaring motor vehicle horns streaming past her. She had searched underneath the front passenger's seat—starting to cry now—and found the can of warm beer. She had just popped the tab to take a sip and try and calm down, when suddenly there was a cop standing outside her car window.

"I hate driving in the city," Tilly said, loading her fork with blackberry pie.

"I wouldn't call Atchison much of a city," said Kearnes. "It's only about ten thousand people."

"Well compared to Mercier, it is," she said.

"It is pretty here though," said Kearnes. "People keep nice lawns. And they grow some really beautiful flowers, too."

"You like flowers?" Tilly asked, surprised.

"Yeah, I do," said Kearnes.

Tilly paused with a mouth full of pie and for the first time since she'd seen Kearnes, hastily glanced at his left hand for a wedding ring. She didn't see one, and her heart sank a little. She quickly swallowed her pie and said, "Why do you like flowers so much? You aren't gay or anything are you?"

Kearnes laughed and took a drink of his coffee before answering her. "You think I might be gay? Just because I like flowers?"

"Well, most straight guys could really care less," she said.

"Sorry to disappoint you," said Kearnes, "but I *do* like flowers, and I am *not* gay."

"Whew!" said Tilly. "That was a close one! And I'm not disappointed…just a little surprised is all."

"Well," said Kearnes, "I like other things, too. Guy things, if it helps any."

"What kinds of guy things?" said Tilly.

"Oh," said Kearnes, "like playing poker, and fixing things, working in the yard outdoors. Pheasant hunting…helping my Dad and my Uncle on their ranch…going to the movies."

"Hmm," said Tilly, pushing away her now empty, berry smeared plate. "Okay, out of all those things I'll pick two: flowers and going to the movies, because I love both of them."

The waitress came by to refill their coffee cups, asking them if they wanted anything more, and to Kearnes' amazement and amusement Tilly said yes and ordered another piece of pie; this one coconut cream.

Kearnes drank his second cup of coffee and Tilly was quiet as she waited for her pie to arrive. When the waitress set it down in front of her along with a fresh napkin and clean fork, she remained still until she had hustled away out of earshot to some new patrons three booths away who had just been seated.

"By the way," she said. "I can't pay for this. I left my overnight bag with all my clothes and my shoes and my wallet in it, back at the Pow Wow. I was like a hundred miles from there when I noticed it was gone. But I stopped and called them; they'll box it all up and mail it to me."

"No problem," said Kearnes. "I invited you, and so I'm buying."

"Give me your phone number," said Tilly. "I come to see my sister Gracie sometimes in St. Joseph. I can meet you here again, and pay you back."

"No, that's okay," said Kearnes. "Just add it to your list of the things you like."

"What?" she said.

"Pie."

"Oh," she said, looking past Kearnes, her face beginning to blush with the color of burnt sienna.

"I thought you meant...*you*."

Kearnes looked at her until she made eye contact with him again, thinking how crazy this was all getting. He didn't know this woman, couldn't even check her driver's license—that she'd supposedly left with her wallet and all her clothes and shoes in another city—to see if she was who she claimed she was. For all he knew she could be wanted, or have a suspended driver's license, or had maybe just killed somebody and was fleeing across the central Plains States. But she was so beautiful and talking with her, just being with her, so comfortable and easy...he didn't want his dinner break to end.

"Sure," said Kearnes. "I'd be happy to be on your list, too."

"So, if I was a flower," said Tilly, "what kind of flower do you think I'd be?"

Kearnes thought a few seconds before answering her. "Definitely a wild-flower," he said.

Tilly's lips formed into a mock pout. "Hey," she said, "I was thinking more like a rose, or an orchid or something. Why do I have to be a plain old wild-flower?"

"Because they are always the most beautiful," said Kearnes.

"Would you ever pick me wildflowers?" asked Tilly. "Or take me to the mov-ies?"

"Maybe," said Kearnes, grinning at her. "But I think I'd take you shopping first for a new dress, before we ventured out in public."

"Hey!" cried Tilly. "This is a Kickapoo Princess's dress. You'd better watch the insults, buster, because I've got some big ass brother's at home!"

"Sorry," he said. "I didn't know you were Royalty."

"Well I am," she said, stabbing a piece of his pie crust off his plate with her fork.

"And," she said, "I've got a good job at the B.I.A. and I've almost got my car paid off…but I think I am going to trade it in on a new Mustang first. Got my own place, too."

"It's a beautiful dress," said Kearnes, "but just not something I think you would want to wear on a date."

"Oh," said Tilly, "so we're dating now?"

"That depends," said Kearnes. "On whether or not I give you a ticket. I doubt you'd want to go out with me after that…if I did."

Tilly's eyes grew wide as she stopped a forkful of coconut cream pie in mid-air, halfway to her mouth. "You're going to give me a ticket? For what?"

"For the open container of alcohol," said Kearnes.

"I didn't even drink any of it!" said Tilly "It's not even my beer! Some guy at the Pow Wow who was hitting on me left it in my car, so I stuck it under the seat."

"Did you hit him back?" said Kearnes, trying to show her he was joking about the whole matter.

"No," said Tilly. "I just kicked him out of my car, the fat slob. I should have kicked his drunk ass for him too though, while I was at it." Tilly's face contorted in ugly remembrance of the quiet and shy male Kiowa dancer she'd met late Friday evening; who by Saturday night had morphed into an aggressive, threatening drunk in the back seat of her Firebird out in the dusty County Fairgrounds parking lot, trying to jam his hands inside her buckskin dress that had no real openings anywhere. Tilly, and many of her girlfriends who danced at the same weekend Pow Wow's, occasionally referred to them as "Paw Waw's," after their attempts to meet and socialize with men they met there sometimes turned into unfortunate incidents of unwanted pawing, or even outright sexual assault…always fueled by alcohol.

"*Please* don't give me a ticket," said Tilly. "My Dad is helping me pay off my car. He would kill me if he found out, and my insurance would go up too."

"Do you have insurance on that car?" asked Kearnes.

"No," admitted Tilly, "I can't afford it yet. But if I did, it would go way up. I got a DUI when I was twenty."

Kearnes saw Tilly put her fork back on her plate, and then begin to slide down in the booth where she sat diagonally across from him. He felt the first little brown toe of her foot begin to creep up the inside of his uniform trouser leg like a small animal, searching for its burrow. Then it was joined by her other four toes, and the ball of her foot, silky soft and warm on the calf of his leg as she rubbed it up and down against him.

"Well, finish your pie," said Kearnes, "while I think about it."

"Think hard," Tilly said, sitting back up straight and attacking the last remnants of her pie.

"I don't know," said Kearnes. "An open container of beer, no insurance...and a DUI?"

"That was three years ago!" cried Tilly.

"I'm behind on my quota of tickets this month," said Kearnes, continuing to tease her, but not wanting to let it go too far. "I don't know whether or not I can afford to pass up an opportunity like you."

"I should have known better," said Tilly, now finally realizing he was only kidding her. "My sister Gracie dated a B.I.A. cop for awhile."

"What kind of cop?" asked Kearnes.

"B.I.A.," said Tilly. "Bureau of Indian Affairs. She said he turned out to be a real prick after their first date."

"Why? What was wrong with him?"

"Oh, nothing. Gracie liked him a lot. But he ended up dumping her in the end."

"But you just said she said he was a prick."

"Yeah," Tilly said, "but that's just Gracie's way of saying he was...umm...a really good lover. She said he was a lot better than the average guys from the Rez she always dated, because the only thing they seemed to be able to get up most of the time was their fat asses from the couch. To go get another beer."

"Why did he dump her?" asked Kearnes.

"Because she's too wild," said Tilly.

"Are you wild?" said Kearnes.

"A little," she said. "But not like Gracie. "I'm a Princess, remember?"

Kearnes grabbed the bill from the table the waitress had brought by moments earlier, glancing at the total and memorizing it, and then stood up. He bowed deeply to Tilly, catching the attention of everyone in the restaurant and silencing their conversations.

Slowly he straightened back up, and in a very loud and as artificially deep a voice as he could muster, announced to her: "Princess Tilly of Mercier! On behalf of the City of Atchison, Kansas we welcome you! And in recognition of your royal visit to our community, I hereby void your traffic ticket and grant you safe and speedy passage through our town on your journey home!" He then tore the bill into a dozen small pieces and let them flutter down all around her, a few of them landing in her hair and sticking, like pale green snowflakes.

All eyes in the restaurant were now on them; even their waitress who had been on her way back to their table to collect the bill and her tip stopped in mid-stride a few feet away, a stack of dirty plates balanced in her right hand, a new bottle of Heinz ketchup clutched in the other…staring at them.

Tilly was more than just blushing now; her entire face was a colorful palette of all the emotions—some of them very contradictory—she was feeling for this strange, masculine, funny, and to her, overwhelmingly attractive young man she had met only an hour ago. She was exasperated, *and* amused at his behavior; embarrassed, yet thrilled at the attention he was paying to her.

"Oh my God!" she cried, staring around the restaurant, a horrified look on her face. "*Sit* down!"

Kearnes ignored her, bowed once more, and then offered her his hand to help her from the booth.

"My lady," he said dramatically, his hand outstretched toward her.

Tilly was laughing now, with an incredulous look on her face.

"You prick!" she half whispered to him.

"How would you know that?" said Kearnes. You don't even know me yet."

Tilly smiled broadly up at him, and then reached out her hand to his.

"I'm hoping," she said breathlessly, gazing into the steady brown eyes of her blue knight in shining armor. "I'm just really hoping."

They left the Denney's and Kearnes drove to the police department with Tilly following behind him. He showed her where to park her car in the public lot, and she waited for him to finish his shift, listening to the stereo and scanning through the big FM stations that blasted their signals into Kansas from St. Joseph, Missouri across the river. When Kearnes got off at midnight Tilly followed him home to his apartment on Utah Street.

As they started up the sidewalk to Kearnes' apartment complex he told her to wait under the street light, and then ran across the street and disappeared into the dark of a weedy, vacant field, emerging less than a minute later, clutching a bouquet of wildflowers in his hand.

He stood in blue phosphorescence of the street light, still in his uniform, the burgeoning, fragrant wildflowers in his right hand, a folding knife with a serrated blade and a clip on the side of its handle in his left…and Tilly's heart raced at the sight of this Warrior…*her Warrior.*

Kearnes held the flowers out to her as he pressed the back of the blade of the knife against his thigh, closing it and clipping it back in place in uniform trouser pocket.

"Here, these are for you," he said. "Baptisia australis."

"What?" said Tilly, taking the flowers from him.

"Blue wild indigo," said Kearnes. I saw them blooming over there last week on my way to work one day. I was surprised to see them. They are usually all finished by late June."

"I'm not going to sleep with you," said Tilly.

"I'm not going to ask you to," said Kearnes

Then they went inside, and Kearnes cut the stalks of the wild indigo's off even more to get them to fit in an old fruit jar he'd found in one of his cupboards, left by the previous tenant, while Tilly used his shower. By morning they had both broken the promises they had made to each other in the street the night before—and in their place—made new, more powerful, unspoken ones.

One month after that night Kearnes helped Tilly move from her "place" on the Reservation in Mercier, a battered old silver Airstream trailer that sat forlornly in a cow pasture like a giant spent bullet, next to her parent's home, and into his apartment. She commuted back to her job in Mercier where she worked as a receptionist in the B.I.A. offices for two months until the daily drive, fraught with the dangers of continually having to dodge prairie dog holes and drunk drivers on the road, began to take its toll on both Tilly's Firebird, and her nerves.

She quit her job and took out an "Indian loan" to enroll in night business classes at St. Benedictine College in Atchison. There was a big sign on the highway near the college which read: "Welcome to Atchison, Home of the Atchison, Topeka, & Santa Fe Railroad & Birthplace of Amelia Earhart," and sometimes while Kearnes was on patrol he would meet Tilly there for dinner—sandwiches, and hot soup in a thermos, and Indian fry bread—that she'd made for them at home before leaving for class.

One spring evening Tilly met him there, sticking her head through the window of his patrol car and kissing him deeply, her soft yet insistent tongue probing for his inside his mouth, like a well witcher dowsing for a hidden underground spring.

"Take me for a ride white boy!" she said excitedly. "My class got cancelled tonight!"

"OK," said Kearnes, "but feed me first. I'm starved...what's for supper?"

"Hmm," said Tilly, searching through the old wicker picnic basket she'd set on the ground. "Looks like good stuff tonight. Authentic American Indian cuisine."

"Read me the menu," said Kearnes. It was a standing joke between them that had arisen out of Tilly's insistence that she make all of their meals "from scratch";

and had resulted in largely breaking him of his fast food restaurant addicted eating habits, with the exception of stopping by Denney's on occasion for coffee and pie. It had been months since he'd last bitten into a Whopper, and as long as he had Tilly's delicious cooking in his life, he really didn't care if he ever tasted one again.

Tilly held up the imaginary menu in front of her and read from it. "Tonight's appetizers will be deep fried grasshoppers, dipped in a chilled pate' of pureed catfish guts. This will be followed by a special marinated grilled dog Caesar salad, and then tonight's main entree...baked Buffalo tongue with sautéed prairie dog gonads, a Kickapoo delicacy."

"Ugh!" said Kearnes. "Suddenly, I'm not so hungry anymore."

"Me neither," said Tilly, a look of growing excitement in her eyes. "Still got that blanket with you?"

Every Atchison P.D. patrol car had an old wool army surplus blanket in its trunk, along with a first aid kit, highway flares, and an assortment of other emergency supplies. There was a small grove of trees on the campus just south of the sign, and on the first night of her classes when Kearnes had met her here he'd joked about them taking the blanket from the patrol, car and making love in the dark inside the shadowy shelter of the trees.

"Yeah, I have that blanket," he said. "I thought you wanted to go for a ride?"

"I do," she said, kissing him again. "I want to ride *you*."

"Tilly..." he said, desperately searching for reasons *not* to get out and open the trunk of his patrol car, as the excitement of the prospect of actually doing what she was proposing they do spread to him also. "I can't. I'm on duty. Besides, that blanket is supposed to be for accident victims."

"You're going to feel like an accident victim, when I get through with you buster," she said.

Kearnes got the wool blanket out of his patrol car, and later they ate the food she'd brought as they patrolled slowly through the streets of Atchison, the second oldest city in Kansas, bumping gently over the brick paved streets in some of the historical neighborhoods, past beautiful old Victorian homes. The houses loomed large and white and ornate, above their neatly trimmed lawns set inside perfect white picket fences, soft yellow light glowing from their curtained windows like gold.

In August, on the very same night that had been exactly one year since they had met, Kearnes arranged to have the day off and asked Tilly out on a "date." They went to a 9 o'clock movie across the river in St. Joseph, and on the way home Kearnes stopped at the same Denney's he had brought Tilly to on that first night.

They went inside and nodding to the Hostess at the cash register, who Kearnes had called and spoken with hours earlier on the phone, saw her motion to a waitress nearby…the same waitress they'd had a year ago…who then quickly made her way to the same booth they had sat at one year ago, and whisked away a "Reserved" sign from on top of the table.

Kearnes ordered a cup of coffee and a piece of Dutch Apple pie, and Tilly ordered iced tea and a piece of coconut cream pie. When their waitress set Tilly's pie down in front of her she didn't see the diamond engagement ring half hidden in the whipped cream on top. She scooped it up in her first forkful, and nearly swallowed it before Kearnes grabbed her wrist, laughing.

He gently took the fork from Tilly's hand, and picking the ring out of the whipped cream, dunked it into his glass of ice water until it was clean, its diamond glistening with a clarity even purer than the crystal chips of ice in his water glass.

Then he handed the ring to Tilly, and asked her to marry him.

They moved to Kearnes' hometown of Dodge City Kansas six months later, and he applied for a position with the Dodge City police department. His previous experience in Atchison, along with his degree in criminal justice and his status as a native son, as well as being the nephew of a retired local law enforcement legend, Ben Kearnes, resulted in his quickly being offered a job.

They were able to buy a modest three bedroom home with a large fenced back yard on Sycamore Street, after his dad and his uncle Ben helped him with a loan for the down payment, and Tilly was warmly welcomed into the family; especially by his Mother, who looked upon Tilly more as a second daughter of her own, and not just her first daughter in law.

The years passed and Kevin Kearnes advanced steadily in his career, respected and trusted by his peers, and promoted by the upper echelon of the police department until he eventually reached the rank of patrol Lieutenant. He and Tilly had two sons, Ethan and Alex, born slightly less than two years apart, and their life together as a family then was happy; comfortable and predictable. For Kearnes there were never ending tasks to be completed—material accomplishments and the attainment of professional goals—which were the measuring sticks he used to determine his own self worth. He was the provider and the protector, Tilly was the nurturer; and he saw it as being in his best interest to keep their roles separated, and mutually exclusive, for the sake of his own emotional survival.

Kevin Kearnes had learned how to live at the surface of his life…on the top layer only; and what was most important to him was to look good, to sound good, and to do the things and act in the ways that were perceived by the rest of society as normal and good. The motivating force behind much of his behavior was his compulsion to appear to be just like everyone else. When in truth, inside, he felt he was nothing like them at all.

Others he knew seemed to strive to reveal the truths that existed in their lives, both past and present, in order to help them light the way into their futures. But he denounced and denied the existence of the single most crucial day in his own life, which had happened so long ago, when everything for him had been changed forever.

As an adolescent growing up he had for a very long time punished himself without relief; whipped himself daily inside his own insular mind for being a weak and helpless child who was unable to break free from the grip of a recurring and depraved nightmare he had. The dream was always the same. The boy…the tall young man the boy had met on the twisting banks of the Arkansas River that braided its way through and around the prairie flatland of his hometown, where he'd ridden his bicycle to go fishing one summer day with the new fishing rod and tackle box he'd just been given for his birthday the day before…the unspeakable horror that followed.

The boy in the dream was sometimes himself, and sometimes some other child who he did not recognize; but the tall man was always the same…always did the same things to the boy. At the end of the dream the boy always escaped from the man, although he could not remember exactly how. The boy lived, and came to understand how desperately important it was for him to keep secret what had happened. At all times and at all costs; he must always keep the secret.

But the boy in the dream, who was still alive after the man had finished with him, really wasn't able to live his life again at all. Instead, he only *existed* in a netherworld, which was truly a hell on earth. And so one night before the dream came again Kevin Kearnes, who was by then, twelve, prepared himself. He decided he could not allow the boy to leave the dream another time…alive.

The boy that the man hadn't killed that day in the thick concealing nest of bitter willow bushes he had dragged him into, jerking the new fishing rod from his small hands and snapping it in two as if it were a dry brittle branch, jamming his face down into the black soil of the river bottom to silence his screams with a massive, muscular hand, that closed over the back of his head like an opened catcher's mitt…this was the boy Kevin Kearnes had finally killed through the sheer power of his will. It was if he had reached deep inside a room in his mind and turned a light switch off, casting everything into a quiet darkness.

He'd had to do it. Because it was the only way he was ultimately able to make himself believe that none of it had ever really happened. It was the only way he could give himself permission to go on living; and when he finally did, the dream stopped…and had never come again. But what was unknown to him then, was that the real nightmare of his life had only just begun.

For Tilly, her decision to be with Kevin in the beginning had been based largely on her strong need for safety and security, in an unsafe and insecure time in her life. It was also the reason why she had grabbed so quickly at the rescue line Kevin Kearnes had subconsciously dangled in front of her then. She felt so differently about him now. The years of sharing a life and a bed with him, having babies together, the many nights she spent staying up late worrying about him at work as he patrolled the streets of a city which was once called "The wickedest town in the West," had transformed her feelings for him into what was now a deeply real, and committed love.

And it was at this pivotal point in their relationship, the place where Tilly had finally arrived after years of giving and giving to him of herself, with little or nothing in return, that she finally understood the one thing she desired and needed from her husband the most—himself—she would never be able to have. Their world began to crumble and disintegrate into a failure as fine as dust, as she first watched, and then felt, Kevin begin to withdraw from her more and more, a little at a time.

As Tilly pressed him even harder for him to love her, a storm of unknown origin began to build inside Kevin as dark and inevitable as a bruised and brooding Kansas summer horizon, the air static and heavily charged, signaling the tornado which would soon arrive.

There were arguments. Screaming matches which ended in doors being angrily slammed by both, in precautionary warning of what might result, someday, in a final leaving by one or the other. Tilly began to drink, and threaten—with the greatest disrespect—their family's financial security by running wild with their credit cards.

She bought countless numbers of cheap and unnecessary items which they didn't need, and would never use, and sent large amounts of money to her sister, Gracie, to help her shore up whatever current financial calamity she might be facing as the direct result of the reckless and irresponsible lifestyle she chose to lead. In response, he cut up all of their credit cards, opened his own checking account, and took over completely the task of paying all of their monthly bills…and threw himself even harder into his job.

And so they went forward with the dark process of killing their love for each other, both believing they were in the right, and neither wanting to acknowledge the simple truth that there is no greater destructive power on earth, than to use another persons own capacity to love against them.

But in the end, that is exactly what Kevin and Tilly did to one another. Like two wild animals, each with a leg caught hopelessly in a steel jawed trap, they gnawed viciously at the muscle and bone and connective tissue of their love in order to free themselves…to escape the agony they were both experiencing, and could think of no other way to end.

Tilly, filled with the painful desperation of unending rejection for no fathom-able reason that she could comprehend, felt her love for her husband start to bleed slowly out of her veins, until nothing was left in them but clear, cold, poi-sonous hate. She took their children one night while he was working and fled back to the Reservation at Mercier. Kevin filed for divorce two days later. Retain-ing the best attorney he could afford from a Kansas City law firm, he went after her with a panicked desperation equal to her own, to recover and reclaim the only things in his life that he had ever allowed to take root in his heart…his two little boys.

But the tribal lands of the Reservation Tilly had ensconced herself and her two sons within was a citadel of old racial hatreds between Indians and whites. The result of the attempted genocide of the Indians over a hundred years before, had now evolved into a present day steel web of biased, complex, and seemingly impenetrable federal laws that seemed to exist to protect these same native people from both thriving in the modern day real world, as well as from themselves. It was a cultural fortress that built federal walls of protection around Ethan and Alex based on their "blood quantum"…the amount of Indian blood they each were, and worked ceaselessly to lay claim to the two little sandy haired, brown eyed boys that had visited the Reservation only twice in their lives, to meet and visit with their Mother's side of the family.

In the end process, held in the tribal court at Mercier where Tilly's free court appointed B.I.A. attorney had been successful in arguing the custody dispute would be heard, Ethan and Alex were taken from Kevin and full custody was awarded to Tilly, their one third blood quantum Kickapoo Mother. It was as if some ghostly raiding party of Kickapoo braves in full war paint had swarmed down upon him chaotically from all sides, out of nowhere, attacking him vengefully; capturing his children in the ensuing melee and carrying them off as slaves. Leaving him bloody, and dazed, and utterly without hope.

At the height of the custody battle during the divorce he had been forced to sell their home and give half of the proceeds to Tilly, while his half was quickly devoured by his attorney's voracious legal fees. He moved into the old bunkhouse on the family ranch which belonged to his Uncle Ben now, after his Father had passed away several years ago, so he could live rent free; and took a second job as a security guard at a meat packing plant.

But the truth was no amount of money and no amount of sacrifice, would have ever been able to restore his children to his life. Father's are often punished by the Mothers of their children, for their past perceived sins as husbands, and Kevin Kearnes was no different. He lost his sons because Tilly was Indian, and he was not. Because Tilly had a vagina, and he did not. And because Tilly had hated him then…more than she had loved her own two sons.

Kevin and Tilly divorced, and unable to reassemble the broken fragments of the life he had both created for himself, and then systematically helped to destroy, he made the decision to move forward, by moving away. He hadn't so much consciously chosen Cutter Point, Oregon as the place he felt he should be, as the circumstances in existence in Cutter Point at the time, and with himself, had chosen him. He accepted the job as Cutter Point's newest police chief sight unseen, literally hired over the phone after a quick review of his qualifications, certifications, and references. He was a career law enforcement officer who had reached the middle rung of the command and administrative ladder in his career, having climbed to the rank of Lieutenant, and his impressive resume more than met the approval of those hiring him.

But as John Grand would later tell him, running from your past is like running in a race for your life while holding your breath. You can do it for awhile, but like one human heartbeat trying to outdistance the next, it can't be done with the expectation that you will survive to run such a race to the end.

He left Dodge in the early morning darkness of a May morning on the day before the long Memorial Day weekend was to begin. His truck was packed so full the completely obscured rear window blacked out the lights of the city which glowed brightly behind him for thirty miles, shimmering up from the receding prairie horizon which was as perfectly flat as a planed, pine board.

As dawn stirred and the black sky above began to split open and bleed vermillion and gold rays of sunlight down through the thin patchwork quilt of blue and buff colored prairie clouds overhead, he crossed the Kansas border and entered Colorado. He stopped in the small town of Lamar briefly to refill his now empty thermos of coffee before driving the last sixty miles on the back roads he'd chosen to take in order to finally link up with Interstate 25, holding on to the memories of Tilly and Ethan and Alex through Kansas just as long as he could.

He stood outside his truck in the restaurant parking lot for awhile, drinking the hot coffee, watching the dawn breaking on the first day of his new and unwanted life. Behind him now lay everything he had ever cherished, yet never really believed he deserved to have, and on this, the most empty and despairing morning of his life, the truth of the immensity of his loss began to eat away at what was left of his soul like some necrotic disease.

Two thousand miles to the west another man also stood outside his vehicle. High on the trail head observation deck at Seal Rock Wayside on Oregon Coast Highway 101, two hundred miles north of Cutter Point, he watched the red ball of the morning sun burning its way like a laser beam through the impenetrable fog bank that had settled on the cold ocean overnight like a vaporous shroud.

He scanned the still murky horizon of the Pacific Ocean in slow, wide arcs with the pair of 8X30 Steiner Military binoculars he held tightly against his tanned face, the powerful muscles in his angular jaw twitching almost imperceptibly in concentration…and anticipation. He was looking for the tell tale sign of migrating whales; the sharp, sudden geyser of water they shot skyward as they swam which gave away their position. And even though it was near the end of the migratory season for grey whales, he was still very hopeful of seeing what it was he had come here to see.

He let the binoculars hang for a minute from their strap around his neck. He stared down at the yellow and blue nylon tent on the beach below him three hundred yards away; the same tent he'd seen the boy and his two friends erecting just before dark the night before. They were probably local school kids claiming a choice campsite early for the holiday weekend which started tomorrow, before the swarms of tourists arrived tomorrow evening and took them all.

He brought the heavy, green rubber armored binoculars back up to his eyes and resumed his whale watching. Casually, he let the powerful lenses briefly stray to the three bicycles resting haphazardly on their sides around the outside of the tent in the sand, then to the front opening of the tent which was still securely closed.

Patiently, Uriah Daniel Beek waited.

CHAPTER 6

▼

It was the youngest of the three boys who emerged from the tent first, alone, zipping the tent flap shut after him. He watched as the boy—who appeared to be about ten or eleven—walked a few feet away from his friends still sleeping inside the tent, in the direction of Beek, and began to urinate on a clump of beach grass. He brought the binoculars to bear quickly on the boy's slender torso just as he finished peeing, catching a brief glimpse of the boy's small, prepubescent penis as he worked it back inside his cut off jeans with his right hand. The sight thrilled Beek to his very core.

The boy knelt beside what he assumed was his bike, and rummaged inside a daypack that was next to it, taking out a soft drink can and what looked like a box of cookies, or crackers. He sat in the sand, drawing his knees up under his chin and hugging his bare legs with his arms against the chilly morning ocean breeze, alternately munching and drinking his breakfast one handed.

Fat, grey gulls hovered above the boy in the air currents like dive bombers in a holding pattern, and when one would boldly swoop earthward with a screeching cry and land close by; he would feign disinterest in the bird. That is until the stupid creature came close enough; and then he would hurl a short chunk of driftwood or a rock at the gull which would then leap skyward, crying angrily. He watched the boy laughing, having fun, even though he never hit a single bird. And when he got up to leave he saw him deliberately walk toward a group of sullen gulls—that had gathered on the sand out of rock range from him—and shake the remains of the box out on the ground for them to eat.

The boy walked in back of the tent out of Beek's view for a few seconds, then returned with a large plastic pail and a small shovel with a narrow, curved, scoop like blade, used for digging clams. The boy zipped up his windbreaker and then set off down the beach walking south in the direction of the large tide pools a half a mile distant, holding onto the tip of shovel handle and letting it drag behind him, the blade twisting a serpentine pattern into the smooth, wet, packed sand like a wandering snake.

The old urges now began to surge through his body so strongly he felt light-headed, almost giddy; and he was barely able to keep his breathing normal and under control. The calamitous uproar coming from the hundreds of barking Stellar sea lions and seals, and shrieking sea birds, perched or lolling on the small volcanic rock mountain that rose from the water in front and below him known as Seal Rock, was drowned out by the roaring inside Beek's skull as his brain, in anticipation of what he was about to do, went into sensory overdrive. He watched the boy walking slowly on his way, stopping to examine something on the beach, skipping flat rocks into the gently breaking morning surf; wandering here and there with the innocent, nonchalant curiosity of a child explorer.

How *perfect* he was, Beek thought; watching the boy disappear down the beach until he was nothing more than a pinpoint of contrasting color against sand and water. As he walked unhurriedly back across the still empty parking lot of the Wayside to his Van, he remade the promise to himself: he would attempt to teach the boy only, but not touch him. The old days and his old ways were in the past, and he'd found a much higher purpose in his life…to teach, to rescue, and to save. He could do all of this and more without ever laying a yearning hand on another young boy, for his true desire now was not for their flesh, but for their souls.

He opened the rear of the Van, which was packed tightly with cardboard shipping boxes, and moved two boxes from on top of a larger box that was the size of a king size bed pillow. He disarranged other boxes and rummaged through the floor of the Van, which was littered with old invoices and packing slips, until he found the Grape Hook knife that rested near the machete. Using the sharp tip of its ugly, hook nosed serrated blade, he completely removed the top of the largest box in four deft cuts.

Reaching inside the box he moved aside packages of plastic bubble wrapped toys and dug toward the bottom through the white foam packing pellets, finally finding what it was he was after; a much larger plastic package with a white label that had the code "LBW-ST/QTY.12DZ." imprinted in black on it. The significance of that number—one hundred forty four—bore into his brain, and he stared in awe at the label for a moment, seeing so clearly God's purpose in all of this. *Little Blue Whales, Squeak Toy, Quantity Twelve Dozen.* Twelve toys made a dozen, and twelve dozen multiplied by twelve toys…was one hundred and forty four.

He sliced open the package and removed one of the items from it; a small, soft plastic blue whale squeak toy about six inches long. He placed the toy whale inside his left jacket pocket, and put the knife in his right one. He looked for another box; a small square one that had gotten buried a few days before in the Van after he'd picked up and loaded his product in preparation leaving home on his route. It was the box of "Trellistrips", twelve inch long strips of green six gauge vinyl that he used to tie the new grape vines to their trellises as they grew in his small backyard vineyard. He found the box and took a handful of the strips, stuffing them inside the same pocket of his green work jacket where the knife rested.

He got in the Van and started the engine, glancing at his wristwatch. It was 7:05 am, and the boy had been walking for eleven minutes now. But Beek wasn't concerned. He knew exactly where the boy was going.

And how to find him when he got there.

Ricky Cates was on his hands and knees, his face almost touching the surface of the tide pool as he thrust his arm elbow deep into the icy salt water, trying to dislodge a big purple starfish stuck solidly onto the rocks below. He didn't see the man coming down from the highway above the beach a quarter mile away; moving through the bramble of blackberry bushes like a large, supple, predatory cat, on a narrow trail that now led to the area of the tide pools.

When he finally tired of trying to capture the starfish and looked up, he saw the man standing fifty yards up the beach from him close to the incoming tide line, staring out at the ocean through a pair of binoculars he wore around his neck, moving them slowly left, then, back to the right across the horizon. The man didn't seem to notice him at first, but finally he lowered his binoculars and looked at Ricky. He smiled and waved at Ricky…then lifted the big green binoculars back up to his eyes and started looking through them again. Ricky stood up, and taking his pail and shovel, walked toward the man.

Beek could sense the boy moving toward him, but kept his eyes to the binocular lenses and continued to scan the empty ocean. In the few brief seconds he'd had to assess him when he had smiled and waved in acknowledgement to the boy, he had suddenly realized the boy was older than he'd first thought; maybe twelve, or even thirteen, and just physically small for his age.

Disappointment began to darken Beek's mood. The euphoric mental high that had carried him confidently down to the beach from the highway, on the path through the rapidly re-growing blackberry bushes that he'd hacked out with a machete weeks before, began to ebb and fade away. Ten years old was ideal. Eleven was usually acceptable too. But in this, the *end time* of today's world, over-flowing with the fetid, corrupting sewage of false doctrine which threatened to infect all men with the wickedness of the *Great Whore of Babylon*; often by the time a boy had reached even age twelve, and almost always thirteen, it was sometimes already much too late.

This *Spirit of Jezebel*, the "Queen of Heaven"—Mother of Harlots and Abominations of the Earth—was a powerful entity. So powerful that *She* had taken Beek's own Father down in the end. But on the night of his Father's death, eighteen year old Uriah had been brought forth by Jehovah into the "overcoming" against *Her*. At his Father's bedside, as the emaciated and defeated old man rattled out his last breaths, Beek had fallen on his knees with upraised arms and shouted out loudly: "And the ten horns which thou sawest upon the beast, these shall hate the whore, and shall make her desolate and naked, and shall eat her flesh, and burn her with fire!"

Shocked at the strange and previously unknown words which had suddenly and irretrievably escaped from his mouth, Beek had looked at the three men from The Hall who had come to sit with his Father in his dank bedroom during his last hours. But not one of them said anything as Beek stared at them, hard; daring them to oppose him in any way for the barrage of vitriolic words which had just spewed forth from his seemingly possessed mouth. It had been a declaration of his life's mission, pledged in a split second of sociopathic insight and spurred on by both his growing religious fervor, and the last will and testament of misogynistic hate that had been conferred now from Father to son.

None of those present had challenged young Uriah, or offered him hope, encouragement, or friendship of any kind, because he was the son of Franklin Beek; one of their own whom they feared greatly for many reasons, and were pleased to see finally die. As far as they were concerned this boy had the mark of the beast on him, too, and they weren't about to take any steps toward seeing Franklin's bad seed knowingly perpetuated in their midst.

But if only *someone* had done something then…

The boy walked to within ten feet of Beek, then stopped. Beek slowly brought the binoculars down from his eyes, then suddenly turned and looked at him and jumped back a little, as if he had been startled by his sudden appearance.

"Oh!" exclaimed Beek. "Hello! You kind of scared me there for a second. Where'd you come from?"

"Tide poolin'," said the boy, pointing back in the direction from which he'd just come. "Back over there."

"You do any good?" Beek asked earnestly.

"Oh," said the boy, setting his bucket and shovel down on the sand, "I got two red rock crabs, and a couple of clams. You want to see them?"

"Sure," said Beek, walking over to him and looking into the bucket. He was judging the modulation of the boys' voice and could hear a slight difference in the tonality of some of his words, the precursor he was sure, of the close and impending onset of puberty.

"What are you looking for?" the boy asked him.

"Whales," said Beek. "Blue whales."

"No shit?" said the boy, looking out at the slowly heaving sea beyond the line of breakers. "Have you seen any?"

Beek winced deeply inside at the boy's use of profanity. He caught a glint of something coming from the boy's right ear as he turned away from Beek to look out at the ocean, and saw that his ear was pierced.

The boy turned back to Beek. "Shit, I don't see nothin'," he said. "What kind of binoculars are those? They are awesome."

"Oh, these?" said Beek, taking the binoculars off his neck. "These are made by a company in Germany called Steiner. They're German Military field glasses. My squad gave them to me when I retired from the Navy Seals." Beek held the binoculars out to the boy, and he took them.

"Wow," said the boy, hefting their weight in his hands, "these are cool. You were with the Seals?"

"Here," Beek said, moving close in behind him, "put the strap around your neck, and I'll show you how to adjust them to your own eyes." He stood still as Beek moved in behind him and lifted his longish brown hair away from his neck, touching his cool, dry skin as he placed the binocular strap over his head. He could now clearly see the thing sparkling from the boy's ear. It was a small, shiny silver metal Crucifix. Beek had the boy point the binoculars back toward the tide pools, and helped him focus on a rock, adjusting the individual lenses until the combined view through both of them was razor sharp.

"We need to go down the beach a little further south," said Beek. "I'm pretty sure I saw a whale spouting about three thousand yards out, just before you came along…but he was moving south."

"I'll carry these if you want," said Beek, picking up the boy's bucket and shovel. "You keep the binoculars…and stay ready. This is a good spot we're going to; I've seen a lot of them there before. I'll let you know as soon as I see one blow."

"Cool," said the boy. "I've never seen a real whale before. Except for Keiko. Before they moved him from the Aquarium at Newport. But that was when I was just a little kid."

"You live around here?" asked Beek.

"In Newport," said the boy. "I'm camping with my brother and his best friend, back up the beach at Seal Rock."

"What's your name?" said Beek.

"Ricky," said the boy. "Ricky Cates. My Mom and Dad still call me Ricky, anyhow. But I like Rick better."

"Glad to meet you, Rick," said Uriah Beek, transferring the pail and shovel to his left hand as he extended his right one toward the boy, shaking hands with him as they walked. "I'm Dan."

"Will your brother and his buddy miss you when they wake up?" asked Beek.

"No," said Ricky Cates. "My brother snuck some of my Dad's beer out of the house and took it with us. They drank it all last night. I think they are going to feel pretty crappy when they wake up because they both puked," he laughed.

"Good," said Beek. "That's good. I wouldn't want anyone worrying about *you* if you're gone for a little while, because we've got quite a hike ahead of us."

They walked on together, the beach ahead of them as desolately empty as a moonscape. And Beek's uncertainty about Ricky Cates soon began to turn to disgust, as Ricky answered his questions about the junior high school he went to where he was in the seventh grade, some of the drugs he'd already tried; what he and his twelve year old girlfriend did when they were alone.

He felt cheated, robbed. Humiliated. He felt as if he had picked a piece of beautiful ripe fruit with God's blessing from *His Garden*; only to bite into it and taste the bitterness of deception…that meant instead it was rotten to the core.

Yet still, this was the journey he had chosen to travel in his life, to do the Lord God Jehovah's work. He would witness to the boy. He would engage in spiritual warfare against the Deceiver of the whole world—and with the Mystery Woman who bore The Mark upon her face—in order to fight for this young boy's soul if necessary, and cleanse his mind and body of every last trace of the Jezebel Spirit filth that clung to him like a dark and heavy cloak of Judgment.

But first, Beek would try what his own Father had done to him when he was a wayward youth, filled with sinful lust and held captive by *Her* seductions, knowing not who the True Enemy was. When he'd discovered what Beek had been doing to other, younger boys in the neighborhood.

He would beat him within an inch of his life.

The first blow had taken Ricky Cates completely by surprise. The palm of Beek's right hand slammed into the back of his head like the flat side of a garden shovel, knocking him to his knees as he threw his hands out instinctively in front of him, his reflexively splayed fingers clawing frantically at the wet sand.

He had been looking through the binoculars out to sea exactly where Dan had told him to; sure he was going to spot a giant Blue Whale any second...excited at the prospect of getting the "weed" that his new found friend had promised him when they got back to his car...and he could not comprehend any of this now.

Dan had asked him a lot of questions about himself; about his life and what it was like to be a kid nowadays, and how hard it must be. He told him he was cool with kids using marijuana—even he and his Navy Seal friends had smoked grass to relax when they weren't in training or on a mission—but he thought kids should stay away from hard drugs like Meth and cocaine. He asked him about his girlfriend, Allyson, and if he needed any condoms; because he could give him some if he did.

And when he had told him no, he didn't need any, because they weren't doing *it* yet; that she was only giving him blow jobs, and he was feeling her up, and sometimes, when she would let him, putting his finger inside her...Ricky's skull had suddenly exploded inside with a brilliant display of dazzling, multi-colored stars.

Beek looked down contemptuously at the boy on his knees in the sand in front of him, frozen in shock like some stunned animal that had just been struck in the road by a passing car. He bent over him and moved the binoculars around to his back, twisting the strap until they were knot tight on his neck and with one powerful arm jerked Ricky Cates off his knees and into the air.

He carried Ricky that way, extended out in front of him, Ricky's leg's kicking and twisting wildly, to a clutter of broken, piled driftwood that marked the high tide line some sixty yards away. When he dropped him on the ground Ricky was unconscious. He loosened the tourniquet like strap of the binoculars from around his neck, and shook and slapped the boy until he gasped, and his eyes fluttered open.

And then he began.

He witnessed to the boy, bellowing scripture at him in a litany that came so blindingly fast from Beek's brain to his mouth, the terrified boy could not hope to process or retain any of it; could not repeat a single word back to the raving lunatic who towered above him raging and demanding that he do so.

"You're too old! That's the problem with you!" shouted Beek. "You're going to be fourteen in November. Confess to me and to God right here and now for every wrong thing you have ever done, or it will be too late!

"TOO LATE!" screamed Beek. "Do you hear me Rick?"

Ricky Cates had been begging for his life for the last thirty minutes, but he could no longer form any distinguishable words; only terrified sobs of anguish that seemed to be dredged up from the deepest depths of his instinct to survive, spilled out from between his now lacerated and bleeding lips.

Beek struck him across the face again, forcefully, with his open hand. "Shut up! Stop crying! Shut up and *listen to me*!" he screamed. But Ricky could not control himself, could not stop crying. Beek rose up and looked around, making sure they were still unseen, and when he looked back at the child, saw the dark wet circle, widening and spreading out from his crotch.

"Oh, that's just great," said Beek. "Now look what you've done!" He reached into his jacket and brought out some of the green vinyl Trellistrips. Jerking Ricky's head up, he gagged his mouth with one of the strips, tying it off tightly at the back of his head, and then used two more to tie Ricky's hands tightly behind his back.

"And this…what is this?" yelled Beek, roughly grabbing Ricky's ear lobe, fingering the small silver Crucifix.

"Didn't you say your little slut girlfriend gave you this?" Beek demanded. Ricky had acknowledged that fact an hour ago when Beek had asked him; telling him Allyson was a Christian and that she'd given the Crucifix earring to him as a gift when they'd decided to "hook up" and go steady. And how he had pestered his parents into letting him get his ear pierced to wear it; because even though he didn't exactly believe in God himself, he hadn't wanted to hurt Allyson's' feelings.

"So you think Jesus Christ died on a cross?" said Beek. He bent down very close to Ricky's face as his fingers worked at the silver earring, trying to get it loose.

"Well, you…and the rest of those in the world like you, Rick…Ricky, are WRONG!"

"That is false doctrine Ricky. We are held in captivity by *Her* Babylon, when we willingly eat such lies! Do you understand this? Christ did *not* die on a cross…he died on a stake," hissed Beek.

"Would you like to hear some more of the world's lies?" Beek continued. "Celebrating birthdays is an abomination to God, Ricky. *You* don't need to celebrate your birthday every year, because YOU are not that important Ricky! None of us are!"

Beek was beginning to tremble with rage. He squeezed hard on the earring, but it didn't budge. Did it screw on and off? Or had it grown in as a part of the boy's ear now.

"And Christmas?" said Beek. "Ha! It's the biggest lie of them all! Jesus was born in October...not December...and no one brought him *any* gifts, Ricky. Not a single, solitary thing."

Ricky's horrified eyes widened even further when he saw the strange looking knife in Beek's hand, its miniature scythe shaped blade just inches from his face.

"Do you ever touch her when she's on her period?" asked Beek. "And get her filthy, whore girl blood all over your fingers? Well if you ever have...then you need to know how WRONG that is too!"

"The Bible says; *abstain from things polluted by idols, and from fornication, and from what is strangled, and from blood!*" Beek said feverishly.

"What makes you think you can wear a thing like that in your ear?" demanded Beek. "Not only should your little Jezebel have ever given it to you in the first place; you should never have accepted it, either. It displeases God, Ricky. And it very much displeases ME!"

Beek swiftly brought his hands down to Ricky's face, clamping his head between them like a vice. There was an instantaneous burning sensation, and then with crystal clarity Ricky saw Beek recoil away from him; holding the severed, bloody ear lobe with the shiny Crucifix still attached to it up to the sky...studying it as if it were a piece of shrimp he'd just plucked from a bowl of seafood cocktail sauce.

Ricky Cates, the boy who'd never believed much in God, now mercifully heard beautiful music resounding in his unconscious ears. Saw dozens of majestic white winged, golden haired Angels fluttering down from Heaven above, their white robed arms outstretched to him, as Uriah Beek strangled Ricky to death with the strap from the binoculars he still wore around his neck.

When it was done Beek removed the binoculars from Ricky and put them around his own neck. He rinsed his hands off, and the bloody knife and Ricky's ear lobe, in a few inches of salt water from the spent surf where it licked at the thick soles of his work shoes on the sandy beach. He put the knife and the fleshy nub of the boy's ear back into his jacket pocket and walked quickly back down the beach to the tide pools; then carefully picked his way up the steep embankment through the blackberry bushes to the highway and his Van.

He thoroughly wiped the blade of the knife off with a paper napkin he found in the console of the Van and then stuck it as far back underneath his front seat as he could. Tearing in half another napkin, he rolled the tip of Ricky's ear up in it; then opened the Van's clean, unused ashtray, placed it inside, and snapped it shut again.

He had three accounts to service in the small beachside town of Waldport—only ten miles south from where he was now on Highway 101—where he usually ate lunch before finishing the last of his afternoon route stops in the even smaller community of Yachats, and then the tourist attraction at Sea Lion Caves. He would then continue south down 101 to Florence and find a motel room where he would spend that night and most of the next day—depending on the amount of orders he had to write—until driving to his next stop in Reedsport; then in the following two days, North Bend, Coos Bay, Bandon, Port Orford, and finally...Cutter Point.

By 12:30 he was sitting in the parking lot of Vickie's Big Wheel Drive-In just off Highway 101 in Waldport, picking half heartedly at his deluxe cheeseburger basket and pondering why, and how, everything had gone so terribly wrong.

He had set out to teach, but no lessons had been learned. He had endeavored to save a soul, and instead had taken a life. In all the times past he had never killed anyone, and he felt acknowledging this should be having much more of an impact than it seemed to be having on him right now. We are all sinners, he reasoned with himself. We *all* must be saved; but especially the young males, as they were the most vulnerable, the most susceptible to Original Sin. After all, it wasn't Adam who had done anything wrong in The Garden, but Eve, with her weak moral character and fondness for serpents.

He was very upset that he had been forced to kill the boy but he judged him to be a lost cause; a once fertile field that had been overtaken with weeds and in which nothing good would now be permitted to grow. But what was more upsetting to Beek—even disturbing—was that in the heat of the moment there on the beach with Ricky, as he had beaten and berated the boy, he had begun to feel the old familiar sexual urges building inside him and he knew he would have raped Ricky Cates, if Ricky hadn't wet his pants first.

Well, he thought, toying with a cold and rubbery French fry...he would pray about it all, and in the future try not to be so hard on himself. Because God's work was never easy.

And never done.

CHAPTER 7

▼

Thud Compton and his family lived on Sea Horse Drive, a posh enclave of some of the most luxurious and expensive homes in Cutter Point. The private residential access road in was carved into the face and sides of a green forested hill, which rose steeply from the edge of the city's northern limits like a miniature Topanga Canyon, and the predominant architecture on the hill, as well as its population, was decidedly Californian.

In fact all of the residents of Sea Horse Drive, except for Thud and his wife Margie and their two daughters, were native Californians; rich, native Californians. And even though the Compton's twenty eight hundred square foot Spanish style stucco home, with its well clipped and watered velvet green lawn, and terraced flower gardens brimming with roses and azaleas, blended in seamlessly with the million dollar villas of their surrounding neighbors, the Californians still wanted them out. And especially one Sea Horse Drive resident who lived at the last address highest on the hill above everyone else…Mayor Vernon Bouchet´.

Thud had recited the history of his house and the invading Californians to Kearnes one Sunday afternoon in June in his backyard after having invited his new boss to dinner, when it appeared no one else in the department was going to. The new chief had walked the halls of Cutter Point P.D. his first week on the job receiving only cold stares and turned backs from his administrative staff; sometimes interrupting their gatherings in borrowed offices, huddled together and whispering, causing them to scatter upon his approach like cock roaches in a dark room when the lights were suddenly turned on.

The exception had been Thud Compton who'd filled Kearnes' doorway his first morning on the job, introducing himself matter of factly; shaking Kearnes' hand and telling him if there was anything he needed to just let him know. When Thud had told Margie about the new chief; that he was recently divorced and had two young sons back in Kansas, and lived alone at the Sea Breeze Apartments down by the Harbor near Pearl Cove, Margie had insisted Thud invite him to dinner.

"So, here's the ironic twist in all of this," said Thud, jabbing at a blood red steak on his propane grill with a long, wood handled barbecue fork. "All these Californians start flocking to town, buying up every square inch of land they can here on the hill…and Margie's folks, the first one's to ever build a place up here? They retire, sell us the house at what it cost them to build it…and move to California!"

"They felt they had to leave?" asked Kearnes, taking a drink from the chilled bottle of Corona Thud had opened and set on the patio table in front of him.

"No, not really" said Thud, grabbing himself a fresh Corona from the plastic washtub filled with crushed ice next to the grill. "Wes…that's Margie's Dad…Wes owned Pan-Pacific Plywood. That's the Mill here in town? He could have bought this whole damn hill and developed it himself; and now I bet sometimes he wishes he had. I think they just got tired of living around some of these assholes that moved in. Especially our esteemed mayor, Mr. Bouchet´."

"The mayor isn't well liked?" asked Kearnes.

Thud took a long drink from his Corona, and then looked out at the sparkling blue Pacific for a minute before turning back to answer Kearnes. "Well let me ask you this, chief," said Thud. Have *you* ever met a used car salesman you ever liked? Or trusted?"

"That's what he did for a living, asked Kearnes, "sold used cars?"

"No, *he* didn't sell used cars," said Thud, "but he had hundreds of other people working for him who did. You ever hear of The Bouchet´ Group, Ltd.?"

"No," said Kearnes. "That was his car dealership?"

"Dealer-ships," said Thud. "Seventeen of them to be exact. In California, Arizona, Nevada, and Idaho. Old Vernon made his millions selling Chevy's and Fords to Hispanic wetbacks that were usually even more broke than the cars were."

This was all new information to Kearnes. He had "met" the mayor only twice; the first time during his telephone interview and the next at his brief swearing in ceremony shortly after he'd arrived in Cutter Point, held on the day before he was to start work. The ceremony had seemed somewhat perfunctory to Kearnes—a formal chore to be gotten out of the way—and Mayor Bouchet´ had left the city council chambers immediately after administering the oath of office to him. He had shaken his hand with a feeble grip, mumbling "welcome aboard" to Kearnes and apologizing to him for his new boss city manager Roddameyer being out of town and not able to attend the swearing in, before leaving him with the only other people in the room; a reporter from the Cutter Clarion who wanted his picture for the paper, the city clerk who had work forms for him to sign, and Thud Compton, who sat in the last row of seats closest to the door, an audience of one.

"Not to be pessimistic or anything," said Thud. "But did you know you are the fourth new chief in six years?"

Kearnes let this new and unwanted revelation sink in, trying to remain unruffled. But he felt his stomach begin to knot up. He had gambled everything on this job, and could not afford to lose it. He was here now and had to stay, no matter how bad things were, or could get. And the fact that he had been ordered to pay Tilly fourteen hundred dollars a month in child support and "spousal maintenance" had sealed his fate even further.

"No, I didn't," said Kearnes. "What do you think the problem has been?" he asked. "In keeping chiefs here?"

Thud put his beer bottle down and stood up, walking back to the grill with his long handled fork. He was wearing a Hawaiian shirt printed in a kaleidoscope of bright colors that featured a beach scene, swaying palm trees, and naked hula dancers whose bare brown breasts undulated when his powerfully muscled chest moved beneath the fabric. His not yet tanned legs were exposed in the green khaki summer cargo shorts he wore, and Kearnes could see a mass of scars on Thud's bulging left calf that looked like a plate of cold spaghetti someone had thrown against a wall that had stuck and dried. The injury was a souvenir Thud had brought home with him from the invasion of Grenada after an RGP rocket had exploded next to him, and years later it had almost kept him from getting hired with the P.D.

"Agendas," said Thud, spearing the steaks viciously and flipping them over on the grill one by one. "A lot of people at city hall seem to have one; starting in the Mayor's office and working right on down to the police department."

Kearnes saw a shadow fall across the edge of the patio table and turned in his chair to see Margie Compton standing in the open sliding glass door that led from the kitchen of the house to the patio, cradling a large bowl in her arms filled with Caesar salad, and holding tall salt and paper shakers in her hands.

"Thud Compton!" she cried. "Leave the poor man alone! He just got to town and you're already trying to scare him off?" She walked over to Thud who saw her angrily coming toward him, and dropped his basting brush into the container of red sauce just as she shoved the salad bowl hard into his stomach. She took a beer from the tub of slowly melting ice and walked over to the patio table, and sat down across from Kearnes."

Kearnes picked up the bottle cap opener from the table and popped the cap off Margie's beer, then slid the bowl of freshly cut lime wedges toward her, which she'd brought to them on her last trip out to the patio. Margie smiled at him, the spray of red freckles across her nose widening in delight at his courteous manner.

"I have to apologize for my husband," she said. "Thud gets a little bit negative about his job sometimes when he's had a few beers."

"Like hell!" said Thud, dropping the salad bowl on the table. "Look, sir, I have no agenda myself, other than wanting to be a good cop. But we need some strong and lasting leadership in this department. And we're never going to have it if every new chief the city hires gets led down the garden path by Bouchet' and his boozing golf pro buddy turned city manager, Roddameyer…and then gets bent over a career busting log to take the *big one* up the you-know-what if they don't fall in line!"

"Thud…shush!" said Margie anxiously. "I don't want the girls to hear you!" Their two daughters, Selena, who was six, and Sarah, nine, were just inside the kitchen slider seated at the breakfast nook eating the dinners they'd requested; tuna sandwiches, juice, and chocolate chip cookies. Margie quickly got up from her chair and checked on the two girls, then closed the glass sliding door, leaving it open just a crack.

"It's the truth," said Thud. "Bouchet' has tried to politically control every police chief we've had since he took office, and it's only gotten worse since he hired his friend as the new city manager. And if it's not those two, then it's the "Four Horsemen of The Abomination" pulling their crap."

"Who are they?" asked Kearnes.

"*They*," said Thud—the contempt in his voice as thick as the smoke billowing up from the grill—"are our department's version of the Four Horsemen of The Apocalypse; you know, like from the Bible? War, Death, Pain, and Pestilence?" Kearnes wondered if he was referring to some of the same negative appearing employees he'd already had contact with at work.

"But you'll soon get to know them as Lieutenant Edgar Polk, Detective Curt LaMar, Sergeant Byron Downs, and Senior Lead Dispatcher Russell Massey," said Thud. "And they are full blown, bona fide pricks, every one of them!" Margie gave Thud a look when he said this, but it was one more of empathy this time than aggravation.

"I've already met Lieutenant Polk," said Kearnes. "I don't think he likes me very much."

"Like you?" said Thud. "He hates your guts. He's applied for chief the last three times the city has recruited, and has been passed over every single time. And to make matters even worse this time, they hired *you* as a Lieutenant…with no prior chief's experience. And that's got old Edgar so tied up in knots he doesn't know whether to shit or go blind."

"How long has he been with the department?" Kearnes asked.

"Too long," said Thud. "Twenty four years. Edgar Polk used to chase me around this town when I was a sixteen year old hell on wheels kid on my dirt bike. He was a logger when the city hired him; ignorant, crude, and about as unfit a person as you could ever imagine to be allowed to wear a badge. And he still is."

"It sounds like the city should have gotten rid of him a long time ago," said Kearnes.

Margie had left the table and was at the grill, putting the steaks on a platter. "Hey you two," she said. "Enough cop shop talk. Let's eat, okay?"

Thud got up from the table to go help his wife, sensing now that he was on the verge of ruining the afternoon for her and he needed to stop. But before he did, he had one last thing to say to Kevin Kearnes.

"Just watch out for him, chief. I know how this guy works. He's already sticking a knife in your back whether you choose to believe it or not. The problem is you might not feel it going in until it's too late."

The rest of the afternoon passed enjoyably and without any further uneasiness as Thud and Margie showed Kearnes around their beautiful and spacious home. Thud took him into his den, the place he referred to as his "hideout", and they spent nearly hour looking at Thud's old Army scrapbooks and photo albums, his high school football trophies, and inspecting his gun collection which he kept locked away from his two children in a massive steel gun safe that looked as if it might weigh a ton.

And then it was Margie's turn. When she learned Kearnes admired flowers and even had an affinity for raising them himself, she whisked him away from Thud and out to her terraced gardens brimming with voluptuous roses and azaleas. Kearnes admired the roses, especially the Floribundas, which he new could be difficult to successfully cultivate in the sometimes cold and over zealously wet coastal zones of the Pacific Northwest.

But it was Margie's azaleas that blew him away. He remembered that all azaleas were of the genus Rhododendron, but beyond that he'd never had any real experience with them, as Kansas was not generally considered a hospitable environment for the orchid like plants. Margie had row upon row of both hybrid and native azaleas healthily in bloom, their vibrant, chromatic colors suffused by the fading evening light making them appear as if they were glowing incandescently from their rod like stems.

As they strolled slowly back toward the patio where Thud was playing with his two daughters, giving them "horsy rides" on his back on the lawn, Kearnes stopped and looked down at the city below, the lights of houses and street lights coming on now randomly in the gathering dusk.

He could see a small armada of fishing boats threading their way in from the open sea toward the long, boulder strewn jetty at Pearl Cove that would funnel them into the safety of the Harbor, their urgent white wakes trailing behind them on the water like ropes of billowy cotton. He was awestruck by the beauty of the last rays of the day's sun beating down on the ocean, their reflection fracturing the water's surface into a pattern of shimmering, hammered gold. And from his high up vantage point in any direction he looked the horizons were either green or blue; so different from the stark, baked landscapes of summertime Kansas.

"How high up are we here?" he asked Margie.

She thought about it for a moment before answering him.

"I'm going to say…about eleven hundred feet above sea level. I know my Dad used to tell me the top of the hill was right at fourteen hundred."

"It's funny," said Kearnes, still admiring the spectacular view. "You call this a 'hill', and in Kansas, it would be a mountain."

"In fact," he laughed, "come to think of it, I don't think there is any place as high as this in Kansas!"

"We love it here," said Margie. "My folks were so wonderful to us when they let us buy it. And Thud gets so angry when Bouchet´ makes his ridiculous offers on the place!"

"Does he just call you up, and ask you if you want to sell?"

"Never. He'll have some Realtor in town do his inquiring for him; and they never tell us who the "interested party" is either. But we know it's him."

"Why all the secrecy?" asked Kearnes.

Margie Compton looked Kearnes straight in the eye. "Because, that's what Vernon Bouchet´ is all about," she said. "He is a horrible little man who has his grubby little fingers into everything, and everyone, in this town. But he is also a master manipulator; an expert at having others do his dirty work for him…and like Thud said…taking the fall in his place if his plans don't work out."

Kearnes looked up to the top of the steep hillside, where the security lights on the grounds of Vernon Bouchet's palatial single story mansion had also come on. "But he looks like he has all the room in the world up there," he said. "And he's a little too far away from you guys to be thinking about adding anything on to his place I would think."

"It's power," said Margie. "Power, and ego, and greed."

"He wants this entire hill to himself?"

"He wants this hill, The Meadows; the whole town," said Margie. "And he already owns all the land where the new Wal-Mart is located; including the rest of the land the shopping center is on, which is even named after him! Two of his cronies from the city council also live up here, and I'm sure he'd like to have a few more of them move in. To him my husband is just a low level civil servant who makes thirty eight thousand dollars a year, and it galls Vernon Bouchet' to see someone like him…like us, still living here."

"What's The Meadows?"

"It *was* a two hundred and fifty acre parcel of land in the Urban Growth Boundary northwest of the city limits. It was previously zoned for single and multi-family residential dwellings; until Vernon Bouchet' began the process to steal it from the citizens of this community. Now it's going to be a twenty five million dollar golf course resort called "Trident Greens"…once the city council passes a final vote on it next month, and it opens in September."

"He stole the land for it?"

"Yes," said Margie. "That's what Thud thinks he's going to end up doing; he just doesn't know how yet, exactly."

"So how does he manage to keep getting re-elected over and over again, as mayor? asked Kearnes.

"Time, and apathy," Margie answered. "He and every member of the city council are all retired. They have all the time in the world to do what they want, when they want to do it. But the majority of people who live in Cutter Point are working folks. They work hard at their jobs, and then even harder at home, trying to make ends meet for their families.

"And so they let someone else 'take care of things'. They become apathetic about the very institution and process that has so much to do with just how difficult, or easy, their lives in the community in some ways will be."

Kearnes pondered this for a moment. He had been a little worried and more than a little uneasy about accepting the Compton's dinner invitation, because he didn't know Detective Compton yet; didn't know what kind of man or employee he was. But Kearnes could see now there had been no ulterior motive in them asking him to dinner, no "agenda" at all as Thud would have put it, and the enmity both Thud and his wife had expressed about the dire political conditions that infected city hall and the police department had flowed from them naturally, like poison draining from an open wound.

"Hey," said Kearnes, politely glancing at his watch. "I must still be operating on Kansas time. I had no idea it was getting so late here, too. It was a wonderful dinner Margie…I want to thank you both for having me over."

"Well, thank you for coming," said Margie.

Kearnes started to walk over to where Thud was still roughhousing with the girls when he heard Margie say behind him, "Chief Kearnes…may I say something rather personal to you?"

Kearnes stopped and turned around, facing her. He nodded his head yes and waited for her to speak.

"Thud almost didn't ask you over," she said. "I made him."

"Oh?" said Kearnes.

"He was hesitant to ask you to dinner…not because he didn't want to, but because he thought you might feel he was, as he put it, 'trying to kiss your ass'."

"I didn't get that impression at all," said Kearnes. "And I can either tell him so right now, or you can tell him what I said after I leave."

Margie Compton was a very petite woman; much shorter than her husband, who literally towered over her when they stood next to each other. But whatever she lacked in stature she more than made up for through the courage of her convictions.

"Neither one of us has to say anything to him," she said. "I think you are going to find that Thud is a lot of things, chief Kearnes, but most of all he is a man of integrity. And he's a man that if he accepts you as a true friend, he will never turn his back on you."

Having said that, and not wanting or waiting for a response from Kearnes, Margie turned and quickly walked away. She got Thud started on helping her clear the dishes from the patio table and scooted the girls inside to begin getting ready for bed. Kearnes retrieved his truck keys from the kitchen nook counter top in the house where Thud had placed them beside a stack of selected DVD's he'd picked out from the movie library in his den. He had insisted his new boss borrow some of his favorites, not knowing he didn't even have a television set in his apartment, let alone a DVD player, and Kearnes had accepted his offer politely without ever telling him.

They said their good-byes in the large turn around of the Compton's driveway in front of the house—Kearnes thanking them both again for having him over—

and when he started his truck and flicked the headlights on Margie and Thud were caught momentarily in the high beams as they walked to their front door. Thud's hand, which had been on Margie's shoulder, guiding her alongside him up the walkway, slid down the back of her shirt and beneath the waistband of her white cotton summer shorts. She slapped at Thud's huge head, managing only to hit his shoulder, and Thud jerked his hand away for a brief couple of seconds before inserting it into her shorts again. This time Margie barely reacted at all, weakly waving her hand at him as if she were swatting at a buzzing fly with a feather.

Kearnes watched their front door close behind them and the porch light come on, then drove back down the short access road to Sea Horse Drive and turned right onto the blacktop. He carefully made his way down the winding and unfamiliar narrow road, descending into the city below which had now been swallowed up by a massive fog bank.

The rapidly cooling ocean air, carried in on the evening breeze, had collided with the muggy warmth of the day which still radiated from buildings, and houses, and the paved streets. The fog was like Witches brew steaming from a bubbling cauldron; the thick, soupy white vapors swirling all around, cutting his visibility to almost nothing, reducing his speed to a crawl as he tried to anticipate where he thought the stop sign at the intersection to Highway 101 was ahead of him.

Finally coming to it he stopped, and strained to see any traffic approaching from either direction before turning left onto 101. Failing to do so, he took his chances and quickly made the turn, then used the barely discernible street lamps above him as a guide as he ghosted through the downtown center of the city toward the Blue Czar River Bridge, and the Harbor.

At the approach to the bridge ahead of him he saw what at first looked like pastel flashes of pink and orange. But as he drove through the quickly dissipating fog that could not survive very long in the cold air which rose from the river below, the flashes transformed into brilliant red and blue electric strobes of light from a Cutter Point P.D. patrol car parked on the shoulder of the highway, its driver's side spotlight on and shining straight ahead into the rear window of a battered old white Toyota Celica.

Kearnes pulled in behind the patrol car when he saw the lone officer standing in front of the Toyota with a man, talking to him and gesturing at him with his hands. The man swayed on his feet crazily as if he was standing on the deck of a boat in rough seas, and suddenly tipped forward, grabbing at the officer's hands. The young officer grasped the man's wrists, held him still for a moment, then let go and stepped back from him. It appeared to Kearnes that the officer was trying to administer an "FST"—a Field Sobriety Test—to the man; but things weren't working out. He saw the man throw his hands up in the air in exasperation and heard him yell something unintelligible at the officer; then saw him turn, listing heavily to his left as he started to lurch away into the southbound lane of traffic. But the officer reached out and grabbed him by his shirt collar, and the fight was on.

Kearnes shot out of his truck and briskly walked toward the struggle. He saw the surprised look on the officer's face as he looked up and saw Kearnes for the first time, coming toward him; then watched as the officer swung the drunk around in front of him with enough centrifugal force to plant him, face down, on the hood of the Toyota.

"Sir, stay back!" the officer shouted at Kearnes as he bent the man's arm behind his back in a wrist lock, attempting to handcuff him.

"Do you need any help?" asked Kearnes. "I'm an officer."

"No," the young officer replied flatly. "Just stay where you are!" Kearnes froze in his tracks, hearing the trepidation in the young officer's tone of voice. He knew if he reached into his rear pants pocket for his badge and ID case, he would probably be staring into the muzzle of the officer's Glock before he could ever get it out.

The officer got the man handcuffed, and as he half dragged and half carried him toward the rear of his patrol car, he recited the man's Miranda warning to him. He bent the man forward on the trunk of the black and white patrol car and searched him methodically, thoroughly; removing a comb, cigarette lighter, a wallet, and some spare change from the man's pockets before placing him in the rear of the car, never completely taking his eyes off Kearnes the entire time.

Kearnes was close enough to him now that he could read the name tag on his uniform shirt…"S. Sparling." The officer keyed the microphone to his portable radio—which was fastened by a clip to a shoulder epaulet of his dark blue uniform shirt—and spoke into it.

"One Charles twenty one to Central, I am 10-15 with one 10-21 male at 101 and Anchorage…send me the next rotational tow. Also, be advised I am out with a Sam Mary and am 10-4 at this point, no second requested."

The dispatcher back in the 911 Center at Cutter Point P.D. acknowledged the officer's transmission as Kearnes silently decoded it to himself: Officer Sparling had just arrested a male drunk driver at Highway 101 and Anchorage Drive. He needed the next tow truck company on the call out list sent to his location for the man's Toyota. And Kearnes was the "Sam Mary"; the suspicious male still at the scene with the officer, but the officer was 10-4…he was all right and was not requesting a back-up unit. At least for now.

"Sir," said Spenser Sparling, keeping his eyes on Kearnes as he walked toward Kearnes' white Ford Ranger truck, its headlights on and engine still running, "what can I do for you this evening?"

"I saw you on the traffic stop alone," said Kearnes, "and just pulled over to make sure you were OK. When I saw him starting to resist, I got out."

Spenser Sparling stopped and stared at the Kansas license plate beneath the front bumper on the truck, and started to reach for the transmit button on his lapel mike to call the registration number into Dispatch.

"Actually officer," said Kearnes, "I have an appointment with the D.M.V. here in town tomorrow at one o'clock to run my truck through the out of state inspection. I should be able to have the new Oregon plates put on before I leave the inspection center."

Like the vacating fog, the professional countenance on Officer Spenser Sparling's face had slipped away and was replaced now with and expression of the stark realization that he had just yelled at the new chief of police.

"You're chief Kearnes, aren't you," said Spenser, already knowing the answer to his lamely posed question that had been uttered as a statement instead.

"Yes I am," said Kearnes, offering his hand to Spenser to shake.

Spenser quickly shook his hand and then looking down at the roadway, stammered, "Sir, I am so sorry. I didn't even see you pull up and by the time I did…what I mean is: I screwed up and I know it. I never should have raised my voice, it's just that…"

"No," said Kearnes. "I'm the one that screwed up, Officer Sparling, not you."

Spenser stopped his apologetic explanation in mid-sentence, and looked up at Kearnes, dumbstruck.

"I should have approached you with my badge and ID in hand, held high, before I ever took a single step toward you. You took the absolute correct action by challenging me exactly when, and in how you did it. And I expect you to do the same thing again, then next time it happens."

"Well," said Spenser tentatively, "I'm still learning. But that is how they taught us at the Academy."

"Where's your back-up tonight?" asked Kearnes. "Do you have another city unit on with you tonight?"

"No," said Spenser. "There is one county deputy on but he's in the north county area right now, and he goes off at 2am."

"So you're all alone out here, is that right?"

"Yes sir."

"Do you need any help getting your DUI to the jail Officer Sparling?"

"No sir," said Spenser. "I think I can manage him OK."

"Well then," said Kearnes. "You have a good night, and stay safe out here."

"Yes sir," said Spenser, "I will. You have a good night too, chief."

Kearnes started to get back in his truck but stopped, and turned back to Spenser.

"Officer?" he said. "One more thing."

Spenser stood as still as a statue, bracing himself for what he felt might be coming. He did not trust supervisory level officers for the most part—with the exception of Sergeant Compton—because he had never been given any good reason to. He spent his days and nights at the job he loved more than anything else in the world trying his best to avoid people like Lieutenant Polk and his three close friends, who were known in the department as "The Unholy Four", and who seemed to exist only to make his life and the lives of the other patrol officers and dispatchers a nearly unbearable ordeal of continuous ridicule, scorn, chastisement, and; if they felt they had been defied or blocked in any of their efforts to see the police department run in the way they wanted it to be run…retribution.

"Yes sir?"

"I want to thank you for giving me a break on my out of state plates. I know that I meet the requirements of residency now, and that you could have chosen to issue me a citation. I appreciate you not ticketing me, and I promise you will see them on my truck tomorrow."

Spenser Sparling was speechless. He couldn't respond to Kearnes; at least not in words, but the small grin that began at the corners of his mouth and spread to a wide and fulfilling smile as Kearnes drove away, said everything that Spenser could have ever hoped to say at that moment. For months he had been sending out applications everywhere, using his regular days off and most of his accrued vacation time to travel to other cities around the state and test for openings on their police departments because he was so miserable working at Cutter Point P.D.

He had believed that the arrival of another new chief, the third one since he'd started working there, would bring nothing but more turmoil and trouble. But as he watched the new chief's taillights disappearing across the Blue Czar River Bridge, the truck's right amber blinker signaling as he took the first exit on the other side to Harbor Way, he suddenly found himself filled with a rush of anticipation for a dramatic change that may soon come, and now he thought that he might stay here at least through summer, to see how things went.

And besides, summer was not only the most beautiful time of year in the city, but also the busiest; just as it was everywhere else on the entire Oregon coast. Tourists would begin to swell into the beachside towns in wave upon wave as soon as schools began to dismiss for the summer—as most would starting this week—and crime and catastrophe always seemed to follow certain of these vacationers as predictably as the ocean tides. All of the communities from the largest to the smallest seemed to have their own unique annual summer celebrations, everything from wine festivals to whale festivals, and the good times and gaiety—accompanied by the sounds of ringing cash registers and the swish of plastic credit cards being swiped through electronic readers—continued all summer long right through Labor Day Weekend, until they finally all went back home.

It was a fun and exhilarating time of the year for all of the young officers of Cutter Point P.D., and Spenser Sparling didn't want to miss a single minute of it. Especially if this was going to be his last summer working here.

But if he had known exactly *who* it was, that was coming to pay his town a visit…Cutter Point would have been the last place on earth where he would have wanted to be.

CHAPTER 8

▼

The Sea Breeze Apartments squatted forlornly at the farthest end of Pearl Cove Harbor directly across from the boat docks, and situated between an abandoned, rusting salmon cannery and a winter net storage barn. Its outer walls, once painted the color of split pea green soup, had faded to a dull lime green and were blistered and buckled from the winter winds and rain that blew in from the ocean, battering them relentlessly all winter long. The decorative porthole style windows of the individual units, which had originally lent a sense of odd and fanciful whimsy to the building when it was first constructed in the late fifties as a deep sea fishing charter motel, now gave the Sea Breeze the appearance of a decrepit old freightliner that had run aground in a storm and wasn't worth hauling off the rocks.

Kearnes lay awake in his bed in the murky light of pre-dawn, his stomach roiling as if he was about to get seasick, but on land. He had left the small apartment porthole window in the bathroom partially open all night in order to get some air—believing it would be too small for even the tiniest burglar to squeeze through—and now the smell of the morning low tide wafting through it was making him sick to his stomach.

He carefully got out of bed and walked to the bathroom, where he swung the heavy round brass trimmed window inward, and snapped the lock shut. Four days after he'd arrived in Cutter Point and had finally been able to find an apartment cheap enough to rent that he could afford, he'd gone grocery shopping and had purchased a bottle of Pepto Bismol for his newly discovered upset stomach which he'd blamed at the time on the inherent nervousness and anxiety of starting a new job, but had now begun to suspect was being caused by something else.

He opened the medicine cabinet, took the half empty pink bottle from the shelf, and drank the entire rest of its contents; then shuffled his way back to bed.

The dank, clammy smell of the ocean at low minus tide, the exposed rocks covered with slick, green seaweeds, the now bare and glistening sand flats that held the chewed flotsam deposited by the receding surf; all of it congealed to form a purulent odor that assaulted and overwhelmed Kearnes' olfactory senses to the point of nearly causing him to vomit. So what was this about the smell of the sea? He had always thought the way the ocean smelled—or was supposed to any-how—was clean, and crisp; a scent that embodied excitement and adven-ture…just like it was portrayed on the commercials for Old Spice after shave he used to see on TV when he was a kid.

He had been to the ocean only once before in his life; when he was a very young boy and his family had taken a rare summer vacation trip together. His Father had borrowed his uncle Ben's camp trailer and hitched it to their old Mer-cury station wagon, and they spent two weeks driving across country to Seattle to see the Space Needle, and ride in the encapsulated elevator to its windy, swaying top, before traveling on to the Washington coast for a few days, and then back home to Kansas. But it had been so long ago he remembered almost nothing about the trip, including the way the ocean had looked, or even smelled, the first time he had ever seen it.

But he was a grown man now, and apparently one who was for some reason possibly allergic to the smell of the sea. And in addition to being the new chief of police of a seaside city police department that seemed to be rife with political and personnel problems that he wasn't sure he would even be able to begin to address, he might now also have to worry about losing his lunch around others whenever the tide went out.

He lay in bed, listening to the forlorn wailing of the Coast Guard buoy two miles offshore from the tip of the jetty at Pearl Cove. It rode in the gentle ocean swells, hidden by a low lying fog bank, invisibly warning all approaching water-craft of the rocky dangers ahead. Its lonely, resonant sound reminded Kearnes of the sound the cattle made as they were herded through the narrow metal chutes in the meat packing plant stock yard back in Dodge City; their eyes bulging with fear, their voices bawling and hooves kicking backward in panicked protest as they were funneled into the bowels of the huge grey concrete building; and shortly thereafter killed by a pneumatic driven steel bolt through their brains.

Drifting in and out of sleep, he wondered if his life was really turning out any better than those cattle; if he in fact wasn't being herded…driven by circum-stances and events that surrounded him which he felt were completely out of his control; propelling him toward unknown conclusions that he both feared, and inwardly railed against.

He had been nervous when he first arrived at Thud and Margie's house, unsettled; not just because they were strangers to him, but because they were a family and his acceptance of their dinner invitation had felt to him in some odd way as if it were an intrusion. But by the time the evening was over…after he had seen Thud riding his daughter's on his back in the grass of their lawn, the girls shrieking with delight as they dug their little bare heels into the meaty sides of his chest, pulling hard on his ears as if they were reins…after he had watched Thud and Margie walking back inside their house and the way Thud touched her—and she had let him touch her—he realized what he was really feeling was fear.

It was the fear of having to confront exactly what it was he had lost: his home; filled with all the comforting and meaningful sounds and smells and activities of family life. His two boys, who he now understood meant more to him than he could have ever imagined…and even Tilly; whose worst qualities and faults he had begun to see as something to hate so much less as he tried now instead to imbue his memories of her with a sense of tolerance and forgiveness.

Like one of the hapless, ill-fated cattle in the vast and endless herd of divorced and displaced men, he had blundered ahead with the others, into the chute, finally arriving at the slaughtering station where the pneumatic gun descended upon him and the trigger was pulled. But as the steel bolt punched into the top of his head and drove deep down through his body into the chambers of his heart, a truth worse than the searing pain of the projectile itself struck him: It wasn't the fear of having to confront what he had lost…it was the fear of the realization of what he had instead, simply given up.

At 6:30 a.m. his clock radio alarm went off with a steady, droning buzz. In the dream he was having he saw himself hanging from a sharp hook beneath the track of a ceiling conveyor belt with other gutted and skinned carcasses…being whisked along the track into a large, white room where men wearing blood spattered white smocks shoved slabs of marbled, red meat into the spinning, ribbon like blades of band saws. Great ham sized portions of the men's bodies vibrated crazily on the edge of the band saw tables for a few seconds as the blade chewed through the torso, until the operator pushed it off into a large stainless steel garbage can.

As Kearnes' own carcass drew closer to the nearest sawing station, he heard the metallic buzzing of the blade roaring in his ears and he panicked, kicking his legs and swinging his body (impaled at the neck) back and forth in an effort to get free…but it was too late. The sound of the band saw paralyzed him. He stopped struggling and all he could hear, all he could feel, was…Bzzzzzzzzzzzzz!

He bolted upright in his bed and ripped the sheet and blanket away from his body. Slick with sweat, and chest heaving from exertion, he twisted violently to his right and smashed the alarm clock radio on the cheap night stand next to him with his fist. Failing to silence the buzzing alarm he spared it another blow and instead, drug it off the night stand and brought it up close to his face while he fumbled with all its buttons until he hit the right one, and it fell silent. He stared at the clock's red digital display: 6:32 a.m. The alarm had been sounding for two full minutes…acting as the background soundtrack to his deranged and morbid dream.

The queasiness in his stomach had largely subsided by the time he had showered and shaved, and changed into a clean uniform. He made a pot of coffee and drank one cup while he listened to the morning news on the local FM station, KUTR; thankful the clock radio still worked after the beating he'd given it. His shift began at eight but by seven thirty he was in his black, unmarked Ford Crown Victoria and headed into the P.D. which was across the bridge in the center of town, only five minutes away.

Cutter Point was a city of approximately twelve thousand souls—about half the size of Dodge City, Kansas—but another five thousand people, including Kearnes, lived in the densely populated unincorporated area surrounding the city limits.

This conglomerate of older houses, apartment buildings, boat yards, and canneries had held out stubbornly in the face of "progress" and refused to budge when the city had received a multi-million dollar grant to expand and refurbish the Harbor, and build a new city park at Pearl Cove, complete with asphalt bicycle and roller blade paths, restrooms, a whale watching tower, and even palm trees imported from southern California planted in the new grass lawns.

The leaning, weathered, ramshackle old structures residents proudly referred to as "Old Town", or "Old Harbor Town"—some of which had been built in the early nineteen hundreds when Cutter Point was a booming logging and shipping port—seemed to those who currently occupied them to stand out like dully gleaming diamonds in the rough. But to Mayor Vernon Bouchet', Old Town stuck out like a sore thumb; one he was about to make even sorer in the future by lopping it off from the hand of the rapidly growing little city, and replacing it with a few luxury resort hotels, condominiums, and expensive ocean front homes.

Kearnes drove across the Blue Czar River Bridge, glancing at the deep chasm of green trees and vegetation in the canyon far below, and the milky blue channel of the river that curved gracefully through the center of it. The dizzying heights of this new land, the vibrant colors that abounded in the earth, and sky, and sea; all of it was so very foreign to him.

He had lived his entire life in places where endless flat horizons of earth tones and wind blown prairie grass melded together in a directionless vista that was at once both painfully lonely to the eye, and heartbreakingly endearing to the soul. And although his new home was without a doubt very beautiful to look at; he thought about how plain, and simple, could also be very beautiful too.

As the glass smooth concrete roadway of the bridge ended, he felt the Ford's pursuit radial tires bite into the hard chip seal surface of Cutter Avenue; the long, dog legged stretch of U.S. Highway 101 that ran through the center of the city for two miles and comprised the downtown business and shopping district. There were a total of four traffic lights on Cutter Avenue downtown, and while he was stopped at the second traffic light headed north, Kearnes spotted the police department's only other unmarked patrol car—also a black Ford—in the parking lot of a pancake restaurant called The Buccaneer.

It was Thud Compton's detective car which meant Thud was probably inside—either on a case or eating breakfast—and as Kearnes sat at the unusually long red light, waiting for it to change, he was thinking about turning into the Buccaneer's parking lot and going inside to buy Thud a cup of coffee, when his car's previously silent mobile radio suddenly crackled to life.

"Central to One Charles Four…One Boy One and One Boy Two requesting you respond to the end of Walton Nature Walkway, west side of the Wal-Mart parking lot, 6080 Cutter Avenue, for a 10-54…reportedly found on the beach that location."

Kearnes grabbed the small plastic laminated "cheat sheet" from the windshield's visor above his head. It was a listing of all the "Ten Codes"…the radio call numbers for the generic categories of incidents police were most often sent on—most of them slightly different from the Kansas law enforcement codes he was familiar with—and a list of all of the department's assigned personnel "identifier" numbers.

He scanned the list quickly: The "Boy" units were the two summer intern bike patrol officers, Frick and Frack; out early on their first day of summer bike patrol. 1-C-4 was the detective unit, Thud Compton. The bike patrol officers were on the beach at the end of an interpretive "nature path" boardwalk, built and paid for by the new Wal-Mart located on the edge of the city's northern boundary at Bouchet' Plaza; and they were requesting a detective unit respond to their location for a 10-54. A possible dead body.

The traffic light in front of Kearnes turned green, and he saw Thud burst from the front doors of The Buccaneer on a dead run—his shoulder slamming into the wooden pirate statute that stood next to the doors and making it shudder—as he ran to his car in the parking lot. He saw, and then heard, Thud shouting into his hand held portable radio as he ran: "One Charlie Four Central! Get medical and fire rescue started to that location! Notify the Coroner's Office, and I want the M.E. standing by there for cell phone contact when I get to the scene. Put me 10-8 en route...and get hold of One Charlie One and have him respond and meet me there!"

Kearnes drove through the intersection, pulling into the far right lane of the double lane roadway, and when he looked into his rear view mirror he saw Thud's car coming now, rapidly gaining on him. The hidden strobe lights behind the unmarked vehicle's grill and in the two outside mirrors were popping out electronic bursts of red and blue light that each lasted only milliseconds, but jelled into a steady blur of color, and the siren mounted beneath the vehicle's hood screeched loudly with a muffled, yet strident tone. Kearnes had only gotten two blocks from The Buccaneer when Thud shot past him on the left, a streak of color and noise. And like a black stealth jet fighter, he rocketed down the nearly empty early morning downtown street toward the Wal-Mart at the far end of town, his black Ford Police Interceptor leaving a white contrail of heated engine exhaust mixed with cool, wet ocean air in its wake.

Kearnes accelerated his vehicle now also, moving over into Thud's same lane, and switched on his lights and siren. He grabbed the portable radio mike from its holder and spoke into it. "One Charles One to Central...I am in service. Show me responding to 6080 Cutter Avenue also on the 10-54. Have One Boy One and One Boy Two form a scene perimeter and maintain same until I arrive."

"Copy, One Charles One," the female dispatcher answered. "One Boy One and One Boy Two, do you copy that?"

Kearnes could hear one of the bike patrol units trying to answer her back on his portable; but he was cut off by other units "walking" on him...attempting to transmit on their radios at the same time, resulting in a temporary impenetrable wall of garbled electronic white noise that no one could get through.

He heard Edgar Polk and his crony, Sergeant Byron Downs...who supervised the Communications Center, and who really had no business leaving there...responding Code 3 from the police station with emergency lights and sirens—even though the Wal-Mart was less than half a mile away; and listened as another Cutter Point patrol unit on the east side of the city cleared from a traffic stop to respond, and the Fire Department toned out both an engine and a Medi-

cal Rescue unit to the call. Then, two Oregon State Troopers and a Cutter
County Deputy Sheriff also chimed in, notifying Central Dispatch they were
responding too; in spite of the fact that the closest one of the three was more than
forty miles from the city.

The parking lot of the Wal-Mart in the Bouchet' Plaza Shopping Center was
a capacious expanse of black asphalt desert, completely devoid of cars at this early
morning hour except for Thud's, and Kearnes would have never seen the black
vehicle sitting at the extreme western edge of the empty black lot, its passenger
door thrown open, if it had not been for the strobe lights Thud had left them on
in his haste to get down the trail to the beach and the dead body before Frick and
Frack (he was sure) would screw everything up.

Kearnes slowed a little and began to brake as he approached the first entrance
off Cutter Avenue into Bouchet' Plaza, keeping his eye on the red and blue
strobe flashes coming from the taillights of Thud's car three hundred yards away.
He was wondering why he had not yet seen Lieutenant Polk's car even though he
had already passed by the police department several blocks back, when suddenly
his left field of peripheral vision was filled with the sparkling metallic black and
white of Polk's freshly washed patrol unit as it zipped past him, siren screaming,
and then swerved across his path—narrowly missing the front of Kearnes' car—as
Polk now assumed the lead.

As they sped by, Kearnes had seen the lackluster face of Sergeant Byron
Downs staring vapidly at him from the passenger window. He tried to analyze
Downs' facial expression but he could not determine if it was one of sheer stupid-
ity—for being out of his element at the moment and not having a clue how to
act—or absolute terror; from the wild and reckless ride his best friend and men-
tor was taking him on. Or, more probable than either of these two explanations...unflinching blind dedication; because Delbert Downs was a fawning,
flattering parasite who would do *anything* for his superior, Edgar Polk. Including,
apparently, dying in a senseless and tragic traffic accident as long as he didn't
show either any concern or lack of gratitude on his face just before the moment
of impact.

According to Thud Sergeant Delbert Downs was known around the police
department as "Downs Syndrome Downs", and in no way did he truly run the
Communications Department in an efficient, effective manner, so much as he,
instead, just ran it into the ground; and the people who worked there, along with
it. And had it not been for the continuing protection of Edgar Polk who had
orchestrated the hiring of Downs fifteen years earlier on the police department—
because he instinctively knew Delbert would make the perfect toady for him—

Delbert would have long ago been relegated to the rank of parking meter reader. And would have been damn lucky to been given even that job.

Kearnes jammed on his brakes and jerked the steering wheel hard left as the Ford skidded across the dewy wet asphalt, the soft pursuit tires clutching at the slick nubby surface beneath them and expanding from the sudden build up of heat like hot chewed bubble gum. He jolted to a stop and turned off his siren and lights as he watched Polk and Downs closing on Thud's car until they pulled up directly behind it and stopped, deactivating all of their emergency equipment too. And then they just sat there, neither one of them making a move to get out.

"One Charles Two and One Charles Three are 10-97 on scene," Kearnes heard Edgar Polk say over the radio. "I will be assuming Incident Command, Central," Polk continued. "Have all responding units stage at my vehicle and 10-7 with Charles Three...I will advise further who will be allowed scene access after I assess same."

Kearnes was shaken from the near collision with Polk's car, his heart pounding with the gush of adrenalin now coursing through his bloodstream like it had been injected through a pressure fed hose. This inevitable physiological chain reaction to stress within his body had started as he was responding to the potentially "hot call" because most cops—and Kearnes was no exception—more often than not equated the term *dead body* with *homicide*; and things had only become revved up even more after Polk had almost sideswiped him.

But had he really heard Polk say what he thought he'd heard him say? Had his second in command...his Lieutenant...not only actually jumped on *his* call and nearly run him over in the process of doing it, but was now also assuming command of a possible crime scene—maybe even a murder—while the chief of police was obviously present?

He saw both doors on Polk's vehicle swing open as he snatched his own radio mike from its clip holder and mashed the transmit button down with his thumb. "Central this is One Charles One...disregard that last transmission from Charles Two!" he said, barely able to keep the anger out of his voice. "Put *me* 10-97 on scene and assuming Incident Command. Do you copy that?"

There was three long seconds of dead air on the radio. Finally, the dispatcher came back on and answered crisply: "One Charles One is on scene, 6880 Cutter Ave., west side of the Wal-Mart parking lot, report of a 10-54 and assuming Incident Command at 0735 hours." And then she paused again, letting all of the units who were monitoring the radio traffic ready themselves to hear what was about to be a verbal gauntlet thrown down by the new chief, challenging Edgar Polk for command and leadership of the police department. It was the very same type of thing that had, in the end, played a large part in costing Cutter Point's last several police chiefs their jobs.

"One Charles Two," the young female dispatcher—whose name was Shoshana—said very carefully, and succinctly. "*You* are relieved of Incident Command...do you copy?"

There was no response; only a tension filled silence.

"Central to One Charles Two. You have been relieved. Do you copy?"

Still nothing.

Kearnes moved his foot off the brake to the accelerator and throwing the radio mike down in disgust on the passenger side seat, floored the gas pedal and sped across the parking lot, sliding to a stop next to Thud's car and jumping out.

"Central to One Charles Two"...he heard Shoshana saying over the radio as he quickly sprinted the scant few feet back to Polk's car. "One Charles Two...acknowledge please."

Edgar Polk saw him coming, his eyes suddenly growing wide with surprise, and he quickly started to get out of his car. But he had only managed to get his door open about six inches when Kearnes reached the black and white and slammed the palms of his hands against the door just below the window, banging the door shut with such force that the vehicle visibly bounced up and down on its shocks. Edgar Polk snapped his hands back from the door handle it as if it had suddenly become red hot.

Polk's car window was rolled down and Kearnes left his hands on the door's frame where they had impacted—stinging smartly now—and lowered his body until he was looking straight inside the vehicle at him.

"They're calling you on the radio, Lieutenant," he said evenly. "You need to answer."

Edgar Polk put his hands on the steering wheel and looked straight ahead at Thud Compton's detective car. His bony knuckles began to show white through the leathery translucent skin of his hands like square, sharp cornered dice, as he began to squeeze the wheel hard.

Neither man had said a word or even acknowledged Kearnes' presence, and when Delbert Downs started to reach for the radio mike to answer the dispatcher on behalf of Polk, Kearnes yelled "NO!" Delbert recoiled backwards in his seat as if he were a misbehaving dog on a leash that had just been yanked back into compliance by its handler. He cast a bewildered, slack mouthed look at Polk, but Polk ignored him; he would deal with Downs Syndrome later, in private.

"One Charles Two?" said Shoshana over Polk's radio. "Do you copy Central?"

In his entire law enforcement career Kearnes had never personally seen, let alone been the recipient of, such blatant insubordination from a subordinate officer. It was commonplace for police officers to often disagree with their bosses, or even hate them, but such "in your face" disrespect and defiance was akin to career suicide. Police departments were Para-military organizations, based on a set of operating policies and procedures that were adhered to by all, and enforced through a chain of command.

At Dodge City P.D. he had won the respect and trust of all his officers by virtue of his competency, character, and integrity, and his consistently fair, but firm, treatment of them all. Last night at the Compton's he had thought Thud's statement about Edgar Polk "hating" him may have been a little too harsh; perhaps even a little slanted by Thud's own personal feelings of animosity toward the Lieutenant. But now he felt as if he'd wandered into the middle of a pit of vipers in a dark and unfamiliar place, and his first footstep had fallen directly on the head of the biggest and deadliest snake there.

Edgar Polk regained his composure; relaxed his grip on the steering wheel and began to nervously tap his fingers on its pebbled vinyl surface like a musician playing a tune on a silent trumpet. He turned his head toward Kearnes and finally spoke.

"This is the way we've always done things here...sir," Polk said brusquely. "Our chiefs in the past haven't regularly responded to calls in the field. We usually let the patrol command staff do their job, first."

"Then it appears you've been doing things the wrong way, Lieutenant," said Kearnes, his gaze now boring straight into Edgar Polk's yellow flecked grey eyes that seemed to pulse behind their constricting pupils with venomous hatred. "Now you answer that goddamned radio," Kearnes said with finality. "I won't say it a third time."

Polk ripped the radio mike from its holder, clicked the transmit button on the side and snarled into it, "One Charles Two Central I copy! One Charles One just arrived on scene and we've been busy...discussing how to handle this. One Charles One will be the I.C."

"Copy, One Charles Two!" Shoshanna came back gleefully. "One Charles One will be handling, at 0736 hours...Central clear."

"Thank you Lieutenant," Kearnes said, stepping back from Polk's car so he could get out. "And by the way, when you get back to the office you might check the P and P Manual...Section 6.1.A I believe...*"the chief of police, or in his absence, his designee, shall be immediately notified of all incidents classified as felonies or which otherwise upon initial assessment appear serious in nature, and shall person-*

ally respond to same and assume command at the scene"...or words to that effect as far as I can recall, anyhow." Kearnes had taken his copy of the Cutter Point Police Department Policies and Procedures Manual home with him after his first day on the job, and read it in its entirety over the next several nights, twice.

"I know what the Manual says," Polk spat back at him, as he stiffly exited his vehicle. "I helped to write it."

Kearnes jogged back to his own car to get his portable radio, hearing the sirens of the approaching fire units off in the distance growing louder. He made a quick transmission over the handheld to Central, advising the dispatcher to contact all the other responding units and have them cut their response codes from a 3, lights and sirens, to a 2, emergency lights only and reduced speed, and a few seconds later the sirens stopped sounding. If this was going to turn out to be a major incident, he wanted to keep things—and emergency personnel—as calm and quiet for as long as possible.

He walked over to the start of the boardwalk path, which was constructed of thick rough sawn planks of yellow Douglas fir nailed lengthwise across widely spaced matching fir beams, and had raised wooden hand rails on both sides. Stepping up onto the slippery wood surface wet from the morning dew and ocean mist, he grabbed at the rail with one hand when he felt his uniform boots suddenly lose traction, and stopped himself from falling just in time. Falling on his ass would have been disastrous at this point in more ways than one, because he knew Polk and Downs must be watching him.

He turned around to look at them and to his surprise saw Delbert Downs standing a few feet away from the patrol car, facing away from him, talking on a cell phone. Later he would learn Downs had been placing a call to the mayor's office, and not finding him in yet, had called the Dispatch Center and ordered Shoshana to page both Vernon Bouchet' and the city manager, Roy Roddam-eyer.

But Polk stood there staring straight at him; his arms folded pugnaciously, the scowl on his face making him look even more displeased than his body language did.

He was a short, stocky man with a body the shape of a stout tree trunk; obviously once heavily muscled and powerful when he had been a younger man in his prime, but now at age sixty eight, softening and spreading out. He had a head full of snow white hair, and a drooping, old west style handlebar moustache. And when he walked it was with a kind of creaking, slow shuffle, which gave him the appearance of exactly who and what he was: a bitter and negative old man who had long ago forsaken his oath to protect and serve the public, and had instead chosen to study and master the arts of being both a preeminent pessimist, and a malcontent. Edgar Polk was one very unpleasant human being to have to be around, and he had a personality that would curdle vinegar.

"Chief!"

Startled, Kearnes spun around and saw Thud standing a few yards away from him on the boardwalk. His shirt collar was undone, his tie opened in a wide loop around his neck, and the knees of his trousers down to his cuffs, and sleeves and elbows of his suit jacket…and his hands…were covered with freshly clinging wet sand. He was out of breath, and sweating.

"Thud!" he said, "What have we got?"

"I didn't want to put anything out over the radio," said Thud, wiping the sweat from his forehead with a clean space on the inside arm of his jacket sleeve. "So I came back up here to get you."

"Just *please* tell me we still need the Paramedics?" said Kearnes.

Thud solemnly shook his head…no.

"Oh shit," Kearnes said under his breath. Although he had been involved in many homicide investigations in his career over the years—as a patrolman, and a patrol supervisor—he had never been tasked with the heavy responsibility of personally being in charge of one before…and it was the last thing he wanted, or needed. Whether he could admit it to himself or not, he had come to Cutter Point in full retreat from his life and what it had become. It was a place to hide and lick at his painful wounds, which he had begun to realize were much more powerful than he himself was now…and might ever be again.

Murder investigations had a way of drawing investigators into a spotlight which sometimes shined equally as harsh upon them in the eyes of the public as it did on a suspect, and he could no longer afford to be tested. The constant self-judgment of himself and his loss of the sense of who he really was now had brought him to a place where failure was a fear he lived with every day of his life. And even though you couldn't fail at something you chose not to attempt, Kearnes had entered a new realm of his career when he became a chief without understanding that his ability to choose what he did, or did not want to be involved with now, no longer existed. It was one thing to deal with a bully at work like Edgar Polk, but quite another to have to be the one responsible for seeing that final justice was done on behalf of a human being whose life had been taken without justification from this world by another.

"We have a real problem down there," said Thud, glancing back over his shoulder in the direction of the ocean. "We're going to need some people with shovels…and you need to come and see this, chief."

Kearnes looked long and hard at Thud Compton and knew almost instantly what it was that Thud had been doing in those few short minutes down on the beach, while he had been dealing with Edgar Polk and Delbert Downs in the parking lot.

Thud Compton had been digging up a dead body with his bare hands.

CHAPTER 9

▼

The wooden boardwalk nature trail zigzagged through a hundred yards of low lying, undulating sand dunes that were as white as soft spun sugar, before it reached a wall of much larger dunes that stood imposingly like a small mountain range in front of the sea. There, the boardwalk ended and the trail became a narrow passageway that cut sharply through the high sand hills, and was snarled and tangled with unruly waist high clumps of stubbornly growing beach grasses, blackberry vines, and blockades of driftwood logs that had been left at odd angles, and in the most inconvenient locations, by the winter storms.

Thud got further and further ahead as they went; easily but gingerly picking his way in and out, over and around, all of the vegetation and every suit snagging protuberance he encountered, until he finally disappeared from Kearnes' sight.

Kearnes giant stepped over the last knee high impediment that lay directly in his path. It was a gnarled, upended tree stump whose roots had been ground down to short stubs; agitated against the gravelly ocean bottom of a high incoming tide before being tossed ashore. He rounded one last small grass covered hump of sand, parting the long, razor thin fingers of beach grass in front of him with his forearms...and was suddenly standing before an unbroken panorama of blue sea.

The roar of the ocean surf up close sounded like a not too distant freight train; one that was always in motion, traveling toward some far away destination, but never quite finally arriving there. Sea gulls patterned in the sky high overhead around the sultry morning's slowly building cumulus clouds, looking like tiny white specks of fuzz that had become dislodged from giant cotton balls and were drifting slowly, lazily, toward the earth.

He tried to hold his breath for a moment against the foul stink of the seashore which was still largely exposed and laid bare by the low tide, but couldn't do it for very long. And when he was finally forced to breathe in the putrid air he felt his stomach begin to churn and could soon feel the bitter acids down there, mixed with the coffee he'd drunk earlier, beginning to creep up into his throat and burn.

He scanned up and down the beach looking for Thud and the bike patrol officers, but they were nowhere to be seen. This part of Cutter Point's coastline was nearly inaccessible, except for the nature trail, because it was sequestered for nearly a mile on either end by large rocky headlands that jutted out into the water, impassable by foot, and the only other access areas were from private property. There were no roads down to the beach here; the nature boardwalk was the only feasible way in and out and in the summertime this made "Wal-Mart Beach" a very popular place for beachcombing tourists by day, and underage drinking youths by night.

Spaced within the sounds of the crashing surf emptying itself onto the shore, he could hear slices of voices speaking from somewhere beyond a large, dark gray and white mottled volcanic rock formation that sat alone out in the middle of the hard packed low tide sand; not yet reached by the advancing waters. He walked toward the giant, oblong shaped rock and as he got closer, saw the rear wheel of one of the white Raleigh police bikes sticking out from behind it.

As he came around the low corner end of the rock the overpowering stench of the ocean…much stronger than anything he had smelled earlier that morning in his apartment…hit him full force, and he stopped in his tracks, feeling as if he was going to throw up. Fighting to regain control over the involuntary spasms in the back of his throat, he took a couple more steps and the dark colored "sand" beneath his feet suddenly came to life as thousands of black sand flies lifted off in a cloud and settled in the air above the rock, buzzing loudly.

He saw Thud towering over the two bike patrol officers Frick and Frack, who were standing beside their parked bikes, helmets dropped on the sand; pinching their noses from the thickly rank smell which Kearnes now realized was something much more than just the low tide.

"What the hell were you thinking!" Thud yelled at both of them. "*This*," he shouted, jabbing an index finger at the huge barnacle encrusted rock, "is NOT a 10-54!"

Kearnes watched in amazement as the cloud of droning sand flies hovering above the rock slowly descended upon its surface; and then scurried away in every direction as they began to find the choicest spots on which to feed. What he was looking at was not a massive slab of barnacle covered igneous rock; but a forty eight foot long, thirty five ton, barnacle covered…dead…and rotting…gray whale.

"You freaking little helmet headed morons!" shouted Thud. "Don't you even know the goddamned ten code yet?"

"Not all of it," said Frick, briefly unpinching his nose to speak.

"But we know most of it, Sergeant!" Frack piped up, keeping his nostrils closed tightly together with his fingers and making himself sound like a hare-lip…infuriating Thud even further.

"Well, your little pedal pushing asses had better learn it by the end of today!" bellowed Thud. "And get your goddamned hands away from your noses!"

"Yes Sergeant!" cried Frick.

"Yes sir!" Frack chimed in.

To Kevin Kearnes the sight of the gargantuan deceased mammal lying on its back in the sun…its gaseous, swelling torso and belly the length and width of a small city bus, and the empty black cavern of its eye socket—picked clean by gulls and ravens—as large around as a slow pitch softball…was a mesmerizing and surreal vision. They had nothing like this back in Kansas that could compare.

"A 10-54," Thud said, "in the ten code, is a possible dead body. Now, a 10-91…which is what you two should have used…is an animal complaint."

"You could have even used code 10-91 David…a complaint of a dead animal. And that would have been OK too," said Thud, calming down some now. Thud was the police departments training officer in addition to being the only detective, and was therefore in charge of the law enforcement summer intern program; which made him Frick and Frack's direct supervisor.

"Jesus," he said, a tinge of hurt in his voice. "I would have thought you guys had learned all this stuff last summer."

"We were learning the city streets last summer, Sergeant," Frick said helpfully.

"And all the avenues, too," Frack added.

"Well *learn* this," said Thud. "You do NOT use the code 10-54 for the discovery of a dead body, when what you have in fact is a dead animal body! You got that?"

"We're clear on that Sergeant," answered Frick

"Crystal clear, Sarge!" said Frack.

"Because," said Thud, "it tends to cause undue excitement amongst the law enforcement and other emergency responder folks; when they think they have a dead body lying around somewhere. Especially if that dead body might still be alive."

"Sorry for the screw up, Sergeant," Frick said.

"Totally sorry," Frack said.

"You two pedal files have caused all hell to break loose this morning...not to mention that you interrupted my breakfast...and probably the chief's breakfast, too," Thud said, pointing at Kearnes as he walked up to the trio.

"Oh, crap," said Frick as he spotted the four gold stars on each collar point of Kearnes' uniform shirt, recognizing him now as the chief and not just another patrol officer.

"Oh, shit," exclaimed Frack.

"And," Thud continued, "you two are to check with me first at the start of every shift for briefing before you head out. What the hell are you doing out here so early, anyhow?"

"Learning this beach trail area, Sergeant," Frick said.

"Uh...I guess we just got excited," said Frack. "This being our first day back on bike patrol and all."

"Well, *don't* get excited in this job," said Thud. "About anything. It's a good way to get yourself hurt, or worse. You can't think straight when you're excited, and thinking your way out of bad situations is what this job is all about."

"Yes sir," said Frick. "And we're sorry, chief," he said to Kearnes.

"Yeah," said Frack. "Sorry for saying 'shit', chief. And for screwing up, too."

Kearnes looked at their youthful, tanned, exuberant faces, and saw not only the future promise of two very fine police officers in the making...he also saw a reflection of himself as a young officer so many years ago. How wonderful it would be to go back in time to those first years on the force; when he'd met Tilly, and the boys had been born. How differently he would do everything over; given a second chance to build and nurture the love he'd had with his wife and children then...and for that matter, many other people who had come and gone in his life since that time. But what he didn't know was that he would have to go back much further than that; years further. For the trouble in Kevin Kearnes' life hadn't started when he'd met Tilly; it had only metastasized.

"You guys listen to what your Sergeant tells you," said Kearnes, "and you'll be all right."

"Thank you sir," said Frack

"Yeah, thanks chief," Frick said.

Thud used his portable radio to cancel all of the responding units, including Fire and Medical, and told Frick and Frack to get on their bikes and go back to the parking lot and string some yellow "Police line—Do Not Cross" tape across the trail head entrance; and to stay there and not let any civilians or the media down on the beach until given further notice.

"Does this happen often?" asked Kearnes, reaching out and touching the whale's skin, which felt like the surface of a peeled, hard boiled egg. "An animal this size…washing up on the beach?"

Thud knelt down in the sand, examining a long tooth rake mark in the skin of the whale next to its upturned paddle shaped flipper, which had probably been inflicted by an Orca—a much smaller but deadly whale species.

"Hardly ever," he said. "I can't remember the last time we had one beach itself around here. In fact, this whale shouldn't even be here this late in the migration. We saw the last of them pass by going north almost a month ago."

Thud Compton had been trained as a homicide investigator to look for and establish a preliminary cause of death at crime scenes, prior to a Coroner's final findings. But in the case of this dead body he didn't have a clue as to either how, or even where to begin, so he set his portable radio down on a driftwood log, removed his suit jacket and hung it from a short snaggy branch of the same log, and began feeling his way along the side of the whale's body with both arms outstretched like a blind man feeling his way down the wall of a strange and unfamiliar hallway.

"It's…big," said Kearnes, still trying to comprehend the bizarre, noxious smelling scene in front of him.

"You think?" said Thud a little facetiously.

"Thud, how in hell are we going to get it out of here?"

"Damn it!" said Thud, quickly pulling his hand back from the whale after he'd sliced the tip of his right little finger open on one the of the sharp barnacles. He reached into his back pocket and pulled out a clean, white handkerchief, and wrapped it tightly around the wound.

"Well, I can't tell what killed it," he said, "or why it died." He stood up, being careful not to lean against any more of the razor sharp barnacles on the whale's skin as he did. "But I know it's beginning to decompose, and something this big could actually pose a health threat…maybe even get this beach closed for the summer by the State Department of Environmental Quality."

"There are not any roads in or out of here," observed Kearnes. "And where could we even find a truck big enough to haul it out of here if there were?"

"Not to mention," said Thud, daubing at his cut finger with the now red spotted handkerchief, "this thing is probably on an endangered or protected species list of some sort. So I doubt we can even touch it until we get the go ahead from about fifty federal and state agencies."

None of this had even occurred to Kearnes. He had only seen, and been concerned with, the immediate immensity of the problem at hand; how to remove the whale from the beach...and what to do with if after that.

"But there's this guy I know who could be very helpful," Thud said. "Let me call him first, chief, if that's all right with you?" Kearnes told Thud to go ahead and make the call, and as Thud got his cell phone from his jacket hanging on the driftwood log branch, Kearnes walked away from the dead whale toward the incoming tide line. There, the cool morning breeze traveling in on the ocean waves was a respite from the stagnant, polluted, fly filled air around the whale; and although it was refreshing by comparison, the smell of the sea by itself caused his stomach to lurch slightly.

He heard Thud calling to him; turned and saw him gesturing for him to return. When he reached Thud he found him talking on his portable radio to one of the bike patrol officers back in the parking lot. He finished the conversation and turned to Kearnes.

"Oh how lovely," Thud said, his voice thick with sarcasm. "I have just been informed the mayor and the city manager are on their way down."

"Who called them?" Kearnes asked.

"Not positive," said Thud. "But I would imagine that asshole Polk...or Downs. One of those two. I did manage to get hold of this park ranger...Connelly...and he's on his way down from his office. I think we'd better get back out to the parking lot before any of them get here, chief."

The morning sun was becoming more dominant now; beaming down through the slowly dispersing clouds and ocean mist and starting to somewhat dry the surface of the nature trail boardwalk, although Kearnes could still see the faint knobby pattern of mountain bike tire tracks in places left by Frick and Frack.

As Kearnes and Thud stepped off the last board onto the sand and trudged toward the blacktop of the parking lot—lifting up and passing under the barrier of yellow plastic tape Frick and Frack had tied to scrub bushes across trail head—Kearnes saw a white Cadillac Escalade pull to a stop next to Edgar Polk's cruiser; and directly behind it, a white Dodge pickup truck with an Oregon State Parks decal on the door.

Edgar Polk got out of his car and moved swiftly to the passenger window of the Escalade and began talking excitedly to the person sitting there, but Kearnes couldn't see who it was; only a small silhouette which appeared to be that of a child and he thought Roddameyer must have brought one of his kids with him to see the dead whale.

A tall, lanky man with a neatly trimmed full beard wearing a khaki uniform stepped out of the pickup and walked over to Thud. They shook hands and Thud introduced him to Kearnes as Steve Connelly, Chief Park Ranger at Musselshell State Park—the southern most tip of which touched the northern city boundary of Cutter Point less than a mile up the beach from the site of the dead whale—and a local expert on gray whales as well.

"Chief, I'd like to let Steve go down on the beach and take a look at our large friend there first and try to get an idea of what we've got," said Thud, "before any of these other people get involved with it." He nodded in the direction of Polk and the white Escalade. "If you know what I mean?"

"I know exactly what you mean," Kearnes said. "Steve, you need anything from us before you go?"

Connelly pulled his own portable radio from its holder on his leather gunbelt which held the radio, handcuffs, and mace, but no gun; because for some idiotic reason Oregon state park rangers were not allowed to be armed. He switched the frequency knob to the Cutter Point channel; then clicked the transmit button twice to test it.

"Nope," he said. "I'm good to go. I'll give you a shout and let you know when to come on down." In a few effortless, lengthy strides he was at the trailhead stepping easily over the yellow tape; and soon after that, was far down the boardwalk and out of sight in the dunes.

Kearnes heard the door of the Escalade open behind him and turned around to face for the first time, the man who was directly in charge of him—his boss, the city manager Roy Roddameyer.

Roddameyer was of medium height and build with an undefined body musculature that bordered on pudginess, and oily, black hair that was slicked back from his forehead in perfectly equidistant comb strokes. He was wearing expensive cotton linen slacks the color of a vanilla milkshake, a pale violet silk shirt open at the collar, and a double breasted wool navy blue blazer with large gold buttons; each containing a fancy script letter "R" on them raised from the metal in high relief.

His sunburned complexion was dark and ruddy and had a reddish tinge to it; like the red clay back in Kansas Kearnes and his Father and his uncle Ben used to kick and scrape from the bottoms of their boots after leaving the muddy spring wheat fields of their ranch, before walking through his Mother's immaculate country kitchen on their way into the dining room for lunch.

The rest of his attire—Nautica designer sunglasses and Bruno Magli Italian shoes—completed his look of pure affectation, and made him appear as if he'd just left a party at an exclusive Country Club somewhere; having had cocktails and witty conversation after a leisurely day of golf on the links. In actuality, that was not very far removed from the truth.

Roy Roddameyer took one step toward Kearnes, extending his hand; then abruptly stopped…forcing Kearnes to walk all the way to meet him and shake his hand.

"Chief Kearnes," he said, shaking Kearnes' hand. "Roy Roddameyer. I'm so glad to finally be able to meet you. I've been out of town the last couple of weeks on business for the mayor."

The "business" Roddameyer had been on was an all tax payer expense paid junket to five different destination golf course resorts on the coasts of Oregon and Washington; sizing up the competition for Cutter Point's own soon to open Trident Greens by playing these other courses; analyzing their market strategies and studying, in depth, their food and beverage operations. Especially their cocktail lounges…where Roddameyer had spent the majority of his time both day and night; tipping up rather than teeing off.

"Kevin Kearnes," he said, shaking Roddameyer's hand…which felt remarkably the same as Vernon Bouchet's hand shake had the day he'd met him at his swearing in: limp, feeble, and cold.

He noticed a long strand of dark blue thread that had come undone from one of the gold buttons on the cuff of Roddameyer's jacket sleeve; and on his pricey silk shirt just below the fourth button from the top, a small food grease stain. Now in close proximity to him Kearnes could smell a faint scent—like dried pine needles—the residual burn off from the three gin and tonics Roy Roddameyer had consumed in the lounge at The Buccaneer during breakfast just before eight o'clock that morning, soon after he'd arrived back in town.

"So," said Roddameyer, "Lieutenant Polk informs me we have a dead whale down on our beach?" Kearnes looked for Polk to see if either he or Downs were going to insert themselves into this, but they were on the other side of the Escalade, helping the child out.

"That's correct," said Kearnes. "We have the beach access sealed off from the public, and we have a state park ranger…who knows quite a lot about whales I'm told…down on the beach right now, examining it."

"Yes, yes," said Roddameyer. "That's good. But Lieutenant Polk tells me you refused to let him and Sergeant Downs view the whale?"

"Absolutely not," Kearnes said a little heatedly. "Lieutenant Polk and I both arrived here at the same time and I assumed command of the incident. I didn't tell him he couldn't go down. In fact, I wasn't even aware he was still up here in the parking lot."

At that moment Polk emerged from around the front side of the Escalade, shuffling forward toward them, his hand guiding the shoulder of the child who had been sitting inside the vehicle…except that it wasn't a child at all: it was mayor Vernon B. Bouchet´.

They moved procession like toward the rest of the group—the expression on Polk's face towards Kearnes switching back and forth between a glare and a smirk—as Delbert Downs brought up the rear like a circus clown in a parade following along behind the animals, shoveling up their shit.

Polk and Downs looked like giants next to the diminutive mayor, who stood only five feet four inches short. Whatever help he had originally either wanted or needed in getting out of the high sided luxury SUV was abruptly terminated as he shrugged his thin, bony shoulder away from Polk's hand saying, "That will do, Edgar," and then stopped in front of Roddameyer, ignoring Kearnes entirely.

"Roy boy," he said softly, "what's the situation?"

"The chief tells me we have a dead whale that has washed up on our beach…just discovered this morning, I believe. And we have Ranger Connelly down on the beach right now, examining it."

Vernon Bouchet´ wrinkled his nose in the light breeze that was wafting in off the ocean. "That the stink I smell?" he asked.

Roddameyer himself took a whiff of the air and said, "I would imagine it is."

Bouchet´ turned to Kearnes. He was one of those unfortunate little old men now who earlier in his life had also been a little young man. His huge oversized eyeglasses, thick, white bushy eyebrows, and loose fitting knit turtle neck shirts in which his debilitated body swam around inside of, and that he wore nearly every day along with equally too large sport jackets and slacks, gave him the appearance of a wary little barn owl sticking its head out of the shell of a snapping turtle.

"Chief Kearnes, do you have any idea yet how or why this whale managed to beach itself? Any plan for removal? Because in my estimation we cannot let something like this linger. It would be bad for our city's image, and extremely bad for business."

"That's what we're waiting to hear from ranger Connelly," Kearnes said. "Sergeant Compton tells me he's very knowledgeable about these whales. But we've also discussed the fact that there may be some additional things we have to take into consideration before taking any action, because these creatures may come under the jurisdiction of certain federal or state laws."

"I can guarantee you they absolutely will," Thud spoke up, "but I can't say exactly what laws those are."

Bouchet' grimaced at hearing Thud's voice and shot a quick, contemptuous look at him.

"Thank you...*detective*," he said, arching his owl eyebrows at Thud.

"But, gentlemen," he said. "I can assure both of you of one thing. That whale *will* be gone from this beach...today...before the sun goes down."

It took them almost ten minutes to navigate the nature trail back to the beach with Bouchet' and Roddameyer leading the way, after Connelly had called Kearnes on the radio and told them they could all come down.

Connelly was kneeling in the sand near the whale's upside down head when they arrived. He was examining the baleen plates on its upper jaw; the long fingernail like material called keratin which hung down curtain like from the top of the whale's jaw. They acted like the teeth in a giant comb, filtering out particles of amphipods—miniscule sea organisms—from the thousands of gallons of sea water passing through the whale's gaping, cavernous mouth as it fed.

He stood up and brushed the sand from his hands and his uniform pants as Kearnes walked over to him; while the others, standing some distance away, stared in awe at the dead behemoth; breathing through their mouths or fanning their faces with their hands in an attempt to mitigate the overpowering stench.

"She's a female," said Connelly, "probably between four and six years old, forty eight and a half feet long...and probably had a live weight of around thirty five to thirty eight tons before she beached here."

"What do you estimate it weighs right now?" asked Kearnes.

"Not a whole lot less than that," said Connelly. "She's been here at least a week, and whatever she's lost due to decomposition has probably been offset by water saturation of the tissues and internal organs. But once they reach this stage they begin to break down fast; helped along by the seabirds opening chunks of flesh on the top that get exposure to the sun."

"How do you think it ended up here?"

"We have about twenty thousand of them pass by here yearly on their migration route from the lagoons in the Baja Peninsula to the Bering Sea in Alaska; and then back to Mexico again. That's a twelve thousand mile round trip. It's like traffic on a heavily traveled freeway. Statistically, you know some of those cars are going to be involved in accidents and crash...but you just don't know which ones."

"So nothing killed it?" asked Thud.

"No," said Connelly. "See how the elevation of the beach drops off a little all around this point? We call these "sand domes". They are carved out and then smoothed around in a circular pattern by rip tides…which are like underwater funnel clouds. It's like turning a dinner plate upside down on a table. Right now we're standing in the raised center of that overturned dinner plate."

"In other words…this whale is just swimming along the shore here, in about twenty feet of extra water at high tide, and it hits this raised sand dome and gets high centered?" said Thud.

"Pretty much," Connelly said. "Whales are a lot like people. Some of them just don't pay enough attention to where they're going."

Kearnes saw Bouchet', Roddameyer, and Polk huddled close together in conference. Polk was doing all the talking. He took a small notebook from the pocket of his uniform shirt, wrote something on it, and then handed it to Delbert Downs. Downs looked at the piece of paper; then took a cell phone from his own uniform shirt pocket and walked a short distance away in the dunes and started dialing a number.

"Steve, is this whale a protected species of any sort?" asked Kearnes. "Is it on some endangered list of any kind that we should know about?"

"Protected, yes," said Connelly. "Endangered? No. Grays were taken off the federal endangered species list in 1994, after they started to make a comeback from being nearly totally wiped out by nineteenth century whalers. They are actually doing quite well these days. Their numbers, overall, are up."

"What should our next move be then?" said Kearnes.

"We definitely need to notify the U.S. Fish & Wildlife Service in Portland; I need to notify my own head office in Salem, too…and I have a friend who is a marine biologist at the Hatfield Marine Science Center in Newport. I'd like to give him a call. I know he'd want to come down and gather some stats, take some pictures. He could probably be here by late this afternoon."

"Sure," said Kearnes, "go ahead and give him a call."

"And if you have that number for U.S. Fish & Wildlife or know the particular person there to contact, I'd like you to make that notification for me if you could?"

"That won't be any problem at all, as long as someone lends me a phone; I left mine back in my rig."

"Here," said Thud, handing his cell phone to Connelly. "And after we make all the calls and all the scientist types come and have a look at it…I mean, her…then what?"

"Then we get a crew of about twenty guys down here with chainsaws and ATV's and start cutting her up and hauling the pieces out to the parking lot; then into trucks for transport to the landfill. It should take around ten days to two weeks to remove every trace of her and entirely clean the beach."

Connelly had just started to punch his friend's number into Thud's cell phone when Roy Roddameyer walked over to him. "Mayor Bouchet', Lieutenant Polk, and I have had a discussion and we believe we've come up a strategy more suited to the immediacy of this problem," said Roddameyer. Connelly stopped just before entering the second to the last digit of his biologist friend's number. He hit the "clear" button on Thud's phone and snapped its cover closed, looking at Kearnes; who was staring intently at Roddameyer as if he were some sort of strange alien life form.

For some reason Roddameyer was sweating now, even though the freshening ocean breeze had increased slightly. He carefully removed the Ray-Bans and pressed with his handkerchief at the thin line of perspiration oozing out in tiny singular beads from his hairline; and as he did Kearnes was shocked to see that Roy Roddameyer was noticeably popeyed. His bulbous white orbs looked like some of the dead bottom fish Kearnes had seen being hoisted from the boats at the docks near the Sea Breeze in big aluminum containers; their cold dead eyes bulged and nearly blown out of their heads from the extreme change in pressure as they were jerked from deep ocean water to the surface, caught hopelessly on sharp steel hooks.

He wondered if the sunglasses were to protect Roddameyer's painful looking eyeballs from the sun, or to conceal the red spider web sea of broken blood vessels that permeated them. Either way, his eyes were a garish billboard advertisement for Roy Roddameyer's obvious problem with alcohol.

"Lieutenant Polk suggested we tap into one of our very own local volunteer resources, and use The Patriots to assist the city in disposing of…all of this," said Roddameyer, extending his hand that held the damp handkerchief toward the whale carcass, the white monogrammed cloth rectangle fluttering in the breeze like a flag of surrender.

Thud and Connelly were both local veterans. They knew who the "Cutter Point Patriots" were; a loosely organized group of disabled or otherwise retired military veterans ranging from the Vietnam era right on up to Desert Storm. Thud didn't know about Steve Connelly, but The Patriots had asked him to join their organization at least once a year, every year, since he'd left the service and come back home to Cutter Point. But he had politely declined their offer every time, reasoning that he already had enough lunatics to deal with in his job and didn't need to voluntarily be around any more on his days off.

The Patriots marched, armed, in every parade the town had, sold red paper poppies on thin stems of wire in front many of the stores in the city and at the post office entrance every Memorial Day weekend; and held Fish Fry's, Spaghetti Feeds, and Truck Washes year around. All to raise money for their single biggest event of the year—one which they and they alone were totally in charge of—the fireworks display at the city's combined summer "Fourth of July—Whale of A Celebration!" festival. Many of them were bored, some of them were bitter, but all of them seemed to be, to some degree…crazy.

"What!" said Thud. "What the hell are they going to do? Have a benefit "whale wash" or something?" Kearnes was completely in the dark now; he had no idea who The Patriots were, and got the feeling neither Roddameyer or Bouchet´ were going to waste any more time with explanations.

"Relative to this…shall we say, very pressing situation, detective, I think they are our best option at the moment," said Bouchet´, with unconcealed annoyance.

"And Lieutenant Polk has a liaison within that group, so he will be handling this incident from here on out. To free up the chief for more important duties, you see." Bouchet´ smiled benignly at Thud, then glanced at Kearnes for any sort of reaction, but got none. And directly behind Bouchet´, Edgar Polk let a smirk as wide as the beach they were all standing on fill his face as he hooked his thumbs inside his gunbelt and rocked back and forth on his heels in the sand, his chest swelling with this type of delusive pride of accomplishment he apparently thrived on.

Kearnes realized now just what and how much was at stake in dealing with these three in their rapidly expanding power play. Their utmost need was to establish and maintain dominance within the group at any cost, and he would never stand a chance of surviving by simply trying to defend himself from them. So instead he would join them; support them wholeheartedly in their ideas which they were going to force on him anyway, and gamble on the fact that whatever they were thinking or proposing would be, in the end, both wrong, and a disaster of some sort. But he wasn't sure how, or if he even could, get Thud on board with him in time.

"Lieutenant," said Kearnes, "I'm not familiar at all with this volunteer group. What, specifically, do you see as their role in our mission?"

Polk instantly perked up; the smirk on his face melting away and being replaced with a mild look of surprise at the genuinely respectful sounding tone in Kearnes' voice.

"Uh…they, uh, do a lot of good in the community; holding car washes and all. To raise money for the big Fourth of July blow out every year…for which they supply all the fireworks. About five thousand bucks worth."

"Blow out is right," said Thud. "They blew up one of the docks at Pearl Cove two years ago, after they got drunk and upended a barbecue grill full of hot charcoal on some cases of sky rockets."

Polk glared at Thud and started to say something, but thought better of it. "In more than twenty years," he said, "that's the only accident they've had I'm aware of…and besides, it didn't involve any unsafe handling of pyrotechnics. A grill full of hamburgers and hot dogs got accidentally tipped over."

"Jesus Christ!" said Thud. "They burned the dock down! The entire goddamned Harbor nearly went up in flames!"

"That's enough detective!" squeaked Bouchet'

"Two of the drunken morons went to the hospital with second and third degree burns," Thud said to the group, ignoring the mayor. "And their fearless leader…Sparky…lost three of his goddamned fingers trying to dump one of the burning boxes of rockets in the bay instead of getting the fuck out of there!"

Kearnes saw Polk start to move around Bouchet' toward Thud; and saw Bouchet' beginning to vibrate with rage like a little wind up toy at Thud's insubordination. He spun around to face Thud, blocking Polk and Bouchet' with his back, and quickly told him in a whisper…"we have to get off the beach with these assholes, Thud. I need your help, so ratchet it down until we're clear…okay?" Thud nodded yes, never taking his eyes off Polk who he could still see over the top of Kearnes' head.

"I know I still have a lot to learn," said Kearnes. "About both the P.D. and the community in general. But as I have just explained to detective Compton, I think the task in front of us is what we all need to concentrate on right now. So Lieutenant, what is your plan?"

Polk stared at Thud for a few long seconds, hoping he would open his mouth again and so could suspend him; but he didn't. Roddameyer, Downs, and Connelly had all remained wisely silent during the heated exchange. Connelly, because it was none of his business at that point. Downs, because he knew better than to interrupt his boss as he moved in for the kill on a subordinate employee—including himself when he was the frequent victim of Edgar Polk's tirades. And Roddameyer, because he had been busy staring out at the ocean horizon, trying to concentrate on not letting the tremor in his hands start to build because it was getting so close to the lunch time Bloody Mary he could already taste, but so badly needed right now. A double.

"Well," said Polk, "I had Sergeant Downs call Sparky...that's Jerry Sparks; he's elected Commander this term. Anyhow, Sparky and a few of the guys will be down here about one, one thirty, to start on preparations to demo this thing."

"Demo it?" asked Kearnes.

"Yeah," said Polk. "Demolition. Blow it up into small enough pieces and chunks to break it down, and the tide will carry it all out to sea."

"You're proposing to blow up this whale carcass?"

"Yeah. Well, not *me*," said Polk. "Sparky. Jerry Sparks. He's a Vietnam vet, and I've known him for years. We used to work together back in the sixties, logging. He was a powder man and a damned good one, too."

"Oh shit," Thud groaned, unable to contain himself any longer.

"You got any better ideas, Sergeant?" Polk shouted. "Because if you do, I'm waiting to hear 'em!"

Kearnes looked at Thud with a *not another word* expression on his face, and Thud quickly looked down at the ground, shaking his head in disgust.

"And what kind of explosives will they use," said Kearnes.

"I don't know, dynamite I guess," said Polk. "Don't worry; they'll get the job done. Sparky is a licensed pyrotechnician; he knows what he's doing"

"Well, I think it's an excellent idea!" said Bouchet', rubbing his little gnarled squirrel like paws together.

"After all, this is really nothing more than one big garbage clean up job! I expect to have over five thousand cars in the Plaza over the weekend, and at least half of them will be tourists who want to stroll down on our beaches. Can't have forty tons of decaying dead animal waiting there to greet them now, can we?"

"The city is going to need a permit from the feds to move this whale carcass; in *any* manner," said Connelly. "And that's only after they come here in person and inspect it. And even after that, I seriously doubt they are going to let you blow it up as a means of removal."

"Mayor Bouchet'," said Kearnes. "I have some real concerns about the potential for liability by the city in letting civilians set off high explosives within the city limits...especially when we don't have any trained personnel to monitor them."

"Bullshit!" cried Bouchet' "Do you know what I have concerns with chief Kearnes? Flooring."

Kearnes didn't know what he was talking about. Maybe the old man was getting senile and his mind had somehow skipped a gear in the conversation, and he'd lapsed into thinking about the new carpet color he and his wife just couldn't agree on for their house.

"Flooring, gentlemen, in the automobile sales game, is the amount of physical space available at any one time on your showroom floor to display and sell your product and the inventory to go with it.

"You never want it totally empty because you're not making any money then; and when it's full, you want to get it empty again as soon as possible.

"This dead whale on our beach…on our showroom floor…is going to ruin our flooring; which are the tourists who come to our town to walk on it! We want them here in droves, new ones every day, walking these beaches and walking in and out of our retail establishments, buying, buying, and buying!

"And they're not going to do it with either a gruesome, negative sight like this…that *smells* like this…waiting for them as soon as they step off this beautiful interpretive trail. Or, if the goddamned beach is closed for two weeks while we get the thing moved by permit!"

Vernon Bouchet′ had gone off like a tea kettle that had been set on a hot stove to boil. His vitriolic litany advocating commerce and capitalism over public safety had poured out of him in one long, continuous shriek; and when he had simmered down…finally boiled dry…it was unknown who, if anyone would speak next or even ever again.

To the amazement of everyone present, it was Delbert Downs.

"I blew a frog up once when I was a kid," he said. "I stuck an M-80 between its hind legs and then tied them together with string. Then I lit the fuse…and just barely got away in time."

"Really Delbert?" said Thud. "What happened then?"

"Blew him up. Couldn't find even a piece of him anywhere; and this was a big frog too. A big pond bullfrog, that weighed about two pounds."

"Well, there you go Lieutenant!" Thud said to Polk. "Sounds like Delbert here has enough demolition background and experience to meet your "trained personnel" criteria…at least at the level you're looking for."

"I'm warning you Compton. You'd better zip it!"

Thud grabbed his jacket and portable radio from the driftwood log and retrieved his cell phone from Connelly. Then he walked over and stood nearly toe to toe with Edgar Polk, and got close to his face.

"I know this is *your* operation now, Lieutenant Polk," he said. "But I figure I might as well put my two cents worth in before I leave…so here it is."

"Why don't *you* hold the fuse in the whale's ass…while Delbert lights it."

"I'm putting you on report Compton!" Polk roared at him.

Thud only smiled.

"No," Thud said quietly. "The only "report" I'm going to be a part of is the one I'll be writing up when all of this shit is over. And I'm not the one who's going to be in it either, Polk. You are."

Kearnes watched Thud and Connelly walking away down the boardwalk trail back to the parking lot until they disappeared from sight around a turn in the sand dunes. It was only a little after nine a.m. now but he was already exhausted; mentally drained by the mind games and toxic personalities of his second in command officer on the police department, and the two most powerful men in the city.

Apparently Cutter Point was a town so unusually routinely quiet that even insignificant events could rapidly take on a life of their own and spin hopelessly out of control, when driven recklessly forward by some who were supposed to be in charge. It made him wonder why people like Polk and Roddameyer, and Bouchet´ found it so difficult to just use common sense and follow the rules, and what might happen if anything serious ever occurred…like a murder.

He only hoped the rest of his day would pass quietly, peacefully, and uneventfully.

But for Kevin Kearnes this day was about to become one of the most eventful days in his life. And peace and quiet would not be playing any part in it.

CHAPTER 10

▼

Jerry "Sparky" Sparks, Todd "Frog Man" Caswell, and Larry "The Rat" Luebcke were sitting at a front table in the dining room at The Buccaneer at lunchtime getting drunk on White Russians and being pissed off about having been run out of their favorite watering hole, "The Gang Plank", which was The Buccaneer's spacious, low lit cocktail lounge that took up the entire back half of the huge restaurant. The bi-weekly noon time meeting of the Cutter Point Rotary Club was the reason they'd had to move. Sparky, Frog, and Rat were not Rotary Club members, nor had they any aspirations ever to become members because they liked their own club, The Patriots, just fine.

At eleven thirty a waitress had tried to shoo them out of their cool, dark hiding place in a booth near the band stage. Getting no response from them—other than an order for another round of White Russians—she had gone to get the assistant manager who was finally able to remove them from their vinyl upholstered grotto, like three angry and evicted moray eels; after telling them their next drinks would be served to them in the dining room…or not at all.

Since Sparky had gotten the initial phone call from Delbert Downs in the lounge a little over two hours ago, the three men had been engaged in a high level strategic planning session; scribbling notes and drawing diagrams in pen on stacks of cocktail napkins; making call after call from the pay phone in the lounge to mobilize other members of The Patriots in town and around the county until all three had run out of change, and Sparky had asked to use the cordless phone kept at the bar…which they had now appropriated and taken with them to their table out front.

There was a lull in their planning session as the waitress arrived at the table with their lunch orders: two BLT sandwiches with fries, one Reuben on rye bread with a side of clam chowder...and three more White Russians. They stopped talking until she'd asked them if there was anything else they needed and when Larry Luebcke told her that there wasn't, she left, and they started talking again.

"I fucking lied to her," said Rat, reaching beneath the table and patting the sunken crotch of his camo pants. "Should have told her to come right on over here and sit on it for awhile!"

"Fuck you Luebcke" said Frog. "Sit on *what* needle dick?"

"On *it*...dipshit," Rat said, indignantly.

Larry Luebcke had come by his nick name the hard and honorable way; as a twenty one year old Army private scuttling silently on his bare belly through the pitch black maze of Vietcong tunnels dug deep below ground at Cu Chi in the Iron Triangle of Vietnam in 1966...an olive drab goose neck G.I. flashlight in one hand, and a Smith & Wesson Model 10 .38 special in the other.

Larry had been five foot eight inches tall then, had weighed one hundred and thirty five pounds, and had been in possession of a mean, boastful, and sometimes reckless disposition; all of which had made him the perfect candidate for being a "Tunnel Rat"...one of an elite all volunteer group of soldiers who purposefully slipped beneath terra firma in order to kill the enemy face to face in the dark. Now all these many years later, plagued with a host of medical and psychological problems that ranged from hypertension, to prostatitis, to chronic depression and the middle stages of acute alcoholism, Larry had shrunk to five foot six and lit up his electronic digital bathroom scales at an even one hundred seventeen; but his disposition remained unchanged. And everyone still called him Rat.

"Bite me," said Frog, exposing his Marlboro ravaged teeth, then puckering up his lips and making a few sloppy, suction like kissing sounds.

"Oh, don't *even* tempt me," Rat said. "I'd show you right now, but I don't wanna' see a grown man cry in public."

"Rat, you scrawny little fuck," said Frog. "Go ahead and whip it out. I'll bet it looks like a peeled carrot! Long and skinny, and orange...from you jacking it all night long."

"Ha!" cried Rat. "If want to talk garden vegetables...then we're talking cucumber here! A big, fat juicy one!"

"You two stand down," growled Sparky Sparks, reaching his deformed right hand across the table which had the last three fingers missing from it and looked like a freshly boiled, red lobster claw. "One of you idiots please pass me the ketchup...and let's get back to business here."

Jerry Sparks and Todd Caswell were Vietnam vets also, but Jerry was the oldest of the trio by nearly two years and unlike them had been an officer by the time his Vietnam experience ended.

Todd had been with the Marine Corps' 1st Force Reconnaissance Team in 1969, when his small unit had encountered and then been overrun by a Company of North Vietnamese regulars; forcing him to take refuge in a nearby swamp. He'd stayed almost totally submerged in a thick stand of water bamboo for eight days in the swamp, drinking the disease infested water and so hungry he'd eaten small spotted green frogs, whole and alive, that swam by. While the enemy camped on the shore only twenty five yards from him, cooking rice over open fires; laughing, and urinating and defecating in the water.

When he'd finally been rescued he'd had to be pulled out of the water with ropes, his quivering legs buried to his knees in the black, sucking mud. His skin was water logged and wrinkled and covered with green slime from the swamp; and in combination with his soaked and now rotting green and black tiger stripe fatigues, he'd looked more amphibian than human when they'd finally gotten him on dry land. And after he'd made the mistake of telling his Captain for the official after action report how he'd managed to stay alive—by eating the frogs—the "nick" his unit immediately gave him was a no brainer: Frog Man.

Jerry Sparks had had it a lot easier. He'd been a tall, angular built kid from the woods of southern Oregon who had two years of community college and knew how to set a dynamite charge—having paid for his schooling by logging in the summers—when he was drafted into the Army and assigned to the 84th Engineer Construction Battalion.

He'd built roads and dikes around Saigon and worked on the expansion of the airport there. After his first tour of duty he'd re-upped for a second one; this time as a newly promoted first Lieutenant working in an air conditioned office and signing requisitions for construction supplies. During the war he'd never crawled into a tunnel, never been forced to eat or drink from a jungle swamp while the enemy lurked nearby, looking to kill him; and the only shots he had ever fired were on the skeet range at the Officer's Club on the Base.

Brains, savvy, and a little college had made Sparky officer material then and still made him officer material now; and his ability to direct men like Rat and Frog, and get things done, had only been enhanced by his selfless act of bravery two years ago during the fireworks incident at the dock. Polk had mentioned that Jerry Sparks had been elected as Commander of The Patriots this year; but the truth was Jerry had been elected Commander *every* year since he'd first helped to found the group nearly twenty years before.

But what neither Polk or anyone else knew was that when Sparky had lost his fingers in the explosion on the dock, he'd been trying to rescue an unopened case of Corona beer which had been sitting on top of the blazing box of fireworks, and not trying to dump the fireworks themselves over the side into the bay.

Frog grabbed one of the bottles from the condiment tray within his reach and handed it to Sparky.

"Todd," said Sparky. "That's A-1 Sauce. I asked for the ketchup. For my fries."

"Yeah, Caswell," said Rat. "Ketchup is the stuff in the red bottle. That shit is brown...like the dung water you drank out of that swamp for eight days."

"Shut the fuck up, Rat!" Frog yelled. "If I hadn't lost my rifle when I hit that water, it would have been a totally different story for those gooks!"

"Yeah, right!" said Rat. "Bet you would have come out of that swamp shootin' and a scootin'! You'd have taken out that whole Company of NVA by yourself!"

Frog carefully put the bottle of A-1 back on the tray and picked up a bottle of Heinz; hefting it in his hand a few times as if it was a frag grenade he was considering tossing at Rat.

"I watched those bastards every move for eight long days and nights," Frog said. "And now it just dawned on me...I know what *they* had in common with you, Rat."

"And what would that be?" Rat asked.

"When they'd drop their pants and squat at the edge of the swamp with their backs to me to take a shit? I could see their little balls, the size of marbles...just like yours Rat!"

"Fucking fuck YOU man!" Rat screamed, coming up out of his chair...but Sparky shot his already extended arm forward and jabbed his two red pincer like fingers into Larry's windpipe, driving him back down into his seat.

Sparky quickly surveyed the rapidly filling restaurant. Luckily, the din of clattering dishes and orders being shouted out for pick-up at the grill window, and the sounds of laughter and loud voices coming from The Gang Plank where the Rotary Club members were beginning to pour in from both the front and rear entrances all helped to drown out the ruckus at The Patriot's table which, if repeated, would probably guarantee their ejection from the establishment sometime in the next two minutes or less.

"Je...sus, Spar...ky," wheezed Rat, holding onto his throat, tears streaming down both his eyes.

"Serves you right," sneered Frog "I still have nightmares about that shit you know!"

Sparky deftly turned toward Frog who instantly recoiled, thinking he was going to get his wind pipe crushed too. But instead Sparky snatched the bottle of ketchup from his hand, and then slammed it down hard on the table."

"Look!" he barked at them. "We've got a mission to complete. You two knock this crap off…NOW! Frog, what's the SIT-REP at the Bunker concerning materials on hand?"

"SIT-REP" was military talk for situational report, and the "Bunker" was The Patriot's enclave; a Quonset hut surrounded by a ten foot high fence of electrified concertina wire on ten thickly wooded acres located high in the Siskiyou Mountains, twenty miles from Cutter Point. It was where they held their monthly meetings, stored their ordnance and fireworks supplies; and where at least one or more members of the group could usually be found in residence at any given time…hiding out from wives, outstanding child support orders, or just reality in general.

"The SIT-REP is very positive," said Frog, smiling at Larry Luebcke, who was now massaging his throat with both his hands. "We've got a case, case and a half of industrial dynamite in burial storage that we can dig up, but it's pretty old. We have plenty of detonating cord and caps, and we've still got a decent stockpile of the *good stuff* on hand…although I'd hate to have to use it for this."

"Well, we're going to have to," said Sparky. "Nobody uses dynamite any more for commercial blasting, and what we have is probably as unstable as hell by now anyway. We need to do this job right. The first time. Call the Bunker and tell them to dig up and load all of the good stuff on the truck…and tell them don't even go near that dynamite."

There was the sound of a small brass ship's bell being rung three times in a long, slow cadence, and the noisy clamor of voices coming from The Gang Plank slowly began to subside.

Then a voice, which sounded like Roy Roddameyer, announced: "Okay everyone, let's get started. Please follow along and repeat after me: What is the 4-Way Test? Of the things we think, say or do, One…Is it the truth? Two…Is it Fair to all concerned? Three…Will it build Goodwill and Better friendships? Four…Will it be Beneficial to all concerned?"

It *was* Roy Roddameyer, the newly elected chairman of the Cutter Point Rotary Club, reciting the opening invocation of "The 4 Way Test" that began every Rotary Club meeting that took place anywhere in the world. He sounded as put back together and smooth now as the double Bloody Mary which sat, already more than half consumed, in a tall frosted glass on his table next to the bony little elbow of his boss, Vernon Bouchet´.

"Fucking twink do-gooder Rotarians," said Rat, staring wistfully at the Reuben on Rye on his plate, wondering if he'd even be able to get a few spoonfuls of clam chowder down his throat, which now felt like it was on fire.

From The Gang Plank lounge Roddameyer's voice boomed out a hearty introduction over the public address system for the scheduled guest speaker Mayor Vernon B. Bouchet′ and his topic: a construction update and progress report on the anticipated opening in September of the crown jewel of all his accomplishments so far…the Trident Greens Golf Course and destination resort.

"Hey," said Frog. "They aren't all bad guys. And besides, they have the deepest pockets in town. They're the best shot we've got at getting The Flame."

"The Flame" was the project nearest and dearest to The Patriots hearts at the moment; other than putting on a bigger, better, and therefore inherently more dangerous fireworks display every year at the concurrently running Fourth of July—Whale of A Festival! celebrations.

Five years before Vernon Bouchet′ had granted The Patriots a small plot of grass on the lawn in front of city hall on which to erect a black granite Veterans Memorial. Not only were the names of Cutter Point's war dead engraved on it, but also the names of the still living who had served in any capacity in the armed forces, including Jerry Sparks, Todd Caswell, and Larry Luebcke. And now in addition to the two towering flag poles that had recently been added to the Memorial…one for the American flag, and one right next to it for the Missing P.O.W.'s flag…both paid for by the Rotary Club, The Patriot's now wanted a propane gas fed "eternal flame" torch installed there and burning 24/7 as the finishing touch.

"Not bad guys?" said Rat. "Vern Boo-Shay is a first class old asshole, you ask me. That old bastard thinks he owns this town, but he don't."

"You want an 'eternal flame' so much, you ought to just plant his buddy Roddameyer in the ground next to the Memorial…and light a match over his head, the fucking alkie."

"Well, he *did* give us a place to put the memorial," Frog said.

"Oh whoop-de-do, Frog!" said Rat. "Little postage stamp sized piece of grass! He could of set aside a real chunk of ground in one of the parks, you know. City's got fucking three of them!"

Jerry Sparks had always believed one important quality of leadership which should always be adhered to was to let the men under your command use the foulest language possible with one another while keeping your own squeaky clean, as a means of demonstrating that you had endless amounts of self control and were the one who was truly in command.

But Larry Luebcke and Todd Caswell were really pushing his buttons today…really pissing him off. They had now forced him to the very threshold of breaking his own rule with their non-stop bickering and badgering of each other; and sitting around just talking about things wasn't going to make it any better. They needed purpose and action in their purposeless, somnolent lives…needed to be "back in the shit" as Larry Luebcke would have put it, and his friend Todd Caswell would have for once, without argument, probably agreed.

He picked up his White Russian; upended it and downed it in three long, deep gulps. Then he set the empty glass on the table and began to violently spear individual french fries from his plate with his fork, as if he were engaged in bayonet practice on the rifle range.

"You men hurry up and eat your lunches, and finish your drinks," he said.

"And that's a goddamned order."

"We've got a whale to go blow up."

Kearnes had assigned Frick and Frack to security duty the rest of the day at the trailhead and in and around the Wal-Mart parking lot, then returned to his office for the rest of the morning before leaving for his lunch time meeting at The Buccaneer with the Rotary Club. Mayor Bouchet' had mandated he be at the meeting and he had also been informed he should prepare a short talk.

His introduction to the club membership—which was nearly one hundred percent of every business owner and management employee of every business in the city—came after Bouchet's long, tedious, drawn out presentation on the Trident Greens project; from its inception as a personal dream of his, to its impending grand opening on Labor Day weekend.

The program was elaborate to say the least and in addition to the prepared speech, even included a power point presentation. But Kearnes noticed Roy Roddameyer didn't miss a beat in pulling it all off; having acted as writer, producer, and now floor director of the show for the mayor. He wondered if Roddameyer came by his talent naturally, or had found it in the contents of the now four empty Bloody Mary glasses which were still at his table, waiting with the dirty lunch dishes and silverware to be picked up.

When it was finally Kearnes' time and Roddameyer introduced him as the new chief, he got up and walked to the podium. He said a few very positive general words about how glad he was to be there, how beautiful the city and surrounding area was but at the same time, so different from what he was used to in Kansas, and how he hoped in the future to be able to meet with every business owner or manager to see what their law enforcement needs or questions might be.

At the conclusion to his very brief, by comparison, speech, the room erupted in applause…even a little louder and a little longer applause than Vernon Bouchet´ had received at the conclusion of his speech. Looking down at the front row table where Bouchet´ and Roddameyer were seated he saw the old man's small, white, wizened head sink down into the collar of his turtleneck shirt, his displeased eyes behind the telescope sized lenses of his glasses narrowing into slits as he glared up at Kearnes.

Although he had never been a chief before Kearnes had worked around enough chiefs in his career, and attended enough functions like this with them, to know what to do next. He quickly left the podium and walked to the exit which led out to the main portion of the restaurant where the cashier's station was, and where everyone would be paying their bill. Standing there, he shook every damp and dry hand of every Rotary Club member as they left; all eighty two members. He was shaking the hand of member number forty when he saw Roddameyer and Bouchet´ exiting through the back door of The Gang Plank, out into the rear parking lot.

It was late in the afternoon when twenty of The Patriots finally arrived in the parking lot of the Wal-Mart in three different vehicles; Sparky Sparks black Hummer2, a beige Dodge Caravan, and a surplus camouflage painted half ton Army truck.

Although Polk had told Kearnes the group would be assembled and on scene with their equipment by approximately one o'clock, it was now four thirty. Polk had also promised to call Kearnes on the radio and let him know when The Patriots arrived, but that hadn't happened either. It had been Frack who'd called Kearnes as soon as he saw the small rag tag convoy turn off Cutter Avenue into the entrance of Bouchet´ Plaza. Kearnes had only been a few blocks away and pulled up right behind them, seeing the look of disappointment on Polk's face when he realized he wasn't going to get the chance to talk with them first without Kearnes around.

The men riding in the beige van were the first to get out, walking to the back of the Army half ton and starting to offload materials being handed down by those above them in the truck's canopy covered rear cargo area.

Kearnes had both of his front windows rolled all the way down in the muggy late afternoon air, and Frick and Frack silently rolled up to his unit on their patrol bikes, each one stopping and grabbing the base of a window for balance.

"Hey chief," said Frick, "are these guys from the Army or something?"

"Used to be," said Kearnes. "They are all ex-military from different branches of the service, I guess."

"Whoa!" said Frack, pointing to the black Hummer2 stopped at the head of the convoy, as three men emerged from it. "Now those dudes look scary."

All three of the men wore camo pants, sneakers, T-shirts, and headgear of varying types

The tallest man was wearing a camo Fatigue cap, and a white T-shirt that had the words "BOMB SQUAD" screen printed on the front in black lettering; and on the back…"IF YOU SEE ME RUNNING, YOU BETTER CATCH UP!"

The medium height, stocky built man wore a camo jungle "Boonie Hat" and a black T-shirt with white lettering on the front which read: "9 OUT OF THE 10 VOICES IN MY HEAD TOLD ME TO STAY HOME AND CLEAN MY GUNS TODAY".

And the skinny, nervous looking little guy with the narrow set eyes and ferret like face, had a cotton camo "Do-Rag" skull cap pulled tightly across his clean shaven head, which was knotted snugly at the back of his scrawny neck. He was also dressed in a black T-shirt. His said: "THE BULLSHIT STOPS, WHEN THE HAMMER DROPS!"

The three of them walked straight over to Edgar Polk. Polk and Sparky talked briefly; then Sparky adjusted his Fatigue cap, pulling it low down over his eyes, and calling out to the men at the truck, assembled the group.

They all knelt down on one knee in a semi-circle around Sparky; with Polk, Frog, and Rat standing beside him. They listened intently for the next fifteen minutes as Sparky outlined the plan. When he'd finished they rose to their feet, talking to one another excitedly. They gathered their boxes, spools, bundles, tools, and military rucksacks full of equipment—some of them donning military surplus gas masks against the very noticeable odor of the whale—and with Rat on point leading the way in front of Sparky and Polk, and Frog at the rear…marched single file down the wooden boardwalk trail toward the beach.

Kearnes was standing outside his car talking with Frick and Frack, who were showing him all the features and equipment on their police patrol bikes, when he saw the column of Patriots come trudging back to the parking lot and dump their loads on the ground at the trail head.

In their haste to reach the objective, lay the charges, and then set them off before it got dark; no one, including Edgar Polk, had thought about the tide. Which had been coming in ever since Kearnes and Thud had first surveyed the dead whale earlier that morning and which—when Polk and The Patriots had excitedly stepped off the boardwalk and made their way on the rough sand trail to the beach like a horde of conquering Conquistadors—had all but submerged the whale entirely when they got there. And low tide wouldn't be until seven thirty.

He got a certain sense of self satisfaction, but didn't show it, when Edgar Polk approached him and semi-admitted fault in the tide fiasco; yet still tried, in his way, to lay the blame off on The Patriots. The tide factor hadn't even crossed Kearnes' mind at all; but why should it? It was as foreign an idea to him as seeing a herd of Longhorn steers trotting down Cutter Avenue would have been to Edgar Polk.

But he decided to use the time caused by the tide delay wisely. He asked Frick and Frack to stay over on overtime, then gave them a one hour meal break to go eat anywhere in the city they wanted to pedal to while he assumed their security duties until they got back. His concern over evacuating at least this half of the lot before the blast was set off had largely taken care of itself, as this remote portion of the parking lot was now completely deserted, and the cars in the rest of Bouchet' Plaza were beginning to thin out now, too.

At six o'clock he heard Officer Spenser Sparling and another night shift officer sign into service for their six p.m. to four a.m. patrol shift. He contacted Spenser on the radio and had him call him on his cell phone. He told Spenser to go to the Fire Department and ask them to bring a couple of their engines and one Medic ambulance unit down to stage in the parking lot just in case; and to also bring with them all of the generator operated flood lights they had. He cautioned Spenser to keep all of this off the police radio and to tell whoever was in charge at the Fire Department to please do the same.

Although Kearnes knew next to nothing about ocean tides he *was* familiar with the concept of darkness; and from what little he'd already seen of The Patriots he didn't feel he could afford to have them operating in the dark any more than they already appeared to be.

He would arrange for the ability to have the area lit up like a Friday night high school football stadium, before Edgar Polk realized that detonating a forty ton whale at night might just pose an operational problem…and they were all stuck out here until midnight while Edgar thought up a way to solve it.

At nine twenty p.m. Kearnes saw the powerful beam of Spenser Sparling's rechargeable Mag-Lite flashlight pierce the shadowy darkness of the dunes, as Spenser returned to the parking lot after having spent over an hour down on the beach, viewing and photographing the whale.

Spenser had been very curious and wanted to see the giant creature up close, but confided to Kearnes that he feared the wrath of Lieutenant Polk if he walked down to the beach to look at the whale. So Kearnes had taken the digital camera from the crime scene kit in the trunk of his car and given it to Spenser, ordering him to go down on the beach and officially photograph the scene; and telling him that if Polk gave him any trouble, to tell Polk to call him on the radio immediately.

But much to Spenser's surprise, Polk hadn't said a word to him when he got there. In fact he had even ignored him...as he focused on all the action at the moment that was unfolding under the several banks of hot, white, generator fed flood lights.

Even Polk had been awestruck as he watched Rat enter the mouth of the whale—jacked open wide and held in place by the Fire Department's "Jaws of Life" hydraulic apparatus—tugging along two bulging olive drab military canvas bags with one hand, and shining a flashlight ahead of him with the other. Two long black wires trailed behind him, uncoiling off their wooden spools like startled snakes.

"Thanks chief," said Spenser, handing the camera back to Kearnes. "That was awesome. I've never seen anything as big as that in my life!"

Spenser liked this new chief...a lot. It was inspiring to see him out here in the field working on a case, wearing the same uniform that he himself wore; and not just any case, either. The chief was going up against Lieutenant Polk and from what Spenser had heard about it earlier in the day before he'd come to work, and had now seen for himself, the chief was definitely at least holding his own so far.

Because he was kind of a gun nut, like most young rookie cops were, he was intrigued by the handgun in Kearnes' holster. It was an older, sleek and slender blued Colt semi-automatic pistol with what looked like white ivory grips. The initials "**B.L.K.**" were inlaid in fancy cut sterling silver wire script lettering, vertically on the outside grip panel, from the top of the grip to the bottom. On the opposite inside panel, done in black scrimshaw, was carved the head of a Longhorn steer, its wild eyes made of two small, deep red, translucent rubies. He wanted to ask Kearnes about the unusual looking gun but he didn't know him well enough yet to presume using that level of decorum. He was just happy he was here, on the department, and for Spenser Sparling that was more than enough for now.

Twenty minutes later the firemen and some of The Patriots who were helping them came down the boardwalk trail, lugging the two portable generators and now dismantled flood lights, and began packing the equipment back into the fire trucks, followed by Polk and the rest of them. All of them except Jerry Sparks, Larry Luebcke, and Todd Caswell.

After all the charges had been set the three of them had begun playing out the main detonation wire...which would transmit an electrical charge from the firing box to the blasting caps imbedded in the explosives…back to the parking lot but off of the boardwalk trail, taking a straight route through the dunes. But the wire had quickly run out.

"What the fuck?" Frog said, looking first at Sparky and Rat in the pale moonlight, then down at the empty wire spool in his hands.

"Don't look at us, dumb ass," said Rat. "You're the one who said we had enough wire."

"Shut the fuck up!" hissed Sparky. "Both of you!"

They were only seventy to eighty yards from the whale in the low lying sand dune terrain which would offer little protection from even a moderate blast, so Sparky thought it best to weigh their options.

He could send some men back to the Bunker for more wire. That would take another hour or longer and make them look even more like dumbshits then they already did; for not thinking about the incoming tide. Or he could blow this thing right here and right now. And because of the amount of the "good stuff" he'd ordered wired up to the whale, he *knew* with absolute certainty that it was going to go up…big time.

But then he thought about the dock down in the Harbor, and what had happened there two years ago on that Fourth of July evening.

He turned to Frog and Rat; handing them one of the two collapsible G.I. shovels he'd carried down to the beach lashed to the sides of his rucksack…keeping the other one for himself.

Then he checked the glowing green luminous face of his watch dial.

"Dig yourselves a hole in the sand," said Sparky…taking a Leatherman tool from one of the multitude of pockets in his camouflage Battle Dress Utility pants and snipping the detonation wire free from where it was attached to the empty spool; then starting to hook it up to the firing box.

"A big one," he said.

"You've got fifteen minutes. At exactly twenty two hundred, I'm pressing the switch."

CHAPTER 11

▼

After Jerry Sparks had called Edgar Polk on the portable radio Polk had given him to use and informed the group back in the parking lot that zero hour would be at 2200 hours, Kearnes had been keeping a close eye on his watch. At one minute until ten, he ordered everyone to get down behind their vehicles.

Even Edgar Polk wasn't going to argue with this logic after what he'd just witnessed: The Patriots unwrapping what looked like maybe a hundred bars of soft, white clay like material—each twelve inches long, two inches wide, and one inch thick—from their olive drab cellophane wrappers. Mashing them together in huge lumps and then inserting blasting caps in the lumps that were connected to black wires. Sticking these lumps in, on, over, and around the whale as if they were elves happily trimming a Christmas turkey.

It had made Polk nervous, watching it all, and he was now even more nervous; waiting to see what was going to happen. If there was any way he could lay all or even some of this off on Kearnes, he would do it. But he couldn't think of anything; it was too late. He was the one who had been in charge of The Patriots down there on the beach. He should have at least asked Jerry Sparks what it was they were using…and why the hell they needed to use so much of it. But he hadn't said a word.

Ten o'clock…2200 in military time…came and went without any explosion; at least according to Kearnes' watch, which he kept precisely synchronized with the 911 Dispatch Center's clock. Others around him began checking their own watches and poking their heads up over the vehicles they were hiding behind, peering out into the darkness in the direction of the beach.

Then Kearnes heard Frack say, "Oh crap…our bikes!" The two bike officers had forgotten to move their patrol bikes which sat out in the open, resting easily on their kickstands and still blocking the entrance to the boardwalk trail fifty yards distant.

Frack stood up from where he'd been crouched behind the right front wheel of Kearnes' car and began to trot across the parking lot toward the bikes as Kearnes, seeing him, scrambled to his feet from where he'd been kneeling down behind the car's trunk and sprinted after him, yelling "NO!" at the top of his voice.

Frack stopped in his tracks when he heard the voice yell at him and had just started to turn and look back toward the chief's car when Kearnes tackled him from behind, plowing into the young bike officer's muscular, tanned legs directly behind his knees and folding him up on the ground like an accordion.

And at that exact moment the two parked white police patrol bikes disappeared from sight…hurtled across the asphalt parking lot's surface sideways and sent skittering out into the sand dunes by the shock wave from the explosion's blast that slammed into them traveling at over eight hundred miles an hour.

Night now literally turned into day as the horizon of the beach and even the parking lot itself was seared with an illuminatingly brilliant white hot light; as blindingly bright as the flame from an arc welder's torch.

The sound from the enormous explosion boiled across the surface of the ground toward them like a sonic tornado; rattling teeth and puncturing a few eardrums of some of the men who'd unfortunately still had their heads popped up when Jerry Sparks, lying in his shallow grave like hole in the sand more than a hundred yards away out in the dunes and unseen by them, had depressed the switch on his detonator box.

Every store front window in the Wal-Mart—which had closed for the night only an hour before—vaporized into powdery, crystalline shards of glass as the blast wave arrived at its front doors. And in seven of the other retail establishments in Bouchet' Plaza which also sat directly in the radius of the explosion's outward cast, or in near enough proximity to it, the front glass windows imploded like soapy blow bubbles being popped with the poke of a child's finger. In the enormous and mercilessly empty shopping center parking lot the tall, brightly painted steel light poles swayed back and forth from the force of the explosion until their thick globes shattered; plunging the parking lot into immediate total darkness, the broken fragments of glass and electrical sparks falling from them like an unexpected early winter snow.

Kearnes let go of Frack's legs and pushed himself up from the asphalt. He looked into the kid's wide eyed, stunned face, and was glad he had still been wearing his bike helmet when the explosion went off. He reached down and pulled Frack up to his feet then bent over at the waist, putting his palms on his knees, trying to shake off the ringing in his ears which seemed to only be growing louder.

But it was a very strange sound; more like a long, drawn out whistling that turned into a buzzing shriek as it got closer. Almost like the sound effects in those old war movies on TV when they opened the bomb bays of a squadron of B-29's high over Germany on a night raid, and let the huge lumbering airplanes belly's full of five hundred pounders loose on the unsuspecting citizenry sleeping below.

Kearnes was looking straight ahead at Edgar Polk, who was still kneeling down by the front of his marked patrol car a short distance away, a look of dazed incomprehension on his face, when a twelve pound bowling ball sized chunk of rotting whale blubber that had been blown nearly a quarter of a mile up into the sky landed on Polk's car...cratering the sheet steel of the hood as if it had just been struck by a small meteorite.

Kearnes stared in disbelief at the lethal sized piece of animal flesh that would have probably killed Edgar Polk if it had only landed a couple of feet closer to the front fender of his car. The air around and above him began to fill with more of the buzzing, shrieking, whistling sounds. He saw a small, white, golf ball sized piece of whale bone strike the top of Frack's bike patrol helmet and glance off to one side with a loud *ping!*...like a ricocheting bullet and finally realized what was happening. "GET DOWN!" he screamed. "Get underneath the vehicles!"

The "good stuff" The Patriots had dug up at various different locations around the compound of their Bunker property and brought to the beach and planted on the dead whale from its nose to its fluke, and even down into the decomposing, slimy, acid filled well of its belly where Larry Rat Luebcke had crawled, had been ninety one bars of military "C-4" plastic explosive. It was every single last bar of C-4 that The Patriots secretly and illegally owned...and which Larry Sparks had just touched off; rocking the foundation of every building, home, church, and school in the city and blowing a hole in the beach where the whale had been only seconds before the size of a back yard Olympic swimming pool.

As the night sky began to rain down whale—and bits of driftwood, sea shells, rocks, and sand—all of the men in the parking lot dove beneath the police cars, fire trucks, ambulance and the van and the Army truck The Patriots had arrived in; incredulous that such a thing could really be happening, but frightened enough that they genuinely feared for their safety and even their lives.

Kearnes grabbed Frack by the chin strap of his bike helmet and jerked him to the nearest vehicle, which was Polk's, and together they jammed themselves beneath the undercarriage of the patrol car as far as they could; ignoring Edgar Polk who was still kneeling at the front of his car, mesmerized by the sight of the gelatinous mass on the hood which looked and smelled like a large bucketful of rancid, tapioca pudding.

The eerie shower storm of mixed debris accompanied by the sound of things wetly going splat in the asphalt parking lot and punctuated here and there by the sharper metallic sounds of harder objects glancing off steel and cracking window glass, seemed to go on forever; but within thirty seconds it was all over with.

Then there was an almost equally long period of absolute dead silence; a quiet so still that in spite of his ringing ears Kearnes could hear every wave breaking down on the beach, and the crunch of every shoe and boot against the fallen detritus on the ground as the men began to slowly extricate themselves from underneath the vehicles like Hermit Crabs leaving their host shells.

Then…all hell *really* started to break loose.

On top of the fire department building, which was located next to city hall and the police department, there was a Tsunami Early Warning Alert System siren. It was tested twice yearly in pre-announced city wide emergency drills to simulate the approach of a tsunami, or tidal wave. Cutter Point sat on a land mass directly above the Cascadia subduction zone; a section of the North American continental crust deep inside the earth that butted up against the subducting plates of the ocean floor, occasionally snapping loose in "seismic events" which scientists more commonly referred to as earthquakes…and a very bad place to be when that happened if you were a city. The last great Cascadia subduction zone earthquake had occurred on the southern Oregon coast in 1700; coincidentally almost exactly where the current day community of Cutter Point had eventually been built. It had had an estimated magnitude of 9.0 and two hundred and sixty four years later in 1964 the small seaport town of Crescent City, California, located fifty miles down the coastline from Cutter Point, had been inundated by a giant tsunami driven wave from a much smaller magnitude earthquake that nearly washed away the entire downtown area and twelve people had died.

The electronic sensors located in two of the permanently anchored buoys maintained and monitored by the National Oceanic and Atmospheric Administration…bobbing in the ocean waters several miles offshore from Cutter Point…now mistakenly recorded the perceived "seismic" activity from the blast as a tidal wave producing earthquake, and transmitted a radio signal to the fire department. Living in Cutter Point there were a certain percentage of people somewhat knowledgeable on the subject of tidal waves—some of whom who'd survived the Crescent City disaster—and whose blood now immediately ran cold as the five thousand decibel warning siren atop the fire department was automatically activated.

The alarm raised from the window rattling explosion began to spread contagiously throughout the city, and overwhelmed the available inventory of local emergency services in a matter of a few short minutes. Many of the citizens in their homes who had heard and felt the massive explosion believed that the Mill had blown up or that an airliner had plummeted thirty thousand feet down from the sky above and impacted in the middle of town.

But as the Tsunami Warning siren began to blare out, non-stop, its ungodly rising and falling, shrieking pitch, public alarm turned into full blown public panic. Every one of the six 911 dedicated emergency phone lines in the Cutter Point 911 center lit up almost simultaneously, jamming and disabling the system after only the first couple of hysterical callers could blurt out their anguished pleas for help, or information about what was going on.

This was followed almost immediately by several neighborhoods in the city as well as all of the street lights and traffic signals that ran the length of the downtown business district on Cutter Avenue blacking out, as many of the residents who had just gone to bed turned the lights back on inside their homes at virtually the same time and the resultant power surge blew the electrical grid that fed power to those areas.

Kearnes got out from underneath the car. He heard the first emergency calls start to come in over his portable radio, and the other night shift patrol officer on duty with Spenser being dispatched to them. Their was an apparent heart attack victim on Ruston Street, a report of more explosions on the south side of the city which were probably panic evoked and false, but had to be checked out, and an injury traffic accident at the intersection of Cutter Avenue and Bouchet' Way…which was the entrance to the shopping center from Coast Highway 101 less than three blocks away.

He saw Spenser Sparling running to his patrol car, telling the Dispatcher over his portable he would be responding to the traffic accident, and saw Frick and Frack disappear at the edge of the parking lot into the shadows of the dunes to look for their bikes.

"Lieutenant Polk," he said to the stupefied man who was still down on his knees, staring at the object on his car's hood which had made a dent in the steel three inches deep.

"POLK goddamit!" he yelled, finally jolting him out of the trance he seemed to be in. Polk looked up at him,

"Get a team together…with paramedics…and get out there and start looking for those men!," Kearnes said, pointing in the direction of the sand dunes; where he was sure they were ultimately going to find three dead bodies…or at least whatever remnants were left of them.

"Have the bike officers cordon off this area: no one gets in or out without *my* say so. And you will NOT, under any circumstances, let any member of The Patriots leave; is that understood? You are to consider this a possible death investigation scene…starting now."

Polk indicated that he understood by nodding "yes" to Kearnes but it was done with a heavy effort, as if his head had been blasted full of sand in the explosion. Then he slowly struggled to his feet and staggered off in the direction of the Fire Department ambulance.

Kearnes jumped in his own car and raced out of the parking lot toward the intersection at Cutter Avenue, clicking on the windshield wipers and the washer control as he drove. The vehicle's wipers labored to clear away a smeared, glossy layer of pulverized whale blubber and soapy water and after several passes he could see the red and blue strobes from Spenser's patrol car radiating from the middle of the darkened intersection. The street lights and signal lights were completely dead from the power failure.

Although traffic was usually fairly light at this intersection late on a weekday night it was still U.S. Route 101, the Coast Highway—which ran from Seattle to Los Angeles—and there was never a time when vehicles of some sort weren't present, going somewhere, for some reason. This night was no exception.

As Kearnes slowed to enter the intersection he saw the spotlight from Spenser's patrol car trained on a Silver Lexus LS 430 with Washington State license plates. It was halfway up on the sidewalk adjacent to the southbound lanes where it had crashed, dead center, into the steel base of a street light pole.

Spenser was standing next to the trunk of the Lexus upon which he had spread out most of the medical supply contents from the First Responder bag that was carried in the trunk of every Cutter Point P.D. vehicle. And he was clamping a huge white, diaper sized trauma pad bandage around the bare upraised forearm of the most beautiful woman Kearnes had ever seen in his life…trying to get her bleeding stopped.

Kearnes saw the long line of vehicle headlights which were beginning to back up in the double south lanes of the highway. He swung his vehicle past Spenser's—which was ahead of the Lexus and blocking traffic coming from the north—and put his unmarked Ford with all its emergency lights operating diagonally across the south lanes. He grabbed his own First Responder kit from the trunk of his car and ran over to Spenser and the woman.

"How bad?" Kearnes asked Spenser, staring at the red dots of blood that were starting to blot through the trauma pad. The woman had been looking at her arm, watching the blood beginning to seep through the thick cotton bandage, but turned her head away from them now. He could tell she was starting to cry, but very quietly.

"It's a pretty nasty cut, chief," Spenser said, keeping pressure on both sides of the pad. "It's on the inside of her forearm, but it looked pretty clean when I first got a glimpse of it. She said she had the green light here and was going through the intersection when something hit her windshield and she lost control of her car."

Kearnes dug into his bag. He found a fresh trauma pad and tore it from its wrapper. "Are you hurt anywhere else ma'am?" he asked. "There's an ambulance on the way." She shook her head no, keeping her face turned away from Kearnes and Spenser.

They coordinated their efforts in changing the woman's first bloody trauma bandage for the fresh one Kearnes had opened, and somehow in the process Kearnes was the one who now ended up keeping the pressure on her wound with his hands.

"Get on the radio," Kearnes told Spenser, "and find out where that ambulance is!"

Spenser called Dispatch on his portable and asked for an E.T.A. on the ambulance to their location; but was asked in return to give an assessment of the injuries at his accident scene. And when he told the Dispatcher they had a single female victim, approximately thirty five to forty years of age, with a four inch long cut to her left inside forearm, and that they had now been largely successful in quelling the bleeding from her wound by applying trauma pads with pressure; he was told no ambulance would be coming.

The City of Cutter Point had a total of four ambulances available in any given emergency situation. Two belonged to the city's fire department and two to a private ambulance company; and all four of them were tied up at the moment on "priority" calls that continued to flood the 911 Center non-stop. When Kearnes heard that news over the radio his heart sunk, because he knew it meant the one fire department ambulance in the parking lot not five hundred yards from where they were couldn't respond either. By now they must have found casualties down in the sand dunes near the explosion site.

He felt the woman's body suddenly go tense and he realized how hard he had been squeezing her arm. Slowly, he relaxed the pressure on the bandage a little and in turn, felt her relax too.

"Have I hurt you?" he asked. "If I did, I'm sorry. I'm trying to get this bleeding to stop."

She turned her head and looked directly into Kearnes' eyes. And as she did he felt something suddenly, startlingly, crack wide open deep inside his chest...and then soar up and out of him like a flight of small frantic birds; beating their wings furiously toward a point of light in the distance as if they'd just been released from a place of caged darkness.

Britt McGraw was one of those very rare and special women who caused men to instantly look away from her as their first instinctive reaction to her implausible beauty...their second instinctive reaction being their inability not to immediately look at her again.

And at that moment Kearnes was, for some unfathomable reason to him, unable to hold the gaze of this woman's dark brown, amber flecked eyes. He quickly looked away from her back toward his car, as if he was checking to see if it was still where he had left it.

"No, you haven't hurt me," she said. "Not yet."

When she spoke it forced Kearnes to turn and look at her again. What had she meant by *that* last statement?

"Actually, I'm a doctor," she said. "They must train police officers very well in first aid because both of you have done exactly what needed to be done...and I thank you.

"But I think I need to go to an E.R. for some butterfly closures, or I'm going to have some noticeable scarring."

He tried to retain his professional persona by staring directly at her for a few seconds with his most serious and inquiring expression before he spoke; but Kevin Kearnes was rattled by the overpowering attraction of this woman, and he could not think of what to say next. He felt like an accident victim himself; dazed and shocky.

The alluring scent of her perfume, her lioness eyes, the long blonde flaxen hair and seductive, beckoning form of her near perfect feminine body...all of it combined to make Britt McGraw an unexpected and unavoidable obstacle suddenly placed in his path who he could not, and did not want to, get out of the way of.

At that precise moment in his heart Kevin Kearnes crashed headlong into her, not yet knowing or even caring, who this woman really was.

Finally he managed to speak. "Can you tell me what happened?" he said.

"I was coming to the intersection," she said, "when I heard...and felt this terrible explosion. It literally shook my car so hard I pulled over and stopped. Then I got scared, and when I saw the light up ahead of me turn green I tried to speed through it. I almost made it when *that* thing hit my windshield," she said, pointing toward the front of the Lexus with her free hand. "I couldn't see anything and I lost control of the car, and crashed."

Kearnes bent slightly and peered ahead through the rear windshield. He saw the front windshield was broken; starred in a large, spider web pattern directly in front of the driver's area. But the safety glass was still held together by its thin layer of urethane plastic bonded in between its two outer glass sheets, and sagging heavily in the center of the broken spider's web from its own weight was a piece of the whale's carcass nearly the same size, shape, and weight as the one that had nearly killed Edgar Polk only moments before.

It had traveled in a long, arcing, mortar like trajectory over a thousand yards from the beach to this intersection where it had struck the windshield of the rapidly moving fifty six thousand dollar luxury car; that now sat crushed up against a steel light pole with steam rising from ruptures all around the edges of its crumpled hood. A quarter million dollar laser guided smart bomb couldn't have done the job any better.

"What is it, anyway?" she asked Kearnes, who had now started to wrap the trauma bandage tightly in place around her forearm with a roll of gauze tape.

"Believe it or not," said Kearnes, cutting the last strip of tape free from the roll of gauze with his folding knife, "that is part of the body of a gray whale."

"A...whale?"

"Yeah, a whale. A dead one that was found down on the beach. And the explosion you heard was how it got here...or part of it, anyhow. It was blown up."

Britt McGraw examined the taping job Kearnes had completed on her arm, and then hugged her arms tightly across her chest as she began to shiver in the cold and misty night ocean air. She walked to the front of her destroyed Lexus and bit her lower lip when she saw for the first time the full extent of the damage done to it for the first time.

Angrily, she stalked back to Kearnes, who was trying to look like he was busy putting the medical supplies back in his First Responder bag and had not been watching her as she faced away from him, drinking in every incredible hollow and contour of her body beneath her dress; the lightly tanned and firmly muscled calves of her legs, her perfectly shaped toes in the white open topped summer sandals she wore.

"What kind of idiot…or idiots…blow up a whale?" she demanded. "Look at my car!"

Kearnes stuffed the last of the first aid items into his bag and zipped it shut. "The police, I'm afraid," he said.

"*What?*" she said, incredulously.

"The police department blew the whale up. With a little help from some friends."

Britt's face flushed with anger. Red splotches of heat appeared in irregular patches on her already reddened face. The skin below her chin on her throat and on her bare shoulders and on her chest where the top of her dress ended was the color of fresh milk, but some of her face was red and chafed appearing; almost like the start of a bad sunburn.

"Oh, well that's just great!" she cried. "I can't believe this! I want to speak to the chief of police right now to file a complaint! I would appreciate it if you would call him for me, officer…" She leaned forward to read the gold metal name tag above the right pocket on Kearnes' uniform jacket.

"Officer…Karns?"

"*Kearnes*," he said. "Chief…Kevin Kearnes."

Britt got even closer to his name tag and looked at it again…this time seeing the much smaller black engraved words, "CHIEF OF POLICE", directly beneath his name. She was beginning to shiver violently now from the cold but straightened up, threw her shoulders back, and stared up at him.

"Oh," she said. "Then I guess I should apologize. I had no idea *you* were the police chief. I'm Britt McGraw…but I'm not quite sure whether I am pleased to meet *you* or not."

Kearnes took his patrol jacket it off and brought it over the top of her head and down onto her shoulders, easing her bare arms into the oversize sleeves one at a time, and then zipping the front of it up to just past the top of her breasts. Britt didn't say anything but she didn't protest, either. The jacket was already warmed from his body heat, and the gleaming silver and gold oval police badge that was pinned through a metal eyelet on its left chest felt heavy and substantial through the nylon fabric where it rested against her breast.

"Don't worry about it," he said. "There are quite a few other people in this town who don't have any idea I'm the chief, either."

"Come on…we can't wait any longer. I'm going to transport you to the hospital in my vehicle."

Kearnes put Britt in the front seat of his car and turned the heater on for her. Then he returned to the Lexus and from the front seat he retrieved her purse and a pair of sunglasses he found on the floor hidden beneath the vehicle's deflated airbag. As he started to back out of the driver's seat area a jagged piece of plastic trim jutting out from the door molding grazed his cheek. It had flecks of blood along its razor sharp edge, and was probably what had caused the cut to her forearm.

With her keys he opened the trunk of the Lexus and found one large black Cordura nylon suitcase and a much smaller matching travel bag. He put the large suitcase in the backseat of his car but Britt insisted he give her the smaller bag which she then placed in her lap, wrapping her arms firmly around it.

Spenser and the other patrol officer, who had just arrived at the scene, were setting out bright flaming cherry red tipped safety flares on either side of the still dark intersection. They would use them to define two temporary single lanes of travel—north and south—to funnel traffic through and get things moving again in a few minutes after Spenser finished his measurements and sketch of the accident scene for his report, and then awaited the arrival of a tow truck.

Kearnes tapped his horn once to catch Spenser's attention and motioned for him to come over to the car.

"I'm taking this lady to the E.R.," said Kearnes. "Do you need any more help here officer Sparling?"

Spenser gazed inside the chief's car past the chief to the beautiful professional looking blonde haired woman who sat next to him on the passenger side of the front seat, her face turned toward her window. She was old enough to be his Mom but he was glad that she wasn't because she was one *very* hot lady, and Spenser immediately felt conflicted about even having such a thought. Seeing the two of them sitting next to one another—even though he knew they were total strangers—he had the odd impression that they looked like they naturally belonged together…like a couple. But he guessed it was probably just the chance pairing of two very physically compatible looking people which gave that impression.

"No, we're fine here chief," said Spenser. "We've got a tow truck on the way and I'll have this report knocked out in just a few. I don't see any fault here, obviously, so no citations. I'll let you know which impound yard her Lexus ends up at…but it'll probably be Priced Right Parts. That's about a mile north of town on the right."

OK, good," said Kearnes. "Have you heard anything further from down on the beach?" He knew there had been a flurry of radio traffic but had been too busy getting Britt's things from her car to stop and listen to it all.

"Yeah," said Spenser. "I just heard them calling for a second ambulance to respond…it sounds like they have some injuries down there."

"Will that ambulance be coming this way?" asked Kearnes

"Yes," Spenser said. "They'll have to in order to get down into the shopping center parking lot."

"Then hold all of this traffic," said Kearnes, "until that ambulance comes through here. Then you can start letting the cars move."

"Oh, right," said Spenser. "Got it."

Actually, Spenser hadn't gotten it at all. He hadn't stopped to consider the potential for disaster posed by letting both lanes of traffic go at once; bottlenecking them down into two narrow, backed up ribbons of roadway crawling at a snails pace as the responding ambulance on its way to the parking lot at Bouchet' Plaza screamed toward the blacked out, clogged intersection.

But at least the chief hadn't screamed at him and called him an "idiot" like Lieutenant Polk surely would have, either. For the first time since officer Spenser Sparling had set foot in Cutter Point P.D. the department seemed to have a true leader…one with intelligence, tact, compassion, and guts; and Spenser found both his admiration for this man and his sense of loyalty towards him steadily growing stronger.

"All right, Spenser," Kearnes said, "I'll be on the radio. Call me if you need me."

And then Kearnes drove out of the intersection northbound with his emergency lights and siren on, splitting the center of the two lanes of backed up north bound vehicles straight down the middle for three blocks until there was no more stopped traffic; punching the Ford Police Interceptor up to seventy as he rushed the injured woman to Cutter General Hospital.

CHAPTER 12

▼

Uriah Beek sat calmly behind the wheel of the windowless, white Ford Econoline delivery van with his engine shut off; the fifth vehicle in line from the front of the north bound lane of stopped traffic at the blacked out intersection.

He pressed another fresh wad of napkins from Vickie's Big Wheel Drive-In tightly against the wound on the right side of his head. It had started to bleed even more profusely soon after he'd left the Wal-Mart and gotten back into the van. When he had removed the baseball cap he'd worn inside the store to hide the first emergency compress made from the left over fast food napkins he'd found in the glove compartment of the van...and found them soaked through with blood...he realized he was going to need to see a doctor. But it would have to wait.

There had been a traffic accident in the middle of the intersection just up ahead of him immediately following the sound of a thunderous explosion that had jolted his van. He'd seen a silver car, which had been almost all the way through the intersection, veer off the roadway and slam into a street light pole. Then all of the street lights and the traffic signal lights had flickered a few times, and gone out. At first he thought a ship must have blown up in the Harbor, or maybe even a natural gas pipeline. But whatever it was he was now certain it had been God's way of shouting at him...showing his extreme displeasure at how Uriah had apparently failed him once again tonight.

He had been sitting there for more than twenty minutes now, watching the three male police officers and the blonde female slut in the intersection up ahead of him through his Steiner binoculars; listening to them—and the other officers and fire fighters in the city urgently talking on their radios—with the police scanner he'd purchased at a Radio Shack store in Coos Bay soon after he'd killed Ricky Cates.

He had the scanner on the passenger seat of the van, lying beneath a folded up copy of the local newspaper he'd bought earlier in the day but hadn't yet a chance to look at. Off and on he softly stroked the hair of the bound and gagged ten year old boy he had jammed between the opening of the two front seats in the van, where he'd hidden him from view by covering him with his jacket in an attempt to try and keep him quiet.

The boy was whimpering and moaning softly, so Beek turned on the van's radio to help cover the sounds of his pitiable terror. If he saw any of the officers start to approach his van, he would take a handful of the child's hair and slam his head against the steel floor of the van again until he was unconscious...like he had done earlier when he'd been forced to leave the boy alone in the van for a few minutes while he went into the Wal-Mart to buy the shovel.

He'd thought it would look suspicious; a man buying a standard garden shovel at almost nine o'clock at night and he didn't want to be remembered by some bored but nosy store clerk...so he'd bypassed the store's Garden Center and had instead gone to the sporting goods aisle. There, he'd picked out a short handled, curved blade clam digging shovel that looked like an oversized ice cream scoop, just like the one Ricky Cates had, and when he went through the check stand with it he was paid the same amount of attention as any one of the thousands of other Oregon beachcombing tourists visiting the southern coast...which was none at all.

When he'd returned and hidden the clam shovel beneath the mountain of empty cardboard boxes in the rear cargo area of the van which he had intentionally saved this time on his route, and not discarded, the boy was still unconscious.

But it didn't appear that any of the officers would be contacting his van. The oldest of the three had left less than a minute before with the blonde whore in the front seat of his black car; speeding off into the night with his siren blaring after he'd bandaged one of her arms and even given her his uniform jacket to wear. And right after that the other two younger officers had waved an ambulance through the intersection which had come from the north at such a high rate of speed, that when it had swerved left at the intersection to proceed down the road toward the same shopping center where he had purchased the shovel, it had rocked over onto its two left wheels, nearly tipping over.

Now a tow truck had arrived, its flashing amber emergency lights radiating sunbursts of orange hued color out to all four corners of the intersection as it backed up to the damaged silver Lexus. One of the officers was already letting the east and west bound vehicles sneak across the intersection one at a time, because there were so few of them waiting, while his partner spoke to the tow truck driver.

As soon the tow truck had the Lexus hooked up and cleared from the intersection, Beek knew traffic would start moving again. He was only one vehicle of a hundred waiting in his lane to go, so he felt the officers should have no reason to approach him. That is unless the boy had been reported missing by now to the police, and someone had somehow seen his van and given them a description of it.

But just in case one of them did approach he had the grape hook knife concealed inside his folded vehicle registration and license papers and if he was asked to produce them he would feign confusion or misunderstanding to the officer. And when the officer stuck his head inside Beek's open driver's window to look at the papers Beek had produced...to see if they were what the officer was requesting...Beek would grab his head, slash one of the jugular veins in his throat open with the knife, and then take his weapon away from him and kill the other one.

At five thirty p.m. on his second and last scheduled day on his route in Cutter Point, he had finally finished servicing his last account. It was a small gift shop located in a large and raucous restaurant and bar on the city's main drag called The Buccaneer.

He disliked the place intensely. Especially at this hour of the day...happy hour...when it seemed as if most of the painted harlots of the town seemed to suddenly materialize out of thin air in the cocktail lounge, moving stealthily through the groupings of men perched atop high bar stools like cheetahs stalking prey in tall jungle grass. More than once when he'd mistakenly chosen to take his evening meal at the overcrowded restaurant he'd been rudely shunted off into the cocktail lounge by a waitress to sit on a stool at the bar, and choke down his hamburger in a silent, cold rage as the most abhorrent examples of female slutdom paraded their barely covered flesh past of him, debasing themselves with dimwitted, lusting men who'd come to meet them.

But today he had worked straight through his lunch hour in an attempt to finish early so he could get to his real work; God's work. He hadn't eaten anything all day and he needed to satisfy the hunger in his body first so that he would have the physical strength and clarity of mind in turn to satisfy the other growing hunger he felt deep inside; for contact and connection with another boy.

So he'd conceded to eating a quick dinner at The Buccaneer. And this time he was fortunate enough to get a tiny table in the restaurant dining room itself, tucked into a corner against a back wall. It was far enough away from the entrance to The Plank Room…the disgusting cocktail lounge…to avoid exposure to the never ending parade of provocatively dressed whores who passed through its ornately carved, fake pirate ship's door, desperately seeking a half priced Marguerita or White Bacardi and Coke, before Happy Hour ended at six.

He'd hurriedly wolfed down his cheeseburger, coke, and fries. By six forty five he'd driven thirty miles north on Highway 101 to the little private playground located at the edge of an isolated five block long strip of expensive ocean front homes called Nesika Beach, just past the small town of Gold Beach.

On his way out of Cutter Point he'd taken a quick detour through Musselshell State Park, but the only kids he'd seen there had been a group of sullen, troublesome looking teenagers standing around their cars in the otherwise vacant day use parking lot. They were skateboarding, smoking cigarettes, and throwing their empty fast food containers and other garbage on the ground all around them like dogs marking their territory. Some of the boys were pushing each other and "slap fighting" in testosterone fueled displays designed to impress and titillate the young female Jezebels who stood nearby, watching them.

When he had slowed his van and stopped next to the group as if to check and see if the combatants were actually fighting or just playing around, one of the boys with orange and purple spiked hair, and who was wearing a black tee shirt with the words FUCK THE WORLD, MAN…BECAUSE GOD'S SURE AS HELL GOING TO! printed on it, stepped out of the melee and walked towards Beek.

"Can we help you dude?" he asked.

"Are you kids all right?" said Beek.

Now the others stopped what they were doing and walked over to the white van where their friend was.

"Well, what's it to you?" the kid said.

A girl of about fifteen walked up beside the kid and hooked one of her thumbs through an empty belt loop of the kid's carpenter's jeans. She wore black Capri pants, cut so low to her pelvis Beek could see the beginning line of her pubic hair, and her fingernails and toenails were painted to match. Her nose, lips, both eyebrows, and both ears held brightly gleaming metal piercings, and through her braless, black fishnet tank top shirt he could see that both her small breasts had also been pierced; the circular metal rings through the nipples giving them the appearance of two small hand grenades with the pins still in them.

"I just didn't want to see any of you kids getting hurt," answered Beek. "That's all."

The kid quickly made eye contact with the six or seven other boys standing around him…seeing if they had his back in what he was about to do.

When he felt confident that he did, he took a couple of steps towards the door of Beek's Van and said, "Why don't you mind your own fucking business, and go harass someone else? Before we kick your ass."

"That kind of language isn't pleasing to God," Beek said quietly. "And neither is that shirt you are wearing."

"What?" laughed the kid. "What the fuck are you talking about?"

"Take it off, please," said Beek. "The shirt."

"Ha ha ha!" brayed the kid, looking around at his friends; a few of whom started to mimic him. He had no idea who this freak was in the bogus white delivery Van, wearing what looked like some kind of a work uniform; green pants and work shirt and a matching green jacket with the name "Dan" embroidered on it in red. But there were far more of them than him, and he'd had enough of this guy's shit.

"Hey, what the fuck are you man?" the kid asked. "Some kind of fucked up Maytag Repairman or something?" He laughed at his own joke, and the group began to laugh at it too.

"I *said* adios, amigo…before we stomp your balls in the…"

The door of the Van flew open as if it were on a spring loaded catapult, hitting the kid full force in the chest and knocking him backwards, arms flailing. But before he could fall to the ground the tall muscular man burst from the Van and was on him, grabbing the kid by the throat as he careened backwards, twisting the neck of his tee shirt into a steel tight knot.

With his left arm Beek lifted the terrified teenager six inches off the ground, his hundred and fifty dollar skateboarding shoes wind milling in panic against nothing but empty air as he tried to run. He pulled the grape hook knife from his jacket pocket and inserted the tip of it just below the twisted knot of tee shirt and sliced downward, opening the front of the shirt, and the kid spilled sideways out of it like a freshly peeled banana, landing on his face naked from the waist up on the hard chip sealed surface of the parking lot.

Beek stood still, holding the cut open rag of a shirt out in front of him as if he were offering any of the rest the chance to come and take it from him. But none of the kids made a move. They stood frozen in fear at both the fury, and speed, of what they had just seen happen.

"What pleases God," he said, dropping the shirt to the ground, "also pleases me. What displeases God…displeases me." He put the knife back into the pocket of his jacket and started to get back into his Van.

The shirtless kid, who was eighteen, and whose name was Derek Downs, now sensed that this Jesus freak delivery man with the super human strength probably wasn't going to gut him with his knife.

So he rose to his feet and screamed at Beek: "YOU FUCKING ASSHOLE! My Dad's a cop! You are NOT going to get away with this shit!"

Beek stopped at the Van's door. He turned around and walked briskly back to Derek, who saw him coming and tried to back away from him so quickly that he literally tripped over his own fashion statement—his untied, over length skate-board shoe laces—and went down to the asphalt again. This time hard on his ass.

Beek grabbed him by the neck and hoisted him back up to his feet, then roughly spun him around facing away from him and with his right hand started to rifle through the dozen or so pockets of Derek's carpenter's jeans, turning them all inside out.

The accoutrements of Derek Downs' post adolescence world spilled out onto the ground: a cheap blue plastic comb, two Trojan condoms, a half smoked pack of Marlboro Lights, a yellow plastic Bic lighter, eighty two cents in change, his parents Shell gas credit card. And a plastic baggie containing about a quarter of a gram of high grade marijuana.

Beek bent over and picked up the baggie of pot. Opening it, he held it directly above Derek's head.

"Do you know what my Father would have done if he'd found me with *this* when I was your age?" Beek asked him.

He upended the baggie and the marijuana sifted down on top of Derek's spiky head like finely mulched lawn mower grass clippings. "He would have killed me," Beek said.

"You go ahead and go get your dad," said Beek. "I'll wait here with your friends until you come back with him."

But the kid hadn't said anything further, and neither had any of his friends. He had just stood there, bare chested, clenching his fists, tears of humiliation, anger, and fear rolling down his cheeks; his ridiculous hair and what clothing he had left on making him look like the sad faced circus clown in the center ring who had just been pushed out of the miniature exploding car by his other clown friends.

Beek had gotten back into his Van and driven out of the state park, turning onto Highway 101 and heading north to Nesika Beach and the private play-ground where he had stopped several times before in the past few weeks as he traveled through the area on his route.

He parked the Van at a "Historic Viewpoint" pull out on the highway less than a quarter of a mile from the playground, and with no one there to see him he went over the steel guard rail, down a gently sloping sandy hillside, and out into the grassy sand dunes…walking in the direction of the playground.

The Steiner binoculars were slung around his neck. He still had the knife in his right jacket pocket along with some Trellistrip ties, and in his left jacket pocket he carried the little blue whale. The same one he'd originally taken down to the beach with him to entice Ricky Cates with, but ultimately never used once he'd discovered Ricky was far too old to be attracted any longer by a child's bath tub play toy.

This time it had been so easy. There had only been a single child at the playground; a perfect ten year old boy who was standing on the top of the park's only forlorn and nearly broken down slide. He had been noisily rolling large rocks down its battered, dented surface from a supply he'd carried up to the top of the slide with him one by one all afternoon and stacked in a precarious pyramid shape, like a pirate's cache of cannon balls.

Beek had purposefully not paid any attention to him at first. But when he felt the boy staring at him as he excitedly scanned the ocean's horizon through the binoculars, and the boy's natural curiosity had finally prompted him to ask what he was looking at, he'd told the boy he was looking for whales…gigantic blue whales. The largest, most magnificent creatures on the entire earth.

The boy, whose name was Tyler Dunne, was intrigued when Beek told him he had been following a huge pod of blue whales…maybe as many as a hundred…down the coast all day where they had been swimming just a little ways out from the shore. But they were so fast he had to keep driving to try and get ahead of them; and then run down to the beach in hopes of intercepting them before they all swam by. He told Tyler he had seen the last of the whale pod from the highway as they passed by in the water not more than a hundred yards offshore from where the playground was. He was surprised that Tyler hadn't seen any of them; they were so huge!

Then Beek pulled the little blue toy whale out of his pocket and gave it to Tyler…to show him what they looked like. He told Tyler that a real blue whale was probably even bigger than his own house was, and asked Tyler to point his house out to him; just so he could see it to compare. Tyler pointed to a small three bedroom Cape Cod house painted bright lemon yellow with white trim, that was on the right side of the street three houses away from where the path to the playground began. Beek looked at the house for a long time with his binoculars and then told Tyler…yes…a real blue whale was probably twice as long as his house, and almost as high as the roof was.

Beek asked Tyler why there weren't any cars in his driveway, and Tyler told him his mom and dad both worked in Cutter Point and didn't get home from their jobs on most week nights until it was almost dark. He had no brothers or sisters, and his parents couldn't afford a babysitter to watch him until they got home. They had only moved to Nesika Beach in March from California, so Tyler hadn't really made many friends yet in the neighborhood either.

Five minutes later Beek and the boy were hurrying through the sand dunes in the descending dusk toward the highway and his Van. If they went fast enough, Beek had told him, they could get ahead of the pod of whales by driving down the highway just a few miles to a secret spot that he knew. He could show Tyler the whales as they passed by…and then he could drive him back to his house before his parents got home.

But once they were in the Van and traveling south on 101 things had started to go badly. Beek had given the boy his binoculars; showed him how to use them and instructed him to watch out his window at the ocean and let him know if he spotted any of the whales while he drove. But it was getting darker now, the ocean's horizon growing dim and gray; the evening breeze shearing the tops of the ocean waves into frothy white caps, and soon Tyler let the heavy binoculars fall into his lap.

He had put his head down and quietly asked the man if he could home now. It was starting to get dark. His parents would be worried if they got home from work and he wasn't there; and he would be in trouble. But the man told him no. It was just a little further. They would keep driving and if the blue whales weren't there when they arrived, he would turn around and take the boy straight home.

Beek watched the endless expanse of wide open beach unfolding to the right of the highway and ahead of him for as far as he could see; with only isolated, black spire like rock formations rising from the sand in places like random obelisks. It was not a place for a lone man and child to be seen strolling alone by a passing motorist; maybe someone who might also remember having seen a white Van parked alongside the highway too.

He had screwed up by getting too late of a start in the day and now he was running out of time and to find a hidden place to take the boy for his instruction. When he began to think about the feral group of teenagers back at the state park, and the kid whose tee shirt he'd cut off, he felt a cold ball of anger in his stomach begin to solidify like a block of rock hard ice.

He'd wanted so badly to smash that arrogant kid's smirking face in; wanted to stomp on his orange and purple head on the ground until it was an unrecognizable mass of leaking colored jelly. Had wanted to force him to get down on his knees in the parking lot and piece by piece, make him chew and swallow every last shred of the blasphemous, God damning tee shirt he had been wearing.

But what Beek *had* done to him instead, he knew, was more than sufficient. His little black haired Gothic dressing slut girlfriend who he was undoubtedly defiling himself with on a regular basis...and the other Jezebel whores in his life yet to come who would only deceive him further with "the strong delusion" of their wicked charms...would eventually finish him.

Women were Satan's takers in this world, and weak willed, stupid, godless men, were the taken. It was why adolescent boys committed suicide six times more often than girls did, or grew up to be men who lost their children, their property, their dignity, and their souls as the price ultimately paid for choosing to lay with a whore of the Serpent from The Garden.

But I suffer not a woman to teach, nor to usurp authority over the man, but to be in silence. That is what God had to say in the Bible about the place women were meant to occupy in the world. But in the end, Beek knew, it would be this kid who would be the one to have his authority as a man usurped...by the women who would inevitably come to infect his life.

As a young boy growing up Beek had watched his own barfly Mother do this to his Father. The affairs she openly had with other men while he was away on his sales route, her departures for weeks and sometimes even months from their lives, her tearful, forgiveness begging returns. Until the day had arrived when she finally found *the* man and left them both for good; destroying his Father who had then turned completely inward to God...and leaving young Uriah, who was only eight, no choice but to follow him.

It was getting very dark when Beek had finally turned the Van off the highway just a few miles from the outskirts of Cutter Point, and they had bounced their way up along the western slope of the foothills of the coastal mountain range on a rutted, narrow logging road. Tyler had been intermittently begging him to take him home, and to stop the Van to let him pee.

Since honoring the boy's first request was an impossibility, Beek had stopped the Van at a place on the logging road that was enclosed, tunnel like, by a fifty yard long corridor of closely growing together young spruce trees on both sides of the road that hid the Van's headlights, which he'd turned off as soon as they'd left the highway. He shut the engine off and switched the headlights back on, then got Tyler out through his door and walked him in front of the Van into the soft twin yellow beams of the headlights. He unzipped the zipper of the trembling boy's jeans for him.

He had stepped back to let the boy take it out, and then like he had done with Ricky Cates he watched, fascinated, as the boy began to urinate. But Tyler was shaking so hard with fear that at first only a dribble of urine leaked out…then a short, sporadic spurt, followed by another…and finally a powerful, long flowing stream began.

He had been so ashamed. He wasn't a little kid any longer. *No one*, including his Mom, even ever saw him naked any more, let alone going to the bathroom. But he had instinctively understood that he'd have to force himself to do it in front of this man. Who had at first stared straight at him, at his *thing* when he began to pee…but then closed his eyes shut tight, his lips moving in a whisper, mumbling strange and unintelligible words…almost like he was in church praying or something.

And Tyler also knew what every ten year old boy knew…that you never tried to run in a race against someone if you had to go *really bad* without peeing first, and he knew he had to run *now*…while the crazy man was in his trance or whatever it was. As he'd felt the release of pressure from the last of the urine emptying out of his bladder, and without zipping up his jeans, Tyler Dunne had suddenly bolted and ran for his life.

Beek had been praying to God so hard…beseeching *Him*, begging *Him* to give him the strength to not do what he now felt the overpowering urge to do to this boy…when he heard Tyler's body swishing away through the maze of low lying branches of the Christmas tree sized spruce trees as he ran. He tried to lunge through the trees after him but the taller tangle of tree branches snapped back in his face like the spines of a huge umbrella, suddenly raised too far and popped inside out.

He could hear the boy careening through the underbrush, sobbing as he plunged wildly forward into the dark woods. So he'd stopped and listened; hearing the sounds of the escaping child at first start to recede in the distance…then grow stronger again, closer, and closer…and he'd realized the boy was running in a wide circle and about to emerge back onto the logging road up ahead.

Beek had sprinted up the road…twenty yards…thirty…thirty five, and suddenly the boy flashed across right in front of him, the fleeting shape of his form illuminated in the Van's headlights briefly like a rabbit in full flight from a fox. Beek had swiped at the boy with his hand, just missing catching the sleeve of his tee shirt but knocking him slightly off balance, causing him to trip in a rut on the dirt road; and he went down on the ground, hard.

Beek had been shocked and angry. None of his other victims had ever tried to escape from him and nothing like this had ever happened before…except once, a very long time ago. And that hadn't been an escape. It had been an attack on him. Because he had been finished with that boy but the boy had come back, looking for him. And now this boy—who was about the same age—had tried to get away from him; and nearly succeeded too.

He had reached down and grabbed the end of one of Tyler Dunne's pants legs and began to pull him along the ground on his stomach back to the Van. Tyler splayed his arms out in front of him, clawing at anything he could with his hands to try and stop the man from dragging him back. One of his hands closed on a fist sized, jagged edged piece of shale rock, and when the man released his pants leg as they reached the front of the Van, and clamped his huge hands on the back of Tyler's shoulders to pull him to his feet, Tyler twisted his body around and with all of the strength he had left, smashed the rock against the side of the man's head.

And the man had let go of him.

Beek had backed away from the boy, his right hand reflexively going up to the side of his head, just above his ear, feeling the warm, sticky blood oozing out from the three inch long lateral gash in his scalp the rock had made.

He'd told Tyler to get on his feet, and the boy rose slowly on wobbly legs, silent tears weaving liquid streaks down his dust covered cheeks. Beek asked him which school he went to; what the name of it was, which town it was in. And Tyler had told him.

Then Beek had taken a quick step toward the boy and struck him hard in the chest with the open palm of his huge right hand, and the boy collapsed, the breath knocked completely out of him.

Beek had carried him with one arm like a sack of garbage to the rear of the Van. He opened the two rear cargo doors and beneath the Van's weak overhead light moved several empty cardboard boxes out of the way and then laid the boy down on the Van's ribbed steel floor. He took the Trellistrips from his jacket pocket and tied the boy's ankles together tightly, then tied his hands behind his back the same way, and used two of the strips to gag his mouth open. He climbed inside the Van, picked the boy up by the back of his leather jeans belt, and jammed him into the space between the two front seats, face down.

As he'd driven back down the mountain and got back onto Highway 101, heading south again, he'd thought about Ricky Cates and how killing him had actually been an accident. He hadn't really meant to do that. His level of frustration was already too great. Trying to reach out to still innocent, virgin boys; to instruct and warn them, individually, of the inequities of the spirit and ravages of the heart soon to be visited upon them in their lives by the she-devil, Jezebel whore beasts of this nearly fallen world…was proving to be too daunting of a task.

He needed to cast a much broader and wider net, if he was to do any good in the end. Jesus had once found himself on a mountain top, surrounded by five thousand people who had come to listen to what he had to say, but with no way to begin to feed them all. A small boy in the crowd offered him a gift of two fish and five loaves of bread, which he blessed and then commanded all who were present to eat from; and as they did, all of them were fed.

Ricky Cates had been an unfortunate accident, and a regrettable waste. But now he saw that his calling was to feed the masses; to spread his message and teachings to the many by sacrificing the few. And so he would begin anew…with this boy.

Yes, he'd thought to himself then; maybe that arrogant punk kid at the state park with his disparaging tee shirt, and attitude to match, did have somewhat of a point. Maybe he was more right than he was wrong after all.

Why not fuck the world?

Because God surely *was* going to do exactly that, just as soon as he got around to it.

Beek had sped up then, pushing the old delivery Van up to eighty, its front end starting to shimmy like a washing machine with a large load of clothes that had become unbalanced.

He'd needed to get to Cutter Point fast.

To buy a shovel before all the stores closed for the night.

CHAPTER 13

▼

Kearnes waited for Britt in the emergency room at Cutter General Hospital, which was filled to overflowing with "patients." Most of them were not truly emergency cases but elderly people who had been nearly frightened to death by the blast, and had rushed themselves or their friends—and some of them, even their pets—to the hospital seeking medical attention for problems both real and imagined.

All of the on call physicians had been paged at their homes and summoned to the hospital to help out in the E.R., as well as several additional nurses. And since forty percent of the population of Cutter Point consisted of retired people over the age of sixty five, the line of stooped and snowy white haired triaged patients waiting to be seen—that had now grown so long it spilled out of the E.R. into the hospital's rear parking lot—looked more like the crowd waiting to get into Saturday night Bingo at the Community Center than victims of a local natural disaster.

Frick and Frack, who referred to these older residents of the community as either "Q-tips", or "Cutter Codgers", spent the majority of the summer on their patrol bikes doing one of two things. Either talking to girls, or trying to dodge these old kamikaze drivers in busy downtown traffic…who sometimes steered their five thousand pound Cadillac Coup Devilles and Lincoln Continentals through the city streets as blindly and blissfully ignorant of their immediate surroundings as the captain of the Titanic had been.

The drive to the hospital with Britt had taken only a few minutes at the speed Kearnes was traveling. On the way they passed the ambulance that was headed in the opposite direction to the parking lot at Wal-Mart. He saw her wince as the box shaped Medic Response Unit bore down on them and then screamed past in the opposite lane only a foot and a half away, the sirens from both vehicles melding into a painful, ear splitting shriek.

Kearnes slid through the left turn off of Cutter Avenue and onto West Medical Way, and began accelerating up the steep grade toward the old hospital which sat on the bluff of a hill that rimmed the south end of the city. He glanced over at Britt as he drove and saw that she was bleeding from her nose.

Great, wet drops of crimson were spattering down onto the front of her dress, and the small black travel bag she still held tightly in her lap. The left side of her face was now a puffy, swollen red, and he suddenly understood why it was she had been crying back at the accident scene; other than having been thoroughly upset and frightened after being in the collision.

When the air bag in the Lexus had deployed upon impact it had caught her on that side of her face as she had instinctively turned her head away from the windshield, and she had been trying to avoid showing the pain from it ever since Kearnes had first walked up to her. In addition to being heartbreakingly beautiful, and obviously intelligent enough to have finished medical school, this was also one very strong woman Kearnes thought.

The hospital was only three blocks away but he made the decision to stop now, and quickly pulled the car over to the side of the road. He switched on the overhead dome light and undid his seatbelt.

Britt stared down at the blood dripping onto her dress.

"Oh my God," she said.

Kearnes saw the corner of a small package of Kleenex sticking out of the open top of her purse on the floor of the car where it sat between her ankles. He grabbed it and tore away its cellophane wrapper, then gently leaned her head back against the vehicle's headrest. Cupping her neck underneath with his right hand, he pinched some folded over tissues firmly against her nostrils with his other.

The back of her slender neck was warm, almost hot; and was slightly damp with perspiration. He could feel the taught cords of muscle in her neck beneath her skin begin to relax into his fingers as he held her there with his hand...and as he looked down at her he had a sudden and completely irrational impulse to kiss her slightly parted lips. But he didn't.

"Does it feel like your nose may be broken?" he asked.

Slowly, she shook her head no, letting Kearnes keep the tissues pressed tightly against her nose as she moved her head from side to side.

Like he had done with her arm back at the wreck, he kept the pressure steady without letting up, watching for signs of blood seeping out from beneath the tissues; and all the while stealing quick looks at her. As he did he saw that her eyes were locked onto him in an unbroken and intense gaze…but like a man staring directly into the sun, he was soon forced to look away from her.

Britt lightly pushed the Kleenex away from her nose with her left hand, and he could see had stopped bleeding. Then her fingers rested briefly for a moment on the top of his hand and looking at them he could see the white banded impression left on the skin of her third finger by the recent removal of a ring.

"Do I look as terrible as I feel?" she asked him.

"Worse," he said, smiling at her.

And she smiled back at him.

"I'd like to apologize for the way I acted toward you back there," she said. "At my car."

"Not necessary," he said, daubing at some blood smeared near the tip of her chin with the Kleenex. "I think we've got it stopped now. We'd better get you into the E.R."

"I've had a very bad day," she said, staring up at the headliner of the car, keeping her head titled back.

"Well, you know what?" Kearnes said, wadding up the bloody tissues and throwing them in the plastic litter bag that hung from the knob of his car's cigarette lighter. "Me too."

Britt turned her head slightly sideways to look at him better. "Really?" she asked. "And what's been the worst part of *your* day so far?"

Kearnes started the engine of the car and put it in gear, but kept his foot on the brake. With a totally deadpan expression he stared at her for a few seconds…then finally said: "When my alarm went off this morning."

Britt stared back at the handsome, confident, and obviously capable man…who was also very funny in a dry and reserved kind of way…and for the first time that day she was able to think about something other than her own overwhelming problems; of all the things that had gone wrong so far for her that day, and more, since her own alarm had gone off at four a.m. in the bedroom of her Seattle condominium.

And then she burst into laughter.

She laughed so hard that she began to cry, and then cried so hard that she started laughing again and couldn't stop. And she was still laughing and crying as Kearnes had carried her in his arms through the wide open doors of the emergency room at Cutter General; holding onto him tightly around his neck with one arm while she held the black overnight bag to her body just as tightly with the other.

The heart attack victim from Ruston Street—a seventy one year old man who'd been frantically trying to load his very obese wife and two poodles into their car to evacuate from their home after the tsunami siren had started to sound—was already in the first bay of the emergency room when Kearnes rushed through the doors with Britt in his arms.

An E.R. nurse saw his uniform and badge and immediately ripped the white sliding cloth curtains open on bay number two open wide, helping Kearnes to gently lay Britt down on the examining table. When the nurse tried to take the black travel bag from her Britt held onto it with a firm grip, and then told the nurse that she was a doctor and began rattling off the list of medical supplies and instruments she would need to get in order for her injury to be treated.

The nurse looked questioningly at Kearnes. He shrugged and said, "She's a doctor." Even though he had no proof yet himself that she was.

Britt sat up on the table and slipped off his uniform jacket, then handed it to him. "I hope I didn't get any blood on it," she said.

From an instrument tray on a nearby counter within her reach she took a pair of small, stainless steel scissors and began to cut away the adhesive gauze tape on her bandaged forearm.

"I'll be all right now," she said, not looking at him. "I'm sure you must have plenty of other duties to attend to." Her voice and her entire demeanor seemed to have suddenly and drastically changed. She seemed aloof now…distant; and in turn Kearnes could feel himself pulling back a little from her, too. He realized they were both professionals, trained to act in certain ways in a professional working environment…which a hospital emergency room certainly was; but in the car when he'd made her laugh he'd thought a genuine connection had been made between them. But now he wasn't so sure.

"Yes, I do" said Kearnes. "I've got to make some phone calls. "I'll be back to check on you in a few minutes." Britt continued to cut away at the tape and didn't look up at him; didn't respond to him.

He went out to the parking lot to his car and took his cell phone from its charging cradle, and speed dialed Thud's home phone number. It rang only once before Thud picked up.

"Thud?"

"Chief?"

"Yeah," said Kearnes. "I need to call you into work. Grab your gear and bring a jumpsuit to wear if you've got one. We've got a very messy potential crime scene down on the beach I'm afraid."

"I was just on my way out the door," said Thud. "What the hell happened? Our place shook like it was going to collapse any minute, and Margie is still trying to get the girls calmed down. They went completely hysterical and they're still crying!"

"I don't know exactly what went wrong," said Kearnes, "But my best guess would be that Lieutenant Polk's ex-military friends may have used a little bit too many explosives."

"Those stupid assholes," said Thud. "I knew something like this would happen. Did anyone get killed?"

"I don't know that yet either," Kearnes said. "There was already one ambulance staged in the parking lot when the explosion was set off, just for safety's sake. And after it went off a second one was requested Code 3 so it doesn't look good but I don't know, I wasn't there. I had to respond to an injury traffic accident."

"I swear to God," Thud said. "If we've got any fatalities in this thing I'm charging all of the idiot Patriots involved *and* Polk, with reckless endangerment and manslaughter."

"Well let's hope we don't, Thud", Kearnes said. "Get down there as fast as you can. And call me on my cell...not the radio...as soon as you have anything for me. I ordered Polk to secure the scene and not let anyone in or out, except medical personnel."

"Where are you?" asked Thud.

"I'm at the E.R.," said Kearnes. "With a woman from the accident. There weren't any more available ambulances so I transported her."

"OK," said Thud. "I should be on scene in less than five...I'm 'outta here now!"

As he started to walk back to the entrance doors of the E.R. Kearnes heard the siren of an ambulance wailing far off in the distance down below in the city. He listened as it worked its way south on Cutter Avenue, getting closer to the turn off on West Medical Way, and trailing behind it was the sound of a second ambulance, trying to catch up.

Soon he could see the reflection from the red and blue lights of both ambulances bouncing off the brushy hillside as they wound their way up to the top of the bluff, traveling cautiously in the oncoming lane only because the funeral like motorcade of fear stricken seniors on their way to the hospital, all trying to get there at the same time, had occluded the roadway ahead of them like a diseased heart artery.

Kearnes watched as the first ambulance roared into the parking lot, turning in a hard semi-circle to end up perfectly in line with the E.R. doors, then backing up to within a couple of feet of the sidewalk. The rear doors of the ambulance flew open and four paramedics jumped out; two from the front cab of the vehicle and two from the back.

They slid a yellow painted steel gurney out of the back of the ambulance and scissored its four hinged legs to the pavement. There was a man on the gurney covered with a bright orange blanket; a tall man wearing camouflage pants, whose long legs stuck out nearly two feet from the bottom of the blanket.

His left hand and arm were wrapped with white bandages and the hand—or at least what was left of it—was wrapped with so many thick layers of bandages it looked like cotton candy on a paper stick. Red stains were starting to appear through the bandages about where the man's wrist was and as one paramedic held the injured arm elevated straight up in the air, and another dangled an I.V. bag connected by a clear plastic tube high over the man's body, all four of them rushed the gurney into the E.R., shouting out assessments of injuries and vital signs to the squad of doctors and nurses who had come running to help them.

Kearnes recognized the tall man on the gurney from earlier in the day at the Wal-Mart parking lot; he was the leader of the group of Patriots.

A minute later the second ambulance arrived and pulled up parallel to the first one, also backing in as closely as possible to the E.R. doors. But when the paramedics driving the ambulance parked, and got out, they approached the rear doors warily.

They swung the rear doors of the ambulance open and Kearnes could see two men…at least he thought they were men…lying on their backs on separate gurneys and punching at one another.

"Hey!" yelled one of the paramedics to Kearnes. "We need some help over here!" Kearnes ran from his car to the back of the ambulance.

Both of the men's tee shirts and camo pants were coated with beach sand and small fragments of driftwood and bits of grass clung to the hair of their mud caked heads like wild bird nests, making them look like two bodies recently exhumed from shallow graves. But they were still very much alive, and yelling at each other at the top of their lungs.

"You asshole!" Todd Caswell screamed at Larry Luebcke, throwing an ineffectual sideways punch at the skinny man across from him. "You could have gotten us killed!"

"Fuck you!" Rat screamed back, wincing as Frog's knuckles drove into his cadaverous arm. "That fucking hole saved *your* sorry ass out there man!"

"Hole?" yelled Frog. "HOLE?"

"That wasn't a *hole* you dug dipshit…it was the Holland freaking Tunnel!"

When Jerry Sparks had ordered both of them to dig in before he set off the explosion, Rat had grabbed the shovel he'd handed him and in a matter of minutes excavated a tunnel deep into the side of a sand dune with a right hand, dog leg turn at its end which would have made even Hoh Chi Minh proud.

Frog had been right behind him, throwing out huge scoops of loosened sand backwards between his legs like a dog digging for a bone, and when zero hour had come at ten p.m. they were both hunkered down inside the cave, safe and secure. That is until Jerry Sparks touched off the massive combined charge of C-4 explosives and the shock wave rolled through the sand dunes, collapsing the tunnel and completely burying them. When the search team of rescuers had arrived only the tip of one of Frog's tennis shoes sticking rearward out of the sand had saved their lives.

Jerry Sparks, on the other hand, had not been quite so lucky. With only one arm to dig with, and Rat and Frog quickly disappearing from sight into the ground like a couple of subterranean moles, he'd only managed to scoop out a low depression in the sand. It had allowed his lanky body from the head down to sink somewhat below the horizon, but forced him to raise and extend his arms forward because he hadn't had enough time to finish digging before zero hour arrived.

He had been lying flat on his stomach, reaching forward and holding on to two clumps of beach grass on a little hump of sand in front of him when the C-4 detonated. And an empty, splayed open razor clam shell lying on the beach near the whale—the size and shape of a small hot dog bun—was sent buzzing through the air at several hundred miles an hour and had clipped off the last three fingers of Jerry Sparks' good left hand as neatly as if they had been chopped off with a meat cleaver on a butcher's block…leaving him with a matching pair of lobster claw hands for life.

"Oh yeah?" shouted Rat. "Well I noticed you had your fat ass about as far in there as you could get it! I couldn't even hardly breathe you were so fucking close!"

"Fucking army retard!" yelled Frog.

"Marine moron!" Rat yelled back at him.

Kearnes climbed into the back of the ambulance and shouted at both of them to stop, and as soon as they saw his badge they instantly shut up. He could now smell both men, who reeked of the strange combination of alcohol from their day long bout with White Russians, and cyclotrimethylene trinitramine; remnants of the chemical compounds from the plastic explosive. As soon as he was sure he had made his presence known to Rat and Frog and that he'd communicated to them the need to de-escalate their hostilities toward one another, he backed out of the ambulance and the paramedics unloaded the two belligerent patients and wheeled them into the E.R.

It took almost ninety minutes for Britt to be treated and released.

The cut on her forearm wasn't as bad as first thought. And even though butterfly closures were ruled out by the E.R. doctor who'd seen her as not being effective enough, and he'd wanted to quickly sew her up using traditional stitches, Britt had insisted she be given a tissue adhesive closure…a kind of medical super glue…and had waited until one of the younger physicians who had been called in and who was familiar with the technique, could treat her.

Kearnes had stayed at the hospital the entire time and when she emerged from the curtained treatment bay, carrying the black travel bag, she seemed shocked to still see him there.

"You didn't have to wait for me," she said, with a slight tinge of annoyance in her voice.

"I just called the tow company who took your Lexus," he said. "The driver thinks it is probably repairable; there doesn't appear to be any damage to the engine but he thinks your frame is probably bent, and of course your hood and front bumper will have to be replaced."

"Here is their name, number, and address," he said, handing her a small piece of paper he'd written the information down on from his notebook. "They said they have their own body shop but they don't work on the luxury cars like yours. But they said they can recommend someone in town to you who does."

Britt took the piece of paper from him and without looking at it, unzipped the black travel bag partially and stuck it inside.

"Thank you," she said. "I'll call them first thing in the morning."

"Speaking of the first thing in the morning," said Kearnes, "where are you planning on staying tonight?"

"A motel, I guess," she said. "Someplace quiet though; not a tourist trap and not with any busy, noisy streets running right past either."

Cutter Point was filled with tourist trap motels, and most of them were downtown, strung out along busy, bustling Cutter Avenue…U.S. Highway 101…but he had seen one place like she was describing; down in the Harbor District and not too far from The Sea Breeze Apartments where he lived.

"I know of one, he said. "It's quiet and off the beaten path, and right on the ocean, too. But it is older looking and I've never been inside it; so it could be a dump. And I wouldn't want you any more pissed off at me than you already are now."

So, here it was again, she thought. The precise moment of relationship conception…*if* she wanted it. In a way it seemed so negligible; inconsequential and almost unnoticeable…all but invisible to those women who chose to, or out of necessity needed to, remain blind to it. But for those who used more than just their eyes to see with it was also rife with the promise of the possibility of the most searched for and sought after dream they all held in common; a life of everlasting love with, and for, just one man.

Sadly, Britt McGraw could no longer be counted among *them*. Her duty now was to herself, and she had sworn to guard her heart at all costs. To wall herself off from every distraction, every temptation that would serve to prevent her from doing what needed to so desperately be done. Her new found clarity of vision had opened her eyes to the reality of the world, and what her life had amounted to so far in it. Men were the takers of this world, and women were the taken; but for Britt McGraw all that was about to change, finally…forever.

In her black travel bag she had seventy eight thousand dollars in cash in rubber banded stacks of twenty, fifty, and one hundred dollar bills, and at the bottom of all the money, in a small, zippered black leather case, a five shot .22 caliber stainless steel mini-revolver not much larger than a pair of fingernail clippers; loaded with five rounds of .22 long rifle hollow point ammunition.

If it wasn't for the bizarre happenstance of the traffic accident she would have been asleep in a Eureka, California motel room by now, waiting for morning; when she would walk into a nearby downtown dentist's office just before it opened at nine a.m.…warmly greet the man there with a surprise smile and a warm hug. And then place the short, inch and a quarter long barrel of the tiny gun to the man's head…just behind his ear. Cock the hammer back. Pull the trigger.

Britt took a deep breath, and then let out an audible sigh. She looked at Kearnes with an expression of pure exasperation.

"Okay," she said. "Let's start all over. First: I am not "pissed" at you. I don't even know you well enough yet to be pissed at you! It's just that I have had an unbelievably shitty day…I think we both have…my arm hurts, my head hurts, my car is wrecked, and it looks like I am stuck here. At least for tonight.

So…what is the name of this place…and would you be able to call a taxi for me?"

Even with a look of undisguised irritability on her face, Kearnes still thought she was the most beautiful woman he had ever seen. He said nothing for a moment; just kept looking straight into her eyes which was very hard for him to do, but needed to be done. He was searching for something; something important he required before he would say another single word to her. Because he had just heard her tell him she didn't know him well enough. *Yet.*

And then she gave in to him, her pained expression slowly melting away into a shy smile.

"Please?" she asked him. "Just this one last thing and I promise I won't be bothering you again."

"It's called The Sand Dollar," he said. "And I'm taking you there myself."

CHAPTER 14

▼

Beek drove cautiously through the crowded parking lot at Cutter General Hospital, searching for an empty parking space as far away from the three cop cars he'd already spotted there as he could. But the small lot was jam packed with vehicles and he was forced to park only two stalls away from the one unmarked, black cop car...the same one, he was sure, that had been at the accident scene.

He climbed out of the Van and brushed the sand from his pants and jacket; still damp from where he had lain on the wet beach earlier...even though he had turned the Van's heater on as high as it would go, and had left it there all the way on his drive in to the hospital.

He walked to the Van's rear doors, opened them, and with his last bloody saturated napkin—which he had been pressing tightly against the loose flap of skin on his scalp since he'd left the beach—he generously smeared his own blood all over on one of the upper door hinges.

That would be his story: he had been at his motel, rearranging the inventory in the back of his Van when the explosion went off, startling him. He had jumped upright, hitting his head on the steel door hinge. He had tried to stop the bleeding himself for the past couple of hours but couldn't; and so he'd come to the hospital for treatment.

He would allow a doctor to suture the wound shut, but nothing more. And if they attempted to transfuse his own blood in any way he would refuse...to the point of violence if necessary. Because he believed fervently what the Bible said in Leviticus: "*You must not eat the blood of any sort of flesh.*" Uriah Beek would choose death first before ever committing the sin of allowing the blood of another to enter his body.

As soon as the police had let traffic start moving through the intersection again he had driven straight through town and across the Oregon-California border which was just a few miles past the south city limits of Cutter Point, finally turning off Highway 101 at Smith River, and there, still twenty miles from Crescent City, he'd taken an unimproved beach access road down to the ocean.

He'd used a small flashlight and the light of the moon to find a suitable driftwood log—a smooth, barkless, reddish brown limb torn loose from a Madrone tree—long enough and stout enough to support the height and weight of Tyler Dunne. Then he'd gotten Tyler out of the Van, along with the shovel, and carried both him and the log through the sand dunes down to the surf line, where the slack low tide was reversing to an incoming flow of water as the high tide began to build.

He had put Tyler face down on his stomach on the cold black sand and pulled his jeans down to his ankles, penetrating him from behind, closing his huge hands around the boy's neck and throat, squeezing tighter and tighter the faster he thrust himself into him.

As the moment of his release had drawn near he'd opened his eyes and thrown his head back, staring wide eyed at the stars and the nearly full moon blazing overhead in the almost cloudless night sky. And as Uriah Beek felt himself losing all control, his body taking charge now and the flood of liquid heat pouring forth from him in unstoppable spasms, he had begun to scream and rage at the moon and stars and the heavens above…his screams eventually blending into one long and mournful howl like some tortured, rabid dog; pleading to be put out of his misery.

Beek had screamed so loudly his voice had drowned out the sound of the close by and relentlessly pounding ocean surf in his own ears, and had completely covered over the crackling sounds of the bones in Tyler Dunne's neck being crushed as his large hands twisted, auger like, harder and harder around the boy's throat.

Then Beek had lost consciousness and fallen; toppling over onto his side across the Madrone log which he had laid on the sand next to him. Everything at first for him was black, and quiet. And then from deep inside the pitted, abscessed, hate infected recesses of his brain; the psychotically delusional dream had come to him once again.

Silver winged angels with hair of spun gold held onto to his outstretched hands and bore him weightlessly upward from the earth toward a blinding white light high in the blue sky above, taking him to his rightful place to wait in line as one of God's chosen. He was one of the one hundred and forty four thousand mortals who were to be allowed to live with Him in His Kingdom. To walk beside Him for all of eternity as his reward for all of the good and difficult work he had done on God's behalf down on earth. Defying the army of whores of the Jezebel Spirit while denying them their young victims at the same time. Teaching young boys of the wickedness and evil of feminine ways; at great personal risk, cost, and sacrifice to himself.

And all of the one hundred and forty four thousand chosen by God…men, children, and even women, would live happily at peace and in harmony with each other. Cleansed; absolutely untouched by the impurities of mind, body, and spirit that had ravaged their souls and hearts in their lives back on the earth like a black, relentless cancer. Maybe even Beek himself would then find love; because that was part of the dream too. He didn't hate love…he only hated the imperfection of it.

He had been brought back to consciousness by the incoming tide washing over his work boots. He'd raised himself up groggily to a sitting position, and saw Tyler Dunne's body a short distance away from him beginning to bob away gently at the edge of the surf. He'd jumped to his feet, grabbed the boy's body, the shovel, and the fence post sized piece of Madrone, and retreated back twenty yards on the beach from the advancing ocean water.

On his knees and digging like a mad man, he had soon been able to sink the first three feet of the Madrone tree branch into the hole in the sand he had dug. He had hurriedly filled the hole back in and then pounded the sand flat around the base of the thick branch with the bottom side of the clam shovel. When he'd wiggled the branch back and forth, it had hardly moved.

His head had started to bleed again. He had seen drops of his blood in the moonlight spattering blackly onto the sand around the boy's body as he used his knife to cut away the Trellistrips that still bound Tyler Dunne's hands behind his back. After he'd cut those ties away he had lovingly picked up Tyler's lifeless body and with more of the vinyl strips, tied him to the Madrone branch; hands together tightly and arms stretched high above his head, feet together and legs pulled straight downward.

Beek had finished tying the boy to the improvised wood stake as the incoming tide had started to lap at the soles of his work boots. He had taken the shovel and walked to the edge of the beach and climbed up onto the top of a small sand dune. Squatting there, he had watched the tide slowly surging toward the boy; coming up to his ankles, then his knees, then his waist.

He had been in awe at the sight of the boy tied to the Madrone branch as the ocean waters rushed over him, and had dropped to his knees in prayer and sanctification of what he had created, guided by God's reassuring and never erring hands.

To Beek, Tyler Dunne had looked just like the crucified Jesus...the *real* Jesus. The Jesus who had died on a simple stake driven into the ground, and not on a cross.

Kearnes walked Britt back out to his car. They passed by a tall man standing beside a white delivery Van, holding what looked like a blood soaked piece of cloth against his head.

He put her in the front seat and started the engine so he could turn the heater on and keep her warm; because she had refused the offer of his jacket to wear again. His cell phone rang just as he started to get in the car, so he stayed outside and took the call. It was Thud.

Thud told him the scene down at the beach and in the Wal-Mart lot was contained; that there had been no further casualties other than the three men already transported by ambulance to the hospital, and that everyone at the scene had been interviewed except for Lieutenant Polk, who had refused to speak to him.

But Thud had anticipated this and had saved interviewing Edgar Polk for last, and he was satisfied he pretty much had the whole story anyhow; piecing it together bit by bit from all the others involved at the scene. The Patriots had somehow gotten their hands on a powerful—and illegal for them to possess—military explosive known as C4...and a whole hell of a lot of it. And Polk had stood by and watched, unquestioningly, as they'd tamped the dead whale carcass full of it and then set it off. He was sure there was enough probable cause for both state and federal criminal charges against Polk and some of The Patriots, too, but he'd have to wait until after he'd conducted interviews with the three injured men. Meanwhile, property damage in the shopping center from the explosion and in some other close by areas of the city was mounting into the thousands of dollars.

Thud asked Kearnes how to handle the barrage of media questions which were starting to come in even at this late hour from both the local and regional newspaper, radio, and television stations; most of them wanting to know if Cutter Point had been shaken by and earthquake, then struck by a tsunami wave. Kearnes prepared a brief press release for Thud, dictating it to him word for word over the cell phone.

The City of Cutter Point had *not* experienced a seismic event of any type. An explosion of unknown origin near the waters edge in the city had possibly been the catalyst for the accidental activation of the tsunami warning system...although this was still being looked into. There had been some temporary confusion in the community by some of the local populace, but calm and order had quickly been restored. Meanwhile, three people were being treated at a local area hospital for injuries possibly related to the mysterious explosion. The source of the explosion itself was still under investigation.

Thud Compton's forte was not writing; unless it was done in the structured, formula like police narrative reports which he cranked out by the hundreds each year in his office at the P.D. So he was grateful for both the chief's help, and skill, in composing the press release that would get the media vultures off his back...seeing as how Polk had already abdicated his responsibility as ranking officer at the scene and gone home for the night. But Thud wasn't much good at taking dictation either and as Kearnes had to pause several times in order to let him catch up in copying down what he was saying, out of the corner of his eye he saw the man at the white Van watching him.

He finished and got off the phone with Thud, then opened his car door a few inches and told Britt he would be right back. He walked over to the man at the white Van.

"Are you okay sir?" Kearnes asked. The tall, well built man was dressed in light green work pants and shirt. On the left chest of his matching jacket, embroidered in red thread, was the name "Dan"; but there was no company name or logo. Kearnes could see now that the bloody cloth he was holding pressed to his head was actually a wad of paper napkins. He looked a little vacant, disoriented, and was holding onto the Van, just below one of the top rear door hinges, as if it was propping him up.

"Yes," said the man. "I'm OK. Just a little dizzy at the moment."

"Looks like you got quite a whack on the head," said Kearnes.

The man pushed off the Van and stood to his full height and Kearnes saw that he had to be at least six four, maybe even six five.

"What happened?" asked Kearnes.

"I was re-stocking my product in the back of the Van when whatever it was went bang. It surprised me; I stood up too fast and hit my head on a door hinge."

"Ouch," said Kearnes, looking now at the Van's rear door hinges. "You deliver here to the hospital?"

"What?" said the man. "Here? Oh, no. I was at my motel for the night, actually, when it happened."

"Let me give you a hand into the E.R.," said Kearnes, scrutinizing the door hinges closely now. "Or I can go in and have them bring a wheelchair out here." On the outside of the right side door hinge there was a large quantity of blood...fresh blood. But the man had said he'd been inside his Van when he'd hit his head. And the blood looked almost as if it had been smeared onto the metal.

"No...thanks. I can make it fine. Just needed to get my sea legs here for a minute."

"You waited a long time to get in here," said Kearnes.

"I tried to stop the bleeding myself," the man said quickly. "You know what they say about head cuts though...you get one and you bleed like a stuck pig. What the heck was that explosion anyway?"

Now Kearnes was scanning the man's clothing. There were dark areas of what appeared to be dampness. Fine grains of sand clung to the cuffs of his work pants in tiny, irregular clumps. His brown leather work boots were soaking wet.

"We had a little trouble down on the beach with some local pyrotechnicians," said Kearnes.

"What were they doing?" asked the man.

"Practicing for the Fourth of July, I think," said Kearnes.

"That's quite a gun," he said, quickly changing the subject and pointing to Kearnes' holster. "Is that a Colt .45?"

"No," said Kearnes. "It's a .38 Super."

"But it is a Colt, right?"

"Yes, it is. But in a little known caliber."

"My dad had a Colt .45," said the man. "He brought it home with him from the Korean War. He was a traveling salesman. Went everywhere with him on the road for almost twenty five years. "B.L.K. What does that stand for?"

"What?" asked Kearnes.

"B.L.K. The initials on the grips."

"Oh...I forget they are even there," said Kearnes. "This was...still is...my uncle's gun. Benjamin Lincoln Kearnes. He was a pretty famous officer back in my hometown when I was a kid. He gave it to me to use when I graduated from the academy, and I've carried it ever since."

"He must have been very proud of you," said the man.

"I was proud of him," said Kearnes. "And still am. He's the real reason why I got into this profession in the first place."

If it was even a possibility for a cold blooded killer's own blood to ever run cold, now was the time it should have registered on Beek's face; like the brief, shadowy passing of a fast moving cloud across the sun as he recognized the gun by its unusual grips, and the lettering on them. But instead he only smiled at Kearnes; a smile filled with remembrance, confirmation...and anticipation.

"Well, thank you anyhow, officer," said the man, smiling at him. "Looks like there are a lot of people in there so I'd better get going." He walked away from Kearnes, headed for the still wide open doors of the Emergency Room.

Kearnes returned to his car. He never looked back at the man who had paused now, halfway to the E.R. entrance, watching him as he got into his black unmarked police vehicle and drove out of the parking lot.

Beek was no longer smiling. You presumptuous, weak little child, he thought to himself. Your uncle wasn't the reason you became a policeman.

I was.

Kearnes drove them back down the hill into the city and onto Cutter Avenue, then crossed the Blue Czar River Bridge and took the Harbor Way exit. They rode in silence, getting closer and closer to The Sand Dollar Motel and Beach-front Cabins; while he tried to work up the courage to speak to Britt who sat motionless in the dark seat next to him, almost as if she were a statute in a wax museum.

The synchronicity of the circumstances of how he had met Britt tonight— standing outside her crashed car—and how he had also met Tilly so many years ago in almost the same way; as she had sat in her car with her flashers on, lost on the freeway near the Amelia Earhart Bridge, was both mystifying and disconcert-ing to him. He decided that fate or some sort of divine intervention had traipsed into the emptiness and uncertainty of his life at both these times, offering him the possibility and perhaps even the promise of love just when he needed it most...if he could only find the courage to act quickly and without hesitation before the moment passed. Or, if it wasn't that; maybe he was just painfully pathetic when it came to relationships, and had a tendency to easily fall in love with women in disabled vehicles.

But the truth, still so hidden from him that night, was that broken hearts were like broken birds, falling from the sky. Plummeting to the earth where they walked about, wingless...seeking one of their own kind in the hopes of one day finding them; and somehow being restored, made whole again, and able to soar high among the clouds once more.

They were getting closer to The Sand Dollar and he could smell the acrid odor of the ocean air as Britt finally stirred to life and rolled her electric window down halfway. He fought back a small initial wave of nausea as the smell of the sea overtook him, and he forced himself to speak to her because it was now or never.

"Where were you on your way to?" he asked.

Britt turned and looked at him.

"What?" she said.

"Where were you going?" he said. "Before the accident. Where were you headed?"

She hesitated for a moment. "San Francisco," she said. "I'm on my way to San Francisco. To attend a medical convention."

"Oh," said Kearnes. "I thought you were on your way to San Diego. On vacation."

"What?" she said again. "No. Why would you think that?"

"Officer Sparling mentioned it to me," he said. "Back at the accident. But maybe he got it wrong." In fact it was exactly what Spenser had told him after Kearnes had finished bandaging her hand and had put her in his car. Cops at investigations never forgot such elementary information once they'd learned of it because they were the clues which were sometimes used as the building blocks for foundations of theories, which sometimes led to solving a crime. Now it appeared that he may have caught her in a lie, but he didn't know why.

"Yes," she said. "Yes. He probably did. Get it wrong."

"Either one is kind of a long drive from Seattle isn't it? Why didn't you just fly?"

An expression of disquiet appeared on her face.

"How do you know that I came from Seattle?" she asked.

"Because that's where you live," Kearnes stated matter of factly.

Britt looked out her open window again. Squat, flat roofed wooden houses with weedy, sand lot yards and yawning, broken down silver gray weathered fences glided past. The street lights in this part of Old Town were unreliable. They either burned out and were ignored by the city public works crews for months, or local kids shot them out with their BB guns soon after they had been repaired. And so what was a kind of charming, eclectic sea side neighborhood by day, took on the look of a foreboding ghetto in some areas at night. She had asked him to find her someplace to stay a little off the beaten path...but not necessarily at the very end of it.

"How do you know where I live," said Britt; not asking a question but instead making a statement...one which she wanted an answer to. She hadn't shown him any kind of identification because he hadn't asked.

"Your license plates," said Kearnes.

Her heart sunk when she heard him say this. How stupid, naïve, and utterly amateurish of her, she thought to herself. They were the police...*he* was the police! Your "privilege" to drive in any given state was directly tied to the driver's license they ultimately issued you, and the data collected prior to it being issued, including your registered vehicles—which was cross stored with a hundred other different government agencies; disseminated, shared, updated, and frequently checked—was the functional equivalent of your electronic DNA; easily obtained, and easily verified. Now she realized that tomorrow, after she'd killed the man, they would have had her in custody in a matter of hours, if not minutes.

The car stopped. "We're here," said Kearnes.

Britt didn't hesitate for a second in getting out, and before Kearnes could get to the car's trunk, open it, and take her suitcase out, she was already standing on the red stained wooden porch deck of The Sand Dollar, clutching the black travel bag in one hand and buzzing the night manager's call button.

There was an old green fluorescent sign above her head the color of a watermelon rind that glowed dimly in the darkness; barely defining the outlines of the motel office door. It hung from a rusted steel bracket attached to the front of the log wall of the motel office, and some of the individual letters were burned out, making it read: "SAND DOLL—MOTEL and CABINS…WEE—LY—ATES." Watching her, he thought she looked particularly vulnerable now…and sad; and he felt embarrassed at having brought her here.

By day and from a distance, The Sand Dollar looked impressive; its solid red stained, log walled, and balconied main building rising up two stories into the air from the sandy ground like the wooden bulwark of some long ago sailing ship. The twelve summer rental log cabins, stained the same dull brick red, were scattered out away from the main motel building in an asymmetrical line down the beach; each one nearly hidden from its neighbor in the rise and fall of the sand dunes and the sturdy scrub pines and wind waving clumps of beach grass that grew waist high all around them.

With his luck she would probably get inside her room and find out it was dirty, or it was a dump; or it was both dirty *and* a dump. And her opinion of him—if she still had one—would sink even lower beneath the horizon of what he imagined it would take to maintain in her even the slightest bit of interest in ever seeing him again after tonight. This motel, like all of the rest of them in town, were usually booked solid throughout the summer…at least that's what he'd been told…and even tonight the parking lot of The Sand Dollar was more than three quarters full of cars, so they couldn't possibly be hurting for money. They should fix their goddamned sign, Kearnes thought.

A light came on inside the motel office. Then another. A puffy eyed, middle aged man, in a well worn and faded blue flannel bathrobe slowly swung open the front screen door. His thinning, but still full head of gray hair was a disheveled bird's nest of sleep bent, tangled locks. To Kearnes, the man didn't look so much like he'd been sleeping when they woke him, as he did having been passed out.

Britt spoke briefly to him in hushed tones; then gave him a credit card she took from her purse. The man went back inside the office but almost instantly reappeared. Handing her a room key and a blank registration card, and glancing askance at Kearnes, he told her to fill it out and bring it back to the office in the morning after they opened up at seven. He pointed to the middle of the lower level of the main log building, indicating the approximate location of her room, and then disappeared back inside the office.

Kearnes heard the deadbolt from the office door click into place, and then saw both of the lights inside blink off as Britt walked down from the Motel porch to where he was standing with her single suitcase.

"It's Room 142," she said, "on the bottom floor." And then without another word walked straight past him almost as if he weren't standing there. He followed her, effortlessly carrying the large suitcase that felt as if it were almost empty…something loose inside rolling around and bumping periodically with a soft and hollow thud as the side of the suitcase banged gently against the side of his thigh.

Britt reached the room well ahead of him and unlocked the door, sweeping her hand up and down on the wall just inside the door until she found a light switch and turned it on. She took a couple of steps inside the room, set the black travel bag and her purse on the floor, then quickly moved back to the middle of the doorway and stood there facing out; her body language making it clear that he was not to come any closer.

Kearnes set the suitcase down in front of her open door. His heart was pounding wildly now and his mouth had gone dry. He could hear the ocean surf in the background of the night reverberating through the darkness, and its powerful sound felt like the blood pumping forcefully through his arteries now as everything backed up, rapidly building up the physical and emotional energy he needed to do what he was about to do.

They stood looking at one another, neither one even daring to breathe.

"Would you have coffee with me in the morning?" asked Kearnes.

"No," she exhaled, a look of relief spreading across her face as if he had just pulled a splinter from her finger after telling her repeatedly it wasn't going to hurt…and in the end, it hadn't.

"You're right," he said, looking down at his uniform boots. "That's pretty dumb of me, since it already is morning. Would you like to have lunch instead?"

"No," Britt said again. "No, but thank you anyway. I'll be on my way long before lunch."

Kearnes looked up at her and searched her eyes with his own. Britt was only able to hold his gaze for a few seconds, and then it was her turn to look away.

"I need to see you again," he said plainly.

"No," she said.

He started to speak, but abruptly cut himself off. He was quiet for a moment longer, giving her time to think. He had known what her answer was going to be before he ever opened his mouth; but he had also known there was no way on earth that he could stop himself from asking her. "No" was an answer, but it was *not* an explanation and to him the only explanation he could, or would ever accept for never seeing this woman again would be the fact that someone else already was, or still was, in her life and in her heart.

"Would you be willing to stop here on your way back through? I would like to take you to dinner."

Britt reached down for the handle of her suitcase, and slid it inside the door. Then she moved further back inside the room, grabbing the handle of the door.

"No, no, no," she said. "No coffee, and no lunch. I am not interested in dating you...or any man!"

"I have to see you again," said Kearnes.

She looked at him, shaking her head no, tears of both exhaustion and confusion beginning to brim in her eyes.

"No," she said firmly. "I do appreciate you helping me tonight, but that's all. I really don't want to see you again."

She slowly closed the door on him, and after a few seconds of silence Kearnes heard the door's deadbolt click into place, making the same identical sound the night manager's door had.

He stood there for a minute longer, trying to will his hand to close into a fist, and knock on her door...but he couldn't do it. Whatever similarities tonight's chance meeting of Britt McGraw had in common with the way he had also first met Tilly, ended when Britt had closed her room door in his face. Yet still, some things were constant in life and the way people were, and never changed.

He returned to his car and got his flashlight out of his equipment bag. There was a large, empty field skewered with realty "For Sale" signs just down the road from The Sand Dollar that he'd noticed as they had driven past, and he walked in the direction of it now, sweeping the beam of the flashlight along the sides of the roadway as he went.

When he reached the first realty sign he left the road and walked out into the open field in the direction of the ghostly apparition of the sand dunes, which he could just barely make out in the darkness. The field was probably about ten acres in size, he judged, and had at one time no doubt been some local farmer's alfalfa, or mint field. But now the ugly realty signs sprang from the flat ground as if they were warning signs in some war torn country that had been planted with land mines—and in a way, they were. The sand dunes served as a final line of demarcation not to be crossed by the "goddamned Calogornians", as Thud called them; a warning to them that although they might try to gobble up every square foot of private property left in the state—inflating the prices of houses and raw land to the outer stratosphere of absurdity—the beach lands were still sacred, and were held in trust for perpetuity for all the citizens of the state. At least for now.

The ground beneath his feet began to turn spongy as he walked into an area of knee high weeds; the remnants of minority crop seeds, still trying to take hold in the sandy soil and grow, the tangle of wild strawberry vines crisscrossing the toes of his boots, trying to trip him and bring him down. Stopping, he closed his eyes and breathed in the ocean air, deeply, and through the dizzying tang of cold salt and spoiling matter that tugged at his body's gag reflex, making him want to retch…he could still smell the raw, fresh sweetness of wildflowers.

He stood where he was, resting the long body of the flashlight on top of his shoulder as he turned in a slow circle, shining the beacon of intense white light out into the weeds like a miniature lighthouse until he caught the reflection of waxy, almond shaped leaves on a green plant. He took out his knife, unfolded the blade, and went to this first group of wildflowers. They were Blue lupine, and he cut a thick bunch of them, leaving the stems overly long for trimming. Searching the same area further he found a small patch of white Lady Slippers and cut some of them; then a handful of delicate Chocolate orchids, and he took them, too.

As he returned to the parking lot of The Sand Dollar he saw a discarded paper soft drink cup sitting upright on the curb. He rinsed it out at a drinking fountain near the motel office, then filled it up halfway again with clean water and cut the stems of all the wildflowers off equally to fit; arranging them in a swirling, tapestry patterned bouquet of mixed contrasting colors, and light

He walked back to Britt's door. All the lights were off inside the room. He knelt down and carefully placed the bouquet of flowers in the middle of the worn rubber door mat in front of her door, but out far enough so she would see them in the morning and not trip over them. Then he got in his car, advised Dispatch that he was going 10-10…out of service for the rest of the night…and drove home to the Sea Breeze.

Utterly exhausted, Kevin Kearnes stripped off his gunbelt and uniform and fell into bed; sleep overtaking him before his eyes had even fully closed. And unlike the night before, he slept soundly, deeply, without dreaming; without thinking of anyone or anything, not even Britt.

It was almost three a.m. when Beek's white Van pulled into the parking lot of The Sand Dollar Motel. He took the police scanner from the passenger seat of the Van where it was still hidden beneath the newspaper, and shoved it underneath the seat on the Van's floor. He grabbed the unread, folded newspaper— The Cutter Point Clarion—then locked the Van and went into Room 144, his room; the same room he had a standing reservation for every two weeks when the near southern end of his route brought him to this town.

He took a hot shower and then changed into his pajamas; leaving the room briefly to walk to the vending machine near the motel's office to buy a diet Coke.

When he returned he settled in the chair in front of the ridiculously small table in the middle of the small room and carefully opened the newspaper, smoothing out his pages.

The front page was dedicated to world headlines and breaking statewide news stories, but the second page was all local news and even before he turned to it, he somehow knew he would find the officer there…and he did.

There was a picture of Kearnes, who was not just a police officer, he learned, but the city's new chief of police. He read the short bio on him; how he had been on the job only a week, that he was a single Father of two, and that he had come from Kansas.

Kansas.

The gun…with the white grips.

The initials on the white grips.

Beek took his small suitcase from the room's open closet; opened it and changed into a fresh set of work clothes. He packed his pajamas, dirty clothes, and his shaving kit; and then put the carefully folded newspaper back into the suitcase last. Then he switched off his room lights and sat in the dark, waiting for dawn and the motel manager or his wife to wake up; so they would see him when he left.

As soon as he was on the outskirts of town he called the office of Sea World in Crescent City from a gas station pay phone where he stopped to fuel his Van, and left a message on their voice mail. He lied and stated that their re-stocking order of one gross of the little nylon fish net bags of assorted dried and polished sea shells from the Philippines for their gift shop had not arrived—even though they were still in the back of his Van, neatly packed in a sturdy corrugated box filled with plastic foam pellets—but he was sure he would have them in stock when he returned in two weeks.

He drove south on Highway 101 for a short distance, passing the non-descript road he'd taken down to the beach to kill Tyler Dunne. At the junction with Highway 199 he turned left and traveled across the Siskiyou Mountains to Grants Pass and got on Interstate 5 northbound; driving non-stop to Portland, where he then turned west to Astoria.

At Astoria he passed over the four mile long Astoria-Megler bridge, crossing the wide, lake shaped mouth of the Columbia River into Washington state. He finally completed the four hundred and fifty nine mile journey thirty minutes later as he drove through the small town of Long Beach and then pulled into the driveway of his house on Sandridge Road, which was on the northern outskirts of the quaint and quiet little sea shore community.

He unloaded and cleaned out the Van, then walked out into the small grape vineyard he had behind the house; turning on the irrigation sprinklers and drenching the burgeoning, heavy bunches of still ripening grapes with life affirming water.

It was late in the evening when he'd finished watering and weeding the vineyard. He went down to the basement of the house, into his gym, and stripped down to his shorts; then worked out mercilessly for two hours, repeating every free weight station twice as he always did when he returned home after being gone on the road for so long...the rippling, rock hard defined muscles of his body screaming for relief when he was done.

He went back upstairs, showered, changed into his pajamas, then fixed himself a light snack in the kitchen; allowing himself one glass of his own home made vineyard wine to go with it.

Returning to the basement he pensively picked at the crackers and cheese he'd tastefully arranged on his plate in a neat, horseshoe shape, and took periodic, short sips from the glass of sweet red wine; timing his bites and swallows so that he consumed everything equally, and finished it all at the same time.

He put the empty plate and wine glass on the workbench he'd been leaning against while eating, and walked over to a darkened corner of the basement where the ancient, hulking, oil furnace stood. From behind the furnace, where he had hidden them years ago, he pulled out a nearly waist high stack of musty and moldering elementary school yearbooks, and then began to delve through them.

He had collected yearbooks from the schools of every boy he had ever molested; writing to the schools with a note saying he was a relative of one of their students, and enclosing a money order. But now he was searching for one in particular; the only yearbook in his thirty year collection that he had from Kansas. Looking for that defiant little boy from so long ago…who had now become a man.

CHAPTER 15

▼

Curt LaMar, The Drug Czar, was a walking exoskeleton of a man and poster boy for the reason why cops should not add chain smoking three packs of cigarettes a day to the list of all the other deadly stressors they placed on their bodies and minds just from pinning on the badge. At six foot five and one hundred fifty eight pounds he was as thin as a thread. His broom stick sized legs ran down the insides of his ironed and sharply pressed Wrangler jeans like the wires inside the hollow cores of two electrical cords, and as Kearnes walked through the pre-dawn, dimly lit lobby of Cutter Point P.D. on his way to his office, LaMar materialized from a darkened alcove off to his left as he passed by like a tall, spindly coat rack come to life.

"Chief Kearnes," he said, stepping out ahead directly into the path of Kearnes. He thrust a pallid, white hand toward him; the back of which was sprayed with red freckles and looked more like a rubbery, undercooked fish fillet that had been dusted with paprika than a human appendage.

"Curt LaMar, Drug Enforcement Administration. On assignment to your agency...for the past two years. We didn't get a chance to meet last week chief; I was tied up on case investigations and grand jury."

Kearnes knew that was a lie. LaMar had been one of those he'd seen congregating in the hallways of the P.D. in his first week on the job; scattering upon his approach. And it wasn't as if you could ever miss, or soon forget seeing, the gaunt and gawky Ichabod Caine like officer who was, Kearnes thought, probably the most visible undercover drug detective he had ever seen in his career. He wondered why he was at work so early, and what the hell he wanted.

Kearnes shook the detective's cold and clammy hand, and lied too. "Chief Kevin Kearnes, detective. It's nice to finally get to meet you."

LaMar pumped Kearnes' hand only twice, then pulled his right hand away and with his left, brought up a carefully folded copy of the just delivered morning paper, The Cutter Clarion, and unfolded it to display the front page.

Kearnes read the bold, black headlines, and the two sub-headlines that filled the full top third of the newspaper's print area just below the masthead:

MASSIVE MIDNIGHT BLAST ROCKS COMMUNITY!
LOCAL MAN LISTED IN CRITICAL CONDITION
POLICE INVESTIGATE SOURCE OF EXPLOSION

"I have a theory about this," said LaMar, dropping his voice to a near whisper. "But I think we should discuss it in your office."

"Sure," said Kearnes. "That's exactly where I was headed."

They walked to Kearnes' office where he turned on the lights and opened the blinds of the spacious bay windows that looked out on the city and Cutter Avenue below, the normally bustling street still quiet at this hour of the morning and freshly washed; glistening from the remnants of overnight ocean mist. The blue Pacific lay on the horizon; flat, dark, and placid…the morning fog boiling up from its surface like steam from a cup of freshly poured hot coffee. Kearnes switched on his computer, and then glanced at the red blinking digital display on his office phone, telling him he had twelve voice mail messages waiting.

"Have a seat detective," he said, motioning LaMar to sit in one of the three generously upholstered guest chairs that were placed in a semi-circle a generous distance in front of his office desk. LaMar eased himself down into the middle chair, his long legs extending out so far the toes of his shoes touched the front of the desk.

"OK," said Kearnes, "let's hear your theory."

"It was drugs," LaMar said, without hesitation.

"Drugs."

"Yeah," said LaMar. "I've been hashing it over with Lieutenant Polk and the bottom line is that this group, The Patriots, have a significant number of users among them and possibly even a few dealers."

"I've already assigned the investigation to Detective Compton," said Kearnes. "I discussed his preliminary findings with him late last night on the phone, and he advised me it appears to be a case of too many explosives and too little common sense."

LaMar shifted forward in his chair; reached back and pulled a small, black leather covered notebook from his jeans pocket. He flipped through a few of its pages until he found the one he was looking for.

He began to read from the page he'd paused on: "Jerry Sparks...Todd Caswell...Larry Luebcke."

"Any of these names ringing a bell with you chief?"

"Sure. These three were all down at the scene. They were the ones who set the blast off. Caswell and Luebcke I met at the hospital when they were brought in for observation. They were going at each other in the back of the ambulance. But I only saw Sparks briefly, as they were taking him into the E.R."

"Todd Caswell...they call him The Frog...he's got a D.U.I. from 1994, followed by two marijuana possessions...both less than an ounce violations. And Luebcke, the one they call The Rat? He's got one prior for possession of marijuana, less than one ounce, from 1986, and he's also a registered marijuana medical card holder."

"And Jerry Sparks?" asked Kearnes.

LaMar flipped the notebook shut and placed it in his lap. "He's not a person of interest in any of this," he said.

"But Caswell and Luebcke are?" said Kearnes. "Why? Because they've both got a couple of minor past marijuana charges? As you said, detective; those are violations...they're like traffic tickets. You pay a fine. You can't even get jail time for those according to Oregon law. That is if I've read the statute right?"

"It's my understanding," Kearnes went on, "that Jerry Sparks is the actual leader of this group...president of their organization in fact...so I would expect that you have run his criminal history also. Did you find any priors for drugs on him?"

LaMar squirmed uneasily in his chair, trying to regain the original comfort zone he had entered Kearnes' office with just moments earlier but was now hard pressed to find. "I have talked this over with Lieutenant Polk, and we don't think Sparks has any culpability in this event."

"You mean Lieutenant Polk, or Edgar Polk, close personal friend of Mr. Sparks?"

Another Marlboro wanted LaMar so badly it could taste him; even though he'd sucked the last one he'd had right down to the filter in the Men's restroom just seconds before ambushing Kearnes in the hallway on his way to his office. He unconsciously swiped a hand across the chest of his black tee shirt which was emblazoned with a Harley Davidson logo on the front and a winged skull shooting flames from its eyes on the back, patting the spot where he would have normally kept his cigarettes; if the tee shirt would have had a pocket to keep them in. But his cigarettes were back in his office and he didn't dare break off contact with Kearnes now before putting the spin on the beach debacle the Mayor's office wanted—and Polk had ordered him to do—just so he could go and have a smoke.

LaMar deftly changed the subject by avoiding answering Kearnes' question. "The Patriots are believed to be a radical and possibly even subversive organization," he said. "They were responsible for the local V.F.W. Post choosing to close down a few years back, and they are doing God knows what up there on that mountain top "Compound" of theirs at any given time. As with most of these types of groups; trafficking in and use of controlled substances usually goes hand in hand with these types of activities."

"What types of activities?" said Kearnes.

"What do you mean?" asked LaMar.

"What types of activities?" Kearnes repeated.

LaMar stared blankly at Kearnes but did not immediately answer him. This was definitely not the way things were supposed to be going, and he began to wonder if the new chief was just stupid, or stubborn, or maybe a little of both. Local, state, and national media would be all over the story this morning, expecting answers, and the police department had to be ready to name names and outline the suspected motives and methods of the guilty parties. And Detective Curt LaMar was just the man to get this job done, and done right. That was why Vernon Bouchet' and Edgar Polk had sent him.

"My understanding of the activities of The Patriots in the community," said Kearnes, "consists mainly of some of their members warming bar stools at The Buccaneer while they plan their next spaghetti feed or car wash to raise money to buy fireworks for the city's annual Fourth of July show."

"I don't think what was set off down on the beach last night was fireworks," LaMar said sarcastically.

"Obviously not, detective," agreed Kearnes. "They had access to some pretty powerful explosives…and apparently a lot of them. But drugs didn't blow that whale carcass sky high, take out windows in the shopping center, and send this city into a panic. The Patriots did."

"Yes," said LaMar. "Yes! That's my point exactly! And where could they have gotten such explosives…obviously illegal. How could they get their hands on them? How could they pay for them? Drug money."

"You didn't let me finish, detective," Kearnes said. "It *was* The Patriots who blew up the whale…and it was also The Patriots who caused an explosion and fire down in the Harbor two years ago on the Fourth of July. But it was the *police department* who allowed this near disaster to happen last night…and we are going to take full responsibility for it happening."

Kearnes watched LaMar's reaction to this slowly start to sink in, and wondered why Vernon Bouchet' hadn't sent someone more apt at the art of closing a deal. Roy Roddameyer, with his direct authority over Kearnes as his boss, combined with his used car salesman skills, might have been a better choice. But he was beginning to understand that this was not how the man operated; head on, direct, and to the point. He was like an arrogant General, sending his foot soldiers in first as cannon fodder directly into the front lines, just to test his enemy's strength.

"Do you understand what I'm saying here detective?" asked Kearnes. "It was Lieutenant Polk's recommendation to the mayor to use these people to clear the beach of the whale carcass. Mayor Bouchet' wanted it gone, immediately; and against the advice of myself, detective Compton, and a state park ranger who seemed very knowledgeable about marine mammal regulations…it was done."

"Actually, I do understand what you are saying chief Kearnes," said LaMar. "But I'm not so sure that you do, sir. I think what we have a need to do, in order to mitigate the potential for any needless bad publicity for the city and possibly even some trouble down the line with a few federal agencies, is to approach this thing from the standpoint of a more global type settlement."

"Global type settlement?" Kearnes said incredulously.

"Meaning what, exactly? That out of all the players involved in this farce we pick the two that are the lowest on the food chain, have minor past offenses on their records or associations with controlled substances, and portray them as Columbian drug lord type cowboys who like to spend their hard earned illicit dope dollars on restricted explosives which they like to use to blow up things in public because they are such civic minded, upstanding citizens?"

When Curt Lamar became stressed he smoked, and he was definitely stressed now. He started to lift himself in segments out of his chair, rising in jerky, angular movements; like a giraffe clumsily trying to get to its feet from the ground up.

He was going to politely excuse himself from the chief's presence and run to his tiny office down the hall, where he would lock his door and turn on his air purifier, and then suction the carcinogenic smoke from three Marlboro's—one right after another—through his lungs as quickly as he could…like a jet engine at full acceleration gulping air. *Then* he would get on the phone to Polk and tell him that none of this had worked.

Kearnes waited until LaMar was halfway up and out of the chair before he slammed his palm down on his desk and yelled at him, "SIT DOWN!"

Stunned, the ungainly detective froze in mid-air for a second like a limbo dancer halfway under the bar, back arched, ropy, underweight arms sprung rearward; then sank slowly back into the chair. He glared at Kearnes, letting him know as far as he was concerned the gloves had just come off.

"You are making a big mistake," said LaMar, the threat in his tone of voice clearly evident.

"Maybe," said Kearnes. "But it doesn't change the fact that I have a real problem with your *theory*; two problems as a matter of fact. Would you like to hear them, detective?"

LaMar didn't answer him. His insides were screaming for a cigarette. The beginnings of a migraine were forming in the back of his skull; the all consuming need for a fix of nicotine chipping away at his skull to get to his brain like a sharpened steel chisel being driven in with hammer blows.

"Good," said Kearnes, smiling at him. "Here they are: first, your theory is asinine. It doesn't fit and it doesn't make any sense. And second…just the fact that you could seriously attempt to sell such a pile of garbage to me, let alone the public, makes me suspect that maybe *you* are the one on drugs detective."

Something had been sparked deep inside Kearnes from the moment he'd first seen Britt the night before. It was like the weak flame of a single tiny candle being lit in the absolute darkness of an infinite, black cavern; guttering in the currents of unseen breezes, fighting not to be extinguished. But still…it was light and heat; and for the first time since he had lost Tilly, his sons, and in turn his way in the world as a man, he caught the briefest glimpse of the person he used to be in the flickering shadows of its dim glow.

He stared at the pathetic persona of Lamar The Drug Czar; the "undercover" drug detective in his freshly ironed blue jeans, dry cleaned biker tee shirt, and the "Willy Nelson" bandanna tied across his forehead; which helped to hide the receding line of his wiry red hair that was pulled backward and tied in a short ponytail. Thud had told Kearnes that the federal grant program Lamar was hired under was called "Federal Officers On Loan To States," or F.O.O.L.S., and that LaMar had basically been deported from the San Francisco D.E.A. office after blowing some big undercover drug case somehow and nearly getting two agents killed.

"I've got physical evidence," wheezed LaMar, the poisoned air escaping from his ravaged lungs as he spoke with a rattling sound; like tin cups in a prison being raked back and forth across iron cell bars. "Proof!" he gasped.

"Really," said Kearnes, unaffected. "Let's hear it."

"I've got urine samples," said La Mar. "Taken from Luebcke and Caswell at the Hospital last night."

"And you had a search warrant to obtain these samples?" asked Kearnes.

"No."

"Signed consent forms then?"

"No."

"How then, detective?"

"Let's just say I have a "friend" who works at Cutter General."

"'A friend'" repeated Kearnes. "In other words detective, you have a confidential informant who works at the hospital?"

"Yes."

"And this C.I. He or she is someone you have used in the past on cases and is considered reliable?"

"Yes."

"Have you sent these samples off for analysis yet?"

"No. I just got them. An hour ago."

"I thought you said they were taken 'last night'?"

"Well, they were. I meant that I just picked them up."

"Where are they now?"

"In my office."

"Let's go," said Kearnes, getting up from his desk.

"What?" said LaMar. "Where?"

"Your office. Now. I want to see them."

Kearnes followed LaMar to his "office" in a remote corner of the police building; a small storage room that at one time had been used to keep janitorial supplies and equipment in. The city had hastily converted it to office space when they'd found out two years before they would be receiving a hundred and fifty thousand dollars in federal grant funds through the F.O.O.L.S. program, and needed immediate, non-existent office space for the fool they would soon be getting in order to be in compliance with the grant.

There was no name plate on LaMar's plain non-descript office door, announcing who or what his position was, and Kearnes noticed for the first time that it was a steel door...and appeared to have a series of aftermarket multiple deadlock bolts installed on it. The clandestine detective, whose second favorite nickname around the P.D. after "The Drug Czar" was "Secret Squirrel," fumbled with his last key in the last lock and then they stepped inside...but just barely.

The small office was hardly big enough to turn around in, and in the dark all Kearnes could see was the carbon blue glow of water in a large illuminated glass aquarium on a table against the near wall. He watched as a few radiantly colored tropical fish weaved their way in and out of a cascade of rising silver air bubbles that burst from an aerator at the sandy bottom of the tank like miniature depth charges exploding toward the surface. And then the smell hit him.

It reminded him of when he was a kid back on his family's ranch in Ford County in the spring. His Father and his Uncle Ben would pull a net of long steel cables that had been chained in tandem between two of their tractors, across the dusty earth around their house, and barn, the hired hand quarters, and grain silos; scrubbing hundreds of tenacious tumbleweeds from the already bone dry ground by their roots…and then piling them up with pitchforks in thorny mountains higher than their own heads.

In the evening when the afternoon winds had finally died down they would walk among the mountain range of weeds, lighting each mound at its base with a hand held propane torch, and in minutes the prairie horizon would begin to glow orange and red from the fires, merging with the oranges and reds of the sunset.

The bitter, acerbic smoke from the burning tumbleweeds would eventually reach him where he sat on the top step of the high wood porch of his house, watching the fires rage fast and hot. And as it did it made his eyes sting and water; dehumidified his nasal passages into thin, stretched parchment, and made him choke and gasp for a breath of fresh air.

But the smell of residual cigarette smoke that hung in the air of Curt LaMar's tiny newsstand sized office; that permeated the fabric of his few meager pieces of office furniture and dripped down from the beige painted ceiling and walls of his office like a fine glazing of melting caramel…made Kearnes want to gag.

LaMar turned on the office lights, and then took a half step in the direction of his desk. He bent down and nervously flicked on his Ionic Breeze air purifier that sat on the floor next to the desk, and the unit began to sound a high pitched electronic hum. It sounded like a single unseen mosquito buzzing around annoyingly in the cloying air of the restricted office space.

Kearnes began to feel the walls closing in on him as he fought to keep breathing now through his mouth. There were ashtrays full of cigarette butts everywhere he looked; on LaMar's desk, on top of his file cabinet, on the windowsill of the small window which had been cut out of the wall facing the parking lot—which LaMar kept covered with black plastic garbage bags—and on the small spaces of the table not taken up by the aquarium. The carpet on the office floor, which had once been an industrial blue color, was now a dull grey, and plumes of ash rose from its nylon fabric and coated the toes of Kearnes' uniform boots when he moved as if he were in a moon walk on a lunar landing.

"The police department is designated as a smoke free building detective," Kearnes said.

LaMar was sitting at his desk, toying with the desk drawer. He had pulled it open a couple of inches and Kearnes could see the red and white corner of a box of Marlboro's inside. Reluctantly, he closed the drawer again before he spoke to Kearnes.

"I have restrictions on my movements," he offered in response. "I can't be seen out back in the parking lot with uniformed officers taking a smoke break. I have to be careful about even being seen in this building."

"So you decided to break policy and smoke in your office instead," said Kearnes.

"Yes," LaMar admitted. I do smoke in here. Occasionally."

"Occasionally?" said Kearnes, tracing a finger across the top corner edge of LaMar's desk in the burnt cigarette ash that coated its surface like fine dust. "It looks like Mount Saint Helens exploded in here. I'm not sure the word 'occasionally' quite fits the bill."

"I bought that," LaMar said defensively, pointing to his air purifier, "out of my own pocket."

Kearnes ignored his comeback. "Where are the samples?" he asked.

LaMar opened a large side drawer of the desk and brought out two small, clear plastic cups filled with amber liquid—their lids taped on with white hospital adhesive tape—and sat them on the desk.

Kearnes picked them up and examined both of them. Both of the cups still felt almost body temperature warm.

"These aren't labeled as evidence," said Kearnes. "What's the reason for that?"

"I'd just picked them up and returned here to the P.D. when I saw you pull into the parking lot. I put them in my desk drawer, locked my office, and went to find you," said LaMar. "To notify you of what I had," he added.

Kearnes put the urine samples back down on the desk in front of LaMar. He leaned over and jerked opened LaMar's center drawer that was filled with pens, pencils, paper clips, and six crush proof box packs of Marlboros, causing LaMar to straighten up abruptly and suck in his slightly pot bellied gut beneath his Harley Davidson shirt. Kearnes rummaged through the desk until he found a black fine point Sharpie marking pen. He removed the tip of the Sharpie and handed it to LaMar.

"Label them."

LaMar took the pen but only stood there with it, holding it in his hand as if it were a cold, dead cigarette.

"Date, time your informant seized these as evidence…and your initials. On each cup, detective."

"I know how to label evidence," LaMar said sullenly.

"Then you should also know you should have labeled it when, and where you found it," said Kearnes. "Immediately. Even if the source is a C.I."

"Any fourth rate defense attorney could rip you a new one on the stand under cross examination about just exactly what *may have* happened to this evidence while in transit from point A to point B before it was officially recorded as evidence in the field."

Kearnes watched as LaMar carefully printed the required information onto the white tape on the tops of each cup with the black indelible pen. When he had finished he picked up both cups and read the times the urine samples had allegedly been taken from Luebcke and Caswell at Cutter General; 0530 and 0545 hrs. The only problem was Larry Luebcke and Todd Caswell hadn't been held for observation. Kearnes knew they had been released from the E.R. a good half hour before Britt had been released, because he'd seen the wives of the two contrite men who'd come to pick them up, screaming at them in the hospital parking lot and threatening divorce while he waited for Britt.

Kearnes ripped the adhesive tape off of both the urine sample cups and removed their tops. Then he took the cups and stepped over to LaMar's aquarium with them.

"I hate to piss all over your case, detective," he said, dumping both cups full of urine into the open top of the aquarium, "but I'm going to anyhow. Because that's the only thing this type of 'police work' rates."

LaMar sat dumbstruck in his chair for a few seconds, unable to mentally process what he had just seen Kearnes do. He saw his tropicals inside the tank begin to streak back and forth in the oxygenated, and now panic frothed water; slamming into the sides of the aquarium's thick glass walls with noiseless thumps as the chemically tainted urine began to spread out around them like golden amber ink. He watched in disbelief as a delicate Marbled Angel fish in the center of the tank suddenly went belly up, and began a slow ascent to the surface, its long and delicate wing like fins folding together like hands clasped in prayer.

"What the fuck do you think you're doing!" he screamed. He began to struggle up out of his chair but Kearnes lunged at him and shoved him back down and when he did, LaMar's right hand instinctively reached down for the forty caliber Glock pistol he wore in a high ride holster on his belt.

"NO!" Kearnes yelled, knocking his hand away from the weapon and pinning both of LaMar's wrists to the armrest of the chair.

He put his face down close to LaMar's and could see real fear in the man's eyes. The stink of his rancid cigarette breath permeated the scant few inches of air between them.

"No, detective," Kearnes said calmly, now fully in control of LaMar—and even more importantly—himself.

"In this department we don't illegally gather fabricated evidence during investigations that we know will later be suppressed and thrown out of court. We don't conduct illegal searches and seizures in order to make false accusations against citizens."

"I don't know what you're talking about," said LaMar, "I haven't..."

"Shut up," said Kearnes. "Just shut your lying mouth and listen; because I swear to you detective this is your first, last, and *ever* opportunity you're going to have with me to get your shit together."

"We don't do these kinds of things in this police department Detective LaMar...not anymore...starting today," Kearnes said.

Kearnes relaxed his grip on LaMar's wrists and then let go of them and straightened up. He backed a half step away from LaMar; keeping his eyes locked on him and letting his right hand fall naturally to his side where his palm rested lightly against the ivory grips of his holstered Colt.

"One last thing detective; and probably *the* most important thing I need to stress to you. We don't make hostile, threatening gestures toward fellow officers of this, or any other department. If you ever put your hand near that weapon around me again, outside of the qualification range...you are going to be goddamned sorry."

Without taking his eyes off LaMar Kearnes picked up one of the overflowing ashtrays on his desk, stepped backwards with it to the aquarium, and dumped its contents in.

"This is a non-smoking office in a non-smoking building," Kearnes said. "I want your office cleaned up and disinfected. Today." Then he opened LaMar's door, stepped out into the still quiet and empty hallway, and closed it gently behind him.

LaMar ripped open his middle desk drawer and clawed at one of the packs of Marlboros with trembling fingers until he had one of the cigarettes out of the pack and in his mouth. He lit it with his chrome Zippo, taking long, nearly unbroken drags from it while he watched another one of his fish pop to the surface of the aquarium, bobbing among the floating cigarette filters and black, gummy ash like some tiny casualty of a submarine attack.

He finished that cigarette and then two more before he was able to dial Edgar Polk's home number. Lieutenant Polk was just on his way out the door on his way to work, and answered on the third ring.

"Ed?" LaMar said into the phone. "This is Curt. It didn't work. We've got a real problem. This guy is totally out of control!"

"What happened?" Polk asked.

"I can't smoke inside my office any more!" said LaMar.

"What the hell are you talking about?" said Polk.

"Just get down here!" LaMar shouted into the phone.

He slammed the phone's receiver down. And then quickly lit another cigarette.

CHAPTER 16

▼

Kearnes went straight back to his office and locked his door. Of the twelve messages that had been left on his voice mail, one was from Thud saying he planned on going to Cutter General as soon as he came on duty at eight to try and interview Jerry Sparks, one was from Roy Roddameyer, notifying him of a ten o'clock meeting with the mayor, himself, and Edgar Polk in the mayor's office for a "strategy meeting" on how best to handle the media concerning last night's "incident."

The other ten calls were from the media themselves. All kinds of media: radio, network television and their affiliates, local and regional newspapers; all of them clamoring for something to expand on from the brief, almost terse press release Kearnes had dictated to Thud a few hours before, and which had finally hit the AP news wire about an hour ago, triggering the flood of inquiries for more information. Enough information, both old and new, that would amount to a story.

But if there was one thing Kearnes had learned in all his years in dealing with the media while he was a command officer with D.C.P.D., it was that you *always* gave the local home town news hounds first crack at any local story first; and to not do so, intentionally, was to invite certain disaster in dealing with them again sometime in the future. While most cops either hated or feared the media due to either their ignorance or built in prejudices of them—or both—smart cops recognized the media for what they really were. Sometimes a help, sometimes a hindrance; but *always* a powerful force that when used shrewdly, and at the right time, in the right ways, could bring remarkable results and help, just when it was needed the most.

He sat down at his computer and booted it up, already composing in his head what he needed to translate onto paper in the form of a new, meatier press release; and he new he had less than twenty minutes to do it in before Edgar Polk, Roy Roddameyer, and Mayor Bouchet' all converged on city hall and the police department, because he was sure Curt LaMar had called someone by now.

He began to type and this time he added his name as the chief of police in some direct quotes, whereas the first brief release hadn't even referenced the exact name of the police department...only the city the incident had occurred in.

He made the gray whale washing up on the beach the focus of the story; its massive size, how it had posed a potential health threat to the local marine life environment, and how city hall officials had overseen the disposal of the whale's carcass by demolition, and had enlisted a local civic volunteer group with some experience in such matters to do the actual job.

After reaching that point in his new press release he left the incident in a state of suspension; giving the standard "still under investigation" ending to it, but clearly putting the onus of further developments and information in the hands of city hall...and giving the mayor's office telephone number for further contact.

In the 911 Dispatch Center room emergency dispatchers Candy Brewer and Shoshanna Perry had just relieved the one graveyard shift dispatcher, who had already left the police department building and gone home. They were enjoying the pre-dayshift quiet, sipping from paper Starbuck's cups while seated at their twin dispatch consoles beside one another and engaging in some serious girl talk gossip, when Shoshanna looked up and saw Kearnes approaching them through the large, rectangular clear glass windows that exposed the insides of the dispatch room from three sides.

"Oh crap," she whispered to Candy. "It's *him*! He's coming in here."

Candy froze in her high backed, ergonomically designed dispatch chair—too late to feign looking being busy—as their door swung open. Kearnes stepped inside the cramped and confined space that was filled with computer screens, boom microphones, a giant copier and Fax machine, telephones, and the two separate console boards that had row upon row of L.E.D. lighted buttons, jack receptacles, switches, a digital dedicated multi-phone line recorder, and base station radio controls.

Candy quickly set her cup of coffee down on her console "Good m...m...morning, chief," she managed to stammer. "Can we help you with anything...sir?"

Kearnes had never met either of the young women yet. He had only seen them through the glass windows of the Dispatch Room during peak radio traffic times;

peering intently at the multiple array of computer screens in front of them while their fingers flew across their keyboards, typing madly while they spoke at the same time to the police, fire, and other emergency service workers in the field.

But he did think he would recognize the voice of the female dispatcher who had handled the whale call the previous morning when Edgar Polk had raced him to the scene. He wanted to thank her and to compliment her on a job well done, but the dispatcher who had just spoken to him was not the same woman; of that he was sure.

"How are you ladies this morning?" Kearnes asked both of them. He leaned over toward them a respectful distance…just close enough so he could try and read their uniform name pins, and so they would know that was what he was doing, and nothing more.

"C. Brewer, and…S. Perry?" he said. "I'm chief Kearnes. 'K Kearnes', actually," he said, pointing to his own uniform name pin and smiling at the odd Cutter Point P.D. practice of using both a first initial and last name on employee name pins instead of just a last name. "The 'K' stands for Kevin by the way," he said.

Candy, the skinny, long faced one with the limp, drab colored hair that fell across her bony shoulders like a well used kitchen mop, and who wore too little, if any, make up; looked at Kearnes as if he had just struck her between her overly close set brown eyes with a two by four. No one in the department who wore a gold badge *ever* spoke to the people in Dispatch with any degree of pleasantry, civility, or genuine kindness; let alone a sense of humor.

Candy and Shoshanna were accustomed to the tyrannical tongue lashings of Sergeant Delbert Downs who moved among them during their workdays like the Master on an African slave ship; cracking his whip of verbal abuse and offering up only cold negativity as fare for their sustenance as employees wanting to do a good job, instead of the few little words of occasional encouragement, or thanks, they so desperately craved.

"And you are?" Kearnes asked her. Candy was still not able to respond; her thin lips were slightly parted and moving, but no sounds were coming out.

"Her name is Candy," said the other girl; the one with the long, flowing, burnished auburn colored hair, and eyes the color of a pale blue China cup. "Candy Brewer. And I'm Shoshanna Perry." He recognized her voice instantly. She was the dispatcher from yesterday.

Kearnes did not shake their hands, and instead nodded at them and said, "It's nice to meet you both." He usually found shaking hands with women to be an awkward task, one which he was never quite sure as having done right when it was over with. And with the exception of Britt, whose hand he had shaken out of politeness, but also just to be able to touch her; to feel the texture and warmth of her incredibly alluring female skin—he usually did his best to try and avoid it. Just like he was doing now. Because it made him somehow uncomfortable.

"I'm looking for a media contact master list," he said. "Something we might have that has all the usual media contact phone numbers and Faxes for releasing department announcements to. Do we have anything like that already drawn up?"

"We do," said Shoshanna. She rose from her chair and walked over to a part of the room's back wall that was taken up with several rows of elaborately built custom bookshelves which held volumes of bound manuals and three ring binders, and extracted a clear vinyl plastic report cover that held several sheets of white paper inside. She brought it to Kearnes and handed it to him. He thumbed through the few pages it contained, quickly scanning its contents.

"Yeah, this will do," he said. "In fact it's perfect."

He could see that these two women were good friends, diverse in looks but probably very close emotionally; and courageously protective of one another as women often were. He didn't want to hurt either of their feelings but he needed to choose one of them for an assignment that would have to be carried out without fail; if he was to keep both the political ground he had gained in the department in the last twenty four hours as well as his job. He chose Shoshanna.

"Here," he said, handing her the press release he had written in his office. "I need you to Fax this to every media organization on this list, except for the Clarion. I'm going to be taking them by a copy myself."

Candy finally spoke. "Chief Kearnes?" she said meekly. "We could have some trouble with our supervisor...doing this I mean. Sergeant Downs never lets us put out releases to the media without his direct authorization. He watches us like a hawk, and he's going to be here in the building in the next twenty minutes."

"Really," Kearnes said dryly. "And why am I not surprised to be hearing this about Sergeant Downs?"

"OK, look," he said. "We are going to get back to basics in this department, but it's going to take a little courage on all our parts to do it. Can I count on you two ladies join me on this?"

Candy looked at Shoshanna, and Shoshanna looked at Candy. Then they both looked at Kearnes and nodded their heads yes.

"Good," said Kearnes. "Now, there is nothing more basic or more important in a police organization than the chain of command, and from what I've seen so far of this agency the chain of command has been broken; probably for a very long time now. But we are going to rebuild our chain of command…link by link…starting right here in this room, today."

"Shoshanna, I need you to Fax this press release out, like I said; and Candy? I need you to watch her back while she is doing it."

"Yes sir," said Candy. Shoshanna didn't answer; she was busy reading what Kearnes had written.

"If Sergeant Downs, or any other ranking officer questions you as to what you are doing, you are to tell them that the chief of police gave you this assignment directly, himself…and you are to continue doing what you are doing.

"And if anyone orders you to stop doing what you are doing, then I want you to stop. I want you to excuse yourself from the Dispatch Center; go to the ladies room, or to the break room…whatever. But I want you to get to a phone and call me immediately on my unit's cell phone. I will have it with me at all times, even when I'm out of the car."

"Oh my God," breathed Candy. "Downs would have our asses…and so would Lieutenant Polk!"

Shoshanna jabbed her dispatch partner and friend on the arm with her fist, and glared at her in exasperation over her lack of decorum while speaking to the new chief of police.

"Ouch!" yelped Candy. "Well they would!" she cried, rubbing the tender spot on her arm just below her shoulder where a red knot was beginning to swell from the impact of the knuckles of Shoshanna's doubled up fist.

"No," Kearnes assured her. "Not in the end they wouldn't. In fact it would be *their* asses; for trying to reprimand or discipline you for doing the right thing and following the chain of command.

"But I need you to both be brave, and stick with me on this…all the way. OK?"

"OK," said Candy, looking like she was nearly on the verge of tears.

"Yes," Shoshanna said, confidently.

"Fantastic," said Kearnes, grinning at both of them. "And now I need you to give me something to do. I want you to put me to work, and keep me working all day long."

"You want to take 911 calls?" Candy asked, puzzled. "In here all day, with us?"

"No," Kearnes laughed. "Not that I wouldn't enjoy your company, and probably learn a few new things in the process. I want you to keep me busy out in the field; answering calls. And when there aren't any calls pending, I want you to *find* me some…understand?"

The city didn't provide Kearnes with a private secretary. All calls to the office of the chief came in through Dispatch first on the police department's business line, and were then transferred to the chief's office by one of the dispatcher's. If Candy and Shoshanna were good enough at their jobs, and creative enough, he should be able to avoid the city manager and mayor for the entire day, while his press release gained more and more momentum with the media and eventually took on a life of its own. And he knew when it became a strong enough story; Roddameyer and Bouchet' would have no other choice but to go with the flow of it, or be sucked under by the lies and subterfuge of their own version of the events.

"Who do we have on right now, and what do we have pending?" Kearnes asked.

Shoshanna took her chair again and hit a few keys on her computer keyboard. The large color C.A.D. screen on the monitor in front of her came to life in a rainbow display; the screen dividing into blocks of different colors highlighting the individual fire and police agencies, their calls for service pending, and the name, location, and current status of the units in the field on duty.

"We have Officer Webb, the graveyard shift, at the station right now," said Shoshanna, "and about to go 10-10, off duty. And at 0800 shift change we will have Officers York, and McNeil as dayshift patrol...and our two bike patrol officers in the downtown area." She typed a few more keys, and the screen changed colors again. "We have zero calls pending at this time, chief."

"It's usually real dead around here this time of the morning chief," Candy offered. "Graveyard didn't get a single call last night," she said, peering intently at her own C.A.D. screen. "It looks like the only incoming calls we got went directly to your office voice mail. Ten...no, twelve of them."

"Come on girls," Kearnes said. "Think hard."

"I know!" said Candy. "You could work traffic."

"No, not busy enough. Especially when we're already going to have two patrolmen out there doing the same thing."

The phone at Shoshanna's console rang and she picked it up. "911 Center," she said, "what is your emergency?"

Kearnes watched as the caller's phone number automatically popped up on the Computer Aided Dispatch screen. Shoshanna hit a single key, and the address the 911 call was originating from was immediately displayed.

"No sir," she said. "No, I'm sorry; that is *not* an emergency. Yes. Yes, I do hear what you are saying. But this line is for emergencies only. Hold one, please."

Shoshanna double checked the address on the screen, then looked up at Kearnes and said, "We have a male caller on 911 Primary at 7277 Dearborn Drive who is calling about a 'severe case of chapped lips'."

"You're kidding," said Kearnes.

"No, I'm not," said Shoshanna. "He's almost in tears. Says he can barely speak, they're so cracked and dry. And he does sound almost as if he's whispering, the poor thing."

Candy grabbed her purse from underneath the console. She dug through it, down to the bottom, until she found a small, half used tube of Blistex. "Here!" she said, handing it to Kearnes.

911 had to be the most interesting telephone number in the world, Kearnes thought to himself. At least for those people in the business of answering the calls on the other end of the line that came in on it. After all of his years in law enforcement, thinking he had long ago already "heard it all", he could still be amazed, on occasion, at the outlandish abuses some people still perpetrated upon this iconic symbol of American culture…the simple, three digit number we were all taught from pre-school on to call if we were in trouble and needed immediate help.

"What would be your usual protocol in handling a 911 like this?" Kearnes asked Shoshanna.

"Get back on the line with him; try to steer him in another direction. Like suggesting he make an appointment with his family doctor, for one. But if he persists we would have to dispatch Medical or Law, or maybe even both. If for no reason other than to avoid a potential lawsuit."

"OK," said Kearnes, "I'll take it."

"Uh, sir?" said Candy, looking at the Incident History Module on her screen. "It looks like we've been to the residence several times in the past on similar type calls. The fire department, too. A bunch of times. This old guy looks like some sort of super hypochondriac. Maybe we should just dispatch C.P.F.D."

"No, I'll go," said Kearnes. "It's a start, so put me in the computer as in service and en route to that address."

"And thanks for this," he said to Candy, holding up the tube of Blistex as he started out the door of the Dispatch room.

"If he wants you to put it on for him chief, I wouldn't if I were you!" Candy called after him.

"Don't worry," Kearnes said, just before the door closed shut behind him. "If he does…*then* you can send in the fire department."

They watched him through the windows of their glass fortress until he turned the corner in the hallway and was gone, heading for his vehicle in the back parking lot.

"Wow," Candy said. "What an awesome guy! And good looking, too."

Shoshanna had wanted to tell Kevin Kearnes what an incredibly brave thing it was that he'd done yesterday; standing up to Edgar Polk, Delbert Downs, and the rest of them. And she'd wanted to thank him for trying to make a difference at work for her, and Candy, and all of the other good employees who had waited so long for a boss like him to come along. But at thirty two and a single mom of three, with two failed marriages behind her with men who had not only each destroyed a part of her heart before they'd left, but had also destroyed her ability to believe in men in general; she had withdrawn and buried her trust of them like a valuable treasure, hidden deep from sight.

"I hear he's divorced and has kids," said Candy. "Don't you think he's cute?"

Shoshanna looked plaintively at the much younger woman who was her good friend, hoping she would never have to experience even half the pain she herself had in the name of love; but at the same time knowing full well that she someday would.

"No," she said. "I think he's beautiful."

Kearnes didn't have to worry the rest of the day about being kept busy. After clearing the man with the chapped lips call—an elderly gentleman who had lost his wife of half a century a few years back and who greatly appreciated the surprise of the new police chief appearing on his door step and having a morning cup of coffee with him, and just talking about life for awhile—the calls began to pour into the dayshift.

They were almost all related to the events of the night before; still frightened and curious citizens, angry business owners…all of them wanting answers about what had happened down on Wal-Mart beach. He hurriedly stopped at the offices of the Clarion first and spent five minutes with a reporter, going over the copy of the press release with him, before he began responding to the calls in the order in which they came in.

Thud called him on the cell phone just before noon to report that he had been able to interview Jerry Sparks earlier in the morning a little after nine, and that he was going to be closing out the case investigation with a final disposition of "accidental by negligence." Kearnes asked him to get a copy of his report to him as soon as he could, and then told him about the incident with Curt LaMar in his office at the department. He thought Thud was going to come unglued.

"What! he yelled into the phone. "He did fucking what? That shit for brains! That's Official Misconduct and Falsifying Evidence…just for starters! And I can think of about three other good felony charges to go along with those. I say we go to the P.D. and pick his skinny ass up right now!"

"No," said Kearnes. "We need to wait and see how all this plays out in the end. Besides, I poured his "evidence" into his fish tank…so the falsification charge would be down the drain anyway…so to speak."

"Why did you do that?"

"To see if the urine samples were drug toxic."

"Were they?"

"Yeah, they were. The fish in the tank started going belly up in just a few seconds. My guess is that he dumped some ground up Crystal Meth into the sample cups; and the urine was probably his own. It was still warm."

"Jesus," said Thud, "he shouldn't have had to use any of his confiscated dope for that. The nicotine level in his system alone has got to be enough to kill a horse."

"He definitely put something into that urine," Kearnes said. "It was *hot*, and would have easily tested positive. But I can't figure out why the idiot thought he was going to be able to frame two innocent men based on evidence he obtained illegally in the first place."

"Chief?" said Thud. "You remember what I told you that night when we had you over for steaks? About things being bad in the department and all?"

"Yeah."

"Well…it's been bad all right; in the past. But it's never been *this* bad before. I just don't think they give a shit anymore about what they try to pull. And trust me: they expect you to go along with it; whatever it is, or else."

"Where are you right now?" asked Kearnes.

"I'm on the road," said Thud. "Northbound on 101, heading up to Nesika Beach. County S.O. is requesting mutual aid on a missing person case they took a report on late last night."

"Who's missing?"

"Don't know exactly. Some ten year old kid I guess. His folks both work and he was gone when they came home; and he's still gone."

"I was going to see if I could buy you lunch. Is this boy maybe a runaway?"

"Unknown," said Thud. "It could be a possibility. They moved here a few months ago from where else but California, of course."

Kearnes thought of his own two young sons; so far away from him now back in Kansas. Alex, his youngest, was almost ten now himself and as unbearably painful as it was to wake up every day and know that they would not be there to share his life with him, but instead, would be with their Mother; he could not begin to conceive of what it must feel like to have no idea where your child was, or what had happened to them.

"That sounds a lot more important than lunch, Thud," Kearnes said. "Let me know if you need any help."

"I will," he said. "It's Brad Dekker's case. You haven't met him yet, but he's a detective with the Sheriff's Department, and is also kind of their one man SWAT Unit. He was a Marine sniper in Operation Desert Storm, and is one hell of a rifle shot."

"I'm working patrol today," said Kearnes, "so I'll be available."

"Yeah," said Thud. "I'll keep you posted. And thanks for the lunch offer. I'll rain check you on that one. You staying out of the office all day then chief?"

"All day," said Kearnes.

"Harder for Bouchet' and Roddameyer and the rest of them to hit a moving target, than one behind a desk huh?"

"Harder," said Kearnes. "But not impossible."

CHAPTER 17

▼

Even though he was surprised to find himself actually getting stomach growling hungry for the first time in longer than he could remember, Kearnes skipped lunch and worked steadily through the afternoon to the end of his shift at four o'clock. In his travels as he had traversed the city going to call from call, he had passed by The Buccaneer twice in the span of an hour and a half and had thought about stopping there for a quick burger. But he had seen Roy Roddameyer's car parked there both times, unmoved from the same spot, so he'd kept on going.

There had been no communication from city hall; not from the mayor, or Roddameyer, or even Polk. Only Candy and Shoshanna had periodically called him on his cell phone to relay information about a behind closed doors meeting in the mayor's office that had been in progress since nine a.m. Shoshanna told him Mayor Bouchet´ had called once, asking about his whereabouts, and she had politely told him it was very busy and was in the field "helping patrol out and answering calls."

Candy, when she had talked with him, had mentioned how strange it had been that Sergeant Downs had only popped his head in the Dispatch Room door and gruffly told both women he would be in a meeting in the mayor's office—and not to bother him for anything until the meeting was over—instead of beginning the day with his usual reign of supervisory badgering and bullying. She told Kearnes an eerie silence had settled over the police department and the adjoining offices at city hall after the meeting had started...like the solemn quiet that descends after a hornet's nest is struck with a large stick; just before the stunned and enraged insects inside mobilize, and boil out of it.

After answering the last call of his shift, which he'd stolen from Frick and Frack—contacting and breaking up a group of skate boarding juveniles downtown near the Senior Center who were running elderly pedestrians off the sidewalks with their boogie boards on wheels—Kearnes called in "10-10", out of service, with Shoshanna over the radio.

"Copy Charles One," she acknowledged him. "10-10 at sixteen zero five hours. Have a good evening, sir."

Kearnes signaled her back with two quick clicks of his radio mike. It was an electronic version of cop semaphore, referred to as "mike breaks," and was used on police radios across the nation to convey "I agree," or "I get it" when using plain voice language over the airwaves wasn't advisable. What Kearnes wanted to convey to Shoshanna and her partner was, "Thanks for you help. We did it." And he hoped that was the message that had gotten through.

On his way home he cruised through the back streets of a neighborhood called "Connelly Heights", a heterogeneous cluster of buckling wooden two story duplexes named after some long ago forgotten Admiral that housed the Coast Guard families whose members were assigned to the Cutter Point Station. The units sat on the furthest lip of the land plateau which contained the mass of the downtown area businesses and homes, and the very last row of duplexes were pushed so close to the ocean's edge that they had no back yards. Instead, they had adjoining eight foot high steel cyclone fences with posts drilled into solid rock. They were meant to save people from the fifty foot fall off the end of the Heights cliffs to the jagged basalt spires below; the tips of which disappeared and reappeared as the ocean swells cajoled their highest points.

It was a generally quiet neighborhood filled with squealing kids who darted in and out of wetly pulsing, yellow plastic lawn sprinklers that were set on the small, neatly squared front yard patches of brown, burnt grass. Summertime charcoal grills sent long plumes of white smoke skyward from the inexpensive cuts of fatty meat being hotly grilled on them, and there were children's bikes and toys strewn everywhere on the sidewalks and in the driveways; and here and there a lawnmower sat forlornly idle next to a grass rake propped against the side of a house, or an empty red gasoline can.

For Kevin Kearnes, who now found himself to be a stranger in a strange land both geographically and emotionally, his almost voyeuristic glimpse of family life from the front seat of his police car both soothed and seared his soul at the same time. In his mind he began to rewind and play back old movies of Tilly and him and their two boys back home in Kansas; vignettes of the most simple—and at the time—seemingly mundane days in their lives when they had been a family and were all together in the unquestioningly eternal way and manner all families automatically assumed they would be forever. Until one day, suddenly, they were a family no more.

He passed out of the neighborhood, turned around on a side street, and went back through it again; a deep feeling of melancholy pulling him into an almost intractable orbit around the outer circle of these stranger's private family lives. He wondered if they knew how truly lucky they were—even with all of their recurring everyday life problems—to have each other in sight, in sound, and within physical touch of one another every single day of their lives. And sadly; he thought that they probably did *not* know that. That they were more likely to be just like he himself had been all along when he'd been a husband and a Father; standing in the shadow of greatness while he cursed what he thought instead was darkness descending all around him. Blind to it, deaf to it. And indifferent to it all.

When he reached the same side street again and began to turn around for yet another trip back through the neighborhood, he wrenched the car's steering wheel back straight and drove in the most direct route possible until he reached Cutter Avenue, crossed The Blue Czar River Bridge, and turned onto Harbor Way.

He wanted to hold onto, as long as he could, the satisfying feeling his small victories from the day had brought him. And with the exception of having to force himself all day long to try and forget how he had acted like a complete idiot at Britt's motel room; lurking in the dark like some stalker, putting flowers that looked more like a bouquet of wild weeds in a used soft drink cup on her doorstep…it had been the best day he could ever remember having had in a very long time. Tonight, when he was alone in the dark of his apartment, would be reserved for wrestling with the demons of loss, and regret; but at the moment he actually felt as if he was among the living once again.

His plan during the day to stay busy and out of his office after openly defying the mayor and city manager, and Edgar Polk; by sending their messenger, Curt Lamar, back to them in completely demoralized, chain smoking pieces, and wet up to his Harley Davidson tee shirt armpits from trying to rescue a few chemically saturated tropical survivors from the bottom of his fish tank…had worked perfectly.

And it had also helped him resist the urge to drive to The Sand Dollar and knock on Britt's door. An urge which he had fought against long and hard all day long; even though she had made it clear she never wanted to see him again. Ever.

But there was a force within Britt which he felt so strongly; pulling him away from the expected and acceptable course of events in his life…and aiming him instead at the completely unknown quantity of her. It was as if a compass needle embedded inside his heart had suddenly swung in magnetic declination toward hers at the precise moment they had met; not pointing him in the true direction he should be taking…but the one he was compelled to.

He was halfway home to his apartment when he saw The Sand Dollar off in the distance; framed against the white dunes, the green pines, and the rolling blue ocean surf of the Pacific. Without thinking…but also without hesitation, he veered off of the paved roadway and onto the dusty access road that led to the motel.

Their was a small blue Geo Metro parked in the parking space in front of Room 142, Britt's room, but the parking spaces on either side of the car were empty, and Britt's window shades were all drawn tightly shut.

He pulled into the empty space to the left of the ugly little blue car, got out, and walked up to Britt's door. He pressed his ear against the door for a few seconds but could hear nothing coming from inside the room. The only sound he heard as he listened was the muffled roar of the surf buffeting against the rocks of the south jetty at Pearl Cove a few hundred yards away, and the pounding of his own heart inside his chest.

He tried the door knob. It was locked.

He was suddenly overcome with the urge to turn and quickly walk away. To get into his car and drive out of The Sand Dollar's parking lot before anyone saw him; before anyone knew he had even been there.

But he stood his ground against the subconscious voice in his head now telling him to leave, to get out…before he made an even bigger fool of himself with this woman than he already had the night before. With his feet firmly planted on the spot where he'd left the flowers he'd picked for her, he wiped the sweaty palm of his right hand on his uniform trousers; then closed his hand into a fist, and knocked on the motel room door.

There was no response.

He waited for a moment before knocking again, but there was still no response.

A corner section of the metal Venetian blinds of the room's front window were bent slightly upward at the edge near the windowsill, allowing a small space to look through. He stooped down, peering inside the room, and saw that the bed was neatly made, as if it had not been slept in; and through the open bathroom door he could see white terry cloth towels crisply folded and draped over the towel rack in perfect rows. His heart sunk into the pit of his stomach at the sight.

Quickly walking to the other end of the long log building, he stepped up onto the porch of the Office, pulled the rickety screen door open, and stepped inside. He heard the sounds of a television coming from a room hidden from his view somewhere in back of, and around the corner from the front desk, which was unoccupied. There was an old fashioned chrome service bell on the desk counter in front of him, and he banged its top with the palm of his hand.

The same rumpled looking man that had given Britt her room key tiredly appeared from the back room, wiping his hands on a white paper picnic napkin, his dinner having been apparently interrupted.

"Help you?" he said.

"Yes," said Kearnes. "I'm looking for the lady staying in Room 142. I brought her here. Very early this morning?"

"Not there any more," said the man.

The man's words shattered his resolve. What the hell was he thinking coming down here to see her again? What the hell was he *doing*? He had to think of something quick; to turn the situation around and give it the appearance of an official visit. But his mind was quickly going numb with the fact that he wasn't ever going to see Britt McGraw again…and that, he just could not accept.

"She in trouble or something?" asked the man.

"What?" said Kearnes. "Oh, no. No trouble. She was involved in an accident, and I needed to get some additional information from her for the report."

"Yeah," said the man. "Doesn't seem the type to be getting in any trouble. Pretty smart lady…and quite a looker, too."

Kearnes ignored the man's last comment. "What time did she check out?" he asked. "And did she say where she was going from here?"

"Checked out about ten this morning," the man answered. "Don't know that she went anywhere, though. Looks like her car is still here."

Kearnes paused for a moment and looked at the man, puzzled; confused about what he had just heard him say…or *thought* he'd heard him say.

"What car?" he asked.

"That car," the man said, pointing past Kearnes' shoulder to the open screen door and the parking lot beyond. "The little blue rental. They brought it by a little after eight this morning, and she came in here, checked out of her room and rented one of our cabins."

"She's…still here then?" Kearnes stammered.

"Should be," the man said. He turned and grabbed a clipboard hanging from a steel hook on the wall behind him. He was wearing glasses now—a change from when Kearnes had first encountered him while checking Britt in—and pushed them down low on his nose as he looked over the top of their fairly thick lenses and read from the clipboard.

"Cabin number six," he said. "The Cypress. One of our best. She paid for the whole rest of this month. In cash."

Kearnes felt as if he was strapped into some sort of crazy runaway carnival ride, driven by pure emotion. Like he was being whipped back and forth; then soaring high into the sky, plunging back toward the ground in a gravity grabbing rush as the experience of having both lost—and then again found—Britt McGraw all within the space of ten seconds compressed inside his chest until he felt like his heart was about to explode. He let his words come out slowly…carefully…like releasing steam from a pressure cooker.

"And where is that?" he asked the man. "Cabin number six."

"Straight out the door and to your right," he answered. You can just see the corner of the first cabin through the trees once you get on the path. The others are spread around as you go, right out into the dunes."

Kearnes thanked him, and then walked back outside. He glanced at the Blue Geo and made a mental note of the license plate before he started down the beach path. When he came to the first cabin, which did not appear to be rented, he looked for a number but found none. Instead there was a varnished wooden plaque attached with wood screws above the front door which read "The Magnolia." The second cabin looked identical to the first except for the same type of sign, obviously made with a wood burning tool, which said "The Sycamore."

By the time he reached cabin number three, "The Willow", he realized none of the cabins were numbered; they were all named for trees and they were dispersed as randomly through the narrow line of woods and the sand dunes as acorns which had fallen from some giant Oak in a windstorm. He passed up the next two cabins, not bothering to approach close enough to read their signs, when he saw beach chairs, half deflated air mattresses, and multiple pairs of muddy, sand caked tennis shoes strewn around the ground near their front doors and on their short, two step porches.

As he moved further out into the dunes through the stubby pine trees, he could feel the repetitive pounding of the surf on the beach two hundred yards ahead. The quickly cooling late afternoon salt air smelled to him like a metal bucket filled with dirty gray mop water; a scummy, sharp detergent smell that penetrated deep into the membranes of his nostrils and made his eyes begin to water, his stomach begin to sway.

The little red log cabins were even more spread out now and from the corner of his eye he caught sight of one in the distance that was different from all the others. It was larger, and taller; almost as if it had a second story to it, which was probably a loft of some sort, and wrapped around its front, extending a short way on either side, was a full raised wooden deck, covered by a gently slanting roof of green painted cedar shingles that gave the cabin a substantial and homey appearance, as if it offered much more potential than just a place to spend the weekend at the beach in. The minute he saw it he knew it was Britt's cabin and he hurriedly left the path, cutting through the dunes toward it in as straight a line possible as the grass choked terrain and bristling pines would allow.

He reached the cabin and stepped up onto the deck, feeling its salted, weather beaten boards creaking beneath his weight. He rapped lightly on the front door with the decorative anchor shaped brass door knocker, but there was no response. He grasped the door knob and holding his breath, turned it so slowly that it appeared to be slipping through his hand, not actually moving; testing her door just like he would a suspect's before he made entry. Her door was locked.

The curtains of the small living room window were drawn tightly shut. He moved down the deck a short distance to another window; this one higher up and even smaller. It had the same green and white checker pattern gingham curtains as the other window, but these had been left slightly apart. He cupped both hands against the sides of his head and peered into the gloom of the darkened room.

There was a well worn green sofa in the small living room that had a colorful rainbow banded Navajo throw blanket draped over its back. He could see Britt's suitcase, open, sitting on the sofa; with many of her clothes strewn around it...some of them lying on the floor. Directly beneath his view was a small round kitchen table with only two chairs; and on top of the table, a half empty bottle of Grey Goose vodka. Next to the bottle of vodka sat a cheap, empty water glass furnished by The Sand Dollar. Its hygienic paper wrapper had been wadded into a spit ball sized lump, and sat neatly balanced on top of the blue, foil covered vodka bottle cap.

He looked around the interior of the cabin a second time—as much of it as he could see—but her black travel bag was nowhere in sight. There was no other direction left for her to go, no other place left for him to check; except for the beach. He walked down the short steps of the deck and began to look around at the sandy earth in front of the cabin, and soon found the fresh imprint of a shoe, small in size. Then he found another one, and another one after that; all of them leading out into the sand dunes toward the sea and he followed them, repeatedly swallowing hard…trying to ward off the growing gag reflex which was trying so hard to coax him into throwing up from the feculent ocean air now filling his lungs.

The contour of the land suddenly dipped away through swales of grass covered sand hills. The shallow, trough like depressions that cut around the base of each one, connecting it to the next, created a labyrinth of separate pathways. They twisted and turned like the broken shaped borders of jigsaw puzzle pieces, but eventually all led to the same place…the edge of the sea.

He had now lost her footprints in this maze. So he let his eyes search out the most natural course ahead of him, as free from obstacles in his way and as straight as he could travel, for nearly being forced to walk in circles. And when he spotted an opening in the dunes through which he glimpsed shimmering blue water tipped with white, he headed straight for it.

He walked through the opening and there was Britt; standing in cold sea water that rushed in around her bare ankles, holding her sandals up in one hand while she tried to keep the hem of her pale blue linen dress from getting wet. She had her back turned to Kearnes as she stood there in the ocean only a few feet from the dry shore, her legs spaced apart for stability; looking out across the horizon at something he could not see.

The lowering sun's intensified rays glanced off the water's surface and into the front of her dress, backlighting the outline of her firm calves and thighs and the slight pear shape of her hips beneath the sleek linen fabric, like shadows thrown from inside a softly glowing paper lantern.

Kearnes stood absolutely still as he watched her watching the shimmering blue horizon, not daring to either move or speak…not wanting to break the genuine spell he had once again fell under the moment he saw her. He realized he was holding his breath in his effort to remain motionless and when he was forced to finally relent, and breathe in the now too close putrid ocean air, he was shocked to find that it was now suddenly sweet and fresh—for the first time since he'd arrived in Cutter Point. He wondered if he was, in some way, starting to lose his mind.

Slowly, Britt turned around and faced him. It was almost as if she'd known the entire time that he'd been standing there, watching her. The expression on her face was calm; an unbroken serenity which revealed neither surprise, or shock at his sudden appearance.

"Hello…again," he said too loudly, trying to be make sure he would be heard over the thundering peal of the ocean surf.

Britt only stared at him for a moment. And then without saying a word she walked out of the water straight toward him, dropping her sandals onto the beach as she came.

Kearnes began to back up slightly; at first just to give her a little more dry land to stand on while they talked. But as she continued to advance toward him he realized something was wrong, and he stopped.

Britt did not. She kept coming at him and as the distance between them closed to within touching, her right hand lashed out and she slapped him hard across the face.

The blow took him utterly by surprise.

At the last second he had seen her eyes narrow in anger and had been sure she was going to shout something at him; scream at him to go away and leave her alone. But instead she had hit him; and hard. He tensed, waiting for her to slap him again, but instead she let her hands fall to her sides, and he saw her shoulders slump in resignation. She began to cry.

Kearnes reflexively touched his hand to the left side of his face where she had struck him. The skin of his cheek felt raw and hot, and his left eye began to water. Britt looked up at him through her tears, searching his eyes for some kind of a reaction, but the only thing he could think of to do was to walk away from her.

He turned around and started back toward the dunes, but heard her approaching from behind. He felt her hand grasp his elbow and begin to tug at his uniform shirt sleeve.

"No," she said softly.

Kearnes stopped.

"No!" she said again, but forcefully this time; coming around the side of him to stand face to face.

"If you came here to say something to me," she blurted out, "then just say it!"

"I came here to see how you were doing today," he said. "I had no idea what I was going to say to you."

"You have ruined everything for me!" she sobbed. "Can you even begin to understand that?"

He reached out and gently took her face in his hands, clearing the tears away from beneath her eyes with his thumbs.

"So," he said, "would you feel better if you hit me again?"

Before she could answer, Kearnes brought his face close to hers and kissed her; and she responded instantly, hungrily pushing her tongue deep inside his mouth, probing...clutching at the back of his head with her fingers in his hair, pulling his mouth down harder against hers.

He closed his eyes as she kissed him back, and deeply breathed in the scent of her skin, the smell of her hair, the now sharply clean, and unoffending ocean air; and he felt something inside him begin to pull loose, and start to slip away...like a boat tied to the shore slipping its moorings in a sudden surge of current.

And his heart, like a long and meandering river having finally run its course to the sea...flowed effortlessly into the terminus of Britt McGraw.

CHAPTER 18

▼

Thud Compton stood on a small hillock of sand above the beach near Smith River, California with Brad Dekker, looking fifty yards out to sea at the bobbing, black wet suited heads of the Del Norte County Sheriff's Department Dive Team as they recovered a body tangled in a thick bed of kelp just offshore. It had been spotted floating there two hours earlier by a man walking along the shore, digging clams.

The divers looked like black seals, their heads popping up unexpectedly in different places on the surface, and then disappearing again, as they surfaced and submerged while they hacked away at the thick jungle of aquatic vines with their sharp knives that had trapped the corpse.

When they finally managed to free it and swim toward shore, then struggle out of the surf and stand up, those waiting on the beach were shocked to see that the body was tied, hands and feet, to a long wooden pole. And lodged horizontally underneath the shoulder blades of the body, perpendicular to the pole, was a shorter, flat piece of smooth driftwood that had become tightly jammed in place with knotted sections of torn kelp and seaweed. It forced the divers, in order to preserve the integrity of their forensic find, to carry the body ashore and deposit it on the beach with the cross like looking wooden device still intact.

The only two details which were missing and prevented the apparent manner of death being assigned the preliminarily eerie, and bizarre classification as a crucifixion by drowning, was that fact that the hands had not been nailed to the crosspiece, and the feet were not nailed to the bottom of the pole. Which now, upon closer view by Thud, appeared to be a large piece of a branch from a Pacific Madrone tree.

The two Del Norte County sheriff detectives, who had been photographing the recovery from the beach with their digital cameras at different angles, took a few quick shots after the divers laid the body down, then gloved up and moved in.

They both got down on their knees in the sand and huddled over the small, lifeless form and starting at the feet, one of which was still encased in an ankle high tennis shoe—the other one missing both shoe and sock—carefully began to palpate the body, feeling their way along up toward the shoulders and head.

At the buttocks they stopped. The bigger of the two detectives, who wore cowboy boots, and a white dress shirt with pearl snap buttons and a black string tie, gingerly reached a blue rubber gloved hand inside one of the body's rear jeans pockets, and extracted a thin, water logged brown leather wallet that had now turned black from being in the water overnight.

The detective looked inside the wallet, devoid of contents except for a shiny plastic laminated student identification card. He got to his feet and then removed the card from the wallet, holding it up to the fading light of the evening sky…looking at the small color picture of a young boy and the logo of the Gold Beach Elementary School Bobcats next to it.

Thud and Dekker approached him.

"Tyler…Dunne," said the big detective, reading the name on the card. He turned the card over so it faced his two Oregon counterparts, then held it out toward them. "This your missing kid?" he asked.

Brad Dekker moved in a little closer to the I.D. card, and pulled a small color snapshot from his shirt pocket that he'd obtained from Michael and Paula Dunne of their son, taken on "make up" day at his new elementary school when he'd enrolled there a few months ago. It was the same exact photo that appeared on the card.

"Yeah," said Dekker. "The name and the picture are a match. "It's Tyler Dunne."

"OK," said the beefy detective, returning to his partner. "Let's roll him."

Thud and Brad Dekker watched as the two detectives carefully eased the body first over onto one side; feeling, looking, and checking as they went. Then onto its back to identify it by facial features.

Except there were no facial features.

Because there was no face left.

What the churning, abrasive action of the rip tides had not erased from Tyler Dunne's face, the palms of his hands, his kneecaps, and his chest cavity, as he was scraped along the rocky, sea shell strewn bottom of the ocean, the crabs hiding in the kelp beds had taken. The scent of human flesh being shredded in the water had caused them to rise from the green depths below by the dozens, with greedily snapping, outstretched pincers.

Involuntary gasps simultaneously escaped from the mouths of all four men. The two more seasoned veterans among them of homicide investigations, fatal car crashes, and gory suicides made their best attempt at disguising their horror at the sight of pink ribbons of muscle tissue and bleached skin still clinging to pure white, polished bone, open sinus passages, and empty eye sockets; but their own intact, living faces, betrayed them.

But Brad Dekker was *not* one of them. Like Thud, he had never yet had occasion to investigate a homicide—they were more than a rare occurrence in Cutter County—and he had actually seen very few dead bodies thus far in his career. And like Thud, he too had children, two boys and a girl. And his youngest boy, who was nine, was also a "Bobcat" at the same elementary school in Gold Beach where they lived. He dropped Tyler Dunne's picture on the ground and lurched away from the scene toward a broken tangle of driftwood logs and debris a short way up the beach, vomiting his lunch as he went.

Thud stood rigidly still, looking down at the body, his mind racing through different possible scenarios which might explain this...the completely unexplainable. What kind of human being could do something like this to someone else, and why? What kind of monster could do something like this to a child?

It wasn't proven yet that *this* was Tyler Dunne. Or if it was him that he had been either killed here, or back across the state line somewhere in Oregon between here, and Nesika Beach. But of course in his gut he knew it probably was the boy, and the one thing he was absolutely sure of was that this was a murder. And whoever had done this had to have driven right through the middle of Cutter Point to get here.

The understanding of the reality of this began to spread throughout Thud's body like a cold, poisonous chemical concocted from equal parts of fear and rage...violently injected into his nervous system and freezing its way through his veins and arteries, until it reached his heart and began to turn it to stone.

Whoever he was, wherever he was, this was someone who had to be stopped, and stopped *now*. And he knew instinctively, just like all the times he had known when he'd been in combat, and had been right...someone was going to have to kill him, to stop him.

He wondered if he might be the one to have to do it.

And he wondered if he was still good enough; if he still had what it would take, if that's what it came down to in the end, after having now led such a soft life of unrestricted banality for so many years in his safe little city by the sea.

"You...motherfucker," he said tightly under his breath to no one in particular, as he watched a small red sand crab the size of a poker chip quickly scuttle inside the shoeless pant leg of the dead boy, and disappear from sight.

"You motherfucker."

CHAPTER 19

▼

Tyler Dunne's body was positively identified twenty four hours later at an autopsy conducted at the Oregon State Police Crime Lab in Central Point.

Thud had called Kearnes' and asked his permission to accompany Brad Dekker to the Crime Lab. They had both left from the crime scene in California without first returning to either their offices or their homes.

They followed closely along behind the pearl grey unmarked Ford of the Del Norte County detectives on the two hour drive along the Redwood Highway, which wound its way from the California coast up into the Siskiyou Mountains, then back down again into the Rogue River Valley in Oregon. Ahead of all of them a black hearse from a Crescent City funeral home, which was under contract to the Del Norte County Sheriff's Department, carried what remained of Tyler Dunne.

After securing the body at the Crime Lab at a little past eleven p.m. that night, Thud and Dekker split off from the two Del Norte detectives and found rooms for themselves at a Super Eight near Interstate-5. The motel, which was new, was only a few miles away from Oregon State Police Headquarters in Central Point— a small bedroom community on the outskirts of Medford—where the Crime Lab was located.

After checking in at the front desk Thud said a quick good night to Brad Dekker and as soon as he was in his room, called Margie at home and woke her up.

He had her visually inspect all of the doors and windows in the house to make sure they were secure; then had her test, and re-set their security alarm system to see that it was working.

And then he asked her to get his off duty gun—the Smith & Wesson .38 Airweight—from the top shelf of his closet. Made her open the cylinder and confirm that it was still loaded with the five rounds of +P jacketed hollow points that he always kept in it.

He told her to put the gun underneath her pillow every night, and to keep it with her at all times, wherever she and the girls went…until he returned home.

The news of the murder of a local child found strangled to death on a California beach and tied to a wooden cross, both shocked and horrified all of the communities in Cutter County, large and small. And when it became public knowledge that the police were unable to determine exactly where Tyler Dunne had been killed, and that the murder, theoretically, could have occurred in any one of these same towns; the horror about what had happened was quickly replaced with the sheer terror of the possibility that it might happen in one of their communities next.

A regional Task Force to investigate the homicide was quickly formed, made up of personnel from the Cutter County Sheriff's Department, Cutter Point Police Department, Oregon State Police, and the Del Norte County Sheriff's Department. And when a possible connection was soon made by investigators between the murder of Tyler Dunne and that of another young white male victim named Ricky Cates, who had also been strangled to death a few days before Tyler had, but on a beach two hundred miles south of Cutter County in Lincoln County, that Sheriff's Department came on board the Task Force too.

The "connection" in the two cases, besides the fact that both victim's were young males and both had a cause of death ruled by two separate Coroner's offices as ligature strangulation with a similar shaped thin, strap like object; and in spite of the fact that one boy had been brutally raped while the other had apparently not been sexually molested at all…was the sign of the cross.

A crucifix.

A small silver crucifix earring had been cut away from Ricky Cates' ear—and part of the ear along with it—presumably taken by his killer. Perhaps as a trophy of sorts. While the killer of Tyler Dunne had chosen to leave the external integrity of his victim's body intact.

And so in addition to the vicious beatings administered to both the boys prior to their deaths, followed by the soul destroying invasion of Tyler Dunne's body from the rape, it was the unexplainable, watery crucifixion on the crude wooden cross, and the violent taking of a piece of symbolic religious jewelry from a child's head that piqued the public's interest and whetted their appetites for more, once the media began to package the story and found just the right spin to put on it.

It was this clue, the crucifix symbols, Thud wanted to either minimize, or hopefully keep out of the harsh spotlight of the media all together. He knew that holding back one or two key facts in a case—things about the crime known only to the suspect himself—was often like finding a secret map leading to buried treasure. And that if you kept that map a secret long enough, the treasure would ultimately be yours.

But it wasn't to be. Investigators in Lincoln County, where Ricky Cates had been killed, revealed early on the cut off and missing silver earring from the boy's body, and foolishly…stupidly; one of the Del Norte County detectives at the Tyler Dunne crime scene had shared with a crime beat reporter from the Cutter Clarion the fact that they had found a piece of driftwood wedged underneath the boy's back where he was tied tightly to the Madrone wood branch.

Like a cross.

And even though the detective had made it clear to the reporter that this cross like piece of wood had not been either tied in place or nailed to the upright piece of Madrone driftwood; and may have, in fact, only been lodged there by the action of the waves and tide…it didn't seem to make any difference.

That "fact" was quickly mentally discarded by the reporter as he sped back to his office in Cutter Point with the story, giddily making the connection with the other murder of a young boy which had just recently occurred up the coast at Seal Rock Wayside. And by the time he appeared in his editor's doorway, he had the name for the manner of the murders and in turn, the murderer: "The Cross Killer."

But even life after murder went on in the City of Cutter Point, and the soft, languorous days of summer on the southern Oregon coast continued to turn over, one after another, like the measureless waves washing ashore and expending themselves on the beaches.

The controversy involving the blowing up of the whale on the beach by the police department, which had locally come to be referred to as "a little commotion, by the ocean", began to die down as the city's insurance carrier settled property damage claims with individuals and businesses, and the city attorney prepared to argue the city's case, and defend against, violation notices and fines being levied against the city by the E.P.A. and The U.S. Fish & Wildlife Service, as well as a lawsuit that had been filed by Green Peace.

And there were no more killings.

The city held its annual Whale of A Celebration!; starting on the Fourth of July and continuing for a full week, which swelled the city to over capacity with out of town visitors and plugged the local beaches and whale watching towers with droves optimistic people, looking anxiously out to sea. And even without the involvement of The Patriots this year it was generally considered to be a financial success; thanks in part to the local Kiwanis Club chipping in at the last minute and hiring a pyrotechnic company from Eugene to put on a modest fireworks display.

A section of downtown Cutter Avenue had been cordoned off with brightly painted orange saw horses from the Public Works Department, so no one traveling through Cutter Point could possibly miss it. Traffic was diverted through the side streets around the encaged throngs of tourists and residents alike who wandered up and down the crowded rows of plywood booths which sold everything from hot, doughy Elephant Ears, to gaudily framed pictures of Elvis painted on black velvet.

There was a small garish, and very noisy carnival in the middle of it all, complete with a Ferris Wheel, kiddy rides, and even a sampling of a few of the much bigger, and more gut wrenching amusements like The Hammer, The Rocket, and The Terminator.

Kearnes had taken Britt there on Saturday night, the Fourth of July, when the carnival had opened; on their first real date. They had spent nearly every night together in her cabin at The Sand Dollar since their first kiss on the beach, delirious together in their futile quest to find some point of final satisfaction, or understanding, or even boredom with each other's bodies, and the ever increasing pleasure they gave to one another. But that hadn't yet happened so Kearnes had asked her out on a date, and much to his surprise, she had readily accepted.

Mayor Vernon Bouchet', dressed in a fire engine red wool blazer, white flannel pants, and a bright blue knit turtle neck shirt, gave a gaseous, opening ceremony speech from an elevated podium on the parade entrant's judging stand which was draped with a huge American flag. A fidgety and perspiring Roy Roddameyer, wearing a blue turtle neck knit shirt identical to that of his boss, but beneath a double breasted chocolate wool blazer, sat on a wobbly steel folding chair behind Bouchet' to his immediate left. Behind him were several more rows of folding chairs containing all the members of the city council, a local State Representative and his wife, and several prominent business owners and civic booster types; most of who were Rotary Club members.

Bouchet' went on and on and on, the words from his high pitched little man's voice droning out toward the half listening crowd from the speaker's of the public address system like angry captive bees suddenly released from a glass jar. He spoke about the history of Cutter Point; named for the graceful Cutter sailing ships that once anchored in the city's deep water Harbor at the turn of the century to take on fresh supplies, and deliver cargo to the logging companies, on their way to different destinations all over the globe. He spoke about how logging and the timber industry had built the town and had sustained it through the economic hardships of the depression, two world wars, and several recessions. He spoke about what it meant to be an American: to be resilient, inventive and to be able to take risks in order to change with the economic times.

And then he turned and spoke to the city council members and others seated with them about the importance of the upcoming Special Land Use Election just a little over one week away, which would determine the ultimate fate of the already scheduled September Labor Day weekend opening, and final ownership of, the massive, sprawling, world class destination golf course project known as Trident Greens.

Bouchet' and Roddameyer, along with a few of their silent partner investment cronies, had rushed to judgment in putting together the financial packaging for the deal; minimizing one slight detail along the way. Half of the land for the monster sized project was currently within the city, while the other half, the most expensive half to develop, containing the Resort Hotel and Condominiums, was on county land. Anything less than a majority vote by the full city council to annex the county half of the land into the city, and Vernon Bouchet' and his friends stood to personally lose millions on the deal; splitting the ownership of the Resort, and its profits, with Cutter County in perpetuity.

Vernon Bouchet' had cooked up the idea of Trident Greens all by himself more than two years earlier, and hadn't given a second thought to the possibility of any one member of his city council giving him trouble by ultimately casting anything other than a "yes" vote on the annexation issue. Those on the council he could not charm, he would intimidate. Those he could not intimidate, he would buy. And those he could not buy...well; he would leave them to Roy Roddameyer, his closer. That's why he had fired the previous city manager and had installed his old former employee and golfing buddy in the position in the first place.

He expected nothing less than perfection from Roy...his seemingly ever increasing appetite for alcohol these days not withstanding. And he did thoroughly enjoy sharing a bottle or two, or three, of fine wine with him, along with some good conversation at home some night before they both retired for the evening. But he was going to have to speak to him, and soon, about his drinking.

He wanted it be just like the good old days again when they were in the car business together. Like selling a used, over priced, rusted out Camaro with a cheap new paint job to a Mexican who had no green card, no credit history, no job, no driver's license, and no down payment. And *still* getting him financed somewhere, by some sucker lending institution, so Roy could close the deal.

Then they would be out on the links of a local golf course by one o'clock; sipping gin and tonics while Roy drove the golf cart, chasing their balls around. Roy Roddameyer was very adept at finding his boss's balls, and he knew what to do with them once he'd found them. And *that* was another, more personal, reason why Bouchet' had wanted him as his city manager.

But to a handful of citizens in town, and one stubborn old councilwoman named Hattie McElvey, who had once, years ago, when her beloved Longshoreman husband Jewell was still alive, had even served one term as mayor of Cutter Point herself; there were some cold hard facts to be spread out on the table about what some people considered to be a boondoggle of the tax payer's money, and a future threat to the very survival of the city.

On a good day for Hattie, a day of lucidity when her onset Alzheimer's hadn't hazed over her mind like an evening fog wisping ashore; she knew that no resident of Cutter Point, not even the most affluent among them, save for Vernon Bouchet' himself, would ever be able to afford the three hundred dollar a day greens fees being proposed for this golf course, or even a one night stay in one of the Resort's "economy" suites for one eighty five, plus the five percent local room tax.

Hattie was eighty two and lived alone in a modest little white clapboard home in the hills overlooking Pearl Cove with her two Manx cats, and on those good days for her at city hall—when she was in her right mind—she was an elderly lioness prowling the halls; roaring and spitting and displaying her claws at whatever she thought about what was going on that was not right, or was wasteful, or just plain stupid. She was the nemesis of Mayor Vernon Bouchet', having run for a council position just so she could bedevil him, and she knew that he knew it.

She had railed at Bouchet' for firing the last city manager; who had been, in her opinion, a good man doing a good job. And she had also flared up at him over the firing of several previous police chiefs; one of whom she had been particularly fond of because he was such a fine figure of a man, and had reminded her in a way, hauntingly, of her now long ago gone husband Jewell.

But then days, or sometimes even just hours would pass, and Hattie would start to forget things. She would forget what she had been angry about, and why. She would forget people, and their names, and what they did; and who they were, if anybody, to her. And sometimes she even forgot who she was, and where she was, too.

But tonight her mind was sharp as a whip as she stared back at the ugly little man in the turtleneck who was staring down on her from his podium, the harsh glare from the spotlighted stage reflecting off the oversized lenses of his glasses like twin search beams seeking her out in the night.

You goddamned old ugly, goggly eyed snapping turtle! she thought to herself; broadcasting a look directly at Vernon Bouchet' that had it had the potential to be lethal, Vernon would have been dead before he hit the judging stand floor. *I know exactly how I am going to vote...you crooked bastard. And believe you me, you are not going to like it!*

She would hold onto that thought, she pledged to herself, like the anchor of a ship lodged in solid rock on the bottom of the sea. Hattie McElvey was nobody's fool, and she hadn't survived thirty five years in the Cutter Point School District as a sixth grade elementary school teacher by being a pushover and not learning how to successfully deal with difficult people. She had straightened out more than one unruly, "lost cause" student of hers in her time—Thud Compton having been one of them—and look what a fine policeman and credit to his community he'd turned out to be. In fact, she planned on talking to Thud soon about some of the shenanigans this so called mayor and his oily, Italian looking city manager were up to!

She looked away in disgust from Mayor Vernon Bouchet' as he began to wind down his yammering, self-serving speech, and let her old cataract plagued eyes begin wander out over the crowd. Near the front she saw a tall and quite handsome man with dark hair, standing close beside a slender woman with very light blonde hair. The young woman was stunningly beautiful, and the man had one arm subtlety, protectively, circled around her waist. Not an overt display of public affection, but something else. Something much more powerful. And meaningful.

Who was that man? She tried to remember. She had seen him before, she was sure. In fact she even remembered being introduced to him; just couldn't remember where, or when, or what his name was. She concentrated hard, looking intently at his face, his eyes, and his height.

Oh...of course! It was the new chief of police! She had met him at city hall the day after he was sworn in, and had even gone to talk to him once at his office since then to file a complaint over some young ruffians who lived next door to her, for shooting at her beloved cats with their BB guns.

How silly of her not to recognize him; but of course it must have been because he was not wearing his uniform. What a nice man he was to look at, just like her

Jewell had been; a fine figure of a man, tall and strapping, with a chest of solid muscle like the trunk of an oak tree. She so missed him.

Hattie blinked her eyes at the memory of him, and her softening, fuzzy vision began to cloud over in concert with her mind. She started to cry quietly to herself with joy, hoping no one would notice the one errant tear sliding down her cheek which she could not hold back, now that the crowd was applauding the end, finally, of that ass, Bouchet's, speech.

How wonderful this was…that her husband would come back to visit her after all this time! She would never forget this moment—as brief and fleeting as it had been—as she watched her beloved Jewell turn and slowly walk away…then disappear among the herds of people making their way toward the carnival midway.

What a loving, thoughtful gesture; to let her see him again like this! And in the way she liked to remember him best; when was as a younger man…healthy, virile, and very much alive.

But who was that woman he'd been with?

Kearnes tightened his hold a little around Britt's waist and guided her out of the path of several people stampeding away from the conclusion of Mayor Bouchet's overly long speech, and now charging toward the rapidly forming lines at the carnival rides with their kids in tow.

He saw Roy Roddameyer impatiently bail off the rear of the elevated judging platform where all the city dignitaries and their guests had been sitting. Unwilling, apparently, to wait any longer in the slow as molasses line of mostly elderly people who were shuffling single file down the one and only narrow set of stairs from the judging platform to the asphalt blacktop of the street.

He watched as Roddameyer's shiny, oil slicked head of black hair was quickly swallowed up in a sea of other bobbing heads as he made his way in the direction of the two "Beer Garden" stands, just up the street, that Kearnes had noted were already open and dispensing tap beers into plastic cups as he and Britt had passed by on their way in to the opening ceremonies speech.

Vernon Bouchet' had been watching Roddameyer's hasty exit too…and disapprovingly…from where he still stood at the podium. Like a little barn owl perched atop the highest branch of a bare leafed tree, he watched the crowd below him disperse as if they were field mice running for cover in the maze of a cornfield.

The previously idling motors of the carnival rides suddenly came to life, almost in unison, with a collective chain rattling roar just as Kearnes started to speak to Britt, and he found himself having to practically shout at her now to be heard.

"What rides do you want to go on?" he asked her loudly, leaning down close to her ear.

She was wearing Tommy blue jeans and a soft V-neck sweater that let the top half of her belly button just barely peek out at the world. Her candy apple red lipstick matched her toenails perfectly. She'd painted them an hour before they'd left for the carnival, and in the open toed brown leather clogs she wore he worried about some oaf in the crush of the crowd stepping on one of those exquisitely formed, beautiful feet of hers.

"What?" she shouted back, putting her hands palms in to the sides of her mouth like a make shift megaphone.

"Which rides?" he repeated again, just as loudly as before. "So I'll know how many tickets to get?"

"Oh...no," she said. "Don't buy any tickets. I don't like rides." She shook her head "no" at him for further emphasis, just in case he wasn't hearing her.

"Well how about the Ferris Wheel?" he said, pointing in the direction of it where it had been stopped while the operator loaded passengers into the bottom cages, two at a time, then sent them skyward.

Britt looked in the direction he was pointing and saw the cage at the top of the stopped wheel rocking violently back and forth; a teenage boy with a maniacal grin on his face causing the motion while his girlfriend shrieked at him, pummeling his arm to tray and make him stop.

"I can't," she shouted back. "I'm afraid of heights."

Kearnes looked around with uncertainty at the mass confusion of people with their kids, packed tightly within the confines of the amusement event, and trying to do everything with them all at once. As he himself tried desperately to come up with his own quick solution for fun that would keep his date interested, amused, and still liking him.

The way she was dressed right now, Britt looked years younger. She looked more like a high school sweetheart than the coolly professional, somewhat aloof and distant, yet still very beautiful stranger he had met only a few short weeks ago, and was now starting to fall in love with. The only problem with that distorted vision was that Kevin Kearnes had never had a high school sweetheart. He had not been allowed one; or any other kind's of girlfriends for that matter when he was growing up. The world had seen to that.

It was impossible to carry on a conversation where they were standing, so Kearnes led her away from the rides; down the row of food booths and concessionaires until they came to a cotton candy stand.

"Do you like this?" he asked, nodding his head in the direction of the cotton candy stand.

Britt's eyes lit up when she saw the spun sugar candy behind the glass window of the stand playing off the big stainless steel shank of the cotton candy machine in long, billowy ribbons, as a man in a splotchy stained white apron wound them expertly around, and around, onto white paper cones.

"Oh my God," she said. "I haven't had that since I was a little kid!"

"Then I'd say you're long overdue," said Kearnes. "What would you like...pink, or blue?"

"Pink, please," she said.

Kearnes approached the man behind the glass, who stopped what he was doing, and wiped his hands on his apron before accepting the six one dollar bills Kearnes held out to him for one pink cotton candy, and one blue.

Britt bit into her cotton candy with hungry relish, and Kearnes did the same but not as carefully; managing to get a strand of his cotton candy stuck to the outside of his upper lip.

"Here," she said, holding her pink cone out to him. "Let's taste each other's."

"OK," he said, offering his own candy to her, too.

She pushed his hand aside. "Uh, uh" she said. "I didn't mean like that. I mean like this." She reached her right hand up around his neck and pulled him toward her, then licked the blue cotton candy from above his lip, and then the tiny blue flecks that were stuck to the corners of his mouth.

Then she kissed him; very long, and very deep.

When she had finished he pulled back from her and looked around; wondering if they should have just done that...recalling the very crowded, and at the moment, very public place they were standing in the middle of.

She had taken him completely by surprise with her spontaneity; had shocked him actually. Because to this point in their relationship the only place she had ever acted spontaneous toward him, and with him, had been in her bed. And the nature of the things they had been doing with each other there, could only have been best described as spontaneous...combustion. But he was still fairly new in town and he doubted that few, if any, citizens would recognize him yet when he was out of uniform.

"Mine was delicious," Britt said, grinning at him. "How was yours?"

"Very sweet and very pink," Kearnes replied. "And, very warm," he added, smiling back at her.

"So, was that your first cotton candy in twenty years?" she asked him. "Like me?"

"Nope," he said. "Three years ago to be exact...at the Ford County Fair in July. Back home in Kansas. Ethan and Alex used to love the stuff. It was the first place they always headed to when my wife and I...well...I mean, when they would get to the Fair. That's what they always wanted first. Cotton candy."

Kearnes had suddenly, and naturally, let their names slip out...Ethan, and Alex, in the way all parents do when they use their kids to illustrate what usually amounts to a significant, if not the biggest portion of their everyday lives. And he had spoken of them, he now realized, in the past tense. As if they were only a memory now. As if they might have died.

Their first night together he had volunteered to Britt that he was a divorced Father of two young sons, who lived back in Kansas with their Mother. But only that much.

And then he had then braced himself for an onslaught of in depth, womanly questions he was sure she would then barrage him with after his disclosure. But there had been none. Wasn't this what most women wanted to know about a man; even more than he knew about himself?

The only conclusion he was left with was that Britt McGraw, for some reason, was not "most women"; because she did not ask any questions of him. And it was obvious to him that she did not care to have questions asked about her. But in truth, he was relieved; like a man being led up the rotting wooden steps of a gallows, and every step breaking under the weight of his feet as he went.

She had not even told Kearnes what kind of doctor she was. And how could she suddenly decide, supposedly on her way to a medical convention in California, to just stop at an unplanned and remote location on the map because her car was involved in a traffic accident? How she could afford to stay in the two thousand dollar a week beachfront cabin, week after week, with no apparent departure date either planned, or even in mind?

He hadn't forgotten the mark he'd seen on her ring finger the night of the accident. It had faded now with time, but he knew it probably meant that she was either currently married, or recently divorced. No woman on earth who was even remotely close to the type of woman Britt McGraw was could ever be anything other than one of these two things.

And since he knew he couldn't ultimately deal with the reality of the existence of either, he chose to deny, for the moment, even their possibility, and to bury them as deep as he had the existence of his own children, and even Tilly. Simply to avoid the pain of remembering them, and what they had all had together, and meant to one another.

"Which one is older?" she suddenly blurted out, and her words froze him in place.

He tried to pretend he hadn't heard what she'd said, and quickly looked away from her at the man behind the glass in the cotton candy booth, who had started up his noisy machine again.

"Kevin?" she said. "Which boy is the oldest? Ethan, or Alex?"

He kept his eyes locked on the man behind the glass window, shocked by her question and hoping she would drop it now that the whirring din of the cotton candy machine filled the air around them. She was probably only being polite; in asking about them. Or maybe she felt the need to reciprocate to him on some small level; to try and meet him in this place of pseudo-intimacy he had brought her to on this date...at least halfway.

But the absence of his sons in his life was like a knife sticking in his heart, and he didn't want that knife moved; didn't want it touched by anyone, no matter how helpful they might think they were being. Because he was certain that the pain of it being pulled out, would be even greater now than when it had first been thrust in.

"Kevin?"

"Hey...chief!" Thud Compton's voice suddenly cracked like a sonic boom in the air overhead above them, nearly drowning out every other sound, and saving him from having to answer Britt.

He turned around and saw Thud moving in on him through the crowd like a linebacker coming in for a block.

"Chief!" Thud called to him again, hurriedly motioning to Margie and the girls, a few steps behind him, to catch up.

"Thud," said Kearnes, unsure of whether or not there was a problem. "Nice to see you guys out on a Saturday night having some family time. Hello again, Margie."

"Hi Kevin," Margie said, eyeing Britt warily.

"I've been looking all over hell for you. Dispatch said you'd be down here. I've got news."

Kearnes turned toward Britt. "I'd like you to meet a friend of mine. This is Britt McGraw. Britt, this is Thud and Margie Compton. Thud is one of my best guys down at..."

"We've got the analysis and identification report back from the crime lab on the vinyl strips used to bind Tyler Dunne!" Thud interrupted.

"Thud Compton!" Margie shouted at her husband, jabbing him in the ribs. "That's just plain rude!"

Thud brought himself up short, then caught his breath and said, "Sorry honey, you're right. Hello, Miss McGraw. I hope you're feeling OK after your accident, and everything. Like the chief said, this is my wife, Margie, and these are our two daughters, Selena and Sarah."

"It's nice to meet you," said Margie, extending her hand toward Britt. I think what my husband is trying to say, is that he needs to talk with his boss. Girls, would you like some cotton candy...like Britt has?"

"It's delicious," said Britt, tearing two small pieces off her cone and offering one to each of the girls, who instantly responded with eager, open hands.

"Thud, give me some money please," said Margie, who had left her purse in their car at Thud's request, so she could keep a tight grip on each of their daughter's hands as they walked through the crowd, looking for Kearnes.

Kearnes could see the slight bulge beneath the right side of Thud's windbreaker at his waist—the outline of his holstered Glock pistol—but when he lifted open his jacket to get his wallet from an inside pocket there, he saw he was wearing his Smith & Wesson Airweight in a shoulder holster as well. It wasn't unusual for police officers to carry off duty weapons—Kearnes himself had his little Kahr nine millimeter tucked in the back pocket of his jeans with his own jacket covering it—but carrying two guns off duty? Any cop found to be doing that, without a damn good reason, was probably ready for a little visit to the department shrink.

"Here," said Thud, handing Margie a twenty dollar bill. "Give us just five minutes. We'll be right here while you get your cotton candy. Don't go anywhere else."

Thud waited until Margie and Britt and the girls were situated in the long line of cotton candy purchasers before he spoke.

"I've been bugging them over there at the crime lab for weeks, trying to get them to put a rush on things, and they actually called me at home this afternoon."

"What did they find out?" asked Kearnes.

Thud searched inside his jacket pocket again and brought out a small notebook, then opened it. "OK, first of all, it's not any sort of plain generic vinyl material like we first thought. It's a very specific six gauge, green, one hundred percent virgin vinyl plant tie material...brand name of "Trellistrip."

"What is it used for?"

"Exclusively? In vineyards; to tie the new growing grape vines to those cross wire things. To support the grape plants and keep them up off of the ground, in the sun and air."

"So, you could use them for other things though," said Kearnes, playing devil's advocate. "Like in flower gardens? Or maybe even for some kind of garden crop?"

"You could," said Thud, "but you'd have to have a hell of a lot of new flower stems you wanted to tie up, or whatever, because they're only sold two ways: a card of fifteen hundred, or in a box of twenty five thousand. And in two lengths only...ten inches, or twelve inches."

"But are there other, similar products out there on the market?" Kearnes asked.

"There are," said Thud, "but "Trellistrip" is the big player in the vineyard industry, and the manufacturer of them has, I am told, about a ninety percent market share cornered for their own product. If you're a grape grower, then you're going to have a few boxes of these things lying around somewhere."

"And it was definitely these "Trellistrip" ties that were used in the Dunne murder?

"Definitely," said Thud. "Several of them; the twelve inchers."

"How about them as a match as what used to strangle the Cates boy in Lincoln County?"

"Negative on that," said Thud, staring intently now toward Margie and the girls...or at something in the crowd just beyond them.

"They weren't used to strangle him. They are made, like I said, with one hundred percent virgin vinyl; so they stretch right along with the new plant growth, and you basically never have to replace them. If they had been the ligature weapon used to kill Ricky Cates, they would have stretched to leave an imprint almost as thin as a wire...like what was left on Tyler Dunne's ankles and wrists. What was used on the Cates kid was something more like a small diameter cord; or some type of thin strap, that didn't give much when it was tightened. And it was made of nylon; it left olive drab and black colored fibers embedded in his neck. Still no word on that, yet."

Now Kearnes saw what is was Thud was staring at.

Frick and Frack had entered the congested carnival area, wheeling their police mountain bikes alongside of them because it was impossible for them to ride through the crowd. They had stopped in front of a booth where a group of juvenile boys were hurling weighted softballs at stacked pyramids wooden bowling pins; showing off for their girlfriends who stood nearby. But the girls, who appeared to be thirteen or fourteen years of age, had now turned their fickle attention instead to the "hot" looking young uniformed officers in blue shorts and white helmets who had just arrived with their cool bikes.

"Excuse me a minute chief," Thud said, glaring in the direction of his two summer goof off, officers. "I'll be right back."

Frick was standing next to his mountain bike, showing some of the girls where his emergency tire pump was attached to the bike's frame, and Frack was adjusting the strap of his helmet on another girl's head, letting her try it on, when they both felt a bone crushing hand of their sergeant's clamp down on the wedge of flesh located just above their shoulder blades, and swiftly drag them backwards away from their young teenage admirers.

Thud spun them around, facing him, and roared into both their faces "What the hell do you two think you are doing!"

"Sergeant Compton!" yelped Frick. "What are you doing here sir?"

"We're...we're patrolling the carnival...and downtown area," stammered Frack. "Like you told us to, sir."

"The hell you are!" Thud shot back at him. "I got eyes, moron!"

"We stopped for a short break, sir" offered Frick. "These young ladies were asking about our bikes, and some of the equipment. I was showing them how I get pumped up."

"Yeah," Frack said cautiously. "We weren't going to let them ride us or anything...I mean them. I mean let them ride them. The bikes I mean, not..."

"I told you both that you were to keep moving...in and out of this crowd...and to keep you goddamned eyes open at all times!" Thud was practically breathing fire at them, he was so angry.

"But we didn't think it would hurt to..." Frick started to say, but Thud cut him off immediately.

"That's right! You didn't think!" seethed Thud. "There is a fucking maniac on the loose somewhere, and he could just as easily be here in our town as any—fucking—where—else! If he snatches another kid...right from underneath your noses...I guarantee you are not going to like having to live with that fact the rest of your lives!"

"Yes Sergeant," said Frack. "We gotcha'."

"Yeah," agreed Frick. "We're cool with it."

"Good," said Thud, derisively. "Now you two pedal files get back on those bikes, and get back to work."

Frick and Frack walked back to their patrol bikes; rolling their eyes at the girls apologetically for the scene their psycho supervisor had just created. Frick squatted down and clipped his tire pump back into place in its holder on the bike's frame, and as he stood up he noticed the sergeant was still standing in the same place. But he didn't look pissed now. He looked worried, and somehow even a little sad.

They started to wheel their bikes past him, with Frick in the lead, when Frack abruptly stopped in front of Thud.

"We're really sorry, sergeant," he said to Thud.

Frick said, "Yeah, sarge. We'll do a heads up job the rest of our shift. We promise."

"And we have qualifications at the range first thing tomorrow morning, starting at zero eight hundred hours, so *do not* be out all night after your shift…partying your asses off as usual."

"Those are only vicious rumors about us Sergeant!" cried Frack.

"Yeah!" Frick chimed in. "By other officers in the department, who are jealous of us for some reason!"

"You guys just get out there, please," said Thud, "and start circulating."

"Just one thing," said Frack. "What is it, exactly; we are supposed to be looking for sir?"

Thud didn't answer for a long time; just stared at the two young officers who he knew would never stand a chance going up against someone like the person who had murdered Tyler Dunne, and—he was sure now—also Ricky Cates. He was afraid for them, for his family, for the town…and even for himself. And it was starting to show.

Finally he said…in a voice so quiet that both Frick and Frack had to strain to hear him, "You look for someone…who is looking back at you."

CHAPTER 20

▼

Kearnes woke in the bed to the reverberant sounds of the pre-dawn ocean surf blustering ashore, and to Britt softly snoring; naked and lying on her stomach beneath the fluffy white goose down comforter, her body snuggled in close to him.

He lay awake in the dark on his back, smelling the cold, dank, ocean air coming in through the open window of the bedroom loft, less than a foot away from his head; perplexed by the fact that the heavy smell of the sea was no longer making him sick, since he had been with Britt. Not even a little bit nauseous. He lifted the comforter slightly above his chest and the warmth from their body heat, mixed with the redolence of their lovemaking from the night before, escaped into the cold, unheated air of the room like thick exhaust.

The amber drops from the small black bottle of Paloma Picasso which she'd dabbed on her forearms and on her shoulders and throat the previous evening before they'd left for the carnival, had absorbed deep into the pores of her skin now, mingling erotically with the slightly sweet, tangy scent of her sweat.

And like a precursor to a scent of even higher refinement and calling, the perfume and perspiration commingled with the dulcet, musky odor which now emanated from between the silken triangle of her partially opened legs. He lay there next to her, smelling her smells, and fighting back his growing primal urge to open her legs even further; and thrust his face between them until he could taste her scent with his deeply probing tongue.

The timer beeping on the coffee maker downstairs in the small kitchen area, signaling the end of its brew cycle, caused him to suddenly bolt upright in bed, and Britt stirred next to him.

"What time is it…you are doing," she said groggily.

"Shhhh." he said. "It's only six. Go back to sleep. Today's Range Day. I have to clean my gun before I go."

They'd stopped by his apartment at The Sea Breeze—a place he rarely ever frequented any more—on their way home from the carnival, so he could get his gun cleaning kit. He'd laid it out on the small kitchen table downstairs in the cabin before going to bed, where it waited for him now.

Britt rolled onto her side, facing him, and pushed the comforter away from her shoulders where he'd just tucked it around her before he stood up, looking for his pants and shirt in the dark.

"I thought we already cleaned your gun last night," she said, sleepily. "Several times."

Kearnes found his jeans on the floor in a tangled mess, his shorts knotted and twisted inside one pant leg. He sat on the edge of the bed, facing away from her, trying to get them free.

"I meant my other gun," he said, gingerly plucking at the pair of white jockey shorts deep inside the pant leg, as if he were trying to remove a hook from the mouth of a fish. "The one I carry on duty."

"I thought you were doing your duty pretty darn good last night," she said, throwing the comforter off of her, and getting onto her knees behind him; letting one small, turgid nipple intentionally graze his shoulder blade as she did.

"Why in the world do all of you have to go do this shooting thing on a Sunday? And why so god awful early? I think it's horrible. And it should probably be illegal."

"Because Lieutenant Edgar Polk is an asshole," he said, "who seems to enjoy disrupting everyone on the department's lives by holding firearms qualifications twice a year on Sundays. And because he's the one currently in charge of the firearms training program; and I wasn't smart enough to take that away from him. Yet."

"Also," Kearnes added, "I hear that he wants to show me up somehow today…that's why he's scheduled the shoot a month early. He's supposedly an excellent shot, too. I'd say I am only about average, I guess, when it comes to hitting paper targets."

"Come back to bed," said Britt, encircling his bare waist with her arms.

"I can't," apologized Kearnes, in more ways than one. "I've got to get some coffee in me, and get started."

"Oh, shoot," pouted Britt; wanting to play now; both with her words, and with him.

"That's the general idea," said Kearnes, popping the pair of Jockey's free at last from the jeans and hurrying to get them untwisted, and on, before she discovered what it was she had already done to him.

But her wandering hands found him first; her fingers closing around him, clamping down on him, moving both her hands up and down now over his pulsing hardness in a steady, rhythmic, milking action…and within seconds he began to groan.

"Oh…what's this?" she asked innocently. "Your cleaning rod?"

"Britt…stop…please," he pleaded; but she only pumped him harder, faster.

He tried to stand but she reached one arm around his neck and pulled him backwards down onto the bed, keeping her free hand tightly gripped around the throbbing protrusion below his waist. And he didn't resist her…he couldn't. There was a small touch lamp on a night stand on Kearnes' side of the bed, and with her leg, Britt reached toward it, bumping its motion sensitive base with her big toe, suddenly diffusing the room in the soft glow of its forty watt bulb.

She grabbed onto him with both hands again, and using his hardness like the horn of a saddle, faced toward his feet and swung her leg up over his head; then opened herself wide to him as she hovered in the air above his face. He felt her take him inside her mouth and he reached up and spread her slender buttocks apart, then thrust his tongue deeply up inside her, feeling her body shudder, and he heard her emit a muffled groan.

Britt could feel him beginning to well up beneath her fingers, a river of molten lava rushing up through a crack in the earth, seeking a point of release. The now involuntary thrusting of his hips was increasing in intensity and urgency, and she knew he was going to explode inside her mouth any second. She eased him out of her and rolled off the bed, onto the floor, standing in front of him now, panting, the red blush of desire spreading blotchily across her chest and the taut nipples of her breasts like a scarlet fever.

"Do you want it from behind?" she asked him.

"Yes," he rasped.

"I know you like that," she said.

She climbed back onto the bed and laid on her stomach, then brought her knees up sharply underneath her chest, so her buttocks were thrust upward and outward.

When she was in position he came behind her and placed a hand on either side of her hips, holding onto her lightly. He eased forward and just barely made contact with her; then held himself still.

Gazing down at her wondrous beauty and the absolute miracle of her body, so open to him now beneath him, no fear in the world existed for him at that moment. And for the first time in his life, Kevin Kearnes knew what it was like to feel the weight of nothing.

"Are you ready for this?" he asked her softly, pushing forward ever so slightly.

"Yes," she gasped.

"Yes, yes…"

And when it was finished, when they were through, they lay in each other's arms in a broken heap on the bed; like things that had been borne toward land on a rough and storming sea, and then tossed upon the rocks of the shore.

Kearnes played with a damp tangle of her hair, gently twisting the end to see if it would form into a curl, and stay like that. Britt had her ear buried against his chest hair, listening to the reassuring thump of his heart, while she let her hand wander below his navel to cup the warm, round, firmness she found there.

Long moments of silence passed before Kearnes finally broke their spell, and spoke to her.

"It's Ethan," he said. "He's the oldest of my two sons…and he's ten now. Almost eleven."

Britt lifted her head from his chest and stared at him momentarily, as if maybe she wasn't sure what it even was he was talking about.

"You asked me last night. At the carnival," he said.

"Oh," was all she said.

"*Oh.*"

CHAPTER 21

▼

Kearnes poured himself a cup of coffee and sat down at the kitchen table. He set the coffee cup away from the Colt .38 Super that he'd already laid out on some old newspapers; to catch the oil and solvent from the cleaning. He removed the gun's magazine and shucked out the nine gleaming, high velocity brass cartridges from inside it, and lined them up in a row on the table, standing on their bases, their odd looking, Space Shuttle shaped bullets pointing upward toward the bedroom loft of the cabin where Britt was sound asleep and snoring softly again.

Sharply, he pulled the blue steel slide of the gun rearward and the round from the chamber went flying. He locked the slide open and set the gun down while he retrieved the round from the carpeted floor, putting it on the table next to the others. He opened the hard plastic cleaning kit box and took out two small bottles; one containing gun cleaning solvent, and the other, gun oil. He screwed a slotted plastic tip into the end of the short aluminum cleaning rod, and holding it by its black plastic handle, pulled a cotton cleaning patch tightly into the slotted tip.

Picking the gun up and releasing the slide again, he let it go forward all the way into "battery", then moved it back slightly about one quarter of an inch while at the same time pushing down on the recoil spring plug located just below the muzzle, then rotated the barrel bushing clockwise about one quarter of a turn. His practiced fingers moved deftly across the surfaces of the weapon, and in a few more seconds the Colt lay on the table in front of him, disassembled into its major component parts, ready for cleaning.

While he cleaned the gun he thought about the picture that hung in the squad room of the Dodge City, Kansas police department. It was a reprint from an old photograph, taken in 1883, of the Dodge City Peace Commission, and it had been put there in 1957 by his uncle, Ben Kearnes, two years after he'd been hired on D.C.P.D. as a young patrolman fresh off his family's wheat ranch just outside of town.

Nearly every day of his working career on the Dodge City force, Kevin Kearnes had stopped and stared at that old photograph of the eight stoic, and steely eyed lawmen dressed men in black frock coats and black hats, except for two of them. Charles E. Basset had chosen to wear that day, instead. a butternut colored duster over his white shirt; but with a black hat. While Luke Short had sported a black jacket, topped by a cream colored, flat, broad brimmed hat.

The men in the picture were posed in two rows, with a fake painted scene of the Roman Coliseum in the background, as was the practice in photographic studios of that era. In the front row, seated from left to right, were Charles E. Basset, Wyatt S. Earp, Frank McLain, and Neil Brown. And in the back row, standing, from left to right; W.H. Harris, Luke Short, William B. "Bat" Masterson, and William "Bill" Tilghman.

Formally organized as a town in August of 1872 and named Buffalo City, until it was discovered another town was using that same name, the settlement was quickly renamed Dodge City, after the nearby military installation of Fort Dodge, and by September of that same year the shiny steel rails of the newly formed Atchison, Topeka, and Santa Fe Railroad had stretched into view.

By the year 1876 the population of Dodge had swelled to 1,200 souls, and there were nineteen businesses within its city limits that were licensed to sell liquor. And soon, Dodge City had become the buffalo hunting capital of the west.

From the years 1872 to 1878 an estimated one million five hundred thousands buffalo hides were shipped from Dodge to points east. The reeking hides, sometimes stacked along the railroad tracks in town higher than a one story building while they awaited shipment out, coined the original term "stinker", which is a part of our American vernacular to this day.

By 1875 the buffalo, as a source of revenue, were largely gone, and on the verge of nearly complete annihilation; but longhorn cattle driven from Texas arrived, and Dodge City flared up like a wind driven prairie fire.

The first city jail—a fifteen foot hole dug in the ground into which drunken and unruly miners and buffalo hunters were lowered by a rope, until they sobered up—was soon replaced by a wood building with iron bars on its doors and windows. Shootings in the streets and saloons between cowboys, soldiers, and buffalo hunters were quite common, day and night, and a hasty place to warehouse the aftermath of such violence—in which men usually died with their boots on—needed to be found by the city. So a local burial place, Boot Hill Cemetery, was quickly plotted on city land.

At its zenith of violence, when it had become known far and wide across the nation as "the wickedest town in the west," the city Father's of Dodge passed an ordinance prohibiting guns from being carried north of the "deadline", which was the railroad tracks; dividing the community into two distinct districts with two separate streets, each, named Front Street. The north side of town was reserved for respectable folks and their families, and businesses. But the south side, where "anything went," remained wide open.

But eventually law and order came riding into Dodge City, along with all that trouble, in the form of men like Wyatt Earp and Charlie Basset; Ham Bell, Bill Tilghman, and Bat Masterson. And as far as Kevin Kearnes was concerned, you could add the name Ben Kearnes to that list, too…only just a little farther along in the history books.

Although Kearnes grew up idolizing his Father's younger brother, Ben, there were memories of times spent with his dad he still cherished too.

Pitching horseshoes with him in the back yard on hot summer Sunday afternoon's after church. Going to the stock shows with him in Topeka and Wichita. And the time he scooped his little family up in the middle of a heat searing summer drought that all but destroyed their wheat crop, borrowed Ben's camp trailer, and drove them out of Kansas and across the country to the blue Pacific ocean; to try and get his Mother to stop crying and not think of how they were now going to survive until next year's harvest season.

But his dad had been a two legged work horse, enslaved to their land and the do or die living he forced from it year after year. Up before dawn every morning and out in the fields, or the machine shop, and in bed and wearily asleep most evenings before the sun had fully set.

Until one late summer day, when Kevin was fourteen, and they had found his Father; slumped over behind the wheel of their old grain truck at a neighbor's silo where he had gone to help with the harvest, but hadn't come in for lunch at noon with all the others…so the neighbor had gone looking for him. After his dad had passed away, it was Ben who had taken care of him, and his Mother and his sister, and who had eventually retired from the police department and the job he loved, in order to care for them and work the ranch.

He finished cleaning the Colt, reassembled it, and buffed its exterior with a soft flannel cloth until he could almost see his image reflecting back at him from the glossy blue steel of its slide. Ben had sent the gun back to the Colt factory twice over the years to have it re-blued from the holster wear it had suffered, and it looked more than brand new.

He rubbed his thumb across the smooth ivory grips, feeling the outline of the silver initials cut into the outside one; **"B.L.K"**. Benjamin Lincoln Kearnes.

In the course of his long career as a lawman, Ben Kearnes had killed two men in the line of duty with this weapon; both of them highly deserving of it. One man, Ben had interrupted in the act of robbing a gas station with a pistol; and the other, engaged in trying to beat to death a woman with a tire iron in the back parking lot of a downtown honky tonk.

He had asked Ben once why it was he had hung that old photograph in the police department's squad room, and Ben had answered: "Because those were the kind of men, I aspired to be like."

And Ben had gone on in his career and in his life to do just that, and much more. Keeping the family ranch going, taking good care of his brother's wife and kids, and teaching young Kevin how to hunt, and shoot; how to work hard in life to get what is was that you wanted, and how, when it was absolutely necessary, and only then…"to fight the devil with fire."

Kearnes wondered what his uncle would think of some of the so called "lawmen" in the Cutter Point police department; like Polk, and Downs and Curt LaMar, with their aberrated personalities, overblown egos, and woefully missing sense of honor, ethics, and integrity. *Probably not as much as a plugged nickel*, he imagined hearing him say.

He left Britt a note and drew her a crude map of how to get to the Range, as she had requested, and placed it on top of her empty and waiting coffee cup next to the coffee maker; then loaded the Colt back up, snugged it into the holster of his duty belt, and grabbed the two boxes of ammunition from the kitchen table which he had also brought with him from his apartment.

He closed the cabin door behind him quietly, making sure it was locked, and walked down the trail in the early morning mist to where he'd left his truck in the parking lot of The Sand Dollar.

The sound of the wind driven waves, drubbing against the giant boulders of the close by jetty at Pearl Cove like liquid thunder, was ominous, and unsettling to him.

And he knew at that moment, without a doubt, that he was on his way to fight the devil…but with his own brand of fire.

CHAPTER 22

▼

Russell Massey swaggered up and down in front of the next six shooters on line at the firing range, shouting garbled and nearly indistinguishable commands through his electronic hand held megaphone. For Russell, this was one of only two days every year in the Cutter Point Police Department when he could feel like a "somebody" again, and actually have a modicum of power and control, as he directed the semi-annual firearms qualifications for the entire force as the Range Master.

Russell had started out some years ago on the department as a patrolman, but various acts of misconduct and ineptness on the job, coupled with the fact that he was, when you got right down to it, a real jerk, through and through, eventually began to move him on a downwardly mobile scale towards termination.

But his best friend, and old high school buddy, was Delbert Downs. So a place for Russell was found in the Dispatch Center—still wearing a C.P.P.D. badge but minus his gun—where he occupied enough chair space for enough time to outlast many of the other, mostly female staff of Dispatchers; some of whom he personally drove out with his boorish behavior on the job, and chronic lack of personal hygiene…resulting in several sexual harassment suits and stress claims filed because of him against the city over the years.

Russell was eventually promoted to Lead Dispatcher, by default, of course; but that wasn't good enough for him. He missed being out on the streets; missed bullying, cajoling, and intimidating people…not that he didn't get to do some of that in the Dispatch Center whenever he wanted to. But mostly he missed carrying his gun.

So he had pleaded his case to his friend and immediate supervisor, Delbert "Downs Syndrome" Downs (he liked calling Delbert that, but only behind his back), who in turn talked to his supervisor, Lieutenant Edgar Polk.

And because they both agreed that Russell was somewhat of a valuable commodity, in that Russell could pretty much harass and destroy any bitch Dispatcher at work they didn't like, or wanted off the department entirely, and could take up the slack for Delbert when he had already done pretty much the same thing with one of the targeted women, but had already pushed things to the limit; they put their inbred heads together like two Siamese twins working off of only one brain, and came up with a brilliant solution. They would send Russell Massey, the worst shot on the department, to Firearms Instructor School, and swear him in as a Reserve police officer, so he could legally pack a handgun again.

"Okay gentleman!" Massey blared through his megaphone, "we have one round of qualifications to go, and then we will have annual prize competition match for one day off with pay, as authorized by the chief!"

"What's that about?" Kearnes asked Thud, who had finished qualifying with his Glock and was packing his range bag to go home. "I don't remember authorizing anything like that."

"You didn't," said Thud. "It's something we've done for years. Supposed to be a morale builder for the troops, but Polk always takes top score. Imagine that. Since he's the one that got it authorized, about five chiefs back before you ever got the job."

"No one has ever beaten him?"

"No. Spenser nearly cleaned his clock last year when they tied…both with a 90. But Polk took him in a shoot off with a 96. Spenser ended up with a 95. At least that's how Massey scored it. The prick."

"Shooters to the line!" announced Massey, and Thud and Kearnes both quickly put their "ears" and "eyes" on; the sound deadening padded ear muffs and clear plastic goggles all personnel were required to wear on the range when it was "hot"; when weapons were about to be discharged.

"Ready on the left! Ready on the right!" Massey called out. "Commence firing!"

The row of off duty officers, clad in jeans or cut off shorts and tee shirts but, wearing their full duty gun belts, dropped down to their right knees in unison behind the large plastic barrels in front of them, which were there to simulate some sort of hard object they had taken cover behind in the imaginary gunfight. They drew their weapons and peeked out around one side of their barrels, and began popping rounds twenty five yards down range at the B-27 black silhouette paper combat targets stapled on large rectangles of plywood.

Massey clicked a button on the digital stopwatch he held in his hand, and then shrilled long and hard into the chrome steel whistle he had clamped between teeth, signaling everyone to stop shooting. He spit the whistle out, letting it drop on its cord which he wore around his neck, and screamed into the megaphone, "Time! Reload your magazines, and make ready!"

Kearnes removed his hearing protectors during the lull in the shooting, while Thud ripped his own from his head, and threw them down on the range table they were standing next to inside the open range shed.

"Who the fuck does he think he is?" said Thud. "General Patton? I'm telling you chief, something's got to be done about this guy. The officers have zero confidence in him. And what other department in the *real world*, has a goddamned dispatcher for their firearms instructor?"

"I agree," said Kearnes. "I'm glad I'm getting to see this today, for myself. Don't worry; we'll change it."

"I think Spenser Sparling would make an excellent Range Master," said Thud. "He's a very level headed kid…and boy can he ever shoot."

"You're not bad yourself," Thud. "Have you ever had an interest in instructing?"

"Naw," said Thud. "I've got plenty to do already, what with all my cases, and trying to keep track of the Hardy Boys on their bikes all summer. Give it to one of the young Turks in the department. We've got to try and keep at least some quality officers here."

"Shooter's…ready!" came the command from Massey, and Thud and Kearnes put their ears back on. "Commence firing!" The last six officers dropped to their knees on the line again, but this time the opposite knee, and fired from their make believe cover, the muffled pop, pop, pop of the .40 caliber Glocks, and one 9mm Beretta sounding like caps pistols through the thick, foam latex walls of the hearing protectors.

Two hours had passed since Kearnes had arrived at the range, and every sworn member of the police department, including reserves, had all qualified with the Remington 12 gauge shotgun, The Ruger Mini-14 Government Model .223 patrol rifle, and either their department issued, or their personally owned, hand guns. But there was still no sign of Britt yet. Then in a crowd of people in the parking lot, of what appeared to be mostly women and kids from different officer's families, he saw her standing next to Margie Compton and her two girls.

Shoshanna Perry was nearby them with two adorable little boys clinging to the pockets of her jeans, while she talked with Spenser Sparling.

"Come on," Kearnes said to Thud. "Let's go talk to the ladies for a minute."

Thud stuffed his gunbelt into his range bag and followed Kearnes.

"How did you do cowboy?" Britt asked Kearnes as he walked up to her. "And did you get that gun of yours cleaned OK this morning?" Margie raised her eyebrows at hearing that one.

"I got it cleaned just fine," said Kearnes, "thank you."

"Sorry I didn't get here earlier…but for some reason, I just couldn't get out of bed." She came forward to meet him, and gave him a peck on the lips.

"Well, we both qualified," said Kearnes. "Thud even kicked my butt by a couple of points, I think."

"What did you shoot, Thud?" asked Margie.

"A 94," said Thud. "Chief shot a 92 though, so I wouldn't exactly say I kicked his butt."

"I didn't know this was a family event," said Kearnes, looking around at even more cars pulling into the firearms range parking lot now.

"It's not, really," said Margie. "But the wives and kids like to come out once a year to see their guys shoot for the free day off. Thud nearly won it last year, didn't you honey."

"No," said Thud. "Spenser almost did."

"Yes, but I said *nearly*. It was so exciting, and the girls were so proud of their daddy!"

"Well *nearly* doesn't cut it!" Thud snapped at her. "I'm not sticking around for this crap. I've got some research to do today."

"Thud Compton! You were on that computer until two a.m. this morning!"

Thud ignored her and turned to Kearnes. "Chief, I went online last night, and found out there are over two hundred wineries in this state. Something like two hundred and sixteen, or eighteen…something like that. And starting tomorrow morning I am going to call every single one of them. I could really use some help with this case, and I was wondering if you might be able to give me Spenser Sparling for a couple of weeks, to help out."

Before Kearnes could answer him, Russell Massey's voice came over the range's public address system, and unfortunately, it was clear as a bell this time.

"I have the results of the top four scorer's who will compete in this year's chief's paid day off, shoot off! They are, in order of current score…Lieutenant Edgar Polk, Sergeant Thud Compton, Chief Kearnes, and Officer Spenser Sparling. Gentleman, please make your way to the fifty yard line now!"

"Oooh!" squealed Margie. "You're a finalist, honey!

"I don't want to do it," said Thud, sullenly. "It's bullshit. I'm going home."

He started to walk away but Margie blocked his path, the fiery red color rising in her cheeks beginning to match closely the same shade of color as her Irish red hair.

"If anyone in this police department needs a free day off," she said evenly, "it's *you*, thud Compton."

"Besides, if you win, you can take the day off when the girls are back in school in September. I've got plenty of things for you to do around the house…we can start in the bedroom, and work our way to the other rooms from there."

Thud stared at her for a moment, not comprehending what it was that he needed to fix at home in their bedroom, and then it hit him; and he began to blush heavily.

"Come on Thud," Kearnes said, "it'll be fun."

"And besides, I don't want to get shown up out there by the Lieutenant, all by myself."

The course of fire for the standard P.P.C., or police pistol combat course, was a total of fifty rounds fired at different ranges and in different positions; all of it timed. It started at the three yard line, where the officer just basically drew his weapon as fast as he or she could, and from the hip, thrusting the muzzle of the gun forward almost point blank at the target, fired three rounds as fast as they could pull the trigger.

It progressed from there back to the seven yard line, then the fifteen, then the twenty five; requiring the participants, along the way, to shoot standing and kneeling, strong hand and weak hand, and to reload their pistol magazines or revolver cylinders swiftly when their guns ran dry in order not to run out of time.

Inside the black, man shaped silhouette of the B-27 target was a series of printed oval, concentric, and ever widening rings, which were marked "7" on the outermost ring, followed by "8", "9", and "10"; and then the innermost ring, the exact center of the target, which was marked with an "X". A hit in the "X", 10, 9, or 8 rings scored as a five. A hit in the 7 ring, scored four points. And any other hits outside those rings, but still somewhere in the black silhouette, scored as three points. An officer had to score a cumulative total of 70 points, or they failed the course.

But in the interest of saving time, and expense to the department for the cost of the extra ammunition, the "shoot off" was an entirely different proposition. The contestants would stand at the fifty yard line, an almost unreal distance to accurately shoot with a handgun, and on the command, would draw their weapons and fire seven shots in ten seconds at the now tiny B-27 target downrange. The shooter with the highest total point score would win, even though the scores, overall, were expected to be lower due to the extreme range.

The crowd of civilian family members moved toward the shooting lanes on the range, queuing up behind a large sign bolted to a wooden post in the ground which read, "LAW ENFORCEMENT ONLY BEYOND THIS POINT." Twenty five beyond the sign, Edgar Polk, Thud Compton, Spenser Sparling, and Kearnes readied their weapons in their individual shooting lanes on the line.

From the group of cops who were standing off to their right outside of the range shed, watching, Kearnes heard someone yell, "Hey! If it isn't Marshal Dillon! From Dodge City!"

He turned and looked in their direction, and saw Downs Syndrome and Curt LaMar, The Drug Czar, scowling back at him. Standing next to Downs Syndrome was a teenaged male with orange and purple spiked hair and a black metal stud punched through one nostril, whose dull, banal expression and narrow slits for eyes made him look like the banjo playing kid in the movie *Deliverance*.

He was pretty sure it was this kid who'd made the comment, although he seriously doubted if he even knew who Marshal Matt Dillon was, from the old television show *Gunsmoke*. The kid bore an uncanny resemblance to Downs Syndrome, and if this was his son, then Delbert Downs had obviously told him what to say.

But instead of replying to either Downs, or the kid, Kearnes looked directly at Curt LaMar, whose head was partially obscured in a hazy blue cloud of cigarette smoke, and said, "Hey there detective! Did you get those new fish yet?" LaMar choked on his Marlboro at this, and flicked it to the ground, showing his disdain for Kearnes' comment. But it was no great loss; he'd already smoked it down to a nub anyhow, and quickly took the pack from his shirt pocket and fired up another one.

"Are you ready?" shouted Russell Massey, this time without his electronic megaphone, since he was standing right behind all four of them. The four men on the line nodded. "Holster your weapons…and at the command, draw and fire, from the standing position, seven rounds in ten seconds!" Edgar Polk snapped his Glock into his holster next to Kearnes; then, without looking at him, Kearnes barely heard him say through his hearing protectors, "Good luck. *Chief*. You're gonna' need it."

"Commence!" yelled Massey, then blew a long, shrill note on his whistle for extra effect, and all four men drew their guns and began firing.

After the last shot from the group, which was Thud's, Massey blew his whistle a millisecond later, and then shouted, "Cease Fire! Holster an empty weapon, and remain in place!" He jogged downrange to the targets where he spent a few minutes carefully marking the bullet holes with a piece of white chalk, and recording the shooter's scores on his clipboard. Then he stapled up three new targets and returned to the group with their used targets, and their results.

"Okay, listen up!" he said, reading from the clipboard. "Sergeant Compton...an 86! Officer Sparling...an 88! And Lieutenant Polk...and the chief...both tied, with a 90! In the event of a tie score, between two of a total three contestants, the third, lower scoring shooter, will remain in the match for another round. Shooter's to the line, and reload!"

"Good shooting, Thud," said Kearnes.

"Yeah, thanks," said Thud, rolling up his target. "I'll stick around until this is over. Something's not right here, chief."

The three men shot the second match, with Kearnes and Polk, again, both scoring a 90, and Spenser being eliminated with an 87. In the third match Kearnes shot a 92...and so did Edgar Polk. While a five minute break was called before the start of match number three, Thud left and went to his unmarked detective car in the parking lot, and returned to the range shed with a pair of binoculars.

When Massey summoned the men back to the line for the start of the third match, Thud Compton was watching hard downrange through the binoculars at the two fresh targets; then swung the binoculars lenses over to cover Polk's target only, as Massey gave the command to begin shooting.

At the sounds of the guns being discharged, Thud saw the unmistakable geysers of dirt being kicked up by the bullets from Edgar Polk's gun. But they were hitting the soft dirt not directly behind the plywood backing of the silhouette target, but two and three feet to the left of it.

Then Thud watched as Massey jogged out to the target to score them, and saw him take an empty .40 caliber brass shell casing from his pocket, the same caliber handgun that Edgar Polk carried, and using the expended cartridge like a miniature cookie cutter, punched seven neat holes in and around the "X" ring of Polk's target. "Oh...you son of a bitch!" raged Thud, dropping the binoculars onto the range shed table and running out toward the firing line.

Russell Massey was only half way back to the firing line, waving his clipboard excitedly above his head, shouting, "We've got a winner! Lieutenant Polk, with a perfect 100 points!" when Thud Compton plowed into him, knocking him down on the grass.

"What the fuck!" yelled Massey, as Thud pounced on him, and started going into his pockets.

Kearnes and Polk ran over to the melee, and Kearnes grabbed Thud by the shoulder. "Thud!" he shouted at him, "Get off him!"

"What the hell is wrong with you, Compton!" roared Edgar Polk...and Thud immediately let go of Russell Massey, lurched to his feet, and grabbed Edgar Polk by the shirt collar.

"You lying, cheating, ASSHOLES!" screamed Thud. Russell Massey scrambled to his feet, leaving the two paper targets and his clipboard on the ground, and ran for the nearby safety of the range shed.

Kearnes leapt onto Thud's back and got his arm around his massive, bull dog like neck in a choke hold, and tried to pull him away from Polk, but it was no use. Thud bulled his way forward, dragging Kearnes along with him, his huge hands now squeezing the shirt collar tightly around Polk's Adam's apple while he repeatedly screamed at Polk, "I saw what you did! I fucking SAW, what you did!"

The group of officers standing at the range shed—except for Delbert Downs and Curt LaMar—ran to help Kearnes, and dog piled the enraged Thud Compton; freeing Polk, who lurched away toward his friends Downs, and LaMar, and Massey, coughing and wheezing.

Kearnes knelt on the ground next to Thud. "What the hell did you do that for?" he asked him.

"They cheated," said Thud. "I saw the whole thing through my binoculars. Polk was throwing his shots into the dirt, next to his target...and Massey punched bullet holes in his target for him. With a shell casing. Go look for it Spenser! He probably dropped it right there somewhere in the grass, beneath his target backing!"

Spenser got up warily from his place on top of the pile of officers still pinning Thud to the ground, and began to walk out on the range in the direction of Edgar Polk's target backing.

"Watch out! Get back please! That's my husband...LET HIM UP!" Margie Compton pushed and shoved her way through the human net of police that had been thrown over Thud, and who were only more than happy to get out of her way now, if she was going to be anything like her husband was.

She landed on top of him, sobbing, covering his big, square, crew cut head and face with kisses. "Oh baby, I am so sorry...so, so sorry!" she said, hugging him. Kearnes stood up and saw Britt standing dutifully behind the law enforcement only sign with the other family members, a look of concern on her face, while she held the hands of Sarah and Selena who, like their Mother, were also sobbing now.

Margie and Kearnes helped Thud to his feet, just as Polk, Downs, LaMar, and Massey approached as a group. "Chief Kearnes," Edgar Polk said formally, "I am advising you that I will be referring charges against Sergeant Compton to the Cutter County District Attorney's office tomorrow, for fourth degree assault; against myself, and against Senior Lead Dispatcher Massey."

"And all of you here," Polk continued, raising his voice so even the people standing behind the sign could clearly hear him, "are witnesses to what just happened!"

Kearnes motioned for Margie to take Thud out of the area. She took his hand and led him toward Britt and their kids, and Thud did not hesitate to follow her.

"Well let me ask you something, Lieutenant. What did just happen here this morning? There seems to be some question about a possible impropriety in the way this match was…conducted?"

"That's bullshit!" said Russell Massey, picking both targets up from the ground and holding them up to the group. "What I mean to say, sir…is that Sergeant Compton is full of it, sir."

"Here's the Lieutenant's last target, a perfect score. All seven hits right in the "X" ring. And here's yours…a 98, sir. You even came up one point! And that's damned good shooting in anybody's book, especially from fifty yards. But the Lieutenant wins the day off…fair and square."

"Chief!"

Everyone turned their eyes downrange, to the target stands fifty yards away. It was Spenser, and he was holding up something small in one hand out in front of him, as he walked quickly back toward them. As he got closer, Kearnes could see that Spenser was holding an ink pen, just like the ones he carried at work in the sewn in pen holder of his uniform shirt pocket. And on the tip of the pen, cocked at a slight angle, was an empty .40 caliber brass cartridge casing.

"That doesn't prove anything!" cried Massey, staring transfixed at the shell casing; horrified that he could have been so stupid, or that anyone could have been so smart, as to find it right where he'd dropped it after it was no longer going to be of any use.

"It does if it has your fingerprints on it," Spenser said.

"Shut up, Massey!" barked Polk. Delbert Downs started to say something too, but Polk elbowed him in the ribs to be quiet.

"I'll take that off your hands, Officer Sparling," Kearnes said, reaching for the pen, which Spenser handed to him. Kearnes opened his last half full box of .38

Super's, and shook the .40 caliber casing off the pen, and into the ammunition box without touching it. He handed Spenser back his pen.

"I have a suggestion, Lieutenant Polk," Kearnes said, the huddle of police officers and their family members nearby so quiet now, that he wondered if any of them were even still breathing. "Let's both think about what happened here today. All of it. And tomorrow, you do what you feel you have to do. And if you do…then so will I."

"In the meantime," Kearnes said, "congratulations on your win; that was some excellent marksmanship. I don't know that I've ever seen a perfect hundred score shot more than once or twice before in my life." Then Kearnes extended his hand to Edgar Polk, and dumbfounded, Edgar Polk shook it.

"The only thing I can attribute my second place shooting to today, other then my general lack of skill, is the possibility that the sights on my gun may have gotten bumped in the move out here from Kansas. Might have knocked them off a little."

Kearnes walked over to the dumpster next to the range shed and opened its top. In addition to the small amount of genuine refuse generated by the shooting range itself, people from town liked to contribute their garbage here too, only minus the garbage collection fees the city charged. He rooted around in the top layer of garbage a little, until he found a steel V-8 Vegetable Juice can, the same size, and shape, and weight of the old Hi-C fruit juice cans Ben had taught him with.

Everybody watched as Kearnes upended the can and dribbled out a little of the remaining juice, then walked back to the line where Spenser was still standing.

"Here," he said to Spenser, "toss that out there about twenty feet, and let's just see how far off these sights really are."

Spenser took the can from Kearnes, looked ahead of him, then looked back at Kearnes, unsure what this was all about.

"Go ahead Officer Sparling," said Kearnes. "Toss it."

Spenser wound the can up, like an underhand softball pitch, and sent the can out into the air in front of him in a climbing arc, and from the corner of his right eye he saw the chief's arm flash out, as a blur of blue steel and white ivory streaked from his holster and the Colt went off with an ear splitting *Boom!*

The bullet caught the can in mid-flight, dead center, and spun it, cart wheeling end over end, and the second it touched the ground some twenty five feet away, Kearnes shot it again, and it jumped two feet into the air and a few feet further away from him.

He advanced on the can as if it were an armed human adversary, never giving it a chance of escape. His body was turned to side profile, the Colt extended at arm's length in front of him straight out from his shoulder, and as he walked steadily forward, firing, he hit the steel can with each successive shot, making it jump into the air ahead of him, or bounce to the left, or right, as he came on, discharging the remaining eight shots…never missing the can once.

And then the Colt was finally empty, the slide having locked back, with hot smoke curling up from the exposed interior of its chamber, and from out of its gaping black muzzle. Kearnes stood there, holding the smoking gun in his hand, down at his side now, as the last echo of his last shot rolled back from thickly forested mountains that ringed the shooting range in the rural countryside a few miles from Cutter Point.

The whole thing had lasted only about five seconds, or less, and since no one in the group had been given any warning first, and therefore didn't have their hearing protectors on, many of them just stood there, still clasping their hands around their ears, with their mouths open…awestruck at what they had just seen.

"Oh my God," breathed Spenser, barely able to comprehend what he'd just seen happen right next to him…or at least thought he'd seen, with his own two eyes. "That was Old West style! Just like some of the old time gunfighters used to be able to do!"

Frick and Frack were the first to snap out of it and break ranks from within the cluster of mesmerized police officers, as they raced each other out onto the green grass of the range to get the can.

"Holy shit!" yelled Frick, holding up the perforated, mangled can for everyone to see. It rattled inside with tiny pieces of fragmented copper from the exploding bullet jackets.

"Chief, can we have this!" Frack shouted, pointing to the can. "For a souvenir?"

Kearnes released the slide on the Colt and put it back in his holster, still hot. He gathered his gear up from the line, and put it in his range bag, then walked over to where Margie and Thud, and Britt and the girls, were standing…with dumbfounded looks on their faces.

"I guess my sights weren't off…after all," he said.

All of the officers still present on the range, except for Polk and his crew, had gathered in a tight knot around Frick and Frack, wanting to get a look at the can; to try and count the holes, in and out of it…to just touch it.

Kearnes saw Polk say something to Downs Syndrome; then Downs Syndrome laughed, and so did that kid who was with him. But as he walked away with Britt toward their vehicles in the parking lot, he glanced back over his shoulder, and saw Polk glaring at him with pure, unmitigated hatred.

The man looked absolutely evil; almost like the Devil himself.

Like the Devil who had just been burned...at his own game.

CHAPTER 23

▼

The only thing that Uriah Daniel Beek had ever wanted to be in his life, was a brilliantly shining mirror, reflecting back to the world the glory of God almighty, Jehovah. But unlike his namesake Uriah the Hittite in the Bible, betrayed by his King, David, and sent to the front of the line of battle so that he would certainly be killed, and David could then have this faithful soldier's wife, Bathsheba, for himself; Uriah Beek had recognized the treachery of the world for what it was...and before it was too late.

He could see now that the mistakes of his youth, spent on the self centered pursuit of his own sinful and carnal pleasures, and revenge against, and at, the expense of other boys, were only a prelude to the Revelation of what was be shown to him now in his later years as a man. As a child he had been an ugly little boy because of his huge nose, and the other children in school had teased and tormented him relentlessly, using his initials, U.D., and his last name, to make up a horrible childish chant: "U.D. Beek! U.D. Beek!"...which quickly evolved into "You Da Beek, Danny! Hey...You Da Beek!"

But in a few years he grew into his nose, and a handsome face and the strong body he developed to go along with it, and some of those same, bullying boys hadn't thought it was so funny when he'd had them down on the ground in the thick grass of the sand dunes, sticking that same nose up into the crack of their ass, and threatening to kill them if they ever told.

Now he understood that had only been a period of apprenticeship which he'd been called upon to serve, in order to someday become the true Messenger of God Jehovah he'd always wished to be. And that it had, ultimately, sanctified him as a teacher of adolescent boys on the dangers all females posed, girls and women alike, within whom the innate Spirit of Jezebel dwelled like a dormant cancer.

The killings he had committed of the two young boys on the coast—one with a religious symbol of false doctrine which he had cut from the first boy's ear, using his vineyard knife, and the other, ritualistically and authentically crucified in the same, historically accurate manner as Jesus had been—were meant to send a message, both to all boys, and the non-believing world at large: That original sin—which had been spawned in The Garden by the deceit and disobedience of Eve—was still alive, and well, and flourishing today. And even though the end times were fast approaching, it was still the duty of *men* to put a stop to it.

But apparently the only message that had gotten through to the world so far was that he was a common killer…The Cross Killer, as the newspapers were now referring to him.

And Uriah Beek was enraged over it.

He had methodically loaded his Van yesterday, on Saturday, one day earlier than usual, in preparation for his two week long sales route trip, which he was nearly already a week late in starting.

Carefully, he'd arranged his boxes of product all to the left as far as he could, leaving an open space on the right side of the Van's steel ribbed floor two feet in width, and which ran the length of the floor all the way to the front passenger seat.

At the end of the stack of boxes, and closest to the rear doors, he'd placed the final cardboard shipping box marked *Made in China…LBW-ST/QTY.12DZ*. When he was finished with the packing he had set the now half empty box of Trellistrips, the clam shovel, and two large folded plastic tarps in the open floor space he'd created. And on top of the tarps he placed the long, white, hard plastic insulated cooler he had purchased; the kind local sports fisherman used for tuna fishing.

From a kitchen cupboard he had taken two bottles of the Pinot Noir he had vinted three years ago, from the grapes in his small vineyard in the field behind his house. He found a greasy cotton towel in the garage where he'd been working, and wrapped the unlabeled, dusty bottles inside it, then placed them in the console of the Van. This was for the desk clerk at The Sand Dollar, who liked to drink. Just in case Room 144 wasn't available when he arrived there, and he had to bribe the man to get it.

His own small home town of Long Beach, Washington had been crammed with tourists downtown and on the beaches that Saturday afternoon as the town held its own three day Fourth of July Celebration, and as he'd walked along crowded Pacific Avenue through these confused herds of milling sheep with fat wallets stuffed with traveler's checks, and digital cameras dangling on straps from their wrists, it had taken all the self-restraint he could gather to keep from snatching one of their lambs with smooth testicles from their midst.

He'd wandered into Marsh's Free Museum, a huge gift and curio shop downtown in an old wooden building that featured a two headed pig, a two headed snake, and Jake The Alligator Man in a glass case in the very back of the store—past the rows and rows of bins filled with sea shells, dried hermit crabs, and cheap plastic toys made in China. It was a place of magical oddities that drew kids to it—especially boys—like ants that are drawn to spilled sugar. But it was a business that he serviced, and one of his biggest customers, so he abruptly left when he noticed one of the sales clerks who knew him, staring at him.

And now it was Sunday morning, just before noon, the day after the Fourth of July. God's mandated day of rest for all men. But Beek had no time to rest today. He had spent the early morning hours of this day so far boarding up the windows of his old house with sheets of plywood, emptying all the food from the refrigerator and freezer into the garbage can he'd set out early by the curb; cutting the telephone and cable TV wires. He would be gone longer than usual this time...maybe this time, forever.

But he had one chore left to do. He went into the garage and emerged with the chain saw he'd used the cotton terry cloth towel to work on with yesterday; changing its oil, sharpening and lubricating its blade. He carried it around the side of the garage and into the small grape vineyard in the field behind the house...ripped at the starting cord once, twice, and the gas engine caught, and started up with a roar.

The Pinot grapes he so lovingly nurtured and tried to coax to a fully ripened sweetness in his spare time, usually only grew to stunted, sour, ball bearing sized hard lumps anyhow, in the sun deprived, cold salt air climate. And the wine he made from them was strong, and bitter tasting.

He walked deliberately down the vineyard rows, stooping to cut each five foot high cedar trellis post off at its base; mashing the purplish red clusters of grapes beneath his work boots that fell to the ground as he went. When he was finished, he cut the heavily twisted grape vines and their connecting wires from post to post with the chainsaw, and tossed the naked posts, fifty of them, into a pile.

He went to his Van, opened its back doors, and shoved three of the posts inside, next to the big white cooler; then went back to the pile and took three more posts, but sliced these exactly into halves with the saw. When he was done he put these pieces in the back of the Van too, and then locked its doors. If the world demanded the lie of dead little boys on crosses, then he would oblige, if that is what it took to finally reveal the truth.

He planned on leaving town by one o'clock, and his first stop would be in Seaside, Oregon, just an hour away.

Glutted with parents and their excited children roaming the two mile long paved Promenade that ran along the beach, or waiting in crowded lines at the Town Carousel, or milling around the art galleries, mini-malls, arcades, specialty boutiques, or antique shops; it would be easy to find another boy.

Then he would take his time the rest of week, skipping past half of his normal sales accounts as he made his way up the coast toward Cutter Point; and the only real mistake, he saw now, that he had ever made in the past. The one which God had spoken to him of over the weekend...urging him to go back, and correct.

He grabbed his jacket inside the house as he locked it up; and checked the pockets. The knife was still there, and so was the little blue whale. Uriah Beek's journey of salvation, and redemption, had begun.

And along the way, there was going to be hell to pay.

CHAPTER 24

▼

Because the Fourth of July had fallen on a Saturday, city management employees were awarded the following Monday as their holiday off, while other employees in the rank and file, like Thud Compton, and Spenser Sparling, worked their regular shifts and were paid double overtime holiday pay. But a special meeting of the Task Force investigating the murders had been scheduled for Monday at noon, and the FBI was coming to pay them a visit. So Kearnes put himself back on the schedule; letting Britt know he would use his Holiday day on Wednesday, to take her on a picnic to the beach as he'd promised her he would before the meeting had been set.

And overtime pay or not, Thud Compton would have been at his desk Monday morning anyway come hell or high water, and Officer Spenser Sparling right along with him, because they had places to call, and people to talk to. He knew many of the brass from some of the other agencies, with the exception of his own chief, would grumble about the short notice for the meeting given only the previous Friday…and on a long Holiday weekend, too…but he also knew they would all be in attendance. Politicians, even the ones with badges, couldn't afford to have any egg showing on their faces whether an omelet was ever made from a big case like this or not.

Kearnes had left a still sleeping Britt a note on the kitchen table again before he'd gone to work, telling her he was sorry that he couldn't meet her for lunch today, and to stay away from Bouchet′ Plaza at all costs. Expanding the joke, he'd suggested in the note that she call 911 if she felt herself weakening. She had asked him to take her on the picnic Monday in order to save her from "the Mother of all shopping sprees", which she said she had rapidly felt coming on after seeing all the long Holiday weekend sales advertised in the paper.

Like every woman, Britt McGraw loved to shop, and taking up residence in the cozy, but drably furnished summer beach cabin had so far sent her off to the Bouchet' Plaza Shopping Center on more than one buying safari to redecorate it.

Her first buying trip and purchase was the big white goose down comforter she'd bought for the bed at the Eddie Bauer Outlet store there, to guard against the surprisingly cold summer ocean nights; but that had only been the start. It was soon followed by junkets to Bath & Body Works, for things for the tiny standing room only bathroom, to Pfaltzgraff, to newly outfit the not much larger kitchen, and to the Liz Claiborne Outlet Store of course, strictly for herself. But she had assured Kearnes she wouldn't be going any further today than the Ray's supermarket by the bridge, to get the ingredients, and some instructions, she hoped, to try and bake him his favorite cookies...which were oatmeal raisin.

The luncheon meeting was held in the squad room of the police department, starting promptly at noon, and Kearnes had Spenser run across the highway to the Pizza Hut a half hour before it started and bring back an assortment of large pizzas, and individually packaged salads for those who were not pizza inclined.

After Thud, Brad Dekker, a detective from Lincoln county, and one of the detectives from the pair in Del Norte County—the bigger one with the cowboy boots—had gone over, with a fine tooth comb, everything they knew to date about the abduction and murder of Tyler Dunne, including the recent forensics report from the O.S.P. Crime Lab on the plastic ties used to bind him, and the similar murder of Ricky Cates, the meeting was turned over to S.A.C. Lloyd Rutledge of the Portland FBI Office. The Cavalry, Thud and many of the others were sure, who had just flown in on a chartered government Bell Jet Ranger helicopter to save them and their stalled investigations.

"Thank you, detectives," Rutledge said, addressing the group. "As you all know, the FBI is taking a look at these cases largely because of the suspected kidnapping of victim number two, Tyler Dunne."

Suspected kidnapping? What the hell did that mean? Thud thought to himself. Did this guy in the seven hundred and fifty dollar black silk Giorgenti suit, and perfectly knotted dark blue tie, with his private pilot keeping the helicopter's rotor blades turning and warmed up out at the airport, ready to whisk him back up the coast to Portland in forty five minutes...did he seriously think the Dunne boy willingly hopped a ride with the maniac who eventually killed him? And if Tyler had been lured away somehow from his home to his ultimate death, that was *still* kidnapping, wasn't it?

"But given the lack of evidence in these investigations thus far, I'm afraid the FBI is not going to be able to dedicate the resources to this case, that maybe some of you had been hoping for."

"Sir," Brad Dekker said. "Even the use of the FBI Crime Lab would be a big help to us here. The State Police are doing the best they can, but they're severely understaffed over there in the Central Point lab...and quite a bit back logged on other agencies cases, too.

Rutledge smiled at him benignly, as if he'd just found a maggot crawling out from under a piece of pepperoni on the second slice of pizza on his plate, which he hadn't touched yet. "Ah...yes," he said, exhaling with an audible, weary sigh. "There is a common misconception among local police department's all across this nation, that the FBI Crime Lab has the ability to process those "priority" cases the smaller jurisdictions have which..."

"We've got some green and black fibers which need processing," Thud said, "from Ricky Cates' neck."

"We could FedEx them overnight to your Lab, and I'd bet you guys could have a positive I.D. on them by close of business the same day."

Rutledge was not a young guy, but he was not by any means ancient either, for as far as he'd already risen within the Bureau. He was a snazzier dresser than Roy Roddameyer was, although not by much; but he was just about as good as Roddameyer was at shining people on, Thud was beginning to believe.

Rutledge ignored Thud's interruption, and focused his attention on the group at large. "Look, people," he said, "it's just not realistic to believe that what we have to offer some of the smaller agencies in the way of..."

Thud began to get the feeling this was turning into one of those bad cop movies...where the good cops run afoul of the Fed's, who either try to take over their case in the beginning, or don't believe the local cops have a case at all, and when one is finally developed...then they try to take it from the locals, and all the credit for eventually solving it.

"Well, what *can* the FBI offer us in the way of help on a serial murder investigation like this?" Thud interrupted again.

Rutledge stared at Thud for a few seconds before he spoke. "And you are...again?"

"Detective Compton, Cutter Point P.D."

"I'm sorry, Detective...Compton?" Rutledge consulted his notes on the table in front of him. "I thought Detective Dekker...of the Sheriff's Department, was lead investigator on this case."

"He is," said Thud.

"Yes, I am," said Brad Dekker. "But we're working closely together on it."

"Yeah," said Thud. "We're partnered up."

"And Chief Kearnes," said Thud, nodding toward Kearnes who was sitting a few chairs away from him, "has put one more of our men on it, as of today."

"But this crime didn't even occur in *your* city," said Rutledge. "It doesn't seem like it should even be any of your agency's concern."

"Well, is it *your* concern?" said Thud, getting up from his chair. "Is it the FBI's *concern,* when children are taken from their homes in this country and murdered?"

Uh, oh, thought Kearnes. *Uh, oh.*

"You have referred to this as a *serial murder,* detective. To my knowledge there is absolutely no evidence linking the murder of the Cates boy in Lincoln County, to the case you currently have down here."

"And there's been no evidence found *not* tying them together at this point, either," said Thud. "So, I'll ask you again. Is the FBI going to show some *concern*? Or not?"

"Detective Compton," Rutledge said, measuring his words very carefully now, "you would be well advised not to make more of this case then it presently is...by assigning terms like *serial murder* to it, or, God forbid, *serial killer.* Unless you'd like to see what panic can do to tear a community apart almost overnight?"

"We already saw that last month." said Thud, "When we blew up a whale down on the beach. And set off a tidal wave."

"I beg your pardon?" said Rutledge.

"You're making a big mistake," said Thud. "This is the beginning of a serial killer at work...and he's not done yet."

"Detective. You cannot say that with any degree of certainty."

"Well since you won't...and this is *my* town here I am trying to protect," said Thud, "I feel like I have to."

"Have you ever solved a homicide investigation before detective? Rutledge asked him.

"No," admitted Thud. "I've never worked a homicide before."

"And yet you can stand here, in front of a room full of law enforcement officers, some of them very seasoned and experienced men I would imagine; and with absolutely no evidence, and no previous experience to go on...make a statement like that?"

"I'm not the one making the statement," Thud said. "My gut is."

"And what, exactly, is that supposed to mean?"

"It means…that I have a gut feeling about all this. This is the same guy, and he's killing for a reason. And he's not through with us yet."

"I hate to be the one to inform you, detective," Rutledge said, continuing his dressing down of Thud, "but murders aren't solved, and murderers caught, and convicted, by "gut feelings."

Rutledge gathered up his notes and put them into his briefcase in preparation to leave.

Then he looked straight at Kearnes, not at Thud, and said: "Perhaps both you and your chief could benefit from some formal training in this area, Detective Compton. Chief Kearnes, feel free to call my office. We have some excellent training to offer at Quantico…maybe I can pull some strings sometime in the future, and we can get your man in."

Thud sat back down in his chair as Rutledge snapped his briefcase shut, and exited the squad room.

He was right. This *was* a bad cop movie. And he was starring in the lead role.

CHAPTER 25

▼

Later in the afternoon, when things had finally settled down at the police department after everyone had returned to work upon the conclusion of the Task Force
meeting; the buzz in the hallways of C.P.P.D. and in the offices, and the patrol
squad room, was about this new police chief, Kearnes. The "gunfighter from
Dodge City", as he was now being called; and the spectacular feat of marksmanship he had demonstrated out at the range the day before.

But not only had Kearnes drawn his weapon from his holster so fast that the
eye could scarcely perceive it, and had then proceeded to shoot hole after hole
through a tin can thrown high into the air, hitting it as it fell to earth and then
continuing to hit it, lightning fast shot, after shot; until his gun was empty...he
had demonstrated something even more spectacular.

He had shown the men and women of Cutter Point P.D. who were present,
that "The Unholy Four" were no longer in charge of the department...he was,
now. Because there was, as the old saying went, a new marshal in town. And it
was him. Edgar Polk may have been the victor in the shooting match between
Kearnes and himself, but it was Kearnes who was clearly the winner that had
taken it all that day.

Spenser Sparling was so proud of his chief he looked like he was going to bust,
as he described, to some of those who hadn't been there, what he had seen Kearnes do with that Colt pistol of his. And when he'd called Frick and Frack at their
apartment and asked them to bring the can Kearnes had shot the hell out of
down to the department, and they had balked—saying something about getting
ready to put it up for sale on eBay—Spenser had been on their doorstep in five
minutes. And had left, bullet riddled can in hand, a minute later after that.

So as Kearnes left his office at the end of the day, walking through the police building to Thud's office to check on him and Spenser before he went home for the day, the people that he passed in the hallway either grinned at him or nodded in a respectful and friendly manner, saying "Chief" to acknowledge his presence, as he walked by. He had to admit to himself that it was a feeling he had gone without for such a long time now, that he wasn't sure he would ever experience it again. But he was experiencing it now, and if felt awfully good.

Thud's office door was open when Kearnes arrived, and he could see both Thud and Spenser were hard at it on the phones, working their way through the checklist of ten investigative questions they had developed, and were asking all of the vineyards and wineries they were calling. He took an empty guest chair and waited until both of them had finished with their calls, and had hung up.

"Whew!" said Spenser. "My brain feels like it's about to slip into neutral."

"Are you getting anywhere?" Kearnes asked Thud.

"Yeah," Thud answered him. "I think we're getting near setting a new record...for one month of the city's long distance bill."

"We've called a hundred and three places since nine this morning, chief. Or was mine I did just now, number one oh four?"

"Who's counting," said Thud.

"I am," said Spenser. "You told me to, Sergeant. Remember?"

"Oh, yeah," Thud said. "You don't have to worry about the total, Spenser. Just cross each one off your list after your finished talking to them." But Spenser didn't look like he'd heard him; he was staring at the ivory handled Colt pistol in Kearnes' holster.

"Anything ring a bell yet?" asked Kearnes, "with any of these wineries."

"Naw," said Thud. "The ones we've spoken to so far have had their share of problems with a few misfits; itinerants and migrant workers and such. But mostly just petty thefts and alcohol related stuff...I mean, throw a rock inside a winery and you're going to break a bottle of booze, right? But nobody tying anybody up, or committing any sex crimes or anything like that. Not even any serious assaults."

"Look, Thud..." Kearnes said. "I'm sorry about what happened at the meeting yesterday. With Agent Rutledge. I thought he was way out of line."

"Don't sweat it," said Thud. "I know I was kind of out of line, too. And besides...the guy had a point. I've never worked a homicide case before. I probably don't know what the fuck I'm doing anyhow."

"I think you are doing great, Thud," Kearnes said. "You've put together a solid and logical investigative plan, and you're following through with it. The leads you're following up point in the direction any good investigator should be looking, in order to develop and identify a suspect. You can't really ask for much more than that in an investigation like this. I know I'm not."

Thud's demeanor brightened up a little at hearing his chief's words of confidence in him.

"Well, I did find out one thing," he said. "These Trellistrips are quite the popular item, just like my research indicated they probably would be. I don't think there's been a place yet that we've called, that doesn't use them. Isn't that right, Spenser?"

"That's right, Sergeant," Spenser answered. "Every one, so far."

"Then you are on the right trail," Kearnes said. "Just stick to it."

"I've found five places so far on the coast…farm and feed supply places mostly…that carry the Trellistrip brand. We've even got one store here in town, Cutter Farm Supply, that sells them."

"Have they sold any lately?" Kearnes asked.

"No," said Thud. I went down there this morning after I got off the phone with them. They've got exactly one box on their shelf, all coated with dust, and the clerk there said they've had that one since a year ago last summer."

"Well, keep on it," said Kearnes.

"I gave the guy my card and told him to call me the minute someone so much as looks at that box. And to just leave it where it is, and not even touch it."

"Good," said Kearnes. "Remember, I'll be taking the day after tomorrow off; for my Holiday, today. But I'll have my pager with me all day."

"What are you doing on your day off, chief?" Spenser asked him.

"Going on a picnic, I guess…if I can find someplace on the beach to go."

"With your lady friend?"

"Yes."

"Agate Beach is nice," said Spenser. "Nice, and remote. You've got to hike a little ways to get there…but there's some awesome agate's you can find in the gravel bars in the surf, near shore. Some of them are really beautiful."

"Where is it?" asked Kearnes.

"Just north of Musselshell State Park," Spenser said. "About a two mile hike up the beach."

"I'm sure the chief has better things to do on his day off, Spenser," said Thud, "than hike for miles through the sand up some deserted beach, carrying a picnic basket; just to pick stupid rocks out of the water. And probably get soaked while doing it."

"I wasn't thinking so much about picking up pretty rocks," said Spenser, smiling mischievously.

"It was the "remote" part, I was referring to."

Britt had thought Steve Connelly, the park ranger, was a very kind and considerate man when they'd met with him on Wednesday morning at Musselshell State Park; to get directions on how to reach their picnic site at Agate Beach before they began their hike.

He had been so nice, in fact, that he'd almost sabotaged her morning by offering them a ride to Agate Beach in his state 4X4 patrol truck. Which would have spoiled the view she had at this very moment of Kevin just ahead of her, and the way his long, muscular legs and tight butt looked as they moved beneath his blue jeans, churning up the sand, the heavily laden backpack stuffed with all their picnic goodies he was carrying bouncing up and down slightly on his broad shoulders, with every step he took.

So Britt had quickly turned Steve Connelly's offer of a ride down for the both of them; thanking him, and saying that they both needed the exercise, and that it was such a beautiful morning, anyway. Kevin looked damned good in his dark navy blue police uniform he wore to work every day, but she thought he looked just as good, and sometimes even better, when he was dressed just like any other guy...*her* guy. That's why she had told him the little white lie, about wanting to go on a picnic with him in order to keep her from going shopping.

She wanted to go on the picnic...on another date with him...because ever since the carnival she had craved more of that very rare (for her) and special kind of intimacy which they had shared between each other that night. It had been as addictive to Britt as the sweet cotton candy Kearnes had bought her, and as absent from her life just as long.

The emotional pursuit of each others hearts, by revealing bits and pieces of those same hearts, in very small increments, was what she was desperately seeking now. Endearing words, chivalrous conduct, protective actions...these were the things Britt needed most, as they had either never been given to her before by the men who had come and gone in her life, or required of her from the men, to be given. Because for as intelligent as she was, and as beautiful, kind, compassionate, and caring...she still believed she wasn't deserving; still wasn't good enough.

But it was true that they both really did need the exercise; or at least a *different* kind of exercise...like walking. And it *was* a beautiful morning, too. No, more than just beautiful; this morning was almost ethereal.

The ocean waves were coming ashore softly, like thick folds of light blue frosting overlapping on a white chiffon cake. And mounds of cottony cumulus clouds touched the surface of the sea on the horizon, reaching up into the cerulean morning sky in progressive steps, and you couldn't see where they ended. Like you could walk up them, and eventually find yourself knocking on God's front door.

Gulls and other squalling seabirds zoomed past their heads as they walked on the beach, flaring in the sudden rising and falling gusts of ocean wind overhead. Crying loudly and dipping their wings, they went at one another, as they engaged in aerial combat sorties over food, and dominance, and probably, Britt imagined, even love.

At first there were a lot of other people on the beach; they seemed to be everywhere. Spread out and walking in front of them, or passing by them, going in the opposite direction. But after the first mile or so the people started to become fewer and farther between; eventually thinning out until they disappeared altogether, and Britt and Kevin were walking alone.

"How are you holding up?" Kearnes called back over his shoulder to her.

"Fine," she said. "I'm doing good. How about you?"

"Just peachy keen. That bottle of wine has finally slipped down inside the middle of the pack, and is whacking me in either the third or fourth vertebrae down from my neck, every time I take a step."

"I'm sorry…I guess I should have packed it more carefully."

"No…you should have packed it more lightly."

"Hey, no complaining! I had to bring everything we needed for a nice lunch, and the rest of your cookies, you know."

"Ah, no…you really didn't need to."

"Hey! You said you *liked them*. Even if I did vary from the recipe a little. By mistake, I might add."

"No…what I said was…that I'd never tasted anything *like them*."

When Britt had gone to the Ray's supermarket the morning they'd had to postpone their picnic date, and then returned to the cabin a short time later with a big box of Quaker Oats, a dozen eggs, brown sugar, butter, vanilla, baking soda, salt, and a box of raisins—all the ingredients she needed make him his favorite cookies—she had been so excited and nervous at the prospect of her first ever venture into baking for a man, that she'd had a glass of wine first.

Glass number one had given her so much confidence she had decided a second one probably couldn't do anything but relax her even more, while heightening her culinary instincts at the same time. And as she opened more and more of the ingredients, and drank more and more of the wine, and tried to read the recipe for oatmeal raisin cookies on the back of the oat box with her contacts out…in teeny, tiny little print…well, somehow, one teaspoon of baking soda got wrongly interpreted as one quarter cup of baking soda.

When Kearnes had bitten into his first cookie later that night he'd thought for a second that Britt was trying to intentionally poison him, and he couldn't think of what it was he'd done to make her so mad at him. But as he'd watched her watching him eating the cookie, her face aglow with anticipation, he decided instead that she had simply been telling him the truth before, when she'd said she had never baked a cookie before in her life.

He'd managed to wash the rest of the cookie down with the glass of cold milk she had poured him, while keeping a reasonably normal face. But when Britt had tried one, and promptly spit it out into the kitchen sink…gagging…the jig was definitely up.

As she had verbally recounted her cookie baking experience from earlier in the day to him, consulting the back of the oatmeal box as she went, the mistake was found. And they had both broken out in fits of nearly uncontrollable laughter that continued off and on the rest of the evening, and even into the night, as they lay in each others arms beneath the big white goose down comforter.

After they'd finished making love, and finished laughing one more time about Britt's cookies—that were like biting into a bar of soap—Kevin had suddenly and without warning, began to tell her about his life. About Tilly, and Ethan, and Alex; about Kansas, the ranch he mostly grew up on, and the home and job he had left in Dodge.

She'd listened quietly, not saying a word in response; wishing he wouldn't say another word…but hanging on every word he did say. And although she knew it was the worst possible thing she could do at this point in her life—getting involved with another man, *any man*—she was drawn to him, and she could not help herself. And so she had just listened to him, letting him talk without interruption, and was quiet through it all.

"I think that's it, just up ahead there," he said, stopping, and pointing up the beach a few hundred yards to a wide spit of land that arced out into the sea in the shape of a boomerang. It was starkly dark in color and composition from the black volcanic gravel, and contrasted against the white sand on either side of its borders like a ripple of chocolate sauce poured down the center of a vanilla cone.

"Are you sure?" she asked him.

Kearnes fished out the hand drawn map from the pocket of his jeans Spenser had given him, which he'd folded up with some other information Spenser had printed off the internet for him about agates. He unfolded the map, looked at it, looked at the oddly shaped land configuration ahead, and then said, "Yes, we have arrived. That is Agate Beach…dead ahead."

"OK, onward trailblazer! I need to find a place to go pee. Unless you'd like to stop here for a few minutes…and take a cookie break," said Britt.

"Very funny," he said.

"Well…get going then, Tonto!" she said. "I have to pee…bad!"

Kearnes found a nice flat and grassy spot on the cusp of the gravel bar, just above where it began to split off from the beach. He took the backpack off and set it down on the ground while Britt wandered out into the tall grass of the nearby dunes for some privacy. By the time she returned he had the blanket from the backpack spread out on the ground, and was removing the rest of the items it contained, including a plastic Ziploc baggie of her now famous oatmeal cookies.

"*That* was a first," she said, plopping down on the blanket beside him.

"What?"

"Peeing outdoors, that's what!"

"You're joking…right?"

"Uh…no."

"So you've never just been somewhere, when you had to go really bad, like just now…where there weren't any facilities around?"

"In case you haven't guessed yet, Kevin…I'm not the outdoor type. Or the Betty Crocker type, either."

Kearnes laughed at this. Britt McGraw was no longer quite the same beautiful ice queen that he'd first met. Little by little her cool, and at times distant demeanor toward him, when they were outside of the bedroom, was beginning to melt away. She had a great sense of humor and was even very funny at times; yet he knew she still had a lot of what seemed like blue blood pumping through her veins.

"So, how was it?" he asked, studying one of the internet pages Spenser had printed.

"The grass tickled a little," she said.

"You have your choice," he said, changing the subject. "We can eat lunch now, and go beachcombing and agate hunting later, or we can do that now, and eat later."

"I'm not really hungry yet," she said.

"You're never hungry," he said.

"I want to find some of those pretty rocks Spenser told you about," she said.

"And I've kind of worked up an appetite this morning being your pack mule," he said, pointing to the empty backpack. "I wouldn't mind a sandwich."

"So, you're hungry?" she asked.

"Starving," he said.

She reached for the plastic baggie of cookies, then held them up and dangled them back and forth in front of his face.

"OK then!" he said. "Pretty rock hunting it is!"

Kearnes wasn't a complete stranger to agate hunting. He had been introduced to the semi-precious stones—formed millions of years ago in the earth's crucible from silica mineral and different types and colors of quartz—by his Father, when he was a very young boy. On occasion, when his Dad was feeling a little sinful, they would leave his Mom and his sister to represent the family at the evening church worship service, and steal down to the gravel bars and dry washes of the Arkansas River to look for agates.

Rare fire agates were the ones they prized the most. Holding them up to the still shimmering late afternoon Kansas sun after they found one, they would watch the center of the agate glow inside, like a tiny red hot piece of coal.

If they were lucky they might find a ribbon agate, with straight bands of different colored crystallized iron hydroxide running through a cross section of its center; or an onyx agate, with white bands alternating with bands of black, brown, or red; or maybe a ring eye. Or even the rarest of them all; a moss agate…filled with different shades of green filaments inside, like prehistoric vegetable matter growing in stone for all of eternity.

But never had Kearnes seen agates anything like Britt was now plucking from the cold and slick, sea washed gravel beds of Agate Beach. Shrieking with delight at each new find, like a kid at an Easter egg hunt, she stuffed the lustrous rocks into the wet and sagging, generous sized pockets of her hiking shorts until they looked like they were ready to burst at the seams.

"Look at this one!" she said, holding up a smooth, egg shaped, blue translucent stone the size of the tip of her thumb. Its center was diffused with a delicate pattern of white, crystal laced markings, and it made him think of a Robin's egg, with tiny cracks in the shell. "It is *so* beautiful!"

Kearnes walked over for a closer look. He consulted the printed pages Spenser had given him. "That's got to be a blue lace agate," he said. "The description here fits it to a T."

"This is my best one yet," Britt said. "It is absolutely gorgeous. I wonder if I could have a ring made from it?"

"I'm sure you could. But you'd have to have it tumbled...polished first...and then cut. To finally see what you've really got."

"Well I'm absolutely keeping *this* one," she said, searching for a place to make it fit in one of her pockets.

"That's what you've said about all of them. And you have kept them. Every one. That's why you don't have any room left in your pockets now."

"But I *have* to keep them all!" she cried. "This is like a treasure hunt...and this is all my treasure! I found them, so I'm keeping them"

"Do you know how many pirate ships down through history sunk out there?" he said, pointing to the blue horizon of the ocean. "Based on that very same game plan?"

"Hey!" she protested. "Your pockets are stuffed, too!"

"No," he said, "my pockets are full of *your* treasure." "The ones you asked me to hold onto for you. Remember?"

Britt was soaking wet now after two hours of intoxicating and frenzied agate hunting; and not just her tennis shoes and socks, and hiking shorts either. She had even managed to get the bill of the baseball cap she was wearing wet; dunking it in the quickly rising shallow water of the incoming tide as she had bent over, searching for another prize agate.

The tips of the sleeves and front of her heavy white Nautica cotton tee shirt were also soaked. And because she wasn't wearing a bra, the outline and shape of her breasts was now clearly visible. Her nipples, erect from touching the cold water, stood out firmly in high relief beneath the cotton fabric, like two precious gemstones of her own.

Kearnes was wet too, all the way up to his ankles, and his hiking boots squished water out the eyelet holes of the laces as he walked. "We have to quit," he said. "The tide is coming in now...and fast."

"Five...more...minutes," Britt said, her teeth chattering.

"Nope," Kearnes said, taking her by one arm and leading her back toward shore. "Right now." He could feel the goose bumps beneath his fingers that had risen on her skin.

On the picnic blanket—which Kearnes had secured with large rocks on all four corners to hold it down on the sand in the irregular bursts of ocean winds—Britt emptied out her pockets of all her "treasure", and made him do the same. While he rooted through the backpack, looking for the extra clothing she was to have packed, Britt separated her agates into small piles, according to color and similarity of type. She had a few rainbow color banded agates and some yellow and black flecked leopard skins, some starburst pattern carnelians, a few green apple colored plume agates that were streaked with darker green bands of jasper, and a lot of fire agates. And of course her most prized find of all; the blue lace.

"Did you bring an extra shirt?" he asked her.

"No."

"Any extra socks?"

"No. I didn't think we'd be getting wet today."

"I think whenever you go to the beach," he said, "always assume you're going to get wet at some point, by some means."

She was visibly shivering now, sitting with her knees hunched tightly against her chest, her hands grasping and pulling at the soggy white half socks of her low cut Reebok's.

"I did bring our jackets!" she said.

"Found them," he said, pulling the two light windbreakers from the bottom of the pack where she had neatly folded them square, to fit.

"Take your tee shirt off," he said, stripping his own away and letting fall to the blanket.

"What?…oh, no. Just give me my jacket; I'll be fine."

"No, you won't," he said. "What you'll be is hypothermic…in about thirty minutes from now."

"My jacket will warm me up," she said.

"Not with this underneath it, it won't," he said.

He knelt beside her and slowly lifted her numb arms straight into the air above her head. He removed the baseball cap from her head, freeing her ponytail first from the plastic closure band at the back of the cap she had stuck it through; and then tugged the wet tee shirt up and off her body. One of his hands inadvertently raked across a breast as he did this, and he felt the nipple; as hard as any of the agates they had found on the beach.

Then he picked up his own tee shirt, four sizes larger than hers, but still bone dry, and put her arms through the armholes, and pulled it down over her body.

"Here," he said, handing her the jacket. "Now you can put it on. And zip it up, too."

"Thank you," she said, very quietly.

"I'm not going to fall in love with you, Kevin Kearnes," she said, suddenly. Her heart began to pound inside her chest…both from the lie she was telling him, and from her fear of what he might say back to this. "I don't have the time."

Kearnes didn't say anything. He put his own jacket on over his bare chest, and zipped it up. It was getting cool out now, and the early afternoon wind coming in from the sea was making it even colder. He looked away from her; up the beach to a low bluff of sand dunes that came down almost to the water's edge. At the foot of the bluff was a huge jumble of silver colored driftwood that had stacked up there, thrown against the base of bluff by winter storms.

"Did you pack those matches, and the newspaper?" he asked.

"Yes, I did," she said, waiting for the other shoe to drop. "They're in one of the zippered side pockets."

"We need a fire," he said. "Stay here and keep warm. I'll be back in a few minutes." Without another word he stood up and walked toward the bluff; hurting so badly inside that he wished he could just keep on walking, and never have to come back to face her again.

They ate their picnic lunch in silence, sitting far enough away from the roaring camp fire Kearnes had built to keep the sparks from flying into their food when the wind shifted. And far away from each other, too.

The food was actually good; delicious in fact. And he had wanted to compliment her on it. But they had stopped speaking to each other completely after he'd returned with the wood and built the fire, and then eaten their lunch.

She had gone back to the same place to get the things she'd needed for the picnic, that she had gone to earlier that morning for her cookie baking supplies; the little Ray's store in Old Town beneath the bridge. Ham from the Deli for the thick ham sandwiches on sliced old fashioned white bread, with lots of mustard, she'd made; and a container each of German potato salad and tapioca pudding. And from the other aisles in the small grocery store; fresh fruit, salt and vinegar potato chips, a block of sharp Tillamook cheese, a box of wheat thins, the bottle of wine, paper plates, napkins, and plastic forks and knives.

But the silence between them was so daunting, he couldn't bring himself to be the first one to speak; not even to tell her what a great picnic she had made.

Finally, after half an hour more of working up the courage to do so, he reached over behind the dwindling stack of dry driftwood he'd brought back to their picnic site in three different trips, and picked something up from the ground there.

He walked over to her and sat down beside her. "I have something for you," he said. "Here."

He handed her a small bouquet of blue flowers that looked almost exactly like daisies. They had round yellow centers, like daisies. But their petals, which were long and narrow, and shaped like miniature airplane propellers, were a powder blue, almost lavender in color, instead of white.

"These are Pacific Asters," he said. "I saw them growing on the little hill above where I got the wood."

Britt reached out and took the small bunch of wildflowers from him, holding them gently between her hands as if they were a baby bird she'd just found, that had fallen from its nest.

"You may not be going to fall in love with me," he said, "but I'm afraid I already have...with you."

Britt lifted her face up to him, and looked deeply into his eyes. She wanted so badly to say something to him, anything...that would make all of this all right between them. But what could she say? What could she tell him? The truth about herself, and who she really was?

That she had been married three times; and that each one of those misguided unions had left her more fragmented and less intact as a woman, and as a human being, than the one before? That the very night before she'd met him she had been standing outside on top of the fifty story high Fourth Avenue Plaza building in downtown Seattle, where her office was, trying to find a way to climb over the security barrier to jump to the street below?

That by the end of this month—or maybe even sooner—she would be a murderer; and some policeman, just like he was, would be looking for her?

Or that she had a secret about her life; one which could never be told to anyone?

Britt McGraw had learned how to live at the surface of her life...on the top layer only; and what was most important to her was to look good, to sound good, and to do the things and act in the ways that were perceived by the rest of society as normal and good.

"Thank you...for these," she managed to say, her voice cracking with emotion. "I'm sorry I said what I said to you, Kevin. I mean in the *way* I said it to you; just out of the blue like that. I didn't mean for you to think..."

Britt was stopped in mid-sentence as her face was suddenly bathed in a flash of harsh, bluish white light. And then a giant peal of thunder split the air around them, literally shaking the ground, startling them both. The noise, like an artillery piece being fired right next to them, was followed a second and a half later by another brilliant fractured bolt of lightning—and seconds after that, more earth shaking thunder.

They had been so focused on each other that neither had noticed the rapidly diminishing sunlight, and the sky and clouds turning a dark grey; like the color of pencil lead. Within a few short moments the howling wind began to blast sand from the beach into their eyes, and the picnic blanket ballooned up in the middle, leveling Britt's piles of agates, and threatening to tear free from its rocky anchors and fly away.

"We've got to go!" shouted Kearnes, staring with concern at the roiling white-caps on the ocean's surface that were being whipped to life now by the sudden summer squall. Fat drops of rain began to pelt their faces and Britt hurriedly scooped up her agates from the blanket, unceremoniously dumping them into the backpack as another jagged bolt of lightning snaked down from the sky.

A small whirlwind descended upon the picnic site, kicking up loose paper plates, and napkins, and burning cinders from the campfire; spinning them like a small cyclone into the air six feet off the ground. Kearnes swatted at the airborne refuse in an attempt to bring it down, but all of it was moving too fast for him to catch. He shouldered the backpack, grabbed Britt's hand, and they ran south down the beach toward Musselshell State Park.

It was only five thirty, but for as dark out as it was now it could just as well have been midnight. Now the beach ahead of them was absolutely deserted. Unlike on their hike in, there were no people to be seen anywhere now, even as they made their way to within what Kearnes judged to be less than a mile from the boundary of the state park.

What Kearnes had thought of as being wet earlier in the afternoon after they'd finished their agate hunting adventure, paled in comparison now to the sorry physical state they were both in. Every inch of their clothing was sopping wet, and they both looked like they'd just spent a half hour in the ocean, swimming around.

Except that would have been an exceedingly deadly activity to try at this time. Huge "sneaker" waves crashed on the sand only a few scant feet from them, sometimes throwing rolling driftwood logs called "deadheads" directly up onto the sand and into their path. And these would send them scurrying out into the relative safety of the sand dunes, and the tall beach grass; the wind ripping through the razor thin tips of the grass with the whine of passing bullets. The blasting winds were so deafening, Kearnes never heard the pager on his belt begin to beep now.

There was a small trickle of fresh water called Smelt Creek that sprang from the ground somewhere in the dunes, and traversed the beach before emptying into the sea. As they had hiked out earlier that morning, encountering it fairly soon after leaving the park, its shallow, three inch depth had been easily crossed by hopping across it from rock to rock, without ever getting their feet wet.

But now the rain, and its runoff effect, had turned it into a brown, muddy, raging torrent; nearly four times as wide as it had originally been. They were standing near its banks in the groaning wind, the rain being driven straight into their faces now at a near horizontal angle, and wondering what to do next, when Kearnes saw two bobbing yellow flashlight beams across the creek, coming toward them.

As the flashlights got closer he saw that they weren't flashlights at all, but the twin headlight beams from a truck. It was Park Ranger Steve Connelly's truck.

The truck lurched to a stop on the other side of the creek, its wipers beating furiously back and forth across the windshield, but still unable to keep up with the driving rain.

Connelly got out of the driver's side; he put his hands together up to the sides of his mouth and shouted, "Stay there! Don't try to cross here!"

Then Kearnes saw Thud get out of the passenger side of the truck, his tie whipping backward in the wind as if someone was standing behind him, yanking on it. He was immediately drenched by the downpour, his light gray suit quickly turning a charcoal black color, but he didn't seem to notice the rain at all. He started to walk to the edge of the boiling creek and Connelly rushed forward, grabbing him by an elbow. But Thud wrenched his arm free, and kept on walking.

"He's got them both!" Thud shouted above the shrieking wind, from the edge of the creek.

"What?" Kearnes yelled back to him.

"Two kids!" Thud yelled, reaching inside his suit jacket and bringing out what looked like some white pieces of paper; which he was barely able to hang on to in the wind

"He's taken two more kids…and he tried to take another one, today!"

"*Who* has two kids?" yelled Kearnes. He didn't know what the hell Thud was talking about…or what he was even doing here.

"You don't understand!" Thud screamed back. "We have a witness now!"

We have a witness now.

Oh my God, thought Kearnes.

It's *Him.*

CHAPTER 26

▼

After a largely sleepless night for them both, Kearnes and Thud left early the next morning just after dawn in Thud's car, en route on Highway 101 to the Florence, Oregon police department to interview the thirteen year old male who may or may not have almost been a victim of The Cross Killer the previous afternoon. Normally, it was a three and a half hour drive from Cutter Point up the coast to the small tourist town of Florence, but the way Thud was driving they would make it in two.

Last night's storm had passed through the area almost as quickly as it had come, leaving everything in its path clean and freshly washed. But the storm between Kearnes and Britt had lingered even after they'd returned home to the cabin, so he'd decided to spend the night at his own apartment. When he had awakened to the sound of Thud pounding on his door at five a.m. he'd been dreaming of Britt, and he was more than disappointed when he had reached for her next to him on the bed, and felt only the empty pillow beside him instead.

As the car climbed and dipped on the old and very narrow coastal interstate highway; traveled up, and over, and around the steeply rugged contours, and formidable rocky headlands of the southern coast—the treed landscape outside his window passing by in a blur—Kearnes listened as Thud recounted the events of the day before to him as they had transpired late in the afternoon; just as he and Spenser were about to call it a day.

At eight o'clock that morning he had asked Shoshanna Perry and Candy Brewer to research all missing persons reports filed in Oregon and Northern California involving any persons under the age of eighteen since the abduction and murder of Ricky Cates. Shoshanna had called him at noon to report there weren't any for subjects in that age range; only two adults, and they had both already been located.

But at five minutes after five, Shoshanna had called Thud in his office with a real sense of urgency in her voice, and asked him come down the hall to the Dispatch Center. When he and Spenser got there, she and Candy had shown him two messages from LEDS, the state's computerized Law Enforcement Data System, which she had just received and printed out. One was a statewide bulletin from the Seaside Police Department in Clatsop County, being issued in conjunction with an Amber Alert, for a ten year old boy named Peter Mossbrooker. The other one was a missing persons report on a ten year old boy named Colin Boyer: reported missing without a trace from South Beach State Park, on the coast at Newport, since late Tuesday afternoon.

Peter had been reported missing to Seaside police on Monday, July 6th, at 1:00 p.m.; twenty minutes after his frantic and panicked single parent Mother, Penny Mossbrooker, had given up looking for him in the crowds of summer tourists near the Town Carousel on Broadway Street in Seaside. She had collapsed to her knees on the sidewalk, screaming Peter's name repeatedly to the strangers around her at the top of her lungs, and a Seaside P.D. unit with two officers had been on scene within less than three minutes from the time they received the call.

A report was taken by the responding officers, and a physical description, and clothing description of the boy was ultimately broadcast to all local, county, and state units on the road. And even a recent school photograph of Peter was obtained from the Mother by the investigating patrolmen to be used in an Amber Alert; the nationwide program which was designed to quickly put messages about missing children on TV and radio stations, and even digitally lighted freeway signs, in order to make every member of the public possible the eyes and ears of the police.

But unfortunately, it was at this point which the rapid and caring response of law enforcement began to break down; into a slow motion quagmire of old unresolved turf wars, politics, miscommunication, and even apathy.

Although it was Seaside P.D.'s case, that agency had to rely on the aid and assistance of their local Sheriff's Department in order to have an Amber Alert actually put into effect. And an incident of a kid going missing, in and of itself was not enough justification to have such an alert issued.

There first had to be some evidence, some strong reason to believe that a child had been criminally abducted; whether it was by a non-custodial parent, or a complete stranger...before an Amber Alert could be issued. This was not a mere guideline in investigating such cases; it was policy. And the problem with policies, of course, is that they didn't, and never could, cover every situation an officer might encounter out in the field.

A detective from the Clatsop County Sheriff's Department interviewed Penny Mossbrooker next. And when he found out that she and her husband, Peter's Father, who loved the boy very much, and who had been "stalking" her recently, begging her to let him see his son; that they were having "problems" in their marriage and were currently separated, but not legally…the potential probable cause for the Amber Alert, at least in the mind of the detective, dissolved.

He suggested to S.P.D. that they look for the Father first; because that's probably where they would find the missing kid.

And on Tuesday, just a little after ten a.m. in the morning, they had finally been able to track Kurt Mossbrooker down with the assistance of Portland P.D. He was at his new girlfriend's apartment on Errol Heights in that city where he'd secretly told to a buddy of his at work he would "be taking a few sick days off" from his job.

But his son Peter wasn't with him.

So now, almost twenty four hours after he'd gone missing, there was enough reason to have an Amber Alert issued for Peter Mossbrooker.

But on the other boy, Colin Boyer, there was nothing.

The Boyer family, on vacation from Arizona, had pulled into South Beach State Park on Yaquina Bay just off Highway 101 at noon on Tuesday, after having eaten lunch at a McDonalds in downtown Newport. They had no reservation for this campground and were just driving through before they continued on down the coast in search of a place to pitch their tent, when Colin's Father had stopped at the Ranger Station and inquired anyway. And as luck would have it, there had just been a cancellation phoned in on a tent site.

But it was the worst kind of luck, and would have horrible and tragic consequences. While the parents had unpacked the car, set up their tent, and made a tidy camp; Colin and his twelve year old sister were allowed to go down to the beach together to play…and told, of course, to stay together. Later in the afternoon Colin's sister had returned to the campsite for a snack. But Colin was not with her.

When Thud had read this second message from LEDS, the one about ten year old Colin Boyer, he felt his knees begin to buckle as they turned to rubber, and he had sagged heavily against one corner of the dispatch console desk.

Spenser had seen his sergeant's face turn white as he read the message; like his carotid artery had just been opened with a razor blade, and all of his blood was quickly draining out. Then he saw an odd, painful expression on his face…like he was experiencing a stroke.

Thud knew where South Beach State Park was; he had been there himself before, camping with his own family. It was only a stones throw from the Newport city limits, and only about ten miles north of Seal Rock Wayside, where Ricky Cates had been abducted.

And then incredibly, while all four of them had stood there and watched in disbelief, a third message had peeled out of the LEDS laser printer, about another missing child on the coast. But this was a "cancel attempt to locate/missing persons" which had been sent to rescind an earlier A.T.L. Missing Person message, which Cutter Point's Dispatch Center had yet to receive.

Thud had hurriedly skimmed this message: *white male victim, age thirteen, missing from parking lot at the Sea Lion Caves on Hwy. 101 north of Florence, Oregon, missing only two hours though before being found…on Highway 101, one mile south of location. Unharmed; but a white male adult had possibly attempted to abduct him. End of message: Sheriff's Office, Lane County.*

Thud had shouted at Spenser to get back to their office and phone both the Lane County Sheriff's Department *and* Florence P.D., and get everything he could from them on the incident. And to tell Florence P.D. that if they didn't know anything about this case as of yet they had damned well better get started…because the suspect could be in their city, the next stop down the road, right now.

Thud had hastily folded all three messages together, jammed them inside his suit jacket pocket, and told Candy Brewer to start paging Kearnes and to keep paging him, every five minutes, if there was no response.

And then he had run out of the Dispatch Center, to go and find his chief.

"I *know* it's him, chief" Thud said, leaning into his car door as he slung the Ford around a hairpin curve, then shot into the narrow straightaway just ahead, tires squealing. "I can feel it in my gut."

"Slow down," said Kearnes, "or neither one of us is going to be feeling anything any longer." He had been on Thud about his driving almost since they'd left the city limits of Cutter Point, but it really hadn't done much good.

"I need you to back me on this hunch of mine, chief," said Thud.

"And you need to slow this thing down a little," Kearnes said.

The parents of the boy who had almost been abducted from the Sea Lion Caves parking lot had agreed to wait in Florence for Thud and Kearnes so they could interview him. But because of what had happened to their son, they were cutting their vacation short and returning home today. The Father had assured

Kearnes over the phone that if they showed up at Florence P.D. at even one minute past their nine a.m. appointment time, they would pass their R.V. on the highway as it headed south, back to San Diego, California.

"We *are* going to get there on time, and get this kid interviewed as fast as we can," Thud said, glancing at his watch. "And I can't do that…driving 55."

"Can you do it at 85?" Kearnes asked. But Thud didn't respond to him.

Thud said, "Then we've got to take a look at that parking lot area at Sea Lion Caves…and then haul ass up the road to South Beach Park. Lincoln County S.O. is toning out their Search and Rescue Squad this morning to resume the search for the Boyer Boy."

The Ford ate up the short, empty straightaway in no time at all, and then crested a small rise, bearing down on a string of slow moving vehicles just ahead that were bunched up on each other's bumpers like a wagon train creeping along through Indian country.

"Oh, and just what the fuck is this!" Thud cried, staring at the line cars dead ahead.

"Thud, slow down," said Kearnes. "This is a double yellow line. You can't pass here."

"We're only ten minutes out," Thud said.

"Thud…No!"

"Sorry chief," Thud said, gritting his teeth, as his fingers punched every emergency light, strobe light, and the siren button on the unmarked car's emergency control console to the "on" position. "But we've got to do this. It's important!"

He jammed his foot down on the accelerator and the Ford's police pursuit engine launched them forward. The sudden speed, noise, and sight of the unmarked detective car, seemingly having come from out of nowhere, began forcing each vehicle off onto the shoulder of the highway as soon as their drivers caught sight of it bearing down on them in their rear view mirrors.

In five minutes they were in downtown Florence, still in one piece and driving the speed limit, and Thud was searching for an empty parking place behind Florence P.D.

The boy's name was Christopher Wayne Lawless and he and Thud had butted heads in the interview room only seconds after introductions had been made. Thud asked him to take a chair at the single gray metal desk in the center of the room, and Chris ignored him and kicked the chair out, using it as a step stool to climb on top of the desk and sit down on it instead.

Chris Lawless was thirteen, and was going to be fourteen on his next birthday in October. But he was very small for thirteen and could have easily passed for a boy of twelve, or maybe even eleven at first glance. That was, until he opened his mouth for the first time.

Chris was the epitome of the just barely pre-pubescent southern California skateboarding youth culture; spoiled, chronically bored, a three hundred dollar Razzer custom skateboard clamped casually underneath one arm, an iPod jacked into one ear, and an all knowing smirk permanently set across his face as wide as the line of board freaks waiting in the run out line at the La Jolla skateboard park.

Thud didn't like him, and it was easy to see that the aptly named young Mr. Lawless didn't much care for Detective Compton, either. Thud had literally been on pins and needles while rushing to get here; a knight in slightly tarnished and ill fitting polyester wool blend armor, coming to the rescue of a young child who had almost been a victim of something Thud never again wanted to have to see in his lifetime.

And he was expecting his victim to be...well...more "victim like," and not some clone of Delbert Downs' kid, Derek; whom he hated almost as much as he did his old man. So now, more than half an hour into what Thud considered as being largely a waste of time so far, Thud was getting pissed.

"Look, Christopher," Thud said, "would you mind setting your skateboard down...and taking that thing out of your ear...so we can go over your statement one more time?"

"I told you man," said Christopher, "it's 'Chris', OK?"

"Chris. Right. Now, when you told your folks you were going back to the R.V. because you..."

"And, dude...it's not a "skateboard", OK? It's called a "deck", man. That's what we call them...a deck."

"Let me just summarize, from my notes so far," said Thud, looking at his notebook.

"You and your folks went to the Sea Lion Caves about noon on Wednesday...yesterday. It was real crowded; the parking lot. The lower one, right off Highway 101, was all full. So your dad finds a spot to park the R.V. on the upper lot; on the hill?

"You three...you, your mom, and your dad...you three all walk down from the top parking lot area, cross the highway, and enter the main lobby and the gift shop area. Your dad buys three tickets while you and your mom browse around the gift shop.

"Then your dad comes and gets you both, and the three of you take the elevator down to the caves. You're all three in the sea lion cave for about fifteen or twenty minutes, when you tell your parents you were…what…bored? And that you want to go back out to the R.V. and get your skateboard."

"It was fucking lame, man."

"What was lame?"

"That big cave; and all those stinking sea lions. It smelled like shit in there, man. Sea lion shit, I guess."

"But, you said you were bored. You told your parents you were bored. So were you wanting to leave mostly because you were bored, or because it smelled bad down there?"

"Smelled bad? I nearly fucking upchucked, man."

"Okay," said Thud. "I think I'm getting the picture. You didn't like it down there, and you don't particularly like doing things with your folks, do you Chris? So you wanted to go up top; back to your R.V. and get your skateboard…I mean your, deck."

"My parents are boring," he said. "Just like their lame-o vacation ideas. Fucking Oregon…what a joke."

Thud looked over at Kearnes, blinking his eyes at him as if to communicate to him without speaking: *do you believe this?* If any boy in the future even remotely like Chris Lawless ever came sniffing around either one of his daughters, he swore at that moment he would kill the little bastard on the spot…and worry about the consequences later.

"So, you take the elevator back up to the main lobby, alone, get outside, cross the highway, make your way to the upper parking lot…and you've got the R.V. keys with you now because your dad gave them to you, and you get into the R.V. and get your…deck. And this is when you run into the man?"

"Yeah. He was just standing there when I turned around."

"You didn't see him following you at any time prior to that? Like from the lobby, or across the highway or anything?"

"No."

"And tell me again, Chris. What did he look like."

"I don't know. Kind of a big guy."

"Tall? As tall as me?"

"Taller than you."

"Was he as big as I am?"

"Bigger. Just not as fat, though."

"You think I'm fat?"

"Shit dude…compared to him you are. That guy was ripped."

"What do you mean by "ripped?""

"I don't know. Like a fucking body builder, or something."

"How do you know? You said he was wearing some kind of jacket, and matching pants. Did you ever get to see him with his jacket off?"

"No."

"What color was the jacket, and the pants?"

"I don't know."

"You don't know?" Thud thumbed backwards a few pages in his notebook. "You said…'his jacket was green, kind of like some sort of uniform…and his pants, they were green too…and he had a name embroidered on the jacket'…but you can't remember what that name was."

"I don't know. I guess so."

"You guess so? Is this what you told me, and the chief here, not twenty minutes ago, or not?"

"They could have been brown, too. Like a kind of light brown. The jacket and the pants. I told you, it was some kind of funky uniform or something."

"What kind of uniform? A postman, a delivery man? A gardener, an ice cream man? What?"

"Shit man, I don't know! All I remember was it was green or kind of a greenish brown…and the lettering…on the name…was red."

"Red. And you're sure about that. That is was definitely red?"

"Yeah. It was red."

"And why are you so sure about that?"

"Because. I like red. It's like my favorite color or something, I guess."

"Chris, look," said Thud, "you were gone for two hours. That time is *unaccounted* for. You went with this man, this complete stranger to you; somewhere, to do something. You scared the shit out of your parents; they called the police. A missing persons broadcast was put out for you. And you show up two hours later walking up the highway, back to the Caves, as if nothing had happened."

"Nothing did happen."

"BULLSHIT!" screamed Thud, bringing the flat of his open hand down so hard on the gray steel desktop Chris was sitting on, that it cracked inside the thickly soundproofed interview room like a rifle shot. "This is a goddamned murder investigation, you little twerp!"

The boy jumped in reaction and started to get off the desk, but Thud pushed him back down onto it. If this was going to be the good-cop, bad-cop thing,

Kearnes would be up next. But for now it was all Thud's show, and he hoped his detective would be able to keep his cool.

"Unaccounted for time, Chris," said Thud, completely calm now. "That means there are only two people in the world who know, right now, what was done during that time: You, and him. And he's not here right now, Chris. Only you are. So I want you to tell me now, son…did he take you somewhere…to molest you?"

"What? No!"

"There's no shame in it, Chris. No one else is ever going to know except us…the ones in this room," Thud lied.

"No, nothing like that happened. We just talked and stuff."

"Did he rape you inside your R.V.?"

"No!"

"Isn't that what really happened?"

"NO! He never came inside! He only wanted to borrow a paper towel, or some Kleenex!"

"And was that inside the R.V.? To clean himself, or you up? Afterwards?"

"No! He just wanted to borrow a paper towel or something…for his stupid binoculars!"

"Oh, right. The binoculars," Thud said sarcastically. "We kind of forgot to mention those earlier now, didn't we Chris. So we've got this guy…great big, muscle bound guy, and not fat like me. And he's wearing a green jacket with brown pants, and carrying a pair of dirty binoculars."

"I'm telling you the truth," said Chris, his lower lip beginning to tremble ever so slightly.

"Oh, I hope you are," said Thud. "I really do hope you are telling us the truth. Because do you know what it means when you lie to the police? When you lie to the police, and because you lie, and chose not to tell the truth, maybe some kid, just like yourself, dies?"

"I told you…I'm fucking telling you the *truth!*"

"You watch your mouth!" Thud roared.

"I'm…sorry," whimpered the boy.

"No, you're not sorry; not yet you aren't. But you know something, Chris? You're going to be sorry. Sorrier then you ever thought you could be. Because by not telling us the truth, Chris…all of the truth…you might just get two kids killed. Did you know that, Chris?

This guy…this muscle man…we think he's the same man who abducted two boys, not much younger than yourself, in the last three days. And I think he's the same guy, Chris, who killed two other boys. He beat them both, Chris, and then choked them to death; and in addition to that, he raped one boy, Chris, and cut off an ear from the other one."

"Nothing happened to me," Chris barely whispered, tears streaming down his cheeks now.

"Did this man molest you!"

"No."

"Did he try?"

"He wanted a paper towel. To clean his binoculars off."

"Did he take you somewhere Chris? Did he ask you to get in his car?"

"We went up on this bluff; up above the parking lot. To look for whales...out on the ocean."

"Is that where he molested you, Chris?"

"No! No! He didn't! He tried to get me to go someplace with him...to drive someplace...but I just walked down to the highway with him. Looking for whales; with his binoculars."

"Your dad found you nearly a mile down the highway, Chris"

"I walked to there...down the highway, with him. He said he knew a better spot to look for whales."

"Did you ever get in his car? Did you ever see a car?"

"No, I already told you!"

"And so you walked down the highway with this guy, a very busy highway; and you are looking for whales? With his binoculars? And no one sees you?"

"We went over the side...over the guardrail thing; and down into this kind of a cave in the side of the hill."

"And is *that* where it happened, Chris!"

"No!"

"You're lying. I'm going to have to have you admitted to the hospital. A doctor is going to check you down there, Chris. Between your legs. And up inside your butt."

"NO! I'm NOT fucking lying! I smoked some pot with the guy...OK! We got fucking high...and THAT'S ALL THAT HAPPENED! I SWEAR!"

"Thud, that's enough!" shouted Kearnes, inserting himself between the cowering, sobbing boy, and the hulking red faced detective, whose cheeks were now beet red and slickly coated with a waterfall rush of perspiration.

Kearnes put his arm around Chris' shoulder, comforting him, while Thud took a few cumbersome steps across the cracked tile floor of the small room and collapsed on the sofa beneath the not so discreetly mounted video camera on the wall above it. Thank God the boy's parents had demanded that their son's interview not be videotaped, or right about now they would be contemplating where to find competent counsel to retain for their impending lawsuits.

No one said anything for a couple of minutes, while both Chris and Thud regained their composure, and Chris stopped crying.

Chris said, "Are you going to tell my folks? About the pot?"

Thud looked at him; felt sorry for him, and thankful for him at the same time. It wasn't easy being a kid these days; the peer pressure, the constant competition with others to be better than they were, or at least try and keep up. The reality of homicidal maniac child rapists knocking on your R.V. door, asking to borrow a paper towel.

"No, Chris," said Thud, "I'm not. But only if you promise me you are going to give that shit up. Starting today."

"Yes," said Chris, "I promise."

"Chris?"

"Yeah?"

"Do you remember what those binoculars looked like? Maybe what color they were?"

"Green. They were a green color. Like an army Humvee, or something like that."

"Did they have a strap on them? To wear them around your neck?"

"Yeah. He let me wear them while we looked. It was green, too. Like the binoculars."

"This guy…was he ever mean to you? Did he ever threaten you?"

"No. He was nice. But he kind of creeped me out. Like he was maybe a gay, or something. So that's why I left."

"What do you mean "gay"? What makes you think that?"

"I don't know…he was weird. He was treating me like I was a little kid or something. He tried to give me a toy…so I'd come with him to look for whales…to this really good place he said he had."

Thud, who had been slumped down on the couch, exhausted now, had started to sit upright at the mention of the color if the binoculars neck strap…green…but now he leaped to his feet.

"A toy?" he said. "What kind of a toy?"

"I don't know. It was like one of those rubber bath tub, squeak toys. You know, for little kids? It was *so* fucking lame. I think I kind of laughed, when he tried to give it to me; and it pissed him off."

"Did you at any time touch it?" asked Thud.

"No. I didn't take it; so he put it back in his jacket pocket."

"This toy, what did it look like exactly?"

"I think it was supposed to be a whale. A little blue whale."

"A whale?" said Thud.

"Yeah. It was *so* fucking lame."

CHAPTER 27

▼

Thud burst from the interview room, on his way to find a phone, charging right past the parents of Chris Lawless who were nervously pacing back and forth in the hallway. They were visibly upset and wondering why their son had been in there for almost ninety minutes now, when they'd been promised by the big detective in the suit, who'd just run past them without saying a word, that Chris would probably be out of there in forty five minutes, and maybe even less.

While Thud found his way to an empty back office in the small police department and quickly placed a call to Brad Dekker in Cutter Point, then another call to the Oregon State Police Crime Lab in Central Point, Kearnes brought the boy out to his parents.

He apologized for keeping him overly long, and explained away the redness around Chris' eyes as a natural result of the emotionally draining experience of being interviewed as a victim by the police.

After he got Mr. Lawless' home address and phone number in San Diego from him, and Chris' full name, date of birth, and his height and weight; Kearnes thanked them, and Chris, once more, and told them they were free to go. They had just turned the corner down the hall from the interview room, heading for the building's foyer, when Thud appeared from the opposite direction.

"I called Brad at the S.O.," said Thud, "and filled him in."

"Then I got hold of the Lab, and gave them all the info about the green binoculars, and matching green strap."

"Did they say anything?" asked Kearnes.

"Said it should help some," Thud said, "since we've already got some green fibers to go with it."

"And black fibers, too" Kearnes reminded him.

"Yeah," said Thud, "but damned few of those."

"We've got predominantly green ones...almost an eighty to twenty per cent count ratio...if I remember it right. And when they ran the spectrometer testing and put the color up on the magnification screen, it was a real dark green; almost an olive drab type green."

"The fibers...maybe from the neck strap of a pair of military binoculars?"

"Could be," Thud said. "I told them...again...they really need to make something happen on this; and fast. We've finally got enough to start building a suspect profile. And I need the identity or manufacturer of whatever it is those fibers came from."

"Hey," said Thud, "was that kid's parents pissed? They looked pissed."

"They were a little concerned," Kearnes said.

"He say anything to them?" Thud asked.

"No...not while I was with them."

"You think I was too hard on him, don't you."

"You were pushing him, Thud. And maybe just a little too hard. He's just a kid."

"He *is* our only witness so far, chief" said Thud. "I couldn't let him walk out of there with *anything* being held back. There's just too much at stake here."

Kearnes thought about that for a minute. His own personal opinion of how Thud had handled the interview was that he had been wrong in what he'd done, and how he'd gone about doing it...and at the same time...very right.

Because he had to acknowledge to himself that right or wrong; they had left the interview room with something very important...and something very valuable. Something they hadn't been in possession of when they had walked into the room ninety minutes before.

And that something...was the truth.

It was a quarter to eleven when they barreled past the city limits sign of Florence, heading north on 101, and only five minutes to eleven when they turned off the pavement and into the lower parking lot at Sea Lion Caves. Thud maneuvered the car carefully through the tightly packed rows of parked SUV's, cars, trucks, R.V.'s, and vehicles towing camping trailers.

There wasn't a single untaken parking space and when they drove to the upper parking lot, the situation was the same. Thud pointed out what he believed to be the bluff high above them that Chris Lawless had described, but there wasn't any time to climb it; or really any reason to, either. So he settled for a quick trip inside the main building which was packed elbow to elbow with tourists, and flashed his badge to the manager; asking if there were any video security cameras inside or outside at the facility, and if there were…he wanted to see every video tape they had.

But Kearnes didn't go with him. He stayed in the car, his window slightly down, trying not to let the salt sea air inside; because it was beginning to make him sick. He closed his eyes and leaned his head back against the seat's headrest.

What the hell was wrong with him? He'd just spent an entire day on the beach with Britt, filling his lungs with this same air, and he'd thought it had smelled good. The ocean breeze had been exhilarating, bracing, and crisp; and most importantly, hadn't made him sick. But now he began to feel his stomach start to cramp, and a cold sweat began to dampen the fabric of his uniform shirt under his arms.

He was tired, but probably not as tired as Thud; who had such dark circles beneath his eyes from not sleeping he looked as if someone had just rapped him across the face with a two by four. But he was tired enough to catch a short nap if the opportunity presented itself, and so within a few seconds of closing his eyes he had slipped away into a light sleep, and began to dream.

It was dark inside his dream. Dark; like in a cave. Not the sea lion cave Thud had gone to, but the small cave, where Chris Lawless had gone with the man across the highway…to look for the whales. He saw Chris now in the grayish black light of the cave; saw the man too. Or just the man's jacket. A part of it, dark against more dark. The man stood close to Chris, motioning to him to come farther back in the cave with him, but Chris was shaking his head no.

The man took a step toward the boy, but the boy quickly raised up something that he was holding in his hand. He pointed it at the man, and the man only laughed. Now he saw what the boy was holding. It was a small, broken fishing rod; snapped off at the third guide down from the top.

He saw the boy was crying now, looking at his broken fishing rod. Then the man reached inside his jacket pocket and offered it to Chris; but Chris shook his head no…no, no, no! And then suddenly Chris wasn't Chris anymore. Chris was Kearnes…*he* was the boy now. That was right…wasn't it? He was the boy? He had made the other boy go away…back inside the willows, into the dark cave of willows that grew thickly on the river bank and now his new fishing rod was broken ruined by this man who pulled it out from his pocket and he tried to make him take it in his hand first and to touch it and then take it into his mouth gagging and choking what is it what is it WHAT IS IT!

"What is it!" screamed Kearnes, jerking away so fast from the headrest that he banged his head on the car's doorpost.

"Shit!" said Thud, standing in the open space of the car door he'd just jerked open. "Are you okay? I was tapping on the window…trying to wake you up. You had the doors locked."

"What?" said Kearnes.

"You were asleep. You had all the car doors locked."

"Yeah," said Kearnes. "I felt like I had to close my eyes for a few seconds. I must have dozed off…didn't sleep very well last night."

"I hear ya," said Thud. "I don't think I slept at all."

"Sorry about that," said Kearnes.

"What is *it*?" asked Thud.

"What?"

"You must have been dreaming," said Thud. "While I was trying to get your attention; you were saying, over and over, 'what is it?' 'what is it?'"

"Oh," said Kearnes. "I don't know."

"Yeah; like I've been having these dreams lately where you can hardly remember anything about them…but you *know* that you damn sure dreamed *something*?"

"Yeah," Kearnes said. "Exactly like that."

"The way I look at it," said Thud, "is that I'm actually pretty lucky that I don't remember any of them.

"Because lately…my life has started to turn into enough of a fucking nightmare as it is."

Thud drove like a maniac for the next half hour, not even letting the awe inspiring and spiraling thin air climb on the highway up to the top of Cape Perpetua, and then down its almost vertical far side, get in his way of setting another speed record.

Once they had descended the craggy precipice of rocky land, that stood high in the clouds above the ocean like a castle's tower, they zipped through the picturesque little burg of Yachats and then a few minutes later arrived in the small town of Waldport.

Thud suddenly swerved off Highway 101, which ran through the center of the town, and pulled up to the front of a small restaurant named Vickie's Big Wheel Drive-In and parked the unmarked Ford. Sleep, he could do without, for awhile; but food was another story.

He hadn't eaten any breakfast that morning, and was ravenous now. The meaty morning interview with the Lawless boy had kept his hunger satisfied to this point, but now he needed one of Vickie's deluxe cheeseburger baskets and a Dr. Pepper. He asked his chief what he wanted but Kearnes told him nothing, so Thud went inside to place his order. To go.

While Kearnes waited for Thud to return, he rolled the car windows up tightly to try and seal out the stench of the ocean air. He felt listless, almost completely sucked dry of energy; and any further interest in what they were going to be doing the rest of the day. There was something bothering him; something that he couldn't quite track in his mind. To try and isolate, and examine, whatever it was.

He was upset about Britt, and the fight they'd had. Wishing now he had spoken to her first last night, before he'd just walked out of the cabin and headed for his apartment. Or had at least tried to call her later, just to talk.

But this was something else…something more. His mind was starting to become fuzzy, his thoughts blurred. He knew he should be going over every word, every phrase that Chris Lawless had uttered during that hour and a half interview. He should be analyzing, theorizing; coming up with suppositions, and even good guesses at who the individual was who had tried to lure Chris Lawless into…what?

Instead, Kevin Kearnes slowly began to retreat into a state of emotional and mental numbness. Bits and pieces of the morning's interview began to drift slowly away from his thought processes, like little paper boats set at the edge of the water in a receding sea. It wasn't that he didn't want to remember what the boy had said…he just couldn't force his mind to hold onto it any longer.

What was it? *What is it*?

Thud yanked on the driver's side door handle of the car to open it and he nearly dumped his cheeseburger basket on the ground when it didn't budge. He looked inside the car window and saw Kearnes sitting motionless in his seat, head down, staring at the buckle of his seat belt. He tried the door again; but it was locked. He quickly walked around the car; all the doors were locked.

He rapped on the window next to Kearnes' head, but the chief didn't move. He set his burger basket and drink down on the hood, removed his keys from his pocket, and unlocked Kearnes' door.

"Chief?"

Kearnes didn't respond.

"Chief. You okay?" Thud shook his shoulder. "Hey…wake up."

Lethargically, Kearnes turned his head in the direction of Thud. His eyes were locked in a far away stare; which made them look almost dead.

"You taking another nap?" Thud asked.

"Hmm."

"*I said*...were you taking another nap?"

"Oh. No."

"No...I'm awake," said Kearnes.

"You *must* have had one hell of a night," said Thud, grinning at him. "But I guess with a lady like yours...is there any other kind?"

They got back on the road. Thud was driving with one hand, while holding his dripping, special sauce bacon cheeseburger in the other; trying to keep it from leaking onto his lap.

As they left town the roadway almost immediately shot them up onto the long, expansive, black topped lanes of the Alsea Bay Bridge, and once they had traversed the bay, and were headed north again, it was only a few minutes before they passed by Seal Rock.

It was the location where Ricky Cates had been murdered. Thud pointed it out to Kearnes, and asked him if he wanted to stop at the wayside parking lot for a quick look around. But his chief was staring out his window and didn't appear to have heard him. So he kept on driving toward South Beach State Park, only ten minutes away.

South Beach was a giant campground park, with 227 electrical hook-up sites, three different large group tent camping areas, six primitive tent areas, and twenty seven yurts; which were canvas covered, wood framed, dome shaped camping shelters that looked like igloos on steroids.

The total campground area was huge. It was laced with a network of different hiking trails which ran across each other in multiple places; traveling here and there through mini-forests of shore pines, and around sand dunes of imposing height which were covered with both European and American varieties of beach grass.

The first thing Thud did when they arrived there was to get lost in the maze of doubling back traffic circles, and narrow, arrow signed one way roads, as he drove aimlessly around looking for any sign of a Lincoln County Search and Rescue vehicle, or a sheriff patrol car. After five minutes of fruitless searching he stopped the car next to an interpretive map of the park, found the location again of the park ranger station they'd driven past on the way in, and then headed back there.

Thud went inside the small, square cedar wood ranger station while Kearnes waited in the car again. Looking out across the water from the south jetty side of the entrance to the bay where South Beach was located, he could see an ancient red domed, white lighthouse with brown window shutters standing guard high on a hill overlooking Yaquina Bay State Park on the opposite shore above the north jetty.

Just slightly inland of the lighthouse the old Newport Bridge reached widely across the waters of Yaquina Bay and into the heart of the city. Like almost all of the Oregon coastal bridges it had been built in the early 1930's, when automobiles were much smaller, and narrower.

He watched the cars moving along the top of it beneath the thin, gothic looking, green steel framework of its high center arch. The cars looked exposed, and very vulnerable; as if one could easily slip off the bridge and over the side at any moment, snapping through the steel safety retention cables like they were rotten string and plunging to the deep blue water below.

Thud came charging out of the front door of the ranger office, opened his car door, and hit the trunk release button on the dashboard. "Oh, *this* is bullshit," he said. "They've already been here and left! About an hour ago!" The car's trunk had sprung open and Thud went around to the back to get his briefcase out. Kearnes got out of the car and joined him.

"Thud, look," said Kearnes, "it was probably just a follow up, cursory search. To make the boy's family feel better. I spoke to the local police chief here late last night; they put me through to his home number. He told me they conducted a massive search the morning after the boy went missing. They had over a hundred people down here searching...cops, citizens, search and rescue people...everyone was looking for him."

"Well then let's go talk to that chief," Thud said, "and see what they maybe *haven't* done, yet."

"No," said Kearnes. "We're not going to do that. This is a local county and city case. The Boyer boy disappeared here, in Lincoln County's jurisdiction; and right on the edge of this town's city limits. We're going to let them handle it. We're not going to get involved."

Thud had shut the trunk door and opened his briefcase on it. He began to rifle through layer after layer of paper clipped copies of police reports, newspaper clippings, and sheets of his own notes.

"I've got FAX copies of both the Lincoln County S.O.'s, and Newport P.D.'s preliminary reports, somewhere here in this mess," he said.

"Thud. Did you hear what I just said?"

Thud stopped what he was doing and slammed his briefcase shut. "Yeah, I hear exactly what you are saying, chief. But it doesn't feel to me like you're involved in this investigation anyhow"

"Do you think that's a fair statement?" asked Kearnes.

"I think it's a truthful statement," said Thud.

"I'm here with you right now, aren't I?"

"No! Not really! It's like your head has been somewhere else, all morning. What the hell is going on with you?"

"Nothing," said Kearnes.

"Nothing, my ass," said Thud, staring hard at him.

"We've done what we came here to do. I think we need to get back home now," said Kearnes. "It's a long drive."

Thud opened his briefcase again; found the two reports he had been looking for, then opened the trunk and stuck the briefcase back inside, slamming the trunk door shut.

"Sure chief," said Thud. "Whatever you say; you're the boss. But because you are the boss, I want to say one thing before we leave…and this is going to be for the record."

"Go ahead," said Kearnes.

"That fucking maniac…that muscle man psycho with the binoculars, and the green jacket, or the brown jacket…whoever and whatever he is…has that boy *right now*. Took that boy from the very ground we are standing on. And that kid is either already dead; or will be very soon."

Kearnes started to speak but Thud waved a hand at him in warning; stopping him.

"And don't you dare tell me we don't know that…because even if you really don't believe it…*I do.*"

Kearnes looked into Thud's face. His detective, and friend, was haggard, worn, and undeniably exhausted. The dark circles under his eyes were something guilty to look at, but he noticed that Thud's jade colored eyes within those circles were shining brightly; almost shimmering as if they were being consumed by some cold, green fire. That was because Thud himself was on fire…from the inside out.

But Kearnes didn't want to stay here any longer; didn't want to have to talk about or hear about any more missing boys, or the man who may have been involved somehow with their disappearance.

Lodged deep in his subconscious, the words and meaning of what Chris Lawless had said to them at the end of his interview—about the man, and what he'd tried to do to him—had now broken free like a blood clot inside Kearnes' brain from the place of safety and anonymity he had assigned them. And that potentially fatal clot was now making its way slowly, but surely, toward the center of his reason.

"Do you really feel that strongly about this?" Kearnes asked him.

But Thud didn't answer him. He just stood there like an immoveable mountain, watching Kearnes' eyes; trying to understand what he thought it was he was seeing in them.

"All right," said Kearnes. "We'll have a quick look around, ourselves."

"And then we're going home."

CHAPTER 28

▼

They used a free map Thud had gotten from the park ranger on duty at the ranger station to pinpoint the three main trails in the park and campground area. The Cooper Ridge Nature Trail was a one and three quarter mile loop that circled close to the outside perimeter of the entire campground; sometimes passing within just a few feet of occupied camp sites.

The South Jetty Trail was a ten foot wide, paved, pedestrian and bicycle path, which was heavily traveled, and was a one mile long link between the park's day use area and the South Jetty Road.

The last one of the three, the Old Jetty Trail, was also a mile in length and ran in the same general direction that the South Jetty Trail did. Along the way the two separate trails did sometimes cross paths, but the Old Jetty Trail was narrow and primitive, sparsely used, and in some places appeared to completely disappear amongst the blind confusion of the grass covered sand dunes, and small clusters of tightly growing together shore pines, which made everything look the same from every angle, once a person had lost their way.

This was the trail ten year old Colin Boyer had last been seen on by the last person ever to see him alive, his sister, as they had ventured out on it from the Day Use area parking lot at the south end of the campground.

She had told the detectives that after traveling on the trail for a short way, they could no longer see where to go next, so she had become nervous and told Colin they should turn back. But Colin had only teased her for being scared, taunted her to come with him, saying they could make their own path through the high, grass choked sand dunes. She had become frightened then, and started to cry. Colin had told her to go back to their camp, if she was scared. Then he had turned and walked into the sea of sharply bent, wind blown grass, that was as high as his shoulders…and the earth had swallowed him up.

Thud suggested they split up, and each start at one end of the trail and eventually meet in the middle. He got two plastic evidence bags, two pairs of blue latex gloves, and his portable radio out of the trunk of the car. He gave one of the bags and a pair of the gloves to Kearnes, and then showed him how to set his own portable on a common channel they could communicate together on called "Open." On the map he showed him the spot he would drive to and park first, campsite number 43; and he would need, he calculated, about fifteen minutes from there to walk on the South Jetty Trail to where it intersected with the Old Jetty Trail. Once there, he could call Kearnes on his portable, and the search would begin.

Thud drove the short distance to the Day Use parking area and Kearnes got out. They did a quick radio check with each other on their portables, and then Thud accelerated out of the parking lot, ignoring the posted ten mile per hour speed limit sign as he headed for the north end of the park.

While he waited to hear Thud come up on the radio and give him the signal to start, Kearnes took in his surroundings. Less than two hundred yards away he could see the sparkling blue Pacific ocean rolling ashore on the blond caramel colored sand beach, which was awash with campers and tourists.

There were kids down on their knees digging holes with their hands; mucking out mounds of muddy sand and squealing with mock fear as the incoming waters rushed threateningly close to their fledgling sand castles.

People flew kites overhead in the strong ocean breezes, or walked their dogs; throwing sticks for them to retrieve out into the first line of breakers. And staring in shock when they sometimes saw their beloved pet being carried sideways down the coastline in a rip tide as they swam back in, stick in mouth. But since dogs were instinctively smarter than humans in the water, they rarely drowned. They just swam with the flow until they felt sand beneath their paws, and then could walk themselves ashore.

The Day Use parking lot itself was like a beehive of constant activity. Just like the Sea Lion Caves, every parking spot was taken. Idling vehicles cruised round and round through the lot like circling sharks, just waiting for something to move…anything. The people lucky enough to have already found a parking place made trip after trip to and from the beach to their vehicles and back; getting inside the locked Vans, and SUV's, and cars…then leaving with blankets, inflatable toys, food, coolers, more clothing, less clothing, cameras, reading material…and even some of them; with binoculars.

The sound of traffic passing by on Highway 101, and across the Yaquina Bay Bridge, was a constant whishing, humming sound, and it suddenly struck Kearnes that you never heard car horns any more in heavy traffic. When he was a kid growing up, even in Kansas car horns were a backdrop sound on the rural roads and highways. Somebody was always honking at somebody else for some reason, sooner or later. But nowadays? No; now it was more common for trouble or distress on the highways to not announce itself in any form. Problems, whether by accident or design, just flared up and were suddenly "there"…without any warning. It was as if people had forgotten their cars still even had horns. Or maybe they were just too afraid to use them now, for fear of the unwanted reaction they might bring.

As Kearnes stood there, in full uniform, people passed by him within less than a couple of feet, but no one seemed to notice he was a police officer. In fact, no one seemed to really notice him at all. He wondered if that's how it had been with Colin Boyer. If someone had walked him across this very same parking lot. Put him into a vehicle. Shut, and then locked the doors. And no one had noticed a thing.

"One Charlie Four…to One Charles One," came Thud's voice over Kearnes' portable radio. He took the radio from its holder on his gun belt, and transmitted back.

"Charles Four…go ahead."

"Okay, chief," said Thud. "I think I'm on my end; of the Old Jetty Trail. Where are you?"

"At the trailhead, in the Day use area," Kearnes answered him.

"Copy," said Thud. "Let's do it then."

"Copy," Kearnes said. He put the portable back in its holder and snapped it down.

There was a wind splintered, wooden sign bolted to a steel post in the ground that announced the name of the trail, and the distance it traveled to its end, but little else to mark the trail as Kearnes made his way past it.

He followed the shallow channel in the sand that was the Old Jetty Trail; catching a glimpse of the much wider and paved South Jetty Trail off to his right, which he was also walking parallel to now. Its south end trail head was located in the Day Use parking area too, but after traveling less than a hundred yards it disappeared from his sight as a barrier of sand, beach grass, and stunted pines rose like a wall from out of the earth.

For supposedly being a mostly untraveled trail, he curiously began to find signs of quite a few people having been on it; and recently.

There were a few fresh cigarette butts from three different brands; all in a little pile in the middle of the trail, as if a small group had stopped to smoke, and talk. Next, he found a candy bar wrapper, from a giant sized Snickers. And not far from the wrapper, a cheap plastic fluorescent green retractable ink pen, with the logo of McGruff the Crime Dog printed on it in black, and the words "Lincoln County Sheriff Department Crime Stoppers—Take A Bite Out Of Crime."

This was the obvious scat that had been left behind by the Search and Rescue Team who had been through the area the first morning after the Boyer boy had been reported as missing. Or maybe even earlier today. A trail of thrown down garbage and accidentally dropped minutia that even a blind man could have followed at night.

Search and Rescue members were dedicated people all right; volunteers with some training, but not enough to know that a search for a missing child under suspicious circumstances could also be a search for a crime scene…just as Thud had said. And a crime scene was never something that was meant to have things added to it. The goal was to find the things there that weren't supposed to be there; then carefully package them up and take them to the crime lab, where the real work of investigation would begin.

But as he began to move further into the dunes, they started to get higher— some of them thirty or forty feet high—and the clumps of beach grass grew broader, deeper, and much denser. What had once been a twelve to eighteen inch wide identifiable groove in the sand, devoid of any vegetation and twisting and turning ahead of him in a definite if uncertain direction, now seemed to have vanished into the anonymity of the surrounding landscape. And he found no further trace of any human being having come this way.

He could hear the steady belching of the ocean surf off to the west of him, but as tucked as he was deep down inside the soft little valleys of sand, with the rustling grass, and the green Christmas sized trees all around him, the ocean sounded hollow, and fuzzy, and very far away. Like the same sound you heard when you picked up a dry seashell and held it tightly to your ear.

But he could still smell the thick, wet ocean air; could almost taste the nauseatingly cloying scent of it at the back of his throat now as he swallowed hard, trying to keep his esophagus from starting to spasm. He stopped and looked around him; looked back in the direction from which he had come…but now he wasn't sure exactly where that was. And then, as silly and ridiculous as it seemed to him, Kevin Kearnes began to feel closed in.

He could still see the bridge from where he was, or at least a portion of it; and could still hear and see some of the cars driving across it. And he could hear the ocean; the crying sea gulls, the sound of the wind filtering through the long, whip thin tips of the beach grass. And now, he could also hear the sound of his own breath as it started to come out of his mouth in ragged, half gasps.

He walked quickly first in one direction, stopped, then turned and veered off another way. He was surrounded by a wall of sand and grass wherever he turned, as if he'd fallen into the cone of a giant dormant sand volcano.

As he began to jog away in a new direction one leg of his uniform trousers was lanced by a low lying blackberry bush. A dozen of its sharp thorns tore into the wool pants fabric and snagged there firmly, like tiny brown grappling hooks, and he tripped and went down to the ground, hard. He landed on his side where the portable radio was on his gunbelt, and felt a sharp pain race from his ribcage, to up underneath his arm.

He sat up, slowly, and felt his side, tender and painful...then removed the radio that had punched him in the ribs, from its leather holster. He saw that the rubber antenna was broken at the steel base connecter where it plugged into the radio's top, and when he touched it, it wiggled slightly, back and forth. He depressed the transmit button, to call Thud, and saw the red LED transmit button light up. But there was no sound of breaking radio squelch noise when he let up on the button...because no signal had gone out through the broken connection in the antenna.

He dropped the radio in the sand between his feet and stared at it as if it were the last link he had between reality—as he thought he had known and understood it for all the years of his adult life—and the cold surge of insanity that he felt spreading through every molecule of his body. It was as if he had been injected with a powerful truth serum that was stripping away the deepest, most stubbornly imbedded lies inside of him; like a chemical peel, applied to the surface of his soul.

For hours now he had been forcing the voice of young Chris Lawless from his head, shouting it down mentally whenever he would hear the young boy's words begin to pound against the thin wall of reason in his brain, demanding to be let in. The local patrol deputy who'd interviewed the boy hadn't suspected anything criminal related to the boy's short and voluntary disappearance from his parents. So why the hell couldn't Thud have just kept his nose out of it, and left well enough alone? Because Thud was a good cop...that's why.

Kearnes was like the patient who went to see his doctor for a routine check up, or a nagging cough, or touch of the flu that just wouldn't go away. And then left the doctor's office two hours later in utter shock, disbelief, and denial after having been told he was actually, instead, dying of some terminal disease.

It was this unique ability of human beings under circumstances and situations which manifested themselves in such impossible levels of stress such as this—to temporarily suspend all disbelief; which had been allowing Kearnes *not* to accept, and *not* to believe, what he had heard Chris Lawless saying.

But the truth is the most powerful antidote against even the greatest of lies; including living your entire life as one. The truth is what really is; and in the end, what shall always be, for all of us. And Kevin Kearnes was no exception.

He grabbed the broken radio and scrambled to his feet. His heart was racing now and adrenalin, mixed with pure dread, poured into his bloodstream as if a dam inside him holding back a lifetime of unreleased horror had suddenly burst; the black waters of panic rapidly rising all around him now. He *had* to find Thud. They *must* leave this place. He remembered now, that he *had* to keep the secret. At all times and at all costs; he must always keep his secret.

Kearnes began to run. He knew that Thud had started on his end of the trail generally north of him; parallel to the south jetty and almost beneath the bridge. So he ran toward the bridge, because it was the only landmark in that direction he could clearly see. He took the path of least resistance, a straight line, as the panic that was surging through him drove him forward. Charging up and over the first sand dune in his path, and then stumbling and falling in the weight shifting sand, he got back up and continued to run on the sheer blind faith that just over the top of the next sand dune he would see Thud, and they could leave, and this would all be over with.

He saw the wall of blackberry bushes looming up ahead, fanning out on each end of an even bigger dune in his way for at least twenty yards. It was a massive growing fence of the green, sweet fruit laden vines that rose from the ground like rolls of razor sharp prison wall wire…but it didn't look all that deep to Kearnes and so he plowed straight ahead into them, and was immediately caught.

It had been cold and foggy earlier that morning before they had left Cutter Point so Kearnes had decided to wear a long sleeve uniform shirt, and now it was his only saving grace as he writhed and twisted against the cutting vines that had penetrated his clothing everywhere, from his ankles to his wrists.

Both his arms were imbedded with thorns at the elbows and as he ripped his right arm free to reach for the knife in its sheath on his gunbelt, he saw the dark blue fabric of his shirtsleeve open as neatly as a surgeon's incision, and beneath it the flesh of his forearm sprouted bright red with blood.

He cut and hacked at the thick vines with the knife and when one would be chopped loose, it would spring forward or back and plunge deeply into his clothing or skin again, attaching itself in another spot. He used both his hands now as he worked frantically to back himself out of the impossible trap, and both were becoming a shredded, bloody mess as the thorns hooked deep into his flesh, and then gouged out channels of tissue as his movements became more and more violent.

And then, just as suddenly as he had been caught, he was finally freed. He ran to his right, down the length of the line of the blackberry bushes and well past the end of them, and then cut sharply back to the left to go up and over the big dune. His uniform was in tatters and he could feel the blood trickling down both his legs beneath his torn pants as he pumped his way through the deep sand to the crest of the big dune, the muscles of his thighs burning.

He staggered down the other side of the dune, and saw a much lower landscape of rolling sand and beach grass ahead. He glimpsed a piece of sparkling, blue ocean water as he ran; saw the bridge ahead, growing larger, and could hear the tires of the vehicles now skimming across its asphalt surface.

He cleared the next sand dune, and then went over another, and one more after that; gaining momentum as he went because the running was much easier now. And so as he neared the top of the next sand dune in line he was moving fast…much too fast to stop when he saw Thud kneeling in the sand with his back to him near the bottom of the dune.

He tried to get his weakening legs under control but it was no use; they folded beneath him like the legs on a cheap card table and he pitched forward on his face, tumbling end over end down the steep side of the sand dune and coming to rest just a few feet away from Thud.

Thud had taken his suit jacket off and spread it out on the sand next to him. On top of it were the clear plastic evidence bag, and the empty black nylon case for the small digital camera he carried in his briefcase. He was wearing the blue rubber gloves and holding the digital camera in one hand, but put it down on top of his jacket next to its case, as if he had just finished using it.

"Don't come any closer," he said, glancing up at Kearnes, and then pointing to something small sticking out of the sand in front of him.

Kearnes was breathing hard. A blackberry vine must have whipped him across his face at some point because there was a small lateral slice beneath his left eye, which was bleeding profusely now, the blood flowing down his cheek and beginning to drip from his chin and onto the white sand.

But Thud acted as if he barely noticed Kearnes kneeling there next to him, and didn't acknowledge his physical state at all. He was sweating and pale, and his face was as white as the sand all around him.

"I tried to call you on the radio," he said. His voice was dull; devoid of any emotion. "I saw this part of it sticking up. Out of the sand. Just like it is now. I haven't moved it yet. I think it's the tail."

Kearnes looked at the object, half buried in the sand.

"My radio is broken," he offered. "So I never heard your call. That's why I came looking for you."

"He was telling the truth," Thud almost whispered. "I can't believe this is here. It must have just been lying out in the open…and they trampled right over it."

He gently bent over the object, and with his blue latex covered fingers, began to smooth away the sand from around it without touching it.

"We should leave that right where it is, Thud," Kearnes said. "And get Lincoln County down here. This is their crime scene, now."

"Sure," Thud said. "I'll be happy deliver it to them, personally. Along with all of my photos. Just as soon as I get this to Salem first. To the O.S.P. lab there; for latents, and DNA."

"Thud…"

"Goddamit, *his* prints are on this, chief! And probably the Boyer kid's prints, too!

"So, I'm going to photograph it, bag it; and then we're driving straight out of here…to Salem. It's only ninety minutes away. You can take my car back today, and I'll rent a car and drive back tomorrow. But I'm not going to let anybody fuck up this case…any further than it already has been."

Thud had all the sand cleared away from around the object now. He grasped it by its tail with two gloved fingers and picked it up, holding it in the air in front of him, blowing delicate puffs of air on it to remove some clinging sand. The toy whale had a white painted eye with a blue center on either side of its head, and with its long, blue, tooth studded open jaw, it looked as if it was smiling at them.

Thud dangled the whale in front of him as he turned it slightly, and squinted to read the small raised printing in the plastic on its belly.

"Made…in…China," he read.

"Well, that fucking figures."

He laid the whale down on his grey jacket, picked up the camera and turned it on, and began to photograph it next to a small, extended tape measure with a yellow blade that he'd taken from his pants pocket.

Kearnes knelt in the sand, watching Thud take pictures of the little blue whale, and now it looked as if it was smiling only at him. Like an old, long lost friend. Gone forever, but having returned now.

And eager to resume their relationship, where thing's had left off.

CHAPTER 29

▼

The drive to Salem had taken longer than two hours. Instead, it was almost a three hour trip, because Thud had decided, finally, to drive normally.

The urgency he'd had earlier that morning had been replaced by his need to protect the precious cargo he now had on board, and to think about his obsessive premonition—rather than just pure dumb luck—which had led him to stand in the very same few square feet of sand that a killer had, only hours before.

They had taken old U.S. Highway 20 from downtown Newport, twisting through the lush verdant dairy land valleys just inland from the coast, until they ascended high into the timber covered mountains with their great swathes of vacant clear cut trees, that looked like places on a man's beard he had missed while shaving.

As they had rolled through the small towns and villages of Toledo, Eddyville, Blodgett, Wren, and Philomath, both men had been quiet, lost in their separate thoughts about the events of the day, and what the next one might bring.

Just outside of Corvallis Thud had taken the southbound on ramp to Interstate-5 and in less than thirty minutes they were in the Capitol, pulling into the police only parking lot of the headquarters of the Oregon State Police.

Thud had asked Kearnes to find him the highest ranking uniformed guy still in the building, at almost five o'clock, that they could, and to use that magic word, "chief", to make things start happening fast, and keep happening all night long if necessary.

He knew that he was out of his league now and that it was all up to his chief if they were going to get any help, and in turn, any results back on their evidence either that same night or at least by early the next morning.

Kearnes managed to pull himself together mentally for a few minutes and didn't let Thud down; making contact with a lieutenant in uniformed patrol, who led him to the chief of detectives. And he, in turn, after listening to their story about the murders of Ricky Cates and Tyler Dunne, and their interview earlier that morning with Chris Lawless, and their description of how, and what they had found in the sand dunes at South Beach State Park less than an hour after that interview had ended, made a call across town to the Crime Lab and then told both Thud, and Kearnes, that all the resources of the Oregon State Police were now at their complete disposal.

Kearnes had then driven Thud to a hotel close by O.S.P. Headquarters, and had given him his own city issued credit card to use for the hotel and his meals, to rent a car, and for any other incidentals including his flight back home.

Thud asked him to get a room also, and stay…just until mid-morning. But Kearnes told him he couldn't do that.

After Thud had elicited a promise from him to go by and check on Margie and the girls as soon he got back, no matter how late it was, Kearnes took Thud's hand written directions on how to get out of the city and back onto the freeway southbound. And then he left, ending his nightmare of a day at last; wishing he could turn back the clock just twenty four hours and do it all over again, but this time, much differently. And wishing he had never heard of this godforsaken place…Cutter Point.

It was a four hour drive south down Interstate-5, passing through Eugene and Cottage Grove, Roseburg, and Sutherlin, and he drove non-stop until he finally reached Grants Pass. Here, he left the freeway, cutting across the small, clean, downtown area of the little mountain city in light traffic on Sixth Street, and passing beneath the big blue "IT'S THE CLIMATE" sign there. As Sixth Street ran out he turned right onto Highway 199, the beginning of the Redwood Highway, which would take him across the Siskiyou Mountains, through the northern tip of California to just outside of Crescent City, then up the coast a short few miles and across the border to Cutter Point.

But he needed to make a quick stop now, before going any further. He pulled into the first gas station he saw, a Chevron at a strip mall on the edge of town, and filled the almost empty Ford's tank with gas. He took a quick restroom break, and then called Britt on her cell phone from his, letting it ring and ring, but there was no answer. It was only ten o'clock. She should still be up; and in any event he knew she would answer her phone even if she was sound asleep.

Unless she was *that* angry with him, for what had happened the night before? He hadn't called her to let her know approximately when he and Thud would be back from their trip to Florence, and he realized now what a mistake that had been. It had also been a mistake to have waited until he'd driven this far to have only thought about calling her now. But still...where was she? And why wasn't she answering her phone?

Beek turned out all the lights in room 144 at The Sand Dollar Motel, then opened the door a crack to check the parking lot area first before going out to his Van. The lot was medium full with the vehicles of guests; not unusual for a Thursday night in July.

But he knew that by tomorrow afternoon there wouldn't be a single room, or cabin, or parking space left at the popular beach front motel. And since he needed *this* particular room, room 144, until at least Monday morning, it hadn't been too awfully difficult to bribe the motel manager with the two bottles of wine he had brought with him, into calling the people who had already reserved the room for the weekend and tell them there had been an oversight with their reservations...the room was not going to be available, after all.

From the small motel room closet he took the two plastic one gallon buckets, and the bottle of Pine-Sol, that he'd bought at Wal-Mart on his way into town four hours earlier. It was the same Wal-Mart where he'd purchased the clam shovel he had used to dig the hole for the Madrone branch that he'd tied Tyler Dunne to, after killing him, and it had given him an immense thrill to be walking down those same store aisles again; a wolf among the flocks of unknowing, bleating sheep that had been milling all around him.

There were two guest ice machines at The Sand Dollar; one next to the motel office, and another one sheltered in a little wooden alcove built at the farthest end of the first level of rooms. He put the buckets inside each other, and then put the Pine-Sol in the buckets, and slipped quietly out of his room.

Halfway down the concrete walkway to the far ice machine, two young children, a boy and a girl, burst from their room and stood in his way, fighting and arguing over a toy. Beek stopped, waiting for them to become aware of him. And when they did—the boy glancing up at him first, then the girl—he looked at them so malevolently, and with such unabridged hatred, that both children instantly withered under his stare. They dropped the toy that had been in contention and both frantically clawed at the doorknob of the room until the door opened, then ran back inside as quickly as they had come out, slamming the door behind them.

When he reached the old style ice machine he set the buckets and Pine-Sol down, and then opened its thick rectangular insulated door. The inside was full of crushed ice; no need to press any buttons and wait until a small quantity of ice was doled out from an automatic hopper, like on the newer machines. There was a plastic ice scoop attached to the inside wall of the machine by a small chain. He picked up the scoop and grabbed one of the buckets, and soon had them both filled to the brim with ice.

He encountered no one as he walked out into the middle of the parking lot to his white Van, an ice filled bucket in each hand and the bottle of Pine-Sol wedged beneath one arm pit. Setting his implements down on the ground, he unlocked and opened only the right door of the Van, then took hold of the plastic spigot at the bottom end of the long white, plastic insulated cooler, and tugged on it. It came open with a wet "plop", followed by a gushing stream of grayish water spewing out in an arc onto the gravel of the parking lot. Beek stood off to one side, careful that none of the water splashed onto his work boots, or pants; letting the cooler drain completely.

When the water had reduced to a slow dripping, he replaced the plug in the end of the spigot, and then moved the plastic tarp aside covering the top of the cooler. As he opened the cooler's lid, a sickly sweet and redolent odor—like a package of pork chops left too long in the refrigerator and now tinged with green—escaped into the air, making Beek's nose twitch.

He stuck his hand inside the cooler and felt the face of the boy at the top, Colin Boyer. The skin and flesh had the feel and consistency now of cold play dough; a good change from the previously hard and unyielding, wax like tissues of rigor mortis both boys had been possessed of a few hours after he had strangled each of them.

It was after this state of post mortem rigidity had left the bodies of both, that he'd begun his icing ritual; stopping wherever he could at grocery and convenience stores, gas stations and shopping malls...any place that sold bagged, crushed ice, as he made his way leisurely down the Coast Highway, 101, to his final destination: Cutter Point.

He knew he couldn't keep up this temporary preservation routine for much longer. Tomorrow, Friday, it would be four days since he'd killed Peter Mossbrooker—the boy in the cooler underneath Colin Boyer—on Monday evening; at a remote area off Highway 101 a few miles outside of Seaside.

The next day, Tuesday, he had drug Colin Boyer from the sand dunes at South Beach State Park late in the afternoon, to his Van parked beneath the Yaquina Bay Bridge, where he'd strangled him in the front seat. But as he hid the body in the cooler in the back of the Van, he couldn't find the little blue whale he'd given to the boy shortly after he had approached him. He went back out

into the dunes, to search for it, but when he heard voices coming his way, shouting the boy's name, he had left the area, quickly.

But his third student—the one at the Sea Lion Caves—he'd had to let go;
because the circumstances in which he had encountered him were not favorable.
Even though he'd wanted to kill him *very badly* after finding out he was just like
Ricky Cates; small for his age and already too corrupted by the world to be of any
use to either God, or the edification of anyone else.

But no matter what steps he took now, short of fully embalming both bodies,
nothing would stop the purification process; if in fact it had not already begun.

The odor problem was arising from the Mossbrooker boy. He had apparently
evacuated his bowels as Beek had ratcheted the binocular strap tightly against his
throat, crushing the boy's larynx as he lifted him off his feet and offered him up
to Jehovah in the night sky; while he bayed and cried like a mad dog at the moon
that was hidden among the clouds.

Beek opened the top of the cooler door as far as it would go, then spread the
ice from both buckets evenly back and forth across the stacked bodies, as if he was
sowing seeds in a field for planting. It wasn't enough, so he closed the Van door
and made another trip back to the ice machine.

After his third trip to the ice machine he had almost emptied it, but the cooler
was filled with ice to its top, and both of the bodies were nicely packed and completely hidden from sight beneath it. He set the empty buckets in the back of the
Van, and opened the bottle of Pine-Sol. Carefully; he poured it evenly, back and
forth again, across the top layer of ice, as if he was making a giant, amber colored
snow cone, until the bottle was empty. He re-capped the bottle and threw it in
one of the buckets, then bent his head down into the cooler; his nose just an inch
from the ice…and sniffed.

Nothing. Nothing but clean, pine scent.

He closed the lid of the cooler, grabbed the buckets and empty Pine-Sol bottle, and had just shut the Van door and locked it when across the parking lot he
saw the yellow beam of a flashlight bobbing toward him in the dark on the trail
that led from the beach cabins to the motel office.

He slid around the driver's side of the Van, deftly unlocked the driver's side
door, and got inside; closing the door quietly and sliding down in his seat. It was
a woman.

As she came nearer he saw she was carrying a small flashlight in one hand, and
what looked like a plate with something on it, covered in clear plastic wrap, in
her other hand. Her purse dangled from its strap slung over her left shoulder and
bumped gently against her hip as she walked on the uneven trail.

Beek watched as she came within a few cars of where he was parked, then stopped and set the plate down on the hood of a small blue car. She turned the flashlight off, unlocked the car door, and as she picked up the plate and walked around to the opposite side of the car and opened the passenger door, setting the plate and her purse inside on the seat, he got a good look at her face; the pale blonde hair, those eyes…and he recognized her.

It was the blonde Jezebel whore he had seen that night at the hospital…with the policeman. He felt a sudden savage beating inside his head, and his heart; a thousand Angel's wings thrashing wildly, lifting him instantly to new heights of comprehension and enlightenment, as he realized the hand of God himself must have forced her from nowhere out of the darkness, and straight to him. And that she, in turn, would lead him to the policeman.

He saw Britt McGraw get in the car, heard the car's engine start up, and then saw its headlights come on. The little blue car lurched sharply forward out of its white lined parking stall, and drove out of the parking lot, turning right onto the main road.

He took the Van's key from his jacket pocket, and put it in the ignition.

And then turned it.

CHAPTER 30

▼

Britt McGraw was happy on this night. Happier than she'd ever been before in her entire life. Even happier than she believed she probably had any right to be; but she could work on those self-defeating feelings, because now she had time. Time to think about her life, and the possibility of all the new choices she could make. She no longer needed to react to the unrelenting pressure that had finally pushed her to the precipice of taking another human being's life, in order to be able to finally find some peace in her own. She had *him* now…Kevin. Because he had won *her* heart completely, by giving her the precious gift of his own.

She had been right about Kevin Kearnes the night he'd come to her on the beach, and she'd slapped him, and told him he had "ruined everything" for her…because he had. Only not in the way she had thought about it, and meant it, then.

What Kevin had "ruined" was her chance to make the last—and probably most fatal—mistake of her life. A mistake which she had been driven to the brink of making by her inability to any longer stand the pain of living her life without the capacity, and ability, to truly love anyone…or to accept the love of someone else. And then somehow, in some way completely incomprehensible to her, Kevin Kearnes had walked into her life one night; and started loving her. And what was even more incomprehensible to her? She…had now started loving him.

The oatmeal raisin cookies on the plate next to her on the seat were still warm. They had steamed up the plastic food wrap she had tugged tightly down over them, snugging in the edges of the wrap all around the underside of the plate. But their warm, home baked aroma was still able to escape and quickly filled the inside of the little car with a good, rich smell.

And she knew they would taste just as good as they smelled, too. Because she had baked batch after batch of the cookies all day long at the cabin, practicing and perfecting the recipe and trying the results out on Margie Compton and her two girls, who had come to spend the day with her at the beach, until she had received the highest compliment possible from Margie's youngest daughter, Selena, who had proclaimed Britt's cookies to be; "bedderst even than my Mommy's!"

It had been a wonderful and carefree "girls day"; a good way for them both to pass the time and not worry about Kevin and Thud while they were at work far away up the coast, investigating something to do with those two horrible murders. Britt had worked with the police on more than one occasion in her professional life, and she knew how some officers could be consumed entirely with some of their cases; especially the ones involving the death by violent means of children.

She would never have called Kevin's cell phone while he was working on a case as important as this, and risk interrupting him in the middle of something crucial; or at the very least, rudely distracting him. And then there was the added circumstance of him having been angry with her when she'd last seen him, and obviously hurt by what she had said to him. But still, as a woman, she inwardly wished that he would have called her today...just once.

No matter, though. Men were still cave dwellers emotionally, to a large degree, and needed time alone to think things out by themselves during times like this. When Margie had called her a little after eight thirty and told her she'd heard from Thud, who was spending the night in Salem, and that Kevin had decided to drive back to Cutter Point tonight and would probably be home quite late—sometime after midnight—she had baked her last, and best yet batch of his favorite cookies.

And now she was making the short drive over to his apartment at The Sea Breeze, to leave them on his doorstep, along with a note, to tell him that she was falling in love with him...too.

It was almost ten o'clock. If he was home when she got there, her plan was to rush into his arms; smother him with kisses and tell him how sorry she was for the fight they'd had and how it had all been her fault.

Then she would strip off his clothes and put him in the apartment's small and very claustrophobic shower stall, and squeeze in naked beside him, soaping his body all over under the fine spray of hot water, and letting her fingers wander over him to the places they held as sacred between only themselves.

But if he wasn't home yet, she would leave the cookies, and the note, and go back to the cabin; let him get some rest after his exhausting day and very long drive. Tomorrow would come soon enough. After all…she had time now. All the time in the world.

There was no traffic anywhere on the road. Beek could just barely make out the taillights of the little blue car up ahead, but he knew she had to be driving into a dead end area. He cut his headlights, and continued to follow her.

This was where the farthest inlet of the Harbor was located. He could see the beginning of the dark outlines now of the boats tied in their berths off to his left, illuminated very poorly by the sparsely placed lights on steel poles affixed to the wooden docks themselves. A good half of them seemed to be burned out, or otherwise not working.

The road they were on ran down the center of a slender finger of land; with the Harbor on the inland side and Pearl Cove, and the ocean, on the other. But he knew it would end soon, and abruptly, in an area of abandoned buildings and defunct cannery facilities because he had been down here before; but only in the daylight.

He was surprised to see her car stopped at the side of the road directly ahead of him—its engine running but with only its parking lights left on—as he came around a blind corner after having lost sight of her for a few seconds.

She wasn't in the car. His eyes picked up movement and he saw her head floating through a maze of tightly parked cars in front of a big ugly green building on his right; saw the sign, then, at what was the entrance of the building's parking lot: "THE SEA BREEZE APARTMENTS-WEEKLY RATES."

He didn't remember this place. Maybe it had been vacant, and only recently renovated and resurrected for habitation. But that would be hard to believe. It looked like a huge, green bell pepper left unpicked in a garden…going rotten with blight; its roof beginning to blacken, the green paint curling and lifting away from the sides of its buckling wooden walls.

There was a sea of stacked, commercial steel crab pots in an empty field just to his left and he quickly pulled his Van into the middle of them and turned the engine off. As he made his way toward her car, keeping in the shadows as much as he could, he could see her fifty yards away, standing under the weak porch light of one of the lower level apartment doors. She looked like she was taping something to the door—a small piece of white paper, maybe—and as she finished and then bent down, stooping out of his line of sight to put the plate of cookies in front of the door, Beek's hand closed around the handle of her unlocked car door.

He quickly jerked open the car door, suddenly alarmed at seeing the small back seat area of the worse than compact sized car he would have to try and conceal himself in; but just until she was inside, and her door had closed shut.

He reached down and released the front seat adjustment lever, viciously batting the front seat forward with one powerful blow from the open palm of his hand, and had inserted his first leg inside the cramped car...when the whore's cell phone, buried somewhere near the bottom of her saddle bag sized purse in the front passenger seat...began to ring.

In one swift, lithe movement, Beek extracted himself from the car, closed its door shut with a soft, but solid click, and was across the road and into the dark hodgepodge of the stored crab pots before the cell phone had sounded its third, muffled ring.

He could barely hear the phone ringing from his position, and knew that the woman, who was walking back to her car now, wouldn't be able to hear it at all inside the closed vehicle with its engine running. But the phone kept on ringing; over and over.

Crouched down at the edge of the pots, he pressed the small button on the side of the face of his wrist watch, lighting up the watch's dial: it was exactly ten o'clock. She was within fifteen yards of the road and her car now when she stopped, and looked back at the apartment once...and as she turned around and took another step in the direction of the car...the phone suddenly fell silent.

He waited until she had turned around, and driven away, before coming out from his hiding place.

Getting back in his Van he checked his watch; he would give her fifteen minutes to return to The Sand Dollar and wherever it was she was obviously staying there, before he returned to his room. He stared at the apartment door where the woman had been standing. He wanted to go there and see what it was she had left for him, but he knew he could not chance doing that.

He needed everything to go perfectly now, from this point on. No mistakes. No missed steps.

As soon as the fifteen minutes had elapsed he would start up the Van, drive back to Room 144, normally—with his headlights on this time—and then secrete himself in his room. Where he would spend the rest of the night and all of the next day, if he had to, in prayer...asking God Jehovah both for forgiveness for what he had almost done tonight...and an answer to why it was that he had almost done it.

He needed to know from God why it was he had felt as if he was being led to kill the policeman's whore tonight when it was the policeman himself who really needed to be made an example of; so that all men would burn with a great desire to rise up and overcome the Spirit of Jezebel…rather than to be overcome by it.

Most of all though Uriah Beek, who had never touched any female sexually before in his life, nor had ever had the natural desire to do so, needed to know why it was that from the first moment he had seen the blonde woman emerge from the dark on the trail that led down to the cabins at The Sand Dollar, he had gotten an erection.

And why even now, after this female spawn of the Great Mother Whore had gone, his noticeable excitement still lay alongside his leg beneath the fabric of his work pants as hard as steel…like the very blade of Satan's sharpened sword itself.

CHAPTER 31

▼

A giant sugar cookie full moon hung in the cloudless night sky over the Rogue Valley, as Kearnes urged Thud's Ford up the highway toward the summit of the mountain pass at Hayes Hill.

He was over twenty miles now past the once unpretentious little logging town of Grants Pass that had—as he'd read in a newspaper article recently—been "discovered" in just the past couple of years by hordes of invading equity rich, new home building, and buying, Californians.

They had almost overnight driven the cost of the area's housing and real estate market up so high that local, working class people, couldn't afford to buy homes any longer. And the ones who owned their own homes before the boom began, and foolishly decided to sell, became near instant millionaires...but were then forced to move away because they couldn't afford to live there any longer, either. The same thing was happening in Cutter Point; first being invaded, and then degraded, as people like Vernon Bouchet´ moved in and literally took the community over, one expensive and overpriced square foot at a time.

He didn't know why he was worrying about things like this; he knew he would never be anything more than a renter. Tilly would keep him financially and emotionally imprisoned for the next fifteen years of his life, with her constant demands for more spousal maintenance, and more child support. While the months and years of forced estrangement from his two sons—for which she was responsible—would soon grow from a gap, to a chasm, and then finally to an impossible void; that could never be bridged between Father and sons in their lifetimes.

The moon cast a shadowy, vanilla light across the reaching tops of the forest. It made the steep sided mountains all around him shimmer and glow with a quivering effervescence, as the thick carpet of tall black trees seemed to be breathing deeply, in unison; trying to inhale the universe of pin point shining stars high above them.

He tried to concentrate on the solitude, and the solitary beauty of the mountains that was all around him, instead of the ugly revelation he felt inside now, slowly preparing to give birth. He was only barely holding it all at bay through sheer denial, and the slowly dissipating belief that none of what he thought he was beginning to remember, or seemed in some incomprehensible way to him as somehow familiar…was even real. He just didn't know *why* he was having these thoughts and feelings; why they were so persistent. And why they would not go away.

It was past midnight when Kearnes finally drove across The Blue Czar River Bridge and into downtown Cutter Point on a mostly traffic deserted Cutter Avenue; on his way to Sea Horse Drive to check on Margie and the girls as he'd promised Thud he would.

Spenser Sparling was working the graveyard shift, and as Kearnes approached the turn off to Sea Horse Drive he saw Spenser sitting in his black and white with his red and blues overheads on, filling out a citation to a driver he had pulled over in a beat up little beige colored Mazda.

Spenser gave Kearnes the "code four" signal out his open window with his right hand, still holding his pen, and then waved at Kearnes as he drove by. But Kearnes did not wave back to him; only barely acknowledged the young officer—who was really expecting his chief to pull over and shoot the breeze with him for a few minutes—with a slight, weary looking nod…then stared back at the road ahead of him and kept driving.

As he pulled into the long, banana shaped driveway of the Compton residence the automatic sensor operated security lights Thud had just installed in several places the week before along the rain gutter of the garage, and on two opposing corners of the house, came on; drenching Kearnes and the car in harsh, brighter than daylight, light.

Had he experienced the sensory overkill of these banks of brilliant lights the last and only time he'd ever visited here, when he had been invited to dinner by the Compton's—he would have wondered if Thud wasn't maybe being just a little bit paranoid about his personal home security measures. But now, he wondered if even this was enough. Because like Thud, he felt the same bleak and inexplicable chill inside him that seemed to have seeped into the very marrow of his bones, and no matter what he did he could not shake the cold, gnawing premonition…that something terrible was about to happen.

He rang the front doorbell and heard it echo softly inside the big house; then waited politely to see if it would have any effect before ringing it a second time.

It was late and he had really only wanted to drive by the house; to see if everything looked all right from the outside without having to actually wake Margie up. But Thud had adamantly insisted he see her, face to face, and after the day he himself had just personally experienced he was through with second guessing the heightened emotions and intuitions of his detective, and friend.

He had just touched his fingertip to the lighted button of the doorbell to ring it a second time, when he sensed movement on the other side of the door. He heard a deadbolt lock clicking open, and saw the door knob begin to slowly twist.

He took a half step away from the door just as it swung open backwards; revealing Margie Compton standing in the doorway entry wearing her bathrobe and slippers, and holding Thud's Smith & Wesson Airweight in her right hand, dangling straight down at her leg.

Her eyes were puffy with sleep, but suddenly grew wide as she stared at him, blinking rapidly.

"Kevin?"

"Hi Margie. Sorry if I scared you. I was actually hoping you were still up because Thud wanted me to…"

"You're damn right you scared me!" she blurted out. "Look at you! Did you get in a fight with a suspect or something?"

"What?"

"Look at your uniform! You have *blood* on your face. My God, what happened to you?"

Kearnes put his hand to his face, and felt the thin ridge of crusted blood beneath his eye. He had been so completely immersed in his own thoughts on the long drive home—about all that had happened that day—that he'd completely forgotten about his battle with the blackberry bushes. No wonder the attendant and the cashier, and two customers at the service station had been looking at him like they had.

"No," he said. "Not a fight. Thud and I were searching a beach up in Newport, for evidence…and I ran into some blackberry bushes. I kind of had a hard time getting out of them."

"Thud called me; and told me you would be stopping by to check on us. We're fine."

"But come inside, please. There's nothing that will get infected faster than berry thorn cuts; if you don't clean them up right away."

Margie led Kearnes into the kitchen and pulled out a chair for him to sit at the kitchen table; where she laid the .38 down. Then she put on a half a pot of coffee and while it began to brew, went upstairs to the master bathroom to get him a small tube of Neosporin ointment and two clean wash cloths to take home with him to clean his bloody wounds.

As the coffee was finishing its drip cycle she took a small cheesecake from the freezer and popped it into the microwave for a quick, one minute thaw. She cut them each a piece of the cheesecake, which she put on small plates, got two forks and two napkins, poured two cups of coffee; and then put all of it on the table and took a chair across from Kearnes.

He hadn't eaten anything all day; the tightening knots in his stomach had squeezed out the normal hunger pangs he should have been experiencing by now. Nor had he suffered any pain from the blackberry thorns which had hooked him deep, and tore into his flesh. But as Margie set the plate of cheesecake in front of him along with the headily fragrant hot coffee—that had steam curling up from the top of the cup like a Genie just let out of his bottle—Kearnes found himself suddenly both ravenously hungry, and in a great deal of discomfort from his multitude of small wounds that were now beginning to burn, and itch.

Margie let him take a bite of his cheesecake, and a couple of sips of his coffee before she said, "Thud told me on the phone that you two made some real headway in the case today; that you found out some very significant things."

"I think that would be an understatement," said Kearnes. "We really didn't have any sort of case at all when we left here this morning. But we do now. Thanks to your husband."

Margie nodded her head at Kearnes.

"Thud is a good police officer," she agreed.

"And he's a good detective, all right. But he would be the first one to admit how way in over his head he is in this whole thing, Kevin.

"This is little old Cutter Point, Oregon. We don't have serial killers around here. Serial skateboarders, serial parking violators, serial drunk drivers, yes…but not serial killers."

"Well…it looks like we do now," he said.

"I want to thank you for supporting my husband, and the other officers, like you have," she said. "No other chief we've had since Vernon Bouchet' became mayor, has even come close to doing what you have done for the police department."

Kearnes didn't say anything; he took a large bite from his cheesecake, and made sure he followed it with several long drinks from his coffee cup—all the while keeping his eyes averted to the plate on the table in front of him in the hope that she would soon change the subject. If Margie Compton knew the truth about him right now; about how he was "supporting" her husband, she would probably throw her scalding hot coffee in his face.

"Anyhow," she said, "I just wanted you to know how much you are appreciated around here."

"Thank you," he said. "And thanks for the cheesecake, and coffee. I was actually starving."

"You are most welcome," she said. "Britt might already have something better on hand for those cuts of yours…being a doctor, and all. But just make sure you at least get them washed up really good tonight, and treated with something."

Kearnes looked at his watch. "It's really late," he said. "After one already; so I don't think I'll be seeing her tonight. I don't want to wake her up."

"Oh!" said Margie, "I completely forgot to tell you! The girls and I spent the day with her, down at your cabin at The Sand Dollar."

"You did?" asked Kearnes.

"Yes," Margie said, "and we had a wonderful time."

"She baked cookies, and we talked while the girls played outside on the porch. And then later on we all went down to the beach, and Britt took her easel and water colors. Did you know she is a very good painter?"

"No," said Kearnes. "She's never mentioned anything about it."

"I guess she'd just bought the paints and the easel, and other things…the empty bags from the store were still sitting on the kitchen table," Margie said.

"Maybe she just wants to try and keep busy while you're away at work…so she doesn't miss you so much."

"I do know she loves to shop," Kearnes said.

"She is a very beautiful woman," said Margie, "both inside, and out."

"I'm glad I'm getting to know her as a friend."

Kearnes stood up from the table, and rolled the tube of antiseptic ointment she had given him, inside the two wash cloths.

"So am I," he said.

"Thanks again for the late night snack…and for these things. I'll make sure and put some on as soon as I get home."

Margie got up from her own chair. She picked up the Smith & Wesson from the table and slipped it into a pocket of her robe, then began to gather up the plates and silverware and empty coffee cups from the table and carry them over to the sink.

Kearnes had started to walk out of the kitchen, toward the hallway leading to the front door, when he heard Margie say, "Kevin?"

He stopped, and turned around.

"Yes?" he said.

"I just wanted to say good night; and to thank you again for coming by to check on us."

"I was happy to. Good night, Margie."

"Kevin? You really should stop by and see her; let her know you are all right."

"Like I said…it's really late, and…"

"Oh my Lord!" she exclaimed.

"And I thought I was married to *the densest* man in the world!" "Don't you know that when a woman is in love with a man…it is *never* a bother to her when that man *wants* to see her? And that it makes her feel so very special when he does?"

Kearnes didn't want to respond to her; he just wanted to turn around, and leave. But he could see Margie wasn't going to allow that; not by the way she was looking at him now.

"No," he finally said. "I guess I didn't know that. Thank you."

"Well," said Margie, "now you do know; and, you are welcome."

Kearnes managed to smile a half smile, and then waved good night to her and walked down the hallway and let himself out the front door of the house.

He got back into Thud's car and sat there for a couple of minutes; not doing anything. If only he could have just this one day back in his life…to do all over again.

But, he realized, even if he could, it would change nothing. Britt would have still loved him anyhow; whether he had gone with Thud yesterday, or not…whether he'd even let Thud go by himself, or not. But now it was too late.

Because *he* couldn't love Britt McGraw now.

He no longer had that right.

CHAPTER 32

▼

The city was like a graveyard; silent, forlorn, and empty as Kearnes drove through it; heading for his apartment, a hot shower, and then sleep. There was not a single car in sight downtown; not even Spenser Sparling's black and white. He took advantage of the wide open spaces, prodding the big Ford along Cutter Avenue at ten miles an hour over the speed limit; slowing for every annoying red light that seemed to blink on just as he entered an intersection…then running it, and driving on to the next one in his haste to reach the sanctuary of his apartment at The Sea Breeze.

He crossed the Blue Czar River Bridge and took the exit at Harbor Way, descending into the flat alluvial plain of the Harbor where the road narrowed down to two lanes, and skirted the thin crescent shaped piece of land that bowed inward, forming Pearl Cove.

The road straightened out again as it passed by the cove, approaching the wide, abandoned farm fields and groves of pine trees where The Sand Dollar was, and helplessly, he swerved the car off the highway and onto the road that led to The Sand Dollar's parking lot. He had to at least see her car parked there…and then he could go.

The parking lot was only about two thirds full, and not at all anything like it was on the weekends now when some of the overflow cars of guests were forced to park along the sides of the road that led into the motel.

That was why when he spotted Britt's little blue Geo parked in a space near the motel office, with three empty parking spaces open to the left of it, he couldn't understand why some jerk had pulled a beat up old white Ford Van so close to her driver's door that there was no possible way she could ever get in that side of the car.

He circled the two vehicles twice, noting the Van's Washington state license plates and looking for any signs of damage to her car. Then he put the Ford in park, took his flashlight from his equipment bag, and got out to inspect it closer.

He didn't see a scratch anywhere on the Geo, but the white Van had been parked so close next to it that he could barely get his hand in between the two front bumpers of the vehicles before his wrist became stuck.

Kearnes had seen this phenomenon many times before in his career. Only a drunk driver could accomplish such a masterful and precision job of parking. A sober person would have taken out the entire side of the Geo, both front and rear bumpers, and the driver's side mirror to boot.

He climbed back in the car and took the radio mike from its clip to call the Van's license plate in to the Dispatch Center; to find out who it was registered to. But he changed his mind, and replaced the mike on its clip. Shoshanna Perry was the only dispatcher working, and Spenser was the only officer on duty.

It was obviously a dead night, and if he called in the plate he knew Spenser would immediately be en route from wherever he was to see what he had; and that was the last thing he wanted. It was why he hadn't stopped by the department to drop off Thud's car first, and pick up his own. He would wait to check out of service with Shoshana on the radio as soon as he got to his apartment; knowing no one would bother him after that.

He took his notebook from the equipment bag and wrote the Van's license number—DED-696—in it; then replaced the notebook in the bag. He could run the plate tomorrow at work; or just call the office at The Sand Dollar in the morning, give the manager the license plate number, and have him go ask whatever guest the Van belonged to, to move it.

He drove the short rest of the way to The Sea Breeze, trying not to think of Britt, and how much he would miss her tonight…and for all the rest of the endless nights to come.

When he arrived he found a plate of oatmeal and raisin cookies on a plate sitting on his doorstep covered tightly with clear plastic wrap, and a lavender colored note, folded neatly in half, taped to his door. He carefully removed the note, and read it…*I hope these cookies turned out half as sweet as you are. Call soon. I love you—Britt.*

He put the key to his apartment door in the lock, and then opened it and stepped inside; turned on a light and smelled the dank, cold mustiness, surveyed the bare walls, the few pieces of cheap and uncomfortable mis-matched furniture, and the complete lack of anything tangible that spoke to this empty space as being a home…and he understood that he had only finally been returned to his cell…and that here, or someplace very much like it, he would stay…for the rest of his life.

He set the cookies and the note on the kitchen table, then stumbled into his bedroom and without turning on the light, stripped off his gunbelt, and his torn uniform, and let them fall to the floor.

He didn't want the hot shower now, and he didn't care about cleaning up his cuts. He only wanted the mind numbing relief of sleep. He sat on the edge of his bed, naked; and then curiously, felt himself foundering backwards into a boundless blackness…as if he'd fallen into a deep well.

And as he fell; down and down and down…he looked up and saw Ben's face in a small circle of pale blue sky above him…watching him fall.

He did not sleep for long; only two hours. But it was a sleep as deep as anesthesia, allowing the mental shock and strain to his mind and body from the day before to be repaired…to be recharged like a dead car battery that at the end of the day had simply refused to start any more.

He lay on his bed; listening to the distant rumble of the ocean which he could now tell, by the variation in the sounds of the pitch, and timbre of the waves crashing ashore…that the tide was currently coming in, rather than receding. It was close and stuffy in the apartment and his torn and bruised skin was glossy with his own sweat which further irritated some of the puncture wounds, making them burn with pain.

He pulled on a pair of jeans and walked barefoot outside in the cold, misty air to Thud's car, and got the ointment and clean wash clothes Margie had given to him. Back inside, he locked the apartment's door again and then started the shower. He let it run a long time, getting it steaming hot before he eased his tortured body beneath the fine, stinging spray; and stayed there, soaping himself and rinsing off, until the water finally began to run cold.

He toweled off, then carefully dabbed the ointment Margie had given him on the worst of the black berry wounds; the ones that were growing red and puffy, and beginning to weep a clear liquid from their centers. Then he dressed in jeans, and an olive green tee shirt with a black screen printed Pelican design on it Britt had bought him, and from his top dresser drawer, hidden beneath a stack of folded white jockey underwear, he took the Kahr nine millimeter an stuck it in his back pocket.

Kearnes didn't have a phone in his apartment. It was too painful of a proposition for him, having a phone sitting there staring at him day and night that never rang, because no one that mattered ever called him. And largely useless, too; because he didn't know where Tilly had taken his sons, and so he could not have called them. Having a home phone would have only reminded him of all this and the city gave him a cell phone to use for both work, and a reasonable amount of local personal calls, anyhow.

But just in case he ever had a need for it, he'd purchased a pre-paid calling card when he'd first arrived in town, and on some of his loneliest nights he'd taken the card to the small pay phone booth across the street outside the Harbormaster's Office and used it to call people back in Kansas…mostly old friend's of his and Tilly's…trying to find out where she was now…trying to find Ethan, and Alex.

He put his jacket on and went into the small kitchen area where he rummaged through two different drawers until he found the calling card, then left the apartment and walked to the pay phone booth.

It was just a little after four a.m., which meant it was just after six a.m. in Kansas. Ben would have already been up for an hour now…two hours, if the summer wheat harvest had already begun on the ranch.

He picked up the pay phone's receiver and squinting to read the calling car in the dimly lit booth, began punching in the card's 1-800 number, followed by the PIN number, and then finally the area code and phone number to the Kearnes Ranch. The phone on the other end of the line, just outside of Dodge City, Kansas, began to ring.

"Hullo?"

"Ben?"

"Kev boy! That you?"

Yeah…it's me, Ben."

"Well it's just great to hear your voice…finally, son!"

"It's great to hear your voice too, Ben."

"You do know, don't you, that if you were here right now…I'd have to kick your ass, Kevin. This phone call is about two months past due, on your part."

"I apologize, Uncle Ben. I really am sorry. I kept meaning to call, but settling in, learning the new job…"

"Speaking of your new job, chief," said Ben Kearnes, "do they even really have laws out there in Oregon to enforce?"

"We've got a few," said Kearnes.

"Well are any of them worth a damn? I heard you can go to a doc out there and get a free card...for marijuana."

"Yeah. That's true. You can," said Kearnes.

"Well, I'll be goddamned," laughed Ben.

"But," said Kearnes, "believe it or not, driving a motor vehicle without having your driver's license on you at the time in the State of Oregon is a crime. You can actually go to jail for it."

"Oh, well hell then!" Ben laughed even harder. "Then that kind of makes up for the free drugs law, now doesn't it!"

They spent the next twenty minutes, uncle and nephew—which were actually much closer in relationship to Father and son—talking about what had been happening in their respective lives over the nearly past three months, since Kearnes had left Kansas and moved to Oregon.

For Ben, who was now seventy three, the big news was the summer wheat harvest, which had commenced only two days before. And even though he'd had to hire a "custom cutting" harvest outfit from Mankato in recent years to come to the ranch every summer with their fleet of massive wheat combines, and monster grain hauling diesel trucks whose exhausts were vented up toward the sky over their cabs like fire snorting dragons, so as not to set the dry fields of ripened grain on fire with an accidental spark—he still enjoyed the hell out of each and every before dawn, to way past dusk day, that it all lasted.

Kearnes told him about the green mountains and hills of the Oregon countryside; about the ocean, and the dead whale on the beach that a bunch of crazy locals blew up...and nearly took out a nearby shopping center in the process. And he told him about the shooting contest at the range between him and Edgar Polk, and how he'd made that vegetable juice can fly around in the air as if it had sprouted wings, while he fired Ben's old .38 Super Colt at it and bullet after bullet expertly found its mark...just like he'd taught Kearnes to shoot as a young boy.

And when the conversation began to wane, the cadence of their words being drawn out longer, and the stories becoming shorter, Kearnes finally got to the heart of the matter about why he had really called Ben Kearnes on this very early July morning.

"Hey, Ben," he said. "You still got the old ranch hand quarters out back of the house? I remember you said you were thinking about tearing it down, now that it doesn't get used any more."

"Yep," Ben said. "She's still standing. But I've thought better of that rash statement since I made it a few years back."

"Oh?"

"Thinking of doing a little remodeling on it…and renting it out to private pheasant hunters as quarters during the upland bird season."

"To hunt on the ranch?" asked Kearnes.

"Yep," said Ben. "The Lohman's started guided hunts on their spread two years ago. You know how much they brought in last season?"

"How much?" asked Kearnes.

"Twelve thousand," said Ben. "And that was *after* expenses. Didn't include the duck and goose seasons, either. I'd imagine that was another five or six grand they took in, before all was said and done."

"Damn," said Kearnes. "That's more than half of your year's wheat harvest, right there."

"Trouble is," said Ben, "I'll have to get a state guide license first, and they don't exactly just hand those things out on the street corners in Topeka. They have a damn lottery system or something you have to sign up for, to even get on the list to apply for one."

"You still have plenty of pheasants on the land?" Kearnes asked him.

"Ha!" Ben laughed.

"The hens are so thick in the fields after they've been harvested, you'd swear you were looking at acres and acres of brown shag carpet! And the roosters? Well…let's just say there are more cocks here on this ranch, then there are in all the whore houses in Kansas City on a cold winter night!

Ben was seventy three now and lived all alone on the sprawling wheat ranch, but it was plain to see that he was just as much of a maverick as he'd ever been as a younger man. His language was still colorful and his ideas were still as big and bold as the "new" old west that he had grown up in. Kearnes didn't have the heart to tell him that there probably weren't any more true "whore houses" in operation in Kansas City…and that they had largely been replaced by internet escort services, and the much cheaper, less labor intensive bar and cocktail lounge dating ritual known as "hooking up."

"I'm glad to hear that old building is still standing," said Kearnes. "I used to love sleeping out there sometimes in spring when I was a kid; before the summer hired hands moved back in."

"Well, it hasn't changed a lick," said Ben. "I shut the water pipes off a few years ago…so they wouldn't freeze up and burst. But other than that, I haven't touched it."

Kearnes paused for a moment, trying to think of a good way to broach the subject; and then realized there wasn't one—and it was now, or never.

"Ben?"

"Yeah?"

"This is going to sound kind of crazy. But I left something out there…in the ranch hand house. When I was a kid. I hid it, actually."

"Hid what?"

"It's something I'd kind of like to pass on down to my boys. That is if its still there."

"What did you hide, Kevin?"

"Oh…it was a new fishing pole and tackle box that I got for my birthday one summer; I think when I was thirteen.

"I caught the tip of the pole in some willows down at the river the first day I took it fishing, and broke it. So I got scared and ran home, and pulled up a board on the floor in the ranch hand house, and hid them both there.

"I told my dad someone stole them when I was down at the river. That I set them down by the bank while I went to look for some grasshoppers for bait…and when I got back, they were gone."

There was nothing but silence on the other end of the line.

"Ben? You still there?"

"Yeah. Still here, Kev. Just thinking back is all. And I believe you've got it all wrong. I remember that new fishing pole of yours, and the tackle box."

"You do?"

"I'm the one that picked it up for your dad. Bought it at the Western Auto store downtown on Third, the night before you and your mom and dad, and Karen, left for vacation to Seattle that one bad summer.

"Your dad asked me to pick it up and bring it out to the ranch, because he was busy helping your mom pack. It was for your birthday; which would have been about a week after you all left.

"But you weren't thirteen, Kevin. You were only ten…going on eleven."

"No," said Kearnes. "No. I don't think so. You must be thinking of some other birthday I had."

"It was a sweet little Zebco; rod and reel combination," said Ben. "That reel was a neat little closed face, bait caster, with an all fiberglass rod. And the tackle box was a gold colored, plastic. A Plano, I think.

"Your mom and dad bought you the rod and reel, and I filled the tackle box with hooks, lures, split shot, and bobbers for you as my birthday gift. But that was the last time I ever saw either of them. When you came back from your vacation to the Space Needle, and the ocean, you didn't have them."

"I don't remember any of that," said Kearnes.

"What floor board do you think you hid those things under?" Ben asked.

"It was over in the corner, by the woodstove. It had a big knot in it...the board did."

"Well there's only one way to find out," said Ben. "I'm going to get the cordless phone, and a hammer and a crowbar...you call me back in five minutes, Kevin."

"No...Ben? I changed my mind. This is crazy!"

"Ben?"

But Ben was gone; leaving Kearnes with a buzzing phone receiver held against his ear, and the watch on his wrist ticking off the longest five minutes of his life.

When the five minutes was up, all Kearnes could do was stare at the calling card he held up in front of his eyes in his shaking hands.

The tiny phone booth had claustrophobically closed in around him now like a casket. He viciously elbowed open its articulated door, letting in a rush of mucid Harbor air that constricted his throat and pulled at the cheesecake digesting in his stomach that he'd eaten earlier at Margie's house, trying to bring it up.

With trembling fingers he devoted his full concentration to entering all the same numbers from the calling card again into the keypad of the pay phone, as he re-dialed Ben's phone number in Kansas.

As he listened to Ben's number ringing again, he didn't notice the headlights of Spenser Sparling's patrol car wash across the Harbor office a few feet away from the phone booth as Spenser pulled into the shadows off the road up the block and blacked out his unit.

Spenser had been patrolling the Harbor District when he was surprised to see Kearnes walking from his apartment building across the street to the pay phone booth next to the Harbormaster's Office. He wondered why his chief was up so early—it was only four fifteen in the morning—but he would wait until he got off the phone to ask him.

Ben finally picked up on the seventh ring, and he sounded as if he was out of breath.

"Hullo?"

"Ben...I didn't mean for you to go tearing up the floor of the hand quarters...it's not something that can't wait until maybe you start your remodeling."

"Looks like you already got me started on it this morning, son! I found your knot hole floor board, and I've got your old rod and reel, and the tackle box, right here in front of me."

"Oh...no," Kearnes gasped. "I changed my mind, Ben. Just throw them away for me, please. I'll buy the boys all new stuff."

"Throw them away? Like hell I will!" he said.

"They're a little grimy and dusty, but there's not as speck of rust that I can see on this reel. Pretty damned good condition, I'd say, for being underneath the floor of my hired hands bunkhouse for...what? Thirty one years?"

"Just stick them somewhere out in the barn, then," Kearnes said weakly. "I'll have a look at them next time I'm home."

"I have no idea why you thought this pole couldn't have been fixed," Ben said. "All's it needs is the top snipped off, just below the break, and a new guide tip glued on. How'd you say you broke it again?"

"In the willows," Kearnes said dully. "Down on the Arkansas...fishing. The first day I got it."

"Nope," said Ben. "The only place you could have gone fishing that day was down at the ocean, in Washington. Because that's where you and your folks, and your sister were on your birthday that summer. Long Beach, Washington."

"No," Kearnes said in a voice, that was more like a whimper now. "No, no, no...no."

"You were one rambunctious little scamp when you were a kid, I'll tell you," said Ben.

"I believe you must have snuck my Colt out of your dad's camp trailer on that trip, too. I loaned it to him take with him...driving clear on out across country and back like that with a family to protect. But when he gave it back to me, it had one round missing from the magazine, and it had been fired."

"It must have been my dad," said Kearnes. "He must have test fired it, or something."

"Ha!" Ben laughed. "Your Father never fired a handgun in his life! Didn't like 'em. Wouldn't even let me give him a shooting lesson with it before you all left. All he wanted to know was that there was a round in the chamber, where the safety was, and how to get it off."

"I didn't shoot your gun, Uncle Ben," said Kearnes, almost in a whisper. "None of that ever happened."

"Sure you didn't, son!" Ben laughed again.

"And I'll bet it *didn't* scare the hell out of you either when it *didn't* go off, right? Why do you think I started teaching you how to shoot the very next summer when you turned twelve?

"It was clear to me even then, that you had being lawman in your blood...and now just look at you today. You're a chief! I want you to know I am damned proud of you, Kevin. And your folks would be too, if they were still here."

Kearnes' heart was pounding now in his heaving chest, and he struggled to get a breath of foul sea air in the suffocating little booth that he'd shut himself inside again when Ben had answered his phone the second time. He needed to end this now; he could not listen to any more it.

"Ben…I have to go now," he said. "It's been nice talking to you. I'll call you again, soon."

"Hey now, just a minute hoss!" said Ben. "I'm not through checkin all this stuff out for you yet."

Kearnes heard a sharp noise as Ben apparently laid the cordless phone down on some hard object…followed by the sounds of something rattling, and then scraping. Then, a kind of noisy, silence.

"Ben?"

Kearnes heard him pick the phone up again.

"Whoee! We hit the jackpot here, Kev boy," Ben said excitedly.

"Your little tackle box is still chock full of what looks to be all the same tackle I bought for you, for your birthday. Do you know what some of these old lures and stuff might fetch on that internet eBay thing? Hundreds!"

"Please…just put it all out in the barn," Kearnes pleaded.

"Whoa…hold on here a minute…I've got some other stuff in the bottom of the tackle box."

Kearnes heard him set the cordless phone down again…then what sounded like the contents of the tackle box being dumped out onto the floor. Thirty seconds passed, and then Ben picked up his phone again.

"Jesus," he said. "I found a pair of boy's underwear…Fruit of The Loom's. They're all caked with what looks like dried rust…but this is blood. Kevin, are these your shorts?"

"Yes," said Kearnes. "They are."

"Oh my God…you didn't have an accident with my gun, did you?"

"No," said Kearnes. "I cut myself…with a knife. I was cutting up some bait, to go fishing with. And the knife slipped."

"Good lord," said Ben. "Looks like you bled like a little stuck hog! Did you lie to your dad about that, too?"

"Yes," said Kearnes. "I lied about everything. All of it."

"Well," said Ben, "that must have been one hell of an unforgettable vacation! I'm surprised you're having such a tough time recalling it."

"I'm starting to remember it now," said Kearnes.

"It's a bloody mess," said Ben. "There's blood all over that toy, too"

Kearnes felt the blood drain from his face.

"What...toy?"

"I found a toy, rolled up inside the shorts. It's a little blue plastic whale. Squeaks when you squeeze it. It must have been your sister's, huh?"

"Yes," said Kearnes. "I think it was Karen's. I must have forgotten that I put it in there."

"Where'd she get it?"

"Ben, I have to go now."

"Your folks buy it for her?"

"No. A man on the beach...he was giving them out to kids."

"Maybe you should call her; ask her if she might want it...as a remembrance, too."

"Good-bye, Ben"

"Funny, isn't it...the things people keep over the years, to remind them of the past? I remember we had this one officer working in our vice unit, and he..."

"Kevin? You still there, Kevin?"

Kearnes replaced the pay phone receiver gently back on its hook; then let his head fall forward onto the cool chrome metal of the pay phone.

He shut his eyes tightly, trying to squeeze the tears back inside his head that were flowing freely now as anguished, sonorous sobs of pain, and fear, and utter horror began to work their way up and out of him from a place deeper in his soul that he thought could ever exist.

The shock and emotion from the catastrophic conflict warring for so long inside him, and which had finally brought him to this point facing the truth of what his life had been, because of what had happened to him on that beach so long ago when he was a child, split him in two. And suddenly he was at once both that same terrified little boy again, and the fearless, outraged adult man that he had grown to be.

He snapped his head back up, and stood up straight; and then reached out and grabbed the pay phone's receiver and with one powerful jerk, ripped it, metal reinforced cord and all, out of the steel phone box.

He slammed his fist into his own reflection in one plexiglass side of the phone booth and it shimmied from the blow. He punched at it again and again and again, with both his fists, until it cracked, splitting apart into ruler sized jagged shards, and then began kicking at the stubborn pieces which bent outward toward the ground, but refused to be completely dislodged.

The blood from his lacerated knuckles was smeared across the plexiglass and when he saw it there; lustrously, brilliantly red…Kevin Kearnes himself saw red…and went temporarily insane.

He bucked out of the cramped confinement of the telephone booth like a Brahma bull, loosed from its chute. There was a stack of short lengths of iron pipe piled up against the side of the Harbormaster's Office that was used to repair the archaic water system which fed the fish cleaning systems down on the dock.

He ran over to the pile, grabbed a four foot piece of pipe off the top, and then charged the phone booth with it, swinging the pipe against its side as hard as he could. A blood curdling scream tore from his throat as he swung the pipe again and bits and pieces of plexiglass, aluminum, and plastic burst in the air all around him like shrapnel from a bomb going off.

Each blow he landed was like one from an expert woodsman's axe, methodically reducing a once mighty tree to only so many pieces of kindling, as he swung the iron pipe into, and through the quickly disintegrating structure.

Spenser sat transfixed behind the wheel of his parked cruiser, not able to comprehend, or believe, what it was his eyes were seeing. He had his driver's side window down and could hear the chief yelling something as he smashed the phone booth over and over again with some long object he was holding in a two handed grip…like a baseball batter up to the plate.

He slid out of the black and white Ford, leaving his door open a bit, and dove into the shadows of the old cannery building he had pulled off the roadway next to. He crept forward, closer to the chief, and could hear him now, screaming something…the same word, repeated again and again.

"Fuck You!" Kearnes screamed, smashing the top of the phone booth which had now toppled over onto the ground in front of him; cut neatly in two from his blows with the pipe.

"Fuck You! Fuck You! FUCK YOU!"

What had once been the pay phone booth, and one of only two or three left in the city, was now a pile of almost undistinguishable rubble at Kearnes' feet; the dust rising from it like wisps of smoke curling up into the air from a dying campfire.

Exhausted, and completely drained, he lurched toward the nearby dock, dragging the pipe on the ground behind him, and with one final burst of rage induced strength, slung the pipe out over the fishing boats in the Harbor below where it disappeared into the darkness, landing in the water somewhere beyond them with a giant splash.

Spenser flattened himself against the side of the old building as he saw Kearnes turn and walk back to the destroyed phone booth, where he dropped to his knees onto the ground. He could hear him crying…sobbing, really. He coughed, and spat something up, and then Spenser heard him yell…"Fuck!…Shit!"

He saw the chief slowly get to his feet, brush himself off, and wipe the sleeve of his jacket across his mouth. Then he watched as Kearnes shuffled back toward his apartment, his head down, moving like a weary old man who wasn't sure where he was going any more; and no longer really cared.

He waited until he saw Kearnes' apartment close shut behind him, and the lights inside go off, before he got back into his patrol car, bewildered and dumbfounded at what he'd witnessed.

He had just seen his chief commit a felony property crime, and he could not comprehend any possible, rational reasons for his chief's seemingly totally irrational act.

And what was even more disturbing to Spenser was the fact that Kearnes had almost appeared to be committing some sort of criminal act on himself as he raged against the telephone booth with that length of pipe, obliterating it.

He had to report this; but he was damned if he was going to make his report to either Sergeant Downs or Lieutenant Polk. They could go fuck themselves. He would wait until Sergeant Compton got back; even though he knew not immediately reporting the incident would probably cost him his job.

Spenser was halfway back to the station before he realized he was driving with his lights still off. He turned them on, but the way ahead didn't look any brighter.

In fact, what lay ahead of him now in his job, and in his life, had never looked so dark…and now he was no longer sure which way he should go.

CHAPTER 33

▼

Kearnes slept the sleep of the dead, and when he finally awoke late in the afternoon, and remembered all that had happened the night and the day before…he wished he could be among them.

The pager clipped to his gunbelt was chirping every so often, like a tentative cricket in tall grass at dusk. It was what had finally woke him up…the pending messages beep tone that sounded with a short chirp every thirty seconds…and not the five actual pages he had received while he slept in his coma like state.

He got out of bed and checked the messages stored on the pager. Two were from the police department Dispatch Center, and the other three were from Britt's cell phone.

He called the police department's business line on his cell phone, which he'd left outside overnight in Thud's car, and Candy Brewer in Dispatch answered. She informed him that the city was quiet…there was nothing going on. And she told him the two messages she had sent to his pager had both been regarding telephone calls she had received from Sergeant Compton earlier; one at nine a.m. and the other at 2:30 in the afternoon, about two hours ago, but neither one required a call back to him.

In the first call the sergeant was only wanting to let him know that the O.S.P. Crime Lab in Salem had recovered two different sets of latent prints from the item of evidence they had found at South Beach State Park—which appeared to be the fingerprints of both a child, and an adult—but that neither set of prints had yet been positively identified.

When Thud had called the second time, it was to let Kearnes know he wouldn't be leaving Salem until probably late afternoon; and according to Candy

Brewer, who had spoken with him briefly both times when he'd called, Thud had sounded hyped up, and very excited, at the prospect of possibly receiving a positive identification from the crime lab there on the green and black fibers found on Ricky Cates' neck and throat.

Kearnes apologized to Candy for oversleeping, and for sleeping so soundly that he hadn't even heard his pager go off; but he had been exhausted from his all day, and nearly all night drive. Candy apologized for sending the first page so early in the morning but said nothing about the second one, because secretly she had begun to get a little concerned when she hadn't heard from the chief when it had started to get so late in the day.

She didn't know the man all that well yet, but from what she did know, this seemed so unlike him. It seemed even more unlike him when Kearnes told her he wouldn't be coming into the office at all today, and to please make Lieutenant Polk aware of this. Kearnes thanked her before he ended the call, telling her he would see her on Monday; but Candy advised him she would be off that day, and that Shoshanna Perry would be working the dayshift instead.

He started his coffee maker and while it began to brew, stripped the sheets and pillow cases off his bed; the sheets still damp with his perspiration.

They were dotted with tiny pin pricks of his blood from some of the still oozing black berry cuts, and both the pillow cases had wide swaths of dried blood smeared across their tops from where he'd dragged his bloodied knuckles as he'd struggled to escape his night long nightmares.

What Kearnes had thought to be a night of blankly fitful, if not entirely peaceful, sleep; had actually been one of ongoing mental torment and anguish inside his head. Only his body had finally been forced to give in to the impossible stress his mind had subjected it to and when he had awakened, he was like a victim of amnesia in reverse: struggling not to remember who and what he had been in his life before, but now trying to forget who and what he had become virtually overnight.

He wadded up the sheets and pillowcases together and stuffed them into the small garbage can beneath the kitchen sink. Then he took Britt's plate of cookies from the kitchen table, removed the plastic food wrap cover from them, and dumped them into the garbage can, too.

Tilly had only left him with two sets of sheets and some unmatched pillow cases from the divorce, but he could make do with the one set he had left until he was out of this city and this state; and was settled in some place new as far from here as he could get.

And as for the cookies…he had no appetite for them; or for the woman, any longer, who had so lovingly baked them for him. He needed to go to her now…and tell her this.

He wasn't in love with Britt McGraw.

There was no such thing as love…it did not exist in the world.

And neither, anymore, did he.

He showered again, and treated his wounds again—including the new ones on his hands—with some of Margie's ointment; then got dressed. He washed the plate Britt has used to deliver the cookies with and put it in the dish rack to dry while he sat at his small kitchen table, drinking coffee and staring at the note she had left him on his front door.

He read the few words she had written on the paper in her crisp and very legible handwriting…over and over. Words that only forty eight hours ago would have made him immeasurably happy, and could have opened up his life to a future of unlimited possibilities with the woman he'd believed he had been destined to fall in love with all along, after journeying so far in his life, and enduring so much, just to find her.

But now they were just words; meaningless scratches of lavender colored ink on egg shell white note paper…that smelled of her perfume. Bitterly, he crumpled the note in his fist, and then threw it into the garbage can under the sink.

He poured himself another cup of coffee while he sat at the table; thinking very long and very hard about how to end it with her.

It would be so much easier if Britt could feel about him the same way Tilly had felt about him toward the end; after their marriage had suffered from the erosion of their mutual ridicule, contempt, and then finally; real hatred for one another.

If only Britt would hate him, then he could quickly and easily end it, and it would be the best solution for them both. She would be free of him and free to find another man; one much more worthy of her and what she had to offer, than Kevin Kearnes was.

And for his part, he would be free to hate himself…even more than he was beginning to now.

He poured the last half of his cup of coffee out in the sink, and took Britt's plate out of the dish rack. It was still a little wet, so he took the dish towel from where he always hung it through the refrigerator door, and finished drying the plate off with it.

He needed to go. It was starting to get late, and if he didn't leave now he knew she would come to his place as soon as she thought he was home from work.

He got his keys and his jacket; grabbed the nine millimeter from on top of his dresser in the bedroom, and the plate from the kitchen table; and then went out to the parking lot and started his truck.

His heart was like a domino, standing on its end in a long line of other delicately balanced and touching dominoes; representing all of the different segments of who he was as a human being, and who he had become as a man. And when the first domino in the line to be knocked down...the eviscerating discovery about the truth of his past...all of the rest of the dominoes had begun to also fall in a rapid chain reaction, which Kevin Kearnes was helpless to stop.

But as he drove away from his apartment, heading for Britt's cabin at The Sand Dollar, he still didn't know how he was going to do what he had no idea how to do.

Or even why, really, he felt that he had to do it at all.

The Sand Dollar's parking lot was noticeably more crowded now than it had been when he'd left it several hours before. Britt's car was parked in the same exact spot where he'd last seen it, but the old white, delivery type Van that had been jammed up against it was gone now, leaving that parking space open; so Kearnes took it.

The trail to the beach cabins, which also served as the main foot access to and from the beach for those guests staying in the motel portion of The Sand Dollar, was bustling with adults and children.

They moved along the narrow pathway in two long lines like army ants; one column marching toward the promise and excitement of the sea on the horizon, and the other falling back in retreat toward the comfort of the candy and soda vending machines, the in room Jacuzzi's, and the free HBO on their 27" flat screen digital TV's.

Once he had gone about halfway down the trail and had passed the first two red stained guest log cabins, The Magnolia, and The Sycamore, he dropped out of the line of slowly trudging tourists and cut across through the sand dunes in the direction of Britt's cabin approaching it from the rear, and soon its green painted cedar shake roof came into view just slightly above the high dunes out in front of him.

He walked around the side of the cabin and stepped up onto the front deck, the wooden decking beneath his feet groaning noticeably, and as he raised his hand to knock on the cabin's door he froze…it was standing open about three inches.

He stopped, and listened. No sounds came from inside the cabin. The only things he heard were sea birds crying in the distance, the wind filtering through the beach grass and the small pine trees that grew all around the cabin, and the weary, repetitive din of the ocean surf in the background. But there was something else; something unheard…and he reached back underneath his jacket to his jeans pocket, and quietly drew the little Kahr.

He set the plate he was carrying down on the deck, and then with the toe of his shoe pushed the door halfway open and called out, softly, "Britt?"

"Britt?" he said again. "Hello?"

He stepped inside the cabin and remained absolutely still while his eyes bore into every shadow and every object within his field of vision…twice. He swept the living room in front of him and the little kitchen to his right before he took a few tentative steps toward the bathroom door, which was closed.

When he reached it he carefully turned the doorknob, and then suddenly swung the door open and rushed inside, stepping off sharply to one side in the living room, the little 9mm pistol leveled at his waist and tracking straight ahead with his every movement. But there was no one there, or anywhere else downstairs, and the cabin was as neat as a pin; just like Britt always kept it.

There was a small utility porch at the rear of the cabin with its own door that led inside to a pantry, which had a curtain across it that blocked it from being viewed from the cabin's living room area. But he had passed it up on his way in, betting it was still locked—just like Britt always kept it—because she didn't want any mud or sand tracked across her clean hardwood living room floor.

He would have called out Britt's name again before he started up the stairs to the second floor sleeping loft, gun in hand, if he'd thought she might be taking a nap up there; but Britt McGraw didn't take naps in the daytime, or anytime else as far as Kearnes knew.

As he cleared the last step up, and then stood at the foot of their bed, he saw that everything looked as if it was in order. The bed was neatly made, with both their pillows fluffed up beneath the down comforter, and he saw the heels of Britt's slippers peeking out from under the edge of the bed on her side. Her robe was draped across the back of the chair that was pulled out slightly from her small make up table, and on the table in a small cut glass crystal bowl were the agates they had found on their picnic a few days before.

He turned to go back down the stairs but stopped when he saw the small closet door just slightly ajar, and a soft yellow light leaking out from inside it.

Then he noticed the single small, circular shaped, porthole window next to it, almost identical to the windows in his apartment at The Sea Breeze—it was also open, but only slightly.

He scuttled around the far edge of the bed toward the closet, having to bend his head and shoulders to conform to the sharply slanted, low ceiling there. When he reached the closet door he jerked it open, and the light from the single forty watt fixture that hung from the ceiling shone down on Britt's upended, large black suitcase. The contents of the suitcase were strewn all over the floor, and all of the items of clothing that had been hanging on hangers inside the closet, were also on the floor. A small dirty clothes hamper had been overturned, and he saw her still soggy and sand impregnated socks, which she'd worn the day of their picnic, laying on the floor just in front of it.

Britt used the small closet's few narrow overhead wooden shelves as her linen storage; but Kearnes saw that all of her extra sheets and pillowcases, towels, and washcloths, and even a bath robe she had bought for him, were all strewn about the floor of the closet too. The only thing that remained on the highest wooden shelf was her black travel bag. He reached up and brought it down from the shelf, then backed out of the closet and set it on the bed.

He'd told Britt repeatedly how important it was to always keep the cabin locked, even if she just went for a short walk down on the beach. And he had thought she had taken his professional advice to heart, because whenever they'd left the cabin Britt was always the one who had locked it up. But maybe she'd forgotten today, just this once; and that's how the burglar had gotten in—just opened her unlocked front door and walked right in. It was odd, though, that whoever it was had torn the hell out of her closet, looking for things to steal…but hadn't touched this bag. Or maybe he'd taken it down, looked in it, and not finding anything of interest in it…put it neatly back?

No, he thought. That would never happen. And when he unzipped the top of the bag and spread it apart, he knew that had absolutely *not* happened…as he stared at what appeared to be thousands and thousands of dollars…thick bundles of twenties, fifties, and hundred dollar bills, secured with rubber bands.

He dug his hand down inside the bag, but all he could feel was more and more bundles of cash. The bag was heavy, and solid feeling and what he saw alarmed him.

No sane person carried this amount of cash around with them; especially not smart, intelligent, lady doctors. But smart, intelligent, and beautiful lady criminals sometimes did, and his heart sank even further out of sight as all of his unanswered questions about Britt McGraw, and the mystery surrounding her, suddenly gelled in his always suspicious cop mind. And he knew she had to be either a drug dealer, a bank robber, an embezzler…or maybe even all three.

He stopped digging in the bag; picked it up and turned it upside down, dumping everything inside it out onto the bed. The bundles of cash piled up in front of him like a green pyramid as they fell from the bag; but the last bundle to fall out, a black one, was heavier than the rest, and slid down one side of the mountain of cash and came to rest on the white comforter of the bed.

But it wasn't a bundle of money. It was a small black leather zippered case, about the same size and shape as a generous piece of pie. And there was an emblem emblazoned in gold on it; the head of an American Eagle inside a circle, looking to its left in profile, and in gold lettering around its head, above and below, the words "NORTH AMERICAN ARMS."

He unzipped the case and removed the tiny stainless steel gun with the miniature rosewood birds head shaped grips, and held it in the palm of his open hand. It was so small that when he closed his hand into a fist, the gun completely disappeared. Opening his hand again, he angled his palm slightly toward his face, pointing the one inch snout of its stubby barrel in his direction, and he could see three of the five rounds of .22 long rifle hollow points resting inside the lethal little gun's diminutive cylinders.

He was very familiar with the make and model of this weapon. It was a micro sized, last ditch back-up gun, favored by many police officers for its nearly invisible concealment. Because it could literally go unnoticed, stuck in the pocket of some officer's uniform shirt…and some for them had, for an entire week…and then ended up banging around inside their horrified wife's Maytag dryer after having already weathered the permanent press wash and wear cycle

But its underpowered .22 caliber round made it a "contact" only weapon; that necessitated its user placing the muzzle of the gun directly against the body of his antagonist—and only then over a very vital area, such as the heart, or against the side of the skull—before pressing the trigger. Women liked the little mini-guns too, because of their "cute" factor, and because they offered a great deal of protection to a woman alone, for taking up so precious little space in a purse.

But as a defensive firearm, used to protect what looked like maybe even as much as a hundred thousand dollars, or more, in cash…the discovery of the little gun just didn't add up. Neither did a rifled through, and completely torn apart and trashed closet from a residential burglary, with the only thing of value present sitting in plain view, apparently unmolested.

He zipped the gun back in its case and tossed it into the travel bag and had started to replace the cash, when he heard the cabin door downstairs slam shut.

He had been sitting on the edge of the bed, examining the gun, but now quietly stood up and started to slowly walk toward the railing of the open loft, the Kahr held in a two handed grip, elbows slightly bent, straight out in front of the centerline axis of his body. He heard footsteps down below, now...then a skidding, scraping noise on the wood floor...and something crashed loudly.

He leaped toward the rail and as soon as he felt it hit him in the stomach, brought the nine millimeter to bear on the wide open space of the living room below and shouted, "Police Officer you fucking freeze right now!"

There was silence...and he saw something strange lying on the bare hardwood floor directly beneath him; something that he didn't immediately recognize. It had three long, spindly, tri-pod shaped legs...a square shaped part at the top...and some different brightly colored paints had spilled on the floor around it.

An easel. An artist's easel?

He saw Britt's blonde head moving underneath his downward, outstretched arms...right into the sights of his weapon. He slowly lowered the gun, staring down at her.

"Kevin?" she said.

"You..."

"You...had a break-in. Someone's been in here. I came to talk to you. But someone's been in here."

"Kevin," she said. "What's wrong?"

Kearnes didn't answer her; he only shook his head from side to side...either in exasperation, or resignation...she couldn't yet be sure.

"Kevin," she said again. "What's the matter? What's wrong?"

"Nothing," Kearnes finally responded.

But one look at his face told Britt McGraw everything she needed to know; for now. And for now she knew that the only man she loved—the last man she would ever love—was in a great deal of trouble.

And that what he had just told her...was a lie.

CHAPTER 34

▼

Britt came up the stairs slowly. She was wearing an old blue cotton work shirt, its untucked ends tied in a knot at her waist. It was speckled with an array of water color paints, and her hands were covered with dried paint. Some of the paint had even gotten in her hair.

She smiled at him as she climbed the stairs and when she reached the top stair she stopped, flicking her eyes down once at the open black travel bag and spilled money on the bed, then making eye contact with him once again.

"You sacred me," she said. "I had no idea you were up here."

"And *you* scared me," said Kearnes. "I thought you were the burglar, coming back."

Britt looked past him to the open closet door, and the heap of clothing and bedding lying on the floor.

"Oh my God…someone was in here. How did they get in?"

"Through the front door, apparently," Kearnes said. "I found it standing open when I got here."

"I was down at the beach…with my new paints," she said. "For about two hours. I *know* I locked the door behind me when I left."

Kearnes sat on the bed, and laid his gun down next to his leg.

"Kevin, she said, "why didn't you call me back today? I left several messages on your pager."

"I was sleeping," he said.

She walked over to him. "Oh, sweetheart," she said, lightly touching the red-dish purple cut beneath his eye with her finger. "What happened to your eye?"

Kearnes slapped her hand away, and stood up. "Is this what they were after?" he asked her hotly, jabbing a finger at the bundles of money on the bed.

Britt's face registered shock; not at his question but at his rejection of her touch. "I...I don't know," she said. "I don't think anyone knows I have it."

"Really?" Kearnes said, sarcastically. "You're sure some bank hasn't missed it by now? Or maybe the business you embezzled it from? Or your drug dealing partners?"

"Kevin. Please listen to me. This money is all mine; from my practice in Seattle. I sold out...and this was the down payment; which I asked for in cash."

"Oh, yes," said Kearnes. "Of course!"

"I forgot. You're a successful doctor...so it would stand to reason that you would be carrying this amount of cash around in one of your suitcases; on your way to a medical convention. Wasn't that it? Wasn't that what you told me the first night we met?"

"Yes," she said quietly.

"You can stop your lying now," he said.

"You are a goddamned doctor...like I'm J. Edgar Hoover. I want the truth about where this money came from...now!"

Britt backed away from him. "What is going on with you?" she said. "I can help you, Kevin. With whatever the problems are..."

"What is going on with me?" he said, his voice rising. He reached inside the black bag and brought out the small zippered case. He ripped the zipper open and the little gun tumbled out, landing on the bed next to her. "No, Britt. What the hell is going on with *you!*"

Britt reached down and picked up the tiny weapon; and Kearnes immediately wondered if he had made a mistake...his gun was still lying on the bed; and too far away for him to get to in time.

She held the miniature revolver up by its grip, turning it from side to side, examining it. "This is my gun, too," she said. "I bought it a few months ago; at a gun shop in Tacoma. I learned how to load, and fire it; and how to put the hammer down in the little notches in between the chambers...to make it safe."

She leaned forward a little, and then tossed the gun onto the bed, next to Kearnes nine millimeter.

"I was going to use it for something very, very, wrong. But that isn't the case any longer."

She lifted her head and made direct eye contact with him. "I changed my mind," she said. "Meeting you changed my mind Kevin. Actually...meeting you has changed my heart."

Kearnes picked the Kahr up from the bed and stuck it back in his rear jeans pocket; then picked Britt's little gun up and zipped it inside its leather case and put it back in her black travel bag.

"Why did you come to Cutter Point?" he asked her. "Why are you with me?"

"I can't tell you why I came here…not yet. I'm afraid if I do…you might leave me. But I can tell you why I am with you…it's because I want to be. I love you, Kevin."

"Well, I don't want you to love me," said Kearnes. "This is all wrong…it was from the very start. I can't do this anymore."

"Did I hurt you that badly? What I said to you on our picnic?"

"You didn't hurt me at all. You were just being truthful…you should try being truthful again."

"What I said to you the other day…I was scared, Kevin. Just like you are scared…right now. Only, I'm not sure what of."

"The only thing I'm 'scared' of, said Kearnes, "is that I'm close to finding out the real truth about you…and then I'll be forced to have to do something about it. I don't want to be put in that position, Britt."

"Margie Compton called me early this morning," she said. "She gave Thud my number, and he called me later, too. We talked about the case, Kevin…and about you."

"He's very concerned about you, Kevin. And so am I. The day to day stress of your job, these murders you and Thud are investigating…the pain of your divorce…of having your sons torn away from you like that by her…

Any or all of these things combined can bring about tremendous, unseen psychological pressures to bear deep within the mind. And when these eventually manifest themselves, in either a short term or long term response phase, great damage can be done. Sometimes, irreparably."

"Maybe all three of you…should mind your own goddamned business," he said.

"What happened on your trip with Thud?" she asked him, undisturbed by his growing hostility.

He abruptly started to walk toward the loft stairs, but Britt jumped up from the bed and blocked his way. "Tell me," she said. "Please."

"What the hell do you think you are?" he demanded. "Some kind of a shrink or something?"

"Yes," she said. "That's exactly what I am. I have a PhD in Clinical Psychology…and an MD in Psychiatry."

Kearnes stared at her, incredulous.

"I've worked with the police before, Kevin. Both the Seattle, and King County Police Departments."

Kearnes shook his head like a drunk, trying to clear the buzzing from between his ears. The room had begun to close in around him; things were beginning to sway now, and a cold blast of putrid, ocean air streamed in through the opening of the loft's only small window, locking onto his nostrils and flying up into his nasal passages like a heat seeking missile.

He looked at Britt, and saw her face begin to decay in front of his own two eyes. The beautiful hair on her head crackled, and then shrunk down to dry, brittle straw. Then it turned to white salt; and suddenly blew away in the foul wind of her breath as she opened her hideous, rotten tooth stumped mouth to speak to him again.

"Get out of my way," he said thickly, the acid from his stomach burning its way up into his throat.

"I can help you with this case," she pleaded. "This man you are looking for…and the suspect *will* turn out to be a male, when you find him…"

"There isn't any case!" Kearnes shouted.

"Neither of the victims was killed in the City of Cutter Point, so *we* have no case! And after Monday morning, it's not going to matter to me anyhow; because I'm turning in my resignation. And leaving this place."

"What? Kevin, no! You're doing a wonderful job here! People here *need you*. Please don't run out on them…please don't run out on *me*!"

"Move," he said to her, menacingly.

"Just please listen to me…for one minute!"

"He *is* a sexual deviate, and there *are* some thematic religious overtones in the two killings. He either thinks God is speaking to him, telling him to kill his victims…or he may even believe he is God, himself. But the beatings of the young boys, as a prelude to the actual manner of death, strangulation, and the fact that the victims thus far, including the new, suspected ones, are also young boys…

"Kevin, I think this man may be a misogynist…a male with a deeply ingrained, almost homicidal hatred toward women. He hates, but at the same time fears…all women. And he's probably a member, or former member, of one of what we call the "restrictive religious groups"; a Mormon, a Jehovah Witness, or a Seventh Day Adventist, for example.

"His victims are safe for *him*; young, defenseless boys, who he first viciously beats…in a demonstration of his rage against females…but then ultimately murders in a somewhat more humane and painless way. Being strangled to death, if one does not struggle, or has ceased at some point to struggle...can be an almost peaceful way to die."

"Shut up!" screamed Kearnes. "I don't want to hear it! The only sexual deviate I know of is *you*...you fucking little whore! Now get the hell out of my way!"

"Oh, Kevin...please tell me you don't mean this!" she cried. *"Please!"*

And then, just as it had happened at the phone booth after he had abruptly hung up on Ben, he reached his flashpoint and lunged at Britt, intent on total destruction. He grabbed her around her neck with both his hands and slammed her down to the floor where she landed in a broken heap, crumpling over like a rag doll.

Kearnes straddled her, seething with anger. Britt had landed on her stomach and chest, but now slowly rolled over onto her back, silently crying; now staring up, terrified, at the insane man above her who had closed his right hand into the solid steel of a fist and cocked it, spring loaded, behind his ear. He was going to hit her. He was going to smash her beautiful face in.

"Don't you ever touch me again!" he screamed down at her. "Do you understand me? Ever! Or I will fucking kill you!"

Britt squeezed her eyes shut tightly; bracing herself for the blow...which didn't come. She felt the vibrations of Kevin's shoes pounding down the loft stairs and then heard the front door being jerked open; then slammed shut with a resounding crash that shook the entire cabin. She opened her eyes again but the room was spinning and she felt as if she might be sick, so she curled into a ball, tightening her stomach muscles down against a mounting wave of nausea.

She lay like that for awhile, tightly coiled, crying softly; thinking to herself the only horrible truth that was left to her anymore to think: that men were pure fire...*all men*. And she was nothing more than air...the oxygen that fueled them.

She had struck her head on the hard, bare wood floor when she was thrown down. Now her heavy lidded eyes closed, and she began to drift toward unconsciousness, and peace. But as she slipped away she had one last, cogent thought. What had he meant...*Don't you ever touch me again?* She hadn't touched him. Before he'd thrown her out of his way, she had still been several feet away from him.

Was he referring to all the times they had made love since the first night they were together?

No...she didn't think so. How could any human being, after having been touched in the ways they had touched one another, ever wish for such a thing to never happen again?

Who was it, then, that had touched Kevin Kearnes in such a way that he would threaten to kill them if they ever touched him again?

It wasn't me, she thought; as the shock of what he had done to her, coupled with the blow to the side of her head, washed over her mind, and body, like deep water.

No, not me.

But then…who?

It had been Uriah Beek's disdain for confined, stuffy spaces and his fondness for fresh ocean air that had saved Kevin Kearnes' life thirty minutes earlier. Beek had gone to take the woman from her cabin, but found it locked; so he'd forced his rock solid, battering ram of a shoulder against the cabin's small rear door until the door jamb splintered, and gave way.

He was upstairs in the bedroom, going through the blonde whore's things in her closet, when he could no longer stand the sickening smell of her perfume, and the lingering scent of their lovemaking trapped in the air of the loft. So he'd gone to the small window that was shaped like a porthole on a ship, and as he opened it to let in the ocean breeze…had seen Kearnes moving through the tall beach grass and short pines in the sand dunes, walking towards the back of the cabin.

For a few seconds he had contemplated taking his prize, right then and there; but he could not disobey the will of Yahweh, to which all things had a time, a purpose, and an order. It was to be the Jezebel first; *then* the disobedient, and fallen boy…so that he could watch her suffering, and come to know, in turn, the suffering he had caused to himself, and the world, for being with her as a man.

He had taken a pair of her panties from the dirty laundry hamper—pale blue bikini's with little yellow ducks on them, wearing sailor's hats—and ran down the loft stairs to the front door which he unlocked; then quietly closed behind him as he left the cabin and melted into the little forest of pine trees.

Now he was sitting on the side of a high sand dune and directly in front of a large clump of beach grass, two hundred yards from the cabin. His green work shirt and pants camouflaged him perfectly, making him an integral part of the landscape.

Periodically, he stared at the pair of the woman's panties lying on the sand next to him; which he'd taken from her bedroom. He would use these as a sign to the man; a message to let him know that he was near, and was coming to him; soon. To impart to him that the present body is corruptible…but the next body is glorious.

He suddenly clenched his teeth as a searing wave of pain from his groin eddied through him…from the wound where he had shed The Blood of The Lamb earlier in his room…as atonement for his sin of lust last night. The pain made him lightheaded and as he stared at the panties the little yellow ducks on them, that were wearing sailor's hats, began swimming back and forth across the front of them.

Ten minutes ago he had picked the woman up in the crystal clear lenses of his 8X30 Steiner Binoculars; watching her as she struggled up from the narrow beach trail to her cabin carrying a long, collapsed, and ungainly artist's easel, a large beach bag, and a small folding case of artist's paints and brushes.

He saw her enter through the front door of the cabin, setting her things down momentarily while she ferried them inside; then she closed the door.

And now, just a few seconds ago, with his hold on the binoculars rock steady, and the lenses focused with diamond clarity, he had seen the boy…the policeman, Kevin Kearnes…explode from out of the front door and charge down the porch steps; and begin pacing madly up and down in front of the cabin's warped wooden deck.

Beek watched as the man kicked at the ground in front of him, sending geysers of fine sand into the air. He saw that Kearnes was highly agitated, and obviously very upset about something. But as he watched him, he saw it was more than just that.

He saw fear.

He knew that if Kearnes had surprised him inside the cabin, he would have killed him. And God would, of course, had forgiven him…because with God, there were never any surprises. He also knew that he could have gone to the cabin a minute after the woman had entered, and killed them both. And that he could go there right now, and kill her now.

But, no. He would wait, as God had planned; and *this* night would mark the beginning of everything.

His long vigil of prayer throughout the night, and today's excruciatingly painful atonement, for his nearly unforgivable sin of carnal thoughts of fornication with the blonde whore, had purified and cleansed both his mind and his body.

At noon, after he had finished praying, he had left his room at The Sand Dollar for the first time, and driven to the small Ray's Food Place market below the big bridge that led into the city.

There, he had purchased some microwavable, packaged meals, a six pack of soft drinks, some fresh fruit, a box of plastic Ziploc sandwich bags, a newspaper for him, and, as an afterthought, a copy of "O" magazine.

He had tried to load his grocery cart with a normal assortment of domestic looking goods, so that when the two boxes of large sanitary napkins, the bottle of Hydrogen Peroxide, and the two rolls of adhesive bandage tape went through the checkout with all the other items, he might only appear to be an average house husband, picking up a few things from the store for the wife who was feeling a little under the weather today.

Leaving the supermarket, he had returned to his room, put away his groceries, and threw Oprah's magazine in the garbage; and then methodically set out the sanitary napkins, the tape, and the peroxide on the kitchen table.

Then he had gone into the bathroom and removed the mirror from the wall where it hung, and brought it into the kitchen area, which had a sink, a microwave oven, coffee maker, and small refrigerator; and propped it up against the back of one of the two chairs that were also furnished with his "kitchenette" room.

He had taken off his work pants, and his underwear, and hung his jacket on the back of the second chair. He had spread out a layer of the absorbent sanitary napkins on this chair; drug it over to face the chair which held up the mirror, and then sat down on it, facing the mirror, which was pointed directly at his groin.

He'd stared in disgust, for a few moments, at his still semi-hard erection. His member had refused to return to its normal state during the night, no matter how hard he had prayed, and was still, to that moment, filled with a tumescent lust inspired by the blonde harlot whore.

From the table next to him he had taken a sanitary napkin from the open box, folded it in half, and placed it lengthwise in his mouth between his teeth; and then took one of the roles of adhesive tape and taped the napkin tightly in place across his chin and around the back of his head, to gag himself.

Uriah Beek had then spread his legs and lifted them both high into the air; reached back into the pocket of his jacket which hung on the chair, and taken out the razor sharp grape hook knife.

And then, while gazing intently into the mirror…he self-castrated his right testicle with the knife.

When he had completed his grisly surgery and finally staunched the bleeding with pressure from both his hands holding several of the sanitary pads tightly in place—until he could tape the stopgap dressing against his groin—he'd gotten up from the chair and hobbled over to the kitchen counter where he'd left the box of plastic sandwich bags sitting out.

He'd opened the box and taken out one bag, then hobbled back over to where the two facing chairs were; and gingerly he'd bent down and scooped up the slippery testicle from the tile floor, where it had fallen after he'd cut its final membranes loose from his scrotal sac.

Carefully, he'd put the testicle inside the sandwich bag, zipped the bag shut, and then placed it inside the small refrigerator.

A last meal, for the condemned whore.

CHAPTER 35

▼

Thud Compton had not driven away from the Oregon State Police Crime Lab in Salem in his rented red Nissan Altima—which had been dropped off to him there by the rental company—until almost eight p.m. Several hours later than he'd advised his Dispatch by phone, earlier in the day, that he would be leaving. But his last minute waiting around there, before he'd started on his long drive home back to Cutter Point, had, in the end, been richly rewarded with the results of a long overdue forensics report.

The black and green nylon fibers found on murder victim Ricky Cates had been positively identified as having come from a German manufacturer of very popular, and expensive, military and marine binoculars—Steiner—and were proprietary to the production of the company's binocular neck straps. That meant that no other maker of binoculars in the world used this exact nylon material—in the same exact formulation that Steiner did—to make their binocular straps.

To most investigators, this revelation would likely have invoked nothing more than a yawn; because Steiner binoculars were sold and used by hundreds of thousands of military and police organizations, sportsmen, and civilians, world wide. But Thud knew all about the high quality German optics, with their trademark olive drab colored, rubber armored bodies, and he had immediately made the connection to what Chris Lawless had told him and Kearnes during the interview…*"They were a green color. Like an army Humvee…"*

So he considered this to be the second major break in the case in the two days; the first one having been the one in a million chance finding of the little blue whale toy in the sand dunes at South Beach State Park yesterday that had fit the description, exactly, of the same type toy Chris Lawless had described to them used in his attempted abduction.

Thud had been right there in the Lab, hovering around the white coated crime lab technician as he processed the toy for latent fingerprints, blood, saliva, semen, and any other foreign substance or chemical which shouldn't be present on it; and his heart had nearly stopped as two sets of fingerprints, one small, and one large, were lifted from it.

The prints were immediately run through the A.F.I.S. computer; the Automatic Fingerprint Identification System, which contained the digitally stored fingerprints of millions of different people, but neither set of prints submitted, had come back with a "hit"…a positive match.

It was understandable in the case of the smaller set of prints, because children were rarely fingerprinted to begin with, and so hardly any existed in the A.F.I.S. data bank; usually only those children who had been classified as homicide victims, having been fingerprinted in death.

But it was depressing when no match was made with the larger set of prints. It meant that this killer, whoever he was, had never been arrested; or at least not fingerprinted after having been arrested. And even today, in some ignorant and unprofessional backwater law enforcement agencies, this was sadly still the case.

Thud knew that when they eventually found the body of Colin Boyer, they would also find the match for the tiny set of fingerprints on the whale. As for the killer, he still remained largely an unknown quantity; but one that Thud saw becoming clearer and clearer to him as the hours, and then days, of the investigation passed.

He was pushing the red Altima hard, south down Interstate-5, keeping it at just under eighty and fighting to keep from falling asleep behind the wheel, when he realized it was now Saturday morning…as of thirty minutes ago ago. He had been gone from home for almost two days now; away from Margie and the kids, and without a fresh change of clothes. He needed a hot shower, a cold beer, and clean sheets with his wife lying naked on them; and to just be home in the morning when his girls woke up…so he could hug them.

He'd appreciated the chief going by his house and checking on his family as he'd asked him to do, and he knew Margie would sacrifice her own life before she ever let any harm come to either one of their daughters. But he wouldn't feel right until he was back home with them again; protecting them himself. Because the constant sense of foreboding that he'd left town with; the eerie, pressing sense of impending danger that had driven him to push the investigation forward, and to push his chief along with it, hadn't lessened as progress on the case had been made. It had instead, only increased.

He rolled his window down to let some fresh air in as he drove, still now a good two hours from Cutter Point, and his mind began racing as fast as the car was; going over all of the things in the investigation he had accomplished in the intense, two day period while he'd been away, and the things he still had yet to do.

Detectives, especially in the smaller police agencies, traditionally did not work on weekends unless they were called out to the scene of some crime where their expertise was immediately required. But Thud knew he would be working straight through his weekend, and that he was going to enlist the aid of Spenser Sparling and Brad Dekker, too.

Before leaving State Police Headquarters in Salem, he'd emailed the color digital evidence photos of the whale to both his home computer and the computer in his office at work, as well as copied them to a small 128 MB jump drive he kept in his briefcase.

He had nearly worn out his welcome with the O.S.P.; wheedling and cajoling them into rapidly getting the things done for him that he needed done right away, and asking for the types of favors that were usually considered as a little rude, coming as they were from an outside jurisdiction, if not downright outrageous.

But he'd managed to get them to put out an A.T.L., an Attempt To Locate Bulletin to every state police unit on both the Oregon Coast Highway 101, and Interstate-5, for the Lawless family R.V. which was believed to be southbound at this time, headed for San Diego, California; and to email a photo of the whale to every mobile data terminal screen in each one of those state trooper vehicles. If the Lawless vehicle was stopped, Chris Lawless would be contacted and asked to look at the picture of the whale—to see whether or not he could identify it—and the results, one way or the other, could be relayed to Cutter Point P.D. immediately by that unit.

Tomorrow, he planned on getting Spenser and Brad, and doing pretty much the same type of thing. Only they would be emailing pictures of the whale to every sheriff's department and police department on the Oregon coast, and as many down into northern California as they could find email addresses for. And then asking those agencies to print out a copy of the toy whale picture, and have their officers contact every gift shop, toy store, and novelty outlet in there areas, in the hopes of finding someplace where the toy may be being sold.

Right now, the only thing that Thud knew was that the toy was made in China. Like a million other products—toys included—which flooded into the United States each year and were almost impossible to track down as to their specific point of importation; once they were taken out of the boxes they had been shipped in.

Curious as to why a popular bathtub toy would be made to replicate a blue whale, instead of, say, a gray whale, or a humpback whale, Thud had called whale expert Steve Connelly, the park ranger, back in Cutter Point.

Connelly had told him that the word "whale", to most people, was synonymous with the species known as the blue whale because of the creature's romantic place in the history of sea lore and legend, and because of the mind boggling facts surrounding the creatures themselves; the largest mammals on the earth ever...from the dawn of time to this very day.

Then Connelly laid some of these facts on Thud, himself: That not only are blue whales the largest creatures on earth, they are also the loudest; and their underwater squeals, clicks, and groans, emitted at levels as high as 188 decibels, can be heard by other whales up to 530 miles away. That the heart of a blue whale weighs 1,300 pounds, and beats an average of only ten times a minute; versus a human heart, which beats an average of seventy times per minute. That the tail of a blue whale generates 500 horsepower as they swim, that their testicles are as large as a Volkswagen Beetle, and that their tongues weigh more than a full grown elephant.

When Thud had asked Connelly how common it was to see blue whales off the coast of Oregon, like the large numbers of migrating gray whales—the same type as the whale that had washed up on the beach in Cutter Point, and had been blown to whale oil by The Patriots—his answer was succinct and to the point— never.

Blue whales were creatures of the deep, deep, blue ocean; and although there were places along the Mexico, and western North American coastlines where they could occasionally be seen breaching while on their own yearly migratory routes...Oregon was not one of them. And come to think of it; Thud himself could not remember hearing any references to blue whales the entire time he had grown up and lived in Cutter Point; only gray whales.

Yet he could see how easily people could become enamored of these magnificent creatures, even if they'd never personally seen one themselves before. And that probably went double for small children; especially if an adult offered them a toy whale first, then offered to take them to a special place where they could see the real thing.

After Steve Connelly had finished giving Thud his first lesson in Marine Biology 101, he'd thanked him, and then called the chief's girlfriend, Britt McGraw. When he'd spoken with Margie earlier that morning and she'd told him about how Kearnes had looked, and how he'd been acting—strange, and distant—when he'd come by the house to check on her and the girls; Margie had asked Thud to give Britt a call because she was getting concerned about him. And so was Thud.

With more than a little apprehension, Thud had dialed the number of the beautiful—and as far as he was concerned, aloof and stuck up—woman's cell phone number, that Margie had provided him; and much to his amazement they had talked for nearly an hour. By the end of their conversation, Thud had radically changed his opinion about Britt McGraw.

She was warm and earnest; caring, and very down to earth, in spite of her obvious intelligence, and her excruciatingly good looks. And after talking with her, Thud was forced to face the obvious: that *this* was the real problem, or at least, had been the real problem…her unabashed beauty.

He could see why she was with the chief, and vice versa; those two could easily appear on the cover of one of those "Fifty Most Beautiful People Of The Year" magazine issues together…and do nothing but make it look even better than it already was.

To Thud Compton—and ninety nine per cent of the rest of the male population of the world—a woman like Britt McGraw was nothing but total and complete intimidation; an untouchable, and hopelessly unattainable Holy Grail of femaledom, which made average looking men like Thud either keep their distance from her, or turn and run the other way, when they happened to be thrown together in some social setting.

But Thud couldn't have been more wrong about Britt. She was like talking to the kid sister he'd never had. And although it was quite obvious that she cared very much for the chief, and that he was the main man in her life, she laughed and joked with Thud, setting him at ease; took a real interest in what he was saying, and had interesting, worthwhile opinions of her own to add to the conversation.

The original premise for which he had called her was based on his understanding that she was some kind of doctor, and he'd wanted to express his concerns about his chief to her, who appeared to be possibly suffering from exhaustion, or stress, or maybe a little of both; like Thud, and his recent bout with insomnia. Britt had listened intently to him; and had then asked him a few carefully distilled questions of her own about the chief, which were unquestioningly medical in nature.

But he was a little shocked when she had told him, just a few minutes into their conversation, that she wasn't really a "doctor, doctor"; but was actually a psychiatrist. A psychiatrist, who in her practice back in Seattle, had worked with two very large police agencies on several different cases in the past as a consultant.

And when she'd mentioned a particular name from one of these cases she had been involved with—Mary Kay Letourneau; the pretty, former elementary school teacher, who'd served seven years in prison for raping the Father of her two illegitimate children...who had once been a student of hers himself—Thud had been immediately drawn in by the promise of some degree of professional expertise she might possess that could help him.

He'd then told her everything about The Cross Killer case he knew: starting with the day him and Brad Dekker had begun investigating the disappearance of Tyler Dunne; and were then present at the site on the beach near Smith River, California as Tyler's body was retrieved from the sea, tied to a makeshift tree limb cross. And about how the murder of the Dunne boy—as far as he was concerned—appeared to also be tied to the murder of Ricky Cates; even though some dissimilarities did exist.

How he felt *so strongly* about the latest disappearance of two more young boys on the Oregon coast, hundreds of miles away to the north, as being somehow definitely linked to the first two murders, too.

And about Chris Lawless, the boy from The Sea Lion Caves, and the man who had tried to get him to go with him somewhere...to look for whales. And about the little blue whale toy Chris had described to him and the chief, during the interview, that the man had tried to give him as an enticement.

The little blue whale toy which matched the description, exactly, of the little blue whale toy he had found half buried in the sand at South Beach State Park. The same place where the last boy, Colin Boyer, had been reported as missing from less than twenty four hours before.

Then Britt...Dr. McGraw...had given him some rough ideas off the top of her head about who, and what, they may be dealing with as a suspect. Her theories about the killer had excited him; and he was quickly hooked. Would she be willing to help them out on the case, he had asked her? Yes, she would. Thud had made an appointment to meet with her in his office on Monday afternoon for further discussions.

But he knew the number one priority right now in the investigation was to find out where that little toy blue whale had come from. It looked like pretty standard tourist trap fare; cheap, imported crap that was sold in hundreds of gift shops and variety stores up and down the Oregon coast all year around and marketed mostly to guilty, harried parents who found it impossible to deny their little angels a souvenir from their summer family vacation to the beach.

If he, and Spenser, and Brad Dekker hit this aspect of the investigation hard enough over the weekend, they might just find a source from which their little blue whale had come from…and that might just eventually lead to the killer himself. But whatever the outcome of their progress was, he knew that at 0800 hours Monday morning he was going to have to be Faxing copies of his report to the Clatsop County Sheriff's Department, Lane County Sheriff's Department, Seaside Police, Newport Police, Florence Police…and even that prick, Lloyd Rutledge; the SAC…Special Agent in Charge…of the FBI Office in Portland. *Sack* is right, he thought to himself. *Sack of shit.*

He had not spoken to the chief since he'd left him in Salem two nights ago, after having given him directions on how to get back onto the freeway southbound just before he had departed for Cutter Point in Thud's car; and now he was bursting with all this new information he needed to relay to him about the case. He was going to swing by The Sea Breeze Apartment's on his way through town, and if the chief wasn't having any better luck than he was in still being able to get a full night's sleep, maybe there would be a light on in his apartment and he could knock on his door, and they could talk for a few minutes.

As he blew past the little settlement of Gasquet, California on Highway 199, less than thirty minutes from Cutter Point, the thin membrane of cool moisture laden night mountain sky above him collided with a warm summer low pressure system marching in from the ocean, and soon needle thin raindrops began slanting down onto the Altima's windshield. The rain only increased as he dropped lower and lower out of the mountains, and as he approached the Pacific coast, torrents of water were beating so hard against the Altima's windshield that its wiper blades were only barely able to provide him with minimum driving visibility.

He entered the southern city limits of Cutter Point on Highway 101 practically at a snail's crawl, his eyes straining through the rain smeared glass, trying to see the exit for Harbor Way in time. He found it, but nearly too late; jamming the steering wheel hard left and fishtailing through the turn.

He crept the Altima down the steep and winding approach to the Harbor and Pearl Cove below, noting for the first time that his portable radio, which he'd turned on as he'd neared the California—Oregon border, was absolutely dead now—no traffic on it at all. He had heard Spenser Sparling about fifteen minutes earlier on it, calling in a traffic stop to the Dispatch Center. The sudden summer rain squall had increased in intensity, even since then, so Spenser had probably pulled over somewhere downtown to wait it out; or had maybe driven back to the department to have a cup of coffee, and wait it out.

On flat and level pavement now, he picked up a little speed as he came around the wide curve that opened onto Pearl Cove City Beach Park, and suddenly to his right the shimmering glob like shape of a white vehicle, and its two headlights, filled his windshield as it shot out of the parking lot next to the Restrooms, failing to yield the right of way to him. He slammed on his brakes at the same time the other driver did, and both vehicles lurched to a stop, just feet from one another.

Thud sat motionless for a few seconds, gripping the steering wheel as if he were getting ready to rip it from the steering column, the Altima's wipers furiously whipping back and forth across the windshield on their highest setting; but still failing to define the other car as more than just an indiscriminate white blur as it sat there, the other driver probably doing pretty much the same thing.

What the hell kind of idiot would be out driving on a night like this, he thought to himself, unless they had a damned good reason. They were probably kids; horny teenagers who loved to use the parking lot at Pearl Cove for their romantic rendezvous, dope smoking, and illegal skateboarding; even though C.P.P.D. ran them out of their on a regular basis.

Goddamit…now he was going to have to get wet. He reached into his equipment bag that he'd taken from his unmarked Ford and placed in the front seat of the rental car with him, grabbed his flashlight from it, and was just starting to open his door when he heard the other car's engine clatter to life.

He saw the large yellow beams from its headlights wobbling backwards into the parking lot, until they receded to the size of two ping pong balls. Then he heard the sound of tires spinning on water; a high pitched, paper tearing, whining sound, as the white vehicle accelerated forward towards him, veered off at a forty five degree angle at the last second, hit the raised curb with a bang, jumping it, then landed in the center of the roadway and raced away up the hill.

Thud took a second too long to disentangle himself from the Nissan's unfamiliar seatbelt system, then jumped out of the vehicle into the hammering rain. But all he could identify about the fleeing car was that it was white; as he watched its two red taillights blinking away up the road, and then finally be extinguished in the solid wall of water that was falling from the sky.

"God damned kids," he muttered, quickly getting back inside the Altima and slamming his door shut; he was soaked to his skin.

He picked up his portable radio and was going to call Spenser...to have him look for the white car and stop it, if he saw it, as a suspicious vehicle and reckless driver. But then he realized he didn't have any description for it; other than it was white...which would not be enough probable cause for a traffic stop.

He put the portable radio back down on the seat, and turned the car's heater on full blast. "Little bastard's," he said to himself. Then he put the car in gear and got back out on the road, and slowly drove in the direction of The Sea Breeze Apartment's, about a mile away.

When he pulled into the parking lot of The Sea Breeze, he was surprised to see his black unmarked Ford parked in front of Kearnes' apartment. Although the two vehicles were almost identical—Thud's car being only two years older than the chief's—and they were both solid black, he knew *his* car when he saw it. He thought it was strange; that Kearnes had not left his car at the P.D., and then taken his own home with him. But then again, there had been a lot of strange things happening with the chief these past few days, and for his own part, he still could not for the life of him get to sleep at night. Maybe they should both make appointments with Britt McGraw, soon, to have their heads shrunk.

Thud couldn't see any light coming from the windows of the chief's apartment, including the goofy looking porthole windows, that every time he came to this beat up old apartment complex made him feel like he was standing on a dock somewhere, watching a big green ship getting ready to sail out to sea. They used to get quite a few calls at this place before Kearnes had moved in, and Thud had last been here on a boyfriend-girlfriend date rape case about three months before. But ever since the chief had taken up residence here, the calls had dropped off to almost zero.

He decided he wasn't going to knock on the chief's door, and possibly wake him from a sound sleep, which to Thud right now, would seem like a crime, but he did want to check on his car and transfer his equipment bag from the rental car to it. As he opened his car door and got out, the rain suddenly stopped as if on cue, like the faucets of a giant bathroom shower having been abruptly turned off. Not wanting to get caught out in the open if the Heavens decided to dump on him again, he quickly, and as quietly as possible, opened the Ford's trunk and put his gear in it. He hated being without his car overnight, but since it was Saturday he could come and get it later in the morning, after he'd dropped the rental off at the Enterprise office downtown on Cutter Avenue.

Driving the rental back toward Pearl Cove he could see pieces of the moon peeking out in spots through the dispersing rain clouds, which were still low over the ocean; looking like a flickering candle coming from behind a torn and ragged curtain. Globules of clear rain water dripped from the high tops of the street lamps, hitting the standing water on the roadway below with the force of tiny bombs, and as he drove by The Sand Dollar he could see the light from its half burned out green neon sign at the office off in the distance, glowing eerily in the mist.

He hadn't seen any other vehicle's after his near accident with the white car; either on the way to the chief's place, or now, as he drove back on the same road, headed for the intersection where he would turn onto Harbor Way. But as he passed by the area where the parking lot entrance to Pearl Cove was, he saw a box sitting in the roadway up ahead, directly on the white painted broken centerline marks.

His first instinct was to just swerve to avoid it, and keep on going; but it was a fairly large box and the road surface all around it was peppered with shiny fragments of what looked like broken glass, so that made it a traffic hazard…and as a police officer he had a duty to clear this debris from the roadway. He stopped the Altima and switched on its amber flashing hazard lights, leaving the engine running and the headlights on, and then cussing to himself under his breath, wearily climbed out of the car again and walked up to the box.

The first thing he noticed was that it wasn't broken glass on the road all around the box, but instead…ice. Chipped ice. Like party ice; the kind you bought at the grocery store for a buck and a half in frozen, clear plastic bags. He kicked at some of the ice and the pieces went skittering away from him across the asphalt; making a dry, scuttling sound.

The cardboard box was soggy and wet; darkened from the rain and leaning a little to one side, its waterlogged condition having compromised its structural integrity. He didn't want to pick it up; so he drew his right leg back, and just like his former days of glory on the Cutter Point High Pirates…placed kicked the box toward the side of the road…and saw the sides of the box explode apart at his feet, and hundreds of long, thin, green snakes came shooting out of it in coils.

But they weren't snakes. They were individual, twelve inch long strips of green colored, six gauge vinyl; and Thud Compton had seen them someplace before…but his sleep deprived brain just couldn't, at the moment, remember where. He bent down and grasped a corner of one of the barely attached cardboard ends, and tore it free from the rest of the box. He turned the cardboard piece over in his hands, and saw the one word printed on it that meant anything to him…*Trellistrip*.

And then it registered…where he had first seen the long, green, vinyl strips before. They had been tied, tightly, around the wrists, and ankles, of Tyler

Dunne; who had been bound to a make shift cross from a Madrone tree branch when the divers had floated him, dead, through the water, and then carried him up onto the beach near the Smith River in California.

Thud dropped the piece of cardboard and backed away from it, horrified, as if it were really a piece of a box of snakes. He felt every short hair on his arms, and the back of his neck rising in electrified alarm. He turned and ran to the idling Altima, reached inside the open window and shut the engine off, then jerked the keys out of the ignition and grabbed his portable radio and the flashlight from the seat.

Except for the sound of the waves lapping against the rocks of the nearby jetty, and the whispering hiss of the surf touching the sloping, sandy beach of the cove, there was utter silence. His eyes scanned the darkened vista beyond the lighted area of the parking lot; the Restrooms, two volleyball net areas, a kid's playground area, picnic tables, grass, palm trees…and beyond all of these…the outline of two people standing far apart from each other on the beach.

He turned the portable radio down to its lowest volume setting, and then jammed it into one of his rear pants pockets. He drew the Glock 23 from its holster beneath his suit jacket and crouching low, sprinted for the corner of the Restrooms, keeping his eyes locked on the two figures as he ran. Reaching the restrooms, he kneeled on the concrete and took a position of cover behind the wall. They weren't moving; they were just standing there, coming into, and going out of his sight as the fractured storm clouds above moved across the face of the moon.

Thud's heart was pounding like a jack hammer and his hands shook as he took the portable from his back pocket and put it close to his face, never taking his eyes off the two subjects. He pressed the transmit button and whispered into the radio's microphone: "Charles Three to Central…I am two zero seven Adam with two subjects, on view, at Pearl Cove Park…I am 10-99…repeat…10-99…do you copy?"

"Charles Three, Central copies…stand by…Central to One Charles Twenty One…detective unit requesting assistance, Pearl Cove Park, possible kidnapping…in progress…Code 10-99…repeat, he is requesting 10-99."

"One Charles Twenty One copies!" Thud heard Spenser say to the Dispatcher. "En route from Cutter Avenue and Sarasota!."

"Charlie Three to Charlie Twenty One."

"Go!"

"Spenser, grab the shotgun from your unit when you get here…I've got a homicide suspect with a hostage down on the beach…near the Restrooms…I have to make contact with them…now!."

"Copy!" He heard Spenser shout into his radio, the adrenalin clearly detectable in his voice. Thud knew that from the location he was responding from, Spenser would be on scene in less than a minute and a half. Two seconds later he heard Spenser's siren, on the far side of the city, piercing the soggy night sky.

He put the radio back in his back pocket, and holding the small but very powerful Scorpion flashlight down at the concrete, flicked its switch quickly on and off to test it. It was only eight inches long, but generated some 30,000 candlepower, enough to blind a suspect by shining it in his eyes from close range. It was also small, and maneuverable enough to hold in one hand, beneath his gun hand, and act as an excellent shooting light to illuminate a target.

But the only thing Thud wanted in his hands right now was his Glock, because this was going to be a "shock and awe" take down; so he stuck the flashlight in the left pocket of his suit jacket, and then rose to his feet.

Approximately seventy five yards of open sand, with the kid's playground in between, was all that separated him from the two people. He looked up at the sky and as soon as the next batch of purple and black clouds began to slide across in front of the big, nearly full moon, he took off at a dead run toward them, the .40 caliber Glock extended forward in his right hand.

Thud couldn't run nearly as fast, and as far, as he used to be able to when he was a star high school football player, and later, a tough, in shape army Ranger. Age, too much beer, a weight gain of fifty pounds, and a nasty wound to his leg that he'd received in action on the Island of Grenada had seen to that.

But by God he could still yell just as loud as ever, and as he pounded across the heavy sand and closed to within fifteen yards of the two subjects he began to scream at the top of his lungs, "POLICE! FREEZE ASSHOLES! GET YOUR FUCKING HANDS IN THE AIR AND DON'T YOU FUCKING MOVE!"

And then he was right on top of them, running so fast he nearly overshot them as they stood there, frozen, with their arms outstretched rigidly…each of them holding something out to their sides. He had been screaming at them to get their hands in the air as he approached, but was surprised to see that they had already had their arms raised in the air before he'd even opened his mouth, and…

Oh my God.

Oh please God…no.

Thud lowered the Glock, and veered away from them, off to his left; and then angled back around to where he was facing them—the two naked boys that were tied with green vinyl strips to what looked like wooden fence posts, with cross pieces. That had been planted in the sand.

At least he *thought* they were boys. The skin of their bodies was drawn tautly, like drum heads, over their bones; having lost all its elasticity in the icy, chemical brine which they had been packed in for days. Their flesh was puckered, and had been bleached as white as the robes of an angel; but the shriveled male genitalia of both were still visible. He just didn't know which boy was which; which one was Colin Boyer, and which one was Peter Mossbrooker.

The facial features of the one boy's face...that he could clearly see, had been rendered almost indistinguishable from the decolorizing, pickling action of the chemically polluted melting ice and water. The other boy's entire head and face, with nothing but his ears sticking out, was covered with a pair of pale blue panties that had little ducks on them. The ducks were wearing sailor's hats.

But it didn't really matter now. He had found them, both of them; but too late. And now there was nothing he, or anyone else, could do for them. Except find the *thing* that had done this to them...and do even worse to him.

Thud dropped to his knees in front of the two crucified children, hanging from the wooden crosses, as if he were kneeling before the altar of a church in prayer.

He looked up at them and saw a last, few, captured errant rain drops; dripping slowly from the tips of their curled fingers like tears, falling from the eyes of God.

Then he fell face forward onto the sand, and began to sob, uncontrollably...the curious smell of disinfectant thick in his nose.

CHAPTER 36

▼

Kearnes had chosen the small kitchen of his apartment in which to spend the last few moments of his life.

Not because it was any nicer than any of the other rooms in his so called home, but because the "blowback"—the explosion of blood, brain matter, and bits of his skull—that would spray against nearby walls after he pulled the trigger of the Colt, could be more easily contained in there, and more easily cleaned up.

Other officers—some of them his friends—would have to see all of this; would have to process this scene. And he didn't want to make it any harder for them than it already would be.

He had been sitting in the dark at the little kitchen table for more than an hour, listening to a turbulent rain storm; which had sounded like buckets of steel ball bearings being poured down on top of The Sea Breeze Apartments. He had placed the muzzle of Ben's .38 Super flat against his forehead, just before the sudden storm had hit; but had set it back down on the kitchen table as the deafening clatter of rainfall had begun to increase in intensity.

He hadn't wanted to die with the sound of chaos ringing in his ears; he had wanted solitude, peace and quiet. He'd wanted to first say aloud the names of his two sons, and to then pull the trigger; hoping his last spoken words about the only part of his life on this earth that had held any true meaning, or value for him...might travel with him as a great comfort on this unknown journey into eternity...like precious, checked luggage.

When the rain suddenly stopped, he picked the Colt up once again and pressed it to his forehead. He cocked the gun's hammer back, then touched the cold blue steel trigger with his finger...and hesitated. It wasn't the rain that had stopped him the first time; not really. It was his sons, Ethan and Alex, and the thought of what he was about to do to *them*...for the rest of their lives.

He put the gun down on the table again, and stared at it, thinking about how differently his own life may have turned out, if only he hadn't missed with it the day he had shot at the man on the beach.

The man that he'd met in the sand dunes as he'd taken what he thought would be a short cut to the ocean that day; anxious and excited to try out his birthday gift...a brand new fishing rod and reel, and a tackle box full of hooks and lures and split shot and bobbers, to go along with it.

The gigantically tall man with the binoculars around his neck; who'd been so nice to him when they had first met. And who'd given him a little blue toy whale, and asked him if he'd like to go with him to see some real whales...because he knew of a secret place, not too far away, where they could watch them with his binoculars.

The man who had drug him into the tall grass in the sand dunes as they were walking, and when he'd resisted and tried to get away from him, whipping at his face with the fishing rod, had reached out with one massive hand and snatched the rod away from him, snapping off its end. And then pushed him down in the grass, and raped him.

The man who had just been getting into the car that he'd parked on a deserted beach access road—not far from their private camp trailer park—when he had suddenly felt someone watching him. And had then turned around and saw the boy, who was crying, come walking out of the sand dunes toward him; holding the big Colt pistol with the ivory grips in both hands and pointing it at him. Saw the orange muzzle flash from the barrel of the gun when the boy fired; and felt the bullet slam into his flesh like an invisible fist, just below his clavicle.

But what Kearnes didn't know, was that he hadn't missed Uriah Beek that day with his first, and only shot from Ben's Colt.

After Beek had raped him, he had let him go. But not before telling him that if he told anybody about the attack, he would come to his family's camp trailer and kill his Mother, his Father, his sister...and then him.

Kevin had then quickly walked away from the man, who had left in the opposite direction; and as soon as he was out of the man's sight, had run as fast as he could through the dunes the short distance back to the camp trailer park.

His sister, Karen, had been bitten just after breakfast that morning by a rock crab, that Kevin had captured the day before in a tide pool and had placed in a bucket by the trailer's steps. When Karen, who was four years younger than he was, had reached in the bucket to pet the crab, it had closed one of its powerful pincers shut on her finger. And after their Father had torn the crab's claw from its body in a desperate move to break its grip on her, his parents had driven his hysterically crying little sister to the hospital in Long Beach, to have the wound examined, and treated.

So no one had been at the trailer when Kearnes had flung open its unlocked door and rushed inside; had stripped off his bloody underwear, and stuffed them inside his new tackle box, along with the little toy whale, and had then hidden the broken rod and the tackle box deep down inside his sleeping bag, and told his parents later that someone had stolen them at the beach.

And no one had seen him reach into the high cupboard above the make down bed, where his Mother and Father slept, and from beneath the stack of folded blankets and extra bedding inside it, remove his uncle's gun from where his Father had thought he had hidden it so well.

And then young Kevin Kearnes had run like the wind in the direction he'd last seen the man walking. And like a miracle, he had come right of the sand dunes to where the man was standing, just starting to get into a car. And as the man turned around and looked at him, Kevin had already raised his Uncle Ben's gun directly at the man, barely able to hold it steady, even though he was using both his hands…and fired.

The man had flinched; startled by the shot…and had then just stood there, staring at him. Kevin had dropped the gun to the ground, and ran back into the sand dunes; where he had hidden in the tall beach grass until it started to get dark. And then not caring any longer if he lived, or if he died, had found a piece of driftwood, shaped like a club, and a flat rock, with a sharp, jagged edge to it…and with murder burning inside his heart…had gone back to find the man.

But the man wasn't there and neither was the car; and he had found Ben's gun lying on the ground, exactly where he had dropped it. He'd picked it up and brushed the sand from its shiny, metallic blue surface, and clicked the hard to move safety back on. And then he had left the same way he had come.

If he had walked only fifteen feet further straight ahead, from where he had picked the gun up, he would have seen where the man's blood had soaked into the sand. Kevin Kearnes had been eleven years and one day old on that day; and Uriah Daniel Beek had been twenty one.

How differently…his life may have turned out. If only he had not missed.

It had taken only the last twenty four hours, for thirty years of his life to collapse and crumble to dust all around him, in a cataclysmic earthquake of fate, truth, and self realization.

And in that twenty four hours he had committed a criminal act, violated his professional code of ethics, betrayed a friend, lied to a man who was like a Father to him, withheld vital information in a criminal investigation upon which the lives of two children might depend; and for the first time, ever, in his life, had physically hurt a woman...the woman he loved. Another criminal act, for which he could not only be arrested...but also prevented from ever wearing a badge again.

"Fuck this," he said out loud. He snatched the Colt from the table and jammed it to his head, positioning it perfectly between his eyes, and as he began put pressure on the inside of the trigger with the thumb of his right hand...he heard a siren wailing somewhere faintly, off in the distance.

Then a much closer, second siren, joined in; wailing along with the first one. Which was in turn followed shortly by a third siren; then a fourth, then a fifth...until there was chaos ringing in his ears once again. He heard his pager start to go off in his bedroom, and put the Colt back down on the table again; but this time he lowered its hammer first.

As he got up from the kitchen table and started toward the bedroom to get the pager, he heard the loudest of the sirens suddenly blaring right outside his door, and in the darkened living room where he stopped the walls were instantly bathed in brilliant flashing sheets of red and blue light.

The siren was abruptly cut off in mid-wail just as he opened his front door, and he saw a Cutter Point P.D. black and white brake to a stop at the curb in front of the apartment complex with its engine still running and its red and blue strobe light bar going full force. He watched as an ashen faced Spenser Sparling got out of his patrol car, came around the front of it, and walked halfway toward Kearnes' apartment door, then stopped.

Spenser looked as if someone had just knocked the wind out of him. His face was gray, and he was hyperventilating. As he struggled to catch his breath to speak he saw Kearnes' bloodied hands, and his eyes grew wide.

"Spenser...what is it?" said Kearnes. "What's wrong!"

Spenser tried to say something, but choked on his words. He shook his head back and forth as if to tell Kearnes that either nothing was wrong...or he couldn't, for some reason, speak.

Kearnes moved from his open doorway and quickly walked to where Spenser stood in front of the patrol car, frozen in place; unable to take his fear filled eyes away from Kearnes' raw hands...that looked like freshly ground hamburger.

"Spenser? Spenser! Look at me!"

Spenser snapped his head up, and made eye contact with Kearnes.

"Take a breath," said Kearnes. "I want you to take a deep breath; then tell me why you're here...what all the emergency sirens are for. Is there a fire?"

Spenser shook his head. "No," he said, his voice beginning to break now. "Sergeant Compton sent me to get you...he needs you to come to the park. Down on the beach, at Pearl Cove. There are two dead kids there. They're both hanging from wooden crosses."

Now, it was Kearnes, who felt as if he had just had the wind knocked out of him. A cold flood of abject terror rushed through his body; a feeling he had only experienced once before in his life...when he was an eleven year old boy.

His legs began to turn to mush as the tissues of his muscles flushed with adrenaline, and his first instinct in reacting to the almost incomprehensible fear and horror of what Spenser had just told him—of choosing either fight, or flight—was to turn and run away, in any direction, as fast and as far as he could.

Looking at Spenser, he realized for the first time just how really young he was, and saw both innocence, and fear, in the young officer's eyes. And yet he also saw the man in him emerging from the boy; who had just seen death for the first time that had been wrought by the hands of pure evil. And at that precise moment, the light that been extinguished inside the mind and heart of Kevin Kearnes so very long ago, when he was only a boy himself...inexplicably, and miraculously...came back to life, and began to shine again.

"Chief," Spenser said weakly. "I need to use your bathroom...I think I might get sick."

Spenser had started to sway on his feet and as he began to wobble past Kearnes, heading for the open front door of the apartment, Kearnes stepped into his path to stop him.

"Spenser," he said. But the young officer had his eyes to the ground, and didn't appear to hear Kearnes as he brushed past him.

Kearnes reached out and grabbed him by his elbow, spinning him around to face him.

"Officer Sparling!"

"Yes...what?"

"Now, listen to me," Kearnes said sternly. "If you have to get sick, you're going to have to wait until you get to where you are going. Right now, I want you to get back in your car and advise Sgt. Compton, on the radio, that I will be en route to the scene in five minutes...have you got that?"

"Yes," Spenser said. "Five minutes."

"Good...OK. But *you* are not going back there; I've got a special detail for you."

"Chief, Sergeant Compton told me to 'get my ass' back to Pearl Cove immediately after I made contact with you."

"I'll explain everything to Sergeant Compton, when I get there. What auxiliary weapons do you have in your unit?"

"I've got a Remington 870 pump, up front with me, in the rack…and the MP5 is in its hard case in the trunk."

"Are you carrying anything else besides your Glock? Do you have a back up handgun on you?" Kearnes asked him.

"No," said Spenser.

"Get the MP5 out of the trunk…and take all the spare loaded magazines, too. I'll be right back."

Kearnes ducked inside his apartment while Spenser retrieved the Heckler and Koch MP5A2 nine millimeter submachine from his patrol vehicle's trunk, along with two extra fully loaded thirty round magazines. He had laid the spare magazines on the closed trunk of the patrol car and was adjusting the web carrying sling of the submachine gun, when Kearnes reappeared and walked over to him.

"Here," Kearnes said, handing him the small nine millimeter Kahr pistol. "There's one in the chamber, and it's ready to go. Unbutton your shirt, and stick it inside the left side of your vest…leave the top two buttons of your shirt undone; you'll be able to get to it quicker that way."

"Chief," said Spenser, "we aren't even allowed to *look* at our sub-guns, unless we're out at the Range for training. What's going on?"

"Do you know where Miss McGraw lives? At The Sand Dollar?"

"In one of the beach cabins?"

"Yes; but do you know which one?"

"No, not exactly."

"She lives in the very last one; toward the beach. It's also the biggest one. It has a sleeping loft; like a second story?"

"OK."

"All the cabins there…they're all named for trees, and they have signs on them. The name of hers is The Cypress. Can you remember that?"

"Yeah…The Cypress."

"Good," said Kearnes. "I want you to go to her cabin and make contact with her…tell her that I have ordered you to be there; and you are to stay there with her, in the cabin, until you are personally called away from there by me."

"All night?" Spenser asked him.

"Until you are personally relieved from that location by me. And you are to have the MP5 with you, at all times. Your job is to protect Miss McGraw...and any other civilians in the area who may need your help."

"So, you think he's still around here...somewhere?" asked Spenser.

"Yes," Kearnes said, "I do."

"But who is he? Who could do something *like that*? Like he did to those kids?"

"I don't know his name, Spenser; but here is what you need to be looking for: He will be an older white male, probably in his late fifties or early sixties. He could be wearing some type of uniform, matching pants and shirt at least, of the same color; brown or possibly green...and look for an embroidered name or logo on the shirt pocket, done in red.

He is very tall, at least six five, maybe more, and he's very strong...a body builder, possibly. But in any case, he is both extremely clever, and extremely dangerous. He is a sex offender and a murderer, and won't hesitate to kill you if you confront him or corner him...and so there must not be *any* hesitation on your part, to kill *him*. Do you understand me, son?"

"No sir, I don't. Because that's not what we were taught at The Academy. We were taught..."

"I don't give a good goddamn what they taught you at the Academy, Officer Sparling!" Kearnes shouted.

"You are going to follow what I am teaching you right now...tonight...and that's how to stay alive!"

"But what if I can't identify him...what if he doesn't appear to have a weapon?"

"You will know him," said Kearnes. "You will *absolutely* know him, if you see him."

"And Spenser? His "weapon", is himself. It's all he needs, and it is all he's ever needed. If he either approaches you, or flees from you, I want you to shoot...and you are to keep on shooting, until he is down, and stays down."

"Jesus Christ," said Spenser.

"Center mass...is that understood?"

"Yes...I'll shoot for center mass, chief."

"OK, now get going...and call me on my cell as soon as you are with her, and you have the cabin secured."

Before the flashing strobe lights of the patrol car had receded from sight into the distance, as Spenser raced toward The Sand Dollar, Kearnes ran back inside the apartment to his bedroom and put on his patrol jacket and his uniform baseball cap to go with the jeans and tee shirt he was wearing. Then he grabbed his gunbelt, and the keys to Thud's car.

He ran into the kitchen and picked the Colt up again from the table, cocking the hammer of the gun back and clicking the safety on; then placed the weapon in its holster and snapped it down before he strapped the gunbelt around his waist.

He stared at the small kitchen table—where by now, had it not been for a freak rain storm and the mournful concerto of emergency sirens, shrieking in the sullen, night ocean air—he would have been slumped over in a pool of his own blood and gore.

Maybe he would sit at the table again...to finish what he had started tonight; or maybe not. He really wasn't sure any longer about it, or much of anything else left in the disassembled wreckage strewn all around him, which had once been his life.

But there *was* one thing he was absolutely sure of: a homicidal maniac was loose somewhere in this town...in *his* town...and as chief of police; it was his job to find him.

CHAPTER 37

▼

When he got there he found Thud Compton sitting in one of the playground swings, smoking a cigarette and staring at the bodies; which were still hanging from their crosses in plain view.

The chorus of police sirens Kearnes had heard from his apartment were all accounted for now at the crime scene, except for one.

Two Oregon State Police cars and two Cutter County Sheriff Department cars had heard, and responded to Thud's original 10-99 call; the most dreaded call every law enforcement officer feared either hearing, or having to broadcast themselves. All four of the marked patrol cars were parked at crazy angles in the center of the empty parking lot, surrounding a red Nissan Altima, some with their doors standing open, but all of them with their emergency lights still flashing.

The fifth siren—and also undoubtedly the first one he'd heard tonight—belonged to Spenser's car. And although he had not heard from him yet, he hoped and prayed that by now he was with Britt in her cabin, securing all the windows and doors, the MP5 hanging from around his neck by its sling.

Kearnes watched as the two Oregon State Troopers, assisted by one of the deputies, cordoned off a wide area around the bodies with yellow plastic crime scene tape. The second deputy stood nearby, guarding the scene and smoking. He must have been the one Thud bummed the cigarette from, Kearnes thought, because as far as he knew Thud Compton didn't smoke.

Slowly, Kearnes walked over to where Thud was and stood in front of him, blocking his view of the two corpses.

He could see that only one and a half of Thud's butt cheeks fit the seat of the child size swing, and that he had both of his legs locked straight out into the sand; like temporary bracing holding up a wall under construction. His suit and tie were soaking wet and covered with a coating of wet sand, as if he had been down on all fours, rolling on the beach. So maybe that was why, Kearnes thought, he had decided to try and squeeze himself into the swing...to try and dry off a little.

"You look like hell, Thud," Kearnes said softly.

Thud looked Kearnes up and down hard, evaluating him. He expelled a lungful of hazy, blue smoke, and then said to Kearnes, "And you don't? You look like shit. What the hell happened to *you* since I last saw you?"

Kearnes didn't respond to him.

"I put out the *HIMA*," said Thud, "as soon as I realized what we had here. I thought you'd want that done immediately...without wasting any time. You should have gotten the page, too."

HIMA was the acronym for "High Incident Mobilization Alert"; C.P.P.D.'s established protocol for contacting and mobilizing every sworn, and non-sworn member of the police department by any means available, in order to have them respond to specifically assigned duty locations in the event of a major emergency. Even on the night that The Patriots had blown up the dead whale on the beach near Bouchet′ Plaza, a *HIMA* had not been initiated.

"No, you absolutely did the right thing," Kearnes said. "And my pager did go off...just as Spenser pulled up to my place. I've sent him to The Sand Dollar; to guard Britt."

Thud took a long, last drag from the cigarette, making it spark furiously as it burned down against the filter. Then he flicked it away backwards, over his head and away from the crime scene. "Margie's going to kill me," he said. "She made me quit ten years ago...right before our oldest, Sarah, was born. Threatened to divorce my ass if I didn't; and she was serious, too."

"I don't think she's going to hold one cigarette against you," Kearnes said, "not on a night like this."

"It's not just one," said Thud, "that was number three."

"But I'll be goddamned if I'm going to be smoking another one when that shithead LaMar pulls up. I won't give that fucker the satisfaction." Thud was right; soon *all* of them would be down here, swarming over the scene like flies on carrion.

It was obvious that Thud Compton was shaken, and in shock, but he had to get him to start talking about what he had seen; how he had come upon this grisly and macabre death scene.

Kevin Kearnes wasn't a very religious man, but he could still vividly recall how he had felt as a young boy sitting in church with his parents one particular Easter Sunday when the sermon had been about the crucifixion of Jesus outside the walls of the city of Jerusalem on a hill called Golgotha; known to the Israelites as "the place of the skull". How the sight of their savior, torn and bleeding, hanging from a wooden cross in death, had affected his followers who had gathered there to watch him die...and how this moment, for many of them, had been their supreme test of faith.

As he stood looking at Thud now, only a few feet away from the stark reality and horror of their own Golgotha, he saw Thud's shoulders slumped in defeat, and his head held low. He saw a man who had finally run out of all faith and hope; in both himself, and his cause, and was finally beaten. If only he could give Thud what he needed most now; faith...and hope. Faith in Kearnes again...as his leader, and as his friend...and the hope that together; they could stop this madman, and soon.

"Thud," Kearnes asked him, "were you the first unit on scene?"

"No. Spenser was."

"Spenser discovered these bodies?"

"No. I mean, I wasn't responding here as a unit...I was in that rental car; I was on my way to your place and practically ran into the guy. Only I didn't know it was him...it was raining so goddamned hard. He almost ran into me, coming out of the parking lot here."

"Did you take off after him? Or call it in?"

"No. I thought it was kids...just screwing around here in the park. I kept on going to your place."

"Did you get a good look at his vehicle?"

"No. It was raining *so* damned hard. All I saw were his headlights, almost in my front seat with me; then he threw it in reverse and hauled ass around me, going up the hill.

It was a white car...that's all I could tell. Everything else about it was a blur...even my wipers on high couldn't keep the windshield cleared off then."

"So you stopped and got out? And that's when you found them? When you walked down to the beach?"

Thud reached inside his suit jacket and pulled out two cigarettes and a plastic disposable lighter. One of the cigarettes was soggy, and bent. He threw it on the ground; but lit the other one up. Kearnes let him drag on the cigarette a couple of times, and waited for him to answer.

Finally, Thud said, "No. I fucked up, chief. I started to call it in, but I didn't. I let him go; drove to your place. I was going to knock on your door and fill you in on the latest; but all your lights were out, so I didn't. I was passing by here on my way back when I saw something in the road; so I stopped and got out."

"It was that…over there," he said, pointing out toward the center of the road where the two state troopers had already encircled a couple areas of what looked like small piles of debris on the roadway with loops of the yellow crime scene tape.

"It's a box of those Trellistrips," he said. "The same thing he used to tie Tyler Dunne up with…and now these two kids, too, on those goddamned crosses. It must have fallen out of, or off of his car…when he drove away. Right in fucking front of me."

And now here it was; almost all of it had come together, and Thud had been right, all along. Not about the specifics, of course; but his instincts, his "gut feeling", had been as true and as real as the sixth sense any four legged animal possesses, who can feel vibrations from deep within the earth, just before a massive earthquake hits, or smell the build up of ions in the air, just before the sky is split apart by a brilliant bolt of lightning, hurled to the ground in an electrical storm.

"I'm going to have an officer sent to your place, too," said Kearnes. "To protect Margie and the kids."

"I already did," said Thud.

"Is he there yet?"

"Yeah, they're there. It's Frick and Frack. The little shits were actually *awake* when Dispatch called their house…probably still up after partying all night."

"They'll take good care of your family, Thud. And remember; there are two of them."

"I had to have Shoshanna verify that they weren't responding on their damn bikes. I guess one of the knot heads did have sense enough to use one of their cars."

"I think you underestimate them, Thud. I think you've actually scared them straight…they're both coming along pretty well as officers, from what I've seen."

"Chief…?"

"Yes?"

"Who in the hell is this sick bastard? Why is he targeting *us*?"

"I don't know who he is," Kearnes replied. "And I'm not sure he is targeting us; but there's definitely something either here, or around us, that he's after…and maybe we're just in his way."

"No," said Thud. "It's not something he's after…it's *someone*. I've felt it from the very beginning. He's using these kids…these victims…as a way of communicating something. To someone else.

He's not really interested in them; as individuals. These are all random acts. Crimes of opportunity. But there *is* a common theme here. I just can't grasp it yet."

As an investigator, Thud didn't have the world's greatest analytical mind; but he was bulldog smart. When he did come upon an irregularity, or a lead, or a genuine clue in a case, he would seize it and bite down on it and never let it go. He would shake it to death until he had rattled every last ounce of worth from it; then dig a shallow hole close by and bury it, for quick retrieval and using again at a later time. Listening to him now, even Kearnes had the sudden urge to disclose to him all that he knew. But he couldn't. Not yet.

"Let's go over everything you've put into play so far," said Kearnes. "Starting with finding the bodies."

Thud dropped his half smoked cigarette onto the sand, and ground it into oblivion with the heel of his shoe.

"Discovered the bodies. Had Central put out a broadcast to all local patrols, to stop every white vehicle observed, as a possible homicide suspect. But that didn't work; they had already all responded here to the 10-99 I put out when I thought I had two live subjects on the beach, instead of two bodies."

"OK…anything else?"

"Well, yeah…I had the *HIMA* toned out, I sent Spenser to get you, I had Frick and Frack sent to my place, O.S.P. in Central Point notified…they are going to chopper in their Crime Scene Unit, and they should be here in about an hour, they said.

And I called Brad Dekker at home in Gold Beach and woke him up. I'm having him stop by Cutter Farm Supply on his way in. Shoshanna called the manager of the place for me and he's going to meet Brad down at the store. We need some tarps. To cover these kids up with. I told Shoshanna to tell him I would be by later this morning, to sign a charge slip from the city. Was that OK?"

"That was fine," said Kearnes. "Looks like you've thought of just about everything, Thud."

"Chief…I didn't mean to go over your head."

"You didn't, Thud."

"Yes, I did. And I had a reason, then. But not so much now."

"And?"

"And...frankly; you have been scaring the hell out of me, sir.

Kearnes knelt down on one knee in the sand, and looking straight into Thud's eyes asked him, "How am I doing right now, Thud?"

Thud met his chief's eyes with his own and never looking away, said, "Better, sir. You seem a lot...better."

Kearnes extended his hand toward Thud. Thud took it and they shook hands, firmly.

"Thud...Sergeant Compton," Kearnes said. "I want you to know that you are one of the finest police officers I have ever served with in my career. And that I have the highest respect for both the man, and the policeman, that you are."

Thud looked at him, his eyes glistening, and swallowed hard. "Thank you, chief," he said, with the slightest trace of a quiver in his voice. "It's good to know that we still have each others backs."

A set of headlights swept across Thud's back and the front of Kearnes' face. Kearnes saw a pearl gray, unmarked Ford pull to a stop next the other cars, and a man get out, then open the back door on the driver's side and begin piling bright blue plastic tarps, still in their packaging, in his arms.

"That's Brad," Thud said, struggling to free his one now form fitted butt cheek, from the curved hard rubber seat of the swing. "I hope he bought some rope, too."

As Kearnes and Thud crossed through the playground area, walking to where Brad Dekker was unloading the emergency crime scene supplies from his car, three more sets of car headlights slowly descended from atop the hill above them like yellow eyed vultures, riding lazily on warm thermal air currents, down to a kill.

As the vehicles neared the bottom of the hill and began to pass beneath the street lights that were in place there, Kearnes could see that the car in the lead was a white Cadillac Escalade, followed by a Cutter Point P.D. black and white, and then a black, unmarked Chevy Caprice with six or seven radio and cell phone antennas sprouting from its trunk and roof; which practically screamed "federal agent" as it rolled ominously down the road.

The white Escalade ignored the outer perimeter of yellow plastic crime scene tape that had been strung across the entrance to the park's parking lot only moments before by the two O.S.P. troopers, and drove right through it, snapping it apart like a rotten rubber band.

Inside the cars were Vernon Bouchet´, Roy Roddameyer, Curt LaMar, Edgar Polk, and Delbert "Downs Syndrome" Downs. They had all responded to or had otherwise been notified of the police department's mass call for help...the High Incident Mobilization Alert.

But as the vehicles stopped, their doors flew open, and the occupants inside them began to emerge; one look at their faces was all Kearnes needed, to see that the last reason on earth these men had come here for...was to help.

CHAPTER 38

▼

Roddameyer assumed the lead position, with his boss, the mayor, directly behind him, while the other three fanned out around them and then they all began to walk, slowly, toward Kearnes and Thud, gunfighter style.

They were in the classic "showdown" configuration now; one that Kearnes had watched unfold hundreds of times when he was a boy, lying on his stomach on his living room floor on a Saturday night with a bowl of Sugar Corn Pops and milk, as he gazed up at the larger than life image of James Arness in *Gunsmoke* on his family's old Philco black and white TV.

Invariably, the ending of almost every episode of the most popular western in television history had concluded with Marshal Matt Dillon in the final few scenes standing in the middle of a dusty, Dodge City, Kansas street, alone; facing one, or several armed and evil men, who were bent on doing him in.

As they came closer, Kearnes wondered where the number four man of their gang was, Russell Massey; and decided he was probably playing the part of the guy they would have posted in a dark alleyway with a Winchester, or on a rooftop, and whose job it was to try for a back shot on the hero.

But where he actually was, of course, was back in Central Dispatch; where he had been working the graveyard supervisory shift, had heard every frantic radio transmission between Thud Compton and Spenser Sparling when the bodies were discovered, and had then immediately called Edgar Polk at home, and woke him up. Even *better* than a back shot.

"What the fuck?" Kearnes heard Thud say behind him, angrily.

Brad Dekker had seen the group drive through the crime scene tape and get out of their cars; now, with his arms full of tarps and coils of half inch hemp rope, he quickly kicked his car door shut with his heel, and then walked over and stood with Thud and Kearnes.

Without taking his eyes off of the approaching pack of pure, malevolent evil, Kearnes said under his breath: "Thud...you need to let me do all the talking." Even though he already knew before he'd said it, that it wouldn't do any good.

In the poorly lit parking lot, Kearnes thought Roddameyer even looked like a classic western bad guy, with his jet black hair, and dressed in all black clothing. But as he walked up to Kearnes within a few feet, and stopped, he saw that Roddameyer was actually wearing a black silk smoking jacket; and beneath it, dark blue and black plaid pajama tops and bottoms...and bedroom slippers, with no socks.

Roddameyer moved slightly to his left, and the diminutive form of Mayor Vernon Bouchet´ materialized; also clad in an identical, but much smaller sized, black smoking jacket, and wearing the same pajama bottoms and slippers with no socks that looked similar to Roddameyer's. But true to form, old Vernon wore a high necked, turtle neck shirt—this one a maroon kidney color—beneath his smoking jacket; concealing his pajama tops. Kearnes stared at the little owl eyed man, who seemed to be more wide awake than the others, and wondered what horrible and hideous sight must lie beneath the generous folds of his turtleneck.

"Good morning, chief Kearnes...detective Compton," said Roddameyer, nodding at them both, but ignoring Brad Dekker.

"Please excuse mine, and the mayor's attire; but we felt it was incumbent upon us both to get here just as soon as we could, and see what it was that is so important as to have caused a city wide alert?"

"What it is, you pompous ass, is two dead kids," said Thud. "A double homicide...right down there."

"You can it, Compton!" shouted Edgar Polk, who now stepped out of the shadows; and he was *not* dressed in his pajamas. He was in full uniform.

Kearnes felt Thud starting to bull his way past him, eager to get at Polk; but he sidestepped in front of him, and bumped him backwards a little, stopping him.

"Detective Compton?" said Kearnes, his eyes locked on Polk, "you will apologize to the city manager, for that outburst."

"Apologize hell!" shouted Polk. "This man is under my command and I am placing him on suspension! NOW!"

It took Kearnes only three, lightning quick steps, and he was nose to nose with Edgar Polk; who was so stunned by the suddenness of it all that his mouth remained agape, in mid-sentence, as Kearnes shouted at him, "And *you*, Lieutenant, are under *my* command…and I am telling *you* this man is NOT suspended! He is in charge of a homicide investigation right now; and he will remain in charge until I say he is relieved! Do you understand me Lieutenant Polk?"

Polk was speechless. He hadn't been able to stop himself from involuntarily recoiling as Kearnes had rushed over to him. He had, in effect, blinked first. And everyone there had seen it. But the thing Kearnes had also picked up on, was the lack of effect the words "dead" and "homicide" had on the group. Which meant that they already knew of the killings before they had arrived…and that Roddameyer had lied to him.

Delbert Downs, standing next to Polk, slack mouthed, his eyes slowly glazing over, looked as if his medication at the home for the feeble minded where he *really* belonged, had just been doubled. Curt LaMar lit the end of a fresh Marlboro with the stub of the one he currently had planted between his lips; which was glowing cherry red, like the end of a bomb's fuse which had just been lit. Roy Roddameyer didn't say anything. He only began to sweat, profusely, and this time; it smelled to Kearnes faintly like gin. And Vernon Bouchet´ scowled; not at Kearnes…but at Edgar Polk. For losing round one of the title fight they had all come to participate in.

Kearnes took a step back from Polk, and then turned to face Thud."

"Thud?"

"I…apologize," Thud said, noncommittally; looking at Kearnes as he spoke, but never at Roddameyer.

"Detective Compton has been under a tremendous amount of stress," Kearnes explained to Roddameyer. "I don't think he's even slept once in the last three days."

"And whose fault is that?" said LaMar, glaring at Thud. "You're such a one man show, Compton. You could have asked for some help, you know. Especially on a homicide."

Thud had been standing quietly behind Kearnes ever since he'd seen his chief verbally lay into Polk. He considered Detective Curt LaMar to be the second most hated officer on the department, right after Edgar Polk. He absolutely despised Curt LaMar and all that he stood for; and despised him even more for the things that he didn't stand for.

"Shut the fuck up, LaMar," he said, "you walking lung biopsy." "It would be a cold day in hell before I ever let you on one of my cases; just so you could screw it up. And by the way, asshole, there's no smoking at a crime scene."

"Thud," Kearnes said, calmly, "you and Brad get with the other officers, and build a wall of tarps around those bodies until the crime lab people get here.

Check the area for footprints first, and grid off and photograph anything identifiable. Use whatever you have to, to support those tarps; driftwood, tree branches…anything that will work. But I don't want any part of either the bodies, or the crosses showing by the time the media gets here."

"You going to be OK, chief?" Thud asked.

"I'll be fine," said Kearnes. "I need a little time to explain to the mayor, and city manager, what we are going to need here. Then I'll be down to supervise the scene."

Kearnes waited until Thud and Brad Dekker had walked away, out of earshot, before he spoke.

"Lieutenant; I want you, and Sergeant Downs, to return to the station. I want two patrol officers sent back down here for crime scene security. We already have three officers at two different sites, on security details. Dispatch will know how to get hold of them if we need them.

Then, I want you to get every other available officer we have, out on the streets, patrolling, and I want every white vehicle, no matter what make or model…"

"There will be no media down here this morning, chief Kearnes," interrupted Vernon Bouchet'. "And this…this police mobilization, is to be rescinded immediately!"

Bouchet' had stood by and watched as three of the four members of his "dream team" he had brought with him to Pearl Cove—to quickly put a stop to whatever controversial or negative events that were reportedly unfolding here—had been run over and mowed down by Kearnes, and Thud Compton, as if they were stalks of wheat beneath the threshing blades of Kansas combine. And since the fourth and last member of his team, Delbert Downs, was a complete imbecile, he felt it was in his best interest to now make a change in the batting order, and to step up to the plate himself.

"Excuse me, sir," said Kearnes. "I guess I'm a little confused…about what you mean by that?"

"Nothing confusing about it," said Bouchet'.

"We have a vote coming before the city council on Monday night. A very *important* vote; about the economic future and direction of this community. And relative to the upheaval, and commotion, *you*, chief Kearnes, caused less than two months ago, with that whale business down on my beach…well; let's just say that we can't let that happen again, here…tonight."

Kearnes stared at Bouchet' as if he was some alien being who had just been beamed down from his Mother ship to the parking lot at Pearl Cove. And as his words, and the meaning of his words, began to sink in; Kearnes thought that maybe he was.

A murderer, who had killed four boys, was at large somewhere in the area, maybe even now watching from a distance the gathering of forces against him at Pearl Cove…and this man was worried about how it would affect the vote for a new golf course and resort hotel?

"Sir, this is a homicide investigation," said Kearnes "Those are the bodies of two young boys down there on the beach…in the City of Cutter Point. And by the time the sun comes up, this park…the entire Harbor area, will be swarming with media, people just wanting to get a look, and more police."

"Ah, but you see that's where you are wrong, chief Kearnes. Because by the time the sun does come up…and that would be in less than two hours, I would expect…all of this, and all of you…are going to be gone. Poof! Vanished. Like you, or none of it, was ever here to begin with."

"Chief Kearnes," said Roddameyer, "I think what the mayor is getting at, is that we need to think about…"

"Shut up Roy Boy!" screamed Bouchet´. "All of you, shut up right now! And you listen to me!"

"Mayor…this is a crime scene, sir, and I am going to have to ask you and Mr. Roddameyer to leave now," Kearnes said.

"Polk," said Bouchet´, "you get on your radio and rescind that order…now! I want every officer called off this thing, and sent back home."

Edgar Polk hadn't taken his eyes off Kearnes since Kearnes had gotten in his face. And Kearnes had been shifting his attention around to all of them; gauging reactions, looking for signs of trouble, but now, as Polk moved his hand slowly up toward his portable radio's mike, which was clipped to the shoulder epaulet of his uniform shirt, he saw Kearnes zone in on him and him alone…and he froze.

"Touch that radio mike, Lieutenant, and you'll be under arrest for official misconduct," said Kearnes.

"This is outrageous!" shouted Bouchet´.

"No sir. *You* are outrageous", said Kearnes. "This is a *crime scene*, in an official police homicide investigation. You, and the city manager, are to immediately get back in your vehicle, mayor, and leave. Now. Or I am going to place you both under arrest for obstruction."

"Godammit Polk! I gave you an order!" shouted Bouchet´

"You have your orders Lieutenant Polk; from me," said Kearnes. "And the same goes for you, detective," Kearnes said to LaMar. "You go on back to the station with the lieutenant and sergeant; and try to make yourself useful. But I advise you to stay away from Detective Compton."

"This is ridiculous, Kearnes!" said Bouchet′ "I have it on good authority that these two...victims...were not even killed here!"

"We have no proof of that, one way or another yet," said Kearnes.

"Well, relative to the fact that...as Detective LaMar has informed me...these two boys were taken from different locations far up the coast from here, it seems to me the only thing you may have on the party responsible for leaving them here is a littering charge!"

"And how, exactly, would detective LaMar know that?" Kearnes asked, fixing his gaze back on LaMar. Kearnes and Thud had specifically excluded Edgar Polk and his cronies from letting them know exactly where they were going, and what they were doing the morning they had left town to interview Chris Lawless; but it was obvious now that they had been tracked every step of the way.

"Because, unlike you, chief Kearnes, he has friends...and in this case, friends in both the Florence and Newport police departments."

Now, Kearnes' Matt Dillon moment had finally arrived. He stepped over to Vernon Bouchet′, and leaned down toward the little man's face, getting so close to him that he could see the magnified reflection of his own face in Bouchet′s car mirror sized eyeglass lenses. But unlike Polk, the mayor didn't even flinch.

"Tell me, mayor," said Kearnes, "what do you suggest I do with the bodies, and the other physical evidence present here?" "What do we do about these other officers?" he said, nodding his head slightly in the direction of Thud and the others, down on the beach, "and the crime lab team that is already on their way here? What do you suggest I tell them?"

"Well, relative to the potential for confusion and the miscommunications that always seem to accompany these sorts of things...you simply tell everyone it was just a mistake; a false alarm. You can take these bodies to Krume and Sons; our local funeral home. Victor Krume is a close personal friend of mine. You can store them there, until Tuesday morning. And then...you can do whatever the hell you want."

"And the other officers here? Who are now all witnesses?" asked Kearnes.

"I'm sure they are all reasonable men," said Bouchet′. "And reasonable men...can always be reasoned with."

"What about the parents, mayor? You don't think they have a right to even know if their kids are still alive or not?"

"Relative to their knowing that, chief Kearnes," Bouchet´ said, "I fail to see what real difference two days will make to the parents of these two boys. Dead is dead."

Kearnes straightened back up and peering down at Bouchet´, actually laughed out loud at him in sheer amazement at the absurdity of what he was demanding he do because he could not help himself; even though he knew that what he was looking at was a very sick and disturbed little old man.

Vernon Bouchet´ was an undiagnosed megalomaniac, and his psychopathological condition; characterized by delusional fantasies involving wealth, power, and omnipotence, and his obsession with grandiose and extravagant actions, had elevated him, in his own curdled mind, to the same exclusive gated community where God resided. But as Kearnes began to realize just how crazy Bouchet´ was—how crazy this whole situation was and how crazy this entire place was—he began to feel a little better about himself, and his own state of mental health.

"Lieutenant Polk, Sergeant Downs, Detective LaMar…please escort the mayor, and the city manager back to their vehicle…and have them leave this crime scene," Kearnes said. "Immediately."

No one in the group moved. Roy Roddameyer's face was bathed in sweat and was flushed; like he'd just stepped out of a hot shower, or had finished shaving at the sink. He was nervously fingering the lapel of his smoking jacket, stroking at it like it was the smooth surface of a crystal highball glass.

"That's an order," said Kearnes," and I'm only going to give it to all of you once. Disobey it, and you are suspended, with pay, pending internal and criminal investigations for failure to perform duties, and official misconduct."

Edgar Polk reached out and touched Bouchet´'s elbow and said, "Come on, mayor, we need to leave now." But Bouchet´ jerked his bony arm away from him.

"Get your goddamned hands off me Edgar!" he screeched. "Do I look helpless? I can walk on my own, Godammit!" And then with one final, dagger shooting glare at Kearnes, Bouchet´ turned and slowly walked toward his Escalade, with the others falling into line behind him.

Looking out at the horizon and the murmuring sea, Kearnes saw blood red streaks of colored light beginning to lacerate the still dark morning sky, and for the first time after stepping outside of Thud's car in the parking lot of Pearl Cove, he realized the nausea which had been his silent and unwanted companion, had somewhere along the way left him.

He heard a cell phone ringing now and realized it was his; coming inside Thud's car where he'd left it. He sprinted over to the car and retrieved the phone and answered it on the sixth ring; it was Spenser.

"Chief?"

"Yeah, I'm here."

"Sorry about not calling you sooner, but I thought I'd better check Miss McGraw's place out thoroughly first."

"Is everything all right there Spenser?"

"Yeah...everything is cool. We are all locked down and we've been sitting in the living room, with only a night light on. Actually, I just finished having some really good oatmeal cookies, and coffee."

"Where is she right now?"

"In the shower."

"How is she taking all this?"

"Good. She's good with it. She says she understands."

Kearnes heard voices and looked over to where Polk and the others were still standing around outside of their cars. Vernon Bouchet' was shouting and gesturing wildly at Polk, and Polk was nodding his head; apparently in agreement of whatever it was Bouchet' was telling him. But he saw LaMar getting into his white Caprice, and Roddameyer opening the driver's side door of the Escalade now; so they were preparing to leave.

"Oh! She told me about the burglary here...to her place. And we found out where the guy got in...when she went to get some more coffee for her coffee maker."

"You did? Where?"

"There's a small door around back...it comes in from the backside of the cabin; and it opens up into a pantry here inside. Just off of the living room."

"What was the status of that that door?"

"She said she is sure that it was locked, but whoever got in here must have just forced it open with their body. I didn't see any footprints on it, or any pry marks around the door handle or lock; but the door jamb was splintered...and the dead bolt was still in the open position."

"Did you try to get any prints?"

"No. I would have had to go back out to my car in the parking lot for the print kit...and you told me not to leave her alone."

"That's right, I did. Good man, Spenser. We can try and print it later."

"Did you tell her you might have to stick with her most of the day today? Or at least until I can call Margie Compton...and see if she can go and stay with them for awhile?"

"She won't have to."

"Why?"

"She says she's leaving town."

"Leaving for where? When?"

"She was already up and packing, when I got here."

"What time is she leaving? Did she say?"

"She said by ten a.m.."

"But for where?"

"California. She said she wants me to tell you goodbye for her. And to also say goodbye to Sergeant Compton, and his wife. And to tell the Sergeant she's sorry she can't keep their appointment for Monday." Kearnes wondered what that meeting would have been all about; if she'd wanted to meet with Thud to make a report about him and what had happened at the cabin, in his irrational panic to get away from her. But if she really wanted to do that, he knew she could do the same thing right now, with Officer Sparling.

"That's why I waited until she was in the shower to call you...after she told me all of that."

"Oh. OK. Did she say anything else?"

"No. Just that she wants me to tell you goodbye...and...and that she is sorry things didn't work out."

"Oh. Spenser?"

"Yes sir?"

"I want you to escort her out to her car when she leaves. You make sure she gets to her car safely, OK?"

"Yes, sir. I will."

"Spenser?"

"Yes chief?"

"Tell her for me, that I am very sorry...too."

"I will, sir."

"Are you sure she didn't say where in California she is going?"

"She didn't."

"OK. All the way out to her car though, Spenser."

"Yes sir. All the way out to her car."

CHAPTER 39

▼

Uriah Beek was slouched down in the front seat of his white Ford Econoline Van in the parking lot of The Sand Dollar, trying desperately to think of a way he could please God. He had been watching the whore's little blue car for hours now, parked just across from him in the next row of parking stalls, and his worsening vision was blurring it in and out of focus; and sometimes it split into two separate little blue cars.

His one remaining testicle had, in the last few hours, swollen to the size and hardness of a baseball as septicemia, the poisoning of his bloodstream by a virulent bacteria called streptococci, which had quickly formed after his botched surgery, rapidly began to spread to his lungs, and liver and brain.

He had a high fever, and chills; and periodically bolts of agonizing pain would sear through him so strongly from deep inside his groin, that he would have to bite down on the Van's steering wheel to keep himself from screaming out loud, and drawing attention to his vehicle in the early morning quiet of the packed to capacity motel parking lot. He knew that this, too, was punishment from God for his moment of abysmal personal weakness the night he had lusted for the flesh of the grown boy's whore.

He had the vague sense that his condition was serious and growing more so by the minute, and was quite possibly something he may have to, by faith, put in the healing hands of Yahweh entirely; if seeking medical treatment turned out to be scripturally prohibited. He would gladly cut his other testicle off too, if that's what was called for. He would worry about all of that later. Because first he was going to cut off both of Kevin Kearnes' testicles with his knife, while he made his Whore of Babylon watch. Then he would slaughter her with the same knife...in front of his rebellious former student, Kearnes. And *then* the lesson would be complete.

But first he needed to replace his box of missing Trellistrips. His box had fallen out of the back of his Van after the man in the red car—who he now knew to be a police officer—had tried to block his path as he was leaving the parking lot at Pearl Cove; just after he'd finished with the two crucifixions on the beach. There was a definite method to Beek's madness, and using only Trellistrips to tie his victims with instead of rope, or heavy tape, was now an integral part of that madness.

He believed it was the hand of God that had been guiding him, and had sent him forth on this glorious path toward true righteousness these past few days. Jehovah had not only shown him the way he should go, he had also shown him the way things should be done; and so far, it had all been working.

There was a farm and garden store only a little over a mile from here; near the big bridge up on Highway 101. It opened at nine a.m. Saturday mornings and it was eight forty five now, but he was going to wait until at least nine thirty before he went there to make his emergency purchase. He didn't want to be either the first or the only customer in the store when it opened. Besides, he knew that the young police officer with the black machine gun, which dangled from a sling around his neck, was still with her at the cabin. His black and white patrol car sat empty and idle, and illegally parked in front of The Sand Dollar's office.

He had hidden in the dunes the rest of the night since first making it safely back to The Sand Dollar from Pearl Cove; watching the blonde temptress through the windows of the cabin—still awake and scurrying around in there— waiting for her lights to go out, waiting for her to go to sleep before he crashed through her back door again and this time took her. But the young officer with his machine gun and his bright flashlight had suddenly come out of nowhere, knocking on her door, and after a brief time, she'd opened the door and let him in. A few minutes later the cabin's curtains had been hastily pulled shut, and the lights had gone out.

As the sun had started to come up at around five thirty, and began to steal the shadows away from Beek that he counted on for concealment, he had slunk away through the maze of trails and narrow hollows in the sand dunes that were choked with beach grass and stands of gnarled, wind bent little pines; until he had finally popped out on the far edge of The Sand Dollar's parking lot. In the pink hued, pre-dawn light, he had walked casually through the middle of the lot to his Van, unlocked its door, and climbed into the driver's seat…to wait.

The young policeman guarding the whore was not a concern to him. And neither was the short barreled, black machine gun that he carried. The only thing which really concerned Uriah Beek at the moment was how God felt about him now; and what he might be able to do to make things better between the two of them.

The active volcano he felt like he was sitting on suddenly erupted again, sending rivers of red hot molten pain radiating outward from the center of his groin. He grabbed the steering wheel of the Van with both hands as he bit down on it, hard...barely stifling a scream.

When the pain had burned itself out, and finally passed, he straightened back up, breathing heavily, and looked down at the scarred and mutilated steering wheel; shiny and slick with his saliva. The steering wheel was a light cream color, like that of bone, and the dyslexic patterns of the deep tearing, lacerated tooth marks in it made it look like a human femur that had been stripped of flesh by an attacking shark, and then bitten over an over again.

If he couldn't think of a way to please God, to regain his favor once again, and soon; Uriah Beek prayed that he would, at a bare minimum, at least not piss him off any more than he already apparently had.

At nine fifteen Kearnes and Thud were finally able to leave the crime scene. They drove to Kearnes' apartment first, so he could get a clean uniform, and then headed into the station, dropping Thud's rental car off downtown on the way. The Oregon State Police crime lab team had finished processing the scene, and had arranged for the bodies of both boys to be transported across the mountains to the Lab in Central Point by private hearses, where they would first be positively identified by their parents, and then autopsied.

A state police truck with two state troopers followed behind the hearses; carrying the wooden crosses, the bits and pieces of Trellistrips found at the scene, bagged cigarette butts—including the ones Thud had smoked—two dozen or so plaster impressions of foot prints and tire tracks, sand samples, soil samples, samples of the grass and other vegetation in the park, samples of the asphalt roadway, gravel from the gravel parking lot, and two small glass vials of some strange, acidic smelling, amber colored liquid that had pooled in a low spot in the middle of the road, not far from where the smashed box of Trellistrips had been found.

In the rear parking lot at the police station Kearnes gave Thud's detective car and his spare set of car keys back to him, and while Kearnes was checking out his own vehicle, making sure he had all the necessary equipment and forms he might need for what he knew was going to be a long and grueling weekend of investigation ahead, he saw one of the mini-blinds in Curt Lamar's office window just barely raise up a crack, then immediately drop back down. Thud had seen it, too.

"I swear to God," Thud said, disgustedly, "that guy has to be a total paranoid schizophrenic."

"I wonder what he's so afraid of," said Kearnes. "Druggies with Tec-9's lurking around every corner?"

"Naw," said Thud. "I think he's afraid C. Everett Coop will show up here one day, and ask him to donate a lung to The American Cancer Society for research."

Kearnes looked at Thud with a deadpan expression on his face; paused for a few seconds, and then said, "Only one?"

He watched as Thud's face slowly spread into a grin from ear to ear as wide and as brilliant as the rising morning sun sparkling on the surface of the blue Pacific. Then Thud broke into laughter...and so did Kearnes; and the accumulated days of pent up tension within both men, and between them, dissolved.

As Kevin Kearnes walked into the Cutter Point Police Department, shoulder to shoulder with Detective Sergeant Thud Compton, he looked at the sea of expectant and anxious faces of the men and women in uniform waiting for him there. He knew that they were all counting on him now, and knew that the entire community, in turn, was going to be counting on them to do their jobs, and to protect them and their families. He had never been more proud in his life than he was at that moment, to wear the badge of a police officer.

But even as valuable as his badge was to him, and all the years of hard work and sacrifice it represented, he still would have traded it in a heartbeat...for just one more day of being in love with Britt McGraw.

CHAPTER 40

▼

Shoshanna Perry had unplugged her hands free headset from her console position in the Dispatch Center when she'd heard Kearnes and Thud check out 10-19 in the back parking lot of the police department, and was waiting in the hallway outside the Center's door, knowing the chief and the sergeant would have to pass by her location on the way to their offices.

She had asked her best friend and partner, Candy Brewer, if she would be all right at the dispatch console alone for a couple of minutes while she waited to intercept the chief and sergeant in the hallway, to give them their messages, and Candy had told her to go ahead. That she was cool with it, and could handle the 911 console by herself for awhile. Especially after Russell Massey, their prick of a direct supervisor, and Edgar Polk, Massey's boss, had left the Center just ahead of Shoshanna. They had been standing around; nitpicking and harassing the two female dispatchers as usual, when they'd heard Kearnes and Compton on the radio, checking out at the station, and they had practically run from the room as if someone had just shouted it was on fire.

The narrow hallway in the old police building was crowded with jostling, heavily armed police officers, who seemed to be either running, or at least walking very quickly, in two different directions at once. Even though the *HIMA* notification had been made several hours previously; police personnel, including regulars, reserve officers, and officers from other responding agencies, were still streaming into the station to report for duty and receive their assignments, or returning to get additional equipment, or to be given new assignments as the dynamics of the investigation began to evolve.

Some of them were dressed in full, or nearly full uniform, and some of them still wore civilian clothes with only uniform baseball caps and their badges clipped to their belts next to their holstered weapons to identify them as police. Many of them had either assault rifles or short barreled pump shotguns slung over their shoulders which they had just been issued from the weapons lockers in the basement of the building, as they hastily made their way to and from the squad room just around the corner and down the hall from the Dispatch Center.

For Shoshanna and Candy the last two hours had been crazy. The ballooning volume of calls related to the double homicide which had been coming in over the department's regular business lines, and the emergency only 911 lines, were threatening a meltdown of the entire phone system…just as had happened on the night the whale was blown up, and the Tsunami Early Warning Alert System had been accidentally activated. But even though the vast majority of the calls they had been receiving were from panicked citizens, some of whom were in possession of exceptionally creative rumors and misinformation about what was actually going on in the city, and others who were seeing serial killers out their windows standing on every street corner, the two harried dispatchers had managed to screen, and take several important messages.

Shoshanna was now holding these messages tightly in her hand—seven of them for the chief, and three for the detective—while she squeezed herself as flat against the hallway wall as she possibly could; watching the chief and Thud Compton slowly making their way toward her through the throng of bobbing officer's heads and waving gun barrels.

"Chief Kearnes! Sergeant! I've got messages for both of you!" she said, waving the small white pieces of paper high in the air over her head to catch their attention.

Kearnes and Thud stopped in front of Shoshanna, letting the flow of officers in the hallway go around them like two large boulders in the middle of a fast running creek. "Thank you," said Kearnes, taking the messages she now handed him. "Anything really important?"

Shoshanna handed Thud his messages, too, then said to Kearnes: "Yes. There's one from a Special Agent Rutledge; of the F.B.I. in Portland? He wants you to call him ASAP. And both Newport and Seaside police departments have called. They want to coordinate with us on notification to the victim's parents…if these are their children. The rest of them are from Medford and Portland TV stations, wanting any information they can get."

"OK," said Kearnes. "I'll handle the F.B.I. and the media inquiries. Thud, can you call Seaside and Newport, and get that ball rolling?"

Thud had just finished reading his messages. "Yeah," he said, "no problem."

"One of mine is from Margie. The other two are both from Jerry Sparks. He wants to offer the "help" of The Patriots; if we need it," Thud said, crumpling up the message.

"We just might," Kearnes said.

"Are you serious? The guy doesn't even have any hands left," Thud said, as he tried to unwrinkle and smooth out the piece of paper he'd compacted in his fist to the size of a spitball.

"We don't have enough officers to close all of the beaches," said Kearnes, "but we could definitely use some more eyes and ears down there on them."

"OK," said Thud. "Ground rules?"

"Tell Jerry absolutely no firearms, or explosives, are to be carried by any of his people; or in their vehicles either. And they all need to be stone cold sober; and they patrol in pairs…with at least one cell phone for each pair."

"Got it," said Thud.

"Chief, is it true?…that both of them…were just little boys? And they were hung up like that? From crosses?" asked Shoshanna.

Kearnes could see the tears welling up in Shoshanna's eyes. He knew that she had two little boys of her own, and even though they were at the moment safe and sound at home, and being watched by their Grandma, this whole horrible event was obviously deeply hurting her heart.

"We're not sure of much right now, Shoshanna," Kearnes lied to her, mercifully. "The bodies do look younger than adult age; and they are both male. But both victims have been dead at least several days…and there is no way to tell how old they are or even who they are, until we make an attempt at identification, and complete the autopsies." He completely skipped over her question about the boys having been hung from wood crosses, hoping she wouldn't ask him that again.

"All right," she said, "I just hope and pray it's not those two missing boys."

"Me too," said Kearnes. He reached out and took both of Shoshanna's hands, and squeezed them between his own. "Thanks for getting these messages to us. Are you on duty alone in there?"

"No," she said. "Candy is with me."

"You'd probably better get back to her. I'll bet your phones are ringing off the hook."

"They are," said Shoshanna. "I will."

"Thud, I'll be in my office," said Kearnes. "I'd like to call a meeting of the Task Force; here at the P.D. at noon."

"I'll get right on it," said Thud.

Shoshanna had just started to go back into the Dispatch Center when she paused in the open doorway and turned back to Thud.

"Oh, Sergeant...I almost forgot. We got so busy, and I didn't have time to write this one down...but Howard from Cutter Farm Supply called, and said to tell either you, or Brad Dekker, the charges for the tarps and rope came to...oh dammit, I don't remember the exact amount. About seventy five or seventy nine dollars, I think he said. Something like that."

"OK," said Thud, "call him back when you get a chance, and tell him I'll be down in about half an hour to settle up with him. I need to make those calls first. Then I'm going to run up to my place real quick to check on Margie and the kids."

As they made their way past the Dispatch Center Thud ducked into the squad room when he saw Brad Dekker standing in the open doorway there, waving him in; but Kearnes kept on going. Despite several officers who saw him coming down the hallway and looked as if they were going to step out in front of him, to ask him something, he picked up his pace and the grave expression on his face had the desired effect; he reached his locked office door, key in hand, without being stopped.

He slid his key into the door's lock and instantly felt the lack of resistance as he turned it. He was sure he'd locked the door the last time he had left his office, on Tuesday afternoon...but it wasn't locked now. He clipped the office key— which was on a key ring with all the other keys he used at work—back onto the attachment on his gunbelt which was made to hold them. He placed the palm of his right hand flat against the cool surface of the door, and then pushed. The door swung open easily, and sitting behind his desk...was Lieutenant Edgar Polk.

"Come on in," said Polk. "Close the door behind you."

Kearnes did just that, but remained standing with his back against the closed door; training his eyes on Polk's hands, which were both on the top of the desk in front of him. He didn't know specifically what Polk's frame of mind was, but he knew it couldn't be good; and the second he saw either one of Polk's hands leave the desk's top, he understood he was going to have to interpret that movement a threat.

"I could have sworn this office was locked; the last time I left it," said Kearnes.

"It was," said Polk.

"Then I guess the question is," said Kearnes, "how did *you* get in here, Lieutenant?"

"My new boss...and I guess, now, your old one; he gave me the key," Polk said.

"Really," said Kearnes.

"Yeah...really," said Polk.

Kearnes let his eyes dart up and away from Polk's hands for just a split second; to steal a quick glance at his face. And what he saw was Edgar Polk, smiling at him, with an expression of such pure malevolence that he felt his body jerk as the adrenalin kicked into his system; like he'd been suddenly plunged, naked, into a bath of ice water.

"Polk," said Kearnes, "you must be as insane as your loony tunes little boss is. Get up from the desk. And keep your hands out in front of you."

"Not so fast there Sunny Jim!" crowed Polk. "Got something here for you! From the mayor." He pushed a sealed white envelope across the top of the desk toward Kearnes, until it was sitting at the edge.

"Why don't you open it, and read it to me?" asked Kearnes.

"Can't," said Polk. "Mayor says it wouldn't be legal. You go on ahead; open it and read it. The I'm gonna' need your badge...laid right down here on my desk."

"It almost sounds as if you think you're the new chief," said Kearnes."

"Oh...I know I am," said Polk. "Come on over here and get your walkin' papers. Then I'll need your badge."

"Why don't you try and take it from me?" asked Kearnes.

"Whoa there! Hold on just a minute, pardner!" Polk said, putting his hands in the air in a sign of mock surrender. His attempt at ridicule by his usage of what he thought was western slang, was not lost on Kearnes. "We all know how fast on the draw you are, chief. Do I look like I'd do something as stupid as that? Try to pull on *you*?"

"Yes," said Kearnes. "You do." He saw Polk's eyes narrow into thin slits, at his answer.

"Thing of it is, Kearnes," said Polk, "outside trash like you are a dime a dozen...and I know that for a fact. I've seen your type come and go through this department for years."

"Gee, I wonder why?" said Kearnes.

"Well, I'm not going to sit here and debate it with you. Read your letter. You're out...and I'm in."

"I've got a year to year contract with the city. By my count, I've still got ten months left on it."

"Like Vernon says; 'contracts are made to be broken.'

"Then I guess I'll just have to read the bad news for myself."

"OK. Please do."

Kearnes let his right hand drift over to his holster, and slowly undid the thumb break snap that was stretched tightly across the top of the rear surface of the Colt's slide. Polk saw him do it, and the slits of his eyes began to widen with concern. Or was it fear?

It was a perilous situation Kearnes suddenly found himself in, and he knew it. Edgar Polk had waited a lifetime for this moment and although he had not been appointed as chief of police on his own merit, and never would be, an appointment by default—by expediency or through necessity—was still good enough for him. He had transcended his usual mode of pugnaciousness and now, to Kearnes, actually looked like he might be dangerous. He could easily pull his Glock in defense of what he felt in his life had always been wrongfully denied him; but had now been won.

Kearnes remembered a story Ben had once told him when he was a boy about one of Dodge City's most legendary lawmen, Bill Tilghman, who one night had been summoned to Ham Bell's Variety Saloon on Front Street, south of the "Dead Line", where one cowboy had shot and killed another over suspected cheating during a nickel a bet card game called "Chuk-aluk."

As the quiet and soft spoken Tilghman had entered the poorly lit premises and walked toward the ruckus where the surviving cowboy sat stock still in his chair, staring at his friend slumped over onto the card table he had just shot and killed, the cowboy had suddenly looked up at Tilghman, startled, and began to reach for his holstered gun. Tilghman, without breaking stride or pulling his own Colt, according to witnesses had said, "Son, if you reach for that gun, I will burn you down. Right where you sit." The cowboy had taken Tilghman's sage advice, and lived to be both tried, and then acquitted on a charge of murder.

"Lieutenant Polk," Kearnes said, "you and I haven't gotten along from day one. And I know you don't know me very well...you only think you do. But I'm going to walk over to my desk now, and pick up that envelope, and I need you to believe me when I say that if you so much as even make me think you are putting your hand near your weapon...I will burn you down. Right where you sit."

Polk didn't say anything; but slowly he put his hands back down on the desk, flat, and out in front of him; and tried to look calm again as Kearnes crossed the room and snatched the envelope off the desk. Kearnes hooked a finger underneath one raised edge of the envelope's seal, and ripped it open. There were two letters inside and he scanned both of them quickly, keeping Edgar Polk's shaking hands on the desk within his peripheral vision.

The first one notified him he was terminated from employment, effective on the date and time indicated on the letter, which was today's date, at 0800 hours;

and the second letter announced Polk's appointment as chief of police, also on today's date, but at 0801 hours. Both letters had been signed by Mayor Vernon Bouchet', and countersigned by Roy Roddameyer. Kearnes folded them both back up, stuck them inside the envelope, and put the envelope in the back pocket of his jeans.

"Believe me now?" asked Polk.

"I don't believe anything about you," Kearnes answered him. "I guess the only answer to my question about how anyone like you could ever be allowed into this profession, let alone stay in it for over twenty years…would be this place itself. It's not normal."

"What? You don't like our little town?" Polk asked him.

"This isn't a town. Not with people like you, and Bouchet', and Roddameyer running it," said Kearnes. "It's an aberration."

Now that Polk could see that Kearnes was not going to shoot him, and probably wasn't even going to try and hit him; his temper, bolstered by the new found sense of confidence and security his instant promotion this morning to chief had given him, flared.

"Dammit, Kearnes. You hand over that badge. Right now! And before you leave, you to get on the phone to the Dispatch room and tell those bitches in there that you are recalling the alert. You got that? Everyone who has been called out is to go on back home!"

"Sorry," said Kearnes, "but I'm on my way to the mayor's office right now. Stay as long as you like, Lieutenant, but please keep your feet off my desk. It's brand new."

Polk pushed away from the desk in Kearnes' chair, and struggled to his feet; prudently keeping his hands out and away from his sides.

"The mayor isn't in his fucking office!" he screamed.

"You think he gives a shit about you? He's out at his new private golf course! Whacking little white balls around with metal sticks! That's how fucking worried he is about you, you stupid college boy. I'm the one who's in charge now, Kearnes. Now you hand over that badge!"

Edgar Polk's face was pumped up and purple with rage now, and he seemed to be swaying back and forth; like an ancient tree in the forest cut into deeply at its base, starting to topple. He grabbed for the front edge of the desk to break his fall, as he began to pitch forward. His head jerked up and down convulsively, like a fish out of water, and he started to gasp loudly as he tried desperately to gulp in great quantities of air.

Kearnes thought at first that he was having a coronary but after half a minute had passed Polk seemed to be recovering and his breathing began to straighten out; but was still shallow, and somewhat labored. Edgar Polk had been like a fish out of water...for his entire career. And he had gotten away with what he had for a very long time. But it had taken someone like Kevin Kearnes to finally hook him, and haul him up on dry land, so that everyone, including Polk himself, could take a good long look at the kind of man he really was.

"You just keep telling yourself that, Edgar...and maybe some day it will come true," Kearnes said.

"But not today."

Swiftly, he walked out of his office, closing the door shut behind him, and hurried down the hallway to the rear entrance of the building and the parking lot He wasn't quite sure how to get to the Trident Greens construction site; he'd never been there before, but he would manage to find it...and he needed to do so without telling anyone exactly where he was going.

What had just happened in his office, between him and Polk, and what was about to happen at Trident Greens...for the sake of the investigation, the officers involved, and the safety of the people in the community...no one could know anything about. Because he knew if they did, the tightrope they were all balancing on at the moment would snap, everything would come crashing down, and a killer might slip through their fingers. And then soon, he would kill again.

No, he wasn't exactly sure of how to get to where he needed to go; or what might happen after he got there. But he did know one thing: He had to put a stop Mayor Vernon Bouchet', once and for all, and if that included having to make Bouchet' eat his own words—the ones he'd written in the two letters that he now carried in his back pocket—then that's what he would have to do.

Even if that meant cramming the letters into the vile little old man's sewer of a mouth and making him chew, and swallow, until every last trace of them...and all of his raving, deranged, and preposterously pathological abilities to interfere with the law any further...had vanished for good.

CHAPTER 41

▼

As he pulled out of the police parking lot, heading north on Cutter Avenue toward the city limits, he was forced to wait for a break in the constant traffic on his car radio before he could interject to Dispatch that he was "clear"; and after Shoshanna came back over the air, acknowledging that he was in his car and mobile, he gave her no further details.

He remembered the morning he and Thud had left for Florence, Thud had pointed out the access road into the Trident Greens project as they drove by it, which was about three miles past the northern city limits. Even at that very early hour, while it had still been mostly dark out, they had seen an army of construction trucks and cement mixers crossing the highway in front of them and turning off onto the private road.

The way Thud described it, the newly constructed and freshly paved access road jogged back in a southerly direction, toward the city, for almost two miles before reaching the entrance to the resort. The actual two hundred and fifty acre Trident Greens site was situated on a long rectangular strip of land there, which consisted of two diverse halves; high, rolling sand dunes which hugged the ocean beaches on the outside, and on the inside portion, green, grassy meadows which had once been a turn of the century dairy cow farm.

He slowed down a little as he saw a huge white truck approaching him in the oncoming lane. It had a massive white superstructure of some sort built onto its bed, behind the high cab, and at first he thought it might be a construction crane of some type. But as the truck got closer he saw that the "superstructure" was actually a large white dish shaped object…a TV satellite dish…and as it sped past he saw the logo on its door, "KOIN NEWS 6", a Portland television station.

Less than a mile later another satellite TV truck passed him at a high rate of speed, also heading in the direction of Cutter Point. He wasn't able to see which TV station it was from but it appeared to be an obvious competitor of the first one, and was trying hard to catch up. The trucks had distracted him and had blocked some of his view along the left side of the highway as he searched for the access road that was not signed. Thud had told him that Vernon Bouchet' had intentionally left any indication of the roadway which led into his twenty five million dollar, dream of a lifetime project, a secret; in order to keep it virtually unidentifiable to the public. There was also rumored to be private security at different locations along the route in, on construction days, to turn back "unauthorized" people.

He went a little further down the highway after the last TV truck had passed by but soon realized he had gone too far now; four point two miles by his vehicle's trip meter which he had reset to zero as soon as he'd traveled past the city limits sign back in town. He eased the black Ford over onto the shoulder of the roadway and when traffic was clear, executed a tight U-turn and headed back in the opposite direction, only much slower now.

At about the same spot where the first satellite truck had grabbed his attention, he saw the access road—now on his right—which would have been easy to see the first time if he'd only been paying a little closer attention. Sand from the construction site had been carried out to the highway on the undercarriages of hundreds of trucks and deposited on the asphalt of the highway, like a dog shaking droplets of water from its coat, as the trucks vibrated over the top of an old steel cattle guard that was embedded into the ground right where the access road began.

It looked as if someone was building a giant kid's sandbox here, and there were bits and pieces of construction junk littering the ground all around the sand. Plastic wrappers from wall insulation, empty tubes of caulking, small, oddly cut sections boards, crushed beer and soda cans and flattened cigarette butts and empty Skoal cans from the workers themselves…and, obviously…probably a few loosely scattered nails, too. He worried about picking up a nail because getting a flat tire would be disastrous now, but he put the thought of that happening out of his mind as he gunned the Ford across the cattle guard and felt his tires grab onto the surface of the new blacktop like magnets locking onto a sheet of steel plate.

In the distance, back in the direction of where the city was, he could see a dramatically high and thickly forested green hill with something small and white perched atop it. The western edge of the hill jutted out toward the ocean and terminated in a steeply sloping, rocky headland, that cut the beach in two at that location. As he got closer to the hill and began to get his bearings he realized that what he was looking at was the back side of the hill that Sea Horse Drive was located on—where Thud and Margie lived—and the white object on the very top of the hill, which was growing larger and larger by the minute, was Vernon Bouchet's house. He had purchased the highest point of land in the city to build his house on—so he could look down on all that he owned—and now he could do the same with his twenty five million dollar golf course, Trident Greens, by just walking out and standing on his back deck.

As he came out of a sharp turn on a twisting stretch of the road that had gradually submerged the car below the tops of the meadowlands, and the blacktop shot out ruler straight now ahead of him, he caught his first glimpse of the Resort's hotel rising from the middle of a circle of grass that was three football fields long in diameter.

The colossal and extravagant building, which wasn't quite finished yet, looked like a cross between the Hearst Castle and a Holiday Inn Express. Red tile roofed towers and cupolas grew up from its top in places like wild mushrooms on a loamy forest floor, reaching for sunlight. Its angles and curves seemed to be in direct opposition to one another at its most critical junctures, making the flow and fit of its architecture hard to follow, and at the very back of the structure a glass and steel wing of the building—shaped like a mattress that had been stood up on its end—towered high above everything else. It looked exactly like a miniature version of the United Nations building; or a large piece of chrome toast that had just popped out of a toaster.

He was looking too long and too hard at the looming hotel as he drove, and not paying enough attention to what was ahead, and nearly ran into a wooden "ROAD CLOSED" barricade sign that had been drug across the roadway just in front of the entrance to Trident Greens.

He stopped the car and got out and pushed the long saw horse looking sign over into the opposite lane just enough so he could drive past it. Beyond the sign, only twenty yards away, was the high, ornate, black wrought iron gate and fence of the Resort. It was a two section gate, electrically operated, and it swung either in or out, with each individual section supported by the shaft of a giant pitchfork shaped trident spear, pointed upward; the spear of the mythical sea god Neptune. The steel "shafts" of the trident spears were as big around as telephone poles, and their huge, three pronged spearheads were finished in real gleaming, hammered gold leaf.

Both sections of the gate were standing open, inward, and he could see Bouchet's white Escalade, with a golf cart trailer hitched to the back of it, parked in front of the Pro Shop. He got back into the Ford and drove through the open gates and parked next to the Escalade.

There was a barrage of traffic over his police radio; officer's were making car stops on white vehicle's and impatiently wanting the registration read backs as quickly as they could get them from Dispatch; so they could hurry and make another one. And other officers were giving their location changes as they worked in teams, scouring various parts of the city in a high profile effort to either panic and flush out the killer, or suppress him with a blatant show of force and hope he was intimidated enough not to act again; at least not while they were present.

He knew he should check out on the radio with Dispatch, and his every instinct told him to do so, but as he reached for the radio's mike he heard Thud come on the air, notifying Dispatch that he was leaving the station and would en route to Cutter Farm Supply in the Harbor District, and the second Dispatch acknowledged him the transmissions instantaneously started up again. So he left the car radio untouched, but took his portable from his equipment bag with him before he got out of the car and locked it up.

The gargantuan grounds of Trident Greens were deserted—except for the mayor's white Cadillac Escalade—and to Kearnes the place felt emptily eerie. With a grand opening date only two months away, and the Hotel still unfinished and all the parking lots still pure, unpaved dirt, the place should have been a beehive of bustling construction activity; even on a Saturday morning. But there had been rumors recently that since late spring, when the first of the Resort's total of three different eighteen hole courses was finally ready for use, Bouchet' and Roddameyer had shut down construction at times and shooed everyone out just so they could play golf, alone and undisturbed.

Kearnes knew hardly anything about golf. He had only played the game a couple of times when he was in college before deciding that if he was going to be involved in a sport that required a lot of walking, and sometimes trying to shoot "birdies", he would much rather spend his days tromping across harvested fall Kansas wheat fields with a shotgun in his hands, scaring up fat Chinese pheasants. But like almost every boy growing up in the West he'd learned how to track as a rite of passage, and so now he ventured out onto the first fairway, searching for the tracks of an electric golf cart in the shadowed areas of grass that still held the morning dew. He found a set of tracks almost right away, and began to follow them.

When he reached the start of the third hole there was a sign that said "543 yards—par 5", and he wasn't really sure exactly what that meant. The only thing he was sure of was that the golf cart, which he could now see parked off in the distance near the hole's putting green, was a very long way from where he still was. And although he could plainly see the cart sitting there, out in the open, Bouchet' and Roddameyer were nowhere in sight.

It took him a couple of minutes of half jogging and briskly walking in a straight line toward the abandoned golf cart before he reached it, and when he did he saw the two sets of very expensive bagged golf clubs there; one lying lengthwise across the back seat, and the other one propped up and leaning against the small, fat rear tire of the cart. There were no other signs of the two men except for a white cotton gym towel draped over the back of the driver's seat, and a bottle of Crown Royal whiskey, half gone, that was standing up on the front floorboard of the cart beneath the steering wheel, with a red plastic party cup next to it which was empty, but still wet inside.

He surveyed everything around him in a three hundred and sixty degree, slowly turning arc; and besides the sand dunes, and the green, wind scrubbed fairways, and the demonstrable, churning boil of the ocean, which he was not very far away from now—its overripe smell starting to make him feel lightheaded, and hollow inside—nothing seemed out of the ordinary or unusual…except for a very strange sound that he could hear, but could not tell where it was coming from.

Just beyond the edge of the putting green of hole number three, which sat on an elevated plateau of land to begin with, a waist high wall of beach grass and low bush cranberries growing there had created a kind of hedge, from which the earth seemed to drop away on the other side; as if there was a small valley or basin there. And coming from the other side of that natural hedge like growth, he could hear the plaintiff cries and desperate, yowling moans, of what sounded like some small wild animal that had maybe been caught in a trap, or somehow otherwise injured.

He saw what looked like a natural cut through the thick vegetation; the start of a narrow, steeply twisting trail, and he followed it in and then down, the sounds growing louder and more throaty now…starting to sound almost human. The steep ground underfoot soon leveled out and up ahead through the bulky, squat cranberry bushes he could see what appeared to be an open area of lush grass; almost as if a small section of the golf course had broken off and toppled down this sharp embankment.

He turned off his portable radio, silencing it, and as he drew closer to the opening his eyes picked up movement…and a prickling, tingling sensation erupted like small cold flames along the back of his neck and all over his scalp. He put his right hand on the butt of the Colt, firmly, and left it there, as he began to inch his way forward toward whatever it was just ten feet ahead of him that was moaning, and moving, and crying out in the tall grass. He unsnapped his holster, leaned forward in a slight crouch, then rushed out of the bushes and into the clearing.

On the ground in front of him Vernon Bouchet´ and Roy Roddameyer were both down on their knees. Bouchet´ was directly facing Kearnes—his magnified little owl eyes behind the huge lenses of his glasses clamped tightly shut in ecstasy—as Roddameyer, who had his hands on the ground, and out in front of him for support, bobbed his glistening, oily black head up and down at the opening of Bouchet's trouser zipper like a blackbird on a lawn, tugging at earthworms.

Bouchet´ was whimpering with pleasure as Roddameyer worked harder and harder at his task, and he was patting the top of Roy's head, urging him on further; but from what Kearnes could see—and he could see *everything* from where he stood—it appeared to be both a fruitless, and a futile effort.

Bouchet´ must have sensed Kearnes' presence as he stood there, watching them, because his eyes suddenly flew open and his cries of pleasure turned into a shriek of alarm. He pushed Roddameyer's head away, trying to get him to stop, and when he didn't he began to pummel the top of Roy's head with his bony little fists.

"Stop! Stop! Stop it now!" shouted Bouchet´, pounding and pushing on Roddameyer; but Roy only quickened the pace. Bouchet´ reached down to Roddameyer's face and with his fingers, clawed frantically at his eyes. He dug his long, yellow fingernails into Roddameyer's eye sockets, and then raked them down the sides of his cheeks.

Roddameyer howled in pain and slapped his elderly lover's hands away from him. Then he brutally shoved Bouchet´; who lost his balance and fell over onto his side in the beaten down grass.

"Bitch!" he screamed at Bouchet´. He touched his hand to one side of his face and then brought it away, staring in disbelief at the blood he found on it.

"That's way too rough, Vernon. You *hurt* me!"

"Shut up Roy!" bellowed Bouchet´, whose gaze was locked on Kearnes, and who Roddameyer was still unaware was standing right behind him. "*You* are in a lot of trouble right now!"

Roddameyer saw that Bouchet´ was looking past him at something other than himself, and as he shifted around on all fours his watering eyes caught sight of Kearnes at waist level, standing practically on top of him, with his hand on his gun.

"What the fuck?" slurred Roddameyer. Kearnes saw him trying to focus on him, and could tell that he was having a hard time comprehending all that was happening at the moment, and as he attempted to get to his feet he could see that Roy Roddameyer was extremely drunk.

Vernon Bouchet' got to his feet and brushed off his clothes. He zipped his zipper back up and then rubbed the palms of his hands up and down the pant legs of his golfing trousers, as if he was trying to get something dirty off them.

"Chief Kearnes," he said. "Thank God you came along when you did."

"I came to talk to you about these," said Kearnes. He pulled the two white envelopes from his back pocket, and held them up.

"That man attacked me," said Bouchet', pointing a finger at Roddameyer. "I was down here alone, urinating, when he came down after me and made an indecent proposal! Which I rejected!"

"What?" cried Roddameyer, as he staggered to his feet, swaying. "What? That's a lie!"

As Kearnes had left the police department and driven out of the city to find Bouchet' and Roddameyer, his mind had been set ablaze with a hundred different scenarios he might choose to, or be forced to present to them; once they were face to face. Everything from arresting them for obstruction, to threatening to sue them, to begging them to give him just one more chance.

But of all the things he had considered, nothing came even remotely close to the bizarre real life scenario which was now playing out right in front of him; and suddenly he realized that *he* didn't have to say another word. He walked over to Bouchet', dropped the two envelopes on the ground in front of him, and then turned and quickly left the clearing and started back up the trail.

When he reached the top and had crossed the green, he paused near the front of the golf cart and turned his portable radio back on. He needed to call the incident in, and to get a back up officer started his way both for assistance, and as a witness. But the radio traffic was still heavy over the main police frequency and he knew he had have to wait for a lull in the transmission before he could break in. He could hear Bouchet' and Roddameyer, thrashing their way back up through the brush to the putting green, shouting at each other and arguing; but he couldn't really make out what they were saying.

He took the radio from his gunbelt and was holding it up close to his mouth, waiting for his turn to transmit, when he saw Bouchet' hurrying toward him and waving his arms as if he was signaling Kearnes—or ordering him—to put the radio down, with Roy Roddameyer hot on his heels.

"Chief Kearnes! Hold on a minute there now! I need to speak with you," wheezed Bouchet´

"You fucking, lying old queen!" shrilled Roddameyer.

But it didn't seem to faze the little old man. He was determined to get to Kearnes and as he hobbled forward on ancient, bird like legs, he yelled back over his shoulder at Roddameyer, "You stay away from me, Roy! My business is with the chief now!"

"You little cocksucker!" Roddameyer screamed at him. "I am not going to let you do this to me Vernon!"

"Seems to me you're the only one here who knows anything about *that*," said Bouchet´ "Chief! I need a word with you."

Kearnes lowered the radio, which was still blaring away with a frenzy of unbroken communications, and stared at Bouchet´. "I don't think we have anything to talk about," said Kearnes. He turned his back on Bouchet´ but he only scurried around the side of him, until he stood facing Kearnes.

"Relative to what you may have thought you saw down there," said Bouchet´, "it was not what it seemed. This man attacked me...and I wish to prefer charges against him."

"I *know* what I saw," said Kearnes, unable to disguise the disgust in his voice. "And you are finished, Mayor Bouchet´. Both of you are."

"Chief Kearnes...Kevin. May I call you Kevin?" Before Kearnes could answer him and tell him that he could not, Bouchet´ forged ahead.

"You seem like a bright young man, Kevin. You show great enthusiasm and initiative in your work; and I like that. I may just be able to find a place for you on my staff...now that we are about to have an opening. Something more suited to your talents and abilities; and with a commensurate raise in salary to go along with it."

"Vernon...may I call you Vernon? said Kearnes. "I wouldn't work for an asshole like you, if you were the last employer on earth."

What little color Vernon Bouchet´ had left in his face drained away, leaving his brown splotched skin sagging, and transparent. Kearnes could see the cold fury that burned brightly in his eyes now; but he could also see the panic and the fear in them, too.

"Let me remind you," shouted Bouchet´, "that you still work for *me*, sir!"

"Really?" said Kearnes. "I thought I was fired."

"Well...no, of course you aren't," said Bouchet´. "That was simply some very bad advice...which I mistakenly took from our former city manager here. We'll get together first thing Monday morning, Kevin...to talk about your future with the city. About your new position."

Kearnes said, "I won't be able to make your meeting Monday morning...and neither will you. You'll be having your arraignment in court then. You and Mr. Roddameyer are both going to jail...for Public Indecency."

Later, as he searched his memory, living and reliving the incident over and over again in his mind, he would remember hearing the rattling sound in the background; just as he had said the word "jail" to Bouchet'. But at the exact instant everything had begun to happen, he hadn't heard it...had not heard the metallic clanging sound of the golf putter as its metal shaft banged against the metal shafts of the other clubs as Roy Roddameyer had jerked it from the golf bag that was leaning against the rear of the cart...had not heard the ominous, warning rattling noise the club had made as it was drawn out...like the sound a prairie rattlesnake makes just as you step on its tail.

Kearnes saw Bouchet' suddenly raise his hands up in front of his face in a defensive move as he screamed, "NO ROY NO!", and instantly Kearnes felt a tremendous blow to the back of his right arm, just below the shoulder and both heard, and felt, the bone encased inside the flesh and muscle, snap in two. And then he was face down on the ground in the grass, staring at the spiked sole of one of Vernon Bouchet's golf shoes just inches from his nose.

"Roy Goddamit NO!" he heard Bouchet' scream again, and he saw Bouchet's shoe bounce into the air and not come back down again as he hopped over Kearnes' head, trying to push Roddameyer away.

"I'LL FUCKING KILL HIM I'LL FUCKING KILL HIM!" Roddameyer screamed. Kearnes could hear the sounds of the two men as they struggled right behind him, and he felt someone step on his ankle.

"MOVE! GET OUT OF MY WAY I'LL FUCKING KILL HIM...I'LL FUCKING KILL YOU!...GET THE FUCK...OUT OF MY WAY!

Kearnes tried to roll to his right but the entire right side of his body felt frozen, completely numb, and as he threw his weight in that direction, trying to generate the momentum to move that his muscles could no longer provide, he felt the two jagged edges of his shattered humerus grating together.

He saw Vernon Bouchet' fly backward through the air and land on the ground in a sitting position as Roddameyer hurled him away, and his mind finally grasped the fact that Roddameyer was trying to kill him. He had made the mistake—and possibly a fatal one—of taking his eyes off one of his suspects and now that suspect, Roy Roddameyer, had hit him with something, and seriously injured him, and he needed to draw his weapon RIGHT NOW.

Instinctively, Kearnes heaved his body to the left and this time he rolled, stopping flat on his back, just as the ground next to him where his head had been exploded in a giant divot of flying grass and dirt as Roddameyer smashed the head of the golf putter straight down at him. Without thinking he reached, right handed, for the Colt, but his hand—his entire arm—would not move, and Roddameyer, standing directly over him, raised the putter high above his head and let it waver there for a second while he drunkenly tried to line it up with Kearnes' head again.

Kearnes reached across his body, desperately clawing at the Colt in his holster while he looked into Roddameyer's wildly dilated, vacuous eyes, and felt the loosely flapping thumb snap of the holster. He had mercifully neglected to refasten it and now he slid the fingers of his left hand underneath it; felt the smooth, cold steel of the Colt's receiver and began to pull the weapon out—backwards and upside down—but it was too late.

He heard the whistle of the golf club splitting through the air as he saw Roddameyer slam it down toward him, and he twisted his head away as far as he could to the right. The bulbous wooden head of the putter impacted, blowing out a crater of grass in the earth next to him, but the very tip of it clipped the back of Kearnes' neck, sending radiating black shockwaves of pain down his spine to his feet.

"YOU MOTHERFUCKER! YOU MOTHERFUCKER!" screamed Roddameyer, as he brought the club up high over his head for the third, and final blow. Kearnes had the Colt out of the holster now, laying on his stomach. He flopped it over and then scooped his hand beneath it, feeling the weapon's configuration, strange and foreign to him in his unfamiliar left hand...and methodically, he began to push at the hammer lock safety.

"Why us...HUH? Why Fucking US!" Roddameyer raged above him.

He felt the solid, metal "thunk" as the safety disengaged...but the Colt Government Model had another safety, a grip safety, and unless you were holding the weapon firmly in hand, with a tight grip, it would never fire. In some strange part of the back of his mind now he could hear Ben telling him that story when he was a kid; about the gun hands in the old West, and how it was never the fastest man who survived in a gunfight, but the man who was the most deliberate in his actions.

Roddameyer was sobbing now; blubbering, and alternately ferociously seething with anger as he chopped at the air overhead with the golf club, warming up. He was "fit to be tied" as Ben and some of the others of his generation would have described Roddameyer's current mental state...someone who had gone so far off the deep end that they had to be tied up for their own safety, and the protection of others. It was clear to him that Roddameyer was going to kill him; and probably Vernon Bouchet' next.

"YOU ARE DEAD MOTHERFUCKER! DO YOU HEAR ME! DEAD DEAD DEAD!"

Roddameyer raised the club up even higher, telegraphing the beginning of his move, and as he did—and apparently for the first time—he saw the chasmal black muzzle of the Colt rising up from Kearnes' body at the same time in an unsteady, weaving, serpentine motion…like a Cobra being charmed from out of its basket. As his alcohol saturated brain was finally able to process this information…that he was about to be shot…Roy Roddameyer started to turn, to run.

And with cool and calm deliberation…Kevin Kearnes fired.

CHAPTER 42

▼

The sound waves from the blast of the shot pealed across the open terrain of the golf course and slammed into the faraway hill behind the hotel, then bounced back around inside the windowless structure, reverberating like the sound of a hollow iron pipe being struck with a hammer.

Then, there was utter, absolute quiet. Even his portable radio, which lay a few feet away from him on the ground, had fallen silent.

He couldn't see Roddameyer anymore. He tried to sit up but was forced back down by fireballs of pain that were now exploding inside his right arm every time his heart beat, as it pumped the blood through his constricted artery that was being pinched by the fractured bone. He rolled onto to his good side, got his knees underneath him, and struggled to his feet, still tightly gripping the Colt.

Roy Roddameyer had managed to run about twenty feet before collapsing and he lay on the ground now on his stomach, with Vernon Bouchet′ kneeling beside him, cradling his head. The seat of Roddameyer's golf pants was soaked with blood, the bullet having entered the outer edge of his left buttock, traversed completely through it diagonally, and then exited in roughly the middle of his right buttock; where it had blown out a golf ball sized chunk of flesh, and kept right on going.

Kearnes, hunched over in pain, listed toward the fallen radio, with each step forward a multiplying agony. He needed to call it in…shots fired, shots fired and officer down 10-99, 10-99…there is a subject down, no, there are two men down, send medical send medical send medical…this location, is that right?

He saw the radio lying in the grass at his feet now. He saw the jagged white tip of bone poking through the flesh of his arm; *his arm, his bone*, and it was *so* white.

So goddamned, amazingly white. Kevin Kearnes had never been seriously hurt before as a police officer; but he was seriously hurt now. Behind him he heard moaning, someone moaning now, and he thought that it must be Roddameyer, because he could hear Bouchet' saying over and over and over oh honey oh honey oh honey you are going to be all right...you are going to be all right!

There was a unique emergency tone utilized by the Dispatch Center which was broadcast by them if they had any sort of forewarning, and the time to initiate it, that was used to alert units in the field of a serious event in progress...an armed robbery, for instance...or an officer involved shooting, or any shots being fired at a scene. It was comprised of three long, blaring, and equally spaced harmonic tones, and as Kearnes dropped his gun on the grass and picked the radio up to transmit his 10-99, those very same three long tones began to pour from the radio's small speaker.

He was dumbfounded that somehow back at the station they already knew of the trouble he was in, and the immediate help that he needed...and they were broadcasting the emergency tones now, for him, and help would soon be on the way. Or had he already told them that? Did he just call them...on his radio? He was mixing things up in his shocky, clouded brain; sequences, and snippets of time were now being scattered in and out of order, like a quickly shuffled deck of cards.

The last tone died away; then there was a pause, and then he heard Shoshanna's voice come over the air.

"Code 10-99, Code 10-99...officer down, we have an officer down...eleven hundred eighty two highway 101...in the parking lot...at Cutter Farm Supply. We have an officer down, that location...medical is en route."

"He's bleeding! Badly!" Bouchet' shouted at him.

Kearnes put the radio back down, lifted the Colt up and got it back in his holster, then picked the radio up again—which had now come alive with officers "walking" over each other—all of them trying to talk on their radios at the same time and canceling each other out.

"Help him!" cried Bouchet'. "Please!"

The emergency tones came over the radio again, but this time as soon as they had ended Shoshanna's firm, and in command voice broke in: "Central is 10-33, repeat, Central is now 10-33...all units, emergency traffic ONLY! One Charles Twenty One, what is your location?"

"I'm on Harbor Hill! Eastbound!" He heard Spenser instantly, and frantically respond. "I am en route...I'm just a few blocks away!"

"Copy One Charles Twenty One…you are the closest unit…Central copies One Charles Twenty One responding to a citizen report of an officer down…the parking lot of Cutter Farm Supply…eleven hundred eighty two highway 101."

When Spenser heard *that* for the second time, he completely lost both his cool, and his radio protocols all at the same time.

"Is it the Sergeant?" he yelled over the radio. "He was just on his way there!"

"One Charles Twenty One…unknown at this time…have received several reports…of an officer reportedly down at that location…now receiving additional that shots have been fired…suspect left in a white Van…unknown make or model…less than two ago now…last seen westbound…your direction on Harbor Way."

"Please, God help us!" begged Bouchet'. "I can't stop it!"

Kearnes went to the golf cart and grabbed the white towel off the back of the driver's side seat, then limped over to where Bouchet' was and threw down on the ground next to the moaning Roddameyer.

"Pressure," said Kearnes.

"What?"

"Fold that up, and apply direct pressure on the wound!"

A hissing, crackling sound began to spew from Kearnes' radio as Spenser came on the air again. Kearnes immediately recognized it as the sound of a rechargeable, seven and a half volt a nickel metal hydride battery that was about to go dead. He hadn't remembered to put his radio in its charger since the night before they had all gone to the range to qualify, and now he was about to pay a heavy price for that little oversight.

"One Ch—rles Twen—One t—Ce—tral!" he heard Spenser shouting. "Wh—is th—ficer tha—s down?

"Call for an ambulance! Use your radio!" screamed Bouchet'.

Kearnes wouldn't be calling anyone on his radio now; it was completely dead. It had begun to chop Spenser's words to pieces just as the battery gave out, and had died before Kearnes had been able to hear the dispatcher respond back to him…to answer his question about the officer who was reportedly down at Cutter Farm Supply…and who he or she was.

But he knew he wouldn't be needing his radio in order to answer the question that he—and every other officer out there who was listening—already knew the answer to.

The officer, who was down, was Thud Compton.

If Uriah Beek had known that Cutter Farm Supply was much more than just a feed and grain store, an Ace Hardware, and a Dutch Boy Paint Center…if he had known it was the local yokel cracker barrel meeting place, and was considered to be "gossip central" for the entire town…he may have thought twice about making the quick trip there that morning to replace his box of Trellistrips.

Even though the town had grown by leaps and bounds over the years, and most weekend carpenters, backyard gardeners, and amateur landscapers could be well supplied after one quick visit to either the Lowe's or the Big R store, which were located at Bouchet' Plaza, some things in small towns never seemed to change, no matter how big they got. And dishing the dirt down at Cutter Farm Supply on a Saturday morning while standing in the checkout line with your box of hummingbird food or your container of slug and snail killer, drinking their free coffee and chatting with either the person in line in front of you, or behind you; was a time honored Cutter Point cultural tradition.

And that was where Uriah Beek was; when he saw, through the large front glass doors of the store, the sleek, black, unmarked Ford police car glide silently into the parking lot. He immediately recognized this car. It belonged to the police chief and he knew that if Kearnes had come here, intentionally looking for him, then he would be forced to take him right here and right now, and his calamitous whore may have to be an afterthought. He did so very much want Kearnes to see her die, before the lesson had begun, but it would all have to be put in God's hands now.

Beek was the fourth customer in the line of five people. Now, he melted away from the line, keeping his eyes trained on the entrance doors, as he walked casually toward the back of the store. There was a large display of dry dog food there in fifty pound bags which were stacked from the floor halfway to the ceiling in a small semi-circle, like a military sandbag emplacement, and he walked into the open space behind them which concealed most but not all of him…as long as he hunched over.

Resting the box of Trellistrips against his knee, he rapped the perforated top of the box with his knuckles, opening it; and pulled out a handful of the green vinyl strips and stuffed them in his jacket pocket. He still hadn't see Kearnes come through the front doors. He set the box of Trellistrips on the floor, pulled one of the bags of dog food from the top of the stack down to cover it with, and then walked back toward the front of the store.

He took his new place at the end of the line, glancing out the doors at the black Ford; Kearnes was nowhere to be seen. But there was a man in a suit across the parking lot, standing and looking at his white Van parked there. The man;

who was big, and had short, crew cut hair, stood staring at the Van as if he were making mental notes of it. Then he abruptly turned away from it, heading straight for the entrance of the store.

Beek faded away again, suddenly becoming interested in a display of pocket knives at the far end of the long customer counter. They were housed in a large, glass faced locking case that stood upright on top of the counter, and reflected back toward the cash register as perfectly as any living room mirror. As the big man in the suit entered through the front doors, Beek turned his back to him…and watched.

"Hey, Howard," he heard the man say to the clerk, as he walked up to the cash register. "Thanks for opening up so early for us this morning. How much do we owe you?"

"Howard" asked the woman he was helping, to excuse him for a minute. Then he said, "Morning, Thud. Hey, no problem. Glad I could help out. Geez…you look like heck. You been up all night or something?"

"Several nights; as a matter of fact. But thanks for bringing it to my attention, anyhow."

"Uh, hold on just a minute, Thud. I got the invoice in the back." The clerk left his cash register and disappeared into a little cubby hole of a room just a few feet away. In the reflection of the knife display case Beek watched the big man standing still, and looking down at his feet. Although he was dressed in a very nice charcoal gray suit, it was rumpled; covered in stains, and dirty looking…and his unknotted tie, which hung loosely around his thick, bull like neck, looked as if it had been drug through a rain puddle. His black dress shoes were caked with dried mud and sand and he was unshaven, and unkempt; he looked weary, and almost completely worn out.

He brushed back the right side of his suit coat and started to reach into his rear pants pocket, apparently for his wallet, and when he did, Beek saw the Glock pistol in a black leather holster on his belt; and clipped to the belt right next to it, a gleaming, oval shaped badge.

He was a cop. *He* was the one who must have driven up in Kearnes' black unmarked Ford…or in another police car that looked just like it. The big, beefy man dug a credit card out of the wallet he'd produced and let it drop onto the counter next to the cash register, just as the clerk returned with a yellow piece of paper in his hand.

"Let's see here. Looks to be…seventy five, ninety nine, Thud."

"You got something for me to sign? Here's my card."

Howard the clerk, who was also the weekend store manager, put the invoice down on the counter and handed Thud Compton a pen, but the big exhausted detective already had his own pen out of his shirt pocket, signing for the bill, eager to conclude this mundane administrative chore and get back out on the street.

"Hey," Thud said to the clerk, as he watched him swiping his city credit card through the card reader, "would you happen to know whose white Ford Van that is out there in your lot?"

Howard looked up from his cash register, which was slowly disgorging the credit card transaction slip, and surveyed the parking lot through the store's big double glass doors.

"Nope," he said. "Never seen it before. Sure is a beat up old thing though, isn't it?"

"It's got Washington plates," Thud said to himself.

"What?" asked Howard.

"Oh...nothing," said Thud. "Thanks, Howard."

In the reflection of the glass, Uriah Beek saw the big detective vanish.

Thud hoped he had spoken up loud enough about the Van; so that everyone standing in line at the cash register had been able to hear him. But there hadn't been any reaction from the four or five customers in the check-out line behind him. And another customer, a huge white male, who had to have been at least six foot seven, and had been standing with his back to him, looking at a glass display case of knives, hadn't turned around or said anything either when he'd mentioned the white Van. So, if it didn't belong to anyone in the store, who did it belong to?

He walked out of the store and started to head for his car. He needed to get back down to Pearl Cove to check on things. Even though the scene had already been processed, and every bit of evidence and potential evidence removed, it was important that the area remain secured—at least for the next twenty four hours or so—in case new information concerning the murders was forthcoming, and a second crime scene search had to be initiated. But even though he knew it was a white car they were all looking for, still; there was *something* about that Van.

He decided to take a closer look and walked over to it, approaching it from the rear, and as he did, the smell reached him. It was a faintly trenchant odor; like some kind of vaporous chemical fumes hanging in the air. At first he thought it might be something just released from the giant smokestacks of the Pan-Pacific Mill at the edge of town, blown in further landward by the prevailing morning ocean breezes. But this was something different; something sickly sweet smelling, and vaguely familiar.

He pressed his nose against the dirty glass of one of the rear door windows, and the smell intensified. Peering inside the dark interior of the rear of the Van through the window, he saw that it was essentially a bare, and empty steel box. The steel floor was ribbed, but its once white painted surface was scarred and dented, with either shiny bare metal, or red rust having taken the paint job's place now; and the steel walls of the Van were in equally bad shape. Instinctively, he reached for the Van's rear door handle and tried it; but it was locked. Stepping back a short distance, he mentally copied down the license plate: Washington...David Edward David, Six Nine Six.

Thud decided he would take a look through the driver's side window, call the license plate in over his car radio to Dispatch, and then leave. But when he walked up to the driver's door and saw the door's old mechanical lock button on the other side of the window glass, standing straight up, the temptation was too great. Without a search warrant, or any probable cause to even be able to get one, he opened the unlocked door of the Van.

An astringent, antiseptic smell overwhelmed his nose; the same smell he had detected at the rear of the Van, only magnified a hundred times now. The Van's dashboard was faded and cracked, and the camel tan cloth fabric of the driver's seat was so worn in high stress places that the steel seat springs underneath were showing through. But the passenger seat next to it, besides being faded from the sun, looked almost as if it had never been sat in, and the entire front cab area had a freshly scrubbed appearance to it.

He quickly checked the overhead visor, and underneath the seat. Nothing. He checked the console between the two front seats. It was clean, and empty. He leaned further inside the vehicle and opened the glove compartment and it was the same; clean and empty. Now it wasn't so much a search to find something suspicious inside the vehicle, as it was a search to find what *wasn't* there...which was turning out to be highly suspicious in and of itself. And what wasn't there; what he had failed to find so far, but should have found by now, was the vehicle's registration and proof of insurance papers.

He had seen enough...or hadn't seen enough...depending on how you chose to look at it, and he was starting to duck back outside of the Van and shut the door; to back off and get a couple of officers out here to keep the Van under surveillance, when he noticed the closed ashtray. He pulled it open and saw what looked like a white paper napkin inside; rolled up tightly like a cigar shaped wrapper. Whoever owned the Van must not be a smoker, he thought, because the paint on the inside of the ashtray looked factory new.

He took the paper napkin from the ashtray and placed it on the driver's seat. The chemical smell inside the Van was beginning to make his eyes water now, so he used his fingers to pinch his tear ducts to clear his vision, then wiped them dry on the front of his grimy white dress shirt. Carefully, he unrolled the napkin, seeing that it was stained with pink blotches inside, and then stared down at its contents; a purplish, black colored raisin. An overly large, wrinkled raisin...with something shiny embedded inside it.

It took Thud Compton just one second too long to process all of it...that what he was staring at was actually Ricky Cates' shriveled, desiccated ear lobe, which had now shrunk down around the small silver cross earring after weeks of being inside the never opened ashtray, trapping it. That the curious smell that was so thick in his nose was the smell of disinfectant, and was the same odor he had smelled coming from the bodies of the two boys down on the beach. That the tall man in the store, the man who had had his back to him the entire time he was inside...had been dressed in some kind of work clothes uniform; with matching green pants and a green jacket...

Beek's fist smashed into the back of Thud's head like a sledge hammer, driving him forward and down onto the transmission hump. And before he could do anything more than grasp the thought that he now knew exactly who the killer was, and that he was about to become one of his victims, Beek began to bring his fist down squarely against Thud's spine with piston like blows...like a Butcher in a meat shop trying to tenderize a piece of tough steak with a mallet.

But Thud Compton was built like an ox, and Beek would need to get a lot more elevation and momentum behind his strikes in order for the blows to have the rib breaking, spine paralyzing effect he wanted them to. Beek was too tall to operate in such a confined space as the open doorway of the Van, so he stopped the attack and ripped the corner of the detective's jacket upwards, exposing his belt and his gun, and began to drag the stunned Thud Compton out of the Van and onto the ground in order to continue. Thud tried to grab for the Van's steering wheel when he felt the first jerk on his belt, but he was too slow to react, and missed; and then suddenly, he felt himself airborne.

He couldn't break his fall and landed on his stomach, pancaking flat onto the parking lot pavement with the wind releasing from his lungs in an audible whoosh. Groggily, he pawed at his holster for the Glock but felt a stinging blow to his hand, then the release of the gun's weight as Beek jerked the weapon free and hurled it away from them.

Thud watched the Glock skim across the pavement, spinning like a shuffle-board puck, until it stopped twenty feet away from his head in front of the Van. And then all he could do was cover the back of his head with his hands, as his attacker began in earnest to beat him to death.

Beek squat directly over the downed cop, his legs splayed wide, as he again began to smash his huge right fist over and over into Thud's spine, and kidneys; softening him up before he turned him over. Now that he'd gotten rid of the cop's gun there was nothing stopping him from flopping him over and crushing his larynx, and even though this man had the neck of a bull, he knew he could still get his fingers around his throat to do what needed to be done.

He hit the cop a few more times, feeling a rib give way, he was sure, on the last blow; then grabbed the large man by one shoulder and his hip and rolled him over onto his back.

"Hey there!" he heard someone shout. Beek looked up and saw the store clerk standing outside the twin doors of the store. Four or five customers were gathered around him and one of them had a cell phone to her mouth, screaming something hysterically into the phone.

"Thud! You all right?" Thud heard Howard Bell yell. *Jesus Christ*, he thought...*do I look like I'm all right Howard, you idiot*!

Thud looked up at his attacker, who was looking over at Howard Bell and the others in front of the store, and that was when he saw it; less than a foot from his face...the name "Dan" embroidered in red thread on the man's green work jacket. And then with every ounce of strength he could muster, Thud Compton brought his knee up as hard and as fast as he could into Uriah Beek's inflamed and diseased groin.

A long, agonizing scream tore from deep within Beek's throat and he doubled over, grabbing at his groin with both his hands as he staggered away from Thud Compton and the Van. Thud slowly got on all fours and started to crawl forward toward the Glock, but Beek was in his way, so he reversed himself and began to crawl backward instead.

He reached the back of the Van and had gotten two or three feet past its rear bumper, just as Beek finally got himself inside the Van and closed the door. Thud tried to rise up, to get on his knees; but something was broken in there on his right side, so he listed heavily to his left, as he struggled to work the Smith & Wesson Airweight free from the shoulder holster underneath his left armpit. When he'd gone home to check on Margie and his two daughters, he had hastily put the little gun in its concealable shoulder holster on; and he thanked God that he had...and that Beek had completely missed it.

Now he had the little five shot .38 out, and up; pointing at the driver's side mirror, and even with the fuzzy, mind numbing shock of his injuries beginning to creep into his consciousness, he was able to hold the almost weightless little gun out in front of him steadily, waiting for Beek to get back out of the Van.

But instead he heard the stutter of the Van's engine as it turned over; then the engine itself cough to life as a cloud of blue exhaust belched from the tailpipe. He saw the Van jerk as Beek put it in reverse but stepped on the brake at the same time, saw the brake lights flash bright red as its engine began to rev up; could see Beek's face in the driver's side mirror staring back at him, emotionlessly, and horrified, realized that he was about to be run over.

Thud did the only thing he could do to possibly save his life; he lunged to the left and then fell onto his back, so the two left tires of the Van would hit his outstretched legs and not his upper body. He had no sooner hit the ground when the Van lurched violently backwards, and he screamed in pain as he felt the burning, grinding weight of the vehicle drive over his legs; first the rear tire, then the front one.

He braced himself for the Van to run over him again when it reversed course and drove forward. But incredibly Beek continued driving backwards, picking up speed, and he saw Howard Bell and the others standing in front of the store scatter away from the double doors as the Van careened into them, exploding the store's entryway in a shower of flying glass and mangled aluminum.

The Van sat there for a couple of seconds—its rear end inserted halfway inside the store—then Thud heard the engine revving again and it suddenly roared forward in a jackrabbit start, its tires screeching loudly and crunching against the broken glass and metal on the sidewalk. But as it peeled away it swerved around him—where he lay roughly in the middle of the parking lot—heading for the exit to the highway, and Thud got off all five shots from the Smith & Wesson as it sped past in a blur. He had no idea where any of his rounds had gone—except for the last one—because he'd seen that bullet take out the Van's left rear door window, dead center; shattering it and throwing glass everywhere.

If there is a God, he prayed to himself, that last bullet had followed the perfectly straight trajectory he had sent it on, and had struck the suspect...because the window it blew out was directly in line with the driver's seat headrest. Thud Compton knew that bullets rarely flew straight after hitting any object, soft or hard; so the odds were against that having had happened. But then again, what were the odds of walking into a farm and garden store to pay a bill, and encountering a serial killer?

Thud had propped himself up on his left elbow so he could use his right hand to fire his weapon as the Van had passed by—and he was still up on that elbow—but he felt the energy draining from his body now. He laid back down. He had five extra rounds for the revolver in a speed loader pouch that was attached to the leather harness of the shoulder holster, and he knew he should reload now. But his whole right side felt numb, and he couldn't move either one of his legs. He closed his eyes and somewhere, far away, he thought he heard a woman screaming; and then Howard Bell's voice…shouting something unintelligible.

Those were the last sounds Thud heard.

Howard Bell had finally managed to grab the cell phone from the hands of the shrieking, hysterical woman customer, who was continuing to scream and run around in short little circles as Howard tried to yell above her into the phone to the 911 Dispatcher.

"Yes!" he shouted.

"Yes! A police officer!"

"Yes! He's been run over!"

"A Van! A white Van!"

"He went south…on Highway 101!"

"No, HE fired!"

"Because, the man was trying to kill him!"

"Yes!"

"He was trying to kill *us, too!*"

"I don't know if he's dead or not!"

"No!"

"Because…"

"I'm afraid to go and look."

CHAPTER 43

▼

As it turned out, there really was, in fact, a God; just as Thud Compton had prayed about before he lapsed into unconsciousness. And this morning he seemed to be on Thud's side much more than he was on the side of Uriah Beek, because Thud's last bullet *had* found its mark.

It had smashed through the back window of the Van, drilling into the driver's seat headrest, and had then exited; burrowing deeply into the thickly overdeveloped trapezius muscle of Beek's left shoulder, just below his neck, where it had finally stopped, burning like the red hot tip of a heated iron poker.

The pain was immense, and coupled with the daggers of pain stabbing upward from his groin, and into his gut, it was almost totally debilitating. But he managed to keep the Van in his lane of travel, and driving the legal speed limit, as he approached the exit to Harbor Way. He made the turn safely and as soon as he had started down the hill, saw the black and white police car charging uphill at him with all of its lights flashing and its siren screaming.

He caught a glimpse of the car's driver as it sped past him; recognizing the young officer with the black machine gun…the one who had been guarding the blonde whore inside her cabin all night. She would be there now, at The Sand Dollar; alone, and unprotected, and he would take her from wherever she was, the minute he saw her. With his knife at her throat, no policeman would dare raise a hand against him. With her life as the prize…the boy, who was now the corrupted and misled man, would come to him…and the final lesson could begin.

When Kearnes reached his car and unlocked and opened it with his left hand, the first thing he did was take the Colt from his holster, also with his left hand, and wedge its barrel tightly in between the space where the back of the seat and the seat itself met. Then he sat down on the gun, making sure its butt was sticking out between his legs, and angling to the left, so he could draw it quickly with the only good hand and arm he had left.

The second thing he did, was with the car's radio mike. After starting the car first and putting it in gear, and turning on his siren and all of his emergency lights, he took the mike off its hook and stretched the coiled cord out to its fullest; then clamped it against the steering wheel beneath his left hand so that he could drive and talk on the radio at the same time. Once he was set he crushed his foot down on the accelerator and fishtailed out of the parking lot of Trident Greens.

Because of the challenging terrain and narrow width of the access road, made treacherous now by his forced high speed, one handed driving, it was only after he had crossed over the cattle guard and was back on the highway, racing toward the city limits of Cutter Point, that he had finally used the radio.

When he did, he instructed Shoshanna Perry to dispatch medical aid and law enforcement to the third hole at the Trident Greens golf course for a seriously injured man down and bleeding at that location. He didn't bother to tell her the man had been shot and that he had been injured, too. Or that he had been the one who had shot the man; because he didn't want to add to the already prevalent atmosphere of complete pandemonium that had taken over the radio airwaves now.

Even though Shoshanna Perry had announced, several times now, a 10-33 clearing of the airwaves for all but those who were directly involved in the two emergent incidents, other peripheral officers in their fear, and excitement, and confusion—inspired by all of the fear and excitement and confusion of what was unfolding—kept breaking in on the radio traffic and walking all over Spenser and Kearnes.

But as Kearnes entered the north city limits, driving at over eighty miles an hour and just barely able to keep the swerving Ford within his lane of travel, the extraneous radio traffic began to clear away like the cars up ahead of him seeing his approaching lights and hearing his siren.

He gritted his teeth against the pain which pulsated from his shattered right arm, in order to concentrate on the new information coming in over his radio: An officer was down, but apparently still alive. Shots had been fired at the scene, but it was not exactly clear by who. The suspect had fled the scene in a Van.

Spenser was on scene now. The color of the Van was white. The officer who was down was One Charles Four...Thud Compton. The license number of the Van was DED-696.

DED-696.

Kearnes was more than halfway through the downtown business district and almost to the Buccaneer, when he slammed on his brakes, putting the Ford into a long, tire burning slide in the middle of the street. He dropped the radio mike and frantically ripped open the equipment bag on the seat next to him and found his notebook; and opening it awkwardly with his one hand, was filled with dread as he stared at the last entry he had made in it only two nights before: "*Wash plate DED/696, wht/van Sand Dol lot.*"

He threw the notebook aside and picked the radio mike up again. "One Charles One, to One Charles Twenty One!" he said urgently.

"Charles Twenty One" Spenser answered.

"What is the status of the subject you were with?"

Spenser; who was at the moment kneeling in the parking lot of Cutter Farm Supply next to his injured, and unconscious sergeant; reassuring him that everything was going to be all right as the paramedics started to work on him, was confused by his chief's question and mistakenly answered: "It's Sergeant Compton! He's hurt, but he's still alive...and the paramedics are on scene now!"

"Negative!" said Kearnes. "I copied *that*; but I am asking about the location of the subject you were assigned to earlier!"

"The female subject?"

"Affirmative."

"She just left...she was loading her car, just as I got this call."

"Did you see her leave? Where is the *exact* location you last saw her?"

"She was putting her bags in the trunk of her car. She was still there when I drove away. I *had* to leave her chief!"

"Yes. I know you did...but I need you to respond back down there...Code 3!"

"To the Sand Dollar?"

"Yes! Right now!"

"What about Sergeant Compton?"

"He'll be safe enough...I'm almost there myself!"

"Can I wait until you get here?"

"NO!"

"Look for an old beat up white Van, Spenser. It's a Ford Econoline, with Washington plates. David Edward David, Six, Nine Six. Also, I believe...*this is* the homicide suspect's Van. It was seen at that location two nights ago!"

"Copy! I'll be en route!" said Spenser. "Twenty One to Central, I need cover units at the Sand Dollar Motel in the Harbor District, Code 3! Are there any units left down at the crime scene that can respond?"

"One Charles Twenty One," said Shoshanna, "none showing on the screen; those units have just returned to the station...stand by...any unit in the area of the Harbor District...respond to back up One Charles Twenty One at The Sand Dollar Motel Resort, 4888 Harbor Way, for possible suspect contact."

"Charles One, to Charles Twenty One."

"Go ahead!"

"Spenser, I want you to find Miss McGraw first. If you see the Van, call it in immediately...but keep going until you get to the motel...I need you to verify if her vehicle is still there or not. If it's still there, check at the office first to see if they know where she is, then check the cabin...but use extreme caution!"

"Copy! What make is her car again?"

"It's a blue Geo."

"One Charles One to Central," said Kearnes, "in addition to the white Van, we are now also looking for a late model blue Geo, unknown license number; but it is a local rental. We have a possible kidnap victim; white female, blonde hair, five four, late thirties, one hundred twenty pounds...she is associated with this vehicle.

"I want units to respond to the intersection of Highway 101 and Harbor Way, to seal that area off. Absolutely no vehicles are to leave or enter the Harbor area, or gain access to the highway from Harbor Way.

"If the suspect vehicle does break through, units are to execute a rolling road block and to pit him at the earliest opportunity that presents itself.

"Under no circumstances is that white Van to be allowed to leave the city...do you copy?"

"Central copies," said Shoshanna. "One Charles Eleven, One Charles Twelve, One Charles Seventeen...respond to the intersection of Highway One Zero One and Harbor Way...Highway 101 and Harbor Way...traffic to be blocked both ways at that location; if the suspect vehicle is observed, a pit maneuver is authorized per One Charles One...suspect vehicle is to be prevented from leaving the jurisdiction.

"One Charles Seventeen...continue on past location to back up One Charles Twenty One at The Sand Dollar on possible suspect contact...all units, this is a Code 3 response."

The three Charles units all individually acknowledged hearing the directives given to them by Central, then Shoshanna came back on and said, "Central to

One Charles One...I have a read back on that Washington plate when you're ready."

"Go ahead," said Kearnes.

"David Edward David, Six Nine Six," said Shoshanna, "comes back to a 1989 Ford Econoline Van, with a two party commercial registration. Primary owner is Great Wall Imports, Seattle, Washington. The second registered owner is a Daniel Beek, 3611 Sand Spit Road, Long Beach, Washington. Registration is clear, and valid."

Her words sounded surreal to Kearnes. To hear the name of the killer for the first time, and in the same sentence, the name of the very place where this same man had so horribly damaged him and had changed his life forever; was beyond chilling. But it was also a huge infusion of reality.

In some men there sometimes comes a point where fear and panic and pain, will evolve into anger and action; and this was now the point where Kevin Kearnes found himself. What he had once dreaded, he now hungered for, and he knew that the first chance he got he was going to kill this bastard...Daniel Beek. And whether or not it was *legal* would have very little, in anything, to do with it.

Spenser came on the air again. "I'm mobile!" he shouted, the sound of his car's siren coming over the radio nearly drowning out his voice.

"Repeat that last! On the kidnap information?" he said.

"Charles One, to Twenty One," said Kearnes. "Be advised...the suspect has been watching her, and I think he was the subject who burglarized her cabin."

"If you find her; put her in your car, immediately, and take her to the P.D.!"

"You mean Miss McGraw?" asked Spenser.

"Yes! *He* is going to try and take her!" said Kearnes.

"Copy that!" responded Spenser.

But it was too late.

Uriah Beek already had her.

CHAPTER 44

▼

Officer Spenser Sparling had insisted on staying with Britt McGraw all morning while she cleaned out the cabin, and then paid her final bill at the Sand Dollar's office. And after he had helped her carry her things from the cabin out to the parking lot, he'd sat in his patrol vehicle nearby while she packed her little blue car…right up to the point where she had heard three long tones come over his police radio. And then he had suddenly raced out of the parking lot of the Sand Dollar toward the main road with his patrol car's emergency lights and siren on; hastily waving goodbye to her quickly as he went.

She was trying to situate the last piece of her luggage in the car's trunk—the small black travel bag with the thousands of dollars of cash in it—when she began to hear more sirens blaring across the city in the sun washed crystal morning air. The Geo's trunk was small, and she was leaving Cutter Point with a lot more possessions than she had arrived with. Things she probably wouldn't even need in Mexico; if she did manage make it there after what she was about to do in Eureka, California in less that forty eight hours on Monday morning.

Things like the white down comforter she had bought for her bed…their bed…and which still held the sustaining scent of Kevin Kearnes. She could not bear to leave it behind; not like she was being forced to leave the man himself behind. So she folded it up neatly and pressed it into the last remaining bit of space of the clean, hardly ever used trunk of the rental car; using it to hide her black bag full of money beneath it, but unable to hide the true desire of her heart.

She only wanted to get away now; from this place, and the man who had hurt her so badly…and who she still loved, in spite of everything that had happened, so deeply. She could see now that in his own way, Kevin Kearnes was just like she was. She didn't understand exactly why, or how, he had become the man he now was, but she imagined his life had been driven by overwhelming and uncontrollable forces; just like her life had been.

And for him, survival wasn't just a deeply buried human instinct to be summoned forth only in rare moments of true crisis. Survival was his day to day existence. Just as it was her own. Dr. Britt McGraw had compensated for her impediments by throwing herself into her career, and while she had helped many other people along the way, she would never be capable of helping herself.

Where others saw her beauty, she saw only her inner ugliness. Where others saw her strength, she despised her own concealed weakness. And where others saw the bold truth of her, Britt McGraw saw only what a lie her life had become, and would always be; unless and until, she revealed, with a bullet, the truth...for all the world to see.

Physician, heal thyself.

Now it was time for her to do just that.

She closed the trunk of the car and took one last look at The Sand Dollar; and felt very sad. How wonderful it had been to be in love again; if only for such a short time. And to begin to make new friends and do new things; simple, feminine things, like decorating a home, and baking cookies for the man she loved, which had, unexpectedly, brought her so much joy.

And she felt terrible about betraying Margie's husband, Thud. She had promised to have lunch with him on Monday to help him with their murder investigation. And now, after what had happened here overnight, he, and the other members of the police department, would need that help more than ever. But by late Monday morning there would a hundreds of police officers just like Thud Compton, looking for her. And she, herself, would be a murderer on the run.

She shut the trunk and started to get in the car, but didn't see the white Van moving toward her through the parking lot. It came on silently, stealthily...like a shark cruising through the shallows, maneuvering to strike its prey.

Beek had made good his escape without much of a problem, other than having been shot in the back. And he had made sure the officer who'd shot him wouldn't be following; because he'd run over him first with his Van in the parking lot where he'd left him; beaten and bloodied. But now he had to get to the blonde whore, and would have to deal with her young policeman protector and his black machine gun.

Or so he thought until he saw that same officer flash past him at the top of Harbor Hill, driving so fast that Beek could hardly tell that it was a police car he was in, except for the snapping blue and red colored lights and the warbling sound of its siren. So he had continued on down the hill, still driving the speed limit, until he'd arrived at The Sand Dollar again.

Once there he had immediately seen her; alone, and standing at the rear of her car. She was crying for some reason, and hadn't see him coming. And all he had needed was that one second of complete physical immobilization she had suffered once she had turned and seen the horrific apparition of him approaching. A towering, crazed giant charging at her; his face contorted and twisted in pain, and his jacketless shirt now completely soaked black with his blood.

He had grabbed both her wrists first, and then struck her in the face, twice; and she was out. But to Beek her limp body was like air, and in seconds he had thrown her into the passenger seat of the Van, tying her right wrist tightly to the inside door handle with two Trellistrips, and then binding her neck to the seat's headrest in the same manner.

He could hear people in the parking lot—who had seen the attack—shouting now; and as an afterthought he leaned over from his seat and rolled down the passenger window, so the world could see the prize he had captured…Satan's own prostitute. Then, laughing, he started the Van and roared away, the lifeless looking whore tied in the seat next to him bouncing as the vehicle encountered the last set of speed bumps on his way out of the Sand Dollar's parking lot.

He was almost to the top of the hill again when he saw two police cars bearing down on him from above in the opposite lane, and as the first car passed by he saw it was the same young policeman again…and this time he looked straight into Beek's eyes. The intersection with the highway was less than two hundred yards ahead. In his rear view mirror he saw both patrol cars braking, and power sliding in jagged semi-circles in the middle of the roadway; trying to get stopped and turned around in order to pursue him. But he had too much of a lead on them now; and he knew he was going to get away.

Until he saw two more black and white patrol cars just ahead at the intersection with the highway. They were parked directly in the center of the road with their front bumpers just a few feet apart; forming an inverted "V" with no other place to go because of the narrow and steep shoulders on both sides of the roadway there. He saw two officers crouched behind the rear of each car, pointing what looked like rifles at him, and he did exactly what God told him to do. He mashed the Van's accelerator down to the steel floorboard, and slammed into the center of the "V".

If the two Charles units had only parked their vehicles one foot closer together, the ordeal with Beek would have ended right then and there.

The roadblock would have trapped his Van on both sides, and the officer on the left—who had a clear shot through Beek's open driver's side window—could have killed him with a head shot; posing a minimal risk to the hostage. But they had put their cars in position hastily and under extreme duress, leaving just a little too much room between them, and Beek's Van had punched through the center like a giant can opener opening a tin can.

He shot out into the middle of traffic on Highway 101 and swerved to the left, narrowly missing several oncoming cars, who jammed on their brakes and blared their horns at him as he headed for the Blue Czar River Bridge. Looking back in his rear view mirror again he saw two sets of emergency lights, traveling abreast and coming up fast behind him. He knew it had to be the young officer and his friend, because he had seen the front ends of both the patrol cars parked at the roadblock rupture in a geyser of hot steam and flying shards of glass, plastic, and metal.

The bridge across the Blue Czar River which connected the Harbor District to the main portion of the city was three lanes of traffic, and a bicycle lane, in both directions, but even with the generous amount of space allotted for the smooth flow of vehicular traffic, it was clogged with cars this morning, that were moving slowly, as the tourists inside gaped in awe at the endless panorama of the blue Pacific Ocean to their left, and the stunning chasm which fell away to the Blue Czar River below the bridge on their right.

Beek laid on his own horn now as he snaked in, and out, and around the sluggishly moving vehicles, sideswiping some of them as he passed, and ramming into the rear ends of a few others...literally clearing them from his path. The far end of the bridge was in sight now and once he reached it, he could go anywhere; do anything he wanted to do. And nothing on this earth could stop him.

And then he saw the black, unmarked police car coming from the south; speeding toward the same end of the bridge he was trying to reach...and behind it, and along side of it, five more police cars; three of them painted black and white and the other two green, with gold markings.

The first, and only turn off at the north end of the bridge was a street to the left marked Anchorage Drive, and now Beek raced with the oncoming black car to get to it first. And he did; but just barely. He skidded into the turn and then glanced quickly in his mirror and saw the black car suddenly loom into view directly behind him, right on his rear bumper...so close to him that he could feel the blast of the police car's siren vibrating through the chassis of the Van.

Anchorage Drive was a main arterial that bled down a steep hillside through quiet residential neighborhoods for over a mile; paralleling the river beside it and terminating in a dead end at the start of the north jetty, directly across from the mouth of the Harbor and Pearl Cove. But it was a long, straight shot road, and even though Beek was unaware of the dead end ahead, he was traveling too fast to turn onto any of the side streets anyhow; so he kept on going.

He saw the dead end of the street less than half a block ahead, and saw the gray steel vehicle barrier that prevented cars from inadvertently driving out onto the rocks, and the yellow and black steel pole mounted signs warning pedestrians of venturing out any further beyond this point. He locked up the now hot and smoking brakes of the Van, putting the vehicle into a rocking, sideways slide across the dirt pad area that was used as a car turnaround, and then slammed into the side of the vehicle barrier.

Outside of the Van the air was suddenly filled with auditory chaos and thick, rising dust, as the pursuing police cars also slid to stops all around him, their sirens shrieking in an ear splitting din that sounded like chamber music being played in hell. Beek reached down into the pocket of his jacket, which he'd taken off earlier in order to look at his wound, and then set on the console on top of his binoculars...and pulled out the knife. He reached across the woman's lap and slashed its hooked blade against the vinyl strips which held her wrist to the door handle, and when he raised up to cut her neck loose, too, he saw that she was awake now and staring back at him wide eyed, with thick clots of stringy red blood hanging down from the nostrils of her broken nose. He slashed her neck free and then scooped her up around her waist...then climbed out of the Van, propping her up in front of him.

And he was there...Kevin Kearnes...standing less than ten feet away from him. Pointing his big Colt pistol unsteadily at Beek's face as he held it in his left hand. And directly behind him, off a little to the right, was that same young police officer, holding the same black machine gun. He was pointing his weapon directly at Beek, too.

A sea of other police officers washed toward him; all of them with raised guns...and screaming commands he could not hear over the sirens. Kearnes shouted something unintelligible over his shoulder to the young officer with the machine gun, who then began to slowly back away toward the cars, still keeping his weapon pointed at Beek. And then one by one, the sirens on the police vehicles began to fall silent.

"Let her go, Beek," said Kearnes.

Uriah Beek's face showed genuine astonishment when he heard the boy, who had become the man, speak his name.

"You remember me?" he asked.

"Yes," said Kearnes, without hesitation.

"I'm disappointed in you, Kevin," said Beek. "Truly disappointed."

"You're under arrest," said Kearnes. He was trying not to look at Britt, but he had to; and when he did he saw her terrified eyes staring straight back at him.

"Really?" said Beek. Kearnes saw him press the strange looking small knife, with its hook shaped blade, tighter against the side of her neck…directly over her carotid artery. "You have no authority over me, Mr. Policeman. Your beliefs have been corrupted, and are false. Renounce your fornications with this sorceress of a whore right now…in front of all who are present. *Then*, I will let her go."

If his right arm was not broken, and now hanging useless at his side; *this madman would already be dead*, Kearnes thought to himself. Because the shot *was* there; even with Beek holding the knife so tightly against Britt's neck. And if he had still been able to shoot right handed, he would have taken the shot…even now. But in the condition he was in he couldn't chance it. He didn't even have enough strength left to keep pointing his weapon at Beek, and so slowly he brought the Colt down to his side.

"She's not a whore," said Kearnes, looking at Britt. "In fact, she's the farthest thing from it. Now please, let her go."

"Ha!" laughed Beek. "I beg to differ with you on *that*, Mr. Policeman."

"Let her go!" Kearnes shouted. "She's got nothing to do with this! This is between you, and me."

"You see, that's where you are wrong," said Beek. "She has *everything* to do with this."

Then Beek lifted Britt up off the ground in front of him, and scuttled crab like sideways around the vehicle barrier. Slowly, he started to back out onto the first of the huge granite boulders of the jetty. Kearnes took a couple of steps toward them, but Beek shouted "No!" "You drop your weapon first! Right there in the dirt!"

Kearnes released the Colt from his hand, and it fell to the dusty ground at his feet.

Seeing him drop the gun, Beek smiled at him.

"That's just fine," he said. "*You* may follow us now, Kevin. But if anyone else comes past those signs…I will slit her throat…from ear to ear." Then; moving backwards, and using Britt as his shield, Beek began to stretch his legs from rock to rock like a giant spider stepping across mountain tops.

"Lower you weapons!" ordered Kearnes. But most of the officers didn't immediately comply, their wildly pumping adrenalin keeping their guns frozen in place in their outstretched hands and tracking the movement of Beek out on the rocks.

"PUT YOUR GUNS DOWN!" Kearnes shouted...and black steel muzzles at last started to drop.

"Spenser!"

"Yes sir!" Spenser answered, walking quickly over to Kearnes, his MP5 slapping against his side where it hung from its sling.

"I've heard that Brad Dekker is a Sheriff's Department sniper. Is that true?"

"Yes. He's our only one, in the whole county."

"Where is he right now?"

"I think he was on his way to the Hospital...with Sergeant Compton."

"Find him. Tell him to get his rifle. I need him in those rocks over there...on the south jetty. And he has to be able to get in place without being seen."

"Yes sir."

"That entire area over there is to be kept clear of all other law enforcement personnel. Tell him that. It's *very* important.

"There's a good pair of binoculars in the trunk of my vehicle. I want you to get them out when you put my duty weapon in there; before you leave. You are going to be Brad's spotter."

"Chief," said Spenser, "you aren't going out there, are you?"

"I have to," said Kearnes.

"No...please," said Spenser. "He'll kill you if you do."

Kearnes looked into the handsome, but distraught face of the brave young officer, who had been exposed to more horror and danger in the last twelve hours than many cops were in their entire twenty year careers, and saw the tears that were starting to flow freely from his clear, blue eyes.

"And if I don't," said Kearnes. "He's going to kill *her*."

CHAPTER 45

▼

The north jetty at Cutter Point had been built to thrust straight out into the Pacific Ocean from shore for a mile, like a long, defensive spear, and at its tip there was a small Coast Guard aid to navigation light that sat on a square concrete pad about the size of a backyard patio. Kearnes could see Britt and Daniel Beek standing on that concrete pad now, next to the white painted steel housing of the light, and saw that Beek was still holding her tightly; still had the wicked looking little knife against her neck.

He followed the blood spatter on the rocks from Beek's dripping wound; not because he couldn't decide on his own route across the treacherous giant boulders—some of them as large as a small compact car—but because Beek had already done the hard work for him. And in his quickly waning physical state, he needed every advantage he could find if he was going to save Britt, first, and then try to kill this monster of a man. Or die trying.

Where Beek had been able to step from rock to rock with his long legs that were half the length of Kearnes' entire body, Kearnes had been forced to hop, and sometimes take short, running starts, and leap across them. And every time he did, the two pieces of fractured bone in his right arm painfully clicked, audibly; telegraphing a warning signal to him that his body wasn't whole any longer, and that he should stop.

But he didn't…because he couldn't. He knew now that Beek was insane, and that he had meant every word he had said before he'd left with Britt. And that was why when Spenser had begged Kearnes to take his little nine millimeter back up gun with him, and had started to unbutton his uniform shirt to give it to him, Kearnes had not only refused, he had backed away from Spenser as if he had the plague. He knew Beek was watching his every move, his body language, and even a misinterpretation of what looked like one wrong move to him would result in Britt's death.

Now he was close to reaching them; very close. An array of sport and commercial fishing boats, large and small, were motoring or sailing both in and out of the Harbor, passing by on the calm waterway created by the north and south jetties. Some of the people on the boats waved cheerfully to him; completely oblivious to the drama that was playing out on the long granite pinnacle only a hundred yards away from their bows. He waved back when they did, not wanting to arouse any suspicion which could result in one of them calling the Coast Guard Station at Gold Beach with their on board marine radios. He knew that if the Coast Guard showed up in one of their fast moving orange boats, to investigate; everyone would die.

As he labored across the tops of the last fifty yards of boulders, he saw Beek roughly drag Britt over to the navigation light, which was twelve to fourteen feet high and shaped like a miniature lighthouse. There were U-shaped, bent steel rods bolted to the side of the light, starting near its base. They acted as steps, used to access its top housing where the beacon was, in order to perform maintenance, and he watched as Beek tied her hands to the first step with some of the green vinyl ties which he had taken from a pocket of his blood soaked pants. His heart caught in his throat when he saw this, because his plan had depended on Britt being free to move— the split second after he attacked Beek and drew his attention from her, to him—so she could jump from the rocks into the sea and swim away.

He knew she was a strong swimmer because she had told him so. She had grown up near the ocean in Washington State—Puget Sound, actually—and had been on two different college swim teams. It was his only plan; and, he knew, their only hope...*her* only hope, really, of survival. Beek would surely kill him after Britt had escaped; and he would be largely incapable of doing anything about it. Even if he had the use of both his arms and hands, he couldn't see how he would ever be able to stop such a huge and almost hideously physically overdeveloped monster like Beek without some kind of weapon. And preferably one that came in thirty eight caliber, or larger.

All the way out Kearnes had tried to not reveal to Beek that his right arm was injured; but climbing and jumping over the rocks with it swinging free the pain had been too great, causing him to nearly black out, and he'd been forced to go the last half of the way hugging it in close against his body with his left one.

As he walked up to within a few yards of Beek now, he saw the madman's eyes close down to narrow fissures in his face, and his nostrils begin to quiver as if he was some giant predatory cat who had just sensed prey. But there was something different about him now; a slight change in his body posture from thirty minutes earlier in the standoff at the end of Anchorage Drive.

Beek was no longer standing so immensely tall, or looking nearly as confident as he had been back there. He was hunched slightly forward now as if his stomach might be cramping, or he was having a bad attack of gas. He was having a hard time keeping his hands from clutching at his lower stomach. And he was shallowly panting like a dog without shade, stricken by a summer heat wave, as rivers of sweat poured down his face from his scalp.

It had to be the wound he had obviously sustained. A bullet wound, Kearnes hoped; and he prayed that if this was the case, the bullet had come from Thud Compton's gun. Given enough time, his wound could possibly save them. Kearnes needed to stall, and drag things out as long as possible; to engage Beek in conversation, but without setting him off, and pushing him toward a murderous rampage.

"Welcome, Kevin!" said Beek. "Welcome!"

Kearnes chanced a quick look at Britt; down on her bare knees on the cement, her wrists tied so tightly to the steel bar that her hands were starting to turn purple.

She was wearing a colorful summer print sun dress, extremely low cut, which showed her bare tanned shoulders and back, and exposed the top half of her breasts to a very generous public view. Which seemed somehow oddly inappropriate to him, given his knowledge of her innate sense of modesty. The front of the dress was stained with blood and she had lost both of her shoes. Thick gobs of blood had congealed beneath her nose, and the nose itself looked slightly off kilter. It had obviously been broken and above it, her right eye was completely swollen shut.

"I'm so glad you made it," said Beek. "Looks like it was a little difficult for you, though. Something wrong with your arm?"

"It's broken," said Kearnes.

"You don't say," said Beek. "Take a little spill on the rocks, did you?"

"No," said Kearnes. "My boss hit me with a golf club. Is there something wrong with *you*? You look like you might need a doctor."

"Not really," Beek answered him. "I've been shot, is all. And for the second time in my life, I might add. The first time having been by *you*."

Beek grabbed his partially opened shirt inside the left collar, ripping it downward, and the bloody fabric peeled away from his skin with a wet, suctioning sound.

"Right here," he said, pointing to a glossy, quarter sized sunken patch of skin just below his clavicle. "Do you remember?"

"I was just a boy then," said Kearnes. "I wasn't a very good shot yet."

"Your big policeman friend back at the garden store," said Beek, "isn't much better."

"Is he the one who shot you?" asked Kearnes.

Beek studied him for a moment with dark, calculating eyes. Then he said, "You two really are friends, then."

"I'm his supervisor," said Kearnes, matter of factly. "I am responsible for him...and his actions."

"So; then your real question is...was he justified in shooting me?"

"Well, the answer is "yes", said Beek. "Considering that I was trying to kill him, first. And I'm fairly certain that I succeeded, too."

Kearnes' mind flashed back to the day Margie and Thud had invited him over for steaks, and the genuinely warm and loving family environment he'd felt a part of while he was a guest of the Compton's in their home.

The thought of Margie and the girls no longer having their husband and their Father in their lives, and of he, himself, losing such a good friend as Thud—for no damned good reason at all—was almost too much for him to bear. But looking into the demonic eyes of the man who may have just killed Thud, and feeling utterly powerless to do anything about it, was almost as unbearable.

"And those four boys?" Kearnes asked. "You killed them, too?"

"No," said Beek. "No, no, no, no, NO!"

"I saved them!" he said. "I only hastened their passage into The Kingdom! And at the same time held up the virtuous purity of their passing! As a message of hope to those on this earth who would be virtuous, and as warning and condemnation to those who will not!"

"You *saved* them?" said Kearnes. "How? By beating and strangling them to death?"

"The Bible says, 'the mind of sinful man is death, and the sinful mind is hostile to God. It does not submit to God's law, nor can it do so. Those controlled by the sinful nature cannot please God.'"

"Jesus Christ, Beek. Sinful *men*, maybe...but these were just little boys for Christ's sake!"

And suddenly Beek was in Kearnes' face, gripping him by the throat as he screamed at him, "YOU SHUT YOUR FILTHY, BLASPHEMOUS MOUTH! OR I WILL SHUT IT FOR YOU! DO YOU HEAR ME?"

Kearnes' first instinct—which was a mistake—was to try and push him away. But Beek was immovable; like a towering wall of chiseled granite, and when he felt the smaller man's puny one armed resistance he became enraged and struck Kearnes in the face, dropping him to the concrete slab on his knees.

Well, so much for not setting him off thought Kearnes as he felt the warm, salty blood gushing from his lower lip, and then with his tongue pushed against one of his lower front teeth, which wiggled slightly now. Beek grabbed Kearnes by his hair and snapped his head back, forcing him to look up at him, and then let go.

"*For if you live according to the sinful nature,*" he said, "*you will die.*"

"*But if by the spirit you put to death the misdeeds of the body, you will live. Because those who are led by the Spirit of God, are sons of God.*"

It was windy this far out on the jetty, and on the distant horizon ugly lead gray storms clouds were starting to build. There was a chop on the sea, which translated into a very stiff prevailing cross wind. A cross wind that could drift even the heaviest rifle bullet traveling at very high velocity as much as several feet off its indicated point of impact, in the estimated three to four hundred yards of open water that separated the point of the shorter, southern jetty, to where Beek now stood on the northern jetty...out in the open and exposed.

Kearnes intentionally kept his head down, kneeling in front of Beek and spitting blood onto the cement, because he knew if Brad Dekker and Spenser were in position by now, over there, that this was the moment when Dekker would take his shot. But it was a very long ways away, and the wind was blowing hard.

Police snipers in the movies and on TV routinely made spectacularly long shots with their bull barreled, scoped rifles. But real police snipers in real life situations rarely pulled their triggers on human targets any farther than fifty to seventy yards away; and only then when the existing conditions were as perfect as perfect ever gets.

"Is that it, Kevin?" Beek asked him. "Is it that you *want* to die today? Because I had something a lot less drastic in mind for you."

"Untie the woman, and let her go," Kearnes said. "She's a doctor...she may be able to help you."

"I don't believe in doctors," said Beek. "Jehovah is both Savior *and* healer to me."

"That's fine," said Kearnes.

"But how are you planning on getting off of this pile of rocks alive? Walk on water?"

Retribution for the sacrilege came swiftly from Beek as he smashed his knee forward into Kearnes' chest, lifting him up off the cement and throwing him over backwards where he then lay sprawled on the cement, choking as he tried to catch breath.

Britt, who had been silent to this point, now cried out, "Please...stop it!"

"Shut up whore!" Beek roared. "I'll get to you soon enough!"

He stood over Kearnes, staring down at him for a moment, letting him get some air back into his lungs. Then he put a toe of one of his dirty work boots on Kearnes' injured right arm...and rested it there.

"I asked you a question, Kevin," he said. "Do you wish to live? Or die?"

"Go...to hell," Kearnes gasped.

Beek pressed down with his boot, and Kearnes screamed in agony.

"Leave him alone you bastard!" Britt cried, thrashing against her unbreakable vinyl bonds as hard as she could.

But Beek ignored her. He was still staring at Kearnes; fascinated by his level of physical suffering, which had now begun to mirror his own. He wanted Kevin Kearnes to feel what he now felt, and to make the same sacrifices he had been forced to make. Only then, he knew, would Kearnes be able to be sanctified, and become a true believer, like he himself was; and could then renounce the whore, and her Dominion over him, forever.

"Well?" said Beek.

"You can't kill me, Beek," said Kearnes.

"Don't you know that?"

"I already died; a long time ago...the day that you touched me."

Beek ground the toe of his boot into Kearnes' arm and this time Kearnes didn't scream, but instead emitted a pitiful, guttural moan.

Britt was sobbing now. She couldn't stand to watch the torture any longer, so she looked down and stared at the Trellistrips, wrapped tightly with several turns, around her wrists...and at the sharp underside of one of the hexagonal head bolts that had worked its way out a little from the first step bracket on the navigational light.

"Then let me ask you this, instead" said Beek. "Do you want your whore to die? Or to live?"

"Because she lies down with The Beast, Kevin. And as long as you allow her to infect your life, so shall you!"

"You don't have to worry; she's no longer in my life," said Kearnes. "So just please let her go."

"Would you like to know what the Bible says about her?" Beek walked over to Britt and grabbed her by her hair, twisting a long length of it into a knot, which he used to force her head back around until she was looking at Kearnes. Then he put his knife to her throat, and began to recite a passage from The Book of Revelation.

"*Come, I will show you the punishment of the great prostitute, who sits on many waters. With her the kings of the earth committed adultery and the inhabitants of the earth were intoxicated with the wine of her adulteries.*

"*I beheld a woman sitting on a scarlet beast that was covered with blasphemous names and had seven heads and ten horns. The woman was dressed in purple and scarlet, and was glittering with gold, precious stones, and pearls.*

"*She held a golden cup in her hand, filled with abominable things and the filth of her adulteries. And written on her forehead was this title...Mystery, Babylon The Great, The Mother Of Prostitutes, And The Abominations Of The Earth.*"

While Beek was ranting, Kearnes had slowly rolled over, gotten to his knees, and then slowly stood up on unsteady, wobbling legs, to face Beek. Desperately, he looked around him for a weapon...any kind of weapon; but there was nothing he could use. The only thing he had was his canister of pepper spray hidden in its holder on his gunbelt. Beek didn't appear to have noticed it yet, and if Kearnes could somehow distract him he might be able to use it to disable him...just long enough to gain control of his knife.

"I'm not going to tell you this again, you sick fuck," he said. "She's got nothing to do with any of this. NOW LET HER THE HELL GO!"

Beek turned loose of Britt's hair, and walked up to Kearnes. Without warning he struck him in the face with his fist, and Kearnes staggered backwards. Then he advanced on him and struck him again, and Kearnes crumpled to the ground on his stomach, dazed and just barely still conscious.

He tried to resist as Beek rolled him over and began to tug at his gunbelt, but then felt the buckle release, and the belt, with all of his attached equipment, being pulled away from his body. Feebly, he grabbed at the belt with his one good hand, but Beek ripped it away and hurled it out across the water where it landed with a splash, and was quickly swallowed up by the sea.

His eyes were still half open but the world looked gray; gray sky, gray boulders, the dingy gray hem of Britt's brightly colored summer dress. All the sounds coming to his ears now turned into auditory distortions, and hallucinations...the soft hissing sound of the waves cupping against, and then receding from the jetty rocks, was like a jumbo jet coming in for a landing directly over his head.

Kearnes fought against passing out just as hard as he could; shaking his head back and forth to stay conscious—like a prize fighter tries to shake off a blow—as he struggled to get back up on his elbows. But when he did, Beek hammered a piston driven fist into his chin, and he dropped to the concrete, fading away into a consummate blackness; hearing nothing, seeing nothing, and feeling nothing.

Which was quite merciful for Kevin Kearnes.

Because he never felt Beek groping at the top button on his uniform pants or his zipper; or next, yanking his pants down past his hips to his ankles, and then off over his boots. And he didn't feel Beek spread his legs apart and insert the cold, steel curved blade of his grape hook knife beneath the white cotton crotch of his Jockey shorts and jerk it upwards, splaying open the underwear and exposing his genitals. And he didn't have to hear Britt's horrifying, non-stop screams as she witnessed Beek, down on his knees, doing all of this. Howling like an animal, like a mad, wild dog, as he prepared to violate him—for the second time in his life now—in the worst way any man could ever be violated by another.

Britt McGraw saw all of it, and heard all of it. And like the victim she had remained of her own abuse—also suffered so very long ago, but still with her every living, breathing second, of every day—she also *felt* what was happening to Kevin. And at that moment, with a clarity and courage she had never known before in her life, she understood the *essence* of who she really was; and who Kevin Kearnes was, too.

The missing pieces of her soul, which for so long had denied her the right to be a whole and complete human being, and woman, had not just been somehow misplaced by her, or lacking in her from the beginning, or lost to her somewhere along the way…they had been stolen from her. And she understood now that they could never be reclaimed by retribution, or even revenge; but only through rebirth.

Spreading her bound wrists apart as far as she could, she exposed a two inch wide long area of the vinyl ties; which felt as taut as steel cable. Carefully, and keeping her eyes trained on Beek, she lowered her wrists down onto the slightly protruding bolt head on the step bracket. And then bearing down with all her strength, she began to saw the vinyl ties back and forth.

She knew what Beek was going to do to him now; or at least she thought she did. But oddly, Beek still hadn't taken off his own pants, or exposed himself in any manner. As she felt the first layer of vinyl strip break, and then give way, she saw Beek probing with the tip of his knife at the base of Kevin's scrotum. And with a chilling certainty, she knew now that Beek was not just going to anally rape him; he was going to cut him. He was preparing to castrate him.

She looked back at the shore, down the length the jetty, but saw no one. Looking out across the channel of water to the other, shorter jetty, on the south shore…she did see something. It was a reflection, like a mirror; something bright and shiny, flashing intermittently, up and down. But it was very small, and obviously very far away. Probably only a discarded aluminum soft drink can being pushed along the tops of the equally large jetty boulders over there by the gusting ocean breezes.

Another strand of the vinyl broke in two. She was more than halfway through it now. She stopped sawing and shouted at Beek, "Hey! Why don't you come over here, and take me, instead?"

Beek acted as if he hadn't heard her. He was no longer howling, but was whimpering something unintelligible, as he worked at getting Kearnes into just the right position. They were some kind of words, loosely strung together. Maybe more passages from the Bible; or maybe just the nonsensical ravings of a madman. She really couldn't tell.

"Hey, you pathetic faggot!" she shouted at him. "Are you *listening to me*?" She felt the last, thin strand of vinyl stretching; and then suddenly snap in two, and almost immediately the blood start to flow back into her fingers with a pounding rush. She froze in place just as Beek, who had now been distracted, raised his head up from between Kevin Kearnes' open and naked legs, and looked straight at her.

"I am not a homosexual," he said…in a of voice so frighteningly normal, and lucid, that she instantly felt every hair on her body electrify and stand up.

"And I have never been one."

Britt vigorously worked both of her hands open and shut, trying desperately to get some feeling back in them now and knowing that their survival absolutely depended on it. Beek saw that she was free from where he had tied her, but he didn't seem to care.

"Well, you must be," Britt said, as she got to her feet slowly, wiping away the clotted mass of blood from beneath her nose with her bare forearm. "You like men, and little boys, don't you? Isn't it true? That you would pick them first? Even over someone like me?"

"Whore!" he spat back at her. She saw he still had the knife in his hand, holding it somewhere up against the inside of Kearnes' thigh.

"Sure, I'm a whore," said Britt, slipping the narrow straps of her sun dress off first one shoulder, and then the other. "But *all* women are whores!" she laughed.

"Everyone knows that!" Slowly, she let the dress fall to the cement, where it piled up in a loose heap around her bare feet. "Be honest, though. Wouldn't you like to at least just look?"

Beek's eyes were locked on Britt as she slowly moved in a half circle out around in front of him; seductively hooking her thumbs underneath the cups of the bra as she moved and pulling the fabric away from the straining weight of her breasts. She stopped when she was directly in line with him—less than seven or eight feet away—and she could see the point of his knife pressing against Kevin's skin.

She didn't appear to have overly large breasts when she was dressed. But now, completely unclothed, except for the matching black panties she wore with the skimpy, low cut bra, Beek thought her breasts looked like two twin creamy goblets; luxuriously full and swollen to their brims with rich, and secret desires…the sweet, but poisonous milk of The Garden itself.

"Do you want to see them?" she asked, coming a little closer.

"No," he said.

She stopped; now at almost point blank range from Beek.

"Would you like to touch them?"

"N…n…no," he stammered. She saw that his respirations had increased; his breathing was much faster than it had even been before. But it wasn't Beek's wound that was increasing his body's demand for oxygen now…it was Britt.

"Good," she said. "Because I'd rather be dead, first."

She reached her right hand inside the center of her bra, into the deep cleft between her breasts, and when she felt her fingers close around the tiny revolver hidden there she withdrew the gun in one quick practiced, uninterrupted motion, using both of her hands to cock it as she did, leveling it at Beek.

And then she fired.

Beek had been totally focused on her bare breasts when he'd heard Britt cock the little gun; but he had never seen it…before it was too late.

He'd heard two very rapid, metallic clicking sounds as the cylinder had rotated into battery as the weapon's little hammer came back, which had sounded almost like someone cracking their knuckles right next to his ear. Then there was a blinding, blue-white flash, and an ear splitting, concussive blast, and he'd felt the hot little .22 caliber lead pill burrow into the thick sheath of muscle of his right pectoral, just above the nipple.

He knew he had been shot, and by Britt; but he didn't know with what. He saw her hands held out in front of her; balled together and struggling to do something with some small object she was holding in them, but he couldn't see a gun.

Then he caught the glint of stainless steel between her fingers. Saw the black, little round hole of the .22's muzzle peeking out at him from her fist, and heard that same, knuckle cracking sound again as she cocked the weapon for a second shot. With lightning speed he lashed out at her and grabbed both of her wrists in a bone crushing grip, whipping her forearms back and forth until the little gun released, and went flying across the flat cement pad, landing near its edge.

"Crafty serpent!" Beek screamed at her. "Queen Whore of Babylon!"

He pinned Britt's bare arms against her sides, and then viciously threw her backwards, away from him and Kearnes. He stared for a moment at the small, neat hole in his shirt where the bullet had entered. Kevin Kearnes had begun to stir now, and was starting to moan. Beek picked up his knife again; which he'd dropped in the struggle. He put the tip of it at the base of Kearnes' scrotum…and sunk it out of sight into his flesh.

"NO!" Britt screamed, as she lunged at Beek, flying through the air and landing on his back; kicking, punching, and tearing at him anywhere she could. She closed both of her hands around Beek's massive wrist, trying to pull the blade back out of Kevin's groin, but she was like a flea on the back of a raging lion.

It was as if Beek wasn't even aware she was there. She let go of his wrist, and sank her teeth deep into the bloody bullet wound on his back from Thud Compton's Smith & Wesson. A cataclysm of pain pulsed through Beek's entire being. He screamed involuntarily, jerking his arms backward in pure, physical reaction; and as he did he ripped the knife blade down through the length of Kevin Kearnes' leg, opening the muscle tissue and exposing the bone from his inner groin to his kneecap.

Britt saw the long, razor thin incision in Kevin's leg from the knife lying open, and then suddenly disappear in a gushing bath of blood as the major artery inside his leg, which had been cut nearly in half, began to pump uncontrollably.

She sunk her teeth even deeper into the mushy, hamburger like hole in Beek's upper back and he raged to his feet, writhing and screaming in pain. He dropped the knife and reached back, grabbing Britt by one elbow and her hair, and hurled her over his head, off of him, and she landed hard; clear across the other side of the concrete pad. And only inches away from the little .22 revolver, which had four rounds left in it. She picked it up. And then stood up. Cocked the hammer back; and wobbled forward toward Beek.

"You get away from him!" she screamed. She was close to Beek now; but not close enough for him to just reach out and grab either the gun, or her. She saw his huge head dip, as he began to bend over to pick up his knife, and she fired. The bullet slapped into Beek's flat, hard muscled stomach, and he instantly doubled over.

"LEAVE US ALONE!" screamed Britt. She cocked the little gun's hammer back a third time.

Beek, still hunched over, looked at her for a long moment, and then slowly reached down for the knife. There was a loud "pop" as Britt fired again and a patch of pulverized, silvery dust jumped up from between his feet when the .22 slug impacted with the concrete, and then whined away somewhere into the air.

Beek rose up to his full height, knife in hand, and she could see a widening, bloody splotch in the middle of his green work shirt. Next to him on the concrete Kevin Kearnes lay, still unconscious, in a large pool of blood from his waist down; which was also quickly growing wider by the minute.

Then Beek spoke: "*Cursed is the ground because of you! Through painful toil, you will eat of it all the days of your life.*"

He took a step toward her…and Britt jumped back, cocking the gun.

"Stop right there!" she shouted at him.

"*It will produce thorns and thistles for you, and you will eat the plants of the field!*"

"STOP!" Britt screamed at him. But he didn't. She pointed the gun at Beek's head and fired. But the bullet went wild; and Beek only smiled at her…and kept coming.

"*By the sweat of your brow, you will eat your food!*" he bellowed. "*Until you return to the ground…since from it you were taken!*"

Backing away from him, Britt stumbled; and fell against the navigation light. Trapped now, she fired her last round from a distance of two feet away, and the bullet struck Beek in his left cheek; gouging out a channel of flesh the length and depth of a stubby pencil.

Suddenly, he stopped. He touched his fingers to the bloody, gunpowder scorched brand she had inflicted upon him; and looking into his eyes, Britt McGraw now saw that she, and Kevin Kearnes, were both going to die.

"*For dust you are!*," he shouted at her, raising the wicked looking knife up high in the air, directly over her head.

"*And to dust you shall return.*"

"YOU INIQUITOUS SLUT!"

And then Uriah Beek's head exploded, spraying Britt with a pinkish white shower of blood, and bone, and brain matter…as if she had been standing too close to someone mixing an exotic drink, in a high speed blender, when its top had suddenly come loose.

His massive, muscular body stood there frozen in place and almost headless—for just a second—and then Uriah Beek dropped straight down to the concrete with a loud and sickening thud…like a butchered steer hitting the slaughterhouse floor.

A tremendous burst of thunder suddenly came out of nowhere, rolling across the water to her from the opposite shore, its rippling shockwaves prickling along the bare skin of her back as she bent over the corpse and pried the bloody knife from Beek's huge, dead hand.

She assumed that the surprise thunder clap meant another sudden offshore rain squall would soon be upon them, and all she could think of as she ran to Kevin—slashing her discarded dress into long, tourniquet like strips of cloth with the knife as she went—was that she *had to* get his bleeding stopped; and keep him warm, and dry, until help arrived.

Never once did she question how it was that this monster was now suddenly lying dead on the ground behind her…or why it was that she was even still alive.

As she frantically began to work as a doctor, on the dying man, there was no more thunder; and the rain never fell from the sky. But she didn't question any of this, either; because Britt McGraw was through with questioning the world, and her life, and was now ready to start living it.

Only later would she be told that what she had heard at the end of the jetty at Cutter Point…had not been thunder.

It had been the echo from the sound of the single, desperate shot fired from Brad Dekker's police sniper rifle.

CHAPTER 46

▼

The old antique Regulator clock on the wall in Dr. John Grand's office had sounded its digital chimes three successive times at ten minutes before each hour, for three straight hours, by the time Kevin Kearnes had finished telling his story. And this time, as John Grand had insisted, it was all of the story; with nothing changed, and nothing left out.

The bottle of Glenlivet Scotch sat on Grand's desk, half empty now. All of it that was missing, except for Kearnes' two drinks—the first one of which he had smashed on the top of John Grand's desk—had all been consumed by the good doctor himself. While he had listened patiently, and intently to Kevin Kearnes as he talked about Tilly, his two sons, his Uncle Ben, Thud and Margie, Spenser, Uriah Beek...and of course, Britt.

Now the two men sat in John Grand's office, alone; looking at each other across the few feet of open space that separated Grand's big cherry wood desk from the couch facing it where Kearnes sat, tears streaming down his face. Grand opened a desk drawer and brought out a small, square designer box of Kleenex, and walked it over to Kearnes, setting it down on the arm of the couch next to Kearnes' empty drink glass on the coaster. Then he sat back down behind the desk, and began looking at the notes he had scribbled during the session on the large desktop calendar pad there.

Kearnes blew his noise loudly, using some of the Kleenex, and Grand looked up at him, over the tops of the reading glasses he'd just put on.

"I swear to God, Doc," said Kearnes, balling the Kleenex up in his hand for a try at shooting it into the nearby waste basket, "if you ask me 'how I'm feeling' right now...I'll kill you."

"All right," said Grand. "So, how are you feeling right now?"

Kearnes laughed, and only shook his head. He blew his nose again into some Kleenex, and then said, "Like shit."

"It will get better," said Grand. "Trust me. That was the worst of it."

"How does anything ever get better?" asked Kearnes. "After someone screws up as bad as I did?"

"What is it you think you've screwed up?" Grand asked.

"My whole life. My family, my career. My friends. Britt."

"As I told you once before, Kevin…the abuse is what *happened* to you…it's not who *you are*. Unless that's what you let it be."

"I don't understand any of this," said Kearnes. "It was only the one time…and so long ago. I just forgot all about it."

"No. You didn't really forget any of it," said Grand. "A young mind, so traumatized like that, will simply re-label such an experience; and then put it in another place. Out of sight and out of reach…seemingly forever. But, it's always really still there. As you now know."

"Who in the hell did he think he was," said Kearnes. "God, or somebody?"

"Yes," said Grand. "In the end, I believe that is exactly what he thought."

"I lied," said Kearnes. "I knew about Beek…early on…and I didn't tell anybody. And then he murdered those two kids."

"Wrong again," said John Grand. "You had no 'truth', yet, to tell anyone…at the time those two boys had been kidnapped."

"And as soon as you did come into possession of the truth, you chose to take direct action; rather than waste time disseminating a bunch of confusing, and possibly even counterproductive information. That may have served to only slow the investigation down, if not stop it entirely."

Kearnes lobbed the last balled up Kleenex into the wastebasket from where he was sitting; a perfect rim shot. Grand watched it go in, then opened a side drawer of his desk and pulled out a long, legal size manila folder.

"I have nightmares, sometimes," Kearnes admitted. "About Beek. Hunting me down again."

John Grand looked up from a thick sheaf of white paper forms inside the open folder he was perusing. "Kevin," he said, "Uriah Beek was never "hunting" you, in the first place. He was just "there". All along. For more than thirty years. On the Washington and Oregon coasts. And *you* just happened to wander into his territory…twice."

"And became his victim, twice," said Kearnes.

"Exactly," said Grand.

"I let people down," said Kearnes.

"No," Grand replied, matter of factly, "you saved people's lives."

"Who?" asked Kearnes. "Just tell me who in the hell I saved, Doc?"

"I didn't do my job. And people *died* because of that!"

John Grand set his pen down on the stack of papers he had just divided into two separate piles, and had started to sign. He looked at Kearnes.

"You saved Britt McGraw's life," said Grand. "And probably the lives of a few, if not several, more young boys, also.

"In the aetiology of murder, there is a very fine line between a true serial killer, and a spree killer. A spree killer will commit multiple murders in different locations over a very short period of time. But without any cooling off period; much like Beek did.

"But the serial killer, in between his murders, can live and act completely rationally before he kills again…and that makes him ten times more difficult to catch. And that would have been Beek's next progression. So, call him what you will…serial killer or spree killer; it really doesn't matter now. The reality is, Kevin, is that you put a stop to one monster, and prevented an even worse one, I believe, from coming into existence."

"I didn't save Britt McGraw," said Kearnes. "Brad Dekker and Spenser Sparling did."

"If you hadn't done exactly what you had," Grand said, "they never would have been where they were, in the first place. Detective Dekker wouldn't have been there to make the remarkable, life saving shot that he did…and Officer Sparling wouldn't have been there, either, as his second pair of eyes; telling him precisely when to pull that trigger."

"And if Britt hadn't fought him off until they could get close enough for that shot," said Kearnes, "neither one of us would have survived."

"Then you saved each other's lives, didn't you," said Grand. "Dr. McGraw certainly could have leapt from the end of that jetty into the sea; the moment she got free. But she chose to stay and defend you, Kevin; at great risk to her own life. Just like you chose to risk your life; rescuing her."

"I'm still not sure why she did that," said Kearnes.

"I believe that was a completely selfless act of love; nothing more and nothing less," said Grand.

"No, she doesn't love me," Kearnes said.

"How do you know that?" asked Grand.

"Because she's not *here*," said Kearnes. "She's not in my life anymore. She's never tried to contact me…I've never heard from her. At all."

"Have you ever tried contacting her?"

"No."

"Why?"

"Because. I'm not...well."

"Do you have any idea why Britt McGraw had the gun with her that morning? And why she had it on her, concealed?"

"No. I knew she had the gun. I'd seen it once. But she wouldn't talk about it with me."

"You and Britt McGraw, Kevin, were like two halves...trying to make something whole. It is not an uncommon theme among survivors of abuse. And sometimes, it even works out."

Kearnes leaned back into the couch, thinking about all of this for a minute. What did he mean by his comment about him, and Britt? He had disclosed very little about her to John Grand in the past; until today. And even this amount of information, he felt, hardly qualified Grand to make such a comment. After all, he'd never even met Britt McGraw.

But he decided to just let it pass. His bad leg had started to ache again and his hand, which he'd cut on the first drink glass that Grand had given him, was throbbing painfully now. All he wanted was to get this over with, and to leave.

"You have to be psychologically fit...to be a police officer," he said. "And I don't feel that I am, anymore."

"Let me ask you something, Kevin," he said. "Does the horticulturist in you— your fondness for flowers and all things that blossom—also extend to trees?"

"Yes, I like trees," said Kearnes.

"Have you ever seen a tree, maybe like a very old oak, where its roots have grown to the surface above the ground, instead of down deep into the soil?"

"I've seen trees like that before," said Kearnes. "There's a few like that in the park...here in town."

"Well, there are reasons for this," said Grand.

"Tree roots, by design, simply try to seek out, gather, and control resources in the soil. But when the soil lacks the element they need the most...sufficient water...the roots of a tree will sense, and then grow, toward other areas; looking for what they need, there.

"And the same thing happens, sometimes, to victims of sexual abuse. Especially children.

"If you can view the developing sense of self, and the processes of learning about intimacy through socially acceptable, and natural life experiences, that are age specific to a child's developmental state of emotional maturity...as if they were water...then it's easy to see what may happen if that water is denied. Or, as in your own case...the water source is poisoned.

"So the roots grow up and out of the nurturing soil; all gnarled, and twisted. And exposed to things that only tend to stunt their growth even further. Instead of growing healthily deeper, year by year, down into the ground. Creating a strong foundation, that is meant to support the tree for the rest of its life."

"Well, then it looks like my tree got chopped down," said Kearnes.

"Yes," Dr. John Grand said, sadly. "I'm afraid it did."

Kearnes took a deep breath, fighting back his tears as he watched John Grand paper clip together one of the separated piles of paper, and sign its first and second sheets; and then do exactly the same thing with the other one.

When he had finished he picked up his office phone, and called Maggie, his receptionist.

"I have two patient release forms to be copied please, Maggie. Mr. Kearnes is signing his here in my office, right now...can you come and get the other one, and have the patient in the waiting room sign theirs also, please? Thank you."

Kevin Kearnes was stunned at what he heard.

And he was even more stunned when John Grand got up from his desk with one of the paper clipped bunch of papers, walked over to him, and handed them to him, along with his pen."

"What...is this?" he asked.

"A medical release form," said Grand. "You need to sign both page one and page two...where I've indicated. Unless you don't want to?"

"I'm...not crazy?"

"Of course you are!" said Grand. "But no crazier, I would imagine, than any other man or woman who chooses to wear a badge, and do the job all of you are sworn to do."

"What?"

"That was a joke, Chief Kearnes." John Grand smiled at him.

"But you said..."

"Oh...you mean my analogy? About the tree? And its roots?"

"Yes."

"Well; there are also other trees, Kevin. Like the ones that sometimes take root and grow in the human spirit; and are so tenacious in their will to survive, that they can, and will grow back...no matter how many times you cut them down."

"Are you saying...I can go back to work then?"

"I can't say either yes, or no, to that. You've still got some nerve damage in that leg to contend with. But I would say if you'll start using your cane again, as your doctor has ordered, and be diligent in your physical therapy regimen; I wouldn't be surprised if you were back in uniform within six months. Or maybe even a little less."

John Grand's office door burst open and Maggie rushed inside. Tears were streaming down her face and she walked straight to Kearnes, who had stood up from the couch now, and hugged him; long and hard.

"I am *so* happy for you!" she said.

"Maggie, let him sign his paperwork first," said Grand, "before you blubber all over them, and the ink runs."

"Here, take these out to our other patient and get them signed," he said.

Maggie stopped hugging him, and took the other set of papers from Grand's outstretched hand.

"Congratulations, Kevin," she said. "Oh! I mean, Chief!"

"Thank you, Maggie," Kearnes said, just before she rushed out of the office with the other set of papers, and back down the hallway to the photocopier which was near her desk.

Kearnes signed the release papers and then handed them back to John Grand, who looked them over quickly and then said, "Fine. Come on. I'll walk you out."

As they walked down the hallway toward Maggie's reception desk and the waiting room, Kearnes could hear the copy machine in the coffee break room, clanking and humming away as they passed by its open door, and he saw Maggie frantically feeding some sheets of paper into its top; as if the building was on fire and she needed to hurry up and finish her copying job, and get out.

Where the hallway ended, just slightly out of sight of the reception area, but with Maggie's desk partially in view, John Grand put his hand on Kevin Kearnes' elbow, and stopped him. Kearnes looked at him, puzzled; wondering if Grand had, for some reason, changed his mind, and now wanted him to leave the building through the back door.

"One last thing," he said to Kearnes, holding onto his elbow very firmly.

"What?" asked Kearnes.

"And I wouldn't ever tell you this, Kevin, if the doctor-patient privilege prevented it…which in this case; it specifically does not."

"Tell me what?"

"But you *are* also a police officer; in addition to everything else…" John Grand, who was never at a loss for words, and usually had all of the right ones at his immediate disposal to say, seemed confused, and a little flustered now.

"What are you trying to say?"

"She had the gun that day…hidden in her bra like that…because she was practicing to use it…to kill a man in California. In Eureka, California. Her abuser…from the time she was thirteen. It was her Uncle. He's a dentist."

"What?" said Kearnes. None of it was registering with him.

"Who are you talking about?"

John Grand led him by his elbow, forward, from the end of the hallway toward the back of Maggie's desk, until they were standing directly behind her office chair.

"Her," he said, letting go of Kearnes' elbow now, and nodding straight ahead.

Kearnes followed his gaze and there, sitting on one of the big leather tanned cowhide couches in the waiting room, idly thumbing through the pages of a fly fishing magazine…was Britt McGraw.

Kearnes started toward her but John Grand grasped his elbow again, holding him back.

"Wait!" Grand whispered to him. "Give yourself a minute, Kevin. It's important."

"What is *she* doing here?" Kearnes asked, completely dumbstruck; but dropping his voice down to a whisper, to match John Grand's.

"Being released from treatment. Just like you," said Grand.

"But how did she get here?" asked Kearnes. "*When* did she get here?"

"She lives here," said Grand. "In town…just like you."

"But why? For how long?"

"She's been here from the day you were released from the hospital, Kevin. As my patient; and as someone who appears to care very much for you."

"But why didn't you tell me, dammit! Why didn't I know?"

"I couldn't tell you," said Grand. "She was my *patient*; and she didn't want any of her information disclosed to you. Until today. That's why I told you about the gun. Because she wanted me to. She wasn't sure how you would take it. In fact, she's even a little afraid you might arrest her."

"For what?"

"For planning a murder."

"That's crazy!"

"*Not* a good word to repeatedly be using in a psychiatrist's office, Kevin," whispered Grand.

"What are you two whispering about?" Maggie's voice boomed directly behind them and startled, both men jumped.

Britt heard Maggie and looked up from her magazine; and when she saw him, she smiled at Kearnes as he had never seen her smile before. Her hair was cut very short now, stylish and sexy, and her bare arms and legs were bronzed a golden brown from the summer sun.

"I have Britt's paperwork copied," Maggie said, breathlessly. "Here Kevin, you take it to her."

Kearnes turned around, and Maggie handed him the papers. Then he reached out his hand to John Grand, and the two men shook hands.

He walked past Maggie's desk and out into the waiting room, where Britt stood now. He handed the papers to her.

"Keep them for me until we get home, would you please?" she asked him.

"Sure," he said. "But where's home?"

"I rented a wonderful little house," she said, "out in the country." "It's only about a ten minute drive from here."

"That sounds nice," said Kearnes. "Much nicer than my place."

"And I have a flower garden, and a vegetable garden, too!" she said. "I work in them both...every day."

"It shows," said Kearnes

John Grand asked them both to wait a minute while he ran back down the hall to his office to get his box of Kleenex for Maggie, who was bawling her eyes out now. When he returned with it he and Maggie saw them to the front office door, said their good-byes, and then Kearnes and Britt stepped outside into the mid-afternoon blast furnace heat of the summer day.

They started down the walkway made of flat, mortared river rocks, heading toward the sidewalk where Britt had her little blue Geo parked. She had bought it from the rental car company in Cutter Point, a month after she'd left town; unable, for some strange reason, to part with it.

"Wait!" she cried, stopping just a few steps away from where the walkway ended, and the city sidewalk began. "Wait right here for a minute."

Kearnes watched as she carefully waded off into the rainbow colored sea of blooming perennial flowers on their right, which lined both sides of John Grand's office walkway; making her way slowly toward a low stone wall that rose above them, marking their end.

She stooped down with her back to him, briefly; and then stood back up again and came back to the stone walkway. In her hand she held a tightly clustered bunch of small beautiful flowers, each with six perfectly spaced, flat, powder blue colored petals and black on yellow centers that looked like tiny Bumble Bees, frozen in flight. She reached out and handed them to Kearnes.

"These are "Forget-me-nots", she said.

"Yes, I know," he said, taking the flowers from her. "From the genus *Myosotis*, I think."

Britt moved closer to him now, and the familiar smell of her hair, and the scent of her skin, penetrated him…clear through to his heart.

"There is a Legend behind these flowers, you know," she said.

"Really?" he said. "Tell me."

"OK," she said.

"A long, long time ago, in medieval times, a Knight and his Lady were walking along the banks of a river. He bent over to pick a posy of flowers for her, but because of the weight of his armor, he fell into the river.

"As he was drowning, he threw the posy of flowers to his beloved on the river bank, and shouted to her, 'Forget me not!'"

"And did she?" he asked, reaching out for Britt, pulling her into his arms. "Did she ever forget him?"

Britt hugged him tightly, burying her face in his chest and holding onto to him for dear life. And when she felt the wet warmth of his tears against her forehead, she drew back a little…and looked deeply into the eyes of the man she loved.

"No," she said. "She never did."

The End

978-0-595-39000-7
0-595-39000-5

Printed in the United States
50803LVS00003B/58

9 780595 390007